THE
EXPENDABLES

Also by Leonard B. Scott
Published by Ballantine Books

CHARLIE MIKE

THE LAST RUN

THE HILL

THE
EXPENDABLES

LEONARD B. SCOTT

BALLANTINE BOOKS · NEW YORK

The battles within this work happened as told within these pages. Information on United States Army and North Vietnamese units —as well as dates, times, locations, tactics, and casualty figures— is based on U.S. Army declassified technical reports, unit histories, diaries, letters, and personal interviews with the survivors. The names, main characters, and dialogue in this work are fiction. Any resemblance of the fictional characters to real persons living or dead is entirely coincidental.

Copyright © 1991 by Leonard B. Scott

Map copyright © 1983 by Random House, Inc.

All rights reserved under International and Pan-American Copyright Conventions. Published in the United States by Ballantine Books, a division of Random House, Inc., New York, and simultaneously in Canada by Random House of Canada Limited, Toronto.

Library of Congress Catalog Card Number: 90-93521

ISBN: 0-345-37171-2

Cover design by James R. Harris
Cover painting by Glenn Madison
Text design by Holly Johnson
Map by Alex Jay

Manufactured in the United States of America

First Edition: July 1991
10 9 8 7 6 5 4 3

The Expendables is dedicated
to the men who were there and their families who waited.
Your sacrifice will not be forgotten.

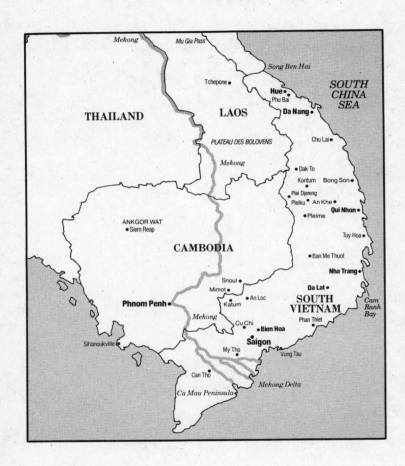

1953

1

KOREA, 23 MARCH 1953

A thin, filthy corporal waited beside the muddy road as an open deuce-and-a-half truck carrying a handful of replacement troops slid to a stop. Artillery shells were exploding on a hill a quarter of a mile away. "This is the end of the line!" the corporal barked. "Get off and form up on me."

Cold and bewildered, eighteen-year-old Private Shawn Flynn stiffly jumped down into six inches of icy mud. He tossed his heavy pack over his shoulder and sloshed over to the corporal. A minute later the vehicle pulled away, leaving Flynn and six other young replacements behind.

The corporal eyed the new men. He couldn't help but feel sorry for them. They had arrived in Korea only the day before, and had already been rushed to the front. If the attack that everyone expected came, most of them would not survive the week.

The tired corporal spoke in a kindly voice. "Welcome to the Seventh Division, 31st Regiment. That arty you hear ain't ours, it's theirs." He motioned over his shoulder toward two distant, adjoining hills. "We're expectin' an attack on Ol' Baldy there, and Pork Chop next to it. You were sent to the front to fill our ranks. We asked for seventy replacements but only got you seven men . . . guess everybody needs expendables. I'm gonna take you to supply, where you'll draw ammo, grenades, and get ya some hot coffee. You'll be assigned to companies as soon as Sergeant Major gets here. Follow me."

Private Shawn Flynn, shivering from the cold, tried to ignore the noise of the artillery landing nearby as he trudged behind the corporal. He was too miserable to be worried. The ride in the open truck had been the worst experience of his life. The two-hour train ride before loading onto the truck had been crowded, but at least the train car had been warm. It was from there that he got his first look at Korea. It was not what he had expected. The first few miles were all he needed to make him realize that the entire country would be the same—depressing. Everything looked dirty brown or dull gray, devastated by three years of war. Houses, countryside, and people were all scarred. No one smiled. There was no color and no laughter, only sad people in a sad land, holding onto a miserable existence.

Shawn sipped the oily, gritty coffee from his canteen cup. For the first time in five hours he was warm. The sandbagged supply bunker got its heat

3

from an empty fifty-gallon drum fashioned into a wood stove. The air was filled with smoke, and his eyes stung, but at least he could feel his feet again.

The corporal poured more coffee into the young soldier's canteen cup. The kid, like most replacements they were receiving, was too young. Probably didn't even need to shave. He had sandy hair, and was average in height, and couldn't have weighed more than 140 pounds. His ruddy cheeks, smooth features, and large, innocent, brown eyes made him look like a lost sixteen-year-old.

Replacing the tin can of coffee on the stove, the corporal sat down on a stack of empty ammunition boxes that served as furniture. "Flynn, being Infantry, you're lucky the sergeant major assigned ya as my assistant. If you'd been like the others and assigned to one of the line units, you'd be freezing your ass off in a foxhole on Pork Chop Hill."

Shawn shrugged his thin shoulders and glanced around the bunker. "This place looks okay. At least it's warm."

The corporal smiled. The soldier appreciated his handiwork. "Yeah, this ain't bad. Where is home in the States?"

Shawn wrapped both hands around the cup to warm his hands. "I was born in Boston, but we moved around a lot. No place special."

The corporal had heard the same story many times. He already knew the answer to his next question but asked anyway. "You dropped out of school and joined up, huh?"

"Yeah, I signed up in Reno."

The corporal glanced at his watch and stood, motioning toward Shawn's canteen cup. "When ya finish your coffee you gotta take some field-phone batteries up to Ol' Baldy. We got a liaison sergeant up there with the Colombos. Take him a bag full, an' that way you won't have ta make the trip again for a couple of days."

"What are Colombos?" asked Shawn.

The corporal sighed. "Sorry, I forget you don't know nothin' yet. Colombos are Colombians. They're part of the United Nations Force and have a battalion assigned to our regiment. The Colombos have a company up on Ol' Baldy. Our guys are next to it, on Pork Chop. The liaison sergeant, Staff Sergeant Quail, talks wetback and keeps in contact with our guys by radio and field phone. The batteries you'll be needin' are in the next bunker. Come on, I'll show where to find 'em and show ya the trail that'll lead ya up to Baldy. By the time ya get back, I'll have ya a bunk in here. It'll sure beat the hell outta where the other expendables will be bunkin' tonight."

Shawn stood looking at the corporal with a puzzled expression. "Why do you call us 'expendables'?"

The corporal stopped in mid-stride and gave the replacement a bitter look. "Cause that's what we are. In the Army supply business, we call something that gets used and tossed away 'expendable.' I've been in this unit for six months and seen replacements come in just like the supplies. They get used up on the front lines, and then we toss their bodies into trucks. We've lost so many, I gave up keeping count. You'll see soon enough what I mean when you help me tag the dead. We're all nothin' but expendable."

Shawn shook his head. "Not me. I'm not expendable."

The corporal couldn't help but smile. He had touched on a strength in the boy. Maybe it would be enough. Maybe believing hard enough would get him through. Maybe.

Shawn clutched his heavy M-1 rifle tightly as he slowly made his way up the snaking trail. When the corporal had said Old Baldy was a hill, he had told a white lie. The hill rose almost straight up from the valley and looked more like a mountain.

Stopping halfway to rest and get his breath back, Shawn turned around to take in the view. The small camp and warm bunkers of his new home were nestled a half-mile below in a narrow, winding valley. He took in another deep breath and looked around. The landscape was desolate. Old Baldy was nothing but blasted stumps, earth, and rock. No grass, moss, vegetation, or any other living thing was visible.

Feeling a shiver run up his spine, Shawn turned toward the hilltop. An eerie gray mist was forming a shroud over the crest. He began to climb the trail. The sooner he delivered the batteries, the sooner he could get back to the warm bunker.

Twenty minutes later, he topped the crest and looked down the barrel of the .30-caliber machine gun that was pointed directly at his face. The Colombian soldier sitting behind the gray weapon spoke softly. *"Buenos tardes, me amigo."*

Flynn shrugged his shoulders and gave the man the biggest grin he could conjure. The gunner waved him on and pointed toward a bunker farther up the hill. *"El americano sergeant es en aqui."*

Shawn kept his grin and quickly made for the distant bunker. He had understood only the words "americano sergeant." He took three steps and slowed to a normal pace to take in the activity around him. He noticed that the peak of Old Baldy was actually a long, narrow ridge of pitted brown and blackened soil. A ragged line of bunkers connected by a trench faced down the narrow ridge's slope to the north. Everything was angled. There was no flat ground anywhere except for the tops of the bunkers, which were dug into the side of the ridge and surrounded by sandbags, rocks, and wooden ammo boxes filled with dirt. Colombian soldiers were standing outside the bunkers, smoking, exchanging equipment, and talking a mile a minute. Ignoring their stares, Shawn hopped down into a zigzagging trench that led to the entrance of the sergeant's bunker.

When he opened the splintered wood door, his stomach immediately revolted. Oh God, it stinks! he thought. The putrid odor was a combination of rotting fish and backed-up commode. On the opposite wall were two huge slanted eyes staring back at him, the firing ports. The east wall, made of wooden ammunition boxes, held a large map. Next to it was a table made from the same type of boxes. On it were three field phones, sitting side by side, and a stack of radios, hissing like snakes. Piled neatly on the floor were ammo cans and boxes of the older K-rations, above which were thick logs covered with sandbags.

He was about to turn and get away from the smell when someone walked up behind him. Shawn turned around and looked up into the bearded face of a smiling staff sergeant.

Staff Sergeant John Quail exposed gleaming white teeth as he smiled and extended his hand. "Man, am I glad to see you. You're my new radioman, right?"

Shawn held up the sandbag full of batteries. "Na . . . no, Sergeant. I'm the supply assistant. I just brought you up these batteries."

"Shit!" Quail blurted. Dropping his hand, he stormed past the young soldier and toward the field phones. "I been telling them bastards for weeks I need a RTO. Don't any of them shitheads listen?"

Minutes later, after talking and cussing on the phone, the dark-haired sergeant tossed down the handset in disgust. "Great! Just fuckin' great! I got another promise." He stared at the young soldier accusingly. "You know how many times they've promised me a body?"

Shawn was about to speculate when Quail shook his head and walked toward the bunker entrance. "At least ten fuckin' times! Ten fuckin' promises in the past three days!" He stopped and peered out the door. "I can't stay awake twenty-four hours a fuckin' day and monitor radios! What do them bastards expect?"

Shawn set the batteries on the floor. The bunker's smell was making him sick. He began to walk past the irate sergeant when the broad-shouldered NCO threw his hand out, blocking his exit. "Where the hell ya think you're goin'? You can't go yet. Bravo Company is relieving Charlie Company and I don't want you gettin' in the way. Just sit your butt down and relax. Make us some coffee. I need it. Captain Valez and his headquarters boys will be here in a few minutes and then you can . . . *Aw shit! Not now!*"

The sergeant glanced up at the bunker ceiling, then outside, while speaking aloud to himself. "Great. Just fuckin' great! Mortars, now . . . while they're out in the open . . . *shit!*"

Shawn's jaw dropped open. He too had heard the sounds, but had not known what they were. The distant thunks sounded like firecrackers going off inside metal drums. He didn't know whether to run, scream, or hide. Instead, he stood frozen in fear to the dirt floor.

The sergeant saw the young soldier's dilemma and gently pushed him toward the sandbagged wall. "Take it easy. You're safe enough in here. Make us some coffee. I really need some."

Shawn didn't move a muscle. He didn't believe a word of the sergeant's assurances. Several seconds passed in silence. Then suddenly the ground shuddered and shook violently with the first impact of rounds. Dirt cascaded down from the roof, engulfing the bunker in a choking cloud of dust. Shawn's chest tightened from panic and lack of air. To him, it sounded as if the thunderous explosions were going off directly on top of the bunker. He tried to scream, but nothing came out of his mouth but a rush of air. With his eyes bulging and his chest about to explode, he frantically bolted for the door, threw it open, ran out, and blindly slammed into the trench wall. Stunned, he staggered backward into the bunker and heard the sergeant yelling. He opened his eyes to see the NCO screaming into the phone handset, but couldn't make out what he was saying over the cracking explosions. Shawn realized he was breathing again. The dust was bad, but he could still suck in enough air.

Sergeant Quail tossed the handset down and ran past him toward the door. Seconds later he stepped back inside, shaking his head dejectedly. The Chinese had timed their mortar barrage perfectly, catching the two Colombian companies in the open. He shut the door just as the intensity of the bombardment increased. The mortar shells were being joined by the throaty, deeper *ba-loom* of medium artillery rounds.

The sergeant looked at the panic-stricken private and yelled over the noise, "Where's my coffee? I need coffee! There's a stove in the corner. And don't worry about this pounding, it'll be over in a little while."

Shawn was not convinced. He wanted to be anywhere but in that stinking bunker. Even freezing in the truck would have been better than this. He nodded stiffly and tried to walk toward the corner to which Quail had pointed. The horrific explosions were shaking the ground under his feet as if he was standing on Jell-O. Even his teeth were rattling. Somehow he had thought he would have been introduced to the war more slowly, like when you first learn to swim, putting a toe in first, then wading in up to the ankles in the baby pool. Instead he had been thrown headfirst into a bottomless lake.

Five minutes passed, then ten, and there still had been no letup. Shawn handed Quail a steaming canteen cup of coffee. "I hope I made it right."

Quail took a sip and his eyes rolled back in ecstasy. "God, that's good. Ain't nothin like good ol' U.S. Army coffee . . . except a good beer." He glanced at his watch and took another sip of the dark, dust-topped liquid. "Thanks, ya did good. We have a little problem here I think you'd better understand. I fucked up. I thought this was a harassing barrage, but it ain't. They're gonna hit us, so get your rifle and break us out some more ammo from the cans on the floor."

Shawn nodded in a stupor. The constant pounding had dulled his senses.

He felt like he was moving in slow motion. The simple act of lifting his rifle took total concentration and proved incredibly tiring. He examined the heavy M-1 rifle as if he'd never seen one before. He felt as if he had been run over by a truck and left semiconscious. Every part of his body throbbed in dull aches. He stared at the rifle, wondering how it had gotten into his hands, and he concentrated on what the sergeant had said. "Get ready and break out ammo" . . . right. The pounding meant they were going to attack. *Attack? Attack who?*

Quail pulled Shawn toward the right firing port. "The captain and his headquarters boys didn't make it back, so we're it. This will be your spot. See down the slope? The barbed wire? Just beyond it the ground drops off. You won't see 'em till they get in the wire. Sit down here and take it easy, but when the arty stops, get up and take up a firing position in front of the portal. You're gonna have lots of targets. Keep your rate of fire steady and aim low. Hit 'em in the balls, it stops them cold."

Shawn shook his head to clear the spinning and looked at the sergeant in desperation. "I'm . . . I'm not supposed to be here. I don't know what to do."

"Snap out of it!" Quail blurted out. "Don't you dare freeze up on me. It's just you and me. Our only chance is to keep them from making it through the wire. Grenades are in the boxes to your right, get some out. If they make it through the wire, toss them out the portal and keep tossing them until you run out. Ya understand?"

Stunned by the thought of impending battle, Shawn could only force a nod.

Quail took a position in front of the other firing port. He opened a wooden ammo box, removed several grenades, and set them on the shooting ledge. Opening another box, he took out a Browning Automatic Rifle. Shawn recognized the deadly BAR from his training back in the States. The weapon could fire like a machine gun for twenty rounds before its magazine had to be changed. Unlike Shawn's M-1, which held an eight-round clip, all Quail had to do with the BAR was hold back the trigger for twenty shots.

Shawn followed the sergeant's example, taking out two handfuls of grenades and setting them on the ledge. He then laid out ten eight-round clips for his M-1. Outside of the portal the ground was blown into a light dust that mixed with smoke and formed a cloud that drifted over the wire. Shawn was shocked to see the sky turning dark. The thought of being in the bunker in darkness was too much. It was all a nightmare. His tongue felt thick and cottony and his heart pounded so hard he could hardly breathe. The artillery shells were hitting farther down the hill, with an occasional mortar round landing behind them. Shawn shook so badly his knees wouldn't stay locked. He shut his eyes and slid down the sandbag wall to the dirt floor, where he could try and regain his strength.

It was only six months before that Shawn had made up his mind and walked out of his mother's trailer to begin a new life. He had failed math, history, and English again, and to make matters worse, his mother had been bringing customers home. It wasn't her fault that she couldn't take care of him. Maggie Flynn had at least tried. His father had abandoned her before he was born, leaving the young woman to make it on her own. It wasn't her fault things had turned out badly.

The Army had been the only place to find the new life Shawn desperately wanted. For the past few years, he had escaped bad times by going to movies and reading books. Within those pages and dark theaters, he could forget he was going nowhere and dream about being somebody else. The Army would give substance to those dreams. It would give him direction and the chance to test himself as a man. He would be like those men in the war movies, who overcame adversity and gained respect. He had joined knowing deep inside he had what it took.

He opened his eyes, praying he had been only dreaming, but his situation remained all too real. His dream of becoming a soldier, a hero like his book and movie idols, had shattered as soon as the first mortar rounds had made impact. He had not reacted like his idols. They would have been steel-eyed, cracking jokes while they waited for the attack, instead of cringing in fear.

The sudden shrill sound of wailing bugles sent a tremor along his spine. He bolted upright. The bugle sound was joined by a chorus of screams that grew louder and louder.

Sergeant Quail stood and yelled over the din. *"Here they come!"*

Shawn stood and squinted his eyes to relieve the pounding in his head and ears. Never had he felt so small and weak.

The sergeant readied his BAR and glanced at his fellow defender. The young soldier was staring at him wide-eyed, as if in a trance. "This is it!" Quail yelled over the screams. "Remember what you learned in basic! Don't jerk the trigger, squeeze! Hit 'em low! It's time, kid."

Shawn nodded stiffly and raised his rifle. He dug his elbows into the firing-ledge sandbags to support the M-1. He couldn't see anyone in the evening dusk and smoke, but he could hear them well enough.

Quail pushed the safety off of his BAR. "In the balls!" he cried out.

Shawn's hands were shaking so badly he was afraid to place his finger on the trigger until he saw something. He had hunted rabbits a few times and shot holes in targets in basic training, but he had never shot a man.

The screams became louder. A machine gun in the next bunker began chattering. Shawn still didn't see anything. A flare popped somewhere above the hill, bathing the slope in a golden glow. Jesus! They were in the wire!

Shawn pulled the trigger twice before he knew what he had done. He had not sighted or even put his cheek on the wooden stock. Fear had overtaken him and caused his finger to involuntarily jerk the trigger.

Forcing himself to take a breath to calm himself, he aimed at the center-most Chinese soldier, who was cutting the barbed wire. The recoil of the weapon slammed into Shawn's shoulder. The soldier pitched backward. Shawn screamed to himself, *One!* Aiming again, he fired. *Two!* Oh God, there are too many of them! I'm going to die! He squeezed the trigger gently after aligning the sights low on his next target. Blam! Three.

Quail held the BAR firmly to his shoulder and squeezed the trigger in controlled bursts. The Chinese soldiers, twenty yards away, were knocked down like rag dolls.

Shawn inserted a new clip and fired two quick shots at a screaming soldier who had made it through the wire. When the attacker doubled over, two more came into view. They were pouring though a gap. With gun smoke filling his nostrils, Shawn shifted his position and fired with surprising calm. Blam, six. Blam, seven.

He picked up a grenade and pulled the pin, then tossed it out and scooped up another one. A bullet creased his helmet, knocking it back on his head. The close call stunned him. He knew he was going to die, but had not thought of how it was going to happen. Suddenly, a bullet seemed too impersonal. He tossed the second grenade out and was about to duck when his first grenade went off in a vehement explosion. Something slapped his cheek, knocking him back a step. His face felt as if it had been set on fire then stung by a fifty-pound bee. Instinctively, his hand came up to feel the damage, but the screams outside were coming closer, so his blood-covered hand came down and grasped the rifle. Bullets stitched the top of the portal as he took up his firing position and began shooting. Blam, eight . . . nine . . . ten. The pain in his face increased each time he laid his cheek against the stock of the rifle, sticky with blood. Eleven. He squeezed again with tears in his eyes. Not me, *not me! Not meeee!*

Quail lowered his weapon and peered out the portal as three flares swayed overhead. The Chinese had ceased their attack and pulled back to regroup. The silence hung as heavy as gun smoke over the hill. He looked out the portal to his right at the stack of bodies lying on the frozen ground. The kid had done good. Suddenly the silence was broken by the young soldier firing his rifle. A Chinese soldier flopped around on the ground, dying.

Shawn fired again at another wounded soldier who had been moaning and was about to shoot him again when he felt a hand on his shoulder.

"Save your ammo," Quail said softly.

Shawn didn't dare take his eyes from the gap in the wire. He had quit counting the number of men he had shot at fourteen. Somehow it didn't matter anymore.

Seeing the blood dripping from the soldier's face, Quail pulled Shawn back from the portal and shined a flashlight, filtered by a red lens, into his eyes. "Ya got a piece of shrapnel in your cheek. Hold still a sec."

Quail popped the iron sliver out as if he were squeezing a pimple. Shawn wiped the tears of pain from his eyes and quickly returned to his firing position.

Quail kicked the expended brass shell casings away from his feet and leaned against the bunker wall. "They'll be back, but the mortars and artillery will come first. Restock your ammo and grenades, then make us some coffee. We're gonna need it. They were feeling us out, trying to find out where we were weak. Next time they'll be going all out. That attack lasted ten minutes, the next one will last till it's over, one way or another."

Quail pushed off the wall, walked over to the table and picked up the field phone. He rang the side handle several times before tossing the phone down. He had known it wouldn't work before trying it but wanted to make sure. The artillery and mortars had cut the wire to pieces. He tried the radio next and immediately got gibberish. He knew they would be jamming, but again, he'd had to try. He glanced at Shawn's back. "The chinks have set this up damn good. The battalion will be sending a relief force from Pork Chop, but they won't make it two hundred yards out of their perimeter. The chinks have got us cold. Looks like we're in this one on our own."

Shawn had started a small fire. He looked up, not completely sure of what the sergeant was talking about. He poured water into the metal canteen cup. "We have plenty of ammunition left."

Quail smiled, as if at an inside joke. "Yeah." The sergeant realized there was no use in making things worse by telling him the truth. "What's your name, anyway? I should at least know your name."

"Shawn Flynn," said the private, sprinkling the instant coffee packet into the cup.

Quail smiled faintly. "Irish, huh? Well, a mick is good as any, I guess. I'm Quail, but vets call me Taco. How long you been in Korea?"

"I got here yesterday."

Quail's eyes widened in astonishment. "Damn, Irish, you've only been here forty-eight hours, and already killed a couple'a squads of commies, got ya a CIB and a Purple Heart, and ain't even had time to sew on the division patch. You're one unlucky sonofabitch, aren't ya?"

Shawn looked at the sergeant strangely. "What's a CIB?"

Quail rolled his eyes. "Damn! Every vet knows what a Combat Infantryman's Badge is. It's given to us dumb-ass infantrymen who've been in combat, and you definitely been in that. Where's home?"

Shawn's face hurt badly. He didn't feel like talking anymore. He was saved from having to respond by voices coming from outside the bunker entrance. Seconds later four Colombians entered, carrying a badly wounded man whose face lay open as if someone had skinned it from his chin up past his nose. In the light of the flashlight, he didn't look human. Two men who had brought him in were wounded as well.

Quail spoke in Spanish, ordering the badly wounded man to be laid on the floor near the K-rations. The sergeant glanced at Shawn. "Walk down the bunker line and count how many we have that can still fight. Don't go more than a hundred yards in either direction, and come back as soon as you're through. If the barrage starts, get your ass in the trench that runs along the crest and stay low, but get your butt back here." Quail motioned to the prone Colombian. "This is the company commander, and the sergeant here says the other officers are dead. He wants me to take charge. Looks like I'm the new C.O. I guess that makes you my first sergeant."

Shawn had his doubts about stumbling around in the darkness, unable to speak Spanish, but his task was made easy. The Army might have been short of covered trucks with heaters, but certainly not of artillery flares. Every thirty seconds three flares would pop overhead, float down under small white parachutes and light the way. The first bunker he had checked only had four survivors, one of whom, Alberto Salvador, clung to him like a long-lost friend.

Shawn had never seen dead men before, except for an uncle in a funeral home. Each bunker and foxhole expanded his education in death and more than satisfied his morbid curiosity. Some of the dead looked peaceful, as if they were asleep, completely unscratched, while of others there was nothing left but pieces of red meat and yellow bone. Death gave off a particular stink. He had not known that. Blood had the smell of a steamroom full of hamburger meat, while death itself smelled like defecation, urine, blood, gunpowder, and fresh-tilled soil all mixed together. The wounded were the hardest to take. The deep gurgling and horrible screams of those who were gut-shot were the worst. Blood steamed in the frigid air, making open wounds look like hot springs. Intestines appeared just like those of animals run over on a highway. The pink, yellowish, soft organs gushed out of seemingly small holes. He had found that he couldn't stop them once they started coming out. It was like opening a box loaded with a steel spring.

Shawn counted the dead and the wounded while Alberto counted those who could still fight. Shawn learned a new respect for the human body. The flesh could be torn, ripped, punctured, or burned, and yet the victim could still function. He had learned a man was hard to kill when he didn't want to die. Some of the wounded fought and scratched for every breath and wouldn't give up, while others wanted to die and end their agony.

Alberto was leading Shawn down the trench to the last bunker when the mortar shells started raining down again. He wanted to lie in the ditch and hide, but felt compelled to return to the bearded sergeant. He needed him.

When he was halfway back to his bunker, artillery shells began crashing in around them in ear-shattering explosions. The initial rounds had landed close, and the lurching ground had knocked him and Alberto to the trench floor. The explosions were deafening, causing his eyes to bulge and his head to pound as if it were about to explode. Under the golden glow of the flares, the trench seemed to sway this way and that as he tried to make his way back. Two more times he was knocked down by near misses. Shawn picked himself up off the frozen earth for the third time. He couldn't hear anything but a constant ringing in his ears. It was an odd sensation and, strangely, made it more difficult to keep his balance as he jogged along. He constantly bounced off the side of the trench wall like a drunk. He began to feel better as he approached the bunker entrance, but then he entered. The entire floor of the fighting position was covered with wounded, moaning men. The smell almost knocked him over. He gagged and quickly backed up, knocking Alberto out of the way, and vomited. He retched until he felt as if his own stomach was coming up as well.

Shawn washed his mouth out with the last of his canteen water, and steeling himself with one last deep breath of fresh air, he entered the bunker to make his report to Quail.

Sergeant Quail's shoulders sagged at the news that only half of the company was able to fight. He spoke softly to three Colombians kneeling by the phones. They exchanged nervous glances and nodded before getting up and moving toward the entrance. Quail's bloodshot eyes shifted to Shawn.

"I told them to hold as long as possible and fall back if the chinks took the flanks."

Having walked the bunker line, Shawn didn't understand the order. "Where do we fall back to?"

The sergeant lowered his head. "Down the hill."

Shawn was shocked. Falling back was no option. Just moving out in the open was suicide, let alone trying to carry the wounded. It would be a turkey shoot for the Chinese. What Quail had really told them was to die in place. The Colombians wouldn't leave their wounded. Shawn's jaw tightened in anger. The corporal had been right. They *were* expendable.

Shawn unsnapped his bayonet sheath and slid the battle knife into place with a metallic clink. His fear was gone, replaced with grinding, seething hatred. He hated everything he had seen and felt in Korea. Blood, bodies, misery, and death were permanently imprinted into his being. He hated his own weakness and his inability to control himself or events. He hated it all. It was all so impersonal. A faceless enemy and exploding shells. Where was the pride and glory of fighting for his country? The movies had lied. The books, stories, and magazine pictures had all been lies! None of them had told him, taught him, prepared him for real war. In the movies, nobody shit their pants. The dark, gushing blood, the screaming of the wounded, the killing, pain, and confusion had not been captured by any camera. War was impersonal, uncaring, unforgiving. There was no feeling in it of elation or satisfaction. There was only the sickly, sinking feeling in his stomach and the knotted stiffness of fear, remorse, and down-to-the-bone weariness. He hated it! He hated the *truth* of war.

Stepping over the wounded, Shawn took up his position by the firing port. He glared at the sergeant with defiance and yelled over the sound of incoming mortar shells, "Not me! They ain't throwing me on no truck!"

Quail couldn't hear what the private had said; the sound of Chinese bugles had drowned out his words.

The supply corporal put down the phone and listened to the battle sounds coming from Old Baldy. Fate worked in strange ways. If the replacements had not come in, he would have had to deliver the batteries to the liaison sergeant and been the one trapped on the hill. What was the new man's name? He had forgotten. It was something Irish, Shannon, Shannagon, Shawn. Yeah, that was it, Shawn. Too bad about that. He was so damned young to die.

The corporal envisioned the soldier's young face and lowered his head. The operations officer had come in for extra radio batteries a few minutes before and said the Chinese had stopped the Pork Chop relief company. Another attempt to break through would be tried tomorrow, as soon as the regiment got tanks. The operations officer knew as well as he did that tomorrow would be too late. When a regiment of Chinese attacked a company, it was all over. The camp had to prepare to move to the next valley. Trucks would be arriving within the next ten minutes to start loading the essential equipment. Expendable supplies would be left behind.

The corporal tried the telephone one more time—nothing. He had a lot of work to do. In a few days another expendable would take the kid's place. Maybe the next new guy would be luckier.

Shawn aimed and fired, ignoring his bruised shoulder and the pain in his face. The screaming men appeared in waves. He methodically shot them left to right as they climbed over their dead. The crumpled stack of bodies were slowing the attackers, making the killing almost easy.

Ping. The M-1 clip ejected and Shawn quickly loaded another, barely breaking his rhythm. A Chicom grenade went off to his front, knocking him down. His face bleeding from stinging bits of frozen soil, he sat up groggily and shook his head. Suddenly a rifle cracked behind him. A Chinese soldier had burst through the bunker entrance, shooting from the hip at the wounded men lying on the floor. Alberto and Sergeant Quail both spun around, stitching the man with bullets and knocking him back through the entrance.

Shawn took a .45-caliber pistol from the stiff hand of one of the dead Colombians and approached the portal. A Chinese soldier had just knelt down in front of the firing port and was sticking his rifle into the slit. Shawn raised the pistol and fired. The bullet passed through the soldier's right eye and blew out the back of his head, taking a portion of the skull. Jamming the pistol in his web belt, Shawn picked up a grenade and pulled the pin. He tossed the miniature bomb out of the portal and grabbed another. He tossed five grenades, one after another, before picking up his rifle.

A shattering explosion rocked the bunker's entrance. Shawn was pitched forward into the bunker wall and slid down, feeling as if he had been hit in the back with a huge ball bat. Chinese infantrymen screamed as they ran shooting into the dust-filled bunker. Again Sergeant Quail met the attackers with a long burst from the BAR, but the magazine ran out before he finished his sweep. The single Chinese soldier remaining fired wildly at the big American, spinning him around. Alberto pulled the trigger of his M-1 but it was empty. Shawn rose up and lunged forward with the bayoneted rifle. The round-faced communist gasped as cold steel sunk into his stomach. Shawn pulled the trigger of the M-1 and jerked the weapon back. Savagely, he jammed the barrel into the screaming soldier's face and fired again. Splattered with blood, brain, and bits of bone, he raised his rifle and fired at another Chinese soldier who appeared in the entrance.

Quail, holding his hand over the bleeding bullet wound in his shoulder, staggered over to Shawn. He began to speak when Alberto yelled, "Grenade!" and threw himself to the dirt floor. The Chicom grenade, tossed in through the portal, landed among the wounded. Shawn made a move toward the deadly bomb but was knocked to the floor by Quail. The explosion lifted both men off the ground, but neither was hit by the tearing shrapnel. It had been absorbed by the screaming wounded, who now felt no more pain.

Shawn jumped to his feet and pulled Quail up. He yelled at Alberto, who was just lifting himself off the floor. "Check if any of them are alive. We're getting out of here!"

Shawn stepped over the dead Chinese soldiers into the trench. He peered over the lip, then quickly ducked down. Under the flare light, he had seen enough to know they were going to die. Men wearing quilted uniforms were streaming over the hill. It was just a matter of time.

Quail took a hand flare from his leg pocket and tapped Shawn's shoulder with it. It was a tubular device. "Shoot this up. It'll signal our artillery to fire on us."

Without hesitation Shawn took the flare and fired it into the darkness. The red star cluster popped only fifty yards overhead.

Firing the flare was like waving a flag telling the Chinese where they were. Immediately a squad crossing the ridge ran straight for the spot where the flare was fired. Shawn cussed and rose up. They were so close, he fired without having to aim. Quail pulled his pistol and joined in the killing. Shawn shot four men before his clip ejected. The fifth soldier shot Shawn from the hip and was about to shoot him again when he was knocked off his feet by a .45-caliber bullet from Quail's pistol.

Suddenly there was a tremendous flash and horrific explosion. Five more artillery rounds landed on the ridge, showering shrapnel and frozen dirt clods.

Shawn's eyes fluttered open as he felt himself shaken violently. The side of his neck felt as if a red-hot poker was embedded under the skin.

Alberto inspected Shawn's wound in the flare's light and yelled over the explosions, "You ees okay!"

Shawn was dazed. He had thought he was dying, and wanted to lie there in peace. Hearing that he was not hurt badly was horrible news.

As he struggled to his feet, the pain shot through his body, weakening him. He sunk to his knees on top of a Chinese soldier whom he had earlier killed. His head began to clear as he picked up the soldier's hat. Using the bayonet, he split the padded material and wrapped it around his neck to cover the bleeding holes. The bullet had passed through the back of his neck. Standing, his head quit spinning, but he was still sick to his stomach. Stiffly, he raised his rifle and inserted a new clip. The artillery had changed to white phosphorous that exploded in brilliant flashes of white light and smoke all around them.

Quail pushed him forward. "Stay in the trench for another fifty yards before trying to make a break down the hill. There's some gullies we can follow."

Shawn tentatively began moving down the zigzag trench. They had made twenty yards when he slowed and peeked around one of the corners. Two feet away a Chinese soldier was hunkered down with his back to him. Shawn stepped lightly around the corner and butt-stroked the soldier in the back of the head. Two more Chinese were in exactly the same position farther up the trench. Shawn butt-stroked the first one and shot the second, who had begun to turn around. He was about to peer around the next corner when he heard voices coming his way in the trench. Backing up a step, he waited with his finger on the trigger.

The Chinese officer, pistol in hand, led his radioman and artillery observer through the trench. As he turned the corner, Shawn shot him in the heart at point-blank range. Quail charged past, stepping on the body, and emptied his pistol at the remaining stunned men, who were turning around.

The last of them took a bullet while trying to scramble out of the trench. Quail slid down to his buttocks totally exhausted. "Jesus! Don't wait like that after you shoot. Ya got to take the corner and hold it or they'll toss a grenade on top of you. How's your ammo?"

Shawn felt his pockets. "I—I've got . . . one clip left for the M-1 . . . and I have the .45."

Quail motioned weakly toward the bodies. "Get what ya can from them." He looked at Alberto and waved him forward. "Alberto, you lead Irish here to the gulley. I'll cover you both and join you after a while."

Shawn spun around. *"No!* You're going with us."

Quail lowered his head, feeling incredibly tired. "I ain't gonna make it. Get the fuck outta here."

Shawn grabbed the older soldier's shirt and pulled him up. *We're all goin'!"*

The explosions of brilliant light and tearing metal burst all around the three men as they crawled down a small rocky ravine. Shawn pulled and cussed the sergeant, whose strength was gone. Exhausted with the effort, they finally stopped to rest. The artillery was making impact farther up the hill, but it was shaking the frozen ground all around them. The biting cold attacked unmercifully. Shawn moved closer to Quail for his warmth and shut his eyes. He didn't care anymore. Death was accepted. Peace, blissful peace, was all he desired. The chance to shut his eyes and forget. The pain, cold, and misery would be gone, replaced by wonderful peace.

Minutes passed. A flare popped almost directly overhead. Shawn opened his heavy eyelids but couldn't lift his rifle. He was too stiff. Alberto lifted his head and started babbling. Shawn forced himself to move. He had made a mistake in stopping. He roughly grabbed the soldier's leg. "Calm down. We gotta keep going."

Shawn shook Sergeant Quail, who moaned loudly. Shawn clapped his hand over the noncom's mouth. "Come on, Sarge, snap out of it. We gotta move."

Shawn called Alberto closer and told him to help the sergeant. Taking the lead, Shawn led the way down the ravine in a low crouch. Unable to feel his frozen feet or see in the darkness, he stumbled and fell on the cutting rocks and hard frozen ground again and again. Each time he got up and kept moving. Halfway down the hill, he heard voices. Someone was coming in his direction. Lifting his rifle, he kept walking. He knew if they stopped again, none of them would be able to move.

The three-man Chinese recon element chattered at what they thought was their comrades from the hilltop. Shawn's M-1 cracked in reply. Shawn had waited until he was only four feet away before pulling the trigger. The first soldier was flung back and knocked down the second man. The third soldier raised his submachine gun and fired a short burst before Shawn's bayonet glanced off his ribs and sunk into his arm. Screaming in pain, the Chinese soldier clawed his attacker, but Shawn withdrew his pistol and shot the man in the face. Spinning around in a rage, Shawn fired point-blank at the second soldier, who had been knocked down and was getting up again. The stocky Chinese was lifted off the ground and knocked back three feet. Shawn replaced the pistol in his belt and yanked the rifle free from the other body.

Alberto had been hit in the stomach and was down, clawing the frozen ground. He was beyond help, stitched from the crotch to the shoulder, but

Shawn wasn't going to leave him. He had bent over to pick him up when the young soldier grabbed the American in a vice-like grip. Coughing up blood, Alberto tried to speak, then abruptly became limp and released his hold.

Shawn stood up wearily and turned around. He pulled Quail to his feet and began walking down the hill again. The sergeant swayed in the darkness and cussed. "Goddamn you. You should have left me."

Shawn kept walking and spoke through clenched teeth. "I'm not dying here, and neither are you."

Shawn didn't stop, although they had reached the valley floor. His eyes were set straight ahead. Every step required all his effort and concentration. His neck was so stiff he couldn't move his head for fear of passing out.

A voice in the darkness suddenly barked, "Halt! Who goes there?"

Shawn painfully turned toward the sound with rifle ready. "Private Flynn and one other from Old Baldy."

A soldier rose up from a foxhole. "What unit you from, Mac?"

Shawn's head was reeling. His eyes wouldn't focus and he couldn't remember the unit's name. His weapon fell from his hands as he spoke in a faint whisper. "We're . . . the expendables."

He sunk to his knees and fell forward into the blackness.

2

WILLIAMSBURG, VIRGINIA, 9 AUGUST 1953

Seven-year-old Blake Alexander slipped his swimming trunks on and tossed a robe over his shoulder. Stepping over the erector set and turning off the new RCA television, he walked out of his room into the large hallway. His bare feet sank into the blues, whites, umbers, and burgundies of the oriental carpet as he walked past a gallery of portraits of his ancestors. His friends called this hallway "Alexander walk." The first portrait was of Seth Alexander, who had been a founding father of Williamsburg, Virginia, and had built one of the first houses there. Now it was one of the homes thousands of tourists visited daily to see how the people of one of the earliest American settlements lived. Seth had also begun to amass the Alexander fortune in tobacco. The next portrait was of Joshua Alexander, who had made his mark as a state representative. The next, Robert Alexander, had proven economically farsighted when he expanded the farm lands to include cotton fields and founded the first Alexander textile mill. Grandfather William Alexander's likeness was the next to last portrait. He had built the family home and had commissioned the paintings. William had been a good state senator but a poor businessman. Had it not been for his son David, he would have lost the family-owned textile plants.

Blake stopped at the last portrait and looked up at the likeness of his father. The artist had captured the look of determination in his gun-metal-gray eyes. David Alexander had extended the textile business into overseas markets and had formed four subsidiary companies, all of which were prospering.

"You wonderin' if there's room for *your* picture?"

Blake turned around with an impish smile. He'd been caught staring at the paintings by the family chauffeur, Hank Matthews. Hank was a retired sergeant who was married to his mother's older sister. Jobs had been scarce when he got out of the Army, and his mother had wanted to do right by her kin. Hank was the only person in the house to remain unimpressed with the Alexander heritage.

Blake motioned to the huge Chinese vase next to his father's portrait. "I don't think they'll move that to put my picture up. What can I do that the rest of them haven't already done?"

Hank took the ever-present Camel cigarette from his lips, letting the ashes fall to the thick carpet. "Don't worry none about it. You're a little young to be thinkin' of how to be makin' money."

Mrs. Harrington, the upstairs maid, stepped out of the guest bedroom. "Hank Matthews! I thought I heard yo' voice. Git out of here rat now. Go downstairs where yo' belong an' stay out of Mr. Alexander's liquor cabinet."

Hank rolled his eyes. "Aw, shut up, Dory. I was just up here lookin' for the boy."

Dorothy Harrington almost fainted away when she noticed Hank's ashes on her rug. She stormed toward the old driver. "Git out of here with that foul cigarette! Stay downstairs where yo' belong!"

Hank winked at the boy and hurried to the ornate staircase to escape the wrath of the rotund woman. Blake joined the craggy-faced man on the stairs. On the second landing, against the wall, was a glass case filled with trophies won by various Alexanders. Resting on shelves covered with green satin were assorted first-place silver cups and bowls for sailing, tennis, equestrian, and swimming competitions.

Blake pointed at the center shelf, which was lighted. "Dad had Dory clear that spot for me, when I win a trophy. One of these days, you'll see my name in there."

Hank grunted without looking at the huge cabinet. He didn't like the boy's father putting on pressure so soon.

"Dad says I have to do my part," Blake reflected. "Maybe I'll finally win my first swimming in the open meet they're holding next weekend at the club."

Hank puffed his cigarette. "Seems like you got a lotta 'have to's' for a young pup. Winnin' and losin' is games older folks play."

Blake looked up with sparkling eyes. "It doesn't matter. I'm gonna do it. You'll see."

Dana Alexander watched her son from the sun porch as he swam laps under the direction of a hired personal coach. Blake was her secondborn and in many ways was very much like her. It made her feel guilty. His older sister Stefne was more like her father. She had the highest grades in her class, while poor Blake struggled just to pass. Stefne and her father saw life in black and white. Things were more important to them than people, and they valued thought more than experience. They both would rather read about France than visit, or hear a review of a film than see it. They preferred the facts and numbers in life to the color and smell of the flowers.

The coach was getting impatient. Dana sighed. Blake was *too* much like her, in that he found so much in the world to see, hear, touch, and feel. By nature he was a dreamer, wanderer, and adventurer. And he was a sensitive boy, who, unlike his father, still snuggled against her every night before going to bed. Fortunately, the Alexander trait of taking oneself too seriously had not yet affected him. David rode him terribly, however, and had already begun giving him history lessons about the family. He would soon be made to understand his place in the scene of things, as well as what was expected of him in the future.

Blake surfaced and climbed out of the pool. The swimming coach shook his head. "You're not concentrating. Keep your head down and get the rhythm. Stroke twice and lift your head just enough to take a breath. Your head is coming way too far up. Get back in the pool and give me six more laps."

Blake flicked water on his older sister, who was lying by the pool sunning herself. "Sis, ya wanna see me belly flop?"

Annoyed, Stefne rose up to her elbows and frowned. "You'd better listen to Mr. Dale, or you won't even place in the country club meet."

The coach barked, "Blake! In the pool! We've got work to do!"

Dana Alexander had seen enough. She waved at the coach for his attention. "Thanks, that'll be enough for the day." She put a towel over her son's bony shoulders and patted his back affectionately. "I think it's time you just had some fun. When Mr. Dale leaves, you can do whatever you want for the rest of the afternoon."

Blake broke into a huge smile, but it quickly evaporated. "What about the swim meet? Dad expects me to—"

Dana waved her hand as if it were not a problem. "Don't worry about your father. He won't even be here next week. He'll be in London at a business meeting. I'm canceling your lessons for the rest of the week. Just enjoy the summer vacation while you can and don't worry about competing."

Blake let out a whoop and ran for the pool.

David Alexander sat at the head of the long table wearing a white linen suit with matching silk tie. Blake could not understand why his father never seemed to sweat. Blake was wearing a dirty T-shirt with cutoff sleeves and Bermuda shorts. He'd had to run to supper from the fish pond, where he'd been trying to catch tadpoles for his aquarium.

David looked up from his green salad and glanced at his son, who was seated to his right. "What happened to your dinner clothes? I might have brought guests."

Blake shrugged. "I didn't have time to change. Sorry, sir."

David's cheeks flushed. He could tell the boy wasn't sorry at all. "How did the swimming lessons go?"

"Fine," said Blake, hoping the conversation was over.

"And the riding lesson? How did that go?" his father asked curtly.

Blake's eyes nervously shifted toward the other end of the table, looking for support from his mother.

Dana patted the corner of her lips with her embroidered napkin. "I canceled the riding lesson today. He's had enough coaching for a while. He's had a schedule to meet ever since he got out of school and it's time he had the opportunity to have some fun."

David's gray eyes were icy. "It's *not* your decision to cancel his lessons. Tomorrow the schedule *will* be followed." His angry eyes shifted to Blake. "Do you understand, young man?"

Blake lowered his head. "Yes, sir."

Dana began to speak, but her husband raised a hand in a warning. "The conversation has ended."

CUSSETA, GEORGIA, 7 SEPTEMBER 1953

Lee Calhoon strained with the weight of two buckets of water as he made his way to the hog pen. He poured the water into the trough and opened the rusty door of the old Buick, which rested on rotting logs nearby. The stripped car was used for feed storage. He scooped one bucket full of corn and fed it to the spotted hogs. Then he headed for the chicken pen.

The sun was just peeking its orange head over the pine trees as he walked back toward the house with eight eggs in one of the buckets. He pumped water to wash off his bare feet and filled the kitchen bucket, which he carried up the steps into the house.

Connie Calhoon smiled at her eight-year-old son as she poured the water into a basin by the sink. "That ol' rooster give ya any trouble this time?"

Lee lifted the bucket of eggs. "Naw, I got me a stick like ya told me."

Connie placed a plate with two fried eggs, grits, a biscuit, and a slab of smoked bacon on the table. She poured coffee into a stained mug and put the tin pot back on the wood stove. "You growin' like a weed, son. Ya daddy be proud, seein' ya do all the chores an' takin' sech good care of us."

Lee blushed as he piled egg on the biscuit. "Taint nothin'. When's Daddy comin' home?"

Connie wiped her hands on her apron. "Next month, when the mill shuts down for the season. You best hurry."

Lee picked up his shoes from the porch, tied the laces together, and tossed them over his shoulder. He carried his schoolbooks in an old army pack on his back. The bus stop was a mile down the red dirt road. He broke into a slow run, throwing rocks at the coon dogs to keep them from following.

Miss Margaret Johnson tapped her desk with a ruler, and her fourteen third-graders folded their hands on their desks and sat erect. She smiled at a young boy with pale blue eyes, sitting on the aisle. "Lee, would you please lead us in the Pledge of Allegiance?"

The sandy-haired boy rose from his chair and waited until the other students stood and faced the small flag in the corner of the room. He placed his hand over his heart. "I pledge allegiance . . . "

Miss Johnson wished she had more time with him than the five hours of the school day. Lee Calhoon was a smart boy, but based on what she had seen, the chances were he would never complete his education. He was one of many in the school that fate had been especially unkind to. What really broke her heart about Lee was his desire. Unlike most of the others in class, he desperately wanted to learn and better himself. For a boy who had never been out of the county, who had never read a paper or a magazine, schoolbooks were wondrous. He would ask a hundred questions and devour the words, pictures, and ideas.

He always wore secondhand overalls and a mended flannel shirt buttoned to the neck. His light hair was long and greased back with bacon fat, but neatly combed. His shoes were too big, but he was obviously proud of them, for he constantly wiped them clean.

Poverty affected Lee Calhoon in less obvious ways, as well. On the second day of school, his teacher had passed out a questionnaire to the students. Lee's paper had revealed a boy who was living twenty years in the past. The only television he had ever seen was the one in school. His house had no electricity, phone, or indoor plumbing. The oldest of three children, he labored during the summer from dawn to sunset, chopping cotton and tobacco in the fields or working in the family garden. Fall was harvest time, and he was one of seven children who had to be released early from class so that he could help in the fields.

A visit to the boy's house the week before had proven the most appalling experience of her life. His father worked in a distant textile mill for the summer, leaving the boy's mother and three children alone and with no other transportation than a sway-backed mule. Connie Calhoon was a frail woman who couldn't read or write, but she tried hard to care for her two "babies." Still, her two-year-old boy was sickly-looking. The four-year-old girl wore Lee's hand-me-down clothes. The house was clean, but small and cluttered with stacked mason jars full of green beans, squash, corn, cucumbers, and everything else cannable from the huge garden that obviously sustained them during winter. The Calhoons' only real asset was the ten-acre plot of soil-poor land, covered by scraggly pine trees, on which their home stood.

Miss Johnson nodded with approval at Lee when he finished the pledge, then she raised an eyebrow toward the small girl in the front row. "Cindy, would you please lead us in the Lord's prayer?"

Lee sat alone on the steps of the schoolhouse reading, while his classmates played on the grassy field. Miss Johnson sat down beside him. "You didn't miss any questions on the math test today. I'm proud of you."

Lee nodded with an embarrassed smile and motioned toward the book she had loaned to him. "Is that Mississippi River Tom Sawyer lives on really that big?"

Margaret smiled. "Yes, it's huge. Are some of the words difficult for you?"

The boy grinned proudly. "I write the big ones down and look 'em up in the dictionary, like you taught us. I learned what a trib-u-tary was today."

Miss Johnson made a mental note to bring in her paperback dictionary and give it to him. "I'm glad you're enjoying the story. You should be very proud of yourself. Most can't read at the level you're at. I'll give you *Huckleberry Finn* next."

The boy's face brightened. "When I learn them hard words, I'm gonna read the story to my sister and mama. They like good stories. I read 'em the Hardy Boys books ya gave me."

The teacher put her arm around his slender shoulders and gave him a gentle hug. She hadn't been sure how long she could bring herself to teach in such squalid conditions, but the boy's beaming face made it all worthwhile. Lee Calhoon might be poor and backward, but he was learning. A whole wonderful world lay before him in pages and pictures. One day, with her help, he would be able to step out into that other world and escape the poverty of Cusseta, Georgia.

CARLISLE, PENNSYLVANIA, VETERANS DAY, 10 NOVEMBER 1953

Eugene Day watched his father shave, wishing he was old enough to smell like his dad, to slap on some of that sweet-smelling water. Old Spice was his favorite.

James Day set down his Gillette safety razor and dabbed some shaving cream on his son's nose. "Boy, you looks like a chocolate dessert. Your sisters is gonna eat you up."

Eugene wiped the white foam from his nose and placed it on his brown chin. "Now I'm like you, Daddy."

James laughed and tossed his towel into the clothes hamper. "Come on. It's a big day today."

The boy followed his father into the bedroom where an old uniform was laid out on the bed. His dad had read in the paper that they were having a Veterans Day ceremony in the town square, and all veterans were invited to attend. Today James Day was going to show the white folks that he had been a soldier and had served his country proudly. He was the janitor at the high school, so most folks thought of him just as a gimp-legged colored man with no education. The staff-sergeant stripes and Purple Heart,

Bronze Star, and Combat Infantryman's Badge would show them differently.

Eugene watched as his father ran his fingers reverently over the badge embossed with the image of a small rifle. "Daddy, how come you never put that suit on before?"

James Day sat down on the bed and looked at the picture of himself on the dresser. The picture was taken in 1944, after he joined the Negro Regiment in North Carolina. "Son, the war is somethin' I wanted to forget. I lost my toes and lots of friends in Italy. I reckon it's time I paid my respects to those friends. I don't want to forget them anymore. The war was horrible, but some of the memories are the best I have. Them friends of mine that didn't come back need somebody to remember. White folks need to know we colored folks were there, too. Sometimes they forget."

Eugene thought about what his mother had said when his father told her what he was going to do. "Daddy, Mama says the preacher told her you shouldn't go."

James's face tightened. "The preacher didn't go to the war." Slipping on his "Ike" jacket, too tight after all these years, James tried to button the blouse but couldn't. "I guess your daddy has been eatin' too much of your mama's cookin'."

The boy smiled with pride. "You look handsome, Daddy."

James walked down the narrow stairway and placed his old overseas cap on his head.

Jewel Day watched her husband from the small living room and turned her back to him to hide her tears. James ignored her and opened the door as Eugene quickly put on his coat and followed his father.

Jewel peered out the window and saw her son walking beside her husband. She immediately ran to the door and yelled at him, "Get back here this minute, Eugene Day!"

James placed his hand on the boy's small shoulder. "He's going with me."

Jewel stepped back out of the cold. "What's wrong, Mommy?"

Jewel looked at her twelve-year-old daughter and lowered her head, speaking softly. "Our men are going to make fools of themselves."

James Day straightened his back and tried not to limp as he walked down the sidewalk past the row houses toward Hanover Street. Once they had passed Pitt Street, they were no longer in Colored Town. This was the part of the community where Eugene wasn't allowed to play. The invisible boundary line between white and colored people was as real as a painted stripe. Eugene didn't understand the arrangement as a younger boy, but later, when he started school, he had discovered he was "different." White folks didn't mind colored people as long as they stayed in their own part of town, but here, in the white neighborhood, things were altogether different.

Eugene pulled up his collar to block out the cold wind as they approached the square. During a school outing, they had visited the historical site of Carlisle and had to read all the historical markers. The square was in the center of town where the two main thoroughfares crossed. On each of the four corners of the intersection, respectively, sat the Carlisle Court House, Cumberland County Court House, St. John's Episcopal Church—built in 1752, and the oldest public building in town—and the First Presbyterian Church, founded in 1734. George Washington had even worshiped in the old graystone building. The ceremony was going to be conducted in front of old Carlisle Court House, where a small park was located. The high school band was playing march music from the blocked-off street, and a platform covered in red, white, and blue banners was constructed in front of the courthouse.

James nodded to several people, refusing to acknowledge their stares as he led his son toward the rows of folding chairs facing the speaker's platform. A sign, reading "For Veterans," pointed toward the rows of empty chairs. James held his head up proudly as he looked around at the hundreds of people gathered around the band.

"We'll sit right here."

Eugene knelt up on his seat to get a better view of the conductor waving his arms in front of the green-and-white-uniformed band members. He pointed at a group of men wearing blue and gold hats shaped like his father's.

"Who are they, Daddy?"

James turned in his seat. "Those are members of the Veterans of Foreign Wars. They're like me, son. They was in the war."

The band concluded its song and the VFW members began filing in behind the chairs. American Legion veterans appeared from down the street and also began marching toward their seats. Many stared with narrowed eyes at Eugene and his father. Eugene quickly snuggled closer to his father, who was watching the color guard approach with the American flag. Eugene wished there was at least one other colored man in the crowd.

A man approached the microphone and said, "Ladies and gentlemen, please stand for the posting of the colors."

James stood and came to attention, and when the band began playing the National Anthem, he brought up his hand in a rigid salute. Eugene, touched by his father's pride, imitated his salute.

The song concluded, and Eugene saw tears roll down his father's cheeks. The boy took his dad's hand and squeezed it tightly as they sat down. The master of ceremonies began speaking again, but a tall man wearing a suit and a blue and gold cap walked up to his father and blocked his view. The man leaned down and spoke in a whisper. Eugene leaned closer to hear.

"Excuse me, but these seats are reserved for the post."

James looked behind him. "How about those seats?"

The man leaned closer. "Look, don't make a show, huh? Just move to the back. All these seats are taken."

James stared into the man's eyes. "I served same as you. I have a right to be here."

The tall man's lips tightened and he spoke coldly. "Don't make this a scene, or you'll regret it. Just move to the back. Negroes aren't allowed in these seats."

James got up slowly and straightened his back. He raised his head with pride, and taking hold of his son's hand, walked to the back. But he didn't stop there. He kept walking. He didn't say a word until he crossed Pitt Street, and only then did he take off his cap, which he dropped into the gutter. He looked at his son and spoke, trying not to cry. "Don't tell your mama."

Eugene stood outside in the hallway, watching through the open door as his dad folded up the uniform and placed it in the bottom drawer of the dresser.

Jewel came up beside her son and put her arm over his shoulder. "Come on, honey. Your daddy wants to be alone awhile."

Eugene looked up at his mother. His eyes were filled with pain. "Why, Mama? Why did they do that to him?"

Jewel Day lowered her head. "They don't understand, honey. One day they will. Come on. I made some hot chocolate for you."

Eugene turned around and walked for the steps. "I'll be back in just a minute. I need to get Daddy's hat. He dropped it."

PHILADELPHIA, 14 NOVEMBER

Vincent Martino strode out through the classroom door, keeping his eyes on the back of Franco Rossi. Vincent waited until the boy walked across the rough asphalt surface of the playground before making his move. Quickening his stride, he grabbed Franco's arm and spun him around. Franco immediately threw up an arm to protect his face, but Vincent's punch was aimed at the boy's stomach and doubled him over. Vincent pushed the gagging nine-year-old out of his way and strutted toward the chain-link fence.

Tony Alvedo lowered his head as his friend approached and whispered, "You're in trouble, man. Whitman seen it."

Vincent sighed in resignation. Mr. Whitman was headed directly toward

him. He paused only long enough to help Franco to his feet before marching directly up to Vincent. "You have a reason, Martino?" he demanded
coldly.

Vincent returned the glare. "Yeah, I got a reason. That punk was talkin'
trash 'bout my sister. He talks, he pays."

Whitman's stare softened. "Franco's brother is going to come looking
for you. You know that, don't you?"

Vincent smirked. "I'm lookin' for him too."

Whitman shook his head. Vendettas were always carried out. In South
Philly, that was as sure as the Bill of Rights. Local neighborhoods were
made up primarily of first- and second-generation Italian-Americans, to
whom honor was the most important virtue. Vinny Martino had done what
his father had probably told him to do. Now Franco's older brother,
Alberto, would have to regain his own family's pride by roughing up
Vincent. For boys like Vinny Martino, pride was all they had.

Whitman sighed and turned around in silence to go back to the elevated
platform known as the "watch tower." There would be more fights, and
his job was to break them up and try to resolve the problems rationally;
but the hard-core cases, like Martino, were beyond reasoning.

Tony slapped Vincent's hand as he assumed his spot against the chain-
link fence. "Ya did it, man."

Vincent stuffed his cold hands into his jacket pockets and glanced over
the paved playground with detachment. "I just wish Rita was worth it. She
been actin' like some nigger whore, man."

Tony nodded in sympathy. It was common knowledge among all the
kids that Vinny's older sister was sleeping with a senior who had his own
car, but if Vinny's pop found out, he'd kill her. So Vinny had to pretend
to be outraged and defend her honor anyway, just to convince him the
gossip wasn't true.

Tony spat over his shoulder. "Ya want me to maybe go wit' ya after
school?"

Vincent knew Tony would ask. He was a real friend. That was good to
know. But it was better to get it over with as quickly as possible and settle
the matter. "Thanks, Tony, but I gotta go over to the market for my mom."

Tony nodded, keeping his eyes on the watch tower. "Yeah."

"Yo, Vinny, my brother says you hit him wit' a lucky punch."

Vincent had seen the bigger boy leaning against the wall of the flower
store, waiting for him.

Vincent stopped one pace in front of the thirteen-year-old, who seemed
to tower over him. "Yeah, I hit him . . . an' I been lookin' for you too."

Alberto Rossi smiled. "I'm here, ya punk."

All day in school Vincent had thought about what he would do at this
moment, but now he couldn't remember a single move. He shrugged his

shoulders and suddenly lashed out with his foot, striking the taller boy just below the shin. Alberto's leg buckled with the blow and he fell to his knee. Vincent threw his forearm into the boy's face, going for the nose. The padded jacket cushioned the impact, but still jerked Alberto's head back.

Vincent hesitated from striking him again, when he saw the kid's nose begin to bleed, and he realized too late that he had made a mistake. Alberto shook his head in rage and swung wildly, glancing a blow off Vincent's forehead that knocked him to the sidewalk. Next, a fist hit him above his right eye and slammed his head against the cement. Dizzy from the blow, Vincent kicked upward, catching Alberto between the legs and doubling him over in pain. Pushing himself off the cold pavement, Vincent repeated the forearm smash into the groaning boy's face, knocking him back onto the sidewalk. Without hesitating this time, he jumped onto the writhing thirteen-year-old and drove his knees into Alberto's stomach.

"That's enough!" barked Antonio Grasso, pulling Vincent off his vomiting opponent. Grasso, the owner of the small flower store, shoved Vincent back against his store wall and knelt over Alberto. Shaking his head, he stood and pulled the boy to his feet. Supporting him around the waist, Grasso glared at Vincent and motioned with his head. "Get outta here. You no-good kids is bad for business."

With the back of his hand Vincent wiped the blood from the cut above his eye. He snickered. "Alberto, ya don't be talkin' bad about my sister again. Capish?"

Vincent walked up one flight of stairs and down the hall to the third apartment. Opening the door, he saw his father lying on the worn sofa, asleep. His mother was still at work at the beauty shop. Sighing in relief, he crossed the small room to the hallway and went into the room he shared with his brother, Billy.

Rita was sitting on the floor reading a story to Billy. She gave Vincent a faint smile that evaporated as soon as she noticed his swollen eye. Her large brown eyes widened. "The Rossis?"

Vincent ignored her and knelt down by his brother. "Come on, Billy. We gonna go see Uncle Geno."

Rita lifted her hand to touch her brother's face, but Vincent brushed her hand away. "Lea' me alone."

Rita's nostrils flared. "Shut your face! You need that cut cleaned." She held his chin up and looked at the gash. "You're too young to be fighting. Everybody wants to fight. Fight, fight, fight, that's all everybody does. Come to the bathroom, and I'll clean it with peroxide."

Vincent wasn't going to move, but she grabbed the front of his jacket in a surprisingly strong grip and lifted him to his feet before he could protest. "My brother, Vinny Martino, the big fighter, the big deal. He'd fight anybody for his sister's honor. You're a fool Vinny . . . but, I love ya."

Vincent gave his sister a small smile. Rita was a beautiful girl who always spoke from the heart and didn't care what other people thought, which was why she was always in trouble with Mom. Despite her stubbornness, she had always adored him, and became his protector when Pop would drink a little too much and try and slap him around. Rita meant it when she said she loved him. He gave her a gentle hug and let her lead him to the bathroom to attend to his face.

1960

3

FORT CARSON, COLORADO, 1 JULY 1960

The staff car door opened and a master sergeant seated by the driver stepped out onto the sidewalk. The soldier's starched khaki trousers were bloused over black glistening jump boots that reflected the glare of the late afternoon sun. Adjusting the green beret on his head and rotating back his broad shoulders, the master sergeant strode for the door of the post headquarters.

The private first class inside stood up from his desk with a pleasant smile. "Can I help you, Master Sergeant?"

The sergeant flopped down in a chair beside the desk. "Tell Sam his buddy Taco is here."

The private knocked and entered the adjacent office. Ten seconds later Sergeant Major Sam Partridge burst out of his office with the PFC following. He was tall and rangy, with cropped blond hair. The sergeant major pointed at the master sergeant with a sneer. "Jenkins, the next time you see that sonofabitch walk into my headquarters, shoot his big ass before he makes it to the door! I *ain't* his fuckin' *buddy!* The lousy bastard is here to steal my people!"

The paratrooper rose from his chair with a warm smile and extended his hand. "Good to see you too, Sam."

The sergeant major broke into a grin and warmly shook the sergeant's hand. "Goddamn, you look good, Taco . . . ya sorry sonofabitch!"

Private First Class Jenkins made a wide detour around the two senior NCOs, knowing to cancel the rest of the sergeant major's appointments. It was war-story time, as it always was when Partridge's old war buddies stopped by. From the look of the ribbons Quail wore, he must have seen plenty of action. Quail's top ribbon was the DSC. A Distinguished Service Cross was lower only to the "Medal" itself—the Medal of Honor. Quail had definitely seen some shit.

Quail leaned forward in his chair. ". . . and the kid says 'the expendables,' and then passes out cold. I swore that night that one day I'd take care of that kid. He saved my ass. The DSC should have went to him instead of the Silver Star they gave him. I wrote him up for the Medal, but the lousy division fat asses downgraded it. We served six months together with the Seventh Division on the front line before I joined you guys for that last year."

Sam Partridge grinned. "Ya didn't have to tell me his fuckin' life story. You told me the same shit back in Korea. I know you're going to ask for him and probably twenty other of my best NCOs."

Quail raised an eyebrow. "Only ten of your best, plus Flynn."

Partridge sighed but kept his smile. "Shit, Taco, I know you get your pick, and there's nothing I can do about it, so let's cut the bullshit. How many you headhuntin' for altogether?"

Quail leaned back in his chair. "The group needs to put seven A-teams together. With your eleven men, that should do it this recruiting trip. I got the rest I needed from other posts. The big brass is still treatin' us like ugly stepchildren, but we have a few friends in high places who still pull a few strings."

Partridge chuckled. "Yeah, I'll say. The old man heard you were comin' for bodies and tried to fight it, but he got a back-channel message that said shut the fuck up and give you whatever you need. Christ, I hope I can get back to Group once I leave here. I've enjoyed the job but I miss jumping . . . and the pay."

Quail looked at the post sergeant major with sarcasm. "You fuck up, they kick up. You're one of the big shots now. There's not much left after playing God of a post. You'll probably be assigned to the Pentagon next, with the rest of the dying elephants."

Partridge threw a pencil at him. *"Thanks a'fuckin' lot, asshole!* You better pray I ain't never sent there and get ta make some decisions on careers. 'Cause if I do, your ass will be on the way to bum-fuck Egypt!"

Quail laughed and stood up. "Come on, God, how's about buying me a beer. I need to find me some strange."

Partridge patted his fatigue pockets. "Fuck you and your 'strange.' I don't have any money. Plus ain't no 'strange' women in the club gonna screw around with vets from Korea. They know our peckers froze off years ago."

Master Sergeant Quail lowered his beer and put his arm around the attractive woman sitting beside him. "Martha, when I told that no-good husband of yours I was lookin' for wild women, I sure as hell didn't think he'd call you."

Martha Partridge looked across the small table and gave her husband an accusing glare. "He remembered this time. I told him if he went to the club, he calls me or he doesn't go. There's too many divorced krauts in here lookin' for second husbands. I didn't want him gettin' any ideas."

Quail glanced toward the bar, where a middle-aged blonde was giving him the eye. He looked back at his friend's wife. "Martha, Sam deserves a good woman like you . . . but, uh . . . you sure are messin' up my strange hunt. Ya think you could lug Sam out to the dance floor for some belly rubbin' and give me a chance to meet some of them kraut women you're talkin' about?"

Martha frowned and took her husband's hand, pulling him to his feet. "Come on, Sammy, let's show these kids how to belly rub."

The sergeant major rose grudgingly and saw a familiar soldier enter the club door. Partridge tapped Quail's shoulder and motioned toward the buck sergeant. "Looks like you got some business to attend to. There's Flynn, but I don't think you're gonna convince him to jump out of airplanes and eat snakes. He's in love. I'll bet ya a six-pack he says 'shove it.' "

Quail was still in shock. He hadn't seen the "kid" since Korea, and had envisioned a slightly older version of the thin soldier he had known. The man Partridge pointed out was most definitely *no* kid. Sergeant Shawn Flynn had gained forty pounds of muscle and looked like a halfback for the Green Bay Packers. The ruddy cheeks were the same, but his face, like his body, had filled out and hardened. He had the look of a professional written all over him. He could have easily been a model for a recruiting poster, with his muscular body, crew cut, and square jaw.

The master sergeant stood without taking his eyes off Flynn, who had walked up to the blonde at the bar. "You're on. I bet he volunteers."

Shawn patted Gretchen's leg. "You ready to go?"

A menacing voice boomed out behind him, "Get your hands off my woman!"

Shawn spun around, ready to swing, and looked into strangely familiar eyes. The face had weathered, but the laughing, piercing brown eyes were still the same.

Quail hugged the startled soldier, lifting his 180 pounds easily off the floor. Shawn returned the embrace, thrilled to see the old bastard was still in the service. When he had been recovering in the hospital after the attack on Old Baldy, John Quail had personally pinned the Combat Infantryman's Badge on his hospital gown. Weeks later he and Quail were discharged from the hospital and served six months together on the front lines, struggling to stay alive, before Quail had moved up in rank and out to another unit. That had been the last time he had seen his friend.

Quail bellowed to the bartender, "Two cold beers for two frozen vets . . . and whatever the lady is drinkin'."

Shawn thumped the older NCO's chest. "God, you look good, Taco . . . and a damn snake eater at that. It's hard to believe . . . damn, I'm sorry. This is my fiancée, Gretchen."

Quail took her hand with a smile, though he knew the glances that she had been throwing him earlier were from no woman who thought she was about to be married. "Nice to meetcha, Gretchen. Shawn and me are a couple of the frozen chosen who gave guided tours of a hill called Ol' Baldy and a couple more I've forgotten the names of. Your fiancé saved my life, and I love him for it. And so do a thousand women coast to coast."

Gretchen smiled and squeezed his hand a little too warmly. "Et es a pleasure, Sergeant."

Quail recognized the German accent, and couldn't help but think about what Martha had said.

Shawn picked up one of the beer mugs the bartender had just set down and handed the mug to Quail. "Bullshit. John is the one who saved me. I was a green replacement, new in-country, and didn't know up from down."

Quail eyed the young sergeant from his flat-top haircut to his shined boots and let out a grunt. "Damn, if you didn't fill out. That Chinese bullet in the neck must have had grow food in it. Jesus, if you don't look like S.F. material. It just so happens we need some weak minds and strong backs. You wanna join us?"

Gretchen leaned closer. "Vas es dis S.F.?"

Shawn laughed and picked up the other mug of beer. "He's talkin' about Special Forces, honey. They do too much traveling for my blood. We need to stay in one place and raise some kids."

Quail noted the discomfort in the woman's eyes when Shawn had said "kids," and hated himself for what he was about to do. It was going to be easy for all the wrong reasons.

Quail lifted his mug. "A toast to us. You said it in 'fifty-three, and it fits us perfect. To the expendables."

Shawn smiled; he had not thought of the word in years. He lifted his mug. "To the expendables."

Quail sat down beside Sam Partridge and stuck his hand out. "Pay up!"

The sergeant major's eyes narrowed. "You didn't?"

Quail smiled faintly. "Yeah, I did. You owe me one six-pack, and another for doubtin' my abilities as a gen-u-ine recruiter of the green beanies. He's goin'."

Partridge seemed stunned. "How? How in the hell did you do it? I would have bet a month's pay he wouldn't leave that woman of his."

Quail smirked. "I told Gretchen about the extra jump pay and TDY trips he'd be makin' . . . and the money he could expect to stash away. I also mentioned the fact that Fort Bragg had the swingingest NCO club this side of the Atlantic. *She* joined him up. They're gonna get married there."

Martha leaned forward with an accusing glare. "You should be ashamed of yourself, John. That woman is after one thing, and you know it. She'll collect her alimony check as soon as she's tired of him, and be out lookin' for another sucker."

Quail's smile dissolved into a serious frown. "I *am* ashamed, but I need him. We need him. She'd do the same thing here just as well as she'll do it at Bragg. I can take care of him there and make sure the fall ain't that bad. He's good people."

Partridge caught the serious implications of the "we need him," and spoke quietly. "You think we're in for some trouble, Taco?"

Quail stared grimly at his beer mug. "I left Southeast Asia six months ago. If there's any place spoiling for a knockdown drag-out, that's it. It's turning bad, Sam . . . real bad."

WILLIAMSBURG, VIRGINIA, 4 JULY 1960

Blake Alexander wiped the sweat from his brow with the back of his hand and gripped the racket tightly. Robby Hancock tossed the ball high and smashed it in a shattering serve. Blake could only block the white blur as it skipped up at him off the clay court. Then the ball sailed over the net in an easy setup that Robby attacked ruthlessly in an overhead smash to the corner of court for a put-away.

The court judge, seated in an elevated chair at the edge of the net, announced in a monotone, "Advantage, Mr. Hancock. Match point."

Blake glanced toward the audience and saw his mother nod her head in support. He winked, ignoring his father's look of displeasure.

Positioning himself a little farther back from the serving line, he readied himself. Rob would hit the ball to his backhand, as he had done the entire game.

Rob served another bullet, but Blake had anticipated the placement and hopped to his left to use his forehand. Meeting the ball with a powerful stroke, he hit a passing shot down the line.

Robby lunged toward the ball and managed to hit a weak return backhand that sailed toward the center of the court. Blake was already at the net, and swung at the ball as it crossed the net for the easy put-away. As soon as he hit the ball he knew he had blown the shot. He was looking at where he was going to place the shot instead of the ball, and put too much force into his stroke.

The line judge barked, *"Out!"*

Blake extended his hand toward Rob as the judge rose up from his chair and spoke over the applause, "Match, Mr. Hancock."

Blake shook the older boy's hand, then went to get his racket cover and a cup of water.

Dana walked up beside her son and gave him a gentle hug. "You were wonderful, honey. You made him work for it."

Blake smiled, elated over his playing. Robby Hancock was sixteen, two years older, and was playing in the junior circuit.

An announcer's voice boomed over the loudspeakers, "Ladies and gentlemen, the annual Chesapeake Country Club awards ceremony will be conducted at three o'clock on the clubhouse lawn. Everyone is invited. Thank you."

Dana glanced at her watch. "You'd better hurry and take your shower. You don't want to miss receiving your silver cup."

David Alexander strode up behind his wife with a scowl. "Forget it. You know the rules. Alexanders don't take second-place trophies."

Dana spun around. "What are you talking about? Blake played his heart out. Robby Hancock plays number-one for Edison, and Blake played him magnificently."

David brushed past his wife, heading for the clubhouse. "He lost. *First* is all that counts."

Blake had ignored the discussion and zipped the protective case around his racket. He had known he would not be able to accept the trophy. Over the years, he had come in second or third in almost every sporting event he attempted. He was good, but never quite good enough. The first-place trophy for the Alexander case still eluded him. Today he had been lucky to get as far as he did. He had played just for fun. Surprisingly, he had played the best tennis of his life.

Dana glared at her husband's back as Blake put his arm around her shoulder. "Forget it, Mom, it's not important. I'm gonna have Hank drive me to the house."

Dana patted her son's hand. He was as tall as she was. During the game, she hadn't been able to get over how much he had grown and filled out the past year. He had truly been a pleasure to watch, for he was so graceful, yet powerful. His grit and determination on every shot had won the crowd over after the first few points. She had noticed how the girls in the crowd especially had cheered for him. Her son had become a strikingly handsome boy, whose strong square jaw and dark hair made him seem older than his fourteen years. She gazed into his brown eyes and didn't see her little boy. He was becoming a man. "I'll go with you."

Blake smiled, exposing gleaming white teeth. "Naw, Mom, you have to mingle. The Alexanders must be sociable, remember?"

Dana couldn't help but return his happy-go-lucky grin. It was common knowledge that David was going to run for the State Senate next year, and he had constantly reminded her to be as nice as possible to their old country club cronies. They represented campaign contributions. Dana gently pushed her son toward the sprawling clubhouse. "Hit the showers, Ace."

Hank opened the car door with a smile. "I saw ya play, Ace. Ya done real good."

A compliment from Hank was a rarity and really meant something. Blake patted the old man's back. "Thanks. Next time I'll do better."

Fifteen minutes later the Mercedes pulled into the long drive of the

estate. Hank stopped the car at the steps of the front door of the huge
house, and Blake hopped out so that Hank wouldn't have to open his door.
"I guess you'd better go back and wait for Dad and Mom."

Hank rolled down his window. "I was proud of you today, Ace. You
deserved that trophy."

Blake shrugged his shoulders. "You know the Alexander rules."

The grizzled retired sergeant shook his head and pulled away, but Blake
heard him mumble, "Fuck da rules."

His sister was standing in the sun-room door. She hollered toward the
pool, where a young woman was sunning herself. "I'll see you this evening.
I've got to drop by the landing and pick up the *Witch*."

Blake leaned against the doorframe behind her. "You can't sail her by
yourself."

Startled by his voice, Stefne spun around. "You scared the pee out me!
Don't do that." She composed herself then, and said, "And yes, I can sail
her by myself."

Blake sighed. "Sis, you can't get her out of the harbor, and you know
it. You want me to help you?"

She gave her brother a guilty smile. "Julian is going to help me. Don't
you dare tell Mother."

His mother disapproved of Julian, a sophomore, but Blake went along
with his sister in this instance, as he suspected his mother's feelings came
from some sort of anti-Semitism, even though she tried to hide it.

Stefne walked up and surprised him by giving him a light kiss on the
cheek. "Thanks. How'd you do?"

"Second place, but I at least went three sets with him."

The dark-haired girl nodded in sympathy. "Next year, then." She picked
up her purse and quickly made for the door.

Blake found a pitcher of sun tea in the refrigerator. He took a long drink,
then strolled into the sun room. Just outside the large, mullioned windows
Sally O'Donnel was rising from her lounge chair. The top of her bathing
suit had been pulled down to her stomach so that she could tan her back.
Her breasts were large and firm, just like the pictures in the magazines
Hank hid in the garage.

As Sally reached for a bottle of lotion, she saw the handsome young man
watching her from the sun room. She laughed aloud and seductively placed
one breast at a time into its cup. Looking back toward him, she called out,
"Don't just stand there watching! Come out here and put some lotion on
my back."

Blake stood frozen to the floor, embarrassed and aroused at the same
time. Sally lived just down the road, and he had known her all his life. She
was a sophomore and his sister's best friend, although he had overheard
his mother warning his sister about spending too much time with the girl.
Word had gotten around that Sally was as wild as a march hare, after she

had been picked up drunk by the local police on the beach one night during a wild party.

Blake gathered his strength and pushed open the door. Sally smiled coyly, noticing that his tennis shorts were bulging. She lowered her top again and lay down on the lounge chair. "Rub some lotion on my back, please."

Blake's hands shook as he poured a spot onto his palm, and shivers ran up his back as he touched her soft, warm, brown skin. He felt himself sweating as he spread the cream lightly over her shoulders. He was about to take his hands away when she moaned. "God, that feels good. Rub it in lower . . . and do the backs of my legs too."

Blake obeyed, and she began purring like a cat. Her thighs seemed twice as soft as her calves. She spread her legs, allowing his hands to explore all the way up to the edge of her bathing suit. She raised her buttocks as he stroked her inner thigh with the warm lotion, and she began to tremble. Suddenly she turned over and said huskily, "Now the front."

By now, Blake was past his embarrassment. He wanted more than anything to touch her white breasts. He poured lotion directly from the bottle onto her pink nipples and gently began to stroke her white mounds. Sally writhed with pleasure and reached for his shorts. "Come closer so I can put some lotion on you—no don't stop. Keep touching me. Lower . . . lower . . . yes, there."

Blake worriedly looked around the pool as she unzipped his shorts. "This is dangerous."

She gave him a sly smile. "It's better when its dangerous."

Blake began pumping faster, but Sally dug her fingernails into his bare buttocks. "Slow. Take it slow and make it last."

Blake bit his lip trying to regain control. She had been in charge since she had taken off his tennis shorts at the pool. They had moved to the upstairs hallway floor and lain on the ornate oriental carpet. From the hallway they had a view out of the large cut-glass window and could see if anybody drove up the driveway. To Blake, it was sort of like all the other lessons he had taken in his life, but a hundred times better. She had been coaching him through every step, and had him doing things to her he wouldn't have guessed would be satisfying to a woman.

Sally began grinding against him harder and she gasped for breath. "Now. Now. Now, oooooh, *now!*"

Blake felt her tense and shiver spasmodically beneath him, then suddenly go limp. She took in a deep breath and felt him push deeper. She smiled impishly. "You're wearing me out."

Blake's expression changed to one of concern. "I'm sorry."

She chuckled and leaned forward to kiss him. "Don't be sorry. That's a compliment."

Blake touched her nipple. He was still fascinated by its pink softness. "Have you done this a lot?"

Shuddering at his touch, she shut her eyes. "This is only my second time, but I read a lot. Lie on your back. It's my turn to be on top."

Minutes later Blake strained upward and felt himself explode as she furiously slapped her body against him. She opened her mouth, gave a sudden yelp, and shuddered, then collapsed onto his chest. They lay motionless for a full minute before she spoke.

"I can't move. Oh shit, my knees. You've ruined me, Blake."

He opened his eyes and stroked her perspiring back. "What'd I do?"

She giggled as she wiggled on his chest. "I'm going to have to wear slacks for a month. My knees are rug burned."

Hank Matthews knocked on Blake's bedroom door.

Blake was lying on the couch, watching television. "Come in!" he called.

Hank stepped inside and tossed a pair of tennis shorts to the bed. "I picked those up from the pool. Thought you might want them before someone asked embarrassing questions."

Blake turned beet red. Hank gave him a wink. "Maybe somebody gives trophies for it."

Blake finally took a breath. "I . . . I just jumped in the pool when I got home and—"

Jake nodded with a knowing smile. "That's what I thought. And you took off your jock too and went in buck naked." Hank took the jockstrap from behind his back and tossed it toward the young man. "Get some sleep. I think ya need it."

Hank closed the boy's door behind him. It was bound to happen sooner or later. In a day or so he would have to have a little talk with Blake about protecting himself—in more ways than one. His father had hired coaches to teach him everything but what he would most need to know: how to be a man.

CUSSETA, GEORGIA, 15 AUGUST

Lee Calhoon slowly raised his rifle and took aim. The buck raised its head and turned toward the three does. The buck's huge black eyes caught a motion to his right, and he began to bolt. A shot rang out.

Roy Calhoon stood up in the shooting pit with a smile. "Ya got him."

Lee hopped out of the pit and pulled his knife. He hated killing animals, but ever since his dad had been laid off, he had had no choice. He had killed at least one deer a week for the past year, and still it turned his stomach to see their lifeless eyes. He quickened his stride. He wanted to get the chore over quickly and to get off government property. If they were caught poaching out of season, they could get in a lot of trouble.

Lee cut the animal's throat and tied a rope around its back legs. Roy glanced around at the trees and motioned toward a distant pine. "Ya can hang 'em yonder."

Lee began dragging the carcass. He knew better than to throw the body over his shoulder, because of the ticks. Deer were covered with them this time of year.

Roy grabbed the rope and helped pull. He was proud of his eldest son. With his good shooting, the boy was providing both meat and extra spending money for the family. "I reckon this un 'ill go a little over ninety pounds dressed."

"Yup, he's a heavy un," Lee said, appreciating his father's help. His dad had come home early from Columbus, as there wasn't much work. The mill had fallen on bad times and had laid half the workers off almost a year before. His father had since been able to get only a few part-time jobs, which didn't come close to paying all of the bills.

Lee threw the rope over a low-hanging branch and with his father's help pulled the deer off the ground. In minutes the carcass was skinned and gutted. Lee heaved it over his shoulder.

Roy wiped sweat from his forehead as he walked alongside his son toward the old pickup. "I think we oughta check your turkey line on the way home. Haskell says he'll pay eight dollars a bird."

Lee, fighting off fatigue, only nodded. The turkey line had been his idea. School was going to start, and he wanted time to study, but he wouldn't be able to if he had to do the chores and hunt in the late afternoons. Turkey, unlike deer, were no problem to sell out of season, and he could make enough money to get his family by until his dad found a job.

The pickup was still some distance off, and the carcass was feeling heavier with every step. Lee clenched his teeth and set his eyes to the front. Just a little farther.

Lee held his breath as he topped the crest, praying his idea had worked. Roy, a step ahead, shook his head in amazement. "I'll be damned."

Lee had been spreading corn for several days in the draw where a flock of turkeys roosted. Earlier that morning he had staked a trout line along the ground and placed soaked corn on the fishing hooks. He had hoped the turkeys would eat the corn and catch the hooks in their throats. He saw ahead four of the large birds lying on the ground and sighed in relief. The turkey line was cruel, and if caught, he would go to jail, but he had no choice. Government unemployment checks were too small. He needed extra money to keep the family together.

Mrs. Swinton was sitting on the porch with Connie Calhoon when the pickup pulled up to the house. Lee hopped out with a big smile. Mrs. Margaret Swinton, his third-grade teacher, had become a close friend of the family over the years. She had married a soldier from Fort Benning, changing her name from Johnson. She had been gone for the summer to visit her husband's relatives and get settled in her new home. Before her marriage, she had come by the house weekly to visit and had always brought books along for Lee. "Afternoon, Mrs. Swinton."

"Hello yourself, Lee. My goodness if you don't look like you've grown a foot." Margaret smiled warmly. She couldn't believe how much he had grown over the summer. He still wore overalls, but he seemed at least three inches taller and was finally filling out. He put her in mind of a young Abe Lincoln, with his extravagant height, long nose, and insatiable appetite for learning.

"Nice ta see you, Margaret," Roy said, walking up the steps and taking a glass of water from his wife. "Ya got the smile of a hitched woman. I guess your soldier boy is doin' right by ya."

Margaret nodded with a smile. "He's coming by to pick me up in a few minutes, and you can meet him for yourself." Her eyes shifted to Lee. "I brought you some books by C. S. Forrester. It's the Hornblower series. You're going to really enjoy them."

Lee beamed.

The uniformed soldier got out of the car and strode straight for the house. Lee sat in the shade of the porch, mesmerized by the approaching stranger. The week before, Lee had had an old buck in his sights, but one somehow different from any he'd seen before. Its eyes were like black marbles, and he walked with such authority and confidence that Lee couldn't find it within himself to pull the trigger. The buck had an air about it that had caused a tingle to run up Lee's spine. As soon as the soldier stepped out of the car and began walking, that same tingle had run up Lee's back. The man had that same confident air about him. He stood up ramrod straight and held his head high, as if he owned the world. Like the old buck, this man was special.

Lee felt the soldier's strength when he shook his hand. He couldn't remember if he had even spoken as he sat on the porch steps looking at the man's uniform. From the conversation among the grown-ups, he found out that the three stripes up and two down meant he was a sergeant first class. The reason he was wearing shiny boots was because he was a paratrooper and taught Airborne Training on the post.

When Lee finally took his eyes off the sergeant, he realized what he wanted more than anything in the world. One day he wanted to walk with an air of confidence just like that soldier's. He wanted to be one of the special ones.

CARLISLE, PENNSYLVANIA, 1 SEPTEMBER

Eugene Day pushed back the glasses on his nose with one hand and dribbled the basketball with the other. He hated his new glasses. They made him look too thin. But at least the headaches had gone away, and he had been shooting hoops better. Pivoting around, he faked right and stepped back for a jump shot. The ball swished through the net without touching the rim.

James Day leaned on his dust mop and clapped his hands. The sound mingled with the echo of the bouncing ball in the empty gym. "You hittin' them every time."

Eugene picked up the scuffed basketball and walked over to his father. Every weekday evening, he helped his dad to sweep the classrooms and empty the trash cans. When it came time to clean the locker rooms, however, his dad insisted that Eugene practice and get the feel of the high school court.

James limped to the mop closet and put up his cleaning equipment. "You gonna make the junior varsity for sure. The practice is tellin' on you."

Eugene smiled. His father was right. He was always the first one chosen in the park pickup games. Being selected by his peers meant he was the best player, and knowing that always made him play harder. If he would grow taller and gain more weight, he would have a shot at making the varsity team the following year.

James picked up his lunch pail and put his arm around his son. "You gonna make me and your mama proud watching you play this year. Keep your grades up, though, or you'll be just another dumb colored boy."

Eugene was used to the warning and patted his father's back. "I'm doin' good, Dad, don't worry. I'll hit the books soon as I get home."

James locked the side door and looked at his son. "It's time you started on your homework earlier and not help me. You can do it here, then get in some practice. That way you'll have less to do when ya get home."

Eugene pushed the glasses back up on his nose. The bifocals had cost his family a part of their savings, and his father had to work at a second job to make ends meet. As soon as they returned home and had dinner, his father would walk to the mill where he worked as a night watchman. Eugene shook his head and headed toward the old Chevy. "I like working with you, and I have plenty of time to get my homework done. I'd never see you if I didn't help."

James smiled to himself. He couldn't imagine a better son than Eugene.

James pulled the car into a parking spot in front of the food store and gave his son a five-dollar bill. "Your mama needs some flour and baking soda."

Eugene glanced at the storefront then back to his father. The food store was located in the white part of town and they would stare at him like he was from outer space. "Not here, Dad."

James sighed. "I know, but our store is closed and Mama needs to bake a cake to deliver to the church tomorrow. Terrance Phillips died, and the church is taking food over to the family."

Eugene took the money. He didn't want his father to have to go in. "Be back in a minute."

Quickly finding the items, he walked up to the checkout stand. A large, red-faced woman behind the cash register lifted her tired eyes. "You're out of your neighborhood, aren't you?"

Eugene stiffened, but nodded his head. "Yes, ma'am."

The woman waved at the assistant manager, who was talking to a customer. "Bobby, do we let his kind shop here?"

Eugene shook with rage and embarrassment. Three customers, including the one the assistant manager had been talking to, turned and stared. He began to turn around and leave the store when the manager stepped closer, speaking to him.

"I'm very sorry she said that." He scowled at the cashier. "Don't you *ever* say anything like that again or you're gone. This young man is a customer. Give him a twenty percent discount to make up for your lack of courtesy."

Eugene nodded in thanks toward the young manager, but returned his stare to the woman. A minute later he opened the car door, waking his father, who was lying back in the seat.

James backed up and in minutes was crossing Pitt Street. He glanced at his son. "You're awfully quiet. Something wrong?"

Eugene forced a smile. "I was just thinking about making the team." Eugene didn't like lying to his dad, but telling him what had happened would serve no purpose. The woman had had the exact same look of the man years ago who had told his father to get up from the front chairs at the Veterans Day ceremony. It was as if she were seeing something repulsive. He had been called names at school, and many of the students wouldn't talk to him, but few ever looked at him that way.

His hands were still shaking with anger. He closed his eyes and made up his mind. He wasn't going to let anyone talk to him that way again. The manager had been nice enough, but he couldn't expect whites to protect him from other whites for the rest of his life. Tonight he had only been a fraction away from confronting the woman and asking for an apology. She would never have given it, but at least she would have known that her words had hurt him.

Eugene pushed the glasses back on his nose. He felt better. The time had come to make a stand. His father had tried to do the same thing by wearing an old uniform. Now it was his turn.

PHILADELPHIA, 4 SEPTEMBER

Vincent Martino led four of his friends to the concession gate. A ruddy-faced guard stepped up to block their path. "Where you think you're goin'?"

Vincent pulled the pass from his pocket. "We're 'ere for da jobs."

The guard studied the pass with a frown and handed it back. "You just gonna cause trouble. You know the colored got it sewed up tight."

Vincent brushed past the guard. "Not anymore."

A second guard, in a brand new uniform, approached as the boys passed through the gate. "What was that all about?"

The ruddy-faced man pursed his lips. "Local kids hawk the concessions at the ball games. They show up early and get in line at the concession office in a first-come, first-ones-get-the-jobs arrangement. At least that's the way it's supposed to work. This year the coloreds have taken over and been keepin' the whites out."

"What's that piece of paper you looked at?" the new guard asked.

"That's a pass signed by their school principal that says the boys are fourteen or younger. The job program is for the youth in the neighborhoods. Them eye-ties showing up means trouble. We best keep an eye out."

Tony nudged his companion. "Here they come."

Vincent pushed off the office door as the group of Negro boys approached. He spoke softly to his four friends, "Hold your ground."

A tall Negro youth wearing a knit cap stepped forward. "You wops on our turf, man. We the hawkers for the game."

Vincent stared coldly into the Negro's eyes. "We're inna line first. We ain't gonna move."

The tall boy spat at Vincent's shoes. "You muthafuckers done fucked up, man. We gonna have ta teach you fuckin' wops a lesson."

Vincent smiled and stepped closer to the taller youth. "You talkin' big, man. Bet you ain't so tough wit' out your friends backin' ya up. How about you and me settlin' da matter by ourselves? I win, we stay. You win, we're gone."

"Fuck you!" the black youth blurted. He didn't like the confidence the stocky Italian was showing.

Tony Alveda held his hands out to the surly group of blacks. "Yo, if we rumble, the cops are gonna come an' none of us are gonna work. Dem going one on one is the only way ta make it, man."

A young man stepped out of the group pointing his finger at Tony. "You fuckers be takin' our jobs, man!"

Another youth elbowed his way to the front and held up his hands. "The man is right. If we go ta knuckles, the cops will come and none 'a us is gonna work." The Negro's eyes shifted to Tony, then locked on Vincent. "But . . . the wop fights *me.*" Vincent kept his smile despite the boy's size. He was his height, but outweighed with twenty pounds of muscle.

Tony worriedly looked at his friend. "Vinny, you still sure, paisan?"

Vincent sized up his opponent with a sidelong glance. "We need lookouts."

Two outposts were stationed, and the fighters moved behind the concession-office trailer. Tyrone Washington took off his jacket and began bouncing around like Sugar Ray Robinson. Vincent calmly tossed his jacket to Tony.

"Come on, wop," Tyrone said, holding up his fists like a trained boxer.

Vincent stepped forward with his hands at his sides. Tyrone bobbed and lashed out with a right jab. Vincent stepped back, avoiding the punch, and quickly shifted his weight to the right, then left, ducking and slipping a series of combination punches. Tyrone lost patience and stepped in, throwing a roundhouse right. Vincent had been waiting for the opening. He blocked the swing with his left arm and came straight up with his right fist in a jolting uppercut. Tyrone never saw it coming.

The tall black in the knit cap cringed at the blow. It was over for Tyrone before he hit the ground. If they had been wearing gloves, he might have gotten up, but with fists, he never had the chance.

Vincent took his jacket from Tony and whispered with a smile, "Another nigger down. Be humble, man. Real humble."

Tony placed the strap around his neck and lifted his tray. *"Hey yo, soft drinks here . . . fifty cents!"* He looked at Vincent with a grin. "How'd I sound?"

Vincent smirked. "Dumb. Real dumb." He walked up and gently slapped his friend's face. "Ya didn't listen ta me. I tol' ya to sell the pennants, not the drinks. Ya don't listen to me, Tony—the drinks are heavy, dummy."

Tony shrugged his narrow shoulders. "Aw, Vinny, I was thirsty, man. I just came ta see the game anyway, man." Looking around to make sure it was safe, he lowered his voice. "Ya busted that nigger good, paisan. When he came out like he knew what he was doin', I got worried. Ya set him up just right."

Vincent raised his swollen hand. "If 'at spade hadn't gone down, it woulda been over for me. The nigger's jaw was a brick. My hand hurts bad."

Tony shrugged, showing no sympathy. "It was your idea, man. Next week the Eagles play here again. Don't be lookin' at me to fight then. Them guys are gonna come back ready next time."

Vincent picked up his bundle of pennants. "I know."

———————

Vincent got off the bus and waved farewell to his friends. The neighborhood smells were a welcome relief after selling the stinking hot dogs during the second half of the game. The job had made him cigarette money and increased the size of his wardrobe. He had found two pairs of gloves, a wool scarf, a thermos, and a stadium blanket left behind by fans. It had been a good haul but a lousy game. The Eagles lost by two touchdowns.

As Vincent passed by a soft pretzel stand and a fruit vendor, his stomach growled. He was in desperate need of a South Philly hoagie smothered in olive oil.

Gina Cantelli caught her breath at the sight of the good-looking boy approaching her father's hoagie stand, and she quickly brushed back her raven-black hair. Vinny Martino lived only a block from her house and they had known each other all their lives. He had grown into a handsome boy, but needed someone to settle him down. He was barely passing in school, and he got into constant trouble because of his fighting.

Gina ran her tongue over her lips to wet them before speaking. "Hi, Vinny. You want the usual?"

Vincent nodded without looking at the attractive girl. "Yo, lot a oil, huh?"

"Vinny, my brother says you could make the boxing team. I could help you with your schoolwork if you want?"

Vincent's eyes slowly lifted to the radiant young woman. "I been doin' all right."

Gina arched an eyebrow. "I'll feed you too."

"How about feedin' me now, huh? I'm hungry."

Gina's face tightened. "You're goofy. Ya can't talk nice, I don't give you nothin'."

Vincent's jaw dropped in surprise. "Who you callin' goofy?"

Gina leaned over the table. "You, that's who! Goofy, goofy, goofy!"

Vincent waved his hand at her as if shooing off a pest and began walking down the sidewalk. He took three strides before looking over his shoulder. "Hey, yo, smart mouth! I'll come by your house at seven, a'right?"

Gina tossed down her apron. "Sure, goof, you come by." Her glare softened and she gave him a bright smile. "Like I said, I'll feed you, Vinny."

Vincent winked. He turned and strode halfway down the block before smiling. He could tell she liked him.

1964

4

WILLIAMSBURG, VIRGINIA, 4 JULY 1964

Priscilla Edwards leaned back in the lounge chair. Her sorority sisters would die with envy when she told them about her weekend.

Stefne Alexander sat up, noticing how the attractive blonde was staring at her brother. "So, you just happened to be in town, huh?"

Priscilla broke her stare from Blake Alexander, who was talking on the outdoor phone. "Heavens, no. My folks and I sailed down yesterday and I happened to see Blake on his boat. Lucky for me I did, because our yacht's small outboard had just broken its propeller. Blake towed us to the docks. I don't think Dad could have managed the harbor under sail."

Stefne eyed the girl with suspicion. "Where are your folks now?"

Priscilla took a sip of her iced tea. "They're in town visiting friends for the Fourth of July weekend. I'm lucky Blake rescued me from them by inviting me over, or I surely would have died of boredom. . . . I just love your home, Stef. It's beautiful. I just wish I could have met your parents. Blake talked about them at school all the time."

Stefne squirted Sea and Ski suntan lotion on her stomach. "Did you date Blake at school? You seem to know each other so well."

Priscilla hid a smile. She knew more about Blake, in some ways, than his sister would ever know. "Blake and I went out a few times just before the semester ended. I just love him. Everybody on campus does."

Stefne smiled. Of course, Priscilla meant that the girls loved him. She had to admit that Blake was handsome, but he was also a spoiled playboy, with no real substance. He hadn't read a paper, magazine, or watched the news since coming home for the summer from the University of Virginia. Her brother seemed oblivious to the real world. He cared only about where the next summer party would be held. His high school grades had been terrible, and her father had pulled powerful strings to get him accepted at UVA. College had not changed his study habits. Blake had barely passed his freshman year, though the courses he had taken were the easiest he could find. As usual, he had failed to apply himself, concentrating on the school's party life instead. His only accomplishments were learning to sky dive and, down in the Bahamas during spring break, to scuba dive. He knew more about every fraternity president at UVA than he did about Barry Goldwater or Lyndon Johnson, who were running for the presidency of the United States. Knowing her brother, if it wasn't cute, wearing a skirt, willing to screw on the first date, dangerous, or fun, he wasn't interested. Blake was smart, a natural leader, but in school he would do only enough work to get by. She had seen a few just like him at William and Mary, where she was attending college.

Stefne leaned back in her lounge chair and adjusted her sunglasses. "Yes, he's always been fun-loving . . . too much so. He doesn't seem to want to grow up."

Priscilla didn't like the other girl's tone of voice, but what else could she expect from a Willy and Mary coed?

Forcing herself to be pleasant, she smiled. "Blake tells me you're a political science major. Are you going to run for office like your daddy?"

Stefne brushed an imaginary fly away from her face. "Daddy lost the election. I'm going to apply for a State Department job. How about you? What's your major?

Priscilla responded after sipping her drink. "I tried art, but it was boring, so last semester I changed to fashion design."

"That's nice," Stefne said, rolling her eyes behind her glasses.

The conversation was obviously over, so Priscilla turned her attention to her host. She thought Blake looked like an aristocratic version of Elvis Presley. His deep-set, sexy brown eyes and sensuous smile were just like those of the rock and roll idol, but his deeply tanned body was even better. At just under six feet tall, Blake had broad shoulders, a narrow waist, and perfectly round, tight buttocks. His legs, like his arms, were muscular and well-defined, like those of a sleek racehorse. Everything about him was first-class, from the clothes he wore, to the red Corvette he drove, to the hotels where he had made love to her.

He put down the phone and clapped his hands. "Pris, it's all set up. Let's drive to the club and pick up the boat. We'll sail over to Tommy's for the party."

The young woman bubbled with excitement. "Really! Oh, this is going to be so much fun!"

Stefne rose from her chair and lifted her glasses so that her brother could see her glaring at him. "Just because Mom and Dad are in Europe doesn't mean you can run off wherever you want. I don't want you drinking if you're going to take the *Witch.*"

Blake laughed as he pulled on a pair of white cotton slacks. "Okay, little mother. I won't drink a drop."

Stefne maintained her stare. "You promise?"

Blake licked his fingertips and raised his hand. "Promise."

His sister couldn't help but smile. "Damn you, Ace. You be careful."

Blake tapped the steering wheel to the beat of the music on the radio and accelerated the red Corvette up to seventy miles an hour. Priscilla rocked her shoulders and sang along with James Brown, "I feel good! Dada da . . ."

She leaned closer to him and ran her hand over his stomach. "I feel like being bad."

Blake went to put his arm around her, but just then, as they reached the crest of a small hill, he saw a semi trailer truck up ahead. The truck's brake lights suddenly lit up, gray smoke billowing from its rear tires as the driver tried to stop. A car had stalled trying to cross the intersection only a quarter-mile ahead, and he was headed directly for it. The truck's fully loaded trailer began fishtailing like a flag in a breeze and struck the rear fender of a blue Ford sedan coming in the opposite direction. The surprised driver of the sedan jerked the steering wheel to his left to keep from running off the road. That put him directly into the path of the braking Corvette.

Blake tried to avoid the onrushing car by steering hard left, but it was too late. Priscilla had only time enough to let out half a scream before the Ford, going fifty miles an hour, plowed into the right front of the skidding Corvette.

During his eight years in the Virginia Highway Patrol, Officer James Osborne had seen plenty of carnage, but he had to admit that this wreck was particularly nasty. The officer with him, a rookie, had never seen anything like it. Osborne didn't blame him for throwing up. The young woman passenger in the Corvette had been almost torn in half at the waist, and her head had been grotesquely flattened on one side. The driver of the Ford had been partially thrown through the front windshield and had lost his face to the shattered safety glass. He had bled to death from gashes on his neck. The crushed front of the Ford was covered in his coagulated blood.

Officer Osborne walked upwind to get away from the smell of blood and ruptured intestines that still lingered in the air around the twisted wreckage. He approached the ambulance driver, who was shutting the back doors of his vehicle. Inside was the only survivor of the crash. "Here's the boy's billfold. He's a somebody, so take good care of him. His daddy is David Alexander, the guy who ran for Senate a few years back. I'll call ahead for you and let 'em know."

The blood-smeared driver took the billfold without speaking and ran to the cab.

As the ambulance sped off, Osborne looked at the plastic card in his hand. He had kept the boy's ID. He would need it when he filled out the paperwork. It was too bad. The kid had been a good-looking young man. Maybe his father's money could make him look like the picture again, though Osborne doubted it. He doubted there was enough money in the world for that.

CUSSETA, GEORGIA

Exhausted, and soaking with sweat, Lee Calhoon lowered his axe and stepped back from the tree. Dizzy, he sank to his knees to rest. The humid, 100-degree heat had gotten to him again. He was on a rise just above the swamp, so that sticky air stagnated beneath the thick forest canopy and made it feel like a sauna.

Lee lowered his head. Either he had to slow down or he would pass out long before chopping down the old oak. He would have to adjust his work schedule during the hot days and only cut down four trees an afternoon instead of six.

Wincing from the soreness in his shoulders, Lee closed his eyes to rest and find the inner strength to continue working. Since graduating from high school, a month before, he had lost ten pounds. The backbreaking schedule of working in the fields during the mornings and chopping down trees in the afternoons had taken its toll on his body, but he had no choice. If he wanted to fulfill his dream, he could not begin feeling sorry for himself now. He was too close.

A sudden breeze rustled the leaves in the canopy above, and Lee sighed in relief as it caressed his face.

Over the years, the forest had given up its wealth to help his family through rough times, and had given him a chance for a new life. It had given up its deer and turkey to pay the family bills until his dad went back to work at the mill, and now it was giving up its hardwood trees to pay for Lee's college education. The townspeople of Columbus had been buying all the firewood he could cut, haul, and stack. He had to help out at home with some of the money, but he had been able to save half. If he could keep to his schedule, he would make enough to start school in the fall.

Lee grasped the axe with determination. He started to rise, but an ominous noise sent chills running up his spine and froze him in place. He couldn't see the snake, but by the sound of the rattling tail, he knew it was close and big.

Trying to control his shaking, Lee moved his eyes to the limit of their corners and almost gasped aloud. He couldn't see the snake's head, but saw a portion of the huge coiled body. It was an Eastern diamondback, at least five inches thick.

The huge, deadly snake was three feet to his right rear, with nothing in its way to obstruct its strike. Based on its size, the head would be as big as an open fist and would hold enough venom to kill a horse.

Lee couldn't help but feel justice was about to be served. He had killed a five-foot rattler only two days before and had nailed its skin to the chicken coop door. He had felt guilty about killing the old snake, which probably had seen as many years as his father, but there hadn't been much choice. The rattler had decided to make the chicken coop his home and had killed two hens. Now, the ol' boy's bigger relative was about to get even.

Lee tried to concentrate on his options. If he fell forward and tried to roll away, the snake would strike as soon as he moved. With its reach, the reptile would hit him easily in the back of the legs or buttocks. Maybe if he pitched over to his left and . . . no, it would still get him. Damn! He couldn't go forward, to the side, or back, and he sure couldn't fly.

Lee felt the smooth wooden axe handle in his hands and knew there was only one option left, and it wasn't a good one.

He slowly slid his hand down the handle to where he could swing powerfully and quickly with one hand. The only chance he had was to swing the axe and spring to his feet at the same time. The snake would strike at his sudden movement. If he was real lucky, the broad axehead would block or at least deflect the snake's attack long enough for him to get away.

The rattling tail sounded like marbles in a cracker can. Lee tightened his grip on the handle and took a breath.

Praying for luck, he swung the axe and sprang to his feet. A blur shot past the axehead as he jumped back. He felt as if he had been hit by a fast-pitched baseball just above his left ankle. He stumbled backward, but to his horror, hit the tree trunk he had been chopping.

Seemingly in slow motion, the thick, seven-foot snake recoiled like a steel spring and immediately lunged at him. Lee closed his eyes, waiting for the pain, but instead of his leg, the snake struck the axehead with such force it knocked the handle from Lee's hands.

Again the snake recoiled and struck. Lee was hit in the back of his leg as he ran down the rise. He pitched forward, then rolled to his feet and stumbled down the rise to the edge of the swamp, where he fell against a pine tree. Shaking and out of breath, he waited for the first effects of the venom. He knew he was going to die, and this was just as good a place to do it as any. There was no use in trying to make it back to the road. He would begin convulsing before he made it fifty yards.

In the distance the huge snake slithered over the axe, heading up the hill. Lee slid down the tree trunk and sat on the ground, wondering how long it was going to take. Where the snake first hit him there were two round, wet spots on his faded jeans. Trembling, he pulled back his jean bottoms, exposing his heavy workboots. Clear liquid was dripping down his boot from the two puncture marks in the leather. He quickly unlaced his boot and held his breath before pulling down his sock. He let out a sigh of relief. There were no puncture wounds. The combination of jean material and thick leather had saved him. A rush of hope flooded through him as he realized he had been moving his left leg without pain. The last strike had hit him in the back of his left calf. Praying, he pulled the jean leg up farther and checked for fang marks. Nothing. *Nothing! Not a scratch! Thank you God, thank you!*

Lee slapped the ground and sprang to feet, feeling wonderfully light and powerful. Suddenly his eyes narrowed and he looked up the hill. Now it was his turn.

He jogged to the top of the rise and bent over to pick up his axe. He immediately saw why the strike had not penetrated the back of his leg. Both two-inch fangs were hanging from the side of metal axehead, attached by blood, venom, and skin tissue. The bastard had knocked his own teeth out.

Lee found the snake a minute later. It was trying to hide under a fallen small tree, but its fat, curled body was extending out on both sides. Lee poked the coiled snake with the axe handle to get it to expose its head. Obliging slowly, the reptile unwound and made its way to find better concealment. Lee readied his axe and stepped in to finish it off, but he changed his mind at the last second. He struck the earth only inches from the reptile's huge head.

As the old snake slithered away, Lee whispered after him, "We're even, ol'-timer."

CARLISLE, PENNSYLVANIA

Regina Davis leaned back on the park bench and guiltily shifted her gaze to the young man crossing the street toward her. She had first noticed him on the basketball court when Carlisle played her school in Harrisburg that winter. He had been painfully thin then too. At only five feet, nine inches, he had also been the shortest man on his team. Bespeckled, awkward-looking, he had not impressed her as someone who could play, but his looks had been deceiving. On the basketball court Eugene Day was a star. Something magic and wonderful happened when he played. He had been so fast and so filled with determination that he had ruled the court. His outside shooting and quick passes had devastated her school's team. He was far from handsome, but his fiery eyes set him apart from any other boy she knew. She had told her father about him, and within two days Eugene had been recruited for the cause. Her father had realized that, because he was a well-known ball player, people would listen to him. Now she felt guilty because people *did* listen and he was becoming a leader. Because of her, the young man approaching her would probably get hurt. He was becoming *too* well known.

Eugene smiled as he came up to her. "Is everything set up?"

Regina lowered her eyes. "Yes, but there's going to be trouble. Somehow the word leaked out and a group is already there to stop us. Daddy told me to tell you he would understand if you wanted to wait."

Eugene motioned toward his slacks. "I've got my bathing suit on underneath. I'm ready for a dip."

Regina rose slowly and stared into his eyes. "I don't want you to go. It's dangerous. Wait, Eugene. We'll do it later, when they aren't ready for us."

Eugene's smile vanished. "Let's go. Your father is waiting."

Minutes later Regina started up her white Chevy Corvair and pulled away from the curb. Her passenger stared blankly out of the window. She had known she couldn't stop him. He was different from the others. He was driven by something much deeper than the desire for civil rights. It was something very personal to him. The others had been upset hearing about the killings in the South and of Martin Luther's arrest in St. Augustine. Not Eugene. He had taken the news without emotion. His views were known by everyone in the chapter. The majority of the association's effort was aimed at the South, but he didn't think that the chapter should worry about those so far away when there were segregation problems here at home. Carlisle was one of the oldest towns in the state, and a protest here would receive statewide attention. It might even make Governor Scranton take action. Regina's father, Reverend Willis Davis, had agreed. The swimming pool at Carlisle's community park would be the start. It, like most of the restaurants, barber shops, grocery stores, and public gathering places in town, was segregated. To Eugene, a swimming pool on the Fourth of July was the perfect place to begin.

Regina turned toward the park. "Eugene, please don't do this. For me, don't do it."

Eugene slipped off his shoes and unbuckled his slacks. "This is for my father, not you."

Reverend Willis Davis, standing before eighteen chapter members, held his hands skyward in prayer. Two local newspaper photographers moved closer to get pictures of him and the screaming whites in the background.

Eugene strode directly for the angry mob that blocked the entrance to the swimming pool. The first few people standing in his path moved, still yelling, to the side, but three large, young men stood firm, blocking the chain-link fence gate.

Reverend Davis moved forward. The chapter members followed. Davis put his hand on Eugene's shoulder and spoke with authority over all the noise. "This boy has the right to enter. Stand back or be in violation of the law of this nation and our beloved God."

The young man in the middle, who was wearing a white T-shirt with a cigarette pack rolled into a sleeve, spit into the reverend's face. *"Get out of here, preacher! This is our pool!"*

Davis wiped the spittle from his cheek and stepped closer. "Yea, as I walk through the valley of death I will fear no evil . . ."

The three youths backed up a step, letting Eugene pass, but quickly blocked the others. One youth snickered to the big-chested young man wearing the white T-shirt. "He's yours, Tim."

Just as Eugene stepped through the gate, Timothy Huggins turned around and slugged him in the back of the head. The screaming crowd of whites became instantly silent while the chapter members shrieked in horror.

With tears streaming down her face, Regina broke through the crowd to the fence. "Don't hurt him!" she screamed. "God, please don't hurt him!"

Eugene had been knocked to the cement by the blow, and scraped his knees, hands, and chin. Bleeding from the abrasions, he picked up his glasses and got to his feet. He put on his glasses and started again toward the pool.

"Nigger, I'm warning you, don't go any closer!" Timothy barked. *"Stop, goddamnit!"* He ran forward, grabbed Eugene's arm and spun him around. "You're not going in! Get back with the rest of them."

Eugene spoke softly. "I have the right."

"Right, *hell!"* The bigger youth slugged Eugene in the stomach and shoved him toward the gate. *"Get out!"* Gagging, but keeping his feet, Eugene painfully pushed off the fence and began walking for the pool again. Reverend Davis and his daughter pleaded for him to come back, while the chapter members screamed and pleaded for mercy from the attacker.

Timothy blocked Eugene's path and pushed him back, but Eugene only stepped to the side a few paces with the shove and once again headed for the pool. Timothy shoved him back once more, yelling, "I'm warning you! I'm not telling you again, nigger!"

Eugene kept his eyes focused on the pool, ignoring the pleading, the crying, and most of all, the warnings. He had to reach the pool.

Timothy waited until the Negro was a step away before swinging with all his might. The resounding pop was barely heard over the gasps and screams as the youth was knocked backward off his feet.

Eugene felt as if his jaw had caved in and been shoved up to his nose. The horrific throbbing in his head and the pain in his face combined to make him feel sick and disoriented. He sucked in air through his numb mouth, but choked on blood and began to gag. His stomach jerked in spasms, and he thought his intestines would come up each time he threw up more bloody bile.

Timothy, cradling his injured hand, felt faint. The Negro's jaw had felt like a concrete wall. The pain in his hand and wrist was almost unbearable. He started for the gate, trying not to show his discomfort, but the Negro had already rolled over onto his stomach and was trying to get up.

Eugene made it to his hands and knees and grabbed the fence. Regina cried out to him and reached through the mesh toward his face. Ignoring her touch, he grabbed higher and pulled himself erect. Turning around, he began a wobbling walk toward the pool.

Timothy looked to his friends for help but none would look back. Everyone had their eyes on the Negro as he struggled to keep his balance with each step.

Eugene stopped at the edge of the water and put his hands out to steady himself as he sat down. He slid in slowly, savoring the cool feeling, and began to wade out deeper. He stopped when the water had reached his waist, and he turned toward the staring crowd. He had practiced what he wanted to say, but couldn't. His tongue and jaw wouldn't respond. It didn't matter. His tears spoke for him.

SOUTHWEST PHILADELPHIA

"Yo, Vinny. How ya doin'?"

Vincent Martino nodded casually to the approaching young man who was dressed identically to himself. Sleeveless T-shirt, black slacks, white socks, and black stiletto-toed shoes. It was the dress of almost all the young Italian men in the neighborhood. Vincent took the cigarette from behind his ear. "Gimme a light."

Tony Alvedo leaned against the brick wall beside his old friend and handed over a pack of matches. "How'd ya do on the test yesterday, Vinny?"

Vincent inhaled on his cigarette while smoothing back his long black hair fashioned in a pompadour. "I tried, Tony, I really tried. The teacher said come back next time. Don't make no difference. Mr. Santani says I'm doin' good, and he's gonna add four more stands to my route. He says in two maybe three years I'll be a supervisor."

Tony covered his disappointment with a nod of understanding. Vincent had flunked summer school again. He had not made the grades required for graduation a year ago, and had tried for the past two summers to get his diploma by taking summer makeup classes. It wasn't that his friend was dumb. He wasn't. The unforgiving system had beaten him. The troubles he had gotten into during his early years at school had continued to haunt him. He never had a chance to catch up.

Gina, his girlfriend for four years, had tried to help, but Vinny had been on a slippery slope. Working full-time after school to help support the family had taken time away from studying. The system didn't understand that the family came first.

Tony took a pack of cigarettes from his pocket, knowing his friend was hurting. Vinny had a good job with Santani's wholesale produce company, but disappointing his mother must have been eating him up inside. She had been counting on her oldest son to be the first male in the Martino family to receive a high school diploma.

Shifting his feet in discomfort at Vincent's silence, Tony shrugged his shoulders. "What we gonna do tonight? We gonna go up on the roof and see the fireworks show or what?"

Vincent kept his distant gaze. "Sure, we do whatever you want. It don't make no difference to me. We'll watch the fireworks like old times, huh?"

Tony noticed the welt under his friend's eye. His father must have come home drunk again. "I see your old man popped ya again. Why don't ya knock him on his ass once and for all, huh?"

Vincent blew out a cloud of smoke. "He called me tough guy. He likes ta hit tough guys, he says. I let him hit me. He hits me, he leaves Billy alone. I don't care when he hits me, as long as he leaves Billy alone. Billy's a good kid."

"Ya ought to bust your old man's face," Tony said, lighting his own cigarette. "I think ya oughta bust him."

Alfredo Mancini strutted up the street toward the two men and called out, "Yo, bozos, you wanna pitch for double?"

Tony smiled and dug in his pockets for his pennies. Pitching pennies against Alfredo was like taking candy from a baby. He had no touch. "You want double or nothin', you gotta show your money, Al."

Vincent ignored the two men as they began tossing pennies toward the building, trying to see who could get the closest to the wall. He didn't feel like doing anything but absorb his neighborhood. He needed the smells, people, and friends of his home. The neighborhood provided everything. So what, he flunked the classes and had a drunk for a father? Vinny Martino could still make it and be respected.

A new Chevrolet Impala rolled to a stop at the curb and Rita stepped out. She walked straight toward her brother with a somber expression.

Vincent tossed his cigarette to the pavement. She had been coming home at least twice a month since getting married a year before. She had married to escape the neighborhood, but somehow she couldn't ever really leave. She had probably left her husband again.

Rita stopped two paces from him. "Mama called me. She's been looking for you. It's Pop."

Vincent's eyes widened and he pushed off the wall. "Did he hurt Billy?"

"No, Vinny. Pop is dead."

Vincent took the manila envelope filled with his father's personal effects from the police officer at the morgue. "You sure he didn't feel anything?"

The policeman shook his head. "He was so intoxicated when the car hit him, he didn't even know what happened. You and I should be so lucky when we buy it."

Vincent nodded coldly and headed for the door. His only regret was that his father had not suffered as he had made the family suffer for the past few years. The bastard had quit being a father years ago—when he started becoming a drunk. Never once did Johnny Martino hug his eldest son, play ball with him, or say anything good about him. Vincent loved his mother, but could never understand why she always let that bum come back. The bastard had drunk up her savings and beat her unmercifully, only later to beg forgiveness. Why had she put up with him?

Vincent walked down the steps to where Rita was waiting in the car. He saw her expression, grave and dignified, and he smiled to himself. There was only one possible answer—pride. The church wouldn't allow her to divorce him, and there was nothing she could do but work twelve hours a day and support the family. Pride would never allow her to do anything else. She would not let her children do without because she was married to a bum.

Rita pulled away from the curb and glanced at her brother. "Was it bad?"

Vincent didn't pretend any feelings he didn't have. After all, Rita hated their father as much as he did. "Yeah," he replied to his sister, and smiled.

5

REPUBLIC OF SOUTH VIETNAM, 5 JULY 1964

Sergeant Major John Quail strode out of the briefing tent, behind a full colonel who was wearing starched stateside fatigues. Quail noticed a familiar-looking sergeant leaning against a parked Jeep and quickly caught up to the colonel.

"Sir, I'm going to talk to an ol' buddy. I'll catch a ride back to the villa and talk to you later."

Preoccupied with the heat, and sweating profusely, the colonel nodded and tossed his briefcase to the waiting driver. "Get me to the villa fast. This weather is killing me."

Quail broke into a smile as he approached. The sergeant first class wore scuffed white jungle boots, faded jungle fatigues, and green beret. "Irish, you lost a little weight."

SFC Shawn Flynn pushed off the jeep with a scowl. "I'm gonna kill your fat ass. You got me into this fuckin' quagmire."

Quail kept his smile. "You're lookin' good, Irish. How long has it been? Year? Year and a half?"

The corners of Shawn's lips began to turn upward in a smile. "Not long enough, you old bastard." He extended his hand. "Good to see you, Taco. You ain't lookin' half bad yourself."

Quail pulled the sergeant to his chest in a bear hug. "Damn if you don't even smell like a field soldier. How ya been?"

Shawn backed up, waving his hand in front of his face. "Yeah, well, you smell like a Pentagon pussy. Good ta see your ugly face too. I'm doin' okay. What brings ya back ta Nam? You lookin' for some Viet strange?"

Quail laughed and threw his arm over Shawn's shoulder. "I'm over here on a fact-finding mission with the colonel, and the briefing I just heard was bullshit. Typical MACV dog-and-pony show with no substance. Tell me what the fuck is really happenin', will ya?"

Shawn looked around to see if anybody was watching, and motioned toward the tent. "I hope you got some time and can fix this fuckin' goat screw. We got serious problems, and everybody is covering them up. We were all told to avoid you and the colonel, but fuck 'em. I had to see my frozen Ol' Baldy buddy. I didn't trust the paper shufflers giving you a briefing. They have a funny way of seeing things the way they want to see them." Shawn lowered his head in frustration. "Taco, things are screwed up. We're expendable again, and I don't like it."

Shawn cleared out the assistant operations sergeant and stood at the wooden podium while Quail took a seat in a folding chair to his front. "It's been going downhill since MACV put us under their control and told the CIA to kiss off. When we were working for the Company, we had problems, but they at least understood what our mission was. Now, under MACV, it's totally fucked up. They don't understand, or don't care, about what the Special Forces is designed to do. Instead of training an army of locals who can protect their homes and villages, we're playin' the same game the French played of establishing remote outposts on the border for surveillance purposes."

Shawn motioned toward the large wall map behind him. "We're expected to detect and stop the dinks from infiltrating into the country. Shit, we're spread so thin, it's thirty klicks between camps. They want us to train the locals in the area to do the fighting, but you know how much the mountain tribes—Montagnards they call 'em—hate the Vietnamese, and vice versa. The South Vietnamese government is only paying lip service to the Montagnard Civilian Irregular Defense Group. The CIDG forces ain't gettin' shit for support from the Viets. The outpost program is screwed up 'cause they're sending CIDG forces from their home area into a completely alien environment. They ain't fightin' for their homes anymore. They're just hired mercenaries, sent to die like the French. On top of all that, we have to deal with the South Vietnamese Special Forces. They call themselves the Luc Long Dac Biet. The LLDB. If you remember, when you were here they were the palace guard for President Diem, and nothing but a bunch of political-appointed pretty boys. They still are, for the most part. They're the ones who are supposed to be in charge of the outposts, with us advising them, but it's all bullshit. They cause trouble rather than help the situation. We got us a rebellion going on right now between the pretty boys and the Montagnards. The pretty boys treat the 'Yards' like shit and cheat them every chance they get. The Yards have had it with their treatment, and are only devoted and loyal to our Special Forces teams. The Yards could give a flying fuck what the South Vietnamese government or LLDB want."

Quail lowered his head at the distressing news. The briefing he had heard earlier had been nothing but positive, watered-down mush, though there had been a brief mention made of "challenges facing the program." What Shawn was telling him about were not "challenges"; they were major problems that could get good men killed. Quail looked up at his friend. "How's your leadership?"

Shawn frowned. "They put a colonel in charge to tighten the noose on us. He's got no S.F. background and pushes the MACV program like it was the only game in town. He's really a pretty good officer, and he's doing his best, but the Viet government boys are playing big-time politics over his head. We're stuck in the outposts without anybody understanding what the fuck is going on. We're doing the best we can, but our hands are tied. It's fucked up, Taco. The border posts are nothing but targets. The damn of it is—the program could work. We could actually do the mission by changing around some things and people, and by doing some aggressive patrolling. But the LLBD, the pretty boys, are lazy. They don't like getting out their bunks, let alone their outposts. And they won't lead patrols or break down their strike forces into smaller, more silent units to find the dinks. See, the dinks move in the evening and at night, but the pretty boys don't like going out at night. Like I said, it's fucked up."

Quail stared blankly at the map. "I gotta tell ya, Irish, I don't know if I can do a damn thing. The colonel with me isn't here looking at the Viet government's problems. That's way above his pay grade. He's here at MACV's request. Your MACV bosses think the green beanies are gettin' over, sending A-teams in-country for only six months and drawin' extra pay. They think you should be like everybody else and stay a whole tour. The thing I'm trying to stop is that they want to rotate the S.F. on a one-for-one basis and break up the cohesion of the teams."

Shawn's jaw tightened. "Taco, they can't do that! Damn, our teams are good 'cause we've worked with each other for years. If we break up the teams, we aren't Special Forces anymore. The whole thing will fall apart for sure."

Quail stood up, obviously dejected. "I know, Irish. But ever since Jack Kennedy bought it, the big brass has been trying to get rid of us. I think this is just another nail they're trying to pound in our coffin."

Shawn's shoulders sagged. "You know, when you got me into this four years ago, I wasn't sure if it was for me. Jumpin' out of planes, the qualification course, and time away from Gretchen kicked my ass, but I've grown to really love the S.F. In the Berets I learned what being a professional means. I've learned the difference between half-assed and first-class, and Taco, this war is being run half-assed. We're nothing but expendables again."

Quail put his arm around his friend, feeling his frustration. To lighten the conversation, he changed the subject. "How is Gretchen?"

Shawn led Quail out of the stifling tent. "She's fine. We have an apartment just off Lumpkin Road outside of Bragg. She's working in the jewelry department at the post exchange and doing great. She looks better than ever."

"You have kids yet?"

Shawn's eyes seemed to sadden. "No, not yet. Gret says maybe after this tour." Shawn lifted his head, remembering something Quail would want to know. "Hey, did ya hear Pop is over here? He's runnin' a team up in Nam Dong."

Quail could not believe what he'd just heard. He and Pop Alameda had served together in World War II and had been close friends back at Bragg. "They got that old fucker runnin' a team? Hell, he's older than dirt."

Shawn laughed. "Yeah, he's your age. I've only seen him once, but he looked good and has lost some weight . . . which, I might add, might do you some good too."

Quail smiled reflectively. "I'll try and get out and see the ol' bastard. His missus keeps sending me letters telling me to get my wagon hitched. She's a real lady. Never could understand why she'd marry that old fart."

Shawn grinned. "She's trying to get you married? She ought to know better than— Aw shit, trouble."

Quail glanced to his right and saw the major who had given him the briefing earlier walking directly toward them. By Shawn's reaction, Quail knew something was wrong.

The major halted and gave Shawn a frigid look. "I insist on knowing what you said to the sergeant major. Sergeant Foley said you gave him a briefing of some kind."

Quail stiffened. "Beggin' your pardon, sir, but *I* asked my *friend* what his impression of the situation was."

The major shifted his attention to the big sergeant major. "Sergeant Flynn is *not* the briefing officer. I am. If you wanted more information, I would have appreciated your going through me. Sergeant Flynn does not see the big picture as MACV does."

Quail noted that the major wasn't a paratrooper and wasn't wearing the Combat Infantryman's Badge. "Excuse me, sir, but when was the last time you visited one of the outposts?"

The major's face flushed. "I . . . I had the opportunity to visit, ah . . . I can't remember the camp's name, but I visited it two months ago. Personal experience in camps is irrelevant. The information we receive and evaluate is what is important. I can assure you and Colonel Denton the briefing I gave you reflected our most recent information. We know what we are doing."

Quail spoke with a tinge of sarcasm. "Yes, sir, I can see where your presence in a camp would be irrelevant. I mean, of course, the information you analyze is much more important."

The major's eyes narrowed, realizing he was being made a fool of. He shifted his glare back to Shawn. "What did you tell the sergeant major?"

Shawn's eyes bored holes through the major's. "The truth . . . sir."

Quail had enough. "Sir, it's my mission to obtain information. I asked Sergeant Flynn for his opinion, and I got it. I am sure Colonel Denton would be surprised to hear you were upset and objected to me asking an experienced veteran for his views. It might almost sound as if you were trying to hide something from the fact-finding mission. I'm sure you don't want that as the perception."

The major was visibly shaken. "Uh, no, of course not. I . . . I mean we have nothing to hide. But I must insist you go through me as a matter of courtesy before asking any more of your friends for their opinions. It would be unfair for you to leave with a distorted view of the program."

Quail spoke with detachment. "Yes, sir, I understand, and I thank you for your 'view' this morning. Was there anything else, sir?"

The major shook with anger. The sergeant major ended his conversation as if dismissing a field-grade officer. Had the senior noncom not been sent from Washington, he would have charged him with insubordination. In light of the sergeant major's position, however, nothing would be gained by a confrontation. It was obvious Flynn had talked too much.

Controlling his anger, the major spoke quickly. "No, I have nothing else, but Sergeant Flynn, I would like to see you in my office as soon as you finish with your conversation."

With that said, the major spun around on his heels, ignoring the salutes that he knew would be rendered, and strode toward his air-conditioned office.

Quail lowered his salute and looked at Shawn. "That's what you have to put up with?"

Shawn rolled his eyes. "Yeah. Now you know what I mean. We're led by paper shufflers who don't know what's really going on. Major Cummings is the MACV representative and gives all the briefings. He's playing head honcho now because the colonel is in Da Nang. They both have to make the information the Special Forces gives them fit *their* program."

Quail put his hand on his friend's shoulder. "I think I just made things tough on you. Sorry, Irish."

Shawn smiled. "What's he gonna do? Send me to Vietnam? Fuck it, Taco. Somebody had ta tell you what's going on."

Quail saw his friend was putting up a front. "I'm gonna be here a week. If you run into trouble just let me know. I can fix things. I'm serious. You let me know if he hassles ya."

Shawn winked. "Is my fairy godmother tryin' to help me again? I ought to kick your ass for gettin' me in this mess in the first place. . . . Take care, Taco. I wish we could drink some beer tonight, but I'm headin' upcountry back to my team. It was good seein' you again. I guess I'd better go see the paper shuffler and take his ass chewin'."

Shawn turned to go, but was roughly spun around. Quail hugged him unashamedly. "Keep your ass down, Irish. Us old vets need each other. Take care of yourself out there."

Shawn watched his friend hop in a jeep, and gave him a final wave. Shawn lifted his hand in a farewell salute and took in a deep breath. Major Cummings was about to have his toy soldier to bash around for fun.

The major sat with a smug smile on his face as Shawn stopped the traditional three paces from the desk and raised his hand in a salute. "Sir, Sergeant First Class Flynn reports as ordered."

Cummings returned the salute without looking at the sergeant and continued reading the file. "Flynn, your personnel jacket reflects a man who has risen through the ranks rather fast. This is of course a reflection of the wartime promotion policies of the Special Forces rather than a reflection of your attributes to the *real* Army. Today you violated your obligation of loyalty to your appointed leaders, and it will be noted. I will make sure of it."

The officer glanced up to enjoy the look on his victim's face. He was immediately disappointed. The sergeant had his eyes fixed on the wall behind the desk.

"I realize you were here at Nha Trang to pick up a resupply for your A-team and were planning to go back this afternoon," the major continued, "but something has come up. I have already made the necessary calls and you are now mine for a week. I realize you Green Beret types don't like working for us staff officers, but your talents, such as they are, are needed by me."

The major rose from his chair. "I'm going to have you as an errand boy for seven days, Flynn. It isn't much, but if by chance you screw up, I will be happy to add an appropriate letter to your file that might interest the next promotion board."

The officer's face began to turn red. The sergeant, showing no expression, was ruining the fun. "Flynn, do you hear me? I'm going to be watching *you!*"

Shawn spoke like a robot. "Sir, the sergeant thanks you for your interest."

Cummings's eyes widened. "Get out of my office and report to the duty officer. I will call him shortly and figure out something for you to screw up. And believe me, you will screw it up. Now, get *out!*"

Shawn executed a perfect salute. The major ignored him, but realized he had to return the salute before he would go.

Throwing up his hand sloppily, Cummings avoided the sergeant's expressionless eyes.

Shawn lowered his hand and executed a flawless about-face. Marching toward the door, he smiled to himself. A week in Nha Trang wouldn't be half bad.

As soon as Shawn opened the door, a sergeant waiting outside rushed into the major's office. Shawn heard the sergeant's excited voice. "Sir, they need you at the operations center. All hell is breaking loose in An Khe and . . ."

Shawn relaxed as he reached the safety of the hall. He glanced down the corridor. Now, where the hell was the duty officer?

The captain broke his gaze from the magazine and glanced at the sergeant sitting in a chair on the other side of his desk. "You sure you don't know why Major Cummings wanted you to report to me?"

Sergeant First Class Flynn shrugged his shoulders. "Sir, like I told you twenty minutes ago, the major ordered me to report to you and said he would call later to tell you what he wanted done."

The captain glanced at his watch. "I guess I'd better try his office again." The officer reached for the phone, but it rang before his hand touched the handset. Lifting the phone to his ear, he spoke loudly. "Captain Circone, Headquarters Duty Officer."

The officer listened for a moment and his eyes shifted to the sergeant. "Yes, I believe I have him right here." Listening for another few moments, he spoke with the same authority. "Sure, he'll be there in thirty minutes. No sweat, glad to help."

Hanging up, the captain again looked at the sergeant. "Now we know why the major sent you over. That was the liaison NCO at the airfield. A civilian scheduled to fly to the outpost at Nam Dong arrived early from Saigon and they need you now. Get your field gear and have the driver take you to the airfield. Looks like you're going to be playing bodyguard for the next couple of days."

Shawn sat up. He couldn't believe that the major would give him such a job. "Sir, I don't think I was sent here for that."

The captain frowned and waved his hand around the empty office. "Do you see anybody else waiting around here? The major must have sent you over here for the job. Get your gear and move out . . . you have field gear, don't you?"

Shawn rose to his feet, not about to argue. It was too good to be true. "Yes, sir."

Shawn leaned back in the nylon seat of the Caribou as the plane's two engines increased their roar. He patted the man's leg beside him. "Buckle up, Doc. We're about to take off."

Dr. Jerry Hickerson quickly buckled his seat belt and shut his eyes. He was terrified of flying. As a doctor of anthropology, he appreciated those who walked, or used more simple means of transportation that didn't require machines. Machines, especially airplanes, were totally beyond his comprehension. They had too many moving parts, of which it took only one to malfunction and cause the machine to stop. Ceasing to function at ten thousand feet meant . . .

Dr. Hickerson blocked his thoughts and grabbed hold of the edge of the seat in a death grip. Please, machine, work!

Shawn saw the doctor's hands turning white, and leaned closer to be heard over the roar. "You ain't changed a bit, Doc. Relax. We'll be there in an hour."

Hickerson opened his eyelids only a crack. "Just tell me when we get there, Irish."

Shawn smiled and patted the doctor's leg for moral support. Hickerson, from the Rand Corporation, was here studying Montagnard cultures. Nam Dong was a good place to study mountain people because several distinct tribes were situated around the desolated outpost located in the jungle-covered mountains thirty-two miles west of Da Nang. Doc Hickerson was no stranger to Vietnam, having worked with many of the Special Forces A-teams to obtain information for a study he was compiling for the government.

Shawn smiled at his good luck. Three days away from the major was too good to be true. The Nam Dong A-team had several of his old buddies from Seventh Group, with which he had trained in the States. A three-day vacation with friends was good news indeed.

A young lieutenant approached the duty officer's desk. "Sir, I'm Lieutenant Zovath. I'm the escort officer for Dr. Hickerson."

The captain set down his magazine. "Who is Dr. Hickerson?"

The young officer set down his briefcase and took out a piece of paper to make sure he had pronounced the name correctly. "Sir, I was told to report here to you. When the doctor arrives from Saigon, I am to escort him to Nam Dong for three days. I—"

"Oh shit!" the captain blurted.

Major Cummings spun around. "You did what?"

The duty officer stood his ground and repeated what he had said before. "Sir, when the call came in, I assumed SFC Flynn was the escort and I sent him to the airfield."

Cummings pointed at his phone in a rage. "Get him back here now!"

The captain kept his eyes directly to the front. "I already tried, sir. The plane left thirty minutes ago. They are halfway to Nam Dong by now."

Cummings sunk into his chair. The loud-mouthed bastard had gotten away from him on a fucking fluke. *Damn!*

NAM DONG, THUA THIEN PROVINCE, I CORPS

"Irish, you sorry bastard! How the hell are you?"

Shawn raised his hand to block the sun's glare as he walked down the rear ramp of the aircraft. He recognized the greeter immediately and broke into a smile. "Pop, you're lookin' old as ever! Hasn't anyone told ya you're too ancient for this shit?"

Forty-five-year-old team sergeant Gabriel Alameda took off his beret and ran his hand through his silver hair. "Yeah, the old lady. Every damn letter I get she reminds me. What the hell you doing here?"

Shawn motioned behind him. "I'm baby sittin' Doc Hickerson. He'll be out in just a sec. He's apologizing to the crew chief for puking on his floor."

Alameda thrust out his hand. "Fort Apache we ain't, but welcome to Camp Alpha 726."

Shawn pumped his old friend's hand. "It's a small fuckin' world, Pop. You'll never guess who's in-country. Taco. I saw him today, and he asked about ya."

Alameda smirked. "He wouldn't dare come and see me. He owes me twenty bucks. How's the old bastard lookin'?"

"He looks mean as ever. Like you. Something about old vets I guess. You dinosaurs don't know your time is up."

Alameda laughed and slapped Shawn's back. "Come on, youngster. I'll send Brownie back for Doc."

The sun was about to set. Shawn listened for a few minutes but felt uncomfortable. He stood up in the back of the hooch and stepped outside. He had been listening to Doc Hickerson's briefing to the team about Montagnard culture when the nagging feeling became too much to bear. There wasn't much time. Since arriving late that afternoon, he and the doctor had been in the mess hall receiving briefings, so he did not have the slightest idea about where to go if the perimeter were attacked during the night.

Shawn took in a deep breath of fresh air and glanced toward the orange sun sinking behind the mountain peaks. It was a beautiful scene, but he sure as hell wouldn't want to be assigned to the outpost. It was too naked. The camp was built on top of a small barren knoll in the middle of a narrow valley. To the east and west the ominous, jungle-covered Annamite Mountains rose almost straight up to three thousand feet. A V.C. with a pair of field glasses could see everything and everyone in the camp.

Shawn was thankful he was just visiting as he shifted his gaze around the fort. The camp was a sitting duck for a large, determined enemy force. Only fifteen miles from the Laos border, Nam Dong sat in the middle of a V.C. guerrilla infiltration route from North Vietnam. The V.C. were trained just above the 17th parallel and walked down the Ho Chi Minh trails through Laos to enter South Vietnam. Nam Dong was situated on one of Uncle Ho's feeder trails and was obviously cramping the V.C.'s style. Pop Alameda had told them in the first briefing that before the outpost was established, the valley had been used as a V.C. training area. The small villages in the valley had been the source of food for the communists, and many of the people were still loyal supporters.

"You snuck out on us."

Shawn turned around with a smile, recognizing the voice. "Yeah, Pop, I needed to get a layout of your camp before it got dark."

Alameda nodded in understanding. He had known Flynn back at Fort Bragg for years, but had not served with him in the field. His coming outside to get the lay of land showed Irish was true to his reputation: he was a survivor. "Come on, I'll show you around so you'll feel better . . . or maybe worse."

The master sergeant took only a few steps and motioned to the rattan longhouse to his right. "As you can see, we have two sixty-foot longhouses built by the Yards. The first one down there houses our orderly room. It's the sleeping quarters for five of us team members and the Nungs. At the other end of the longhouse you were just in is the commo room and more sleeping quarters. That's where you and Doc will be bunkin'. If the shit hits the fan, don't stay in the firetraps. Run to the fighting positions we have scattered along the inner-perimeter fence or one of the mortar pits. We have two 'sixties and three 81-millimeter mortar positions dug inside our perimeter. The small hooches alongside the longhouses are the Viet's mess hall, dispensary, and a few of our sleeping hooches. It's the basic setup, nothing fancy."

Shawn committed to memory the location of the closest machine-gun position and shook his head in bewilderment. "I still haven't figured out what design you used. I've seen star-pointed, triangular, and square camps, but I can't make heads or tails of yours."

Alameda dipped his chin in agreement. "Believe me, I didn't design this sonofabitch. We inherited it as is." The sergeant squatted and used his finger to draw in the dirt. "The camp is shaped like a wide U. The outside perimeter is about five football-field lengths long and 250 yards wide. It's surrounded by a barbed-wire fence and a trench interspersed with fighting positions. The three-hundred-man Yard strike force defends it, along with all the ash and trash. We got laborers, truck drivers, mechanics, and even some strike-force families within the perimeter. You saw their hooches when we first walked into the perimeter from the airfield. With all the troubles we've been having with the locals, and this area being an old V.C. stomping ground, we don't trust the outer perimeter to hold off an attack. We team members stay in the inner perimeter during the night so we can sleep without getting our throats cut. Our egg-shaped inner fort is sorta a fort inside a bigger fort and sits at the bottom of the U. It's a little over a hundred yards long and eighty yards wide. With the sixty Nungs we've got, plus us, we figure we can hold off whatever makes it through the outer perimeter. It's a small area, but we've got a strong barbed fence, trench system, the mortars, and plenty of machine-gun positions."

Shawn noticed a Nung sergeant manning a machine-gun position only a few yards away and felt a little better about his stay. Knowing there were Nungs in camp would allow him to sleep without an eye open. These tough soldiers were mercenaries of Chinese extraction, hired by the Special Forces as bodyguards and special camp guards. Fierce fighters, they were loyal to their assigned S.F. teams, and unlike the Vietnamese, could be counted on when lead started flying.

Shawn turned around and looked at the road leading toward the inner perimeter. "And that road goes to the villages?"

Alameda stood and wiped his finger on his jungle fatigues. "Yeah, it leads straight to Nam Dong and six other villages farther to the south. We've got our work cut out for us here. We've got a little over five thousand civilians in the valley, and they're about as backward as you can get. We spend most of our time on civic-action programs, the basic stuff—digging wells, running sick call for the kids . . . We patrol the valley and the lower mountain slopes, but the district chief won't let us patrol east of the Ta Trach River, even though the sonofabitch is just two hundred yards outside our perimeter. He says it's too dangerous."

Shawn shook his head sympathetically. It was the same old story. The team's hands were tied. Not being able to patrol an entire sector so close to the camp was like giving the V.C. an open invitation to attack.

Shawn pointed at a huge mound of dirt near the main gate. "What the hell is that for?"

Alameda patted his shoulder as he strode in the direction of the gate. "Come on, you gotta see our swimming pool."

The two men stopped at the edge of an eight-foot-deep, rectangular hole. Alameda kicked a dirt clod into the pit. "It's thirty feet long and fifteen feet wide. It's gonna be our operations center and dispensary. The Navy Seabees dug it for us while they were here building the airstrip. They left us those cement blocks stacked behind it and twenty bags of mortar. We're gonna build it as soon as we get a little time, and cover the whole thing with the mound of dirt. It'll be the safest place in Nam once we finish her."

Shawn couldn't help but think to himself his friend would need the underground bunker if they weren't allowed to patrol around the entire camp.

Alameda seemed to be reading his thoughts, and tossed his arm around Shawn's shoulder. "Don't worry about us, Irish. I got these guys squared away. Let's go to the commo hooch. Brownie and Bee-man want to see ya and drink a few beers for old-times' sake."

Shawn nodded with a smile. "Sure, but first I want to find Doc and tell him what to do—just in case. I figure I'd better walk him through a few ways to make it to the closest fighting position."

Alameda's eyebrows raised. "You ain't takin' any chances, are ya?"

Shawn exchanged a knowing glance with his friend. "Nope."

Dr. Jerry Hickerson sat down tiredly on his bunk to take off his boots. It didn't seem possible that the soldier writing a letter on the bunk across from him was the same man he had seen earlier in the mess hall. Nam Dong's team had thrown together a beer call for their guests' benefit, to get acquainted. After the introductions and friendly chat, sergeants Flynn, Alameda, and the two other Korean War veterans drifted to one of the corner tables and began the veteran's ritual of laughing, drinking, and telling war stories. The men's eyes seem to light up in each other's presence, and soon they had become the focus of general attention. The other team members pulled up chairs close to the four men to listen, laugh, and learn. It was a strange phenomenon to observe, but one he had seen many times before among men of their breed.

Hickerson tossed one boot down and began unlacing the other. He realized he was analyzing them again, acting like an anthropologist, but he couldn't help it. The study of man was his job, and these little-understood men were a fascinating breed apart.

Hickerson tossed the other boot and leaned back on his bunk, glancing again at the sergeant. "Irish"—the nickname was perfect for him. He looked like a steel-eyed, ruddy-cheeked, pub brawler who would charm the ladies and intimidate their men. He seemed born for the service, much like the others Hickerson had met from the Nam Dong team. The Special Forces ranks were replete with such men. Alone, their type would perish, or worse, change. The men of the Special Forces were above the Army's parade, dress-right-dress, and spit-and-polish mentality. They judged men not for their looks or education, but rather for their courage, tenacity, and performance. Correct uniforms and short haircuts meant nothing to them. They respected men who were confident in their own abilities, who were not afraid to fight and lead. They were individualists when by themselves and clannish with their own kind. Rebels by nature, they hated depersonalized institutions and systems that ran on rules, regulations, and tradition. The only rule they abided by was common sense. Experience counted more than looking good, and action was paramount to talking.

Team Sergeant "Pop" Alameda, Irish, Brownee, and Bee-man were men who had attained the ultimate goal of all such warriors. They were respected by their peers. They were also members of the elite club known as "combat veterans." The club's membership rules required facing combat and surviving. The dues they paid were only this—mutual respect for one another. Favors could be asked and given without question. If a member had a problem, a fellow veteran could be expected to be there to help. Should a member die, he knew tears would be shed by his fellows, and his wife would be comforted by men who really understood.

Hickerson blew out his candle and took off his glasses. He envied this special breed. They were different and at times incredibly cold, but they were, in their own way, beautiful. Warriors of old, outcasts in peace, heroes in war. They did what others abhorred, and they were the best at doing it.

They were men who understood that there was no glory at the end, but only each other.

Setting his glasses on the floor, Hickerson lay back on his bed to sleep.

Shawn finished writing his letter to Gretchen and placed the four pages into a dirt-stained envelope. He had relayed the good news Pop had given him over a beer. Trudy Alameda was expecting their fourth child within the month. He wanted Gretchen to drive over to Trudy's and check on her and tell his friend's wife her husband was doing well. Shawn also hoped Gretchen would get the hint that he wanted to start a family as soon as he returned in three months.

He threw the envelope to the floor and picked up his Colt .45. Making sure he had a round chambered and a full magazine, he was about to blow out his candle when he glanced at the doctor. Damn!

Hickerson had just dozed off when he felt a hand clamp over his eyes. "Don't move, Doc. You didn't listen to me this afternoon when we rehearsed getting hit. This is a lesson for ya. Keep your eyes shut and get up and move to the bunker I showed you as if we'd just got hit."

Hickerson was so relieved to hear the familiar voice, he obeyed without hesitating. With his eyes closed, he got up and began walking like a blind man, his hands extended in front of him. He stepped on one of his boots and stumbled. In catching his balance, he had also lost his sense of direction. After two cautious steps his legs bumped against a bed frame. He turned around, and walking with more confidence, slammed into the side of the hut.

He sighed, opened his eyes, and faced the sergeant. "I flunked the test, huh?"

Shawn nodded with a look of disappointment. "Doc, you never go to sleep without first laying everything out where you can find it in a hurry and in the dark. You gotta swing out of bed and be able to put your feet in your boots, slap on your glasses, pick up your pistol, and then freeze. Listen before moving, and then move with a purpose toward the exit, checking the door first. Go through the motions in your mind several times and visualize yourself making every move. It sounds dumb, I know, but it works."

Hickerson knew his teacher was trying to save him from himself if the unthinkable happened. "I'm sorry, Irish, I just plain forgot."

Shawn smiled and leaned back on his bunk. "Ain't nothin' to be sorry for. You learned something. It's cheap insurance. . . . Good night, Doc."

Hickerson sat on his bunk and unlaced his boots farther so he could slip his feet in easily. Glancing at the sergeant, he spoke sincerely. "Thanks, Irish."

6

Shawn had seen secret service agents protect the President on television, but he had never appreciated their work—until now. After walking through the villages watching Doc Hickerson's back for the past four hours, Shawn told himself that the special agents earned every dime they made. His nerves were shot and he was physically exhausted. His head had been on a swivel since leaving the camp that morning for the tour of the villages. The team medic, Doc Graig, and the team executive officer, Lieutenant Oberstein, had served as tour guides, but they had been talking, not protecting.

Shawn was relieved when the baby-faced lieutenant finally turned around after visiting the third village and led them back toward the camp. The officer had talked to some local farmers and seemed upset. Reaching the village of Nam Dong, Sergeant Graig made the best suggestion of the day. He asked Hickerson if he wanted to stop at one of the small hooch shops for something to eat. Shawn spoke quickly for the doctor, needing a break himself. "You bet. Let's get a beer!"

Shawn made sure Hickerson sat in a corner, then positioned himself at the only door. For the first time, he had to keep his attention on only one area. Thank God for small favors, he thought. It was funny, but he couldn't recall a single thing the tour guides had said. His concentration had been strictly focused on the countless civilians they had passed or stopped and talked to. He had been looking for suspicious bulges under their clothes or sudden movements.

Shawn relaxed his sore neck muscles and was about to order a cold drink when rifle shots echoed in the distance, from the direction of the camp.

The lieutenant jumped to his feet and ran toward the door with his rifle readied. Shawn blocked the entrance with an extended arm. "Hold it, sir! Don't be exposing yourself!"

Realizing the sergeant was right, the officer took up a position on the other side of the door.

Sergeant Graig had a radio on his back, and quickly grabbed for the handset. A minute later, after calling the camp, he blurted aloud, "Shit! There's a firefight going on inside the camp! The Viets are shooting at the Nungs."

Lieutenant Oberstein sat down dejectedly. "It was just a matter of time, but damn, why now?"

"Would somebody tell me what's going on?" Hickerson asked in confusion.

Oberstein sighed. "We've had problems between the Viets in the strike force and the Nungs. The Nungs have more money, and the local honeys like their company better. The Viets are jealous little guys, and I guess it's finally come to shooting. It couldn't have come at a worse time, with what we heard today from those farmers."

Shawn poked his head out the door to see if they were in any danger and ducked back. "What did you hear?"

Oberstein leaned back in his chair, looking blankly at the wall as if in thought. "It's what they didn't say that worries me. I've talked to those guys before, and this time they were different. They're worried, and they wouldn't tell me what's bothering them. Something is up. I can feel it."

"I felt it too," the medic agreed. "I was in those two villages just two days ago, and the people were all smiles. This time they wouldn't come out of their hooches. Something is wrong for sure. They know something we don't."

Shawn took a magazine from his bandolier and stuck it in his pocket. "Graig, call the camp and get another update. See if it's safe enough for us to move back to camp. It's safer there than here."

Hickerson finished his second bowl of soup and drank the last of his second Coke. He pushed back from the table and, with a contented smile, leaned against the thatch wall. "You all should relax and have some of the soup. It's great."

Shawn glanced at his watch. They had been waiting for over two hours for word from camp that the situation was safe. The last radio message said that the Nungs within the inner perimeter had come to a standoff with the Viets in the outer perimeter. The team captain was still trying to negotiate a peace.

Hickerson sat down by Shawn. "Help me, will you, Irish? I've already forgotten the team members' names."

Shawn kept his eyes on the hooches across the road as he spoke. "The best way to remember is to start from the top. You got the team captain, Captain Dolan, the martinet; the L-tee over there; then Pop Alameda, the team sergeant. Bee-man and Brownee are the vets I was talkin' to last night. The Negro is Whiteside, then there's big Woody, Daniels, Houston, Terrin, Dissner, and Conway, who's an Aussie. Countin' Graig, there's thirteen of them, plus us two."

Hickerson jotted down the names in his small notepad and was about to rise when he stopped and motioned to the holster on the sergeant's hip.

"I noticed you carry that Colt .45 everywhere you go. Is that insurance too?"

Shawn turned and looked at the inquisitive professor. "I was in a situation once where this .45 saved my ass. A supply corporal in Korea gave it back to me before I was shipped to a hospital. He said it had been expendable, like I was. This pistol and me are kind of a team. I aim him and he knocks them down. Yeah, it's insurance. Permanent Life."

Hickerson smiled faintly and got up. He had talked to Pop Alameda at breakfast about Sergeant Flynn. He had wanted to know more about the man whom he knew only as "Irish." Pop had told him that the sergeant had a good reputation in the Special Forces and that they had been friends at Bragg. When Hickerson had pressed him about Flynn's family background, however, the old team sergeant shook his head. "I heard his old man left before he was born, and it kinda went downhill from there. His mother had been hooking in Reno when he joined the Army in 'fifty-two. The Green Machine was his family till he married a German divorcée." Pop had ended the conversation with the words that really meant something to Special Forces types. "Irish is good people."

Hickerson found that he felt safe, knowing the sergeant was looking after him. One thing he didn't need Pop to tell him: Sergeant Shawn Flynn was a pro.

Lieutenant Oberstein lifted his wrist to read the luminous dial of his watch. Damn, it was only a little after midnight. He had almost an hour left on his shift before he woke Captain Dolan. He began to walk toward the second longhouse when a voice in the darkness startled him.

"The dogs usually bark like this?"

The young lieutenant squinted to make out who the man was. "Oh, Sergeant Flynn, it's you. No they don't. They've never made this much noise before. They wake you up?"

Shawn moved out of the shadows, cupping a cigarette in his hand. "Yes, sir. I thought I'd just listen awhile."

"You can come with me if you want," the officer said, glad to have some company. "I'm making the rounds of the inner perimeter. I'm sorry about this afternoon you and Doc having to wait so long and all. The situation was embarrassing for us."

Shawn took a quick drag of the Chesterfield before joining the lieutenant as he walked toward the first longhouse. "It didn't bother me, L-tee. We have the same problems in our camp. Dealing with the Viets is like trying to deal with relatives—ya can't please 'em all."

Oberstein smiled. He liked the stocky sergeant. "Thanks for understanding."

The two men checked the machine-gun positions. Not only were the

Nungs awake, but they were on full alert, with every man in position in case the Viets decided to reopen the argument by throwing grenades.

Oberstein shook his head as they walked toward the main gate. "The damn village dogs haven't let up a bit. What do you make of it?"

Shawn had unconsciously put his hand on his holster. "I think you were right this afternoon. Something's up. A dink unit may be passing through the valley tonight. Or it might be a smaller group trying to scare the people into giving them support. Or they're out there waiting to attack. No way of telling for sure."

The officer lifted his automatic rifle and patted his .357 magnum pistol on his hip. "They'd be fools to try us."

Shawn admired the officer's confidence but thought he was too young and thin to be talking so big. "L-tee, a friend of mine once told me the only good fights are those people talk about in bars. When you're in one, they ain't never what you expect. They're your worst nightmare . . . believe me. Don't wish for one. They ain't good for you."

Embarrassed, the lieutenant nodded, and whispered as he walked back into the darkness, "Good night, Sergeant."

Shawn concentrated on the sound of the barking dogs. Damn, why couldn't the bastards wait till he was gone?

Captain Dolan yawned and looked at his watch. It was 0226. The dogs had stopped barking an hour ago and everything seemed quiet enough. Perhaps the V.C. had decided not to mess with his camp after all. He stopped in front of the mess hall to check the guard, and began to open the screen door. The door moved only an inch when the mess hall exploded in a blinding flash of light and a thunderous blast that blew him off his feet.

Shawn leaped up, hearing the unmistakable ripping thunderclap of mortar rounds, and saw the doctor in the eerie glow already up and putting on his boots. He was doing exactly what he had been told. Good man. The back portion of the longhouse erupted in a vehement explosion, knocking them both to the floor. Picking up his AR-15 and fighting harness, Shawn crawled to the shaking doctor and pulled him toward the door. A fire had started and was spreading up the rattan walls.

Shawn could see across the open ground to the protected machine-gun position—the mess hall was like a homecoming bonfire and lit up the entire camp. To his left, team members were yelling and running toward the commo hut to save the radio equipment. Shawn hollered to be heard over the din, *"Damn, Doc, this ain't a probe! This is an all-out attack!"*

"What do we do?" Hickerson cried out.

Shawn grabbed the lanky man's arm in a viselike grip. "Follow our plan!"

The two men ran for the bunker, but made it only two steps when they were blown off their feet by a nearby explosion. Feeling as if he had just been slapped by a sheet of plywood, Shawn shook off the smoking dirt clods and yanked the stunned doctor back to his feet. *"Run!"*

Making it into the protection of a sandbagged bunker, Shawn pushed the terrified man into a corner next to a Nung soldier who was opening M-60 ammunition cans. "Don't move from here! I'm gonna help the team!"

Shawn began to sprint toward the burning mess hall when the communications hooch took a direct hit and blew up in a brilliant flash. The entire camp was bathed in an orange and gold glow from the raging fires that were consuming the thatch-roofed longhouses. Mortar rounds rained down in sudden flashes of white light, causing the ground to lurch, as in a killer earthquake. *Ba-rooom. Ba-rooom Bloooom Ba-room.* Between the thunderous detonations, small-arms automatic fire made a noise like a hundred roaring lawn mowers running loose in every direction. Shawn suddenly thought of his friend. Jesus, Pop!

Alameda was throwing equipment out of the burning longhouse when he was suddenly jerked toward the door. Shawn had asked the two members outside the hooch where the team sergeant was, and they had pointed toward the inferno.

Alameda fought Shawn's grasp. *"We need the equipment, goddamnit!"*

Shawn pushed the old soldier out the door. They had taken only two steps when they were both violently knocked to the ground by a blast behind them. Shawn moaned and clawed the ground. Alameda grabbed the stunned sergeant under the arms and dragged him to the sniper protection wall.

Shawn jerked free from Alameda's grasp and slapped frantically at the back of his own legs, thinking he was on fire. *Shitshit shit!* . . . "Damn, Pop, I'm hit!"

Alameda pushed his friend over and quickly checked the damage. Slapping Shawn's buttocks, he barked, "It ain't nothin'! A couple of fragments in the back of your legs is all. They'll quit burning in a bit."

Shawn winced as he picked up his rifle. "Damn you, they hurt!"

A portion of the wood and earth sniper wall shuddered with the impact of a direct hit by a recoilless rifle. Forgetting his pain, Shawn jumped to his feet, yelling, " *'Fifty-seven recoilless. Get out of here!"* Alameda joined Shawn as they ran to the communications trench and dived in headfirst.

Alameda raised up and saw their Vietnamese interpreter run across the parade ground in front of the gate and take cover behind the wall they had just left. The sergeant stood and screamed, "Tuan, get away from there! Get a—"

An explosion cut him off. The small interpreter was knocked five feet back from the wall by another recoilless rifle round. His legs had been blown off below the knees.

Doc Graig ran from a bunker, pulled the writhing man to the trench and inspected the horrible wounds. It was too late for a tourniquet to stop the bleeding. He had no blood left.

Alameda pointed toward the north where a nearby firefight was going on. "Irish, check to see if you can help Brownee get his mortar going. We need illumination rounds so the Yards can see the bastards. I'm going to the 'sixty pit and do the same thing. Good luck!"

Shawn stuck his hand out. "See ya in Hell or the Bragg NCO club!"

Alameda slapped his hand. "See ya!"

Shawn followed the trench down toward the bunker where he had placed Hickerson and heard the Nung machine gun chattering. Stepping inside the bunker was like walking into an ear-shattering echo chamber. The machine gunner was hunched over his M-60, shooting through a narrow slit. Doc Hickerson was lying down on his back feeding the belt of 7.62 ammunition like an expert. Shawn knelt down to look out the portal. *Jesus!* The V.C. were visible in the firelight running across the open ground only twenty meters in front of the bunker. They were almost in the inner perimeter's wire. Spinning around, Shawn bolted out of the bunker and belly-flopped into the trench. A flare went off overhead in a pop and flash of golden light. Shawn felt relief. Pop had gotten to the 60 mortar pit. Crawling toward the northern mortar position, Shawn raised up to get his directions. He discovered two enemy soldiers five feet away trying to cut through the wire fence. Lifting his AR-15, he fired a burst that pitched both men backward. He lowered his rifle as a Chicom grenade fell in front of him and skipped into the trench. Shawn jumped out just before the explosion. Immediately, three V.C. rushed toward the wire carrying a satchel charge. Aiming at the closest one's crotch, Shawn fired his rifle and swung the barrel while still holding back the trigger. All three of the small Viet Cong were jerked and knocked backward by the hosing. One screamed in agony and bounced on the ground as if he were on fire. Shawn rolled back into the trench, hoping it was the bastard who had thrown the grenade.

A second flare joined the first one, then another popped in the air off to his left. Shawn heard a thunk ahead and knew Brownee had gotten to his mortar pit. Shawn raised up to see what the last flare had revealed, and gasped. The parachute flare was swaying above the western outer perimeter fence, exposing hundreds of V.C. pouring over the wire. An image of the Chinese attacking in Korea, years ago, flashed into his mind. The only difference was that now he could see the enemy at a greater distance and he was a hell of a lot warmer. The Nungs saw the V.C. too, and their machine guns rattled defiantly. *Yeah! Yeah get 'em! Get 'em! Ye—* Shawn was blown out of the trench by a shuddering explosion that spun him around and knocked the rifle from his hands. Hitting awkwardly on the lip of the trench, he rolled over and fell to the bottom, hitting his head. Stunned, and with his face burning with stinging bits of embedded dirt and gravel, he willed himself to get up, but couldn't keep his balance. He suddenly felt sick, which convinced him to stay on his stomach. He felt for his rifle but realized he was facing in the wrong direction. He turned around and found his AR-15.

SFC Thurman Brownlee took the mortar rounds from the two Nungs as fast as they could hand them over, and he dropped the projectiles down the tube. *Thunk . . . thunk . . . thunk . . .*

Shawn reached the mortar pit bleeding from his scalp and facial wounds. He fell headfirst into the hole and got to his knees. "Brownee, they're in the open to the west 150 meters!"

Brownlee yelled to his Nung assistants. "H-E! Give me H-E! *Charge One!*" He shifted the mortar and adjusted the elevation knob, bringing the tube almost to an upright position. Then he turned for his first round, yelling toward Shawn, *"Adjust for me!"*

Shawn climbed to the edge of the pit and peered over to see where the round landed. *Thunk.*

Twenty seconds later an explosion of light and shrapnel burst at the edge of the outer wire in the midst of the assaulting enemy. *"On target! Shift left and right a few mils, same range!"*

Brownee understood what his friend wanted. By shifting left and right, he could lay down a wall of iron splinters. *"Got it!"*

Sergeant Dissner was glad Pop had joined him at his mortar position to keep the V.C. from tossing in grenades. Pop was positioned at the edge of a parapet, shooting the Viet Cong who were trying to rush the gate. Dissner slid another round into the mouth of the tube and dropped it in. *Thunk.*

Dissner turned toward his Nungs for another round and saw Warrant Officer Conway, the Aussie assigned to the team, calmly walking down the pit steps as if he were taking a Sunday stroll. *"Stay down!"* yelled the sergeant.

Conway began to speak, when his head snapped back and he slowly sunk to his knees. Dissner reached the Australian just as he fell into the dirt. The sergeant turned the soldier over and cursed. There was a small hole between the man's eyes, and a back portion of his skull was blown out, exposing gray matter, but he was moaning. He was still alive.

Dissner gently patted Conway's arm and returned to his mortar. There was nothing he could do but keep firing and try and keep the attackers from taking the camp.

Bleeding from a cut on his forearm and a stomach wound, Captain Dolan dashed toward Sergeant Dissner's mortar position. He arrived simultaneously with Lieutenant Oberstein. Dolan thought he saw figures near the gate and yelled to Dissner, "Light the gate!"

Seconds later a flare popped overhead, revealing three V.C. kneeling by. the gate, taking satchel charges from their packs. The captain knelt down, fully exposed in the light, and fired six rounds. Oberstein saw the V.C. pitch over, and instead of joining in on the killing, he pulled his wounded commander into the mortar pit.

Dolan saw Conway lying by the steps and barked, "Take care of him. I'm all right. Dissner, can you hold here?"

The sergeant nodded. "You'd better check Houston and Terry over by the swimming pool. They were on the dirt mound, holding off dinks in the wire!"

Dolan immediately crawled over the parapet. He had moved only ten yards when a flare revealed his two men lying on the huge dirt pile. First one and then the other would roll and fire a few rounds. They were trying to confuse the attackers as to their exact location. V.C. bodies were stacked just outside the wire only fifteen feet away. Terry let loose a burst and quickly rolled back for protection as bullets thudded into the mound. Houston scooted down a few feet on the far slope, then rolled over into a shooting position. He hosed a V.C. about to throw a grenade, and shifted his weapon toward two more attackers.

Dolan was waiting for him to fire, when he realized something was wrong. Terry sensed the same thing and crawled over to his friend. Grabbing for his shirt, he heard Houston whisper, "I'm hit."

As he pulled the sergeant back, Terry heard the man's last choking sounds. *"Noooo, goddamnit! Noooo!"* Terry screamed in anguish. Standing up, the enraged sergeant spun around shooting from the hip at the attacking enemy, who by now had reached the wire. From behind the cinder blocks to his right came a grenade, tossed by an unseen V.C.

Dolan cried out a warning but it was too late. The blast ripped the AR-15 from Terry's hand and laid open his hand and forearm. Splattered with shrapnel from head to foot, the sergeant tottered back and fell onto his buttocks, still screaming, *"Nooo! Nooooo!"*

Dolan jumped up and ran toward the crazed soldier and dragged him back toward the trench.

"Help meeeeee!" Shawn screamed as he rose up, shooting automatic fire at the wave of attackers climbing over the wire. They had crawled up to the fence and had risen all at once. There were too many for him to stop.

Brownee tossed down the mortar round he was about to drop into the tube and grabbed for his grenades. Shawn fired his rifle until it was empty, then pulled out his pistol and shot a screaming Vietnamese only four feet away. Without aiming, he pulled the trigger again at another man who was running straight for him.

Brownee yelled a warning as the first grenade left his hand, "Grenade! *Down!*"

Shawn ducked and holstered his .45 as the ground shook from the blast. Picking up his AR-15 and jamming in another magazine, he rose up after the second grenade had exploded. Two V.C. were dangling in the wire, and another wounded soldier rolled on the ground directly in front of him. Shooting the soldier in the head with a single round, Shawn ducked back down. "Thanks," he said to his friend.

Brownee nodded and motioned toward his Nungs. "More H-E! Keep it coming!"

Sergeant Dissner stopped firing his mortar and helped the others hold off a wave assault. Chicom grenades were landing in the pit faster than the Nungs could throw them out. Four of the bamboo-handled devices had gone off already, wounding the Nungs, Dissner, Alameda, and Lieutenant Oberstein. A V.C. jumped up at the edge of the parapet holding a grenade, but Dissner had seen his head just before he rose. The sergeant stitched the soldier from knees to neck in a sweeping burst of AR-15 bullets.

Another enemy grenade fell into the pit at the lieutenant's feet and exploded, knocking the officer down. His feet and legs were peppered with shrapnel. Pop Alameda slumped and fell back against the steps. His body was bleeding from countless shrapnel wounds and a fresh bullet hole in his cheek.

Captain Dolan dived into the pit just as another grenade went off. The blast stunned him for a moment, and he shook his head to clear away the horrible ringing. The position had to be abandoned. The enemy were able to hide in a depression just outside the wire and toss in grenades. Dissner, Oberstein, the Nungs, and Pop couldn't take the pounding anymore. They all looked like they had been blasted by shotguns. "Move out of here!" Dolan shouted over the din. "Get to the commo trench!"

Dolan covered his men as they crawled over the parapet. Pop Alameda tried to move but couldn't, so Dolan lifted the old soldier and threw an arm around his waist to support him. As they reached the steps, both men were suddenly propelled upward. An enemy mortar round had made a direct hit inside the pit. Dolan screamed from the burning pain as he flew through space. Hitting the ground with a grunt, the captain passed out. One of the Nungs pulled the officer into the trench as Dissner ran back to the old silver-haired sergeant. The trip was wasted. The sergeant's body had taken most of the mortar shrapnel, shielding the captain. The old veteran had fought his last battle.

Shawn lowered his smoking rifle, the wonderful noise of a flareship finally arriving over the camp. Flares illuminated the area like stadium lights at a night football game. Shawn glanced at his watch. It was a little past four. *Damn, Doc!* He had not checked on Hickerson in over an hour.

Rising, Shawn saw no live V.C. The dead ones were scattered everywhere. "Brownee, I gotta check the Doc!"

Brownee waved him on and motioned for a Nung to take up his friend's position. Shawn had crawled halfway to the bunker when he heard a shrill whistle, then a Vietnamese voice coming over a loudspeaker. Damn, they brought everything but the kitchen sink, he thought as he crawled. When he reached the bunker, he sighed in relief. The doctor was peering out the bunker slit.

"Damn, I'm glad to see you're in one piece, Doc."

Hickerson turned around. "Good to see you too, Irish. How are the others doing? It sounded like they were hitting the main gate area hard."

Shawn's expression changed. "I don't know, Doc. I've been on the other end with Brownee. You stay here, and I'll check on Pop and the others. I'll let you know . . . only, don't move from here."

Shawn heard the loudspeaker crackling again as he made his way to the southern part of the perimeter. The voice had switched to English and was ordering the defenders of the camp to lay down their weapons. Fat chance, he thought. The dinks knew it was over. Once the flare ship arrived, it meant that close air support wasn't far behind.

Shawn passed several Nung positions where many were killed or wounded. The Doc had been right. The southern part of the perimeter had been hit hard. He crawled faster, hearing Doc Graig cussing ahead.

Graig shook his head with irritation at the captain. "Sir, goddamnit, let me tend to your wounds. You're hurt bad."

Shawn reached the pit where the medic was working on the bleeding captain. Wounded with every conceivable type of injury were lying all over the ground. Shawn abruptly stopped in his tracks. Pop lay on the rim of the mortar pit, looking at him with unseeing eyes. Oh, Jesus.

Shawn had lost one friend and did not plan on losing another. Bee-man's mortar position was on the northeast corner of the inner perimeter, and he was the only team member not accounted for. The others said they had heard his mortar firing, but no one could get to him. Shawn crawled along the bottom of the shallow communications trench, popping his head up only now and then to make sure no V.C. were cutting him off. As he turned a corner, he was forced to jerk back. Just ahead, lying in the ditch, were two dinks talking to each other. Shawn didn't dare rise up. He would be seen for sure. He slowly lifted his rifle, extended it around the corner, and pressed the trigger. He held tightly to the bucking weapon. After he had fired the entire magazine, he dropped the rifle and pulled his .45, then peeked around the corner. The smell hit him first. The stink of ruptured intestines was overwhelming. Climbing over the messy bodies would be too much. Fuck it!

Shawn brought his legs up under him and jumped out of the ditch, at a full run. He was ten feet from Bee-man's position when two V.C., lying just outside the inner wire, rose and fired. Shawn stumbled sideways, feeling as if he had been hit in the side by a semi truck. He screamed in anguish, fighting to stay on his feet as bullets cracked by his head. *"Beeeeee!"*

The V.C. sniper hit him again, this time in the leg. Shawn was spun around and fell to his stomach. *"Beeee!"* He clawed toward the mortar pit, feeling as if he were mired in cotton candy. His body didn't seem to want to respond. Finally he closed his eyes and yielded to the cloud that had enveloped him. He knew he would be with Pop soon.

NHA TRANG, 8 JULY

The nurse noticed that the patient in bed four was trying to sit up. She strode straight for him with a scowl. "Lie down this minute, Sergeant Flynn! I told you about those stitches." She pushed him back gently. "Lie back and relax."

Shawn clenched his jaw and stared at the ceiling as she inspected the bandage on his side. Satisfied he hadn't reopened the wound, she checked his leg bandage. "Well, Sergeant Flynn, it looks like you didn't do any damage to the doctor's work. You're one lucky man. It's incredible—two bullets in you, and neither one hit a bone or anything vital. I suspect you'll be out of here in a couple of weeks, and they'll put you on light duty for a while. Some of the others who came in with you weren't so fortunate."

Shawn raised his head with a look of concern. "How are the guys? Are they all gonna make it?"

The nurse smiled. "None of your friends are critical. They'll be fine. General Westmoreland is in their ward right now giving them Purple Hearts and some other medals. He'll be coming down to see you next."

Shawn shook his head with a sneer. "He ain't comin' in here. Why do you think I'm not in their ward? That bastard Major Cummings wants to make sure I'm not seen with them. It was a fluke I was at the camp."

The woman rolled her eyes. "I met the major after he came in and talked to you this morning. He wouldn't do that. I'll bet he—"

The door opened at the end of the ward, and in strode Dr. Hickerson. He approached the sergeant's bed and held out a Colt .45. "I'm sorry, Irish, the general left just a minute ago. I tried to tell him you were here, but Cummings wouldn't let me get close enough to talk. I thought you might want your 'insurance' back. Bee-man said he found it after he dragged you into his hole."

Shawn took the heavy pistol and held it with reverence. "Thanks, Doc. It means a lot to me. I appreciate it."

Hickerson patted his arm. "No, I thank you. I wouldn't have made it without you. If ever you need anything, call me. By the way, you'll be getting your medal despite the major. I had a little talk with the general's aide before he left. You'll be receiving your Purple Heart and a Silver Star by this evening. Take care, Irish. I'll never forget you . . . or your lessons."

Shawn laid the pistol on his chest and shook the doctor's hand. "Next time, Doc, study somethin' a little safer. You keep your ass down out there. You're good people."

Hickerson headed for the door feeling as if he were floating. He had been given the ultimate compliment from a man of a special breed. Irish had called him "good people."

2300 HOURS

Shawn was awakened by the feeling of a cold beer can being pressed against his cheek. "What the—"

"Shuuuu, ya dumb shit. Ya wanna get us both busted to buck-ass privates? Shut the fuck up and drink."

Shawn adjusted his eyes to the darkness and took the ice cold can. "Taco, you crazy bastard. What the hell you doin' here? Hell, I thought you'd be up to your ass in Pentagon secretaries by now."

Sergeant Major John Quail took a long drink and staggered back a step. "I gotta make sure some of us are still alive. I'm sayin' good-bye ta Pop the way he would do for us. . . . Goddamnit! Goddamn this fuckin' war."

Shawn had known his friend would take the news badly. Pop and Taco were very close friends. They had both jumped with the 82nd Airborne Division in World War II and had served together on assignments all over the world. The two old vets were well-known in the Special Forces, for they were among the few who wore two stars above their Combat Infantryman's Badge, signifying they had fought in three wars.

Shawn lifted his beer and took a swallow. Quail lifted his own can to propose a toast. "To one of the best fuckin' expendables there ever fuckin' was. Our friend, Pop Alameda. Pop, we'll see you in Hell, by God."

Shawn lifted his can and bumped Quail's. "To our friend."

Quail emptied the can and tossed it on the bed. Then he took another beer from his pocket and pulled out a pocket knife, with which he stabbed the top. Beer spewed out, showering Shawn. Stabbing the can again, Quail quickly guzzled half of its contents before stepping back and giving Shawn a strange penetrating stare. "I gotta go see her, you know? What the hell am I gonna tell Trudy? What the fuck do you tell a woman whose whole life revolved around her husband?"

Shawn lowered his eyes. Quail, of course, had comforted widows before, but attending the funerals of friends was something he would never get used to.

The sergeant major maintained his stare. "I pulled some strings. You're outta this fuckin' war. You're going home as soon as you get out of the hospital. I lost enough friends for a while."

Shawn's eyes widened in surprise. "But Taco, I got another three months to go."

"Not now, ya don't! You're goin' back to Bragg and be with your ol' lady. I fixed it. I'm Sergeant Major John Fuckin' Quail! I can do fuckin' anything. Don't fuckin' argue! Your ass is outta here. Your wounds are bad enough to shorten your tour. No fuckin' body argues with me. I'm a Pentagon god."

Quail staggered forward and picked up the black case lying on the nightstand. He opened the box and stared at the Silver Star medal for several moments, then shut the case lid. "They gave Pop the DSC. At least I can give something to Trudy."

Suddenly he snapped to attention, facing the nightstand, and raised his hand slowly in a salute. "Mrs. Alameda," he said in a raspy whisper, "a grateful nation wishes you to have this American flag and your husband's Distinguished Service Cross. I . . . I'm sorry and offer the condolences of . . ."

Tears trickled down the old soldier's cheeks. Shawn wished he could somehow ease his friend's anguish.

Quail lowered his salute and took another long drink of beer, then turned and started down the corridor. He stopped at the door and looked over his shoulder. "Irish?"

"Yeah, Taco."

"Take care, huh? I care about ya."

Shawn was about to speak when he heard the ward door close. The sergeant lifted his can toward the door. "To the best damn expendable I know. See ya, Taco."

FORT BRAGG, NORTH CAROLINA, 7 AUGUST

Shawn watched the incoming passengers and smoked a cigarette while he waited for his duffel bag. The older woman whom he had sat beside on the flight from California approached him with a warm smile. "Sergeant Flynn, it was very nice meeting you. It's nice to know that young men such as you are serving our country."

Shawn smiled and put out his hand. "The pleasure was mine, Mrs. Stevenson. I hope your sister gets well soon."

Mrs. Stevenson began to turn away but stopped herself. "Sergeant Flynn, I know it's none of my business, but I really think you ought to call your wife before you drive home. A woman likes to look nice for her husband. You might embarrass her if she's in curlers."

Shawn gave the woman a gentle smile. "It's okay, Mrs. Stevenson, believe me. Gret works on Saturdays and gets off at five." Shawn pointed at his watch. "It's only five-thirty. She'll look fine. I'll be home in twenty minutes. I can hardly wait to see her eyes light up when she opens the door. I've dreamed about that look for a long time."

The woman patted his arm. "Make your dreams come true, then, Sergeant. Take care of yourself."

Shawn parked the rental car in front of the brick apartment building. It was going to take all his resolve not to run up the steps. He got out of the car and wiped his sweating palms on his trousers. Adjusting his beret, he limped toward the steps. Near the top he slowed his pace and took in a few deep breaths to control his excited shaking. It's been too long, he thought. Thank God it's time I got to hold her again. He knocked loudly. He waited. Then, after what seemed like forever, he lost patience and knocked again. Nothing. Damnit! She was probably working late.

Shawn felt behind the outside light fixture and touched the key they always left there. He unlocked and opened the door slowly. Damn, she had changed everything around. The television and his favorite rocking chair were no longer in the living room. They had been replaced with a new stereo and love seat. In the kitchen he found that the secondhand kitchen table they had picked up at the post thrift shop had been replaced as well. She had bought a new chrome table with a glass top and matching chrome chairs. Nice. Real classy. He opened the refrigerator out of habit and was surprised to find beer on the top shelf. She hated beer. He smiled. She must have found out he was coming home. Taking out a bottle of Budweiser, he raised it as if in a toast. Thanks for thinking of me, honey.

He wandered into the hallway, where he stopped abruptly. His pictures, plaques, and award certificates were gone from the walls. When he glanced into the small bedroom that had been his study, he nearly dropped the beer bottle. "What the—"

Shawn turned on the light and suddenly felt weak. The stacked cardboard boxes made his stomach ball up into a knot. The top box was stuffed with broken picture frames that had held photos of his team and his military school certificates. In the other open boxes were his wadded-up clothes. He spun around and limped into the master bedroom. When he flipped on the light, his jaw tightened. Their bed was unmade, and on his side, on top of the nightstand, were three empty beer bottles. Stepping closer, he discovered near the bottle an ashtray filled with crushed, half-smoked cigarettes. Gret didn't smoke. Shaking, he picked up a lighter beside the ashtray. It was a stainless Zippo with crossed sabers embossed on its side. He turned the lighter over. His hand was shaking as he read the inscription.

IF YOU AIN'T CAVALRY
YOU AIN'T SHIT!
Capt. L. Mackey

Clutching the lighter, Shawn stormed out of the room. A minute later he knocked at apartment twenty-three. A young, pregnant woman in bare feet opened the door and gasped when she recognized her old neighbor. She recovered quickly and managed a nervous smile but wouldn't make eye contact. "Sha—Shawn, we didn't know you were coming home. I—I—"

Shawn spoke gently. "Where is she, Marge?"

Margarie Novacks lowered her head. "Shawn, I'm sorry. I tried talking to her but—"

"Where is she, Marge?"

The young woman lifted her head but still wouldn't look at him. "She—She's probably at the Officers Club. It's where she always goes after work." Marge raised her eyes to him as if begging forgiveness. "She wouldn't listen to me."

Shawn wanted to bolt down the stairs but forced himself to put his hand on the young woman's shoulder. Marge had been a good neighbor and friend. Her husband wouldn't be coming home from Vietnam for another three months. "Thanks, Marge. I know you did everything you could."

Shawn's eyes narrowed as he turned away.

Out of habit, Captain Leon Mackey dug into his fatigue pocket for his lighter, though he knew it wasn't there. He had done the same thing all day. He picked up a pack of matches from the bar and lit his cigarette. Exhaling a cloud of blue smoke, he leaned close to the blonde beside him. "Remind me to pick up my lighter tonight. I left it on the nightstand."

Gretchen stirred her drink. "I am hungry. Are ve going to eat?"

Mackey gave a wave to a pilot from his unit who had just walked into the crowded bar, then looked back to the attractive woman. "I gotta change out of these fatigues or they won't let me into the dining room. Hey, I got a idea. How's about you come with me, and after I change, we'll go someplace fancy? The O Club food is gettin' old."

Gretchen smiled and leaned over, touching his handsome face. "You know vat you vill do to me vonce you take off your clothes."

Mackey grinned. "You complainin'? Hell, I hadn't thought of that, but now that you mention it, it's not a bad idea. After, we can go someplace fancy, then go back to your place and do it again. Sound good or what?"

Gretchen picked up her glass. "Let me finish my drink first."

A lieutenant sitting with four other officers raised his hand for the bar waitress. She noticed his signal as she collected empty beer bottles from another table. She had started toward them when she bumped into a stocky soldier, wearing greens, who had just entered the bar. She stepped aside for him. "Gosh, I'm sorry," she said apologetically.

The soldier ignored her as he looked around the bar, obviously trying to find someone.

The waitress was miffed at his discourtesy. Had she noticed he was a sergeant, she wouldn't have been so polite. He was not supposed to be in the club in the first place. "You lost, Sergeant? This is the Officers Club, you know?"

Shawn stiffened. The woman he was looking for had her back to him. She was walking toward a side door with a tall officer.

The waitress's way was blocked by the sergeant, and she was about to tap his shoulder when he pulled what looked like a roll of quarters from his pocket and placed them in his right hand. Clutching the roll tightly, he strode toward the side door as if he were in a hurry. Some people have no manners at all, she thought.

Mackey shut the door behind him and put his arm around Gretchen, giving her a gentle hug as they approached the short flight of carpeted stairs. "Where would you like to eat tonight, honey?"

Gretchen was about to respond when she heard a voice that froze her blood. "You're not going anywhere." She spun around and almost fainted at the sight of her husband.

Mackey turned, looking first at Gretchen, then at the sergeant. Shawn tossed the lighter toward the officer with his left hand. "Is that yours?"

Gretchen gasped as Mackey caught the Zippo in both hands. "Yeah, how'd you—"

Mackey saw the fist coming but had no time to protect himself.

Gretchen cringed in horror as the captain's head snapped back with the crunching blow that knocked him against the wall. She shrieked as her husband pushed her lover back and viciously hit him again, showering them both in blood.

Shawn savagely jerked his knee up into the officer's groin and brought his fist back to knock the rest of his teeth out. Screaming for her husband to stop, Gretchen grabbed his arm. Shawn spun and slugged her in the mouth with his left fist. She reeled with the blow, hitting the banister, then catching herself before she could fall down the stairs. Shawn struck her again with a backhand across the face and swept her legs out from beneath her. She tumbled headfirst down the five steps.

Picking up the lighter from the floor, Shawn lifted Mackey's head and jammed the Zippo into his torn, bloody mouth. "Eat this, you sonofabitch!" Shawn rose and kicked the officer's jaw with his boot. Then he strode down the steps to where Gretchen, still stunned, had gotten to her hands and knees. He brutally kicked her between the legs, lifting her up off the floor. Grabbing her hair, he dragged the moaning woman up the stairs and threw her down on top of the blood-splattered officer. Grabbing her hair, he pushed her face into the captain's mangled face. *"Eat, bitch! Eat!"*

"What are you doing?" yelled a stunned lieutenant, who had just appeared through the side door.

Shawn released Gretchen's hair and stared at the young officer cruelly. "It's payback time. Mind your own business!"

The lieutenant grabbed the doorknob and rushed back into the club for help.

Shawn kicked the woman in the buttocks as a final gesture and strode down the steps. He needed a drink.

The tavern manager quit wringing her hands when city and Military Police cars pulled into the parking lot. She ran to a police officer as he got out of his car.

"He's in the corner! Get that crazy bastard and put him away. He's an animal!"

The officer spoke with detachment. "Calm down and tell me what happened."

The woman began to speak, but the officer stopped her and motioned toward the two approaching military policemen. "Wait. I want them to hear this too."

When the M.P.s arrived, she cleared her throat. "Well, this Green Beret sergeant comes limping in about nine and orders two doubles of Black Jack. I knows something is wrong then 'cause he's wearin' his greens. Nobody wears their Class A's in my joint . . . and then I sees the blood on him. Jesus, he's been in a fight, I says to myself. Anyway, he sits in the corner and had about three more drinks when one of my girls asks if she could join him. The asshole slapped her. Can you believe it? Slapped my girl for nothin'. She just asked to join him, for Christ's sake. Well, a couple of the customers got up to knock him on his ass, but the bastard is real mean and hurts them. One of the boys has a busted nose."

The police officer looked at the M.P. sergeant. "Sound like the one you're looking for?"

The sergeant nodded and slid his nightstick out of his white pistol belt. "Ma'am, we'll handle this from here. All you'll need to do is point out the individual and make a positive identification for us. I would appreciate it if you would also find the woman he assaulted and keep her nearby until we have him secured."

Shawn leaned back in his chair as the M.P.s walked through the door. He wasn't ready to go yet. The sickening images of the captain in bed with his wife were still locked in his mind. He needed just a few more drinks to wash the images away. He lifted his glass and drained the last of his bourbon. Slamming the shooter on the table, he yelled toward the bar. *"Two more!"*

The M.P. sergeant nodded to the specialist fourth class and they separated. Moving slowly toward the table from two directions, they watched the sergeant's hands.

Shawn pushed himself up from his chair to meet the party poopers. He staggered back a step, then caught his balance and shook his head to stop the spinning sensation. Facing the approaching M.P. sergeant, he snarled, "I'm not finished yet. Leave me alone."

"Yes you are," the sergeant said calmly. "You've had enough. I want you to sit down and keep your hands where I can see them."

Shawn shrugged and bent his knees as if he were about to sit, but then spun sideways, lashing out with a side kick. The boot caught the unsuspecting M.P. just above the groin, doubling him over. Shawn turned to strike the second M.P., but his reactions were too slow. A nightstick caught him behind the ear. Everything became blurry, and he felt himself falling into blackness.

19 AUGUST

Shawn walked into the paneled office and stopped three paces in front of the group commander's desk. "Sir, Sergeant First Class Flynn reports."

The gray-haired colonel put on his glasses and looked up. "Stand at ease, Sergeant." The officer leaned back in his chair. "Sergeant Flynn, I asked you to step outside a few minutes ago because I wanted to take some time and think about your case before passing judgment in the Article 15 proceeding. I have made my decision. First, let me tell you I considered the extenuating circumstances concerning the first two charges of assault and battery. Personally, I think you stepped over the line by beating your wife and the captain so badly, but it doesn't make any difference. Neither your wife nor the captain had the guts to press civil charges against you. They knew they didn't have a case. As far as I'm concerned, the military doesn't have a case either. I have dropped those two charges from the Article 15."

The colonel's eyes narrowed. "I understood why you did what you did to your wife and Mackey. I even kind of understand about hitting the M.P.—being drunk and still upset about your wife and all. *But,* I don't understand what the hell got into you afterward. You were picked up by Sergeant Major Sizemore from jail and warned you were pending an Article 15. He told you to keep your nose clean, and yet, you go to the NCO club the next night, get drunk, and destroy five hundred dollars' worth of club property. Then, two days following that, you get picked up downtown, drunk on your ass, and you resisted arrest. The police officer lost his front teeth."

The colonel shook his head and studied the paper in his hands. "Sergeant Flynn, you used to be a good soldier. You know what discipline is all about, and you know I can't condone one of my senior noncommissioned officers making a fool of himself at the club and beating up policemen. The legs and civilians love it when a Special Forces soldier acts like an animal. It's exactly what some of the bastards in this town expect of us. . . . You embarrassed me and the men of this group. You have given me no choice. I must make an example of you. Sergeant Flynn, you are busted down two stripes to buck sergeant. You are fined one-half of your pay for two months, plus you must pay for the damages to the club. You will not be confined or given extra duty, because you're going to be shipped to another post within forty-eight hours. You're out of the Special Forces until such time as you prove to us you can soldier again."

The colonel held out a pen to the sullen sergeant. "You have the right to appeal my punishment if you wish. Do you want to appeal?"

Shawn snapped to attention. "No, sir, I don't want to appeal."

The colonel nodded and pushed a legal document toward him. "Sign, initial, and date the blocks I have the X's by. It says you accept my Article 15 and don't wish to appeal."

Shawn leaned forward and quickly complied, then stood erect again. The colonel took off his glasses and tossed them to his desk. "Sergeant Flynn, I'm sending you off this post so you can start over again. The punishment I gave you is not as bad as it could have been. You used to have a flawless record. Maybe by starting over you can soldier your way back to the Special Forces. The decision is yours. My hope, Sergeant Flynn, is that you decide to soldier. You're dismissed."

FORT BENNING, GEORGIA, 23 AUGUST

When the personnel staff sergeant glanced up at the soldier standing in front of his desk, he noticed his uniform sleeve rank of Sergeant First Class had recently been removed and replaced with the three stripes of a buck sergeant. He smirked before speaking. "So, Fort Bragg shipped you to us because you were a troublemaker?"

Shawn motioned to the folder on the NCO's desk. "You got my personnel record. They sent me here to start clean."

The staff sergeant picked up the folder, keeping his stare on Shawn. "We don't like gettin' other people's troublemakers. You stay right there. I'm gonna let the NCOIC handle your assignment." The sergeant got up and walked into the office behind him.

A minute later the noncommissioned officer in charge strolled out of his office with the other NCO following. The master sergeant eyed Shawn from head to foot as if examining property for flaws.

"Flynn, I heard about you. Your S.F. group sergeant major called our post sergeant major about assigning you to the Airborne Department as an instructor. It just so happens the post sergeant major left yesterday for a new assignment in Germany. That means the deals he made don't count anymore. We have a policy on this post that says a sergeant who's been busted don't instruct students. Just 'cause you were a green beanie don't mean shit to me. I plan on putting you where you belong—a job for troublemakers where you can't screw up anything important. You're going to be assigned to the weapons committee, range maintenance branch. I'm not about to assign you to the airborne job where you'd get jump pay. Let's see how you like being like the rest of us nonjumpers for a while."

Shawn glared at the smug face of the leg sergeant. "I wanna talk to the new post sergeant major and see what *he* says."

The master sergeant's eyes narrowed. "You want to go over my head, huh? Fine. I'll call him right now. I'll talk to him first. Then we'll see. I got the regulations on my side. Plus, you oughta know, the new sergeant major ain't a paratrooper either."

Shawn's shoulders sagged. The bluff had backfired. The rivalry between paratroopers and leg noncoms was like that between Irish Catholics and Protestants—too much bad blood had gone under the bridge. He was doomed.

Two minutes passed when the master sergeant confirmed his suspicion by stepping out of his office with that same smug smile. "Flynn, the sergeant major feels the way I do. You're going to the maintenance branch. You want to call anybody else and go over sergeant major's head?"

Shawn clenched his teeth and shook his head.

The sergeant smiled with his victory. "I didn't think so. Sergeant Danford here, will tell you where to report. Oh, by the way, don't be gettin' in any trouble on this post or you're history, understand?"

Shawn answered with a cold stare.

8

WILLIAMSBURG, VIRGINIA, 10 DECEMBER 1964

Blake Alexander walked into the crowded dining room. His father's annual birthday party was a gathering that required his presence. It was an event where the somebodies and old-money families of the Tidewater area rubbed shoulders and traded plastic smiles. As usual, the lavish, stand-up buffet of exotic foods, ice carvings, and magnificent flower arrangements provided topics for boring conversation. The Maine lobster, king crab, smoked salmon, and jumbo shrimp always drew a crowd, and was a good spot for Blake to mix with the guests.

Blake purposely approached people with their mouths full, as they could only nod or raise an eyebrow to his greeting. It was a way to avoid lengthy socializing. He had to make his presence known for the benefit of his father, then he could escape back to his room.

He was about to greet an elderly couple feasting on crab meat when he felt a tap on his shoulder. Turning around, his stomach tightened into a steel ball.

Sally O'Donnel smiled, having prepared herself for the worst. She had not been home for over a year, and had learned about the accident only when she had returned for the college Christmas break. She was relieved. His face was not nearly as bad as she had heard. "It's been a long time, Blake."

Embarrassed, Blake immediately turned his head so that the injury was not so noticeable. "You're as beautiful as ever, Sally. How's school going?"

Sally furrowed her brow. "Boring. How about you? How's UVA?"

Blake felt his body shriveling. Nobody wanted to hear about his failing his classes. Feeling trapped, he motioned toward the kitchen. "Excuse me, I have to check the caterers. I'll be back in just a minute."

Sally watched him go as Stefne approached. "Hi, Stef. I was just trying to talk to your brother."

Stefne took her friend's arm. "I know. I've been watching him. Sally, Ace has been down lately, so you'll have to excuse him."

Sally could see that Stefne was concerned, and spoke softly. "How bad was he hurt? His face seems fine, except when he . . ."

Stefne nodded. "Yeah. The left side has permanent nerve damage. He has no facial expression on that side. We were just lucky they saved his left eye."

Sally patted her friend's arm. "He looks great, really. He shouldn't be so depressed."

Stefne forced a weak smile. She remembered all too well what he had looked like when she saw him lying in the emergency room. She had not been able to recognize him, except by his build. His nose had been partially ripped off, his front teeth shattered, and the left eye had hung out of its socket. It had proven too much for her to bear, and she had passed out. If it had not been for Hank, she would never have been able to make it until her folks had flown back from France.

The best doctors money could hire had been able to reconstruct her brother's face, and now the scars were hardly noticeable, but the nerve damage could not be mended. His old smile was gone.

"Was he able to go back to school?" Sally asked, realizing she had probably asked him a sensitive question.

Stefne sighed. "He tried. He was in the hospital all summer and went to UVA in the fall. I think he went back to school just to get away from Dad. He had two more plastic surgeries during the semester, which caused him to miss a lot of classes, and he just couldn't get caught up. He flunked out. Dad hasn't changed a bit. He's been riding Blake hard to go to another school out west. The Alexander tradition must live on, you know."

Sally caught the sarcastic tone of the last sentence and looked toward the dining room, where David Alexander was talking to the ex–state governor. "Your dad can be a royal ass at times. How's your mother taking all this?"

Stefne's eyes seemed to soften. "She's coping. Ace is still her little boy and always will be."

Sally raised an eyebrow. "I've got a week before I go back to school. I think I'll stop by tomorrow. Blake and I need to talk about old times."

Stefne lowered her head. "Good luck. If you can get him to say more than four sentences, you'll have done better than I have."

Blake stepped into the bathhouse, closing the door behind him. He just couldn't face telling another person he had flunked out of school. Sally would have given him that same look of pity. He had failed as an Alexander. God, he hated his name.

Blake leaned on the marble sink, looking at his reflection in the mirror. None of them could understand he needed more time. If only things had gone differently. If only he had not been speeding, the young woman might have lived. But he *had* been speeding, and the girl had died, and he had had to learn to live with the guilt and his injuries. He had tried studying, but it had been impossible to concentrate. The theories and concepts were meaningless. He desperately needed something solid to grasp hold of in his life. He needed to find confidence again and succeed in something. His father wanted him to go to school, but he knew he wasn't ready. He could not face failing again. What was he going to do? He felt lost. He had no goals, no desire to get up in the mornings. Nothing seemed to matter.

"Ace?"

Blake broke his gaze from the mirror, recognizing the voice, and opened the door. "What's up, Hank?"

The retired sergeant eyed the young man with concern. "I thought I saw ya sneak outta the house. The party gettin' to ya?"

Blake lowered his chin. "Yeah . . . I'm tired of them telling me how much my face has improved. They'd lie to their mothers if they thought it would get them closer to Dad. They piss me off."

Hank's brow furrowed. "What's really wrong? You've seen this crowd a hundred times. They've always been assholes."

Blake looked into his friend's bloodshot eyes. "What am I going to do, Hank? I can't stay around here. I'm going nuts."

Hank was about to speak when David Alexander strode up behind him. "I can answer that. You're going back to school. Come on back inside. I have some people for you to meet."

Blake glanced at Hank for strength, then shifted his gaze to his father. "Dad, I don't wanna go to school yet. I . . . I'm just not ready."

David's gray eyes narrowed. "Nonsense. You have to go to school. You'll be eligible for the draft if you aren't in college."

Blake realized that this was not the place to argue with his father, and tried to lighten the conversation with a little humor. "At least being in the Army is something an Alexander hasn't done yet."

David did not find the comment funny. His face flushed. "The Army is for losers! Everybody knows it's for people who can't cut it in the real world."

Blake looked sheepishly at Hank, wanting to apologize for his father's remark. The old soldier's eyes shifted to David Alexander with a sad expression, as if he felt sorry for the richly dressed man. His eyes suddenly became set in a strange, expressionless stare. Straightening his back and lifting his chin, he spoke in a tone that unmistakably said he was the man's equal. "Mr. Alexander, I'm proud of my service to this country . . . damn proud."

Hank maintained his stare for a moment before turning and marching for the kitchen door.

"Why'd you say that?" Blake said to his father in a rage. "I was just kidding, and you knew Hank was a career soldier. Does it make you feel good to make others feel small?"

David met his son's anger with a sneer. "I made my point. I'm right, and he knows it. Hank's working for us was your mother's idea, not mine. If it was up to me, he'd be gone tomorrow. He's a loser."

Blake turned his face away in mortification. His father wasn't listening. He never had listened to him or understood him. Blake made for the door to catch up to his old mentor to apologize.

"Where are you going?" David barked. "I'm not through talking to you!"

Blake spun around. "Yes, you are! And you're through talking to me about becoming a great 'Alexander.' I'd rather be a 'loser' than be like you!"

"Get back here!" David yelled at Blake's back as he strode away. "You're not talking to me like that! You hear me? *Get back here!*"

11 DECEMBER

Blake lay spent on the bed. He had forgotten how insatiable Sally could be. He brushed her hand away from his face and spoke tiredly. "You're going to have to give me a break. I'm out of practice."

Sally smiled and propped herself on an elbow. "I'm the one who needs the break. I just wanted to touch the scars. I can hardly see them."

Blake looked into her flushed face and smiled to himself. He had forgotten her radiance. It was strange, but Sally had always had the radiant glow after making love. Just a few years before they had made love in every secluded spot in Williamsburg. During all those "secret deals," as she had called them, he had always loved that glow. It was a special look that warmed him and made him feel good inside. They had never been in love, for they both somehow knew it would have spoiled their relationship. They had been good friends over the years and had always been honest with each other. In their world, where people never spoke their real feelings, their relationship had been very special.

Blake looked into her eyes. "How do I really look?"

She touched his cheek and gently ran her fingertips down one of the thin scars to his lip. "You look mean. Kinda like Humphrey Bogart when he played that gangster role and talked out of the side of his mouth. If I hadn't known you before, I would have thought you were trying to be a tough guy."

She retraced the path up his cheek. "The damaged nerve must run from the eyebrow down your cheek to just above your lip. When you smile, the upper left lip moves just a little."

Blake pointed to his cheekbone and above his left eye. "The last operation shortened the muscles to keep the left side of my face from drooping. It was like a face-lift."

Sally smiled seductively and kissed his cheek. "At least everything else is working fine."

Blake glanced at his watch and patted her bare buttocks. "I've gotta go. I've got an interview for an exciting job."

Sally leaned over so her breasts would touch his chest. "What could be more exciting than me?"

The upper right corner of Blake's lip curled up. "I need to get away for a while. I'm going to join the Army."

Sally fell back on the yacht bed with a moan. "My God, Blake, the Army? Why?"

Blake sat up and looked for his socks. "I guess it's to prove a point."

The young woman stared at him in bewilderment. "What have you possibly got to prove?"

Blake stood and looked into her questioning eyes. "Blake Alexander is not a loser."

CARLISLE, PENNSYLVANIA

"Hey, Gene, you're wanted in the office!"

Eugene Day pushed the dolly stacked with boxes into the back of the truck and gently lowered the load. He waved at the dock boss to let him know he had heard the message and strode toward the office.

The supervisor rose from his chair as Eugene walked through the open door, and just before leaving, said, "Gene, these two cops wanna talk to you for a little while. See me after they leave, huh?"

A dark-haired plainclothesman flashed his badge. "I'm Sergeant Broski and this is Sergeant Simpkins. We wanted to ask you a few questions. Sit down."

Eugene pushed his glasses back up on his nose and sat down with a blank expression.

"Where were you on New Year's Eve night?" asked the dark-haired officer.

Eugene's eyes rolled upward, as if in thought. "Let's see . . . yeah, I was in Harrisburg at the Maclay Baptist Church. We were making posters for an upcoming march. I left there a little after midnight and was driven home."

"You have witnesses?"

"Yes, the pastor can give you a list of people who were there. The pastor's daughter drove me home, so you can ask her too."

Broski took out a notebook from his jacket pocket. "So between ten P.M. and approximately one A.M. you can prove where you were?"

Eugene raised an eyebrow. "No, I can prove where I was from about five P.M. till one A.M. I got there early."

Simpkins spoke for the first time. "Did you hear about the Roadside Café burning down?"

"I read the papers," Eugene replied flatly.

"You were one of those arrested at the Roadside a month ago, weren't you?" Simpkins asked.

"Yeah, I was arrested, but the charges were dropped."

Broski flipped up a page of his notebook and took over again. "To be correct, you've been arrested six times for various reasons."

"I was released in each case without charges being filed. Don't your notes say that?"

"Look, kid," Broski fired back, "we're asking the questions. You happen to be a suspect in the arson of the Roadside Café."

Eugene smiled smugly. "Find yourself another colored boy. I can prove where I was."

Eugene began to get up, but Broski pushed him back into the chair. "Just sit down, boy. We're not finished yet. We're on to you. We know there's a group that's turned renegade. We also know you're the leader, and you order the hits. The four fires we've had in the last two months all have one thing in common. Each place that burned didn't allow Negroes. What happened, Day? You decide it was time for payback?"

Eugene smiled again. "You have a wonderful imagination, officer. Do you have any more stories for me?"

Simpkins lunged from his chair. "You sonofa—"

Broski blocked Simpkins and kept him from grabbing the young man. Simpkins backed off but pointed at Eugene's face. "Day, I'm gonna get your ass! That's a promise."

Eugene stood and rolled his eyes. "I'se be here Mistaw Po-lice."

Broski motioned toward the door. "Get out, Day. Have your laugh today. We're gonna get you real soon, then *we'll* have the last laugh."

Eugene kept his smile. "I'se be waitin'."

Regina Davis was waiting in the parking lot of the trucking company when the final work whistle blew and Eugene came out carrying his lunch pail. She drove the car up beside him and honked. He seemed pleasantly surprised and got in beside her.

"Hi, hon, why you in town? Something the matter?"

She pulled out onto the highway. "You tell me. The police came by the church today and talked to Daddy."

Eugene leaned back in the comfortable seat. "Well?"

She glanced nervously at her passenger. "He said you were downstairs making posters with the rest of us. You were lucky, Gene. If he'd a' known you left, he wouldn't have lied for you. The police are on to you."

Eugene leaned over and kissed her cheek. "Don't worry. We're going to stay low for a while."

Regina kept her eyes on the road. "I love you, but this has gone too far. The last two months has changed you, and I don't like it. You've become somebody I don't know. I want you to stop it, now. Daddy would be broken-hearted if he knew what you were doing. He's worked too hard, and you'll ruin everything he's done."

Eugene lowered his head. "You're right. It's over. There, wasn't that easy?" He smiled and touched her cheek affectionately. "I love you too much to lose you." ~

Regina pulled into a parking lot and stopped the car. "Come here, I need a hug."

James Day walked into his son's room as Eugene was changing out of his workclothes. "Gene, some police officers came by the school today and talked to me. I want you to look at me and say you're not involved."

Eugene pulled on his slacks and looked into his father's eyes. "Dad, I didn't burn down those places. I don't believe in violence."

James lowered his head and limped toward the door. He stopped in the hallway and spoke over his shoulder. "I didn't tell your mother about the police talkin' to me, it would upset her. I want you to quit what you're doin'. She couldn't take you bein' in jail."

Eugene tried to speak, but his father was already to the stairs. He had thought he had pulled it off perfectly. How did his father know?

Eugene felt a sickening, sinking feeling as his father walked down the wooden steps. His father's last look was one of heartbreaking disappointment.

"Gene, back here, man."

Eugene looked up the darkened street in both directions before stepping back into the alley. "You recon the place?"

Rafford broke into a toothy grin. "Yeah, the joint is gonna go easy, man. When we gonna do it?"

Eugene stepped back into the shadows as a car drove down the street. "Soon as I get an alibi. The heat is on to me."

Rafford shrugged his shoulders. "Fuck 'em, man. You done enough. I'll take care of it myself tomorrow night. You be someplace where you got witnesses. It burns at ten, man."

Eugene raised his fist. "The Brothers."

Rafford raised his arm, clenching his fist tightly. "The Brothers!"

12 DECEMBER

Regina leaned over and kissed Eugene's cheek. "The movie was great, thank you."

Eugene adjusted his glasses on his nose. "Too bad James Bond isn't a Negro." He turned the car toward town.

Regina scooted closer to him. "I thought for sure you'd want to park."

Eugene glanced at his watch. "I'm hungry. I thought we'd stop at the drive-in for a burger."

Regina had become more and more aware of his remoteness all evening.

Something was wrong. "What's going on? You've looked at your watch at least ten times since we left the theater."

Eugene yawned. "I'm sorry, it's just I have to get up early tomorrow. We have a big shipment coming in."

"Why'd you call me, then? We could have gone another time." Regina was perturbed.

Eugene pulled the car into a parking place in front of the drive-in. "I'm sorry, it's just that I wanted to be with you. You're on my mind all the time."

Regina felt better at that. "I like seeing you too. Go on, get your food before you starve. I don't want anything."

Eugene secretly glanced at his watch again as he got out of the car, then he strolled over to the outside counter. He gave his order to the counter girl, and after several minutes, a sack and paper cup appeared on the takeout ledge. "A burger, fries, and cherry Coke. Thanks."

To be remembered, Eugene took the sack but fumbled the paper cup and knocked it over on the counter. As the young woman grabbed for a towel, a siren began to blare in the distance.

Eugene got in the car and tossed the sack to Regina's lap. "You were right. I'm wasting an opportunity. Let's park!"

Regina punched him lightly on the arm. "You're terrible! What about your food?"

Eugene started the engine. "You come first."

When Eugene walked into the house, he was surprised to see his mother sitting on the sofa watching television. "Mom, I'm a little old for you to be waiting up for me."

Jewel Day shook her head. "I wanted you to know about Rafford Mills. Ann Washington called me just as I was getting in bed. Rafford was killed by a night watchman tonight. They caught him trying to start a fire at the Trucker's Café."

Eugene felt himself shriveling. He was too shocked to speak. He knew if he had been there as a lookout, Rafford would be alive.

Eugene sunk into the chair across from his mother. Her eyes focused on him. "What makes a boy like Rafford want to burn people's livelihoods? He seemed like such a nice boy."

Eugene lowered his head, unable to bear her eyes. "The Trucker's Café didn't allow us coloreds, Mama. Maybe he was trying to tell white folks something."

Jewel's lips tightened. "Was it worth dying for? Jesus didn't destroy or burn to change the world. He loved his oppressors."

Eugene got up and walked toward the stairs. He stopped at the banister. "They killed him too, Mama."

Jewel lowered head. "There's a letter for you on your dresser. I forgot to give it to you this afternoon when you got home from work. Son, pray for him tonight. Pray Jesus will understand."

Eugene took the stairs two at a time and went immediately into his room. His mother was like the rest of them. They thought praying would bring about a righteous world. But blood and flames was the only way to make the whites understand. Rafford knew that. That's why he died. But even as he told himself that his friend had died for justice, he knew there was no justice in the death. It wasn't a night watchman who'd done the killing—it was him, Eugene Day, Rafford's friend.

Eugene collapsed numbly on the bed, but got up, remembering the letter. He took the envelope from the nightstand. It had a government return address. Probably more forms to fill out for the job. He opened the letter and read the first line. "Greetings from the President of the United States."

No! They can't do this! No way am I going! He tossed the letter to the floor as tears began trickling down his cheeks. Thoughts about Rafford suddenly filled his mind. Oh God, Rafford I'm sorry . . . I'm so sorry, brother. Forgive me.

CUSSETA, GEORGIA, 13 DECEMBER

Connie Calhoon stepped outside the door. "Lee, git in tha house this minute before ya catch your death."

Lee rose from the steps, holding the shoes he was shining, and smiled at his mother. "I'm done anyway, Ma."

Connie held the door open and followed him into the kitchen. "I finished ironing your shirts. Ya gonna look real nice when ya go back ta school. I'm prouda ya, son."

Lee sat at the table and basked in his mother's glowing pride. He was glad she had never come on campus or seen the other students at Columbus College. Most of them drove their own cars and wore new clothes, not shirts and jeans from the Salvation Army. The looks he had tolerated his first semester would have turned her purple with anger. "Thanks, Ma, ya didn't have to iron 'em for me."

Connie sat down across from him. She reached over and patted his hand. "Ya worked so hard. I figured it was the least yo' mama could do. It's hard ta believe ya start again after Christmas. Ya'll ready?"

Lee smiled. "Sure, Ma, I'm gonna do good just like last semester. The courses are hard, but I'll make it."

Connie's eyebrow shot up. "That job don't mess with your study time, does it?"

"Naw, most of the classes are over by one. I have plenty'a time to clean the rooms an' study too."

"Ya came back skin an' bones. Ya gotta take better care'a yourself next time."

Lee rose to his full six feet. "Ma, the janitor job for the school pays for my room and board. Don't ya worry 'bout me. I'm gonna—"

Lee's eight-year-old sister ran crying into the kitchen. He bent over and picked her up. "What's wrong, Puddin'?"

She sniffed back her tears and pointed to the ceiling. "Cha—Charlie is layin' . . . in the floor. He's cryin'. He says he's dying."

Lee gently wiped her tears from her cheeks. "Charlie is too mean to die, Puddin'. Come on. Let's go see what's ailin' him. He's probably funnin' you again."

Connie put her hands on her hips. "Lee, ya tell your brother ta not scare Lisa, or I'll tan his hide good."

Minutes later Connie looked from the ironing board and gasped. Lee was walking toward her with her six-year-old son in his arms. He spoke calmly. "Ma, I think we'd better get him to the doc's. He can't sit up or walk. Somethin's wrong with his stomach."

Connie paced just outside the hospital entrance. She stopped only when she saw her husband walking in from the parking lot. She had called the mill from the doctor's office before they took Charlie to the hospital.

"Roy, Charlie has appendicitis."

Roy's eyes widened. "Is he gonna be all right?"

Connie nodded, but her eyes told him something was wrong. "The hospital folks wanted ta know how's we were gonna pay. I told 'em you was a workin', but they kept talkin' about insurance or somethin' called Blue Shield. I told 'em we didn't have none of those things."

Roy's face reddened. "Is they helpin' Charlie or not?"

Connie's eyes began to pool. "Lee . . . Lee is payin' em. All that money he saved is—"

"Don't start bawlin'. I'll pay him back every red cent. Come on, I wanna see Charlie." Roy took his wife's arm and led her toward the entrance. He squeezed her arm affectionately. "It ain't no problem, so don't be worryin' none. I can work time-ana-half and do some huntin'. Things is gonna be just fine."

Connie sniffed back her tears, but inside she was still crying. She knew her husband didn't understand about college things. Lee would not be able to go back to school until he had money. It would take Roy at least six to eight months to earn enough. She had begged Lee not to pay. They could have taken Charlie to one of the county hospitals. But Lee wouldn't listen. The doctor had told him that moving Charlie would have been risky. All her son's hard work, his dream, was out of reach for at least another year.

Lee strolled down the street, looking in the store windows. He had wanted to get out of the stuffy hospital awhile and to pick up something to eat for his mother. He paused to look at a poster taped to a large plate-glass window. The answers he was seeking were clearly written on that poster. He knew it the minute he read the words.

Lee Calhoon walked into the United States Army recruiting office. A sergeant glanced up from his desk. "What I can do for ya?"

Lee pointed at the poster. "Can you tell me about the education benefits, please?"

The sergeant smiled and stood up. "Sit down and let's talk."

SOUTH PHILADELPHIA

Vincent Martino parked the fruit truck at the curb and stepped out onto the sidewalk. Down the pavement, past the pretzel stand, he saw her. She was slicing cold cuts from a large smoked ham.

Gina glanced up. "Vinny, you off work so early?"

Vincent shrugged his shoulders. "Naw, I thought I'd come and see ya. I got somethin' today. A letter."

Gina wiped her hands on her apron. "Ya know somebody who can write, huh?"

Vincent bobbed his head. "Funny, Gina, real funny. I know a lotta people. I got a letter from the President. He says maybe I should work for him."

Gina rolled her eyes. "Okay, the President, yeah, sure. You want somethin' to eat?"

Vincent pulled a crumpled letter from his back pocket and handed it to her. "I tell you the President, I *mean* the President. He says he wants Vincent Martino."

As she read the letter, Gina's hands began trembling. She looked up at him with tear-filled eyes. "You got drafted? They can't do this to me."

"You? You didn't get drafted. The President is tellin' me I gotta go. Ain't no big thing. I been workin' a long time now, an' I ain't doin' so hot. I talked to Tony an' he thinks it's okay."

Gina tossed the letter toward him. "Tony don't love you. Tony don't feed your ugly face neither. You're not going. You're gonna marry me, now."

Vincent backed up, holding out his hands. "Yo, Gina, you're talkin' crazy. Your old man thinks I stink. How'm I gonna marry you? Come on, Gina, I ain't got no money."

Gina tugged at her apron strings and began to sob. Vincent quickly walked around the stand and put his muscular arms around her. "Hey, ya know I don't like it when ya cry. I love you too Gina, but we can't get married now. Your pop won't let us."

Gina spun around, hugging him. "I can talk to Father Vittari. He'll understand. He'll help us and—"

"Hey, what're you two doin'? Get away from her, Martino!"

Vincent backed up, glaring at Gina's father, who had walked down the front stoop of their house. "I ain't a kid, Mr. Cantelli. You shouldn't be talkin' to me that way."

Franco Cantelli ignored the young man and spoke harshly to his daughter. "You get back to work. Leave the bum alone."

Vincent stepped within a few inches of Franco. "Don't call me no bum. Nobody calls me a bum."

Gina savagely tossed her apron at her father. "Leave me alone! Go back upstairs!"

Franco smiled smugly at Vincent. "I was at the door and heard you guys. You're not as dumb as you look, Vinny. You're right. I'm not lettin' you marry Gina."

"You don't tell *me* what *I* can do," Gina snarled at her father. "I'm twenty years old, Papa. Vinny, tell him! We're gonna get married."

Vincent backed away from Franco and shifted his gaze to the brown-eyed woman. Slowly his eyes lowered and he began walking back toward the truck.

Gina cried out, "No, Vinny . . . tell him . . . Vinny, don't! Don't do this to me."

Vincent quickened his pace. He couldn't marry her. They could never live with her folks, and his mother didn't have room in their apartment. He didn't make nearly enough money to rent a place and pay the bills. There was no way he could take care of her the way she deserved.

Franco put his hand on his daughter's shoulder. "He's goin' nowhere here. He knows that. Let him go."

Gina spun around. "I hate you!"

Franco showed the hurt he felt at her words. "No, you hate the truth."

1965

9

10 JANUARY 1965

Sergeant First Class Gleason knocked once on the trailer door. The light force of his hand made it creak open. One look inside the filthy trailer told him he must have had the wrong address. He reached for the knob to close the door but saw an Army fatigue shirt hanging over the far window, like a curtain. Damn, it was *his* place! Stepping inside, Gleason barked loudly, "Shawn!"

When there was no response, Gleason walked toward the narrow hallway, stepping over beer bottles and cans scattered over the stained linoleum floor. The trailer living room and adjoining kitchen looked like a trash heap. Dirty dishes were stacked on the counter along with countless beer bottles. Trash and rumpled clothes lay in smelly piles. The only furniture in the tiny living room was a beat-up couch with the stuffing hanging out and a small portable television sitting on top of a battered footlocker. Stepping over still more piles of dirty clothes in the hallway, he passed the bathroom and halted at the open bedroom door. Gagging, the sergeant stepped back from the smell and repugnant sight. Shawn was lying naked on filthy brownish sheets. He had thrown up during the night and was covered with vomit.

Gleason backed up farther before yelling. *"Flynn! Flynn, get up!"*

Shawn's eyes fluttered. He moaned and raised his head. "Huh?"

Gleason walked back into the tiny living room to get away from the putrid odor before speaking. "I need the keys to the maintenance shed. The basic course committee needs some targets."

Shawn brought his hand up to rub his blurry eyes and noticed the dried vomit on his arm. The smell hit him a split second later. Sickened, he jumped up and ran to the bathroom holding his hand over his mouth. He barely made it in time to throw up into the toilet.

Gleason felt his own stomach rumble at the sounds of the sick soldier and stepped closer to the open trailer door for fresh air.

He waited several minutes before Shawn came into the living room wearing only underwear. "What'd ya want?"

Gleason tried to breathe through his mouth. "Keys. I need the keys to the maintenance shed."

Shawn tried to focus his bloodshot eyes. "It's Sunday, for Christ's sake.

111

What the hell you—" He spotted his fatigue pants and picked them up to search his pockets. He found the keys and tossed them to his boss.

Gleason caught them and stared at Shawn with disgust. "You looked in the mirror lately? You've put on at least twenty pounds of fat in the past six months. Jesus, you live like a fucking pig."

Shawn felt dizzy and flopped down in the chair. "I do my job . . . ya got a cigarette?"

Gleason's eyes softened. "Look, Shawn, I know the job sucks, but shit, you're still a soldier. Start takin' care of yourself or you're gonna have this shitty job permanently. We're gettin' an officer next week, and he's not gonna put up with you like I do. You've been late to work the past two weeks, and when you did make it in, you smelled like a fuckin' brewery. You gotta get your act together and try, at least."

Shawn raised his bloodshot eyes to the sergeant. "Have ya got a cigarette or not?"

Gleason sighed and walked out of the stink. Flynn was on a downhill slide. He had given up months ago on the first day he had reported to the job. Flynn had reacted like a professional baseball player sent down to a farm team to be the bat boy. He had quit trying.

Gleason walked down the trailer steps and strode toward his car. Stopping at the trailer park entrance, he looked over his shoulder at the rusted, rented trailer. It tore him up inside knowing that there was nothing he could do but watch a pro drink his career away. Flynn needed to play ball soon, or he would never be able to play again. He was running out of time.

19 JANUARY

The newly assigned lieutenant pointed at a heavy-set sergeant getting off his motorcycle. "He's not assigned to this committee, I hope?"

Sergeant First Class Gleason frowned. "Yes, sir, he's ours. That's Sergeant Flynn. He maintains the range targets and our equipment."

The officer stared at the overweight soldier as he walked toward the maintenance shed. "He's fat and sloppy-looking. I want you to square away his appearance and—" The young officer stopped talking in mid-sentence and swiveled his head toward Gleason as if he just remembered something important. "Did you say 'Flynn'?"

The senior NCO nodded and motioned for the lieutenant to follow him toward the range shack a short distance away.

The officer followed as he took a small notebook from his fatigue shirt pocket. "I remember writing his name down when I looked over the men's records. He's ex–Special Forces and has two CIBs. How come he's not wearing his combat patch and badges?"

The sergeant opened the door of the small office. "Sir, Flynn is the most experienced vet in our committee. Sit down, sir, let me give you a rundown on him and the others you have working for you."

The sergeant poured two cups of coffee, handed one to his new officer and sat down. "Sir, the first thing you have to understand is we don't exactly get the best people assigned here to the post. We get the outcasts or those who can't cut it in the line units. You're gonna see what I mean soon enough. Flynn is a good place to start, since you pointed him out. Sergeant Flynn got busted and tossed out of the S.F. about six months ago and was sent here to Benning. He was assigned to the range committee cause they figured he was trouble waiting to happen. He's got no family or friends and doesn't give a shit about much of anything. He's a loner and lives in a trailer just off post. I understand he spends most of his off-duty time in a tavern by the trailer park. Saying all that, I gotta tell you he does his job and never complains. But he's not cut out for being a maintenance man. He needs to be doing something with troops and given a chance to soldier again."

The officer set down the coffee mug after taking a sip. "I thought Special Forces soldiers were all gung-ho types. He's fat and doesn't even wear the patches he's authorized."

The sergeant's brow knitted. "We don't do any P.T. out here, sir. Our hours are the worst of anybody on post. That's not an excuse for Flynn, he just doesn't care anymore. Something happened to him . . . the fire inside him went out. I'll talk to him about his uniform and have him get a haircut. As far as the combat patches go, that's his option. I can't require him to wear them. I think he knows he would embarrass his old outfit by the way he looks."

The lieutenant made a notation in his notebook. "Okay, that takes care of Flynn. I hope you're going in order of worst to best, or this job sounds like I got screwed. Who's next?"

Bob Lincoln heard the motorcycle's distinctive rumbling outside and reached in the cooler for a Budweiser. Seconds later the rider walked into the tavern and strode to his usual table in the corner. Bob, the owner and bartender of the Outpost Tavern, set the beer on a tray and walked around the bar to personally give his best customer what would be the first of many beers that night. "How ya doin', Sarge? What's it gonna be tonight? The wife made up some chili that ain't bad."

Shawn took off his fatigue cap and tossed it to the chair beside him. "Chili sounds good."

Bob set the beer down in front of his customer and took a seat. "You look tuckered. Are you takin' care of yo'self?"

Shawn took a sip of beer and nodded toward the other side of the tavern. "I'm fine. You hire somebody new?"

Bob looked over his shoulder at the small, auburn-haired woman, wearing blue jeans and a cowboy shirt, who was standing by the jukebox.

"Yeah, that's Cindy. She's the wife's little sister. She's had some tough breaks. Her year-old son died last month . . . she took it real bad. Her ol' man ran off just a week before the accident, so the boy was all she had. She showed up this morning with no other place to go. She's broke and stayin' with us awhile to get on her feet. It's too bad, she's a good little gal, but doesn't have a high school diploma or a single job skill. I gave her a job till she finds somethin'."

Shawn nodded absently and lifted his beer bottle. "Bring me another in a few minutes."

Bob got up and looked at the soldier's puffy face with concern. "You sure you're taking care of yo'self?"

Shawn took out a pack of Chesterfields. "Yeah."

Cindy picked up a tray full of beers from the bar and made her way around the crowded tables. Bob had told her they got busy at six, but she hadn't realized just how busy. She was exhausted, and it was only a little after ten. She wasn't sure she could stay on her feet until they closed at midnight. The only good thing about the job was that it kept her too busy to think about Timmy.

After delivering the beer, collecting the money, and picking up the empty bottles, she headed back for the bar. She felt a hand pat her behind but kept walking. Bob had warned her the crowd was rough. They were mostly mill and construction workers who were trying to forget their jobs, wives, and bosses. She had been propositioned and pinched a half a dozen times, and they were getting worse as the night and beer wore on. Their leering looks were the hardest part of the job to take. They seemed to undress her with their eyes, and it was hard to smile like Bob wanted. In fact, her smile seemed only to make it worse.

Cindy stopped near three construction workers who were pounding the table and laughing. One of the men glanced up at her and spoke thickly. "Well, looky what we got here. Honey, you're put together like them houses we build. Every brick is in the right place. How's about givin' us another round and tell us which one of us ya gonna take home with ya."

Cindy maintained her forced smile while picking up their empty bottles. "Sorry boys, but I'm not that kinda girl."

The worker patted her buttocks. "You go with me, I'll make ya one of them kind."

Cindy brushed his hand away, still holding the smile. "Be nice. Three beers coming up." She began to move toward the bar but again noticed the sergeant in the corner. He had been sitting there alone all evening. She had caught him looking at her several times, but not with a leer, like the others. It was a strange look, almost as if he thought he knew her.

She changed direction and walked to his table. "You want another one?"

Shawn glanced at his half-full bottle and shook his head. "Naw, I'm good."

She began to speak again just to be friendly, but he was ignoring her. She shrugged her shoulders and walked toward the bar.

Shawn shifted his gaze back toward the diminutive woman as she strode toward the bar. She reminded him of his mother when she was young. Cindy would have won no beauty contests, but she was still attractive. She was the kind you needed time to study and appreciate. She didn't wear makeup or fix her hair in a fancy hairdo; she didn't need to. Like his mother, the new waitress had a natural sort of prettiness that would have been ruined by rouge and powder.

Maggie Flynn, his mother, had tried hard to make a worthwhile life, but loneliness had finally overcome her. A young boy couldn't give her the kind of love she needed. She had needed a man, but could never seem to hold on. She always believed them when they told her they loved her. They never really did. Maggie had lost her pride after the first couple of years, and then it had not mattered. Her lovers used her up and took away her dreams. Her face turned hard, and the beauty—like her love—was lost. In the end Shawn couldn't stand to be around her. To know what she had been and how far she had fallen was too much for the both of them. He had walked out of her trailer when he was seventeen and never saw her again.

Cindy's delicate features and long auburn hair were like his mother's, but it was her eyes that held the most striking resemblance. The large, brown, innocent eyes were her strength. They showed signs of loss and pain, but also the spark of renewed determination. He could tell she was struggling, trying to keep up a smile of happiness she didn't feel. It was the same look his mother had in the beginning. She was trying to believe again. Too bad. The world was just too cruel for such delicate creatures as this girl or his mother.

Shawn lowered his head, feeling a nagging emptiness clawing at his heart. The anguish and guilt he had felt for leaving his mother—and more, for not being able to help her—had scarred his heart forever. In comparison, the pain he felt at thoughts of Gretchen were minor. He found he could no longer bear to look at the waitress. Just the sight of her seemed to reopen old wounds.

Cindy collected beers for the construction workers and returned to their table. She set the bottles down, when suddenly the biggest of the three men pulled her to his lap. He laughed drunkenly and ran his hands roughly over her breasts as he tried kissing her cheek. She fought to free herself but his grip was like steel. She began to scream, and then saw a blur pass only inches from her face. The construction worker's head snapped back and his body went limp, as if he'd turned into a rag doll.

Shawn stepped closer to the table and faced the two other workers, who had been caught by surprise. The closest shoved his chair back, but Shawn lashed out with a quick jab that smashed the man's nose in a shower of blood. Leaning over the table with a menacing glare, Shawn growled a warning to the other worker. "Don't even think about it."

Bob Lincoln reached the table a second later, holding a sawed-off ball bat. He pointed the blunt end of the club at the unhurt worker. "Pick up your friends," he barked, "and git outta here. Pay for your beers first!"

Cindy turned to thank the sergeant, but he just waved her away and walked back to his corner table. She followed him anyway. Stopping in front of him as he sat down, she extended her hand. "Thank you for—"

Shawn glanced up but wouldn't make eye contact. "Save it," he interrupted icily. "Just get me a beer."

Cindy's eyes narrowed. She slowly lowered her hand and spoke with disdain. "I was wrong. You weren't helping me . . . you're just mean, and you were looking for an excuse to hurt somebody. You're as bad as they are."

In silence and without changing expression, Shawn shifted his gaze to his empty beer bottle. There was no use in saying anything. She was partly right. He hadn't helped her. He'd done it for another woman from his past.

Cindy shook her head as if disappointed, and strode for the bar in the silence.

Cindy looked at her watch and sighed in relief. Thirty minutes to closing and only a few customers were left. She could hardly wait to take a bath and wash away the smell of stale beer and cigarette smoke.

The sergeant was still at his table, smoking a cigarette and staring blankly toward the bar.

She took the five empty beer bottles from his table and began to move to the next table but stopped herself. She had been feeling guilty about what she had said to him and wanted to apologize. Bob had told her the sergeant had come in every night and sat at the same table for over five months. Not once had he made a bit of trouble.

Cindy sighed and sat down in the chair opposite the sergeant. "Hey, I'm sorry about what I said. I was upset."

Shawn nodded without looking at her.

"You don't talk much, do ya?"

Shawn glanced only a second at her before standing up. He tossed a dollar on the table and headed for the door.

Cindy watched him leave. She picked up her tray feeling incredibly tired. "Thanks anyway," she whispered.

29 JANUARY

The lieutenant put down the phone and stepped out of the range shack. "Sergeant Flynn, come here a minute."

Shawn put down the targets he was carrying to the shed and came over to the range shack steps. "Yes, sir?"

The officer put his hands on his hips. "You're to go see the post sergeant major immediately. Don't ask me why, 'cause they didn't tell me."

Shawn nodded. It probably had something to do with the guard detail that the committee had to pull the following week. "Yes, sir, I'll go right now."

The lieutenant shook his head as the sergeant walked toward his motorcycle. As usual, Flynn needed a haircut and his uniform wasn't starched. Flynn would probably get him into trouble if any brass saw him. Damn him.

Shawn stopped at the receptionist's desk. "Ma'am, I got word to see the sergeant major?"

The secretary glanced up only as far as his fatigue-shirt name tape. "Flynn . . . yes, you have a visitor in the sergeant major's office. You're to go right in."

Shawn sucked in his protruding stomach and strode into the carpeted office knowing that whoever it was must be important to rate use of the post senior NCO's office. Shawn abruptly halted. A soldier sat behind the desk. His disapproving look cut through Shawn like a hot knife.

Sergeant Major John Quail stood and tossed a bayonet toward Shawn, who caught the weapon out of instinct.

Quail motioned toward the knife. "Ya might as well do it now and save time."

Shawn's shoulders sagged and he lowered his head. His old friend was the last person he wanted to see. Quail walked around the desk. "Go ahead, do it. Cut your throat now. I can take seeing you die this way rather than watch you kill yourself like you're doing."

Shawn used up the last of his self-respect and tossed the bayonet to the desk. "You wanted to see me, Sergeant Major?"

Quail shook his head. "No, I wanted to see a friend, but instead I'm lookin' at a fat, self-pitying fool. What the hell is wrong with you? Ya look like shit!"

Shawn stared at the wall in silence. Quail raised an eyebrow. "She was a bitch. Ya gave her what she deserved, but you're still letting her fuck you over. I can understand being down for awhile, but damn, it's going on six months. Why the hell did ya decide to let her finish off your career?"

Shawn's eyes shifted toward his old mentor, but he didn't speak. He had no excuses. How could he explain that nothing seemed to matter anymore?

Quail shook his head and sat down on the edge of the desk. "When I heard about the trouble ya got into at Bragg, I called the group sergeant major. He said you were given the chance to soldier your way back. I figured you'd do just that and didn't need my help. That was obviously a mistake. I called here last week to check up on you, and they told me you were out at some fuckin' range as a maintenance man. I blew my stack. That was a mistake too. Looking at you, I'd have given you a nothin' job too."

Quail picked up the bayonet and pointed it at Shawn's face. "Well, I got news. You're not going to be a maintenance man anymore. I pulled some strings and fixed it so you got yourself another assignment. It's one where you won't have time to feel sorry for yourself. This new job will give you a chance to fuck it up real quick and get thrown out on the street. You're gonna work your ass off and become the soldier I knew, or you're out."

Shawn lowered his head, still too embarrassed to speak. Quail stood with a look of disdain. "Irish, I'm walking out the door and I ain't comin' back to play nursemaid for you. You're on your own from here on out. I got ya a job that needs a pro. It's your last chance."

Quail walked out the door without looking back and stopped at the secretary's desk. "Tell Chuck thanks for lettin' me use his office."

Shawn turned around only after he had heard the old soldier's footsteps fade down the hallway. The secretary came in and held out a pack of papers to him. "These are yours."

Shawn took them. They were reassignment orders. He was being sent to the test unit on post. The Eleventh Air Assault Division (Test).

The secretary smiled sweetly. "Good luck."

Cindy heard the motorcycle rumble to a halt outside. She walked over to the bar to where Bob was already setting a beer out for her. "He's awfully early," he said with a hint of concern. "Tell him June is makin' roast beef, but it won't be ready for another hour."

Cindy waited until the sergeant walked through the door before following him to his corner table. As usual he didn't acknowledge her when she set the beer in front of him. Over the past weeks, she had become friends with the regular customers and had learned how to deal with the drop-ins who tried to make a pass or drank too much. She finally felt comfortable with the job . . . except for the sergeant. He would never make eye contact and hardly ever spoke. The few times she did catch him looking at her were unnerving. It was as if he had been looking into her mind, reading her thoughts. She couldn't take it anymore.

Shawn felt uncomfortable with the woman staring at him. He took a long drink and slammed down the bottle. "What the hell you starin' at!"

Cindy raised an eyebrow. He had never raised his voice to her before. She faked a smile. "Tough day, huh?"

"Just get me another beer and mind your own business."

Cindy felt partial success. He had at least looked at her when he'd spoken. Determined, she sat down across from him. "Look, I know I'm not much to look at . . . but I listen pretty good."

Shawn turned in his seat, ignoring her in the hope that she would leave. Having expected this tactic, Cindy leaned back in her chair and made herself comfortable. "I've seen you almost every day for two weeks, and I don't even know your first name." Waiting only a few seconds for a response, she continued, "I noticed you don't talk to any of the customers. You have any friends? Everybody needs *somebody* to talk to."

Shawn couldn't take any more of her rambling. He stood and took out his billfold. Tossing a dollar to the table, he marched toward the bar. "Bob, give me a six-pack to go."

Cindy had followed him and stood next to him as he waited. Now she stepped closer, looking directly into his eyes. "She must have hurt you bad. Who was it, a wife? Girlfriend?"

Shawn ignored her. He took out a five-dollar bill and set it on the bar. Bob put the six-pack beside the money. "You ain't stayin' for dinner?"

Shawn took the beer and looked at Cindy. "It's too damn noisy in here."

Shawn strode toward the door with the now irate woman following him. She followed him outside and spoke to his back. "I don't care, you know? I don't care if you ever speak to me. It doesn't bother me in the least."

Shawn set the beer on the backseat of the motorcycle and used elastic bands to secure it. He got on the bike and snarled at her, "Get out of the way, will ya?"

Cindy returned his glare. "You think you're too good for me, right? Well, you're not. At least I have friends. Where are your friends? Huh? Who do you talk to except a bottle of beer? Who cares that you're even alive?"

Shawn started the bike and rolled past her. He turned onto the road and headed toward the trailer park only a block away. But as he started to turn into the park, he realized it would do no good to go to the filthy trailer. He suddenly changed direction for the open road, and he accelerated. He had no place to go. Quail had given him a job at which he would only fail. They would take one look at him and throw him out. He was a failure, and he didn't care.

He shifted gears and rotated the throttle forward. The biting cold wind tore at his shirt and hair. Fifty, sixty, sixty-five, seventy . . . He kept the throttle forward and roared down the road to get away from the woman, from Quail, from everyone. Eighty, eighty-five, ninety . . . He didn't care what anybody thought or said anymore. One hundred, 110 . . . The stripes on the road were nothing but blurs as he shut his eyes. He only wanted peace and to forget forever. Pushing the throttle all the way forward, he felt the bike leave the road and whine as he flew over the embankment. It didn't matter. She was right. No one would care.

Cindy was behind the bar clearing away empty bottles and dirty ashtrays when a tall mill worker rushed in and began to babble excitedly to Bob about some kind of accident. ". . . And I sees him fly over the embankment like Evel Knievel. He musta been goin' a hundred, easy, 'cause his cycle flew at least fifty yards before it hit the marsh. I almost wrecked the car, watching him fly. By the time I got turned around, two other cars had already stopped and the drivers were out in the mud trying to find his body. Bob, whatever the sarge drinks, you can start givin' to me. He's the luckiest sonofabitch in the world. There wasn't a scratch on him. He musta fell off the bike as it nosed over, 'cause he hit the marsh a couple'a yards past it and sunk in almost six feet. The water and mud saved him. He almost drowned in the crap, but them two guys pulled him out just in time. They drug him to the bank, and I'll be damned if he don't get up and start walkin' back this way. If he comes in here, I'm buying that lucky bastard a beer."

Cindy exchanged looks with Bob, who yelled to his wife, in the kitchen, "June, take over the front!"

Bob and Cindy rushed to the door.

Still covered in mud, Shawn got out of the back of the pickup and waved a thanks to the driver who had picked him up. He was about to walk to his trailer when a car skidded to a halt beside him. Bob threw open the door. "You all right, Sarge? I just heard."

Shivering, Shawn waved him back. "I'm okay. I just lost my brakes. Go on, I'm fine."

Worried, Cindy got out of the car. "You need to be checked by a doctor."

"Leave me alone," he said, and started for his trailer.

Bob shook his head. "Come on, Cindy, he's okay."

Cindy's eyes narrowed as she watched the sergeant walk away. "Go on, Bob. I'll walk back in a little while."

The bartender began to object, but she was already on her way after him. Bob frowned as he backed up. "I hope to hell you know what you're doin'," he mumbled to himself.

Shawn had just begun to take off his boots when she opened the trailer door and stepped in. He gave her a blank look. "I didn't hear you knock."

Cindy glanced around the filthy trailer, somehow unsurprised by the mess. "This place doesn't deserve a knock. You all right?"

Shawn continued unlacing his boots. "Yeah."

Cindy walked into the kitchen. It was cluttered with stacks of dirty dishes. "You gonna try it again?"

Shawn looked up at her as if he had been caught stealing.

"I heard what happened," Cindy said. "I know you tried to end it for yourself." She pushed back her shirtsleeves, exposing her scarred wrists. "This is the way I tried it." Her eyes widened and looked past him as if in a daydream. "My baby suffocated in a crib while I slept two feet away. Afterward, I lived in hell. Nothing but guilt and memories. I hated going to bed, 'cause I would dream, and I hated getting up in the mornings to face another day. When I finally sat in that bathtub and cut my wrists, I felt released, free, like a bubble floating peacefully away . . ."

Her eyes focused and she gave Shawn a serious, thoughtful look. "A friend found me, someone I shut out of my life when Timmy died. See, I didn't want to share my grief with anyone." Cindy stepped closer. "I was lucky, I had someone who cared."

Shawn's eyes narrowed. "Leave. Get out and leave me alone."

Cindy stiffened. "Go ahead, be a bastard, but I've got news for ya. I'm your friend. You can say anything you want, but you're stuck with me. You've sat in Bob's for weeks, and I know you."

Shawn stood and pointed at the door. "Out, now!"

Cindy ignored him and went into the kitchen, sizing up the mess. "I'll be over tomorrow and try to clean up in here." She opened a cupboard and shook her head. "Looks like I'll have to pick up some soap. You don't seem to have any."

The muscles rippled in Shawn's jaw. He strode over to her and grabbed her arm. "You're not doing a damn thing but getting the hell out of here!"

The young woman surprised him with a smile. "It won't work. Get as loud as you want . . . friend."

Shawn held her firmly. "Why? Why are you doing this?"

Cindy's smile dissolved and her eyes began to water. "I owe this world a life."

Shawn released Cindy's arm but kept his glare. "Get somebody else."

Cindy fought the tears that began to cloud her eyes. "I can't change what's happened to you . . . and neither can you. People like us just have to believe in tomorrow. It's all we've got."

Cindy stepped out of the trailer, closing the door behind her.

HARMONY CHURCH, HEADQUARTERS, ELEVENTH AIR ASSAULT, 27 JANUARY

Sergeant Major Chad Twining motioned the heavy-set sergeant into his office. "Come on in, Flynn, and take a seat."

Shawn's stomach was twisted into knots as he watched the wiry soldier's eyes for signs of disappointment. He knew Quail would have built him up to the sergeant major as a pro. His appearance, however, would certainly indicate otherwise. His only consolation was that the senior soldier before him was a master parachutist. He wore a Screaming Eagle patch on his right shoulder, signifying that he had served with the famous 101st Airborne Division during World War II. He might give a fellow veteran a second chance.

Twining sat down behind the desk, his pale blue eyes locked on the sergeant. "Flynn, Taco and I had a long talk about you, so I already know about your past troubles. That's history as far as I'm concerned. I'm not gonna sit here and threaten you with you-gotta-prove-yourself-to-me bull-shit. You know you have to lose twenty pounds, and I won't say another thing to you about it. I'm in a real bind with this bunch of kids they call soldiers, and I desperately need your experience."

Twining glanced toward the open door and hollered, "Angie, get me two cups of coffee, will ya?"

"Right away, Sergeant Major," the secretary acknowledged in a high-pitched squeak.

Twining leaned back in his chair. "Flynn, I'm gonna give you a little history lesson so you'll understand what you got yourself into. It all started in 1961 when Secretary of Defense Robert McNamara got pissed off with the Army. Ya see, he believed the Army needed to think about the future. He figured helicopters were going to change the future of war fighting. The big brass dragged their feet and didn't budget enough money for aviation to meet his vision. Mac changed all that. He directed the Army to get off its ass and come up with a concept of how to use helicopters for war fighting. The secretary directed the big brass to form a task force to come up with new concepts employing air mobility. He even told them who he wanted on the task force and ordered them not to interfere in the study. Needless to say, he didn't make any friends in the Pentagon. The task force under General Howze came up with a plan and a concept. The Eleventh Air Assault is the result of their work. The Eleventh was activated to test the new air-mobility concept."

The homely secretary walked into the office carrying two cups of coffee. "Here ya go, Sergeant Major." She gave one mug to Twining and the other to Shawn.

Twining, in need of the caffeine, sipped his coffee before turning his attention back to Shawn. "General Kinnard took over the unit a year ago and has been working his ass off to make the airmobile program work. It's been an uphill fight. We still have some in the higher Army echelons who want us to fall on our butts. The Air Force is also fighting us all the way. They figure we're getting involved in their turf, and they don't like us flying anything but kites. We just finished a big test called Operation Air Assault Two, which proved air mobility is here to stay. The problem is, we've been reduced in strength while we're waiting to see what the Army wants to do with us. The betting is that we're going to Nam and kick some ass."

Twining took another slug of coffee and pointed to the photo on the wall behind him. "General Kinnard and me served together in the 101st. He believes the airmobile unit has to be made up of paratroopers. He wants his men tough and spirited. That's where you come in. I'm assigning you to an infantry battalion where they can use your jump and combat experience to help refine their training. It's a tough job because things change every day. We aren't using field manuals or the tactics we're used to. We're developing new ones to meet the needs of the airmobile concept. It's a good job for you. It's a chance to help the Army and yourself. You'll also be on jump status, so you'll be getting the additional pay. Taco told me you're one of the best. I'm glad you're with us, and I know you'll do a hell of a job."

Twining stood and put out his hand. "Flynn, ya got a hell of a friend in Taco. You're lucky. Soldier for him . . . and me."

Shawn felt a lump in his throat as he shook the soldier's hand. "Thank you for the chance, Sergeant Major," Shawn said emotionally. "I'm not gonna let you down."

A COMPANY, FIRST BATTALION, 23RD INFANTRY HEADQUARTERS

The first sergeant pounded Shawn's back as if he had known him for twenty years. "Damn, am I glad to have an experienced man for a change. All I got around here are cherry jumpers and nonvets. You're going to be my recon platoon leader and start getting the fuzz-faced punks I got turned into real snoopin'-poopin' recon men. Come on, I'll show you your team room, and I'll introduce you to the company commander. He's gonna just shit when he sees you. None of us are jumpmaster-qualified. He's been cryin' for a master blaster."

Shawn walked into the barracks with his back straight and head held high. He felt like a soldier again.

The young soldiers of his team gaped at him with awe. Being a veteran of two wars still meant something to men who were as yet untested.

A young buck sergeant stepped forward. "I'm Bo Derringer. I was the acting platoon sergeant. The guys and me are ready."

Shawn smiled at the wide-eyed young soldiers assembled before him. "I'm afraid I'm not much to look at right now, but that'll change. As far as your training goes, I need to see your training records and . . ."

Thirty minutes later Shawn marched his platoon outside to prejump training. He'd forgotten how good it felt to have purpose again. It gave him a long-forgotten confidence in himself. Irish was back.

Cindy was picking up empty bottles from a table when she felt a tap on her shoulder. When she turned around, what she saw made her gasp.

Shawn looked directly into her wide eyes and said, "The name is Shawn, and you're right, everybody needs a friend." He held out his hand. "How's about you and I being friends, starting right now?"

Cindy took his hand, and he did something she had never seen him do before—he smiled.

10

Hank shut the Mercedes door and walked around back to open the trunk. His passenger had made his farewells to everyone except his father, who wouldn't see him.

Blake got out and looked down the empty street. It would be a long time before he saw his hometown again.

Hank began to lift the bag out of the trunk, but Blake took the suitcase from him. "That's okay, I'll take it in. I wanna go in by myself."

Hank understood. He let the bag go and extended his hand. "Remember what I told ya. Keep your mouth shut and your eyes open. Do what they say, and do it right the first time, but don't volunteer for nothin'."

The right side of Blake's mouth turned up in a smile as he shook the retired sergeant's hand. "I'll remember. Take care of Mom for me, and take care of yourself. I'll write and tell ya if it's like you said."

Hank chuckled. "I gar-un-tee it ain't changed. It never does. Take care of yourself, Ace . . . I'm gonna miss ya."

Blake threw his arms around the old man and hugged him tightly. "Thanks for everything, Hank. I'm gonna miss you too."

It took all of Hank's resolve to keep his tears back. The boy had become like a son to him. He wished Blake didn't have to go, but knew it was time for him to make his break. Blake's father thought of him as a failure, but he didn't understand or really know his son. Blake had not failed the family. He had made the toughest decision of them all. He was not going to make himself a chapter in someone else's history. He would write his own story.

Hank shivered in the early morning chill and took one last look at the bus station. Good luck, son.

CUSSETA, GEORGIA

Connie Calhoon wrapped a sandwich in newspaper and placed it in a used paper bag. Wiping her tears with the back of her hand, she held out the sack to her son. "I don't wantcha starvin'. I heard about how the Army feeds their boys."

Lee leaned over and kissed his mother's forehead. "I'm only gonna be twenty miles away, Ma. I'll be home when I get a leave, I promise."

Lee picked up his sister and gave her a hug. "Puddin', you take care of Mama and help her like a big girl. I'll bring ya something when I come home."

"How 'bout me, Lee? Ya gonna bring me somethin' too?" Charlie asked, tugging on his brother's jeans.

Lee scooped up his little brother in the other arm. "You bet, partner."

Roy stepped in the front door. "Come on, son, we gotta git ya there."

Lee walked out still holding his brother and sister in his arms. Setting them on the top step, he looked back at his mother. "Don't be cryin', Ma. I'll be back real soon."

Connie rushed to her son, giving him one last embrace. "I love ya, Lee. Ya show 'em you're a Calhoon. There ain't none better."

Lee kissed her cheek. "I will, Ma. I will."

CARLISLE, PENNSYLVANIA

Eugene said good-bye to his mother at the house and walked to the bus station with his father. His dad, wearing his Sunday suit, had sat silently with him while they waited for the silver Greyhound.

James Day stood and reached into his pocket. "Son, it ain't much, but I wanted you to have this."

Eugene recognized the badge from years before. His father had called it a Combat Infantryman's Badge. It was a framed silver musket on a field of light blue, surrounded by a silver wreath. He didn't know what the badge signified, but it had meant a lot to his father.

Eugene closed his father's fingers around the gift. "I can't take it, Dad. It's special to you. I don't feel the same way as you when you went to war. This Vietnam is for the whites. I'll be back. They won't want me."

Tears trickled down James's cheeks as he lowered his head. "Don't come back that way, son. One day you'll understand why. Believe me, don't come home that way. We got problems in our country between races, but times like this brings us together. Do your duty for me."

Eugene's jaw tightened. "They forgot what you did, Dad, remember? They wouldn't even let you sit with the white veterans. The war is *here,* not in Vietnam."

Heartbroken, James turned his back on his son and limped down the sidewalk toward home.

Eugene climbed the bus steps and took a seat next to the window. Despite losing everything he loved, Eugene knew he had been right in what he had done. Regina had left him the day after Rafford had died. She realized that he had lied to her about his quitting the Brothers, and worse, that he had used her. And now he'd had to face his father's sad, disappointed look. The old man thought his son had failed him, but James Day, to Eugene's way of thinking, just didn't understand. His father was the *reason* he fought for the cause. The flag the old soldier had saluted those many years before was a white man's flag, and would remain so for as long as there were people who wouldn't give his father the respect he deserved. One day Regina and his father would understand. One day.

SOUTH PHILADELPHIA

Wanting privacy, Vincent Martino took his little brother's arm and walked with him to one of the benches near the south entrance to Thirtieth Street Station. "Billy, you gotta promise me somethin'."

Billy looked up at his brother. "Sure, Vinny."

Vincent shifted his feet. He was having a hard time finding the right words. "I . . . I ain't no bum, but I let Mama down. The neighborhood, it got its own way. I want you to forget doin' what the other guys do. Don't be fightin' and hangin' out. Be smart. Graduate from school for Mama. Don't be like me, huh. You graduate."

Billy hugged Vincent tightly. "I promise, Vinny."

Vincent patted his brother's back. "I gotta go now. You take care'a Mama for me."

Vincent kept his arm around Billy and walked him back to where the others were waiting. His mother was dry-eyed and raised a penciled eyebrow. "You write your mama and come back soon, huh?"

Gina handed Vincent a paper bag full of hoagies and root beers. "I love you, Vinny. I—" She broke into tears and took his sister's hand. His sister was also crying. "Take care, brother. I love you."

Tony Alvedo stuck his hand out. "You take care, paisan. Don't be playin' no John Wayne horseshit, you hear?"

The driver honked the bus horn. Vincent shook Tony's hand, then put his arms around his sister and Gina, kissing both of their wet cheeks. Backing away, he stepped toward his mother and kissed her forehead. "Bye, Mama."

The sullen-faced woman shook with emotion and threw her arms around her son. "Come back to me, Vinny . . . come back."

Vincent broke from her embrace and ran to the departure stairs. He turned toward his mother one last time. "I will, Mama. I'll be back."

FORT BENNING, GEORGIA, 2 FEBRUARY

An Army green shuttle bus that ran from Columbus, Georgia, to the post stopped in front of the reception station. The shuttle's door opened and a waiting drill sergeant climbed the steps and faced the passengers. "Loosen up, people. I am Staff Sergeant Batis, your reception station drill sergeant. You are now located at the Fort Benning reception station. You will be getting off the bus with your bags and form up on the white lines on the sidewalk. From this moment on, you will not talk until told to do so. If you do not have the packets with your orders in your hands—once outside, secure the packets from your bags. You must have your orders in your hands when you enter the building. Today we are in-processing, so there will be others joining you who arrived yesterday. Once you are formed on the white lines, you will, on my command, march single file into the building and follow the yellow line painted on the floor into the classroom. People, get off my bus and follow my instructions."

Six minutes later the sergeant walked down the front rank of standing men. As usual, it was a zoo. Every conceivable species of man watched him with searching eyes, wondering what horrors were in store. They were tall, short, skinny, fat, black, brown, yellow, and white; long-haired, short-haired, bearded, mustached, clean shaven, and fuzz-faced. They wore everything from suits to overalls. The only thing similar about them was the manila envelope in their hands and the looks of bewilderment on their faces. Four days from now they would all look alike—no hair, same uniform, and dead on their feet. The system was working perfectly. The Army would take away their individuality, decivilianize them, and transform this menagerie into a single, trainable animal.

The sergeant strode to the end of the first row and barked, "Follow me and stay on the yellow line!"

"Welcome to IPB. IPB is Initial Processing Branch, and I am Sergeant Drew from the Military Police. If you have contraband—such as alcoholic beverages, drugs, prescription or otherwise, knives or any kind of weapon, cigarettes, cigars, chewing tobacco, snuff, or pornographic material—on your person or in your bags, throw it in the boxes located at the rear of the room. First row, you're first. Get up and turn in your contraband."

Sergeant Batis stood in the back of the large briefing room, watching with a frown as good cigarettes were thrown away.

Once the M.P. sergeant was finished and the contraband had all been turned in, Sergeant Batis strode to the front of the classroom. "People, cards are being passed around at this time, along with number-two pencils. *You will* address the card to one of the following: your mother, father, stepmother, stepfather, guardian, relative, or wife. The card tells one of those people you are here, alive, and under the care of the U.S. Army. *You will* fill out the card with an address. *I will* collect the cards afterward. The purpose of this card is to keep some mother from writing her congressman saying we lost her son. People, you may look and feel lost, but you are not lost. You are at Fort Benning, Georgia, and I am your nursemaid for the next four days. Hurry up and get those cards passed out! This shouldn't take all day. People, you're on your time!"

———

"Good morning, men, I'm Captain Catton, the Third Training Brigade chaplain. I'm here to help you in the transition from being a civilian to becoming a soldier. I have a chapel service tomorrow morning after you've had breakfast. I will also be conducting a bible study tomorrow evening and hope most of you will attend. The next few days will be very trying, but remember, many have gone before you. If any of you have personal problems and you want to talk, please drop by my office in Building Thirty-seven. Bibles are available in the back of the classroom, and I would like to see all of you take one. My name and telephone number are on the first page. God bless you."

Sergeant Batis waited for the chaplain to leave before positioning himself on the small stage. "People, I follow the chaplain to explain the rules. First, if anybody wants to see the chaplain, you see *me first. And* at no fucking time will you wander around looking for the chaplain. You will *not* have time for chapel service tomorrow morning because you will be getting up at 0400 in the morning. For you beatnik types, 0400 is four A.M. You will *not* have time for bible study tomorrow evening either because you will be in classes on how to make bunks and clean the barracks. If you wanna talk about personal problems, hold 'em till you get to your basic training companies and talk to your drill sergeants. At no fucking time will you use the pay phones located in the reception station area. The phones are off limits."

Batis put his hands on his hips and rocked back on his heels. "People, I know some of you want to quit. That's fine. We have an opportunity for those people on day four. At that time you will be able to explain why the Army is not for you. I don't want to hear of anybody bellyaching, complaining, or not complying with my instructions. You all *must* go through in-processing, even though you have a problem with being in the Army. It is the law. Does anybody here have a problem with that?"

A thin Negro in the second row stood up and pushed his glasses back up on his nose before speaking. "Sergeant, I want to speak to the chaplain now. I see no need in—"

Batis pointed to the back door. *"You, outside!"* The sergeant glared at the audience as if daring another of them to raise his hand. "Anybody else? . . . Good."

Batis walked to a chart behind him and picked up a pointer. "Now people, it's time for your first class—how to identify and address officers and noncommissioned officers. Notice the chart. Officers are identified by rank on their shirt collars and hat. Officers are in the in-processing area, but at no fucking time should you speak to them until they speak to you first. Notice the rank of NCOs is on the sleeve. We run this Army, while the officers command it. If an officer speaks to you, you face the officer and snap to attention and stay that way. You can usually respond with a 'yes sir' or 'no sir.' Example, 'No, sir, I do not have any problems. Yes, sir, I like the Army.' And in case ya get stupid, you can use this one: 'I don't know, sir.' People, you address us NCOs as 'Sergeant.' Example. 'Yes, Sergeant, I am happy here. No, Sergeant, I don't miss my mommy.' I gotta warn you people, us sergeants don't like the dumb response of 'I don't know, Sergeant.' You'd better know somethin' by the time we get through with you. Now take a look at the rank again, you can . . ."

Eugene Day stood in front of the reception-station first sergeant's desk. The Negro first sergeant had his eyes fixed on the young man's chin. "Day, I understand you want out of the Army. Is that correct?"

Eugene spoke confidently. "That's right. The war is unjust, and I feel I don't have to participate in the white man's—"

The first sergeant exploded out of his chair. "Shut up! Listen to me good, boy. You got two options. *One,* you can become a member of the Army for two years, *or,* you can go to prison for *three* years. Let me give you some advice. Take option one. At Fort Leavenworth prison you learn only one thing—how to bust big rocks into small ones. When you get out, your résumé ain't exactly the best for gettin' a job."

The first sergeant strode to the door and threw it open. "You can walk out this door and go back to the classes, or you stand there while I call the M.P.s. Decide, now!"

Eugene spun around, glaring at the sergeant. "I have a right to talk to the chaplain."

The NCO strode back to his desk and picked up the telephone. "I'm calling the M.P.s. Your 'rights' ended when you got off the bus."

Eugene let the sergeant dial three numbers before he lowered his head and walked toward the door. He would go to the classes. There were other ways to resist them.

"Good afternoon, men. I am Corporal Stacy. I am now going to explain mess hall procedures. You will be eating in ten minutes and must understand the SOP. SOP means standard operating procedure. First, you will line up at parade rest one arm's length away from the trainee to your front. You will not talk, fart, grab ass, or burp in the chow line. When the head count yells 'Give me five,' everybody in the line will yell 'Give him five!' At that command the first five men in line will move into the mess hall door, passing by the head count. Each man will count off with, *One, two,* and so on. Once you get to the table where the head count is seated, you will sound off with the following. 'U.S.,' if you were drafted. 'R.A.,' if you were stupid and joined. 'N.G.,' if you are National Guard. The purpose of this is we keep separate records for each group. Once in the mess line you will pick up a tray and utensils. You will take all food we give you. There are no choices except for chocolate or white milk. You will fill the mess hall from rear to front and fill an entire table before filling other tables. You will eat your food without talking. Once finished, you will get up with your tray and all your trash and move to the rear exit. You will place your trash in the trash barrel and leftover food in the food barrel. You will put utensils in the utensil pan and leave everything else on your tray and hand it to the K.P. through the wash area window. Should you not follow the procedure, *you* will be tomorrow's K.P.s. *On your feet!* First row file out and follow the black line to the mess hall. *Do it.*"

After lunch the men were marched back inside the huge classroom, where Sergeant Batis waited for them.

"People, you are looking sleepy. You are not authorized to be sleepy. You have twelve hours to go before your training day is over. I am now going to teach you how to stand at attention, parade rest, and at ease. First the position of attention. At the position of attention you will bring your heels together smartly on the same line. Your feet will be turned out equally, forming an angle of forty-five degrees. Keep your legs straight without stiffening or locking your knees. You will hold your body erect with your hips level, chest lifted and arched, and your shoulders square and even. For you skinny beatnik types that don't have big chests, pretend like you got a chest. You will let your arms hang straight without stiffness along your sides with the back of your hands outward, your fingers curled so that the tips of the thumbs are alongside and touching the first joint of your forefinger. Keep your thumbs straight and along the seams of your trousers with all fingers touching your legs. Eyes will be locked to the front and there is no movement except for breathing. A demonstration is as follows. . . ."

"Good afternoon, men, I am your reception commander, Captain Early. I welcome you to Fort Benning on behalf of the post commander, Major General George Sweet. I realize most of you have been riding buses for a long time and are pretty tired. You will have a chance to get rested up tonight and start fresh tomorrow. For you that came in yesterday from the local area, I suggest you help others get squared away. I am in charge of the in-processing center and am here to ensure you are in-processed as quickly as possible and assigned to basic training units. If you have any suggestions for our program, please fill out the papers that are being passed out at this time. You can turn the suggestion forms into the suggestion boxes in your billet area. That's all I have for now. If you are having problems, please feel free to stop by my office. I am always willing to listen. Thank you."

Sergeant Batis waited until the captain had left before mounting the stage. "People, I follow the captain to make sure you understand the rules. First, you ain't gonna get to sleep tonight until after midnight. We have classes on how to keep the billets clean that you must know because tomorrow morning you gotta clean your area. Second, if you have any suggestions, save them for your mother. Turn in the suggestion sheets the captain gave you to the end of the aisle. Don't be puttin' nothin' in the suggestion boxes or you will all be up tomorrow night until thirty minutes before you gotta get up. Third, at no time will you walk up and shoot the shit with the captain. Nor will you wander around and try and find his office. He is a busy man and ain't got time to hear you snivel. *Now,* for your third class, how to salute. You salute from the position of attention or while walking. The right hand is brought sharply up with fingers extended and joined with the palm down. The wrist is locked, forming a straight line from finger tips to the elbow. The index finger should touch the bottom right corner of the eyebrow when not wearing a headdress. A demonstration is as follows. . . ."

"I'm Corporal Stacy. I'm you guys' barracks NCO. This barracks will be the most squared-away barracks in the reception station. We *will* be number one. We *will* be number one with hard work, spit and polish, and elbow grease. We will not tolerate those who do not give one hundred percent. This building has two floors. The latrine is located at the south end of each floor. The la-trine is *not* a head, can, bathroom, rest room, powder room, cat box, outhouse, or shitter. It is the 'la-trine.' You all will now follow me to the supply room, where you will draw blankets, sheets, and pillowcases. After that, you'll march to the mess hall for dinner chow, eat, then return here for your classes on making a bunk and cleaning the area. Follow me."

Corporal Stacy walked down the line of men waiting in the chow line and stopped in front of a young man wearing a blue blazer and gray slacks. One look at the kid told you he was a blue blood with money. The blazer was obviously fitted and very expensive, but the dead giveaway was the Rolex watch. It was exactly like the one that belonged to the colonel who commanded the training brigade.

Stacy looked the young recruit over from his shined Weejun shoes to his twenty-dollar haircut. "You been to college, stud?"

Blake Alexander came to parade rest. "Yes, sir."

The corporal snickered. "You don't listen too good college boy. I'm a corporal. You don't call me 'sir.' I work for a livin'. And don't talk out of the side of your mouth to me. What kind of watch is that you're wearin'?"

Blake Alexander spoke trying to keep his chin tucked in, as Sergeant Batis had demonstrated. "Corporal, I was in an accident and just talk this way. The watch is a Rolex GMT Master."

Stacy studied the young man's face as he spoke. "Are you medically qualified with that kind of injury?"

Blake nodded. "Yes, Corporal."

Stacy motioned to the watch. "Don't take that off around here, or you'll never see it again. You are now my acting platoon sergeant." Puffing out his chest, Stacy barked, "Anybody else here have any college?"

Four men raised their hands. Stacy walked down the line pointing at each man with his hand raised. "You are temporarily the first squad leader. You are the second squad leader. You are the third, and you—wait a minute, you don't look like you've been to college."

Lee Calhoon snapped to attention and spoke in a syrupy drawl. "Corporal, I went a year to Columbus College."

Stacy's eyes widened, looking at the tall, rangy recruit. "You're a local cracker, huh?"

Lee kept his eyes to the front. "I'm from Cussetta, Corporal. What's a cracker?"

Several men in line chuckled along with Stacy. "Okay, cracker, you're the fourth squad leader. Just talk a little faster or your squad will go to sleep on ya." Stacy backed up and barked again. "You squad leaders move to the front of the line and see me in the billets as soon as you're finished eatin'. I need one more volunteer . . . *you!* The one moving down there, *freeze!*"

The offender quit scratching his groin and froze. Stacy marched to him. "*You.* What's your name?"

The recruit bobbed his head. "Vinny Martino, Corporal. I had to pull my shorts down."

Stacy's eyes narrowed. "Looky here, eye-tie greaseball, get to parade rest when you talk to me. You are going to be my latrine orderly. Report to me after chow."

Vincent began walking to the front of the line when Stacy yelled, "Freeze, greaseball! Where the hell ya think you're going?"

Vincent motioned toward the mess hall door. "I'm goin' to the front like the other guys."

Stacy shook his head and pointed in the opposite direction. "No, dummy, you go to the *end* of the line. Latrine orderly ain't a leadership position. You're gonna be in charge of toilets. Move it, greaseball!"

Blake Alexander had been directed to turn off the barracks lights at ten o'clock because of reception station policy, but they were not allowed to get into their beds. The corporal had explained that "lights out" meant only that—lights out. The term did not mean go to bed. The men were to continue cleaning the floors and making their beds by the light of the red firelights at each end of the barracks. The latrine lights were allowed to remain on, so half of the newly formed platoon was in there cleaning the shower stalls. Blake had made the mistake of pointing out that the following morning they would be using the latrine and would have to clean it again. He didn't see the purpose of cleaning it tonight. "Alexander," the corporal answered with a smirk, "there is the right way, the wrong way, and the Army way. Welcome to the Army way. Don't ask questions, just do it."

Stacy strolled into the latrine at midnight to see how the work was progressing. He saw his victim shining a faucet with a sock. "Greaseball, what did I tell you about the toilet paper?"

Vincent Martino tiredly moved into the parade rest position and spoke with his eyes half closed. "You said to take half of the rolls so the guys didn't use 'em."

Stacy paced in front of the toilets. "Martino, I count six toilets and four rolls of toilet paper. You did not follow my instructions. You will report for K.P. at 0300 hours in the morning. You will pull fire guard at 0200, so you won't miss K.P."

Vincent cocked his head with a confused expression. "What hundred time is it now?"

Stacy's eyes rolled up. "Why do I always get the dummies? *Alexander! Get in here!*"

Blake jogged into the latrine. "Yes, Corporal."

Stacy pointed at Vincent. "Square this greaseball away on military time and ensure that the fire guard roster is posted. Have the men go to bed now. I will see you tomorrow morning at 0330."

Blake made another mistake. "Corporal, according to the schedule that you gave me, wake-up time is 0400."

Stacy shook his head as if dealing with a third grader. "That's the 'lights on' time. Wake-up is 0330. Got it?"

Blake realized the "Army way" had struck again. "Yes, Corporal."

3 FEBRUARY, 0330 HOURS

Eugene Day awoke to the sound of a trash can clattering down the aisle.

Stacy yelled as he strode down the barracks, following the can like a windstorm. "Get out of the those fart sacks, people! Shit, shower, and shave time! There will be no mustaches, beards, or hairy growths on yo face! Move people! You got ten minutes!"

After the breakfast meal, the men were herded into long lines and began the traditional Army routine of hurry up and wait. First they went to a window and were given an advance pay of twenty-five dollars, then marched to a huge barber shop where they paid butchers a dollar for a one-minute scalping. The loss of their hair was also a loss of identity. Everybody looked somehow the same. Medical, eye, and dental exams came next, which included urinating into cups, being prodded and poked, measured and weighed, and having blood drawn and classified. They were shot with air guns for exotic diseases, the names of which no one could pronounce. After receiving their dog tags and individual interviews, they were all issued cardboard boxes and told to strip. All civilian clothing was to be sent home. Holding the boxes filled with relics of their past lives and wearing only underwear and the new dog tags, they gave their possessions over to people who exchanged them for a collection of U.S. Army uniforms, T-shirts, underwear, socks, boots, black shoes, and hats.

Corporal Stacy marched them to chow. Later he reinventoried all their new equipment and rechecked the fit of their boots and shoes. Complete with the screaming and hollering known as "squaring away," they were given classes on how to wear and care for their uniforms. A trip was made to the small post exchange to buy two of everything. Somebody asked why they had to buy two tubes of toothpaste instead of just one, and they got the standard answer. "Just do it!"

Once back at the barracks, it became clear why two items were needed. The Army way was to display one for inspection and keep the other one for real use. A "display" consisted of a white towel pinned down and smoothed over the top tray of the foot locker. A diagram was provided and everyone was to place their razor, toothbrush, shaving brush, boot polish, socks, soap dish, shaving cream, comb, and toothpaste in an exact spot on the white towel. The placement required precise measurement and spacing. They were told an inspecting officer would certainly faint at finding a toothbrush that failed to point the right way, with brush up and placed exactly one-half inch from the toothpaste tube that was aligned on the bottom edge, precisely one inch away from the Kiwi boot polish can. The idea was for everybody to have exactly the same standards.

The corporal explained they would not be inspected at the reception station, but once assigned to their basic training companies, they would be expected to know how to lay out a display. To the horror of the confused men, they were issued four more diagrams. The "display" was just the beginning of yet more impossible standards. Not only was the top foot-locker tray supposed to be precise, but so was the bottom storage area, as well as their wall lockers. Stacy showed them a bunk, footlocker, and wall locker that they were to use as examples. The blankets had to align with a row of folded blanket covers. The laundry bag had to be tied to the end of the bunk with so many twists, wraps, and secured by a special knot. Boots, shoes, and shower shoes had to be aligned just so and marked properly. Wall lockers had a location for everything, and there was to be a specific spacing between hangers and a particular order of sequence of uniforms. *Inches, finger spacing, aligned, dress-right-dress,* and *squared away* were words and phrases that seemed to flow out of the corporal's mouth in every sentence. The recruits looked at each other, each hoping the other had absorbed the mind-boggling instructions. The realization slowly sunk in that the Army was not going to be fun. The Army had rules, regulations, and policies covering virtually everything they did, including urinating. The corporal said that if they shook their peckers more than twice, they would be charged with abuse of their bodies, and their bodies weren't theirs anymore. They belonged to the Army.

Later they marched to the briefing room where two movies were shown covering venereal diseases and the virtues of buying savings bonds. Most of the men slept through the savings bond presentation. Dinner chow was next, where in agony the recruits tried to lift what seemed like fifty-pound forks—the shots had finally taken effect. To try and lift their right arms was torture. The dinner meal was wieners and sauerkraut. After the venereal disease film, the shriveled wieners were too much to bear looking at. Few ate.

The night cleanup was delayed because of boot-shining classes. Blake turned the lights out at ten, but they didn't get to bed until one A.M.

4 FEBRUARY, 0330 HOURS

"Get out of them fart sacks, people, it's test day!" Corporal Stacy yelled as he strutted down the aisle. The weary recruits rolled out of bed, twice as sore as they were the day before. Most of their right arms felt like boils. The shower stalls were taped off so they wouldn't have to clean them again, so most just splashed water on their bodies. After inspecting their uniforms, Stacy marched them to chow and then to the testing facility.

Blake learned that, as acting platoon sergeant, the men complained to him in the hopes that he had an in with the corporal. He knew better but tried anyway, asking the corporal the purpose of giving a series of tests to the men when they were so tired and sore. Somehow he knew what the answer would be. "It's the Army way. Do it!"

The testing sergeant stood in front of the classroom. "Good morning, recruits! The battery of tests you are about to take will determine your future military occupation speciality. I know some of you joined and were told you would be assigned to jobs or branches you wanted. Sorry about that, but that's not how it works. If you score low, you will not be a nuclear weapons expert. It behooves you to do your best to keep from becoming an eleven bravo."

Lee Calhoon raised his hand. The sergeant pointed at him. "Yes, you have a question?"

"Sergeant, what's an eleven bravo?"

The sergeant cracked a smile. "Recruits, an eleven bang is a bullet stopper, grunt, ground pounder, boonie rat, fodder, the queen of battle, or better known as an infantryman. Eleven means infantry, thirteen is artillery, and so on. An example of a military occupation specialty, or MOS, is an eleven B, infantryman. An artillery MOS would be thirteen bravo. Gun bunnie. Communications is a thirty-six kilo. The tests will determine what skills you have. You will also be tested for special aptitudes, such as language, communications, and Officer Candidate School. For those of you who can type, we have a test for you too. Men, you have test books in front of you now. You will have two hours for the first test. Take two minutes and fill out the top part of the test booklet. Remember, *last name first!* Also the date is always written with the day first then the month and then year. Use only the number-two pencil provided. Do it."

After the first hour of the testing, the sergeant kept himself busy by walking around the room and waking up the testers. The high heat in the classroom combined with lack of sleep encouraged the men to nod off. Blake was filling out question forty-nine and had shut his eyes for just a second when he felt a nudge and quickly focused his eyes. He was on question sixty-five and didn't have the foggiest idea what answers he had marked or how he had gotten that far. Lee Calhoon constantly shook his head to keep himself awake and dutifully filled in every answer. Eugene Day began guessing after question seventy with only a minute left. Vincent Martino was sound asleep in the back of the room, having completed only forty questions out of the hundred.

After a latrine break, they were tested on communications. They were told to listen to a series of dots and dashes and write down the sequence of the sounds as they heard them. When the speaker boxes broadcasted the dots and dashes, they also broadcasted a loud squeal. The tests grew more and more difficult, and it became harder and harder to stay awake. Blake came to the conclusion, as did many others, that the MOS of eleven bravo would not be so bad. The testing was obviously a way to convince recruits that they were capable of nothing else.

The lunch chow break was a respite from the much hated number-two pencil that by now seemed to be marking blocks on its own. After chow they went back to the testing center, their stomachs full and the room stuffy as ever. The sergeant didn't even get through the opening introduction before two men's heads hit their desks. Toward the end of the day, Vincent Martino had figured out the secret to the testing. He would open the booklet and block all of the third answers, then go to sleep. Some tried first and third answer alternation. Blake and Lee were among those who attempted the impossible—figuring the *correct* answers.

Corporal Stacy was a welcome sight when the last test was completed. His presence meant they were going to do something they could pass—getting through the mess hall.

5 FEBRUARY

The fourth day began as had the others, in a blur. Blake was amazed how much he could do while he was half asleep. Even breakfast went by like a dream. If anyone had asked any member of the platoon what they had eaten, most would have shrugged their shoulders. Few men talked to each other. There was too little free time. After chow the recruits were totally demoralized when they found out they had two more hours of tests.

Vincent Martino and four others tried the easy out by asking to volunteer for the infantry rather than fight his number-two pencil again. They were told to "shut up and do it."

After the test the men were moved back to the barracks to pack their gear. Assignments to training companies were read out, and they marched to their classroom.

Sergeant Batis explained the do's and don'ts of a basic trainee. The bottom line was that whatever their drill sergeant said was gospel. Then Batis turned over the stage to smiling Captain Early. The officer was thrilled that he had received no suggestions, thereby assuming everything must have gone smoothly. Next came the solemn chaplain, who was disturbed that no one had shown up for his services. He blessed the recruits anyway, and gave them a card with a schedule of services.

Sergeant Batis took the platform for the last time. "People, the vacation is over. In thirty minutes you will be shipping out for your training companies. Good luck and good hunting!"

The men sat in sullen silence. If the reception station was a vacation, they were doomed.

Lee Calhoon stood and rotated his shoulders back. He had been just as tired and miserable many times in his life. They couldn't beat him.

Blake stood tiredly and followed the tall soldier who had gotten up first. Even if it was as bad as they said, he was ready.

Vincent Martino was shaken awake by the man beside him. "What? Where's everybody goin'?"

Eugene Day sat in his chair until the last man had left the classroom. He got up and spat toward the stage. Fuck them. They had cut off his hair and dressed him like all the others, but he would never be one of them. They could change his looks and tell him how to act, but they couldn't tell him what to think. The Army would find out soon enough that it didn't want him.

11

SAND HILL, FORT BENNING

Sergeant Singleton, in starched fatigues and spit-shined boots, adjusted his campaign hat and waited until the second large bus opened its doors. He quickly climbed the steps and stood in the aisle.

"Welcome to Sand Hill, Third Brigade, First Battalion, Charlie Company. I am Drill Sergeant Singleton. Drill Sergeant Cassidy will be your platoon drill sergeant, and I am standing in for him until he returns from main post. I am the operations sergeant, but for the time being, I am responsible for you meatheads. From now on you are the second platoon. You will get off the bus with all your bags and line up in four squads on the four blue lines over there on the company street in front of the pine tree. You will growl like crazed tigers until you get to the blue lines and show me you are enthusiastic. You will have one minute to get off the bus and impress me. Move, meatheads!"

Growling, the men quickly picked up their duffel bags and rushed for the door. As soon as a recruit touched the ground, Singleton was waiting for him and screamed into his face, *"Move, move, move!"* A thin Negro soldier, who wore glasses, was moving too slow and Singleton grabbed him. The sergeant pointed to the ground and screamed, *"Drop, meathead, entirely too slow, ten* push-ups!"

Eugene Day got down into the prone position, and thereby blocked the other men from getting off the bus. Still, the sergeant kept yelling at the others, *"Moveit! Get off the bus! Move!"*

Trying to comply, the men in the rear pushed those in front, and soon trampled over Eugene as they ran toward the company street. Eugene rolled and covered his head to keep from being kicked in the head. Suddenly he was jerked roughly to his feet.

Lee Calhoon kept his powerful grip on the soldier's fatigue collar to keep him on his feet and pushed him along to avoid being knocked down again in the stampede. Growling crazily, Blake grabbed the fallen soldier's duffel bag and dragged it toward the street. Another soldier grabbed the other end. Blake was relieved to have the assistance. The bag was heavy. He looked at the soldier's white name tape, so he would know who to thank later. It was the Italian, Martino.

Making it to the blue lines, Blake tossed the bag to the Negro and fell in. The scene around them was bedlam. Confused soldiers from the other three buses were running in every direction trying to find their platoon locations. Drill sergeants were attacking like sharks, screaming and dropping lost recruits into push-up position. It was obvious that the other busloads had not been told where they were supposed to go. Three bewildered soldiers ran by, and one yelled, "Is this the third platoon?"

A drill sergeant stepped in front of the confused men and yelled, *Drop!* They all fell to the gravel in the street as if a machine gun had mowed them down.

Eugene flexed his hand and looked around him at the buildings. They were of the same World War II vintage as those they had stayed in at the reception station. White, but in dire need of paint, the buildings were arranged in rows surrounded by huge pine trees.

The soldier beside Eugene motioned to his bruised hand. "You all right?"

Eugene nodded in silence, noting the tall trainee's name tape. It was the cracker, Calhoon.

Drill Sergeant Singleton ignored the mass hysteria going on around him as he strode toward his platoon with a scowl.

Blake saw him approaching and commanded, "Pla-*toon,* a-ten-shun!"

Singleton bellowed, "*Who* gave that command?"

Blake reluctantly raised his hand. The red-faced sergeant stepped within two inches of his face and screamed, "*Drop, meathead! You don't give commands while standing in ranks!*"

Singleton backed up and began walking down the front rank pointing at different people. "Gig line not squared away. *Drop!* You, you look stupid! *Drop!* You, your boots are cruddy! *Drop!* You, quit lookin' around! *Drop!*"

Within thirty seconds half of the forty men in the platoon were doing push-ups. Once everyone was back on their feet, the sergeant stopped pacing and rocked back on his heels. "Meatheads, when I say 'drop' you will hit the ground without hesitation. You will go down like you've been hit with a .50-caliber bullet between the eyes. You will count aloud the number of push-ups and remain in the push-up position with head up and back straight and arms fully extended. You will then ask permission to recover. *You,* looking around, *drop!*"

Vincent Martino saw the sergeant pointing directly at him and immediately fell to the ground and began doing the push-ups.

"I can't hear you, meathead! Start over!" Singleton yelled.

Vincent barked, "*One . . . two . . . three . . .*"

Singleton paced back and forth like a hungry, caged panther looking for prey.

Vincent completed the tenth push-up and yelled. "Drill Sergeant, can I get up now?"

The sergeant bent over the prone soldier and yelled, *"Ten more, meathead!* You don't say 'Can I get up.' *You say,* 'Drill Sergeant, request permission to recover!' "

Vincent completed the tenth exercise with ease and yelled, "Drill Sergeant, request permission to recover!"

Singleton ignored him and continued pacing in front of the formation. "Meatheads, you are now on the company street. This is where all formations are held. Directly behind you is your new home for eight weeks— barracks number C-22. First platoon is on your right. Third and fourth platoons are on your left."

Vincent readjusted his hands. His arms were extended but were beginning to shake. He dropped to his knees to the ground to rest a few seconds. Singleton stopped speaking and pointed at Vincent. "You, weak-dick wimp! *Get off your fuckin' knees!* As I was saying, meatheads, this is Charlie Company area. At no time will you leave the company area. You will *not* cross the roads that border our area for any reason unless a drill sergeant tells you." He pointed at Martino. *"Recover, wimp!"*

Singleton kept pacing and explained the different rules of the platoon until he saw the company commander walk out of the orderly room and take up a position on a raised platform in front of the company. Singleton immediately called the platoon to attention and moved six paces in front of the formation.

The baby-faced captain bellowed, *"At ease."* He paused for several seconds to scan the four platoons of recruits before speaking in a surprisingly strong voice. "I am Captain James Dike, your company commander. You are now proud members of Chargin' Charlie Company. Whenever you salute an officer, you will say, 'Chargin' Charlie, sir,' to let him know you are a member of the best. Today you will be meeting your platoon drill sergeants and receiving briefings on how we do business—and our business is making soldiers. The key to your success for the next few weeks is cooperating with your fellow recruits. I have had the best companies in the battalion for the past three cycles. You WILL be the *fourth!* Chargin' Charlie is the best because we do not accept substandard performance. *You will* give me one hundred percent of your mind and body. I do not allow shirkers, malingerers, or whiners. You will become lean mean fighting machines that *want* to kill. Our country is at war. You will most likely have the opportunity to serve your country in combat. For that reason you *must* be the best. In war, there is *no* second place. At this time your drills will be breaking you down into squads and assigning bunks. They then will be briefing you on the SOPs and policies of the company. I will be talking to you again when you receive the orientation class in the theater."

The captain called for the first sergeant, who saluted and turned the company over to the drill sergeants by commanding, "Take charge of your platoons!"

"Re-cover, meathead! Next time watch where you step. You kick another butt can over, I'll kick your ass up and down the aisle!"

Private Calhoon got to his feet as Sergeant Singleton strutted down the aisle motioning toward the large tin cans. "Meatheads, you will always have six butt cans evenly spaced down the center of the barracks aisle on this floor and upstairs. The cans will be kept painted bright red and filled with two inches of water at all times. If I find a butt can with less than two inches, you will all drink the cans dry and then fill them correctly. You have been assigned squads and buddies. Get to work getting your gear unpacked and squared away. Third and fourth squads follow me upstairs, and I'll show you your area."

The sergeant spun around and strode toward the stairs with twenty men dragging their bags behind him.

Vincent Martino sighed in relief at the sergeant's departure and patted his empty pockets. "I'd kill for a smoke right now."

Eugene Day snickered at him. "Shut up, fool. You gonna get us hassled again."

Vincent's eyes narrowed. He didn't like the Negro who had been assigned as his buddy. It was bad enough that he was a nigger, but he was a mouthy complainer as well. Vincent pointed a warning finger at the soldier's face. "I wasn't talkin' to you."

Eugene saw the hate in the man's eyes and glanced over his shoulder toward the other Negro in the squad, who was unpacking his gear the next bunk over. Brushing past the angry Italian, he approached the Negro soldier he had met during in-processing. "Hey, Jerome, how about me and you being bunk buddies, man. I don't want the wop."

Vincent angrily spun around. "Wop? You callin' me a 'wop'? You're askin' for this 'wop' to bust your face, you know?"

Showing no fear, Eugene faced the muscular soldier. "Back off, fool. We trade buddies and everything is cool."

Vincent shook his head in disbelief. "Now you callin' me 'fool'? No colored boy calls me names."

Jerome's red-haired bunkmate walked over and patted Vincent's back. "No use gettin' in trouble over niggers, man. Let the coons bunk together. I'll be your buddy."

Two black soldiers across the aisle in the first squad walked over. "Who you callin' 'niggers' and 'coons,' muthafucka?" one of them snarled.

Blake, who had heard the heated exchange, quickly stepped in front of the glaring men. "Hold it! Everybody just get back to work or we've all had it."

Now that he had allies, Eugene motioned to the redhead and Martino. "The dudes fucked up, callin' us 'niggers,' and they gonna pay!"

Vincent Martino clenched his fist. He would take out the mouthy one first. He growled an invitation to Eugene. "Come on, quit talkin' an' start somethin'!"

Suddenly a shrill wail filled the barracks. The startled men turned around and gasped. Standing in the aisle was a huge black bear wearing starched fatigues and a campaign hat. Sergeant First Class Cassidy returned the brass whistle to his pocket. He looked first at Martino then Day with a stare that froze their blood. "I heard most of it. I'd say we've got a little problem here." He pointed at Eugene. "You! What's your problem?"

Eugene was in awe of the sergeant's size, but he knew he had the giant's ear, because of his color. He quickly snapped to parade rest. "Drill Sergeant, I don't want him as my buddy. He's a racist."

Cassidy nodded, as if in understanding, and looked to Martino. "And you? What's your problem?"

Vincent figured he was dead. The huge Negro drill sergeant would surely take the side of his own kind, so Vincent had nothing to lose. He forgot about coming to parade rest and motioned to Eugene. "The guy was callin' me names, you know? He's askin' for trouble."

"What the fuck is going on?" Sergeant Singleton yelled as he ran down the steps. He saw Cassidy and strode toward him. "What happened, Cass?"

Cassidy motioned the other sergeant closer and whispered. Singleton nodded with a smile and strode for the door.

Cassidy spoke in a deep baritone voice. "I am Drill Sergeant Cassidy. I am the platoon's senior drill. One of you go upstairs and get the rest of the *boys* and tell 'em to join us. We're gonna have a little chat."

Cassidy pushed a footlocker out into the aisle and sat down. "Take a seat on the floor, boys. Make yourself comfortable."

Minutes later the entire platoon was seated on the floor. Cassidy seemed totally relaxed. "Ain't this nice?" he said. "It's like a weenie roast, ain't it?"

Nobody said a word. Cassidy grinned wryly. "Boys, we gonna come to an understanding right now. This platoon is made up of wops, niggers, Jews, wetbacks, spicks, and WASPs, *boys*. Ain't none of you *men*. 'Boys' fight among themselves, and that's what you were doing. This platoon is a cross-section of the U.S. of A. Boys, I don't like training little boys. I also don't like my platoon to be mad at each other and thinkin' bad things about their assigned buddies. We're gonna change all that in about two minutes. First thing we're gonna do is get to know each other. No-body is changing buddies. I'm gonna leave for thirty minutes. When I come back, you're gonna be able to tell me all about your buddy. You're gonna know where he's from, how many brothers and sisters he has, his schooling, his mother's and daddy's name, if he's married, or if he got a girlfriend. What I'm saying, boys, is you best get to know your buddy real quick. If you don't . . ."

The massive sergeant stood to his full six feet, six inches of bad news. "Well, we don't wanna talk about that right now. Just believe me . . . you boys don't wanna see me get angry."

Sergeant Singleton walked through the door carrying an armload of ropes.

"To help you get used to your buddies," Cassidy explained, "I have something for ya. Each buddy team will take a rope from the sergeant and tie the ends around your waists. I call em 'buddy ropes.' You will keep your buddy ropes tied to each other twenty-four hours a day until I tell you to take them off. The *only* exception is P.T. When one buddy has got to go to the latrine, your buddy goes. When you sleep, you stay tied to each other. You will pull fire guard together, clean the barracks and eat together. Boys, get the ropes tied on and get started knowing each other. I'll be back in thirty minutes."

Martino grabbed up a rope and tied it around his waist before tossing the other end to Eugene. "Yo, man, I'm Vinny."

Eugene glared at the barrel-chested private. "You still a fool."

Martino's jaw tightened and he spoke with forced restraint. "I'm gonna know you just like he says. I hafta get to know you, but I don't hafta like you . . . I cleaned enough toilets."

Eugene began tying the rope around his waist. "Tell me about you first."

Martino tugged his buddy down the aisle toward his bunk. "I'm from South Philly and . . ."

Sergeant Cassidy listened to the stories and tried to keep a straight face. The tension in the group had given way to smiles and even laughter. The redhead from Kentucky was relating his Negro buddy's past. "Jerome, here, is from Biloxi, Mississippi. His daddy, Jack, was a travelin' man and his mother's reputation was in doubt. Jerome says he graduated from cotton choppin' to stealin', and flunked. The judge told him it was the Army or jail. He asked for jail, but the judge's brother-in-law was a recruiter. Jerome got four brothers, and he thinks six sisters. He says he don't remember their real names. His mama called them by the number they was born. Jerome is known to his mama as 'Four.' "

Private Calhoon stood up next. "My buddy is from the great state of Virginia. He's Blake Alexander but his family calls him 'Ace.' He was in a car accident and says it's the reason he looks funny when he talks. So if he looks like he's given us an evil eye, he ain't really. He's got nerve damage on the left side of his face. He went to the University of Virginia for three semesters but says the girls and beer were better than studyin'.

The only problem was that the school didn't give grades for partyin'. He thought the Army might help his study habits. He's . . ."

Looking at the faces of the young men made Cassidy feel very old. He had trained hundreds of recruits over the past years, and yet every time he saw a new group, he was stunned at how young they looked. They seemed to be getting younger and younger while he just got older and had to struggle harder to keep up.

The sergeant glanced at Alexander. The kid had been injured, but he was really no different from others. Alexander's scars were on the outside, while most of the others carried their scars on the inside. Most in the platoon were from low-income families, a quarter came from broken homes, and half of them had not graduated from high school. The country's best and brightest were deferred from the war and only worried about their grades so they wouldn't have to worry about dying. These young men were all scarred, in their own way, by being poor and uneducated. Now he, Sergeant First Class Lawrence Cassidy, was going to deprive them of their youth as well, and make them into warriors.

The next eight weeks would change them. They would learn the only thing that counted—how to stay alive. Their confidence would slowly build and they would become a team. He understood them. He knew the sooner they accepted each other, the faster they would accept their new way of life. Alone, a man fought a constant uphill fight. As part of a team, he would always have a friend to help push him up when he was slipping.

Cassidy stood when Alexander had finished telling about his slow-talking buddy, Calhoon. He took a moment to collect his thoughts.

"Not bad, boys," he finally said. "Not bad at all. I think we're gettin' somewhere. I want everybody to take out their ID cards. Good. Now take a look at the photo on that card. Take a good look at that person. Boys, the card you're holding authorizes the person you're looking at to kill on behalf of the United States of America. You are holding a killer card and *you* are the killer. In the next eight weeks, myself and the other drill sergeants are going to teach you how to look, act, dress, march, and talk like soldiers. Once you've got the basics, we're gonna issue you weapons and teach you about killing. Today, you're gonna get your gear stored away and your displays made up. I'm gonna let ya go to bed at ten so you can get some rest. Tomorrow your first formation is at 0500 for P.T. Tonight at nine all work stops and I want you to write your folks. They need to know you're all right and where to write you. That's it for now. You've got gear to store and square away. I'll be back this evening to check on ya. Private Day, untie your rope and come with me a minute."

Eugene untied his buddy rope and ran to catch up to the sergeant, who had walked outside.

Eugene stopped in front of the sergeant and pushed his glasses back up on his nose. "Yes, Drill Sergeant?"

Cassidy stepped closer, looming over the small private. "You watch yourself, Day. I seen your kind before. I can tell you have an attitude problem. I see it in your eyes. You were the only one in there who didn't smile or laugh. You don't like it here. You think you're above all this Army shit. I got news. I'm on to you. Don't *even* think about making trouble, crusading for Negro rights, or going AWOL, or I will have some one-on-one intensive individual training sessions with you. You're in the Army now, and you have a big problem—me. Do I make myself clear?"

Eugene snapped into the parade rest position. "Yes, Drill Sergeant."

Cassidy could tell he had not gotten through, and sighed. "No, you don't, but you will." He turned and walked away, leaving the defiant soldier staring at his back.

SAND HILL, 7 FEBRUARY, 0500 HOURS

Blake Alexander stood at the door waiting, with the rest of platoon behind him in the aisle. Sergeant Cassidy had awakened them at 0430 and had told them to be the first platoon to form on the company street when the whistle blew.

The first sergeant blew his whistle, and Blake joined two hundred screaming men as they poured out of the white buildings into the lighted company street. The first sergeant thought the company had been entirely too slow and dismissed them back into the barracks, proclaiming yet another standard. There was the right, wrong, and Army way, and, he added, the Chargin' Charlie way.

The whistle blew again and the ground shook with screaming, running men. The first sergeant noted with a hidden smile that the second platoon was the slowest to form. It was not because of a lack of trying—they had become hopelessly entangled in their buddy ropes.

Ignoring the second platoon, the senior noncom turned the company over to the senior drill sergeant, known as the "field first," who marched the company to the lighted physical training area.

Blake touched Lee Calhoon's arm and motioned ahead at the two drill sergeants standing on platforms waiting for them. "I've got a bad feeling about this."

Lee sighed, feeling the same tingling sensation running up his back. "It don't look none too good."

The physical training instructors took over the company and introduced them to the Chargin' Charlie way of conducting P.T. It began with a series of commands that extended the company, counted them off, and then uncovered them, so that there was plenty of room between each man, yet left the formation looking military. Everything was done by the numbers to ensure that everyone lined up perfectly.

Vincent Martino thought the primary instructor looked like Tarzan, with his huge chest and narrow hips.

Tarzan bellowed, "Army drill one, exercise one of the Army daily dozen exercises is the *side straddle hop!* My demonstrator will demonstrate three repetitions of the exercise. Demonstrator! Army drill one, exercise one, the *side straddle hop!* Starting position, *move!* Notice my demonstrator did not move. The position of attention *is* the starting position. Demonstrator, *ready, exercise!*"

The demonstrator counted the cadence aloud as he jumped and tossed his arms above his head three times in a perfect exhibition of agility, strength, and grace. Completed, Tarzan motioned proudly toward his demonstrator. "Notice, Chargin' Charlie, that the side straddle hop was a four-count exercise and that my demonstrator counted the cadence while I counted the repetitions. Company *at-ten-hut. Army drill one, exercise one, the side straddle hop! You will count the cadence and I will count the repetitions. Starting po-sition . . . move!* Don't move, idiots! You are in the starting position, *Readddddy . . . ex-ercise!*"

Blake Alexander had thought the instructions were clear, but the men to his front were obviously still asleep, for when half the company were bringing their arms over their heads, the other half were bringing them down, and people were yelling out all sorts of numbers. He cringed, knowing they were in for it.

Tarzan came to attention after the jumping, yelling, and arm swinging had ended. "Chargin' Charlie, you look like a yard full of retarded rabbits. YOU have managed to screw up the easiest exercise of Army drill one. You will now pay the price for not listening and executing the exercise properly. *Front leaning rest po-sition . . . move! Idiots, that's the push-up position, get down!*"

Eugene Day looked up at Tarzan on the platform as he gave commands. By the sixteenth push-up, Eugene's arms were Jell-O. He tried to keep his back straight, but his stomach muscles were too weak. He fell to the ground shaking and looked to his right at Martino. The soldier had a smile on his face. He was doing the killer exercises with glee.

The sergeant finished the exercise and commanded, "Po-sition of attention . . . *move! At ease, shake it out!*"

The company shook their arms and bodies for several seconds before Tarzan bellowed, "Com-pany, *a*-ten-*hut!* Army drill one, exercise two is the *high jumper!* It is a four-count exercise. Observe my demonstrator. Demonstrator, starting position . . . *move!* Notice the demonstrator has spread his feet a comfortable distance apart. His legs are bent and his upper torso is bent over at the waist in the three-quarter position. Notice his arms are extended back and are straight and his head is up. He will, on the command of execution of 'Exercise,' throw his arms forward while bouncing, come down, extend the arms back and bounce higher, throwing the arms over his head. Three exercises at normal cadence are as follows. Ready, *exercise!*"

Lee Calhoon, watching the demonstrator, knew the company would never be able to do it together. The inability of this group to do even simple jumping jacks was still vivid in his mind. It was like seeing an Olympic diver doing a full twist and two somersaults, and then asking a ten-year-old novice diver to do the same thing. They were going to be doing a lot of push-ups after this one.

Sergeant Cassidy stood behind the company formation shaking his head. The company was totally bewildered and demoralized. They had done so many push-ups because of their poor performance that they had no strength left in their arms. It was evident the complicated exercises and precision movements were too much for them to learn in a large group. They needed to be taught in smaller groups and taken through the exercises by the numbers.

Finally, after forty-five minutes of hopping, jumping, yelling, and over 150 push-ups, the instructors gave up and turned the company over to the platoon drill sergeants for the two-mile run.

Cassidy marched the platoon to the road with a grin. "You boys must be livin' right. This morning ain't cold like it usually is this time in February. Boys, we're gonna run two miles at a nine-minute pace. This is just a warm-up run. By next week we will be running two and a half miles, and in three weeks we'll be running three miles at an eight-minute-per-mile pace. Don't be fallin' out of this easy run. If you fall out of three consecutive runs, you can be boarded out of the Army. I have never lost a man because of run fallouts, and I won't lose any of you. We're gonna take it slow and easy and build up your endurance. When I give the command, 'Double-time,' you will growl loudly. When I give the command, on your right foot, of *March,* you will immediately pick up the double-time and sing the following ditty:

"We like it here, we like it here, we finally found a home.
We like it here, we like it here, we're never goin' home."

Cassidy positioned himself to the right of the formation and began calling out cadence. "Hut, two, three, four, your left, your left, *doubbbble-time . . . march!*"

The platoon growled when he said "doubbbble" and immediately broke into the song as they began running. Cassidy waited until they had finished singing before yelling out, "Repeat each verse after me. Here we go!

. . . All the way . . . One way . . . Every day . . . One mile . . . you bet!
. . . Two mile . . . runnin' yet . . . Three mile . . . no sweat!

> "C-130 rolling down the strip.
> Airborne daddy gonna take a little trip.
> Stand up, hook up, shuffle to the door.
> Jump right out and count to four."

The platoon responded enthusiastically by singing each verse. Soon they were in perfect rhythm. Their left feet hit the ground at the beginning of each verse, making the sound of boots an accompaniment.

> "And if my chute don't open wide,
> I got another one by my side.
> And if that one should fail me too,
> watch out below I'm comin' through.
> Tell my mom I did my best
> and bury me in the leaning rest."

Eugene had not sung a word. He was exhausted from push-ups and didn't give a damn about making the run. Cassidy had given him the information he needed to get out of the Army. All he had to do was fall out of three runs and be boarded out. He moaned, grabbed his stomach as if cramped, and staggered to the side of the formation.

Vincent Martino saw his assigned buddy fall out and smiled. His problems would soon be over. He had known the mouthy bastard wouldn't make it. Eugene was going to take the easy way out.

Sergeant Cassidy saw Day leave the formation and bellowed. "The buddy of that fallout go get him and drag him back to the formation. *No*-body quits on my first run!"

Vincent rolled his eyes and peeled out of the formation. Seconds later he roughly grabbed Eugene's arm and pulled him down the road.

Eugene fought his grip. "Lea—Leave me alone."

Vincent kept his vicelike grip. "You heard him! Move it!"

Eugene again tried to fight off his buddy's grip, but Martino increased the pressure even more. He reluctantly gave in and began a slow jog. The Italian would tire of pulling him soon enough.

Blake Alexander was struggling. He had not realized he was in such bad condition until they had turned around at the one-mile marker and headed back toward the barracks. The lights of the company seemed twenty miles away. Lee Calhoon patted his back. "No sweat. Keep yo' head up an' breathe. Watch them lights. You gonna make it, Ace. I'll make sure of it."

Cassidy saw several members of the platoon falling back. "Nobody falls out!" he bellowed again. "Hang tough, second! We're all going to make it together!" He slowed the pace, knowing it was important to build their endurance slowly. Trying to make racehorses out of them the first day would only cause injuries and fallouts.

Eugene tried to stop again, but the Italian's grip was just as strong as when he had first grabbed him. (The bastard didn't seem to be tiring!)

Blake vomited twice but kept running. The barracks were only a quarter-mile away now. His legs felt like rubber and he couldn't seem to get enough air. His stomach jerked into a knot again and he began dry heaving.

Lee Calhoon grabbed Blake's belt and kept him moving. "You gotta keep runnin'. Ya can die when ya get there. Come on, you're almost there."

Eugene finally broke Vincent's grip and sunk to his knees beside the road. Cassidy saw him fall out, and he sprinted to the front of the formation.

"We're not losing anybody, *second!*" he yelled. "*Everybody* makes it or *nobody* makes it!"

Cassidy turned the formation around and headed back down the road. Passing Eugene, the drill sergeant grabbed Eugene's belt and yanked him to his feet. "*Nobody quits!*"

Dragging the black soldier, Cassidy turned the platoon around again and headed back for the barracks. "*Nobody quits in my platoon!*" he hollered.

Blake held on to Lee's arm for dear life. He had no strength left and thought he was going to pass out. The barracks were only a hundred yards away, but he didn't think he could run another ten feet.

Cassidy smiled to himself. With the exception of Day, the platoon was hanging tough. Everybody was helping each other. He slowed the formation almost to a walk.

"*Quick time . . . march,*" he commanded. "Hut . . . two . . . three . . . four. Get your heads up and breathe!"

The sergeant shoved Eugene into the formation and marched the platoon up the street to let them cool down. Then, after turning them around, he halted the platoon in front of their barracks. "Second platoon, you have learned something today. Nobody quits in my platoon. We will never have a fallout, or this platoon will stay out there on the run until every man quits. We finish together or not at all. Now fall out for showers and chow!"

Lee helped Blake toward the barracks. "You'll feel better when you eat."

Blake gagged hearing the word "eat" and began dry heaving again. His gagging caused a chain reaction among the queasy stomachs of the other men.

Eugene Day caught up to Martino as he walked for the barracks and angrily spun him around. "Don't ever grab me again!"

"What you gonna do about it, tough guy?" Vincent said, snickering.

Cassidy had heard the exchange and yelled from the dark shadows of the barracks, where he had been standing. "*Private* Martino, *Private* Day, *come here!*"

Vincent sprinted toward the sergeant, while Eugene walked nonchalantly. Seconds later Martino was at parade rest, facing the hulking sergeant who patiently waited while Eugene strolled up and casually took up the parade rest position. The sergeant looked directly into Martino's eyes while pointing at Eugene. "*This* soldier is *your* buddy. If he doesn't make it, I'll hold *you* directly responsible. A buddy team sticks together, no matter what. He *will not* fall out of any more runs. Do you understand?"

Martino clenched his teeth and nodded mechanically.

The massive drill sergeant shifted his cold eyes toward Eugene and pointed directly at his chest. "I'm on to you! I know you want out, but it ain't gonna happen. The only way out of my platoon is if you go AWOL, *and* you best not even think about that. They'll catch you. They always do. And when you come back, I'll be your worst nightmare come true. Day, you'd better be listening cause I'll take it real personal. *No*-body—I mean *no fuckin' body*—brings dishonor to me or my pla-toon! Martino, here, has my permission to drag your ass up and down the road if you *even* think about falling out again. *You got it?*"

Eugene felt a sickening, sinking feeling in his stomach. He had seen for an instant into the depths of the huge man's soul. It was all too clear that the drill sergeant's pride was at stake. Eugene knew beyond a doubt that the man wouldn't blink while tearing his heart out if Cassidy thought for an instant his pride was in jeopardy.

Cassidy gave Eugene one last baleful look before turning around and disappearing into the darkness.

Angry that he had to be responsible for a loser like Day, Martino grabbed Eugene's shirt and shoved him toward the barracks. "Come on, 'buddy.' "

Eugene knocked Vincent's hand away. "Fuck you, man, keep your hands off me!"

Vincent shook with rage. He wanted to knock the bastard's teeth out so bad he could taste it. Instead, he took a breath, calling on all the self-control he possessed, and walked toward the barracks in silence. In his mind he was obeying Cassidy's order. He was taking care of his "buddy" by not busting his face right there and then.

Blake was so sore and tired he wasn't sure if he could climb up to his top bunk to sleep. The day's training had dragged on forever with old black-and-white films and boring briefings that all seemed to run together. He couldn't remember a single thing he was supposed to have learned, except for the morning torture session known as Chargin' Charlie P.T. The real horror was knowing he would be doing it again in less than seven hours, which was enough to make him want to lie down and cry.

Lee Calhoon was shining his boots when he felt a tug on his buddy rope. He smiled, realizing his tired buddy had forgotten about the rope and was trying to climb up into his bunk. "Whoa, Ace, ya can't get up there until I get up."

Blake turned around with an impish frown. "I guess my brain is as dead as my body. Sorry."

Lee motioned to his lower bunk. "Lay down in mine and I'll get ya up when I finish shining these boots."

Blake collapsed on the bunk and looked up at the bedsprings above him. "Lee, you shine those boots like they're somethin' special. They're shined good enough to pass inspection."

Calhoon ran his blackened fingers over the polished leather as if it were silk. "These are the first new boots I ever owned. They sure are good uns. My daddy sure would like a pair like 'em."

Blake rolled his head to the side to look at his buddy. "Was your dad in the Army?"

Lee shrugged. "Naw, none of my kin served with Yankees but for my uncle Seb who done got shot in World War One. My great granddaddy served with Stonewall Jackson hisself. He got wounded at Chancellorsville. How about your kin? Any of 'em serve in the Confederacy?"

Blake began to reply when Vincent Martino raised up from the bunk beside them holding a piece of paper. "Yo, rebs, how's about some quiet, huh? I'm trying to write to my Gina. I gotta concentrate to say somethin' good."

Blake rolled his eyes. "Martino, there ain't nothin' good about this place."

Vincent smirked. "I know that. I'm tellin' her how bad it is with you guys. I says to her I'm stuck with two rebs next to me an' I'm tied to a colored boy. She's gonna feel real sorry for me and maybe send me some food."

Painfully, Eugene rose up from his bunk and yanked at the buddy rope with the last of his strength. "Knock the shit off, man! I can't sleep with you dudes jackin' your jaws."

Martino grinned and pointed at the glowing light bulb above him. "Lights is on, Day. Lights on means we can talk if we want to." He yanked the rope with a powerful tug, almost pulling Day out of bed. "You can't sleep till lights out, 'man.' "

Eugene felt too miserable to argue. He rolled onto his back and put the small pillow over his eyes to shut out the light and Martino's mocking grin.

"Guess he don't wanna play no more, huh?" Martino said to his two new friends.

To lighten the situation, Lee motioned to the letter in Vincent's hand. "Martino, why don't ya tell that girlfriend of yours ya got two handsome buddies who'd like some purty Italian girls to write em'."

Vincent shook his head with exaggeration. "You guys? You ain't handsome. I can't be lyin' to Gina. 'Sides, nice Italian girls wouldn't write no rebs."

Blake winked at Lee and began singing, "Oh I wish I was in the land of cotton, ol' times there ain't forgotten . . ."

Lee joined in and stood up. ". . . look away . . . look away Dixieland . . ."

Other members of the squad from the South put down their boots and joined in the singing.

Vincent tossed down the letter and stood on his footlocker. He bellowed, *"My eyes have seen the glory of the coming of the Lord . . . He is a . . ."*

Soon all the men in the bay, less Day, were singing one of the two songs, with each group trying to drown out the other.

Sergeant Cassidy strode into the barracks. He had heard the singing as he was heading for his car, and had returned to investigate. He was secretly pleased, despite his scowl, because singing meant his boys weren't feeling too sorry for themselves.

The soldier closest to the door spotted the sergeant and screamed, *"At ease!"* Instantly the singing stopped.

Cassidy took off his campaign hat. "Boys, I like it when my boys sing. *You!"* He pointed at Calhoon. "I heard your voice. You sang good. *Sing me a song!"*

Lee came to parade rest. "What'd ya want me ta sing, Drill Sergeant?"

Cassidy sat down on a footlocker and cocked his head to the side, as if in thought. "Uh . . . let's see. How about both songs? A kind of rendition like Elvis Presley does it?"

Lee lowered his head for a moment to gain confidence, then began singing almost in a whisper. "I wish I was . . . in the land of cotton . . . ol' times there . . . were not forgotten . . ." He slowly raised his head, and his rich tenor grew louder, filling the barracks with the refrain.

Cassidy had meant for the song to be a joke, but immediately realized he'd picked the wrong man. The soldier had a spell-binding voice, so full of both joy and sorrow that it reached out and grasped the heart of every man.

Lee changed octaves and began singing the Battle Hymn of the Republic. Feeling goose bumps raise up on his arms, Cassidy couldn't help himself. He began humming along.

Lee's last note echoed through the barracks, leaving the platoon mesmerized. Cassidy broke the awkward silence by clapping in approval. The rest of the platoon quickly joined in. Then Cassidy got up and stuck his hand out to Calhoon. "Ya done good, troop. That was something." Turning around facing down the aisle, his smile dissolved. *"Hit the sack, boys! P.T. tomorrow at 0430. Nobody goes on sick call, unless they go through me!"*

Blake patted Lee's back. "Damn, Lee, you were great! I'm proud to be your buddy."

Embarrassed, Lee shrugged his broad shoulders. "I sang the same song in church a couple'a times. It weren't nothin'."

Vincent grabbed Calhoon's hand and gave him a teeth-jarring handshake. "Sounds likes you got a little Italian in your family."

Ten minutes later the darkened barracks was quiet except for snoring and an occasional groan.

Eugene Day stared into the blackness. Tomorrow would bring only more misery. But not for long, he told himself. Eugene closed his eyes and clenched his teeth. No matter what it took, he was going home.

12

SAND HILL, FORT BENNING, GEORGIA, 10 FEBRUARY

The second platoon dejectedly walked toward their barracks, having been dismissed from evening formation by the first sergeant. It was the end of the fourth day of their training, and again, because of one man, the men of the second platoon ended up as the "slugs" of the company. The first sergeant had actually singled them out for their poor performance.

Rewards were simple in basic training—if your platoon performed better than the rest, you ate first. If you performed the worst, you ate last, which meant less food, no selection, and one hour less of sleep due to the clean-up detail. Six hours of sleep versus five hours meant a lot to physically and emotionally drained men. The first sergeant understood perfectly that basic training was a matter of survival. Men were reduced to the basic needs. Taking away food and sleep was usually more than enough incentive to improve performance. Today, however, was the second time in a row that second platoon had been designated as last to eat.

The men were sick and tired of the situation, which had been created mostly by one man, Private Eugene Day. The scrawny little bastard, with his 'don't give a shit' attitude, had managed to screw up everything he did. He had not passed a single inspection, had been caught sleeping in classes, had failed to report properly for the mess hall head count, and most recently had failed to salute the company commander.

Johnson, the first squad leader, who spun around at the barracks door, sneered at Blake Alexander, and barked, "You square away Day, or *we* will!"

Blake took the remark as a personal attack. "Johnson," he shot back, "you take care of your squad, and I'll take care of mine."

Not satisfied, Johnson blocked the entrance. "Either you change Day's attitude or this platoon will! We're tired of being called 'slugs' because of him."

The third squad leader joined Johnson at the door. "Johnson's right. You make that sonofabitch soldier or we're gonna take matters into our own hands. He's causing all of us to suffer."

Red-faced, Blake turned away. He couldn't argue with them. They were right. Day was causing extra work for the entire platoon, not to mention the Italian, Martino, who had been doing hundreds of extra push-ups because of Day and had to pull the malingering soldier the entire distance on the morning runs. Martino was in excellent condition, but not excellent enough to do the work of two men.

Still tied together, Blake and Lee headed for the orderly room where the first sergeant was overseeing Day's punishment.

Day and Martino were doing jumping jacks outside the office door, while the first sergeant sat behind his desk finishing paperwork. He looked up briefly at his victims.

"Next time, Private Day, you'd better damn well salute the commanding officer. You made the entire company look like shit!. The C.O. thinks maybe the whole company is like you and don't know proper military courtesy. I know they do. *You, Day, you are the only dumb-ass! You didn't listen, and that pisses me off! Now, knock out push-ups!"*

Blake waited outside until the first sergeant got bored with watching the two recruits agonize and sweat through a dozen different exercises and dismissed them back to the barracks.

As soon as they walked out the door, Blake motioned the two tired men over. "You hangin' tough, Vinny?" he asked sympathetically.

Exhausted, Martino could only nod.

Blake's eyes shifted to Day and turned to stone. His voice was just as hard. "If you don't get your shit together, the platoon is gonna take things into their own hands. Just because you want out doesn't mean you have to make the rest of the platoon suffer. You may not want to be here, but damnit, we do!" Blake sighed. Day had assumed his give-a-shit look.

Blake tried a different tack. He softened his expression and put his hand on Day's shoulder. "Look, there are better ways of getting out than dragging down the platoon. Just look at what you're doing to Martino. Doesn't it bother you?"

Eugene had difficulty lifting his head, but the fire still shone in his eyes. "Fuck the platoon, fuck Martino, and fuck you."

Blake didn't change his expression. By now he was used to Day's attitude.

Lee tugged the rope to get Blake's attention. "Come on, Ace. We gotta git back and make out the clean-up roster."

The first sergeant motioned for Cassidy to take a seat. "Take a load off, Cass, and tell me about your problem child, Private Day."

Cassidy leaned back in the chair. "Top, I've tried everything. I hoped peer pressure would work, but it's backfiring on me. He's bringing down the whole platoon."

"Yeah, well, Cass, you can't make 'em all into soldiers. You're gonna lose some." His eyes locked onto Cassidy's. "The mass punishment bit isn't cutting it. You're gonna lose more than just one shitbird if you don't change your approach. But what the hell am I telling you for? You know that."

"Yeah, Top, I know," Cassidy replied dejectedly. "But I really thought I could get through to him. It's hard to explain, but he ain't a typical shitbird. He's got potential. I just can't seem to reach him. Maybe another couple of weeks and he'll come around."

The first sergeant swiveled his chair around to look out the window that faced the barracks. "Cass, you're one of the best I've got. You know these kids, and you get the best out of them, but you gotta learn ya can't save 'em all. Let him go. There are thirty-nine other men in your platoon who need your help."

Cassidy rose from the chair. "It's funny, I know what Day is thinking. It's like I'm in his head, and I know what he's gonna do and say. I'm close, Top, I know I am. Another week and maybe—"

The first sergeant turned to Cassidy. "The board meets next week. I want his name at the top of the list for termination from service due to unsuitability."

Cassidy's back stiffened and his face lost expression. He put on his campaign hat and instantly became a hardened drill sergeant again. "Yes, First Sergeant," he said mechanically. He executed a perfect about-face and strode for the door.

At midnight the fire-guard team awakened their squad leader as ordered. Within minutes every man on the second floor had moved silently down the darkened stairs. The first squad, already waiting in the aisle, joined the rest of the men as they snuck toward the end of the bay.

Eugene Day was awakened by a towel thrown over his mouth and ropes that were tied around the rest of his body. He tried to fight but he couldn't move. In seconds his buddy rope was removed and he was soundlessly lifted from the bed, trussed up like a Thanksgiving turkey. His mouth was gagged and his head covered with a pillowcase.

Eugene was thrown into the lighted latrine. His muffled screams went unheard as the first fists struck his face. He reeled with the blows and knocked into others, who then pushed him erect and hit him again. There was no sound other than the heavy breathing and grunts of his attackers as they shoved and slugged him.

Dazed and bleeding, Eugene collapsed to the cool, tile floor. He was immediately kicked, then kicked again and again. He tried to ball up to protect his groin, but his attackers grabbed his legs and hands. Suddenly, through a darkening haze, he heard a familiar voice. "*Hey,* whatta you guys think ya doin'?"

"Get out, Martino. The dude is gettin' what he deserves!"

Eugene recognized the second voice and felt an even deeper pain than that he felt from the blows. The second voice was from Washington, a Negro in the third squad.

Realizing what was happening, Martino shoved the nearest man aside and broke into the circle. He stood over the prone soldier and raised his fists. "You fuck wit' my buddy, you fuck wit' me!"

The third squad leader, a big Texan, stepped into the ring to reason with the Italian. "Look, he deserves it. Just back off and let us get rid of him. We're only doin' what's best. He don't wanna be here, so we're making it easy for him."

Martino glanced down and saw the bloodstains on the pillowcase. He raised his eyes and looked at the Texan with a glare. "Yeah, you makin' it real easy. I can see that."

The Texan stepped closer. "Why you protectin' this piece 'a shit? You of all people should want him gone."

Martino backed up a step to buy time while he thought of an answer that would make sense. He remembered what Cassidy had told him about taking care of his buddy, but it was more than that. " 'Cause . . . 'cause it ain't right," he replied.

The Texan shrugged his shoulders, as if giving up, but suddenly lunged at Martino. Vincent was not fooled by the ploy. He struck the squad leader just below the right eye with a jab that jolted the Texan's head back as if he had run into a clothesline. The resounding smack halted further attack for only a few seconds, then the rest of the third squad moved in.

Vincent got two good punches in before he fell under a flurry of fists, but he had gained enough time.

"A sergeant is comin'!" someone yelled.

The crowded latrine emptied in fifteen seconds, leaving Martino and Day lying on the floor. Blake Alexander entered the lighted room, knelt down and took off the pillowcase from Eugene's head. He spoke to Vincent, who was trying to stand. "Nobody's comin'. I yelled the warning. It was all I could think of to do when I saw what was happening. I'm sorry I didn't get here sooner."

Vincent waved away the apology and wiped blood from his nose.

Blake got Eugene to his feet and leaned him over a nearby sink for support. Eugene looked into the mirror through the bruised and swollen slits where his eyes had been. He had wanted to see if he looked as bad as he felt. He looked worse. His face was puffed out to the size of a melon, as if he'd been stung by fifty bees, and his split, bleeding lips were twice their normal size. He ached all over and couldn't take a normal breath without wincing from pain.

Eugene painfully faced Blake. "Wh-Who was it?" he said thickly, drooling saliva and blood.

Blake's brow furrowed. "The whole platoon, except the guys in our squad. You were lucky Martino stopped them before they put you in the hospital."

Eugene shifted his body like a rusted robot toward Martino. "You okay?"

Vincent tore off some toilet paper to stuff up his nose and stop the bleeding. "What the fuck da you care?" he said icily. The Italian turned around, trying to keep his balance, and weaved his way toward the latrine door.

Cassidy walked down the ranks and stopped in front of Day. "What the hell happened to you?"

Eugene painfully straightened his back and stared straight ahead. "I fell down in the shower last night, Sergeant."

Cassidy had sensed something was wrong as soon as the platoon formed up for the morning formation. Their fidgeting had been a dead giveaway. Then he noticed Martino had to hold Day upright.

Cassidy inspected Eugene's swollen face more closely. "Are you sure that's what happened?" he asked softly.

The entire platoon seemed to hold its collective breath. Eugene kept his half-opened eyes focused on the sergeant's campaign hat. "Yes, Sergeant, I fell down in the shower."

Cassidy was genuinely surprised that the 'attitude problem' had the guts not to report what had obviously happened. The platoon had finally taken action. "You be more careful," the sergeant said without sympathy. "Shower floors can get real slick."

He was about to move the platoon to P.T. when he noticed Martino's bruised face. Turning around, he quickly scanned the faces of the rest of the platoon. The third squad leader and two of his men also had black eyes and facial bruises. I'll be damned, he thought. The Italian had made a fight of it. Martino was probably the only reason Day was still standing in ranks.

Cassidy stood behind the company P.T. formation as the men performed their morning exercises. He turned around and motioned for the soldier whom he had excused from participating. Private Eugene Day approached and came to parade rest.

"Day, you win," Cassidy said without emotion. "Next week is the board, and you're going to appear before it. Your performance and attitude are such that you've demonstrated yourself unsuitable for military service. For the next five days all you have to do is stay out of trouble and do what you're told. No more bullshit. You got what you wanted, so don't be screwin' around and messin' up my platoon anymore. When you go before the board, all you have to say is you don't want to be a soldier. You'll be on a bus for home the next day."

Cassidy's tone softened. "I just hope you know what you're doin'. Here, in the Army, you had a chance to make a difference."

Eugene maintained his expressionless stare, despite his joy at the news. He was going home. He'd beaten the drill sergeant and the system. "I know what I'm doin'," he said with conviction.

Cassidy's eyes narrowed. "All right. Just don't be fallin' out of any more runs."

After P.T., Cassidy marched the platoon toward the road and bellowed, "This run is gonna be different. *No*-body helps their buddy if they fall out. It's time we saw who can make it on their own. But, boys, we *will* keep running until every man finishes. If a man falls back, we'll turn around and keep turning around until every man runs, walks, or crawls back to the barracks. *Private Day, that means you! We* are *all* going to finish together! *Doubbbble-time . . . march!"*

A hundred yards short of the halfway point of the run, Eugene fell out. His bruised ribs felt as if they were bursting through his chest every time he took a deep breath.

Martino had been watching Day during the run and knew he was hurting. He was secretly glad to see him suffer. At least this time he didn't have to go back and drag his bony black ass to the barracks.

Cassidy saw his problem child alongside the road and yelled, "Day, join the formation when we turn around."

Suddenly, inexplicably, Martino felt guilty at seeing his buddy kneeling on the road. He was glad, yet he felt as if he had failed him in some way. He had learned something about Day, being tied to him for so long. The guy honestly believed he could make a difference by going home. Day wasn't lazy or a bum. He was fighting the Army the only way he knew how. Vincent sighed and peeled out of formation.

"Get back in ranks," Cassidy yelled. "He has to make it on his own!"

Vincent ignored the sergeant and helped Day to his feet. He spoke quietly, as if they were the only two men in the world. "Come on, just move your feet an' head for the barracks. Don't let the bums know they hurt you. Show 'em. Show 'em you ain't no bum."

Cassidy turned the platoon around at the halfway point and led them up the road back toward the barracks. When he got alongside Martino, he ordered him into the formation but ignored Day.

Eugene saw the looks of disdain on the faces of the men as they passed by, and began to spit at them when he heard Martino yell out, "Show 'em!"

Through all his pain and hatred, Eugene smiled to himself. Martino was such a dumb dago. He actually believed in a system that forced him to take punishment for what someone else did.

Eugene watched the last of the platoon pass by before facing the distant barracks. He was going to run, but not for the platoon, Cassidy, or even his own pride. He was going to run for the dago. The dumb shit had paid out enough. He deserved to get something back.

Eugene painfully began to jog. He was going to show his buddy he could do it.

Cassidy watched along with the platoon as the lone soldier ran up the road toward them. The platoon had finished the run several minutes before and were waiting. Cassidy had changed his mind and let the platoon finish rather than wait for Day. The first sergeant had been right. Mass punishment would serve no purpose other than to hurt good men.

Martino yelled out. "Come on! You can do it!"

"Shut up, in ranks!" Cassidy barked. "Pla-toooon ... *a*-ten-*hut! Fall out* and get showered."

The formation quickly dissolved, leaving only one man to await the arrival of Day. Martino walked up the dark road to meet his buddy.

SAND HILL, 13 FEBRUARY

Sergeant Cassidy stood on a rise that overlooked the obstacle course. His men took off their hats and web gear and were about to move up to the start line, where they would wait in a single file and start the course, one man at a time, at five-second intervals.

The obstacle-course race was a company event, which meant that platoons competed against each other for bragging rights. The company commander had given a pep talk before the event, and promised the winning platoon a streamer and a two-hour pass to visit the post exchange beer hall. The men had been fired up after the speech and hollered challenges to other platoon members.

Second platoon drew the last start time. Cassidy assured his men that the last starting position would give them an advantage, as they would be able to learn from the mistakes of the others, and they would know what time they had to beat.

The first platoon had begun the course first and finished in nineteen minutes flat. The third platoon was next and finished in eighteen minutes and forty-five seconds. The fourth platoon had half their men on course when it started to rain. The red clay turned into a quagmire. They finished in twenty-six minutes.

Cassidy asked the captain that the event be delayed, in fairness to his men, but the protest fell on deaf ears. There was no time in the company's busy schedule for a makeup.

Many of the second platoon members grumbled as they lined up. With all the mud and slippery obstacles, it was useless even to try.

The company commander held up his hand for everyone's attention. "Men, I realize it's wet and muddy, but just do your best. Remember the rules: the clock stops when the last man crosses the line. The time to beat is third platoon's eighteen minutes and forty-five seconds. Remember, if a member of your platoon is injured while negotiating the course, the platoon will not be penalized. If you see an injured soldier, call for a medic and he will be attended to. The obstacles and ropes are slick, so be careful." The officer looked at his watch and pointed at the first soldier in line. "One minute until you begin. Do not go until I tell you."

"What's the use?" the soldier snickered to the man behind him.

Blake Alexander heard the negative comment and stepped out of line. He glared at the sullen, rain-soaked soldiers and bellowed, *"We're the second to none! We don't quit or give up! Ta hell with the rain . . . ta hell with the mud . . . ta hell with the third platoon's time. We're gonna kick their ass and drink beer tonight!"*

"Yeah, let's show 'em who we are!" Lee Calhoon yelled.

The third platoon had formed up behind the second platoon to watch. Their platoon sergeant yelled out, *"Forget it, Second. Give up! You slugs ain't got a chance in hell!"*

"Fuck you," Jerome Davis screamed back, "we're gonna whip your ass!"

Blake had first thought his efforts had been wasted, but knew as soon as the third platoon began yelling insults, the second would respond. The platoon began hollering and growling like mad men, and Vincent Martino began chanting, *"Beer . . . beer . . . beer!"*

Soon the whole platoon picked up the chant. Blake yelled at Vincent to take the last position and keep the platoon fired up as he and Lee moved to the front of the line.

Lee took up the first position and looked at the captain who was beginning the countdown. "Five . . . four . . . three . . . two . . . one . . . *go!"*

With a bloodcurdling rebel yell, Lee bolted off the line and hurdled the log wall in one powerful jump. There were screams of support from his platoon and hoots of derision from the other units. Blake growled crazily as he started the course.

Eugene Day stood in silence in the middle of the line. He knew that all the yelling and psyching up in the world was not going to help. They were dreaming if they believed they could beat the third platoon's time. Anyway, what did he care? He had only two more days before he went before the board. Two more days then home.

Rain dripped off Sergeant Cassidy's campaign hat brim as he watched Martino approach the starting line. He was the last man, and he was beating his chest like a crazed gorilla. The sergeant shifted his gaze to the course and felt a chill run up his spine. His "boys" were going all out, sloshing through the mud and screaming as they ran, crawled, jumped, and climbed over the obstacles. The sight of them made him stand a little straighter and prouder.

Lee Calhoon climbed the twenty-foot rope on the last obstacle, touched the cross pole and slid back down the rope without worrying about burning his hands. He hit the ground and sprinted toward the finish. Out of breath, he crossed the line and immediately threw up. His face was white as a wrinkled sheet. Blake came in only seconds later, followed by another soldier.

The captain looked at his watch. "Twelve minutes and thirty seconds . . . thirty-one . . . thirty-two . . ."

Cassidy tensed. Jesus, they had a chance! He broke into a run and ran down the hill, yelling, *"Come on second platoon! You've got the best time! Come on! Gooooooo!"*

Vincent Martino had passed three men and was making his way across the rope bridge. Almost to the end, he reached for the platform, but lost his grip from the slippery rope and fell. The back of his head hit the support pole just before his body slapped the wet ground. The soldier behind him screamed for a medic and kept going.

Eugene had been loping along, taking it easy, and had completed the second to the last obstacle when he looked behind him and saw he was one of the last men on the course. He had assumed his efforts would not matter to the platoon, but now, seeing only Jerome Davis behind him and coming up fast, he broke into a sprint.

Jerome caught him just as they topped a small knoll, and snarled as he sprinted past. "You been half-steppin' muthafucker!"

Eugene ran faster to catch up and jumped for one of the ropes. He pulled himself up toward the top, hearing the platoon screaming they were still ahead on time.

"Move your ass!" Jerome yelled.

Eugene reached the top, but not before Jerome had already slapped the pole and begun sliding down. Eugene wasn't about to let the jeering man beat him. He released his grip and fell the twenty feet to the pit and rolled to his feet in a dead run.

The captain yelled, "Eighteen minutes and ten seconds . . . eleven seconds . . ."

Eugene crossed the finish line three strides ahead of Jerome, who was met with cheers from the victorious platoon. Blake pounded Eugene's back, yelling they had won the competition, when he suddenly stopped and pointed toward the obstacle course. "What the hell is he doing?"

Vincent Martino was on his feet despite the gash in the back of his head. He had pushed the medics away and was running toward the next to the last obstacle. He was still stunned, and fell over the first of six logs he was supposed to jump. He got up despite another cut on his chin and kept running. The medics called out for him to stop, but he kept jogging and tried to jump over the second log. He pitched over, falling hard on his shoulder. He got up shaking his head like a wounded buffalo, but he kept moving.

Jerome stood in front of Eugene and glanced over his shoulder. "Your Eye-tie buddy is dummer than dirt. He ain't never gonna make it."

Eugene fired back, "He's got more brains and guts than—" He stopped himself. He shifted his gaze back toward Martino, who was swaying like a drunk, trying to jump the last logs. The damn fool! The fool was running for nothing! Shit, didn't he know they'd won?

Jerome snickered as he stepped closer, still watching the staggering soldier. "You two are perfect together, man. Ya both ain't never gonna be soldiers. You gonna get thrown out, and he's too dumb to make it."

Eugene didn't waste time on a response. Instead he broke into a run toward his buddy.

Seconds later Eugene grabbed Vincent's arm. "Quit, man. It's over, we won."

Vincent pushed his hand away, speaking sluggishly. "I . . . I gotta finish."

Eugene grabbed him again. "Why, man? It's over. Come on, you're hurt."

The soldier's eyes became set as he stared at the log in front of him as if it were a hated enemy. "I . . . I gotta make it. I'm no bum."

Eugene felt a lump lodge in his throat and released his grip. The dumb dago was trying to make it because of pride. Vincent was strong as a bull, but was struggling in the classes. He had to succeed now, at the only thing he was good at. Pride. It was forcing him to continue. It was blind, self-destructive, and had nothing to do with reality.

Eugene jogged beside his buddy to make sure he didn't fall over the last log. "Come on, lift your feet . . . get ready to jump . . . *now!*"

Vincent jumped, but his trail foot caught the log and he pitched forward. Eugene tried to catch him but it was too late and both men tumbled to the wet ground.

Eugene got up and helped Martino to his feet. "That's it. You're too tired to climb up the rope. Let the medics see your cut."

Vincent pushed him away and began running toward the ropes, yelling, "I gotta *finnnnnish!*"

Blake Alexander watched in silence, along with the rest of the platoon. Eugene was trying to help the soldier by pushing him up the rope, but Martino was too heavy. Blake ran toward the rope climb to help. Lee Calhoon gave out a rebel yell and also broke into a run.

Jerome Davis exchanged glances with his buddy, the redheaded Kentuckian. They both nodded and followed at a dead run. In seconds the entire platoon was running toward the ropes.

Cassidy smiled to himself as his platoon began to build a human pyramid to help Martino achieve his goal.

The company commander walked over and stood beside the big drill sergeant. "You won more than just the competition. You've got a good group there. I wish I was with them to help that trooper."

Cassidy, thinking exactly the same thing, broke into a run toward the rope climb.

A minute later the officer smiled seeing the platoon cheer as the hurt soldier triumphantly touched the cross pole. Cassidy had gotten on his hands and knees in the mud and had been a part of the pyramid.

Cassidy paced back in front of his platoon holding the first place streamer. He stopped and rotated his shoulders back. "Boys, ya done good . . . ya made me proud today. You demonstrated to me and this company you are not individuals but you are a team. You learned something today . . . and so did I. You're no longer boys . . . today, you became *men*. Men, you're dismissed and can go to the beer hall."

Cassidy spun around amidst the cheers and hollering and strode toward the orderly room. It was on days like today that he knew why he loved his profession.

Vincent Martino picked up a pitcher of beer from the bar and made his way through the crowded beer hall to the back table, where a soldier sat by himself. Vincent set the pitcher down on the table and took a seat beside his buddy. "I never got no chance to thank you for—"

"Forget it," Eugene said. He hoped the Italian would leave him alone.

Martino lowered his head. "It meant a lot to me to make it. I . . . I ain't doin' so hot. I ain't smart like you and the other guys. I try . . . I try hard, but—"

"What you talkin' about, man?" Eugene said emphatically. "You're gonna make it. You're gonna get a new buddy, and he'll help you. Things are gonna get better, you'll see."

Vincent glanced around at the other tables. "Nobody is gonna want me. They know I'm not smart enough to make it."

"That's bullshit, man," Eugene said angrily.

Vincent searched Eugene's face to see if he was sincere. "You really think I can learn all this Army stuff? Tomorrow, for the captain's inspection, we gotta know the first three general orders, and I ain't got 'em memorized. I can't get 'em into my head."

Eugene looked into his buddy's searching eyes and answered honestly. "You can do it, but you gotta work at it. You ought to be practicing right now. Write them down on cards and study them one at a time. Once you memorize one, then start on the other one. You can do it."

Eugene could see the doubt in the soldier's eyes and sighed. He stood. "Come on, let's go back to the barracks, and I'll show you how I memorized poems. We'll write 'em down and practice."

Vincent looked longingly at the pitcher of cold beer. "But . . . how's about just one glass, then—"

Eugene shook his head and pointed toward the door. Feeling strange, he said, "Come on, it's study time."

Only after the Italian reluctantly stood and made for the door did Eugene realize why he had felt so strange—he had been smiling. It was the first time he had smiled since . . . since he could remember.

The company commander walked down the ranks of the second squad and stopped in front of a tall, rangy soldier. He looked first at the soldier's spit-shined boots, and slowly brought his eyes up, checking the brightly shined brass belt buckle, then the pressed fatigue shirt. Finding no fault with the recruit's appearance, he barked into the soldier's face, "What is your first general order?"

Private Lee Calhoon kept his eyes fixed on the horizon. "Sir, the first general order is, 'To take charge of my post and all government property in view.' "

The captain nodded and barked again, "That is correct. You look good, trooper. Keep it up."

Facing right, the captain stepped off and passed the next two men before stopping before a stocky soldier who was sweating profusely, though the temperature was in the low fifties. He repeated his inspection routine.

Sergeant Cassidy, accompanying the company commander, groaned silently. These weekly inspections, held to check appearance and general knowledge, were the captain's method for determining whether his drill sergeants were teaching the soldiers properly.

Cassidy knew his men's appearance would pass. He had checked them daily, and at a morning pre-inspection had found no faults. The problem was that many of the men had not yet mastered the general orders. Especially Martino.

Cassidy sighed inwardly as the captain looked into the sweating soldier's face and snapped, "Private, what is your second general order?"

Cassidy knew the soldier didn't know. Martino had not passed any of the memory work. He was a good trooper with a big heart, but he was as dumb as a box of rocks.

Vincent's mouth was dry and his eyes rolled up. He thought about the white cards that Eugene had gone over with him over and over again. They had spent half the night in the latrine when the lights were turned off, but now his mind was a total blank.

The captain's eyes narrowed. "Private, do you know your general orders or not?"

Vincent's eyes widened and he began to shake his head when suddenly a melody played in his head. Eugene had taught him to think of each of the orders as an individual song. The words didn't rhyme, but the system worked.

He gulped and forced his tongue to move. "Sir, the second general order is, 'I will walk my post in a military manner, keeping always on the alert and observing everything that takes place within sight or hearing.' "

Cassidy was in total shock and barely heard the captain say, "Correct, good job." The captain began to face right, but stopped himself and looked at the cut on the soldier's chin.

"Private," he said, "aren't you the one who was hurt on the obstacle course but kept going?"

"Yes, sir," Martino said sheepishly.

The captain held out his hand. "Private, I want to shake your hand. You did a hell of a job. I'm proud to be your commander. You're going to make a fine soldier."

Martino took the captain's hand and motioned toward the thin soldier next to him. "Thank you, sir, but it was my buddy who helped me make it. You should be shaking his hand."

The captain broke into a smile, finished shaking hands with Martino, and put his hand out toward a very embarrassed Private Eugene Day.

"Trooper," he said, "you two men make a good team. I like it when my soldiers help each other and give each other credit. You two are what this Army is all about."

Cassidy closed his gaping mouth and looked at Day as the captain shook his hand. The thin, bespectacled soldier was grinning!

The captain turned to Cassidy. "I've seen enough, Sergeant. Your platoon looks superb and obviously knows their general orders. The morale and performance I've seen here reflect your superior leadership skills. Keep up the good work. By the way, I'm awarding your platoon this week's best platoon streamer."

Cassidy saluted smartly. He *had* to be dreaming. "Thank you, sir," he heard himself saying. "We're second to none."

Eugene lay on his bunk, staring up at the ceiling and thinking about going home.

Martino looked up from the letter he was writing and tapped the bedsprings above him. "Yo, buddy, how you spell your first name?"

Eugene broke from his reverie and rose up on an elbow. "Why you wanna know that?"

"I'm writing my girl and wanna tell her 'bout my buddy."

Eugene leaned over the mattress and looked down at the Italian. "Man, don't write about me. Shit, man, I'm history. Day after tomorrow I'm outta here."

Martino looked up at his buddy. "You can't leave. You and me are a team. We gonna make it together."

Eugene lay back on his bed, unable to take the lost look from Martino. "No, man, not me. Nothin' has changed . . . I'm going home."

Martino lowered his head, speaking softly. "But . . . but you and me . . . we're buddies. I thought we'd . . ."

Eugene closed his eyes, trying to concentrate on what he was going to do once he got back to Carlisle. A minute passed before he leaned over the mattress and spoke almost in a whisper. "Vinny, you spell it E-U-G-E-N-E."

Martino smiled and picked up his pen again.

Sergeant Cassidy inspected the private's uniform and brushed a piece of lint from his lapel. "You look fine. Remember, all you gotta do is march in and stop three paces from their table, salute, and come to parade rest when they tell you. They're going to ask if you want to be in the Army, and then you tell 'em you don't wanna be here."

Eugene Day nodded and nervously adjusted his black tie. Cassidy eyed the soldier, noticing his lack of confidence. "What's wrong, Day? I thought you'd be thrilled."

Eugene looked up at the sergeant with wide, questioning eyes. "Who is gonna be Martino's buddy?"

Cassidy shrugged his shoulders, surprised by the question. "I don't know. I'll probably put him with Murray and Finch."

Eugene's face showed pain. "Not them. They won't help him."

Cassidy's eyes narrowed. "I run the platoon. And it's none of your concern anyway. You're outta here."

Eugene was about to speak when the office door across from them opened and a lieutenant appeared.

"Private Day, come in and report to the board."

Private Day stood in front of a table where a major, two captains, and two first sergeants were seated staring at him. The major read the performance report aloud to the rest of the board, then looked up at the bespectacled soldier.

"Private Day, based on this report, it is clear that the government would be best served by releasing you from military service for reasons of unsuitability. For the record, do you have anything to say for yourself?"

Eugene lowered his head. He had thought it was going to be easy. It was what he had been waiting for since leaving home, and yet . . .

"Private Day, do you wish to say anything?" repeated the major.

Eugene raised his head. "Sir, I . . . I want to continue training and become a soldier."

———

Cassidy stood in front of the irate first sergeant, whose voice was rising in pitch.

"I thought he wanted out! You said he would tell the board he wanted to go home! And out of the blue I get a phone call from the board that says the shitbird pleaded to stay! The major wanted to know what the hell was going on. He was pissed because we wasted his time!" The first sergeant took a breath and leaned across the desk. "Would you mind telling me *what the hell is going on!*"

Cassidy spoke calmly. "Top, the kid changed his mind. He felt that if he left his buddy, Martino, the chances were Martino wouldn't make it. It surprised me too."

The first sergeant leaned back in his chair, still red-faced. "Well, it ain't that fuckin' easy to 'change your mind.' We sent in a report that said he was a shitbird. The board has delayed its findings until they have our recommendation." The first sergeant's eyes riveted on Cassidy. "What *is* our recommendation . . . can he make it?"

Cassidy smiled to himself but showed no outward signs of emotion. "Top, he's gonna make a good one, or I'll owe you a case of Bud."

The senior NCO sighed in resignation and pointed to his door. "Get the fuck outta here. You've wasted enough of my time." He waited until Cassidy turned around and grasped the doorknob before speaking again. "Cass?"

"Yeah, Top?"

"Cass, you're gonna lose one someday. You can't always save them, no matter how hard you try. One day you're gonna lose."

Cassidy smiled. "Yeah, Top, I know. But not today."

13

A lone Huey streaked over the treetops at ninety knots, heading for a small landing zone nestled in the pines a kilometer away. Newly promoted Staff Sergeant Shawn Flynn saw his checkpoint pass beneath him and unbuckled his seat belt. He motioned to the other members of the recon team to do the same, and he scooted toward the open door. The wind tore at his fatigues as he extended his legs over the edge of the frame and readied his rifle.

The Huey dipped its tail to slow its speed and dropped into a meadow surrounded by tall pines. Without waiting for the bird's skids to touch, Shawn jumped the four feet to the ground and ran ten yards before throwing himself down and rolling into firing position.

The chopper lifted off, and in fifteen seconds the green meadow was left in silence. Shawn studied the woodline for signs and movement for several more seconds before hopping up and running toward the protective pines. Entering the cool shade, he threw himself to the ground and rolled behind a tree. He didn't need to see if his team had followed him; he heard them as they hit the ground behind him and formed a small perimeter. Waiting a full five minutes, Shawn was satisfied they were not in immediate danger. He whispered to the radio operator, whom he knew would be to his right, "Tell 'em we're in with negative contact and will begin clearing."

The last chopper lifted off and banked hard right after unloading the last of the rifle company in the landing zone. The company commander knelt in the woodline and spoke to the recon sergeant, who had joined him a minute before.

"Repeat what you said. I couldn't hear over the choppers."

Shawn motioned to the high ground five hundred yards to the north. "Sir, we found very recent signs of an aggressor company on that small hill. I followed their trail for a little ways, and I think they're trying to circle around and hit the L.Z. from the south. I suggest you get patrols out ASAP and get ready for an attack."

Captain Jim Tomkins smiled with confidence. "Thanks for the advice, Sarge, but they wouldn't dare hit us now. They would have tried to knock us out when we were landing. They pulled back to the defensible terrain farther to the north. We're going to follow the plan I briefed to you this morning. Go ahead and move your recon team out to the north, and we'll follow in ten minutes. Keep me posted if you see anything."

Shawn pulled out his map in a last attempt to show the captain he was making a mistake. "Sir, I don't think they pulled back. If you'll look at the map, you'll see the enemy wouldn't fall back in that direction because of the sparse vegetation and flat terrain. He knows with our helicopter assets we would send in another unit behind them to cut 'em off. The signs are he's—"

The captain shook his head, losing patience, and stood up. "Enough, Sergeant. I'm in charge here. You are attached to this company for this operation only, and you don't understand the aggressors as I do. Move your team out immediately and keep me informed."

Shawn put on his helmet. "Yes, sir, we're on the way."

Shawn and his team had moved two hundred yards when the rattle of gunfire erupted behind them from the direction of the landing zone.

Sergeant Derringer began to turn around, but Shawn stopped him and whispered, "Where you think you're goin'?"

Derringer pointed toward the L.Z. "They're gettin' hit just like you said. Aren't we gonna help?"

Shawn put his finger to his lips, signaling silence, and concentrated on the sound of gunfire. He listened for several seconds and motioned for the rest of the team to close in around him and sit down. When the team was assembled, he whispered, "Listen to the firefight and tell me what you hear."

Derringer spoke first. "Small arms, about two platoons slugging it out."

Two more men agreed with Derringer while the others thought it sounded more like a couple of squads firing.

Shawn knelt down. "The first bursts weren't from machine guns. That tells you it's not a full-scale attack. I'll bet a beer the aggressors hit them with a squad then pulled back to suck them out to where the rest of them are waiting." Shawn pointed at Derringer. "And never rush blindly back to a unit that's hit. Get on the radio and find out what's happening and listen to the firefight. In Vietnam, the dinks are masters at feints. They hit you on a flank with a feint attack then hit ya in the ass or the other flank with the main attack. In this case, I think they hit the company with a light force and pulled back hoping the gung-ho captain would pursue."

Shawn motioned toward the radio operator. "Have you heard anything?"

The RTO nodded, keeping the handset to his ear. "Yeah, the aggressors have pulled back after firing up the second platoon. The captain just ordered the second platoon to follow the aggressors, and told the third platoon to maneuver to the right to try and cut them off."

Shawn shook his head. "If I'm right, it's gonna hit the fan any minute now. The captain fell for it. The aggressors are gonna hit him from the east or west with the main attack. The captain's only got one platoon left to secure the landing zone, and it'll be stretched too thin to stop them." Shawn spoke to the RTO again. "Has the captain requested any fire support yet?"

The radioman shook his head. "Nope, nothing. He's just told the second platoon leader to hurry and get his platoon moving."

Ten seconds had passed when machine guns in the distance began chattering. A roar of small-arms fire and yelling quickly followed.

Shawn stood. "Come on, we'll be able to hit the aggressors in the flank and do 'em a little damage before we die as heroes."

Derringer looked at his sergeant with awe. "Jesus, Sarge, you called it perfectly . . . what would we do if it was real? I mean we wouldn't really go back and get wiped out with the rest of them, would we?"

Shawn chambered a blank round into his M-14. "Yeah, we would, but we'd go in smart. The captain didn't call in arty, gunships, or fast movers. We'd call in everything we could get for him and pick off as many of the enemy as we could. The Viet Cong don't usually stay around a battlefield very long once the fire support starts coming in. We'd have a damn good chance of making a difference. Come on, I wanna see the captain's face."

SAND HILL, 3 MARCH

"Men, this is an M-14 semiautomatic, air-cooled, gas-operated, magazine-fed, 7.62 rifle with a maximum effective range of 460 meters. You will *never* call your weapon a 'gun.' A 'gun' is an artillery piece or that thing between your legs. You will refer to this weapon as a rifle or weapon. You have been issued your rifles and weapons cards. You will memorize your rifle's serial number and take care of your weapon as if it were a willing girlfriend. Your rifle is your best friend, for it will save your life. Kiss your rifle at this time and tell it you love it."

Blake Alexander rolled his eyes but complied, as did the rest of the platoon.

Cassidy watched the platoon kiss their weapons and shook his head with exaggerated disappointment. "I can sure tell you men haven't had much experience with women." His expression changed from a half smile to all business. "The M-14 is a deadly bitch as long as the man pulling the trigger knows what he's doing. She would rather kill than screw, just like you . . . well, some of you anyway. Tomorrow you will be learning to disassemble and assemble your weapon and know its working parts. Today you will learn how to carry your best friend and how to show her off. We call this . . . the manual of arms. The first position is the one you're in now, 'order arms.' The next position is 'port arms.' I have given a soldier some prior instruction and he will be my demonstrator. Give a big hand for Private Day."

To applause and hoots, Eugene stepped out of the ranks and mounted the platform with Sergeant Cassidy.

The sergeant motioned to his demonstrator. "Observe that the demonstrator is at attention. "Demonstrator, *port . . . arms.*"

Eugene executed the movement with precision.

Cassidy nodded with approval and barked, "Or-*der . . . arms.*"

Again the small soldier performed the movement flawlessly. Cassidy puffed out his chest. "Ya see that, men? That was done like a real pro. Give him another hand."

The platoon clapped and hollered their approval. Eugene couldn't help himself and cracked a smile, which caused an even louder outburst. Cassidy grinned. His mission was accomplished. He tossed his arm over the soldier's shoulder. "Men, I think we got us a super-dooper-trooper!"

Martino jumped up on the platform. "I taught him everything he knows!" he yelled.

The platoon booed him. Vincent shrugged his shoulders. "Aw, come on, you guys."

Cassidy pushed Vincent off the platform. "Okay, men, let's watch the demonstrator and notice how he performs the movements by the numbers. Demonstrator, by the numbers, Port . . . arms. Ready . . . *one.* Notice the weapon is brought up diagonally across the chest and the left hand grasps the weapon at the balance and holds it so that it is four inches from the belt. The right elbow is held down without . . ."

Blake Alexander glanced to the right at his squad. In the past weeks the men had all become close friends. They had gotten rid of their buddy ropes long ago, but they still remained close to their buddies. Blake knew more about Lee Calhoon than he did his own sister. They had shared everything together—their food, misery, loneliness, fears, hopes, and dreams. Together they felt they could overcome anything the Army could dish out. Now those feelings had expanded and took in not only a single buddy, but the entire squad. As a squad, the men had mastered displays and layouts, close-order drill, P.T. exercises, first aid, and distance running. They were slowly becoming real soldiers. Blake felt good about himself. He felt as if he were a part of a success story.

Weapons training seemed easy after what they had been through. It was as if somewhere in their minds a switch had turned on. They all could now accept the fast-talking instructions and directions without blinking or worry. They had learned that by listening carefully they could break down the instructions into consumable parts and do everything by the numbers. Even Martino, who had difficulty at first, was learning. The "Army way" actually worked.

"Ready . . . *two.* Notice how he regrasped the weapon with the right hand at the small of the stock with his fingers and thumb closed around the stock. His right forearm is horizontal and the elbows are against his . . ."

COLUMBUS, GEORGIA, 9 MARCH

Shawn opened the trailer door to go inside, and immediately smelled her presence. He was about to drop his helmet and web gear on the floor when a familiar voice from the kitchen stopped him. "Don't you dare! I just cleaned that floor."

For the past two months, Cindy had been coming over on her two nights off to clean his place. They both knew the "cleaning" had been a pretense. They'd really sat and talked, him about his job and she about the future. The past was never mentioned. Neither of them wanted to remember it. They had become special friends with a special understanding of each other. At least he had thought he understood her, until tonight. In all the time he had known her, she had always worn blue jeans. Tonight she was wearing a dress, and her hair was fixed differently.

Recovering from his surprise at her transformation, Shawn shrugged his shoulders. "It's a hell of a note when I can't do what I wanna do in my own trailer."

Cindy glared at his still partially camouflage-painted face. "Just look at you. You're filthy . . . ooh, and you stink!"

Shawn rolled his eyes. "Well, what'd ya expect, I've been in the field for a week."

"Nine days," she snapped.

"You counted, huh?"

Cindy's glare dissolved. She couldn't conceal her real feeling from him. "Yeah, I guess I did. Go ahead and drop your stuff and take a shower. Dinner will be ready in a little while."

Shawn's eyebrow shot up. "Dinner? Hey, what the heck is going on? And why are ya all dressed up?"

Cindy checked the green beans simmering on the stove. "It's nothing, go on and shower and then we'll talk."

Shawn gave her a last questioning look before setting his gear down and heading for the bathroom.

Cindy waited till he was out of sight before turning around. She was trembling. She had done it all wrong. Nothing had happened as she had dreamed or planned it. It was stupid to think things could change between them. She wasn't ready.

Shawn opened the bedroom door and smelled the wonderful aroma of rolls baking. He smiled and strode down the short, narrow hall. "You didn't have ta go ta all the trouble of—" The front door was open. Somehow he knew before looking toward the kitchen she was gone.

Bob Lincoln, as usual, was busy washing beer glasses.

"Whatta ya have?" he said, then looked up and recognized the tall customer. "I'll be damned, it's you, Sarge," he said with a huge smile. "Damned if you ain't lost a lotta weight. Ya don't look near the same."

Shawn offered his hand to the bartender. "It's been awhile, Bob. Have you seen Cindy?"

Bob seemed confused by the question. "She said she was gonna be at your place. June told me she was all dressed up and had said somethin' about you and her goin' out to celebrate. She ain't with you?"

Shawn felt a sinking feeling. "No. Could I talk to June?"

Bob tossed his head toward the double doors. "Sure, go on back. Wonder where Cindy might be? Reckon she's at the store or somethin'?"

Shawn didn't answer. As he pushed through the doors, June put down a wet dish rag and wiped her hands on her apron. "I was wonderin' when you'd show up," she said tiredly.

It was obvious June had seen Cindy since she had left Shawn's trailer. He relaxed and took her damp hand.

"Been awhile, June. I've missed your food."

She didn't smile, but gently squeezed his hand. "Ya lost some weight. By the looks of ya, I'd say you're just as well off without my cookin'." Her eyes saddened. "I was kinda hopin' you wouldn't show up lookin' for her . . . that way I woulda known you didn't care." June picked up a dirty plate and scraped off the food scraps. "Cindy talks to me, so I know what's going on between you two. I didn't like it at first 'cause I thought you was sleepin' together. She said you all weren't, but I thought you was. Only a couple weeks ago did I come to believe her."

June rinsed the plate and picked up another one. "A good friend. That's what she said you were. But I'm no fool, Sergeant. It was written on her face that you meant more to her than that." June put the plate down and looked into Shawn's eyes. "My sister has done fallen in love with you, Sergeant."

Shawn began to speak, but June shook her head. "Don't say anything right now. Let me finish. I don't know how ya feel about my sister and I don't wanna know. It makes what I gotta say easier." Her eyes locked onto his. "Sergeant, she can't love you. I know her and seen her when she was about dead. She's lost too much. When that no-good husband left, she gave all of herself to Timmy. When he died, a part of her died with him. Believe me, I know. She may look and act fine to you, but Cindy is not the sister that I grew up with. Somethin's missing from her—a piece of her heart, you might say."

June hated what she was doing. She moved to a chair to sit down. She needed the distraction to gather strength for what had to be done. Steeling herself, she again looked at Shawn. "She's tried. God knows she works hard and tries to forget. And lately she been actin' more like her ol' self. I thought maybe she was getting better . . . till two days ago. Tonight she came in the back door crying. She said she had been gonna tell you how she felt about ya. She said she'd dreamed about it for weeks. But she couldn't do it."

June reached for Shawn's hand. "Sergeant, Cindy can't afford to lose again at bein' in love. But it takes two to make it work, and right now she doesn't know how you feel. So I'm asking you not to tell her you love her. She has special needs that you can never understand. She needs someone to be there all the time for her. You're in the Army. You know you can't give her all the time and company she can't live without. Let her go. Let her find love again with someone who can be there."

June still held his hand as she stood up. "I want you to see something." She walked to the back door, opened it and pointed toward a distant tree. "See the little mound of dirt in front of that oak? Two days ago would have been Timmy's birthday. Cindy bought him a present, even wrapped it. She buried it out there while singing the birthday song to him."

June turned to him with sorrowful eyes. "You weren't here. She needed you, but you weren't here. Ask yourself, Sergeant. How many birthdays can you guarantee that you'll be there for her?"

By the time Shawn got back to the trailer, he felt completely lost. He had not thought of his feeling toward Cindy as love, because love had once betrayed him. He had never intended to use that word again, not after Gretchen. June, confronting him with his emotions for Cindy, had made him angry and caused him an inexplicable, deep sense of loss. It was a throbbing, aching sense of having lost an essential piece of life. June had been wrong only about one thing. He *could* understand Cindy's needs. He knew what she had done for him when he was down. Her being there, talking to him, listening and caring, had lifted him back up and given him purpose again. He understood what Cindy felt, because his own feelings had not been so different.

A trace of her fragrance was still in the trailer mixed with the aroma of the bread. He glanced at the couch where they'd sat and talked for hours. How clearly he could see her in his mind. He knew the images, like the smell of her past presence, would take time to fade.

He unbuttoned his shirt as he walked through the dark hallway toward the bedroom. He was tired, but he knew he wouldn't sleep. She would be there, in his mind, and he would only hurt that much more.

He stumbled over his old field boots in the dark and threw his hand out to the wall to stop himself from falling down.

"I've been waiting," a voice whispered from the dark.

He knew the voice, and thought he was dreaming. He fumbled about for the light switch, but she stopped him, whispering, "Come to me, Shawn, I need you to hold me."

He made his way toward the bed like a blind man in the totally black room. He wanted to be touching her when he told her they could not continue their relationship. He sat down on the bed and reached for her.

Cindy felt his hands and tenderly pulled him down beside her. "You don't have to say you love me," she said softly. "It doesn't matter. Just make me a part of you tonight and hold me."

Shawn trembled at the feeling of her nude body pressed against him. Her warmth and touch instantly melted away the deep pain within his heart. June's plea faded and disappeared into the darkness, as did his restraint. He could no more have protested her touch than he could have stopped breathing. It was as if he were in a dream, floating in the blackness. Her touch and kiss were real, but like a mist, soft and yielding. He wanted to speak as she undressed him, but he was afraid he might break the spell. They lay back on the bed together. He knew he should not let this happen, and yet he knew he would.

In the magical darkness, they explored together, caressing, touching, feeling, until they had stirred the inner embers of desire into a blinding, burning furnace. They became one, all their senses screaming for and demanding release. Their bodies seemed to toss in a raging sea. Cindy gasped and moaned louder and louder as she desperately pulled Shawn closer and deeper. The fury of their loving built until it suddenly burst in a thunderclap of ecstasy. For a moment, then, they lay breathless, their bodies wet and still tingling. They seemed molded together, as if sharing the pounding beats of a single heart.

Afterward, Shawn drifted into sleep, only slightly stirring as he heard Cindy softly whisper, "Thank you."

A tear fell unfelt onto Shawn's cheek before Cindy lowered her head to his chest and snuggled against him. "I love you, Shawn," she whispered as she shut her tear-filled eyes.

When Shawn awoke in the morning, she was already gone. He moved and felt the dampness of the sheets. So it hadn't been a dream. He smiled and moved over to where she had lain beside him. The pillow still held her fragrance. He laid his head on the pillow and shut his eyes to be with her just a little longer.

14

SAND HILL, 1 APRIL

Anticipation hung in the air as the members of the second platoon stood at parade rest in front of Sergeant Cassidy. The massive soldier held up a clipboard.

"I know you have been waiting on your next assignments, so I'm not going to keep you in suspense. Lookin' at this list, I can tell the Army must be needing infantrymen. Boyce, Thurman, Johnson, and Dickenson, you're all going to the communications school at Fort Gordon. Vetock and Shultz, you're going to the cook school at Fort Jackson. Washington, you're going to be trained as a medic at Fort Sam Houston. Haddock, you're going to Fort Sill to be an artilleryman. The rest of you are staying right here at Fort Benning. You're going to advanced individual training for infantrymen. You're eleven bravos. Congratulations."

The men assigned to training other than infantry hollered their joy as the rest of the "new" eleven bravos exchanged glances of consolation.

Cassidy's brow furrowed at the disappointment he saw in the new infantrymen's faces. "You men not going infantry are dismissed. The rest of you sit down."

Cassidy waited until the others were gone before sitting on the edge of the platform.

"Look up here at me. I don't like seein' you hang your heads. You all graduate next week and can't be going to AIT with an attitude problem. Being an infantryman is what this Army is all about. All the other units in the Army exist to support the infantry. We're the ones who make things happen. You ain't gonna get fat, sloppy, or have ta tell your kids you were just a clerk in the war. The war in Vietnam is a grunt's war. We are the ones who are gonna win it, so get those heads up and be proud . . . I am."

Cassidy stood and came to attention. "On your feet and start actin' like who you are—the best damn soldiers in the world, *United States Army infantrymen!*"

Minutes later in the barracks Vincent tossed his arm over Eugene's shoulder. "You proud, or what?"

Eugene shrugged his shoulders. "I guess so. Are you?"

Martino smiled and motioned to Blake and Lee. "I am if we all stay together. We gettin' good, you know?"

Blake spoke as he took off his fatigue shirt. "What we all ought to do is volunteer for airborne school and become paratroopers. Since we're going infantry, we might as well go all the way."

Martino shook his head. "Uh-uh, not me. Jumpin' outta planes? No way."

Lee Calhoon patted Blake's back. "I reckon we should do it. We'd git fifty-five dollars extra a month, an' that ain't chicken feed."

Eugene lightly punched Martino's chest. "You gotta go now. Like you said, we all gotta stick together."

Vincent's usual smile was replaced with an unnatural frown. "No way. I ain't gonna do it."

Eugene eyed his buddy, realizing something was wrong, and changed the subject. "Vinny, I haven't seen that last package you got from your girl. Have you been holding out on us? When you gonna give your friends some of the chow?"

Vincent's smile returned. "Friends? What friends? All I see is a buncha moochers."

Lee sniffed the air and began walking toward Vincent's locker. "I smell candy bars!"

Vincent quickly blocked his path. "You don't smell nothin' but Ace's undershorts. Get away."

Blake attacked the locker from another direction. *"Food!"*

Lee feinted right and jumped to his left to avoid Vincent's half-hearted attempt to stop him from getting to the locker. Blake had already opened the metal door and found the box. "Damn, Vinny, no wonder you haven't lost any weight like the rest of us. There must be twenty Baby Ruths in here."

Vincent shrugged his shoulders. "She likes me sweet. *Hey, only one apiece, you guys!"*

The first sergeant looked up from his desk. "Come in."

Blake, Lee, and Eugene marched into the small office and came to parade rest three paces in front of the sergeant's desk. Blake took a step forward. "First Sergeant, we want to volunteer for airborne training. In formation this morning, you said you had a list where we could sign up."

The first sergeant motioned to the table to his right. "Over there is a clipboard. Just fill in your name, and we'll take care of the rest. You better be sure you wanna do this, because once you sign up, you'll be goin' right after AIT. They have a test unit here on post that needs paratroopers bad, and they'll take just about anybody to get their strength up."

Blake strode to the table. "I'm sure, First Sergeant."

Blake printed his name and handed the clipboard to Lee, who grinned. "Heck, this is better than I thought. This means I'll be assigned right here at Fort Benning, and I can see my folks." He quickly wrote his name and gave the board to Eugene.

The soldier pushed his glasses back up on his nose, then printed his name. He glanced at his friends, who had their backs to him as they headed for the door, and at the first sergeant, who was busy at his desk. Hesitating for only a moment, Eugene added another name to the list and set the clipboard on the table.

HARMONY CHURCH

"Sir, Sergeant Flynn reports as ordered."

The battalion commander, a lieutenant colonel, motioned to a chair. "Sit down, Sergeant. I called you here because your name has come up several times as being the best recon man we've got. I'm afraid your performance has been noticed, and not just by us within the battalion. I got a call from the division sergeant major's office. It seems the 227th Assault Helicopter Battalion has the highest priority for experienced veterans. The division has ordered you to report to them today."

Shawn was stunned. "Sir, I've just got my platoon trained. Why would an aviation battalion want me? They don't need recon men. There's got to be a mistake."

The lieutenant colonel listened patiently to the exact arguments he had given to the division sergeant major. He leaned back in his chair.

"I understand your frustration. I've been doing my damnedest to train this unit, but every week I get levied for more bodies for Vietnam duty. They're bleeding me dry of my most experienced men, and I get nothing back but green inexperienced replacements. Even so, I'll have to admit that this case is different. The aviation battalion is testing a new concept, and they need your skills. They've practiced it a couple of times, but they have the same problem all of us have—a shortage of skilled soldiers to pull it off. That's why you're being reassigned. I can tell you this, the new concept was important enough that the division commander himself made the decision for you to move. I'm sorry, Sergeant Flynn, because I know what it's like to train a unit to where you want it and then get yanked out. It's not much of a consolation, but think of it as a move up. It's the price of success."

Shawn knew there was no sense wasting his and the colonel's time. The discussion was over the moment the colonel mentioned the division commander. He had been in the Army long enough to know once a commanding general made a decision, the ball began rolling and everybody down the ranks saluted and said "Yes, sir."

That was how the game was played, and Shawn was the last player in the long line that had repeated words similar to those he was about to say as he stood, faced the colonel, and saluted: "Yes, sir . . . I'll report immediately."

The 227th Aviation Battalion sergeant major was impressed. For a change he had gotten someone who had credentials. Flynn had two CIBs and two Silver Stars. He motioned for the sergeant to take a seat.

"Sergeant Flynn, you are now assigned as the platoon leader of our test blue platoon. The new concept will work . . . when we have trained people. Right now, we're on our ass. Our lieutenant has just rotated out, and the platoon sergeant doesn't know his butt from a hole in the ground. You're going to change all that. Go down there and get the blue platoon combat ready. Do you have any questions?"

Shawn leaned forward in his chair, "Yes, Sergeant Major. What the hell is a 'blue' platoon and what the hell is this new 'concept' everybody is talkin' about?"

The sergeant major's face contorted. "You mean nobody told you what we're doing? Shit! I thought you were briefed. I guess I'd better back up and start over. First, the concept. Our new concept is based on the fundamental principles of the offense, the three F's: find 'em, fix 'em, and finish 'em. With our aviation assets, this has never been more possible. Our small scout ships, the OH-13s, called 'whites,' search for the enemy and 'find' them. The whites then call our gunships, the UH-1Bs, called 'pinks,' who 'fix' the enemy by killing them or pinning them down with their rockets and machine guns. Then the 'blue' platoon comes in on UH-1Hs and 'finishes' them.

"The concept requires top-notch training, coordination, and timing. Helicopters make it work, but as always, it takes a grunt on the ground to dig the bastards out and take the objective."

The sergeant major's eyes locked on Shawn. "Flynn, I'm not a flyboy like most of the people assigned to this battalion. I'm an infantryman like you, but I gotta tell ya, I'm impressed by these rotorjocks and mechanics. They're a different breed. They ain't like us, 'cause they don't get in the mud and smell the blood, but they got the spirit. They believe in their machines, and they're stone-cold fearless. They think they are fucking indestructible when they're behind the controls. They're good, damn good. This new concept ain't really nothing new. It's just another way to do the job we've always done—find the enemy and kill him."

The sergeant major stood and pointed out the window toward a lone helicopter that sat just a hundred yards from the headquarters. "That machine out there is going to change warfare as we know it. We don't have to march through a jungle or swim a river to search for the enemy anymore. No more marching for days to find them, no obstacles standing in our way. Those thin-skinned metal contraptions will take us to him. But that's all they'll do. From then on, we're nothing but what we've always been, and we've got the same old miserable job.

"The blue platoon is going to have to be better than just good. It's got to be made up of very special men. I think you can see why. You're not going to have to search for the enemy—when you get off your choppers, they're going to be there waiting for you."

The sergeant major looked for a hint of uncertainty in Flynn's face. What he saw was a hardened veteran staring back without emotion.

"Well, what do you think about the concept?" the sergeant major asked.

Shawn looked out the window toward the helicopter. He thought about what the senior NCO had said for a full thirty seconds before he broke the silence. "It will take a month. I need authority to pick who I want and to get rid of those who can't cut it."

The sergeant major's eyes narrowed. "We have brass coming down from the Pentagon to see the exercise that goes in three weeks. You have to be ready then."

Shawn suppressed a smile. He had known the sergeant major had been beating around the bush as to why he was needed. It wasn't a question of testing the concept. Too much was riding on the entire airmobile doctrine idea for it to fail. The real question was, could he, Shawn Flynn, *make* it work.

"I'm in charge," Shawn said firmly. "Nobody comes down and looks over my shoulder. I'm the one who calls the shots and makes out the training schedule. You give me that and we'll be ready."

The sergeant major knitted his brow and nodded. He had underestimated Flynn. The veteran had seen right through the gung-ho speech and had cut to the chase. The sergeant major looked at Shawn with a new respect.

"You never did answer my question," he said. "What do you think of our concept?"

"I don't know," Shawn replied honestly. "There are a lot of ifs. *If* the dinks are surprised, and *if* they don't have the landing zone covered with automatic weapons, and *if* the gunships support us, and *if* we have good communications . . . *if* everything works, then yes, the concept will work."

The sergeant major studied Shawn's face a moment before offering his hand. "We'll see in three weeks, then."

Shawn shook the sergeant's hand in silence and walked out the door to find his new platoon.

0700 HOURS, 8 APRIL

Thunder rumbled across the darkened sky as the rain beat down in a roar. Sergeant Cassidy took off his wet campaign hat. His men sat on the floor of the barracks.

"Men, I got bad news and good news. The bad news is the graduation ceremony we rehearsed yesterday is canceled because of the thunderstorm. The good news is you won't have to stand for three hours in ranks, waiting around, and then listening to speeches. You won't have to march by the reviewing stand, and you won't have to march back here and outprocess from the company. You will pack your bags now, and we'll begin outprocessing in the mess hall. At 1000 hours we'll march to the theater, where you will graduate, then be released. You can then come here, get your bags, and take off on leave. You'll be on the road by noon, except for those of you going to infantry AIT. As you men already know, you will only have two days before you have to report, so you won't have time to go home."

Cassidy smiled and held up a piece of paper. "I have some more good news. Two members of our platoon will be receiving trophies during the ceremony. Private Calhoon will receive the battalion marksmanship trophy for being the best shooter in the battalion, and Private Alexander will receive the company outstanding soldier award for scoring highest on the training tests. Congratulations troopers, ya done good."

The platoon cheered and applauded, but Cassidy quickly raised his hand to quiet them. "Last, *we* in the second platoon will be given a trophy for being the outstanding platoon of the company. *You all done good!*"

He waited until the riotous noise of self-congratulation died down and then spoke softly. "Men, you've made my job easy. You were an exceptional platoon. We didn't lose a single man. The average loss in the other platoons was five men. You can be very proud of yourselves. I'm going to say farewell to you now, because there won't be time later. I want you to know I'm very proud of you and what you've done. I wish the best to you all. I . . . I . . . ."

The sergeant put on his hat to give himself time to control his emotions before he raised his head with pride. "I'm gonna miss your ugly faces." He spun around and strode down the aisle without looking back. Graduation days always left him feeling down in the end. His men didn't need him anymore. It was like raising children and finally having to let them go to make it on their own.

The sergeant stepped into the rain and paused, looking up the company street, where in a week four buses would stop. Unlike raising children, in seven days there would be forty new "boys" who would need him again.

WILLIAMSBURG, VIRGINIA, 13 APRIL

David Alexander sat down at the large dining-room table and picked up his napkin before speaking. "Who put the trophy in the case?"

Dana put down her fork. She knew the trophy would not go unnoticed for long. "Hank and I did. Blake deserves to have his award shown off. I'm proud of him, aren't you?"

David leaned back in his chair, fixing his wife with piercing eyes. "I took it out. The Alexander case is *not* to be used for something that was probably bought at a pawnshop. I put the thing in his room with the rest of his trash. Don't ever open the case again."

Enraged, Dana tossed down her napkin. "You're a pompous ass! Blake sent the trophy to show you he was living up to the precious standards of your precious family name. He's trying to demonstrate to you that he cares about living up to the traditions that *you* taught him."

David ignored his wife's accusing stare and began cutting his steak. "I understand perfectly that our son elected to rebel against me. The only thing that I will accept from him is an apology. Eat your meal, dear. It's getting cold."

COLUMBUS

Shawn rolled over on the bed and hugged the sleeping woman beside him. Cindy awoke with a smile. "What time is it?" she said.

Shawn got up to take off his boots and uniform. "A little after midnight. I had to give some of the men some training in night land-navigation. They did pretty good. They're gettin' there. I think we're going to make it."

Cindy nodded sleepily, then smiled at what he'd said. "We are too, aren't we . . . I mean 'gettin' there'?"

Shawn tossed down a boot and leaned over, giving her a light kiss. "We've been there for some time, as far as I'm concerned."

Cindy lovingly cupped his chin. "I'm the happiest I've ever been in my life. Thank you."

Shawn patted her hand and sat up to finish taking off his clothes. She had moved in with him the day after they had first made love. He spent every minute he could with her, and missed her horribly when he was away. She asked nothing of him. He had gotten her a job on post in the commissary, and they were teaching her how to use a cash register. In another week she'd be making twice what she had waiting tables at the bar.

He lay back down and felt her snuggle against him. Putting his arm around her, he closed his eyes. The words of warning that June had given him weeks ago had been long forgotten. Cindy had changed. Not once had she been depressed or complained about his being in the field for days at a time. Each time he'd returned to a smile and a kiss. Yes, she had changed. She would be fine if he had to go.

He had changed too. The thought of having to leave her was almost too much to bear. Still, he refused to worry. They would both be strong enough if the day came.

22 APRIL

The light observation helicopter buzzed over the treetops like an angry dragonfly. The pilot had thought he had seen a glint of light, a reflection from something. He had been looking for the elusive aggressor patrol for the better part of the morning. The single glint could have been sun rays catching an old Coke bottle or . . . there it was again. He brought the small craft around and came to hover.

Yeah, there you are, you bastards. You think you're hidden, but I got ya. The guy with the binoculars gave you away.

The pilot noted the location and shot the helicopter forward as he pressed his talk button and spoke into the radio headset. "Pink lead this is White one-three. I've got an aggressor patrol directly below me. Do you have a visual on me?"

Two UH-1B gunships carrying a load of simulated rockets lazily circled high above the small scout ship. The gun platoon leader pressed his talk button. "Roger, White one-three, I got a tally-ho on you. Drop smoke and leave the good part to us. We're going hot now."

The scout-ship pilot darted back over the hidden men beneath the pine trees and threw out a smoke grenade to mark their location. He banked hard left to watch the show and spoke on the radio again. "Base, this is White one-three. Rally Blues. We've got a party for them."

A voice came back through the headphones. "White one-three, this is base, we have been monitoring your transmissions and have Blues on the way. They'll be calling you on your push, in a few minutes."

Sergeant Shawn Flynn leaned forward in the helicopter seat and looked out the door window. Just off the tail of the chopper were three UH-1H Hueys in close formation. Inside each aircraft was one of his squads. They had been on strip alert for two days, waiting for a chance to show off their training. Shawn sat back. It wouldn't be long now. They were losing altitude and going in.

The radio operator beside him had to yell over the roar of the turbine engine. "We're going to land in a field only fifty meters from where they spotted the patrol. White one-three says their location will be at our three o'clock when we get off."

Shawn nodded and held his hands up, signaling the other seven passengers to look at him. He made sure they were looking at him when he yelled over the beating blades. *Enemy at three o'clock, fifty meters. This is it!*

He grinned and held his thumb up. The tense faces of the men changed. Their eyes narrowed and they smiled back as they lifted their thumbs.

The grin had done it. They had no reason to worry after what they had gone through the past three weeks. If they had been weak, they would not have been there. The sergeant with two CIBs had been merciless. He'd thrown out half the men in the platoon in the first two days and brought in green replacements. He had trained them night and day, going through the drills until they could have done them in their sleep. The sergeant demanded perfection, never once letting a mistake go by without pointing it out. He led by example and expected nothing from them that he couldn't do himself.

Shawn yelled one last time. *"Simulate lock and load! Seat belts ready for release. Doorman, ready!"*

Shawn didn't like that the doors were closed, but the aviation battalion's safety rules required closed doors during training missions. He watched the trees speeding by and sat up straighter to see if he could spot the landing zone.

The helicopter was speeding along at ninety knots, when suddenly its tail dipped to slow its airspeed. The skids were still five feet from the ground when the door was pushed back and the door gunner began firing blanks into the distant treeline.

Shawn and his radio operator were out of the aircraft before the skids touched the ground. Shawn fired from the hip as he ran in a zigzag pattern for a nearby tree stump that would give them cover. In the next thirty seconds he would know if the mission was going to be successful. The first chopper's load was to secure the landing zone while the other Hueys landed. If the enemy was not surprised and had automatic weapons sighted on the L.Z., they could decimate the platoon as they unloaded. Shawn watched the treeline for telltale puffs of smoke from rifles and was relieved to see none. They were going to do it!

The last Huey lifted off and he immediately began running toward the treeline again, rifle ready at the hip. Passing the first stand of pines, he hit the ground and rolled. He immediately changed magazines and rolled once more to get behind a tree, then looked behind him. The radioman was behind him along with the rest of the men, just as he'd taught them. They were spread out and watching their squad leaders, all of whom, in turn, were looking at him. He pointed at his third squad leader and motioned toward a spot to his right. The buck sergeant nodded and immediately leaped to his feet and ran for higher ground, with his men following. They ran in four-second rushes, hitting the ground, rolling, then springing to their feet again. In thirty seconds they were in position. Shawn now had a support element with a machine gun ready to shoot at anything that moved. It was just like in the movies when a cowboy would tell his buddy to "cover" him. The rest of the platoon would now be covered when they moved out.

Shawn held his hand out for the radio handset, and seconds later was pushing the handset sidebar. "White one-three this is Blue one-six, L.Z. is cold. Do you have a visual on my party? Over."

The scout pilot was still angry as he pushed the talk button. "Standby, Blue one-six, I'm checking now, out."

The gunship pilots had screwed up the timing and had not been in position to prep the L.Z. with fire before the Blues went in. The Blues had been lucky the L.Z. was cold. Otherwise the umpire with the aggressor patrol would have torn them up in a report.

The scout pilot maneuvered his ship to the location at which he'd last seen the patrol. He cussed under his breath at not seeing them and spun the bubble-nosed craft around to check the area to the north. He didn't have to go far before he smiled. "Tally-ho, Blue one-six. I've got 'em. They're in a stream bed one hundred meters to your north. Three o'clock at the L.Z. was due north, 360 degrees. They are trying to hide in the thick stuff along the creek. Over."

Shawn had his map out. "Roger three-one, we're on the way. Have guns standing by. Out."

Shawn pointed at the first squad leader, then pointed his thumb down, giving the signal for "enemy." He held up one finger and formed a zero twice, then pointed to their front toward a slight rise. The squad leader repeated the silent signal to his two-man point team.

Shawn let the two-man point team move ahead for twenty-five meters before standing and motioning the first squad leader to move his element out. He and his radio operator fell in behind the first squad. The second squad followed. They moved fifty meters when he moved the second squad into a cover position and ordered the third squad, the original "cover" unit, to move up. This was known as "leap-frogging," and ensured that the lead moving element was constantly covered.

A minute later the point team signaled that they had spotted the enemy. Shawn began to crawl forward, realizing that all the silent signals had been a waste of time. The scout ship hovering about would have covered all their sounds from the enemy patrol. He crawled to the lead point man and raised his head to look down into a steep ravine. The eight-man aggressor patrol was wagon-wheeled on the side of a creek. The patrol leader was talking on the radio, obviously telling his leaders he was in big trouble.

Ten minutes later the deadly simulated game was over. The actual fighting lasted less than fifteen seconds, all the time it took for two of his squads to fire up a magazine of blank ammo at the shocked, helpless men. He had simply ordered two squads up to his location and put them on line at the edge of ravine. Once they were in position, he had signaled them that the enemy was directly below, and they rose up and fired at his command. The aggressor patrol didn't have a chance. They didn't even get off a single shot.

———

Shawn walked out of the treeline and saw two Hueys sitting on the L.Z. The shiny paint job on the lead bird told him it had brought some VIPs. "Smitty," he mumbled to his RTO, "it's dog and pony time."

The young radioman had only been in the Army for six months, but he knew the meaning of a dog and pony show. That's what the old salts called all VIP demonstrations and briefings.

A major with a huge smile approached and motioned to his right. "Sergeant, over here, we've set up a briefing for our visitors. We'll need you to talk about your actions and explain how you trained for the mission." The major got closer and whispered, "Lay it on thick."

Minutes later Shawn stood in front of the commanding general of the Eleventh Air Assault Division, the brigade and battalion commanders, and two three-star generals, who seemed uncomfortable in fatigues. The exercise demonstrating the capability of an airmobile brigade had been going on for three days. Shawn's platoon was only one small part of the overall exercise.

The three-star general, a gaunt, severe-looking man with thinning gray hair, asked all the questions. Shawn thought the old boy did a good job trying to pick his brain, and surprised him when he finally said, "Sergeant, I see by your combat patch you've had a tour in Vietnam. Based on your experience over there, do you think that an airmobile division can really operate in that environment? Is it worth the millions we're spending?"

Shawn looked into the general's eyes. "Sir, if we want to find Charlie, we're gonna need choppers. As far as cost goes, all I can say is that choppers can search a hell of a lot of area. We would need four or five divisions to do the same thing pounding the boonies."

The general seemed to ponder what the sergeant said for several moments. "I see what you mean." He smiled and put out his hand toward Shawn. "Very impressive demonstration, and thank you for your candor. My report will use your exact words."

28 MAY

Private Vincent Martino stood before his platoon sergeant, shaking his head. "But I didn't sign up for no airborne training."

The sergeant rechecked his list. "M-A-R-T-I-N-O. You're the only wop on the list. Now shut up and move over to that other formation of volunteers."

Vincent held his ground. "There's gotta be a mistake. I don't wanna jump outta no planes."

Tired of wasting time, the sergeant leaned forward to within inches of the private's face. "Martino, you have orders for the United States Army Airborne School. You will report in one week, as soon as you graduate from AIT. You cannot quit airborne school now. You have to quit when you get there. Now get your ass over there and join those other volunteers and shut up!"

Vincent grumbled as he fell in beside his friends, who were standing outside the orderly room. The airborne volunteers had been called out of training to receive orders and instructions.

Blake nudged Vincent with his arm. "Relax, Vinny, it's gonna be a good deal for us. Plus, we all get to stay together."

Lee smiled in agreement. "Yeah, Vinny, you're gonna do great, just like ya did here. We're gonna have fun."

Vincent shook his head angrily. "I'm not gonna jump outta no planes."

Eugene cringed guiltily at his buddy's reaction. He had thought that with time Vincent would have changed his mind. The Italian had become one of the stars of the AIT company. He was strong as a bull, and he'd had none of the learning problems experienced in basic. In fact he had become so good that the roles had changed; he was helping Eugene make it through the demanding training.

Vincent shook his head with frustration and turned to Eugene for support. "Gene, what am I gonna do? I don't wanna go."

"Don't argue with them anymore. Just take the orders. When we get to airborne school, you can tell them it's not for you. I'll go with you."

Vincent sighed. "Okay, but I still wish I knew how them guys made the mistake."

COLUMBUS

Shawn walked into the trailer and froze. Sitting in his chair in the small living room was John Quail. Cindy sat across from his old friend. She rose with a smile, gave Shawn her customary kiss, and motioned to the sergeant major. "John said you'd be surprised."

Shawn was speechless until the old soldier smiled warmly and stood. The two men hugged and pounded each other's backs. Shawn had forgotten how much his mentor meant to him and how hurt he was to have disappointed him.

Still holding Shawn's arms, Quail pushed him back. "Well, I'll be damned if you don't look lean and mean. I'd thought with all those choppers, you wouldn't be getting any exercise."

Cindy was pleased to see how close the men were, and patted Shawn's flat stomach. "I make sure he gets up and runs his four miles a day."

"I can see you're good for him," Quail said. "I'm proud of him."

Shawn, embarrassed by the direction the conversation was taking, changed the subject. "What the hell are you doing here? The Pentagon throw you out, or are you on a boondoggle, looking for strange again?"

Quail threw his arm over Shawn's shoulder and walked him toward the door. "Come on. I'm taking you two to dinner at the NCO club and we'll talk. We've got a lot of catching up to do, and I need to find out how this airmobile business is working out."

Quail glanced over his shoulder at Cindy. "Sorry about barging in this way, but I needed to see this old Korean vet. Like I told ya, we go back a long ways. We'll probably bore ya to tears."

Cindy laughed and took Quail's arm. "No, I'm really interested. I promise not to be bored."

Quail pushed back from the table and picked up his can of beer. "Now that was one good meal. In Washington I usually end up eating TV dinners. I don't have much time for real meals anymore."

Cindy eyed the sergeant with concern. "You need a woman to take care of you."

"What woman would want to put up with an old has-been like me? Hell, I don't have the time to look anyway."

"John," she said, "I think you're underestimating yourself. A woman would be lucky to have you. Take some time and look around, you'll see."

Quail seemed uncomfortable, and turned to Shawn for help. Shawn tossed his arm over Quail's shoulder. "She's right, Taco, you ought to take some time and start lookin'."

Quail laughed aloud. "You two are ganging up on me. Okay, okay, when I get back I'll check out some of the old crony secretaries in the five-sided puzzle house and see if any of 'em can cook." Quail took another sip of beer and glanced at Shawn. "I've been hearing good things about you and the Eleventh Air Assault. You think you're ready?"

Shawn picked up his can of beer. "Ready for what? The unit is just a skeleton. Your buddies in the Pentagon have been stripping the division of its manpower. We're only at sixty percent strength and strugglin' to keep our heads above water."

Quail lowered his voice. "That's soon gonna change. Don't say a damn thing to anybody, but the powers that be are about to up the ante in Nam. McNamara has approved the activation of an airmobile division. The Eleventh Air Assault is going to be deactivated and given a new name and the colors of one of the regular divisions. Don't ask me which one, 'cause I don't know yet. General Kinnard wants the 101st Airborne Division to be the first airmobile outfit, but it's turned into a political football among the generals."

Worried by the conversation, Cindy leaned closer. "Does this mean Shawn will be going to Vietnam again?"

Quail saw the concern in Cindy's eyes and cussed himself for not waiting to tell Shawn later. He patted Cindy's hand. "Cindy, we're all going back again. The United States is at war. Guys like Shawn and me are old vets. They need us."

Cindy stiffened. "When?"

Quail sighed, knowing he couldn't lie. "Soon."

Cindy closed her eyes and excused herself on the pretense of freshening her face. As she walked toward the entry hall, she hoped Shawn didn't notice her trembling.

Quail waited until she disappeared into the hall. "You're a damn fool if you don't marry that girl," he said to Shawn.

"We have an understanding," Shawn told him.

"Irish, the odds are that you're going back to Vietnam in less than six months. I'm telling you this because it makes a difference on how you should be training. Things are turning to shit over there. I read the reports from Westmoreland, and he's in trouble. The NVA are in it now. They ain't sittin' on the sidelines sending in a few replacements like they used to. They're sending in the first team and they're kickin' ass . . . especially in the Central Highlands. Westy's last report said all the roads are cut going into the Highlands. No traffic can go in or out. He wants more men, and the Army and the President are going to give them to him. Soon you'll be getting new people and this post is going to grow ten times over. The little war we're in is gettin' bigger as we speak. Christ, the whole damn Army is gearing up."

Shawn accepted the information with a faint nod. He had been reading the papers and had read between the lines. "Are the politicians gonna let us win?"

Quail grunted. "Are you kiddin'? We're on our own with this one. We're just gonna have to do our best and hope the country gets behind us. We're gonna have to kick ass early. If it gets bogged down, we're gonna lose it. You and I know 'cause we've been in a 'police action' before and we know where that got us."

Shawn's mind was racing with the implications. He had a hundred things to teach his platoon to get them ready, and— His thoughts were interrupted by Quail's penetrating stare. Shawn returned it.

"What's the matter?"

Quail smirked. "I can see that brain of yours thinking about going, but aren't you forgettin' something? Like the little gal that was sitting beside you. Did you know she was pregnant?"

Shawn stiffened in disbelief. "I stopped in at the bar down the road to ask where your trailer park was," Quail continued. "The bartender said he knew you and told me where you lived. He also told me about Cindy and how concerned they were about her. It seems Cindy had some tests done and gave the hospital her sister's phone number to call with the results. The hospital called today.

"I went over to your place to wait for you and Cindy drove up. I told her we were old friends, and she invited me in. We talked for quite a while before you showed up. All she could do was talk about you. I was hoping to hell you knew this little gal was a keeper."

Shawn shook his head numbly.

"Hell, don't get sour-faced," Quail went on. "This is good news. All you could ever talk about was having your own kid. Marry her and make it all legal. You do love her, don't you?"

Shawn was about to respond when Cindy approached the table. His heart sank. She was wearing her fake smile. She spoke before either of them could get up. "Sit down, guys. I'm sorry, but I'm going to have to leave. I called June to tell her where I was, and I found out some bad news. . . . Our aunt is sick and needs us to be with her. I'll take a cab back and get packed. We'll be leaving tonight. Don't argue with me, now. I don't mind taking a cab. I want you both to stay and catch up on each other's stories."

Shawn stood anyway and began to put his arm around her. She was doing such a horrible job of lying, it broke his heart. She gently pushed his arm away, and softly, but with resolve, said, "No, please sit down. I'll call you tomorrow." With that she leaned over and kissed Quail's cheek. "It was a pleasure meeting you. I'm happy to know Shawn has such friends."

She gave Shawn a last, sad, loving look, then walked toward the club entrance.

Quail looked at Shawn. "Don't stand there, or I'll bust your damn hard head."

Shawn's eyes had not left Cindy. He started after her.

Cindy was waiting outside. She was trying to keep from crying. He came up behind her and spoke softly. "Hey, pretty lady, you going my way by any chance?"

She turned around and began to speak, but he grabbed her and pulled her to him. "You can't leave without me. We're a team."

Cindy fought his grip for only a second before giving in to his warmth and strength. She looked up with tears running down her cheeks. "Everything has changed."

Shawn kissed her forehead and smiled. "The only change is I love you more. I know you're pregnant, and I think it's wonderful. We're going to expand the team to three. What'd ya say? I'll tell Taco and he'll be my best man?"

Cindy didn't return his smile. "I won't marry you, Shawn. I . . . I can't."

Shawn lifted her chin, "Of course you can. I was a fool not asking sooner."

Cindy stiffened and quickly wiped the tears away. "Go back inside, Shawn. It's over."

Shawn couldn't believe what he was hearing, but her look told him she was serious. The deep pain returned and weakened him. "Why?" he asked in a whisper.

She brought her eyes up to his. "I have what I want now. You gave me a child . . . a second chance. I thank you for that, and for much more than you could ever understand. But now it's over. John said you'd be leaving. I can't wait for you, Shawn. I just can't. It hurts too much. I can barely stand it now, when you're only away for a few nights. I fall apart . . . I'm lost without you."

Cindy steeled herself with a deep breath and stared into his eyes. "Let me go, Shawn . . . let me leave you now. You'll only hurt me more later."

Shawn slowly released his grip and let his hands fall limply to his sides. His grief and pain sapped his strength and made him feel helpless. Her eyes only made it worse. It tore through his heart like burning shrapnel.

She turned and walked into the darkness to find a new life. He raised his hand and called out in a raspy whisper, "I—I love you, Cindy."

15

13 JUNE

Privates Martino and Day marched up to the office of the Airborne Ground Training Branch. The training area had seemed deserted, so they decided to check the small, white blockhouse with the sign in front.

HEADQUARTERS
GROUND TRAINING BRANCH
UNITED STATES ARMY AIRBORNE SCHOOL

Through a front window they could see that the offices were empty, except for a sergeant sitting behind a beat-up desk. His gray hair was shaved down to a short crew cut. They knew he was a sergeant because he was wearing a white T-shirt with his name stenciled across the shirt-front.

Martino opened the front door and approached the NCO. He came to parade rest in front of the desk.

"Sergeant Burke, I want to quit," he said with determination.

The sergeant looked up from the report he was filling out. His expression was one of surprise and confusion.

"Huh? What did ya want?"

"I said, I want to quit," Martino repeated.

"Quit what? What are you talking about?"

Vincent wondered if he was in the right place.

"I—I wanna quit airborne school, today," he stammered.

Sergeant Burke leaned back in his chair, studying the stocky Italian. "Let me get this straight. You're an airborne student that's supposed to start training tomorrow, but you're quitting today. Right?"

"Yes, Sergeant," Martino said.

The sergeant looked past Martino to Eugene. "And why are you here?"

Eugene snapped to parade rest. "Sergeant, I want to quit too."

Shocked, Vincent spun around. "No, Gene, you can't quit cause'a me. You go ahead and go to the school."

The sergeant rolled his eyes. "What the hell is going on? Are you both here to quit or not?"

Eugene barked out a yes as Vincent said no.

The sergeant's eyes began to glow, but he still spoke with patience. "Okay, we're gonna take this one step at a time." He pointed at Martino. "You, why do you want to quit?"

Vincent's eyes shifted nervously back and forth as he tried to decide if this sergeant could be trusted to know his secret weakness. He glanced at Eugene, then back to the sergeant. "I—I'm scared'a heights. I used to hawk at the Eagles games, an' once I looked down from the toppa the stadium to the parking lot. I got all dizzy and weak. It scared me real bad. I can't be no paratrooper bein' scared'a heights."

Vincent felt as if a load had lifted from his shoulders. He had carried this secret around for years, and getting it out in the open was like unloading fifty pounds of excess baggage.

The sergeant dipped his chin and shifted his gaze to Eugene. "And you? Why do you wanna quit?"

Eugene nodded toward Vincent. "He's my buddy. If he quits, I quit."

"*No way!*" Vincent blurted. He leaned over the sergeant's desk, pleading. "He don't wanna quit. Don't let him just cause'a me."

Master Sergeant Richard Burke had heard enough. Picking up his black baseball cap from the desk, he pushed back his chair and slowly rose. He put on the traditional headgear of the U. S. Army Airborne instructors and immediately transformed. The hat was blocked and sat low on his forehead, casting a sinister shadow over his weathered face. Centered on the cap's front was a glistening pair of silver, master parachutist wings that sparkled in the light. His eyes narrowed into piercing black marbles and his face hardened to stone. Suddenly his chest expanded and he bellowed, shaking the interior walls. "*Outside,* nasty *legs!*"

Vincent and Eugene had watched the transformation in awe and backed up knowing they had made a horrible mistake. It was like waking up a sleeping grizzly bear. They broke into a run for the door.

Master Sergeant Burke eyed the two men, who now stood at attention in the parking lot. He stepped closer and stared coldly at Vincent.

"Today is Sunday, *leg!* I came in today just to clear my desk so I'd be ready for tomorrow . . . and *you* nasty *legs* waltz into *my* office and snivel to *me! You* have disturbed *my* Sunday! I am the Ground Training Branch *chief instructor!* Do you know what that means, *leg?*"

Vincent took the coward's way out and shook his head.

Burke's ball cap bill touched Vincent's forehead as he looked into the Italian's fear-filled eyes. "I am responsible for changing nasty, filthy legs like you and your nasty leg buddy into paratroopers. I do not have to talk or train nasty legs on Sunday! I am off on Sunday!"

Burke began to speak again, but suddenly took a step back as if summoned and looked up into the crystal clear blue sky. He stood for several moments without moving a muscle. Finally his eyes lowered and locked on Martino. The sergeant raised his hand, pointing a finger skyward.

"A sign! Yes, that's what it is! You legs were sent to me on Sunday as a sign from the big jumpmaster himself!"

Vincent exchanged looks with Eugene. Not only was this sergeant weird, he was crazy.

Burke began pacing in front of the two men, speaking aloud to himself. "Yes, a sign, that has to be it. These nasty legs came to me wanting to quit when the rules say they can't quit until tomorrow. They can't quit today, and now they can't quit at all. The sign was meant for me to make sure these misguided nasty legs have the opportunity to join the ranks of the airborne. Yes, it has to be a sign for me to ensure that these legs see the light and become members of the glorious fraternity of paratroopers."

The master sergeant halted and faced the two men. His eyes turned to marbles again. "Legs, you cannot quit! You will become paratroopers! Tomorrow you start a new life, and I will lead you on the path of righteousness. A path to the heavens that will lift you from the nasty leg life in which you now dwell. Yes, tomorrow a new life awaits you!"

Vincent began to protest when the master sergeant suddenly raised his hand and pointed toward the distant barracks. "Go now, nasty legs, and prepare!"

Vincent and Eugene gave the crazy sergeant one last disconcerted glance before turning around to begin the long walk back to the barracks.

"*Legs!*" the sergeant puffed out his chest and barked. "*Nobody walks in my training area . . . Run, run and prepare to be paratroopers!*"

Master Sergeant Burke saw them break into a jog, and only then did his stone face crack. He smiled as he strode back to his office. He had "saved" two more quitters from themselves. He had heard the same "scared of heights" story a hundred times. It was not uncommon. In fact, he himself still got dizzy when looking down from tall buildings—and he had made over five hundred parachute jumps. Jumping from planes was different. When standing in the door of an aircraft in flight, the ground was 1250 feet below and passing by at 120 knots an hour. There was no dizzy sensation at that altitude, and there wasn't time to worry about it. A paratrooper rarely stood in the door for more than a second before leaping out.

Burke could still see the two running soldiers. They'd both make it. Hell, they had to now; after all, there was the "sign." He laughed aloud. Wait till he told his fellow instructors about this one.

Vincent and Eugene didn't stop running until they reached the barracks. Gasping for air, Eugene faced his friend.

"What . . . what are you gonna do, Vinny?"

Vincent looked up at the sky, then back to Eugene. "Looks like I don't have no choice. I guess I'll go ta training and try ta be a paratrooper."

Eugene broke into a huge grin and mimicked the crazy sergeant's voice. "A sign! Yes, us nasty legs must be paratroopers!"

HARMONY CHURCH

Shawn looked at the training schedule and tried to concentrate on Monday's events, but his mind kept drifting to an image of a small, auburn-haired woman. Day and night for the past two weeks he had struggled to keep his mind off of her, but he had failed miserably. Cindy had become a part of him. He somehow knew that the first time they had made love was when they had conceived the child. He knew it without a doubt. A son—perhaps a daughter, it didn't matter—a child had been conceived in love by two lonely people brought together in the darkness.

Shawn's jaw tightened. He was angry with her. She did not have the right to inflict so much pain. She had taken away both his heart and their unborn child. A child who would not know his father. A child, like himself, who never had a dad to . . .

A lieutenant wearing khakis walked into the office. He seemed surprised to find the staff sergeant behind the desk.

Shawn stood. "Can I help you, sir?"

The lieutenant immediately noticed the sergeant's uniform, white name tape, and the star above the Combat Infantryman's Badge. He walked over and extended his hand.

"I know all about you, Sergeant Flynn. I've been assigned as the new platoon leader for the Blues. I consider it an honor to meet y'all an' have y'all as my platoon sergeant."

Shawn had heard about a new officer coming in but had hoped it was just a rumor. He had gotten used to being the platoon leader and didn't like the idea of moving down to the number-two position. He shook the dark-haired officer's hand and forced the resentment he felt out of his mind. He knew, as a noncommissioned officer, that it was only luck that he had gotten the platoon leader's job in the first place. Officers led platoons, while their platoon sergeants ran them. He was now going to have to step down a notch and teach this new shavetail how to lead his platoon.

The lieutenant backed up, embarrassed. "I'm sorry, I didn't introduce myself. I'm Jim Owens. I reported in to Division on Friday. I'm originally from Lubbock, Texas."

Shawn smiled, feeling better about the officer. Owens was a short, stocky type with a pleasant, perpetual smile. "Likable" was the first word that came to mind. His muscular body and round, strong face would look formidable without the smile. He was like a cartoon, a powerful bear with a teddy bear's face. Shawn knew this was no off-the-street lieutenant. The first clue was the black and gold Ranger tab sewed on the officer's left shoulder. The second was the silver parachute wings pinned on his chest. The Blue's platoon leader position would be a highly sought-after assignment, and the battalion commander himself would have screened all the lieutenants. Obviously this young officer had been picked because he had the best record.

Shawn motioned toward the desk. "Sir, welcome aboard. You must be rarin' to go, to come in on a Sunday. It'll just take me a minute to move my stuff off your desk and—"

Owens held up his hand. "Naw, don't move your stuff now. I just came by to get the lay of land. I didn't wanna get lost when I came to work tomorrow."

Shawn thought of the first question that would come from the troops when they heard about their new platoon leader. He glanced at the officer's left hand for the telltale ring.

"Sir, are you a West Pointer, by any chance?"

Owens's face contorted and he staggered back as if he'd been slapped. "Damn, that hurt! Do I look smart or somethin'? Tell me what made you think that, and I'll change it right now."

Shawn laughed. "I guess that's a no."

"No, that's a *hell no!* I'm a dyed-in-the-wool Texas Aggie who got ta college 'cause I played a little football. Hell, I can't even spell 'Military Academy.'"

Shawn chuckled again, feeling warmth for the young officer. They were going to make a good team. "Sir, I'm sorry I asked, but the troops will be asking me tomorrow. Most of 'em think West Pointers are prima donnas that only go by the book and think of their careers. I'll tell 'em we have an ex–football player, Ranger, who will run 'em into the ground the first P.T. session."

Owens raised an eyebrow. "Don't lay it on too thick about the P.T. I just got outta Ranger school, and I'm still recovering. The course beat the hell outta me. I'm outta shape."

Shawn smiled inwardly. If Owens was out of shape, he wondered what he would look like "in" shape.

U.S. ARMY AIRBORNE SCHOOL, 14 JUNE

Five hundred and two men of the 44th Airborne Training Company, Class 22, arrived at ground training branch of the United States Army Airborne School at precisely 0645 hours. They took five minutes to form up in four platoons with four ranks each, and took another minute to dress right and cover down. They then stood at parade rest, wondering what airborne school was going to be like.

At exactly 0700 the notorious "Black Hats" of the ground training branch made their grand entrance. The loud slap of twenty-five pairs of glistening jump boots striking the pavement in perfect unison was the first indication that they were coming. Seconds later they appeared in a tight formation from over a rise, running in perfect step, their cold unreadable eyes partially hidden beneath their raven hats. They wore white T-shirts and starched fatigue trousers. Their shoulders were back, chests out, heads held high and proud, arms bent at the elbow with forearms horizontal to the ground. They looked like a championship military drill team. The sound of their boots became louder and louder. The silver parachute wings pinned to their baseball caps sparkled in the early morning light.

They turned toward the company of wide-eyed men like a churning, pounding machine. Their ranks suddenly separated, and within seconds four instructors were running in place at the right side of every rank of every platoon, with another instructor in the front and center of each platoon.

The awed airborne students were mesmerized by the performance, until a booming voice broke the spell.

"In-struct-tors . . . halt!"

The Black Hats stopped running in place and came to attention, slapping their sides in a thunderous *pop* that echoed across the graveled formation area.

A Black Hat captain stood on a rise to the front of the formation and refilled his lungs before commanding, "Student company commander, *post!*"

A frail-looking captain wearing horn-rim glasses broke from the ranks and jogged toward the thick-chested airborne officer. The student company commander halted two paces in front of the ground branch committee chief and brought up a shaky salute. *"Airborne Class Twenty-two reports 502 airborne students prepared for instruction!"* he yelled in a squeaky voice.

The Black Hat captain looked with disdain upon the frail officer and snickered loudly. "Pre-pared? Do you really think this ragtag collection of nasty, filthy legs are *pre-pared?*"

The frail captain trembled as he spoke meekly. "I—I think so."

To the men of Class 22 the next hour became a blurry nightmare. The airborne captain had become enraged and fired the student company commander on the spot. Another was appointed and was fired a minute later. In the meantime the company had been told to strip to the waist. They were marched to huge tin-covered sheds and there took an airborne P.T. test. Afterward, they dressed and were moved back into the sheds for briefings from their airborne platoon sergeants, who would be responsible for their training.

Blake, Lee, Eugene, and Vincent had all been assigned to the first platoon, and they had all passed the P.T. test with no problem. Eleven men in the platoon had failed the test and were not in formation when Sergeant First Class Jenkins arrived and climbed a platform.

Jenkins, a small man with a skinny body, seemed innocent enough until he eyed his platoon with a scowl and spoke. "I hate legs . . . I hate them so bad I even refuse to talk to my leg mother. My daddy was a paratrooper, and all my friends are paratroopers! You people are *legs!* You do not know how to talk, walk, eat, fight, or jump like paratroopers. You are dangerously dumb. I get pissed off just looking at your sloppy, leggy, nasty bodies. I am now going to tell you how *not* to piss me off. First, when I talk, you listen."

The sergeant's eyes suddenly locked on a student in the first rank who was yawning. Jenkins exploded. *"You dare yawn while I'm talking? Drop! All of you drop! You have pissed me off!"*

The entire first platoon got down in the front leaning rest position and began doing push-ups. Jenkins shook his head and put his hands on his hips. *"Stop what you're doing! You look like a bunch of kinky monkeys screwing footballs!* Legs, when I say drop, you go down like a lightning bolt hit you. You will *not* pick a spot! You will *not* lollygag and look around. *You will drop!* Legs, do not ever yawn in my presence or pick your butt or nose or roll your eyes. You will give me one hundred percent of your attention or I will get one hundred percent of your funky nasty leg bodies. Is that clear?"

During the tirade, the first platoon had still been in the front leaning rest position, and their arms and backs were breaking.

"Yes, Sergeant!" the men screamed.

Jenkins shook his head. *"No, legs!* You do not say 'yes' to me or any Black Hat. The proper airrr-borne response is 'Clear, Sergeant, Airrr-borne.' Now, Is *that* clear?"

Half the men yelled yes while the other half yelled "Clear, Sergeant, Airrr-borne!"

Jenkins barked, *"Re-cover!"* He saw only three men get up, and shook his head again. "Legs, 're-cover' means get up on your feet, dummies!" He paced back and forth, his face livid red. "Legs, you have demonstrated to me that you are incapable of listening. You are all obviously inflicted with that horrible leg disease known as 'incurable dumb-ass'! Your brain-housing-group is vapor-locked into the ignorant position. The only cure is Airrr-borne P.T. *Drop!*"

The tired airborne students of the first platoon dropped into the front leaning position, "re-covered," and dropped again five times before they got it right. Jenkins finally seemed satisfied. He lowered his voice and gave the platoon their briefing.

He was what was known as a Black Hat, but he introduced himself to the platoon as their *"Airrr-borne pla-toooon sarge-gent!"* The stenciled name on his white T-shirt said STAFF SERGEANT JENKINS, but he had told them they would call him *Sergeant Airrrr-borne.* Needless to say, the men of the first platoon were confused. They were, in fact, more than confused; they were stupefied.

Every student had heard stories about the famous school, and most had prepared themselves mentally and physically for the worst. The problem was that they had no idea what "worst" meant—until they had been "briefed" by the small, wiry terror of a man wearing a black ball cap and a scowl calling himself Airborne Instructor, alias, Black Hat, alias, Sergeant Airborne, alias, Platoon sergeant, alias, SFC Jenkins.

Jenkins had one of those high-pitched voices that gnawed at airborne-student nerve endings. His scowl made his gaunt face look as if he had just drunk rancid prune juice. He seemed to like getting pissed off. "Drop" seemed his favorite word. He gave a briefing that no one understood. The students soon realized that airborne instructors talked in a strange language that only they could decipher. He had used words and phrases that made no sense, like ". . . first stick will perform PLFs while others are donning. Later will be the LDA and the thirty-four-foot monster."

At the conclusion of the briefing, the situation seemed hopeless. Not only did they not know what to call their instructor, they didn't even know how to communicate with him. It had been made perfectly clear they were aliens from the lowly world of legs and unable to understand the higher life form from Airborne world.

Satisfied he had reduced his platoon into a submissive trainable mob of confused and tired men, Sergeant First Class Jenkins pointed to a grassy area to his right.

"Legs, you will now take a ten-minute break. Over there is the break area. When I say 'fall out,' you will *run* out of my pit hollering all the way to the break area. You are the mighty first plaa-tooon! *You will* move like *lightning* and sound like *thunder! Pla-tooon! A-ten-hut! Fall out!*"

Blake Alexander led his three other friends in a screaming, pushing, and running scramble to the break area, trying to sound like thunder. Once at the grassy spot, the four men sat down by a tall pine tree. They looked at each other for several seconds, wondering what the hell they were doing there at the school. All eyes settled on Blake. He felt their burning gaze and held up his hands in resignation.

"I know, I know, it was my idea. I fucked up. What else can I say?"

Vincent lowered his head. "I shoulda quit."

Eugene nudged Lee. "Hey man, wasn't you the one who said this was gonna be fun?"

Lee mimicked Vincent by lowering his head. "I shoulda quit too."

They all laughed and drew stares from the other tired men, who could not imagine anyone laughing at a time like this.

Vincent saw a familiar face approaching and mumbled a warning as he quickly got to his feet.

Master Sergeant Richard Burke spotted his two "quitters" and strode straight toward them. He stopped a few feet from Vincent and dipped his head in recognition. "You passed the P.T. test, I see. That's good. If you and your 'buddy' make it past today, you'll make it. Hang tough . . . it gets better."

Vincent was shocked. The sergeant had spoken to him in a regular tone without raising his voice—and he had been wearing his black ball cap! They could talk normal while wearing the black hat! There *was* hope! They *were* human!

Burke dipped his head again and cracked a faint smile. "Good luck."

Blake scooted over beside Vincent when the sergeant was gone. "Who the hell was that, Vinny?"

Vincent leaned back on the old pine with a smile. "A sign of hope."

16 JUNE

Shawn and his entire platoon sat watching television in the barracks day room. Throughout the post every man, woman, and child was glued to a TV set awaiting the word. The Secretary of Defense, Robert McNamara, was going to make a formal announcement about the authorization of a new airmobile division in a nationally televised press conference. Most of the other citizens of the United States would not notice or know what his announcement would mean, but for the residents of Columbus, Georgia, and the soldiers and their families at Fort Benning, the announcement could change their lives forever.

When the secretary appeared on the screen, all of Columbus and Fort Benning held their breath.

Shawn listened to the slick, bespectacled politician, and decided he did not like having his fate decided by a man who was not wearing a uniform. The secretary announced the forming of an airmobile division and then shocked the local listeners by saying the Eleventh Air Assault Division colors would be retired and that the First Cavalry Division would be named the first airmobile division in the world. The First Cavalry was at present assigned to Korea, and they would send their colors to Fort Benning. The secretary then looked directly into the camera and declared that the new airmobile division would be at REDCON-1, the highest combat readiness condition, in eight weeks.

Shawn nearly fell out of the chair when he heard the last sentence. REDCON-1 in eight weeks was impossible!

The men around Shawn smiled nervously at each other. They knew they were making history, but weren't sure just what that meant. "What does the First Calvary patch look like?" a private asked Shawn.

Shawn didn't hear the question. He was lost in thought. How were they to make the impossible happen? The strength of the Eleventh Division was less than 9500 men. A full-strength division required almost 16,000 men, to say nothing of the additional weapons, equipment, and helicopters. How could the leaders in Washington possibly think they could get that many replacements, train them, and organize an entire division for combat in eight weeks?

Lieutenant Owens stood and quieted the platoon before speaking. "Men, what you just saw means we're going to war. We don't know when yet, but it means we're going pretty damn soon. Today, I want you to go home and think about what that means. Tomorrow we begin training for Vietnam."

Twenty minutes later Lieutenant Owens strode into Shawn's office. Shawn was sitting at his desk making out a list of things that had to get done. Owens tossed a yellow scarf on the sergeant's desk and spoke with pride.

"You'll soon be a proud member of Charlie troop, First Squadron of the Ninth Cavalry. I just heard we'd be changing to the new designation. We're gonna be a part of the new division's reconnaissance squadron."

Shawn leaned back. He could tell the officer was beside himself with excitement, as were the rest of the men. They were untested soldiers looking to their first challenge in combat. It was written all over their faces. Shawn, however, was jaded and incapable of feeling what they felt. He knew all too well what lay ahead.

Owens's confident smile dissolved. "What's wrong, why are you so down?"

Shawn looked up with a sad, distant stare. He could think of nothing but the fact that many of his men would not be coming back alive. He was going to war again. The ugly bitch was again calling. She deceived everyone except the veterans who knew the real meaning behind her seductive sweet words of glory, pride, and victory.

He could not tell this lieutenant or his men what she really was. They would not believe him. The bitch's powers were too strong. The confident faces were filled with lust for her. Soon they would learn for themselves. Soon they would know her secret, that she was an insatiable black widow, hungry to consume the bodies of men.

Owens saw that the sergeant was lost in thought and had not heard him. He turned around in silence. A chill ran up his spine. It was something in the veteran's eyes . . .

18 JUNE

Vincent Martino leaped out of the door of the thirty-four-foot tower and snapped into a tight body position. His feet and knees were together, his hands clutching the ends of the reserve parachute, his chin down, and his eyes open. "Onethousand twothousand threethou . . ." he counted aloud. Suddenly he was jerked upward by the risers attached to cables, and he slid down the greased cables toward a mound of red dirt.

He had performed the door exit flawlessly, as did Eugene Day and Blake Alexander, who followed him out of the door of the thirty-four-foot tower. The fourth jumper leaped but his legs were apart and his head was up. The risers slapped his head and nearly tore off his helmet. The Black Hat grader who was below the tower watching the students placed another red mark by the soldier's name. Lee Calhoon was failing.

For Blake, Vincent, and Eugene, the training had become almost fun. The first day's confusion of commands and strange language had all been made clear, and they now had a foot into the airborne world. They spoke the language of paratroopers and knew what was expected. They had learned what a PLF was—a parachute landing fall, designed to lessen the chance of injury by keeping the feet and knees together and rotating on impact with the ground so that only the fleshy portions of the body made contact with the earth. They had learned how to put on the parachute harness and take it off quickly. They had learned the jump commands that would be given in the aircraft and how to leap out of the plane so that they would not be injured or delay other jumpers. They had learned all that was required in the first week of instruction, and proven their abilities by jumping flawlessly out of the dreaded thirty-four-foot tower.

Lee Calhoon was different. He had learned, but he had been unable to make his body do what his mind wanted. He could not keep his feet and knees together when doing a PLF or jumping from the tower. It was unnatural for a human to jump from a platform and not spread his legs before impact. For those who had played sports, it was easier. They had learned early to control their bodies. Lee had never played sports. He'd had to work after school to help feed the family. His body and mind were unaccustomed to the demands of doing the unnatural, and jumping from the tower was the most frightening thing he had ever done. His mind could not control his fear or his body.

The Black Hat grader motioned toward Vincent, Blake, and Eugene. "You three made *out*-standing exits. Y'all have qualified. Take off your equipment and sit down behind me and watch the hard heads." He glared at Lee, who waddled up, wearing the tight-fitting harness. "*You* had your head up, eyes closed, didn't count, and didn't have your feet and knees together. *Your exit* was *un*-satisfactory. Go up and do it again!"

Lee's face showed the weariness he felt. He had jumped six times that morning, and each time he had failed. The run up the stairs, the jump, and the long runs back from the red mound had drained him of energy. His body was a throbbing boil of pain. The tight parachute harness had rubbed his flesh raw, and the improper jumps had bruised his body to black and blue jelly. He knew that any further attempt would be futile. He had to make three satisfactory exits in a row to qualify and to be allowed to stay in training, and he didn't think he could even get up the tower steps again. The future looked hopeless.

He swallowed and forced himself not to think of the pain. "Clear, Sergeant Airrr-borne!" he yelled.

Sergeant Jenkins stepped up and blocked his path to the tower. The sergeant, who was much shorter than Lee, had to look almost straight up to see the student's face. "You failed again, huh?"

Lee dejectedly lowered his eyes. "Clear, Sergeant Airborne!"

The sergeant sighed, took hold of Lee's harness and walked him toward a sawdust pit. "It ain't gonna do no good for you to go up again. You need to rest awhile and think about what you're gonna do. Take off your harness and sit down."

Vincent, Blake, and Eugene exchanged glances of disbelief. Sergeant First Class Jenkins was actually talking normally instead of behaving like his usual asshole self.

Jenkins spun around and pointed at Blake. *"Come here, leg!"*

Blake jumped up and in seconds was facing the sergeant.

Jenkins motioned toward Lee. "This leg is having problems. I want to see him make it and continue with this class. You two have been good for the platoon. I've been watching you both. You have helped other teams by setting an example. You, leg, have tried to help Calhoon here, and that makes me feel good. It makes me believe he is worth saving. Teams make it in war. Individuals die. You two men are a damn good team, and I don't wanna see it get busted up because Calhoon can't jump."

The sergeant glanced past Blake to the activity around the three thirty-four-foot towers. "We've got more students here than we Black Hats can train effectively. We have to work with those who have it, and we don't have time to train those who need additional help. Calhoon is one of those who needs more help. I'm going to take ten minutes and show you how to help him. Then you're on your own. Listen to me good. In three hours we're going to test Calhoon again. If he fails to qualify from the tower, he's out."

Jenkins had Lee stand in a mock plane door and had him make five door-exits. He showed Blake what to look for and what techniques to use to improve his buddy's performance. "Trooper," Jenkins said to Lee when he was finished, "you're gonna have to suck it up and fight through the pain and fatigue. Most of the hard heads will quit 'cause they aren't mentally tough. They *think* they can't make it. Anybody who thinks they can't, can't. You *think* you *can* do it and sooner or later you can. Your only chance is to listen and do what your buddy tells you."

Jenkins gave Lee something he would never forget: the sergeant cracked a smile and spoke with admiration. "I'll say one thing for ya, ya got heart." With that the Black Hat walked away.

Lee took in a deep breath and faced Blake. "Let's git started."

Three hours later Lee Calhoon stood in the door of the thirty-four-foot tower. Jenkins sat below the monster in a grader shack and watched as the jumpmaster yelled, *"Go!"*

Lee leaped from the tower and snapped into a tight body position exactly as he had been taught. The sergeant marked a second blue S by the hard head's name, meaning he had made his second satisfactory jump.

Lee slid down the cable to the mound some fifty yards away and was unhooked from his harness. He had to make one more jump to qualify. The other eight hard heads had quit, so there was no wait, which meant no rest, between jumps. He looked at the tower and began jogging. His body was weak from the heat and the constant running back and forth and climbing up the steps. As he ran, he fought back dizziness from fatigue. He could do it now. He had learned the secret of a concentration so total that it forced his body to respond to command. He knew he could qualify if he could just make it up those steps one more time.

His uniform, soaked with sweat, seemed to weigh a hundred pounds, and his legs had turned to rubber. He shook his head to try and focus his eyes. *I can do it, I can do . . .*

But the tower seemed ever more distant, getting farther away with each step instead of closer! *Noooo!* he screamed within himself as he felt his legs buckle.

Sergeant First Class Jenkins saw the soldier go down, but before Jenkins could move, three students ran over to the prone trooper. They poured their canteen water into his face and got the soldier to his feet.

"You can do it. You can do it," Blake said softly as he dripped water onto Lee's parched lips.

Eugene and Vincent each grabbed an arm and began running him toward the tower. Blake kept waiting for the sergeant to yell at them to leave Lee alone, but Jenkins seemed preoccupied with his clipboard.

They practically carried Lee to the steps, but still the sergeant did not yell at them. Jenkins still had his head down. Heartened at their luck, they helped Lee up the stairs. Arriving at the top of the mock-up aircraft, the waiting Black Hat jumpmaster bellowed, "Get your hands off that trooper! Get out of here, legs!"

He grabbed Lee and hooked a set of risers to his harness.

"Stand in the door!" he commanded.

Feeling only slightly better, the lanky Georgian lifted his head. A part of his brain was feeling the numbing fatigue and pounding pain that told him he was incapable of continuing. The other part of his brain transmitted a single message: *You're a Calhoon. You're a Calhoon. You're a Calhoon.*

With determination, Lee set his eyes on the door and stomped his foot forward to begin his shuffle. *You're a Calhoon!* Taking up the door position, with his hands extended to the sides of the metal skin, he lowered his butt, raised his head, and stared at the horizon. *You're a Calhoon! You're a Calhoon!*

"Go!" the jumpmaster yelled.

With the last of his strength, Lee sprang up and out and snapped into the tight body position.

Sergeant Jenkins watched, nodded to himself, and turned around in his chair where three students stood waiting for their friend. He gave the men his usual scowl.

"*Drop!* You all owe push-ups for helping that hard head up the steps!"

Blake, Vincent, and Eugene completed the push-ups and jumped to their feet yelling, "*Airborne!*"

"You legs better go help that hard head back here and get his harness off him," Jenkins then told them. He stood and began to walk toward the distant white house, then stopped and looked over his shoulder. "And tell that hard head he qualified."

At midnight Shawn tiredly walked into the trailer, and tossed down his equipment. He turned on the light, and froze. Cindy lay on the couch asleep. His heart raced as he walked over, then gently stroked her cheek.

Cindy awoke with a start and sat up. She pushed back her mussed hair. "I . . . I came by to pick up some things I'd left and . . ." She couldn't keep her hands from reaching for him. Shawn sat down and hugged her to his chest, never wanting to let her go.

She looked up into his eyes with tears running down her cheeks. "I won't marry you, Shawn . . . but—but I'll stay with you till you leave. I've tried to put you out of my mind, but—"

"I know," Shawn said softly.

She kissed his chin and whispered, "I've missed you so much."

Shawn picked her up in his arms and walked into the waiting darkness of the bedroom.

16

Lieutenant Owens dropped into a chair beside his platoon sergeant. "I can't believe this shit."

Shawn lifted his head with an "I told you so" look, which Owens acknowledged with a sigh. "This is ridiculous. The Secretary of Defense himself tells us we're going to be REDCON-One, but nobody has told us how. Jesus, we've only got twenty-one men. We need twenty more. And even if we do get more men, how the hell are we going to train them in time?"

Shawn glanced outside toward the huge field where only a few helicopters sat. "Sir," he said pointedly, "if we don't get more choppers, then we don't need more men."

Owens let his head drop to his chest. The realization of what REDCON status meant had finally sunk in. Now everyone was scrambling for men and equipment. The in-processing center, where replacements reported, looked like a meat market. Sergeants roamed in roving packs, looking for bodies for their depleted units. On July 3 the colors of the First Cavalry were to be unfurled in a huge ceremony. The standing joke among the veterans was that there would be more VIPs, dignitaries, and visitors than soldiers taking part in the division activation ceremony. The sad reality was that the First Cavalry (Airmobile) Division would be a division only on paper unless a miracle happened.

The phone rang and Shawn picked up the handset. After he had identified himself, he listened for a full minute before saying thank you and hanging up. He stood and offered his hand to the weary lieutenant. "Come on, sir, we have some body shopping to do."

Owens let himself be pulled to his feet. "What are you talking about?"

Shawn put on his cap and headed for the door. "That call was the squadron sergeant major. It seems the Army has wised up. We're gonna get us some troopers. But we gotta hurry before word gets out to the rest of the units."

Owens quickly caught up to the fast-walking platoon sergeant. "Where we hurryin' to?"

Shawn pointed to the distant, famous landmarks of Fort Benning—three 250-foot airborne towers erected during the early part of World War II.

They were near the center of the post and could be seen from miles around.

"The airborne school?" Owens said with disbelief.

"Yes, sir. Our cut of the class is ten men. The Blues are well thought of, so we get first pick. The division is getting the men that are in their second week of training, tower week. We get to go down today and pick out the ones we want. When they graduate next week, they come straight to us. We'll have a couple of days to get em' ready for the third of July color ceremony."

Owens glanced at the distant towers. "It's about time we had some new meat."

An airborne instructor walked down a line of wide-eyed students. Each of them had just finished a hair-raising ride up and drop from a 250-foot tower. At first the experience had seemed like a huge amusement park ride. Each paratrooper dangling from a fully opened parachute encased in a steel ring had been raised to the top of the tower. There the amusement ended. From a control booth at the base of the structure, the parachutes were released and floated free. For most of the airborne students the short, six-to eight-second drop to a plowed field would be the scariest thing they had ever done in their lives, and they thought they would never forget it. But they would forget. In just days they would jump from an aircraft in flight at an altitude of 1250 feet.

The Black Hat had just explained to the students that all unassigned soldiers would be sent to the new division on post as soon as they graduated. The news was taken in silence. They had all heard the gossip on post that the division was headed for Vietnam. The Black Hat motioned over his shoulder toward Lieutenant Owens and Staff Sergeant Flynn.

"Legs, there are some men here from the First of the Ninth Cavalry Squadron. They're looking for volunteers. Does anybody here wanna join the cav?"

Not a single soldier held up his hand. They had learned the golden airborne rule early—don't volunteer for nothin'.

Shawn stepped forward. "Thank you, Sergeant," he said, "but it is not a question of volunteering. They are all going to the First Cav Division. It's just a matter of which unit. Me and the lieutenant came to pick the best men for the *best* unit." Shawn centered himself on the formation and barked, "If you're not infantry, fall out to the rear."

Half of the formation of four hundred men quickly stepped back, grateful they were not infantrymen.

Shawn walked down the ranks pointing at the biggest and strongest-looking men. "You, stand over there . . . you . . . and you . . . you."

Shawn stopped in front of a stocky soldier and motioned him to join the others he had selected.

Vincent Martino held his ground. Shawn turned and gave the private a fierce glare. "Did you hear me, trooper?"

Vincent nodded. "Sergeant, I hear you, but I'm not gonna go wit'out my buddies."

Shawn squared himself to the soldier. "Where are your 'buddies'?"

Vincent motioned to the three men beside him. "We been to basic, AIT, and airborne school together. We're a team."

Shawn stepped back and looked at the three men. He nodded and jerked his thumb over his shoulder. "Okay, 'team,' get over there."

Blake watched the sergeant and lieutenant walk away before facing the other three men. "At least we know where we're going when we graduate."

Eugene cocked his head to the side. "Charlie troop, First of the Ninth Cavalry. It sounds cool . . . wonder what it means and what they do?"

Vincent shrugged his shoulders. "Who cares, as long as the team is together."

Lee was beaming. "I still git ta stay right here on post and see my folks."

Blake saw the Black Hat sergeant striding toward them. "Come on, we've got to finish this week and jump five times out of an airplane next week. We'll worry about what we're gonna be doing in the cavalry later."

"*Move it, legs! Fall in!*" the Black Hat yelled.

27 JUNE

The jumpmaster opened the door of the aircraft, letting in the roar of the engines and the howl of the wind. Seated by the door, Martino crossed himself and stared out the opening, praying he could do it.

Blake patted Lee's leg to boost his confidence.

Eugene leaned over to Vincent. "I signed you up!" he yelled over the noise.

Vincent broke his gaze from the door and looked at Eugene. "Huh?"

"I signed you up for airborne school. I gotta clear my conscience."

Vincent's eyes narrowed and he began to speak when the jumpmaster yelled, *"Get readyyyy!"*

Without thinking, every soldier stomped his foot and slapped his thighs as he had done a hundred times during training. They could all do it with their eyes closed and in their sleep. They had performed the drill so many times, it was imprinted in their bodies and brains forever.

"Outboard personnel, stannnnd up! Inboard personnel, stannnd up! . . . Hook up!"

Lee fumbled with the snap hook, trying to release it from his top reserve handle. Blake put his hand on top of Lee's, which was shaking, and calmly unhooked it for him. He winked.

"Relax, this is 'fun,' remember?" They hooked their snap hooks to the cable over their right shoulders and held on to the yellow static line.

The jumpmaster commanded, *"Check static lines! . . . Check equipment! . . . Sound off for equipment check!"*

Beginning at the rear of the waiting line of jumpers, the last man stomped his foot forward and slapped the man's buttocks to his front, yelling, *"Okay!"* The same action was repeated by every man until it reached Vincent at the head of the line, who stomped his foot forward, pointed at the jumpmaster, and barked, *"All okay, jumpmaster!"*

The jumpmaster gave a thumbs up to Martino then stepped to the door. Grasping the sides, he leaned out into the 115-knot wind and looked ahead of the aircraft for the drop zone. Martino was shocked to see the sergeant's face was flapping in the wind. Then the jumpmaster stepped back in and yelled, *"Thirty seconds!"*

Eugene shuffled closer to Vincent. "Vinny, do you forgive me for signing you up?"

Vincent glanced over his shoulder. "I'm gonna kill you!"

Eugene desperately needed his conscience cleared before leaping. He had not slept a wink the night before, thinking about all the errors of his life. The thought of the upcoming jump and all the things that could go wrong had weighed heavily in his mind. It was time to get right with his God. Many of his sins could never be reversed, but the one thing he *could* do was tell his buddy the truth. It had eaten at his insides that he had forced his friend into something he had not wanted.

"Vinny," he pleaded, "you gotta tell me you forgive me."

Vincent glanced over his shoulder again and saw the pleading expression. "I forgive you till we're on the ground," he growled, "then I'm gonna kill you!"

Eugene grinned. He now had a clear conscience. He could jump into Hell, and it wouldn't matter.

Blake looked over his shoulder at Lee's fearful face. The Georgian was only seconds away from jumping out of the first plane he had ever been on.

"Just follow me," Blake said, "and don't think about anything else. You'll do fine."

Lee tried to smile but his lips were frozen in place. Every fiber in his body seemed to be trembling all at once. He didn't think he could move.

The jumpmaster leaned out the door again into the blast of wind. He rotated his head to make sure no other aircraft were below or close by, then he looked at the drop zone for the smoke. White smoke would mean the jump was a go. He saw the white plume drifting lazily upward and immediately stepped back. *"Drop zone coming up."* He pointed at Martino, then at the open door. *"Stand in the door!"*

Vincent gulped and shuffled to the sun-lit door, where he assumed the rigid door position with arms extended, butt down, and head up. The

115-knot winds tore at his fatigues and face. The red light beside the door went out and the green light came on.

"Go!" the jumpmaster yelled, and slapped Martino's rear. The Italian did not hesitate. He leaped and then immediately forgot everything he was supposed to do. His eyes were closed so tightly his head hurt, and he prayed instead of counting the traditional four seconds. The sensation of falling made him feel as if his stomach had leaped into his throat. Suddenly, he jerked upward. His green chute had caught air and blossomed just as they had said it would.

Eugene had followed Vincent, and he too had his eyes closed. The instant his parachute opened, he remembered he had not counted.

Blake leaped, but he was too worried about Lee to be concerned for himself. Lee was in the door with everything in his being screaming for him not to jump. He began to turn around when the jumpmaster's boot caught him in the rear and lifted him out of the plane into the howling windstream. His eyes were wide open and he saw everything in blurry slow motion, the ground, other opened chutes, the ground, his fatigues fluttering, the ground! *Pop.* It was such a sweet sound. The risers slapped his face as the silk chute fluttered open and jerked him upward.

Blake turned in his harness just in time to see Lee's parachute open. *"Lee? Lee, is this fun or what?"*

Eugene was screaming at the top of this lungs *"Airrrborne . . . airrrborne!"* He couldn't stop. It released all his fears to yell and scream out his joy at surviving and enjoying precious life.

Vincent watched the ground coming up without appreciation for the free ride on a cushion of air. He was trying to remember everything he had been taught about a PLF. One rule kept running through his mind. Keep your feet and knees together. Keep your feet and knees together. Keepyourfeetandkneestogether. The ground seemed to be coming up faster. Maybe his chute had collapsed! Keep your feet and knees together. God, I'm going in too fast! Keepyourfeetandkneestogether! God! God! Gawwwwwwwd!

He hit the grass-covered field with his feet together and instinctively rotated his body. He lay on the ground for a lifetime, feeling the chute drag him, but he didn't care. The warm sun on his face told him he was alive. His chest heaved with the pounding beat of his heart, and he opened his eyes to see the beautiful blue sky from whence he had come. What he saw instead was a man only ten feet up hurtling straight down toward him.

Eugene screamed another warning and pulled down on another set of risers. Vincent rolled right just before Eugene hit the ground and tumbled over Martino's legs, then smacked the ground with the front of his helmet and ate grass as he was pulled along the ground by the parachute.

Martino grabbed Eugene's leg to stop him. The parachute pulled. Vincent pulled. Eugene groaned.

Finally the chute fluttered and collapsed. Eugene spit out grass, opened his eyes, then lay still. He was afraid to move and see how badly broken his body was. Finally he moved an arm a fraction of an inch and felt no pain. He moved a leg and still felt no pain. He sat up and still felt no pain. He jumped up and shook himself like a wet dog, and still, unbelievably, there was no pain. He screamed to the heavens, *"Airrrrborne!"* It was then that Vincent tackled him from behind and Eugene Day suddenly felt pain.

"You signed me up for this? You, my buddy, did this to me?" Vincent yelled while slapping Eugene on the helmet.

Eugene couldn't help himself. He laughed hysterically. He was just happy to be alive. *"Yeah, I did, and I'd do it again! Airrrborne!"*

Blake ran to where Lee lay in the grass. He had seen him hit the ground and roll into a perfect PLF, but his friend had not gotten up. He looked down at the lanky Georgian and saw him grinning strangely up at the sky.

Blake leaned over him. "Are you okay?"

"It was wonderful. I've never felt nothin' like it before. It was plum wonderful."

Blake grinned and went back to collect his chute. He knew what Lee was experiencing. It was as if they had been reborn. Everything looked, smelled, felt, and tasted better. Things that before were taken for granted were now treasured. The sound of the wind in the grass, the birds singing in the distant pines, everything was different because the men who experienced the wonderful feeling were different. They had faced death and won.

Vincent and Eugene jogged over carrying their equipment and huge grins. Eugene nodded toward Lee, who was still staring at the sky. "Is he okay?"

Blake nodded. "Yeah, he's just soaking up the feeling."

Vincent and Eugene dipped their chins in understanding. Vincent suddenly cuffed Eugene's helmet again. "Ace, did you know this bum signed me up for this shit?"

Blake raised an eyebrow toward Eugene, who was pushing back his glasses. "Yeah, I knew. Lee did too, but we didn't say anything. We didn't wanna lose you."

Vincent shrugged his shoulders and joined Lee in looking skyward. "I guess the sergeant was right . . . it *was* a sign."

The troubleshooter sent from the Pentagon sat in his new office, which had been given to him by the commanding general of Fort Benning. He had been sent to Fort Benning for the specific purpose of cutting bureaucratic red tape and getting necessary equipment for the new airmobile division. He held a phone to his ear and listened to a high ranking civilian employee tell him it was impossible to ship twenty helicopters in ten days.

Sergeant Major John Quail waited until he had heard all the usual excuses before he put to use all the artful tact that he had mastered while assigned to the Pentagon. *"Look, asshole,"* he skillfully suggested, *"you're feeding me bullshit again!* I've talked to you two times in two hours about what needs to be done, and all I get from you is excuses why you *can't* get the job done. You'd better start telling me how you *can* start shipping me those choppers or I'll have your ass retired without pay! I don't want excuses. *I want those fucking helicopters!*"

Quail slammed down the phone and looked up. Standing in his office door was Major General Kinnard, wearing a stern expression.

"I see you're as smooth as ever, John," the general said, and then winked.

The phone rang and Quail scooped it up. "Quail." He listened for a moment and bellowed, "Bullshit! Tell those sonsofbitches I want the weapons on the southbound train tonight, or we'll pull their damn contract and buy them from the goddamn Germans. And if the union bitches again about transporting the weapons, tell 'em we'll fly the damn things down here on Air Force birds, and they'll all be outta fucking business." He slammed down the phone again and smiled at the general. "I hear you're taking some heat, sir."

Kinnard raised an eyebrow. "Yes, you could say that. I've had to listen to every high-ranking logistician in the country complain about the way you talk to their people."

The phone rang again. Quail answered, listened, then shouted, "Hell *no!* Don't wait till they build wooden shipping crates. Use cardboard boxes and get the shit here the fastest way. What? . . . Don't take that shit from him. I'll be glad to talk to his fucking congressman. Tell him I'll remind the congressman that the ammunition plant in his fucking district is a meal ticket for half of his voters. The sonofabitch doesn't hold up *our* shipment so he can build too-fucking-expensive wooden boxes. Fuck him! Pull his contract and find someone who can deliver on time!"

Quail replaced the phone and faced the general. "Sir, I never said I was a diplomat. I have a mission to get your division ready, and that's what I'm going to do."

Kinnard smiled. "I thought you'd like to know I tell those that complain that you're not under my control. I give them the Secretary of Defense's office phone number. I tell them to call him if they want to persist in their complaint."

Quail faintly smiled. "Sir, we're gettin' too old for this shit."

Kinnard nodded in silence and walked out of the office. He stopped in the hall and glanced at the gruff sergeant major. "Don't let up, John. Get my division what it needs."

Quail began to speak, but the phone rang. "What? . . . You tell that fat-ass sonofabitch he'd better have that ammo on the trucks tonight, or we'll nuke his fuckin' house!"

The general turned and walked down the long hall. He knew that John

Quail would turn the impossible into the possible. They would be ready.

"... I don't care what the fucking regulations say! Get it on the trucks and get it here!"

29 JUNE

The stick of men standing in the shaking C-119 flying boxcar knew that within two minutes they would be called paratroopers for the rest of their lives. They held yellow static lines and stared at the jumpmaster, waiting for his word to go. They all had four jumps behind them, and they were confident in their equipment and themselves. There was no doubt in any of their minds that they would jump from the aircraft. They would go when commanded. Then, no matter what happened, they would receive the coveted silver wings of a paratrooper. Even if they died or suffered injury, a Black Hat waited at the drop zone to pin their wings on them.

The jumpmaster yelled, *"Thirty seconds!"*

Lee was first in the stick. He looked back at his friends, and they all raised their thumbs. His stomach churned with butterflies but he was not scared. He was ready.

Eugene looked over his shoulder at Martino. "Yo, Vinny, we gonna impress the ladies with our wings, man."

Vincent grunted. "Gina is all I care about impressin'."

The jumpmaster backed out of the door and pointed at the Georgian. *"Stand in the door!"*

Lee lowered his head and shuffled to the waiting door and howling winds. I'm a Calhoon! Seconds later the red light went out and the green light flashed on. The jumpmaster yelled, *"Go!"*

Lee leaped and snapped into a tight body position. Seconds later he was under a canopy of silk and looking toward the east. Seventeen miles away, past the countless pines, was his home. His joy at the sight was marred by the sudden realization that he could never adequately share the experience with his family. Words couldn't describe the feeling. Only those who actually jumped and felt the exhilaration could understand.

Lee felt a pang of guilt. He knew things had changed. He had changed. His family seemed a world apart from him now. He would go back to visit them, but he knew somehow that it wouldn't be the same. He found himself thinking that he would rather be with his friends and talk about what they'd done and shared together. They were his new family.

Staff Sergeant Shawn Flynn stood on the edge of Fryar drop zone, watching the C-119s pass over, disgorging paratroopers. The sight brought back good memories. The airborne school had taught him more than the right way to jump out of airplanes. The instructors had impressed him with a professionalism and skill that he later tried to emulate. They were true masters of their profession in teaching and motivated young men to be the best paratroopers in the world.

He broke from his reverie, noticing four men approaching from the drop zone. They walked side by side with their arms over each other's shoulders. He envied them. They were obviously very close, and were sharing a great moment in their lives. He had learned long ago that memories were always best when shared with friends.

Shawn could hear them laughing and kidding each other and he smiled. He wished he could be there beside them and feel what they were feeling.

He looked away but suddenly turned back. He recognized one of them. He shook his head and stepped closer. Yes, it was them, the "team."

"You night-jumped again, I bet."

"You'd lose, man." Eugene snickered. "I had my eyes open and saw everything. I got this airborne shit down cold."

Lee grinned. "I'm gonna start talkin' like them Black Hats, ya know, airborne this and airborne that. I'm gonna put on my airborne boots an' airborne walk and get me some airborne chow, then do airborne P.T."

Blake laughed. "All I wanna do is find me an airrborne honey that will airrrborne my body and send me to airrrborne heaven."

Vincent saw the sergeant first. "Hey, isn't that the sarge from the cav?"

Blake rolled his eyes. "Damn, we haven't even got our wings yet, and he probably wants us to go to work."

Lee's shoulders slumped. If what Blake said was true, he wouldn't be seeing his family as he planned.

Eugene pushed back his glasses in awe. "Check out the ribbons on his uniform, man. He's a super-duper hero, man."

Shawn waved the four men over. When they stood before him, their expressions were full of the fear of impending doom. He laughed and went down their line, shaking their hands.

"Hell, I'm not gonna bite. I just came out to see you graduate and congratulate you on becoming paratroopers." He backed up so he could see all their faces. "I'm proud of you, and I'm damn glad to have you four men in my platoon. I promise you all that I'll put you in the same squad. By the way, you get one day off before you have to report. I know it's not much, but we have to get ready for a big ceremony. Once the ceremony is over, I'll make sure you all get a four-day pass."

Their smiles told Shawn that he was lucky that he had relented and selected all four of them. He waved them away with his hand. "Go on and get your wings. You deserve them. I'll see you day after tomorrow."

Shawn watched them jog to the ceremony site and wished again he could share in their joy.

"Shawn?"

He turned at the sound of the familiar voice. "Honey," he said, "you shouldn't be out in this heat."

Cindy furrowed her brow. "Don't be silly, it isn't that hot. It's better out here than in the car. Who were those boys you were talking to?"

"Boys? I hope they don't hear you call them that. Those were four new paratroopers who will be joining my platoon."

"They're so young . . . too young to be going to war so soon," she said sadly.

Shawn put his arm around her slight shoulders and looked at the distant ranks of paratroopers. "They're the reason I have to go . . . somebody has to take care of them and bring them back."

Cindy felt the sincerity in his voice and knew he had spoken from the heart. She could see why he was so proud of his profession, but she knew she would never fully understand it. The four young men were no more than eighteen or nineteen, boys dressed in soldier's uniforms, trying to look mean and tough but failing. Their smiles betrayed their innocence. They beamed as only boys could. They seemed so young to be away from their homes and the people who loved and feared for them.

Shawn felt her tremble. "Honey, are you all right?"

She couldn't take her eyes off of those young men, all beaming with pride. She spoke in a whisper, on behalf of all their mothers, "Take care of them, God . . . take care of them."

17

3 JULY

Despite the scorching sun and sultry heat, Fort Benning's Doughboy Stadium was filled to capacity. The spectators had come to witness history in the making. Before them stood the sweltering soldiers of the Eleventh Division (Air Assault) soon to be renamed the First Cavalry Airmobile Division. The men were formed in ranks in front of their unit's respective guidons and battle flags. Among the spectators, many an old veteran tried to hold back his tears as an officer mounted on a dark charger entered the stadium. He wore a 1930s cavalry uniform and held in his hand the First Cavalry Division's colors. Minutes before, the Eleventh Air Assault Division colors had been cased and retired. The drums had rolled as the colors had been marched off the field, and then the band had broken into a lively cavalry tune, "Gary Owen," which had been adopted as the First Cavalry Division's official song. It had been a favorite of General Armstrong Custer.

The announcer's voice resonated throughout the stadium. "The First Cavalry Division is proudly the Army's first airmobile division. But this is not the only first for this glorious division. The First Cavalry was also first in Manila, first in Tokyo, first in Pyongyang, Korea, and . . ."

Standing among the ranks of the hundreds of soldiers were four very hot and sweat-soaked men who didn't know or care that they were making history. All they wanted was for the ceremony to hurry and end so that they could get out of the blistering sun and start a four-day leave. The four new soldiers had reported to their platoon only a few days before and had immediately been placed into the ceremony as fillers. All they had done since joining their new unit was rehearse and prepare for the big event.

Vincent spoke from the corner of his mouth as the announcer droned on. "Yo, Gene, ya see the babe on the third row? In the white dress, blond hair? I can look all the way up her dress."

Unable to see because of a soldier to his front, Eugene grunted, "In your dreams, man."

Blake whistled lowly. "You're right, Vinny, she's puttin' a show on for us . . . damn, I don't think she's wearin' anything underneath."

Lee blushed but didn't take his eyes off the attractive girl, who really did seem to be showing more than she probably intended.

"Give me five minutes, no, just two minutes with her, and she'd never wanna leave me." Blake sighed, with sweat trickling down his face.

"We've been with you for months, and we know that's a crock," Eugene said, snickering.

Blake's eyes narrowed. "Fuck you, Gene."

Staff Sergeant Flynn stood behind his platoon listening to the whispers. "Knock it off," he snarled. "The blonde is the lieutenant's girlfriend."

Blake, Eugene, and Martino's eyes had snapped to their musclebound lieutenant, who stood six paces in front of the platoon. Had he heard? The officer balled his hands into fists behind his back. He *had* heard! Ohhhhhhh shit. Their eyes rolled back in their heads, knowing they were going to die slow deaths.

Lieutenant Owens smiled. He'd never seen the girl in his life, but he wished he had.

The team dragged themselves up the stairs into the barracks after marching back from the stadium. Everyone else in the unit had been bussed back, but Sergeant Flynn had thought that, in light of what had transpired, the four new soldiers would want to walk, to avoid a ride with the lieutenant.

Eugene tossed off his soaked khaki shirt and faced Vincent. "You just had to talk in ranks, didn't you? You just couldn't keep your mouth shut."

Blake began to speak in Vincent's defense, but Eugene spun around and pointed his finger in his face. "And you! You gotta talk about what you're going to do to the blonde. *Damn!* How damn dumb can you get?"

"I remember you a'talkin' too," Lee reminded Eugene.

The sudden appearance of Staff Sergeant Flynn dampened further conversation. He smartly strode down the barracks aisle, halted, and scanned the four worried faces. "I hope you all enjoyed the walk?"

Nobody spoke or moved. The sergeant nodded. "Good. I thought you would. I'm afraid I couldn't cool off the lieutenant. He's waiting in his office. I think he wants an apology. If I were you four, I'd go in together, and that way you'd have witnesses if he blew his stack and punched one of ya."

The four men's eyes widened. Shawn continued speaking in the tone of an understanding father. "I know you troops are new and haven't had a chance to meet the lieutenant 'cause he's been so busy. Since ya haven't been around him, let me give ya some advice. The best thing to do is throw yourselves at his mercy and ask for extra duty. He's got a weakness for people who volunteer, so ya might ask if there's anything he wants you to volunteer for. Yeah, that's probably your best chance . . . 'course, you could tell him you didn't mean it . . . Naw, he was too pissed to believe that."

Blake used the last of his inner strength to take a step forward. "Sergeant Flynn, Private Calhoon didn't say a word and shouldn't have to see the lieutenant."

Shawn stepped up to Lee. "Did you look up the lieutenant's girlfriend's dress, Private Calhoon?"

Lee nodded. Shawn clicked his tongue. "The lieutenant thought you did . . . you go in too."

Shawn spun around and walked back down the aisle. "Come on, he's waiting."

Lieutenant Owens sat at his desk with a scowl. He heard the knock and barked, "Enter!"

The four men marched in and came to attention wishing they were anywhere but the small, hot office.

Owens stood. "*Who* is going to report to me!"

Shawn shoved Blake forward. "Sir, this is the one who said he only needed two minutes with your fiancée."

Blake nearly fainted hearing "fiancée." He recovered and raised his hand while staring above the officer's head. He didn't dare look into his eyes. "Sir, Private Alexander reporting for . . . for the team. Sir, I accept full responsibility for what happened and I apologize for my remarks. They were totally uncalled for."

Owens eyed Blake coldly, then the others, before speaking. "What color was her underwear?"

"White, sir." Blake gulped.

Owens shook his head. "Private, I don't think you're telling the truth. What was the color?"

Blake now knew how a prisoner felt when facing a hangman's noose. He lowered his eyes to the floor. "Sir, I don't believe she was wearing any."

Owens backed up and pointed directly at Blake's face. "*Out-standing,* Private. That's why you're in the Blues . . . your powers of observation are excellent. We in the Blues must report what we see so that others can respond. What you men did today is exactly what good cavalry soldiers are supposed to do—*report!*" Owens cracked a smile. "I haven't had the chance to meet any of you because of the hectic schedule, but I can see Platoon Sergeant Flynn picked some damn good recon men. I'm proud to have you in the Blues."

Owens shook the hand of each man—they all seemed to be in shock—and winked at Shawn. "Platoon Sergeant, I think you selected a pretty good bunch. My compliments."

Shawn motioned the soldiers, who were still staring in disbelief, outside and nodded to the officer. "Thank you, sir. And sir, my compliments to your fiancée."

16 JULY

Staff Sergeant Flynn held up an all-black metal-and-plastic rifle that half the men in his platoon had never seen before. "Men, this is the new M-16.

It weighs only 6.3 pounds empty and fires a 5.56 millimeter cartridge with a muzzle velocity of 3250 feet per second. It can be fired semiautomatic or in the automatic mode. In the automatic mode, it has a cyclic rate of fire of between seven to nine hundred rounds per minute."

Shawn inserted a twenty-round magazine and turned toward the targets, which were twenty-five meters away. He fired in the semi mode at one target, then switched to the automatic mode and sprayed the other three. He had obviously impressed the platoon.

"You have all heard about the controversy over this weapon. Well, that's all bullshit! I carried an M-16 in Vietnam on my last tour, and it's a mean sonofabitch, as long as you keep it cleaned and oiled. Our enemy in Vietnam is equipped with Kalashnikov assault rifles, better known as AK-47s. Some say they are the best assault rifles in the world. I can tell you from experience that if you get in a firefight with Charlie and you're carrying an M-14, your shit is in the wind. The firepower Charlie can put down with their AKs is awesome."

Shawn held up the M-16 again. "With this baby, you can match his firepower and beat it. Today you're going to learn all about M-16s. Tomorrow you will be issued one of your very own and turn in your M-14s."

Minutes later the first squad sat in a circle watching their squad leader take apart the new rifle.

"What'd ya think about it, Reb?" Blake asked Lee. Lee was a hunter and would know something about weapons. His opinion mattered.

"Well, it's lighter than the 'fourteen and it ain't got much of a kick. The only thang I'm not sure about is that little bullet. The M-14 fires a bigger bullet that has knockdown power."

Shawn had been keeping a close watch on the first squad ever since a new squad leader had transferred in two weeks before. To date the over-weight sergeant, named Watley, had not impressed him. Shawn had heard the conversation and stepped closer.

"Calhoon is right, the M-16 bullet is only a tad bigger than a .22-caliber, but it carries a hell of a lot more wallop. When the bullet hits, because of its light weight, it tumbles. It messes up people bad."

Lee looked up at him with concern. "But Sergeant, don't that mean the bullet will tumble when it hits branches and other thangs?"

Shawn cocked up an eyebrow. "You know, Calhoon, that's a damn good question. The answer is that you're right. It doesn't penetrate vegetation, but that doesn't make it a bad weapon. You've got to shoot straight and keep in mind the vegetation in front of your target. Remember that in the platoon we have an M-60 machine gun in every squad. That baby can chop down a bamboo forest." Shawn began to walk away and check one of the other squads but noticed the squad leader was having difficulty taking apart the weapon. "Watley, didn't you practice before we came out here? I thought I told you to know how to field strip that weapon?"

Sergeant Watley shrugged his shoulders. "I'll figure it out."

Shawn leaned over, picked up the rifle, and in seconds handed it back in pieces. He looked directly at Lee. "Calhoon, how many men can ride on a UH-1D?"

Lee looked at the sergeant as if he had spoken Portuguese. Shawn shifted his gaze to Vincent. "Martino, tell me the difference between a UH-1D and UH-1B. Which one is the gunship?"

Vincent exchanged glances with Eugene, hoping he knew and would mouth the answer. Shawn wheeled around to the squad leader. "Why don't your cherries know the basics?"

Watley nonchalantly stood. "Look, Sarge, I've been busy. I'll get 'em squared away just as soon as—"

"We don't have time, Watley! You get your ass in gear and teach these men the basics like I told ya two weeks ago!"

The puffy-faced sergeant rolled his eyes, not in the least concerned with his platoon sergeant's threatening stare. "Look, Sarge, I got thirty-six days left in the Army an' then I'm history. I'm not gung-ho like you and—"

Shawn grabbed the sergeant's fatigue shirt and yanked him to within inches of his face. "Don't say another fuckin' word or I'll stomp your miserable fat ass into the ground right here! You are a noncommissioned officer! You have been given the responsibility to train your men . . . *and you have failed!*"

"You can't grab me like this," Watley whined. "I can press charges against—"

Shawn flung the soldier to the ground. "You're relieved! Get your ass back to the barracks and report to the first sergeant. Write up all the charges you want, but you'd better be out of my barracks before I get back or I swear I'll make you eat those stripes you're wearing. Get out of my sight! I can't stand to look at you!"

Shawn spun around and pointed at Specialist Fourth Class Peters, who had been in the platoon when Shawn had arrived. "Peters, you're now the squad leader. Take charge and get these cherries squared away."

Peters stood. "Clear, Sergeant."

It took a full twenty minutes before Shawn finally calmed down. He had gone into the pine forest behind the range to find solitude. He knew he had handled the Watley matter poorly, but he couldn't help himself. It was unfathomable to him that an NCO put in charge of young men going to war would not have done all he could to prepare them. His anger was justified, but it was more than just being mad at Watley, much more. He knew Watley was just the beginning of a larger problem that was building like a thundercloud on the horizon. Of the original platoon he had trained for the demonstration, only half remained. The rest had shipped out to

Vietnam or Germany, or had left the service. He had gotten replacements for the losses (Quail had been right about the post growing five times bigger). In fact, replacements and equipment had been pouring in around the clock, but somewhere the system was broken. Soldiers like Watley were reporting in, short-timers with less than sixty days remaining in the Army. Others turned out to be troublemakers shipped out from units that didn't want them. The blue platoon was only a few men short of being full strength, but twelve were short-timers and six more were cast-offs. It seemed that the Army didn't care who or what they sent to the First Cavalry, so long as they got there to fill the quota. Charlie troop had over forty-five men who were short-timers, many of whom were much-needed pilots and mechanics. If the division were to deploy to Vietnam, Charlie troop would be going over at only two-thirds strength. And of that number, half were green replacements who had not been with the unit for more than thirty days. He was trying to train a platoon, but it was like trying to build a dam with defective materials. He would get one wall up only to have another piece of the wall wash away. He was losing the battle before it started.

LAWSON ARMY AIRFIELD, 18 JULY

It was a sight to behold. Flying at less than two hundred feet over the airfield were thirty helicopters in a tight formation.

Specialist Fourth Class Vernon Peters jerked his thumb over his shoulder. "Those are UH-1Ds, better known as Hueys. They are lift ships, and they carry us infantry types." He turned and pointed at squatter versions of the same type of helicopter parked on the tarmac. "Those are UH-1Bs. They're our gunships. They can carry twin forty-eight tube rocket pods that shoot 2.75-inch aerial rockets. They also hang other weapons on them, like forty-millimeter cannons and Gatling guns. And over there"—he pointed to the other end of the field, where the smallest and biggest helicopters were parked—"is the OH-13 scout ship and CH-47 Chinook. The OH-13s do the snoopin' and poopin' and find targets for the gunships. The Chinook, the big bird, can carry thirty troopers and can sling-load an artillery 105 howitzer. It's the workhorse of the division. The division is designed so a platoon of Hueys—we call them 'slicks'—can pick up a platoon of infantry, and a company of slicks can pick up an infantry company. It's easy to figure out."

The squad members were sitting on a ridge overlooking Lawson Army Airfield. Peters took his new job seriously. He had been marching the squad to different locations to show them what made the First Cavalry Airmobile Division special. The lesson he was trying to impress on them was that the airmobile concept demanded a huge team effort. The infantry couldn't do their jobs without the support of the pilots, who couldn't do theirs without the support of the mechanics, who in turn depended on supplies, parts, fuel, etc.

Having explained the big picture, he now narrowed his focus to the cavalry squadron. "The cav squadron is like a battalion, and the 'troops' are like companies. The First of the Ninth is a true cav unit because it's totally mobile, air-mobile. Every swinging Richard has a seat on a chopper and can move over the battlefield. The cav has traditionally been the eyes and ears of our armies in the past. You've all heard about the exploits of Jeb Stuart. The cav's job is scout to the front or flanks and report what it finds. Since it's mobile, it can cover a lot of area, and if need be, it can hit quick and hard. That gets us down to us, the Blues, and what we do."

Blake listened in fascination. He had learned that his troop had a scout platoon of OH-13s, a lift platoon of slicks, a gun platoon, and of course his platoon, the Blues. Now he understood what piece his unit played in the giant puzzle known as an airmobile division.

Later, during a break, Vincent lifted his head but had his eyes closed as he spoke. "I think I got it. We're in the first squad in the blue platoon of Charlie troop, in the First of the Ninth Cavalry Squadron, in the First Cavalry Airmobile Division."

Peters stood with a smile. "You got it. I know it seems complicated, but it really isn't, once you figure out how the system works."

Eugene sat up. "What I heard you tell us was the scout ships find the bad guys. The gunships come in and blow their shit away, and we go in and pick up the pieces."

Peters sat down in front of his men. "Look, if everything works and you get real lucky, that's what might happen. I can tell you we rehearsed the technique a hundred times, and it's not as easy as it sounds. You have to be good. Everybody, and I mean everybody, has to do their job right to make it work. We are the luckiest Blues. The blue platoons in Alfa and Bravo troops don't have what we have, and you can count your blessings we have him."

"Who?" Blake asked.

Peters looked at Blake as if he'd asked the stupidest question he'd ever heard. "Flynn, of course. We have Staff Sergeant Flynn. He's the best there is."

Staff Sergeant Shawn Flynn could not believe what he just heard, and he appealed to the squadron sergeant major. "My platoon does not have time for this bullshit. I've got green kids that need time on helicopters, not wasting themselves doing stupid details like this!"

The sergeant major's brow furrowed. "You better keep your voice down. If the old man heard you, you'd be shoveling shit for a month of Sundays. Don't argue. You've got the detail. Everybody has their turn, and your

Blues get Maggie for two months. Here's a list of what needs to be done on a daily basis, and you best not fuck this up. Maggie is special to the old man."

Shawn took the paper from the sergeant major and headed for the office door. He had seen a lot of stupid things in his time in the Army, but this took the cake.

Shawn stood in front of his assembled platoon and commanded them to stand at ease. He briefed them on the next day's activities, then casually asked, "By any chance does anybody here have any experience with mules?"

Lee Calhoon raised his hand before Peters could stop him. Peters slumped, dejected. His man, Calhoon, had made the fatal mistake of a soldier in ranks—never ever raise your hand when a senior asks a question of the entire unit. The squad was going to pay.

Shawn's face brightened. "Calhoon? You know about mules, huh?"

Lee nodded innocently. "Clear, Sergeant, we've got one back home."

"Well, Private Calhoon, that's just fine, 'cause the blue platoon has a mission from the squadron sergeant major. One of our jobs for the next two months is to take care of the squadron's mascot, Maggie. Since you know about such animals, you will be her main caretaker, and you will have help from the rest of the first squad. Peters, you'd better move the men to the stables and get on with the mission." Shawn handed the list to the squad leader that sergeant major had given him. "And Peters, don't fuck it up."

Vern Peters sighed and nodded in silence. It was common knowledge that the squadron commander, Lieutenant Colonel John Stockton, loved Maggie. Stockton was said to be crazy, but crazy in the right way. He was totally dedicated to one thing—cavalry. His only problem was that he was born too late. He should have ridden at Jeb Stuart's side or Custer's. Stockton was a throwback to the cavalry days of old. At just under six feet tall, he was rawboned and wore a nonregulation handlebar mustache. He was a fire-eating, tradition-bound, swashbuckling cavalryman from the tips of his cav boots to the top of his black cavalry hat. He had been with the Eleventh Air Assault Test Division from the first and had earned the reputation of being a man who got things done—his way. His style was direct and relentless, but always had flair. His peers disliked him because he was always upstaging them. Stockton's subordinates might have sometimes questioned their colonel's methods, but no one could argue about his results. His squadron had the highest esprit de corps in the division, and it showed in their performance. "Bullwhip Six" was his call sign, and every soldier and family member knew him on sight.

Vern Peters, along with every other soldier who had served for more than a month, knew the story behind the colonel's mule, Maggie. During an exercise in the Carolinas, some of the colonel's officers rented a gray-white mule from a local farmer and staked her out in front of the colonel's tent as a joke on his birthday. The problem was that he thought the mule was a real present. He named her Maggie, after his wife, and proclaimed her the squadron's mascot. The officers who had rented the mule had to go back to the farmer and shuck out sixty bucks. Since that time, Maggie had participated in every exercise and paraded in every post event. Maggie was almost as famous in Columbus and Fort Benning as was her colorful colonel.

Peters dejectedly marched his squad toward the stable, wishing he'd had time to brief the newbies on the colonel and his mule.

Ten minutes later Lee Calhoon met Maggie. He made a quick inspection. Her legs and hoofs were in good shape, but her teeth were only fair. He figured Maggie was close to twelve years old, a youngish middle-aged animal. She had an even disposition and had gained too much weight from too easy a life in the cavalry.

Lee looked over his shoulder toward the rest of the squad. "I figure she needs some brushin', some airborne P.T., and less oats. Ya won't even know her in a couple weeks, she'll be so purty."

Vincent held his nose. "I don't wanna know her now."

Eugene, who had taken particular notice of the size of Maggie's manure piles, shook his head. "No way, man. My great granddaddy might have had to clean up after mules, but not me."

Blake cocked his head in thought. "Wait a minute, this could be the best thing that's happened to us. I read the list. It says early morning feeding and cleaning, and in the evenings we do the same thing. How long can that take? Huh? Don't you get it? No P.T. in the morning! And no formations at night! Guys, we have found us some super get-over time!"

Vincent smiled. "Maggie, I love you."

Eugene gave a sigh. "Okay, maybe, but I don't clean up the shit, man."

Peters silently stepped out of the stable. He didn't want to burst their bubble just yet. They still didn't understand that Flynn was a pro and knew every trick. They'd learn.

22 JULY

Shawn laughed and set down his beer. ". . . and they thought they could get out of P.T. in the mornings too. You should have seen their faces when they found out they had to take Maggie on the runs with us."

John Quail bellowed in laughter and slapped Shawn's back. The other customers in the restaurant glanced toward the table, wondering what was so funny.

Quail finished off his beer and tossed his arm over Cindy's shoulder. "I think this guy likes what he's doing, don't you?"

Cindy smiled at Shawn. "I always knew that, but I'm a little jealous of Maggie. She always seems to be a topic of conversation when he comes home."

Shawn shrugged his shoulders. "I admit it. I like her. She's good for the platoon. We're all going in a hundred different directions, but Maggie brings us together. This kid who takes care of her, Calhoon, he's taken the job seriously and has got her lookin' like a thoroughbred. You just wouldn't believe it. The colonel is thrilled. He comes down to run with us in the mornings and to see Maggie. He really motivates my troops. I thought he was a showboat, but now that I've been around him, I've learned he's really got his stuff together."

Quail nodded in agreement. "The brass don't like him 'cause of his wild ways. Maybe they should take some lessons from him. That's the problem with our Army today. Nobody can be different or they're pegged as rebels. Ol' Georgie Patton himself, if he came back, would be court-martialed in a week if he pulled some of the same stunts he did back in the late thirties or early forties. Where have they gone? Where are our leaders that have flair and you'd *want* to follow?"

Shawn nodded toward his friend. "I'm looking at one, Taco."

Embarrassed, Quail threw his napkin at Shawn. "I'm a dried-up ol' vet who saw his best years long ago. I have to watch on the sidelines now." The old soldier's eyes became serious. "Irish, I can't put it off any longer. I heard some bad news today."

Cindy knew they were going to talk business and lifted her hand. "Whoa, ya know I don't like it when y'all talk shop. I think I'll visit the ladies' room."

Shawn knew better than to say anything, and quickly got up to pull back her chair. Cindy did not want to hear about his leaving. He had honored that and never discussed his future.

"Irish," Quail said when Cindy was gone, "the President is gonna make a television announcement on the twenty-eighth. He's gonna tell us what we've already known—the cav is going to Nam. But what he *ain't* gonna do is going to hurt the division real bad." Quail leaned closer. "I got word from some of my buddies in the Pentagon that he ain't gonna call up the reserves or declare a state of emergency like we thought. That means all the short-timers in the division ain't goin'. And it means you ain't gonna get no reservists to fill their place."

Shawn stared at his friend in disbelief. The division had been counting on a national emergency decree that would extend the short-timers on active duty, especially the experienced pilots who were already in short supply. Pilots just out of flight school had to learn how to fly the new helicopters as well as the new tactics. It took three to four months before a new pilot could be expected to learn enough to survive in combat. The

President, in not declaring a national emergency, was going to send a division to war but was not going to give them the trained men they needed to carry out the mission.

Shawn's face tightened. "Politics. He and the Congress figured if they called up the reserves or National Guard, there would be no way they could get reelected. Goddamn politics . . . what the fuck are we supposed to do for replacements? I've got at least ten short-timers in my platoon alone."

Quail leaned back in his chair. "The First Cav is gonna have to strip the other units on post of everybody it needs. That's not gonna make a whole lot of people happy around here. A lot of guys are going to be getting orders in the next couple of days that they weren't expectin'." He waved at the waitress and held up his empty beer bottle, signaling he needed another.

Shawn guzzled down half his beer to suppress his seething anger. The politicians had started a war but didn't have the guts to make the hard decisions to support it. By not calling up the reserves or Guard, they in effect had told the nation the Vietnam "conflict" was not a real war. The First Cav would have to strip other units of their leaders and experienced vets in order to accomplish their mission. The next division to go over would do the same. So would the next. But there were only so many leaders with experience in the regular Army. Soon the best men would be gone and there would be nobody left to train the replacements. Who was going to patrol the wall in Berlin or the border in Korea? The Army would do its best to survive, and, like a mother coyote, it would eat its young to live if it had to. The problem was that the litter was small. Soon it would begin gnawing at its own flesh.

Shawn shifted his eyes back to Quail. "How long before we ship?"

"Soon, real soon."

"Where to?"

Quail met Shawn's stare. "The Central Highlands, your old stomping grounds . . . the Pleiku and Kontum Province area. The NVA are moving in and the brass thinks it's the start of a big push. Just today we got a report that the Duc Co Special Forces camp is surrounded by an NVA regiment. The brass needs the cav over there fast, before the whole country goes down the drain."

"And they're sending in the First Cav to find the NVA?" Shawn asked.

Quail's eyes seemed distant. "Not just find them . . . you're going over to find 'em and finish the bastards."

28 JULY

The blue platoon sat quietly in front of the day-room television set. The President had just announced he was sending the First Cavalry Division to Vietnam but had decided not to issue an emergency decree and call up the reserves.

Every man in the platoon already knew they were going to Vietnam because for the past week they had been helping the aviation platoons to ship their aircraft to Jacksonville. The President's announcement might have been a surprise in Maine or Washington state but everybody in Georgia had known for weeks the Cavalry was leaving for Vietnam. In fact, that morning the second brigade had gotten word to depart Charleston on the fifteenth of August. Another rumor that had been confirmed that morning was that an advance party of just over a thousand men would fly to Vietnam on the second of August.

Lieutenant Owens turned the television off and faced his men. "So rumors don't start up, I'm gonna tell you what the division policy is on short-timers. Starting today, if you have thirty days or less, you can get an early discharge. If you have sixty days or less left, you're going to be reassigned to a unit on post and probably pull shit details till you get out. Everybody else goes. No exceptions."

Specialist Marvin Williams jumped up to his full five feet, three inches. "Sir, I only gots sixty-two days left. You ain't gonna make me go, are ya?"

Staff Sergeant Flynn pushed off the doorjamb he was leaning on. He spoke before the lieutenant could respond. "Williams, the platoon leader didn't stutter. He said 'no exceptions.' Sit down. You men that have sixty days or less move on out and start packing your gear. Everybody else stay in place."

The team was surprised to see Specialist Fourth Class Peters get up and head for the door along with ten others.

Owens waited until the last short-timer walked out. "You can plan on leaving by troop train on the fifteenth of August. We'll be going to Jacksonville, Florida, where we'll board the USS *Boxer*. It's a small aircraft carrier that will haul the squadron's choppers and most of the people. We should reach Vietnam four weeks after sailing. I suggest you plan on bringing along a lot of reading material. Are there any questions?"

Lee Calhoon raised his hand. "Sir, what about Maggie?"

"Maggie stays here. There's an order that no pets are to be taken overseas. Any more questions?"

One of the married soldiers stood. "Sir, can we get some time off with our families before we ship?"

Flynn stepped up beside Owens to answer the question. Leaves were his department. "Yeah, all married troops will get ten days' leave. Single soldiers will get five days' leave on a rotational basis. Any more questions? . . . Good, we still have work to do packing the shit in the supply room. Move down to supply and take your instructions from Sergeant Bates. Alexander?"

"Yes, Sergeant!"

"Since Peters ain't goin', you're the actin' squad leader till we get some-body else.". Shawn winked. "Don't fuck it up."

Shocked, Blake only nodded and closed his open mouth.

Thirty minutes later Blake was in the supply room overseeing his squad load equipment into boxes when Sergeant Flynn strode in.

"Alexander, come here a sec." Blake followed his sergeant, who stepped back into the hallway to keep their discussion private.

Shawn sighed as if tired as soon as Blake stood before him. "I got bad news. I just got a call from Sergeant Major. Looks like you and your squad ain't gonna get a leave. You've all been given a special mission and will be leavin' the fifth instead of the fifteenth from Lawson Army Air Field."

"No way!" said Blake angrily. "I don't care about going home, but my guys haven't been home since going to basic. Didn't you tell the Sergeant Major that?"

Shawn stiffened. "Look, 'Squad Leader,' I ain't just a fuckin' messenger boy. Hell yes I told him! I argued with him and it still ain't over 'cause I got the lieutenant involved and he's lookin' into it from officer channels. But it don't look good. The special mission came down from the colonel's office."

Blake lowered his head. "I'm sorry, Sergeant. I know you tried . . . it's just that it's so damn unfair. Vinny and Eugene had plans to leave tomor-row for Pennsylvania."

Shawn put his hand on Blake's shoulder. "I know what you're thinkin'. You're askin' yourself 'how am I gonna tell 'em they ain't goin'?' There ain't no easy way, Alexander, bad news don't get better with age. Tell 'em now so they can call or write home and tell their folks and girlfriends."

"It's not fair," said Blake, shaking his head in frustration.

Shawn patted his squad leader's shoulder. "It never is. You just learned the truth of our profession . . . the Army always comes first." Shawn gave Blake a last pat on the back and walked down the hall toward his office.

Blake took in a deep breath to steel himself before stepping back inside the supply room. His previous pride in being given the temporary squad leader position was gone. He wished someone else had gotten the job and was the one to have to look into his friends' eyes and tell them they wouldn't be going home before going to Vietnam.

18

The six men of the first squad of Charlie troop stood by Lawson Army Airfield, waiting for a ride. For the preceding week they had collected lumber, nails, and hand tools. They had been following secret orders that had been written on a piece of paper delivered by the squadron commander's driver. Sergeant Flynn helped them find a truck to haul the materials to the airfield and now stood with them as they awaited final instructions.

Shawn checked their bags and glanced down the runway. "You guys have everything, so it looks like you're ready. Do a good job at whatever you're supposed to do and I'll see you on the fifteenth when the rest of the troop gets there. Stay outta trouble and remember you'll be representing the First Cav."

Frustrated at all of the secrecy, Blake motioned toward the truckload of lumber behind him. "What the hell is going on, Sergeant? Nobody's told us what we're supposed to do when we get to Jacksonville and what this secret mission is."

Shawn took off his cap and wiped the sweat from his forehead. "Alexander, I don't know a damn thing more than you do. I've checked with every buddy I got to find out, 'cause I don't like it any more than you do. All I can say is that this is being run at the top, and nobody knows but the colonel. By the way, Alexander, it's not much of a consolation, but you did a hell of a job organizing the squad to accomplish the mission. I haven't appointed a squad leader 'cause I thought we'd be getting a buck sergeant in. We haven't got one, so I'm making you the acting squad leader."

Calhoon, Eugene, and Vincent all slapped Blake on the back and offered their hands in congratulations.

Shawn turned at the sound of an approaching Chinook helicopter. The big double-rotor machine landed a minute later and lowered its tail ramp. Smiling, Lieutenant Colonel John Stockton marched down the ramp and strode directly toward the surprised men.

Shawn called his men to attention and saluted. Stockton returned the salute and halted before the wide-eyed men of the first squad. He waited until the Chinook engines ceased their whine.

"Troopers, you're probably wondering what the hell all the secrecy is

231

about. Well, the reason is driving up behind you."

The squad turned to see a pickup with a horse trailer pull up beside the truck of lumber.

"In the trailer is the ol' gal. I'm not leaving her behind for these post weenies. Maggie is going with us to Vietnam. I've flown down to Jacksonville and talked to the ship's captain and struck a deal. He's going to haul her for us, but I had to guarantee she would have a stall and that we'd keep everything nice and sanitary. You troopers are going to take Maggie to Jacksonville, build her a corral on board the carrier, and take care of her during the voyage. I know ya might think it's a shit detail, but it's important to the squadron . . . and me. I picked you troopers 'cause you've taken such good care of her, and I think you care about Maggie like I do. What I'm doing is in direct violation of orders, so it must be kept secret until we get to Nam. You're going early, so nobody knows . . . the press won't be snoopin' around until the squadron arrives on the fifteenth. You're gonna have to build the corral and take Maggie on board as early as you can, then take it easy and wait on the rest of us. In the Chinook is hay, oats, and everything else she needs. Three of you will fly down with the load to include the lumber you've collected. The other three will drive down with Maggie." The colonel took out an envelope from his pocket and held it up. "Who is the squad leader?"

Shawn motioned to Blake. "Sir, this is acting corporal Alexander. I just made him the squad leader a few minutes ago."

Stockton smiled good-naturedly at Blake. "Well, son, it's a hell of a day. You make squad leader and your first order is given by the squadron commander himself. Son, this envelope contains a list of all your contacts in Jacksonville and money for expenses. Your mission is to get Maggie to Jacksonville safely and to get her aboard the ship without the whole world knowing about it. Simply put, take care of the squadron mascot and don't fuck it up."

Blake took the envelope and saluted. "Yes, sir."

Stockton returned the salute with an even wider smile and shifted his attention to Shawn. "Make this squad leader a real corporal before he leaves, and promote the others to specialists. I can't have our squadron mascot being cared for by buck privates." He winked and strode toward his waiting sedan, which had followed the pickup.

Shawn waited until the colonel was gone before addressing the squad. "Okay, the mystery is over. The old man is hanging himself out on this one. The order of no pets to Nam was aimed directly at Maggie, so the old man's career is on the line. Alexander, you are now a full-fledged corporal, and the rest of you are now specialists fourth class. I'll square away the paperwork with the sergeant major later and bring down the rank patches when I see ya on the fifteenth. Alexander, ya got your mission. Organize the way you see fit and do it."

Blake nodded with confidence and motioned to the truck. "Okay, let's unload the truck and put the lumber on the chopper. Vinny, you and Smitty and Prescott will fly down with the stuff and . . ."

Shawn saw that he wasn't needed further. He walked toward the parking lot, reflecting on the situation. The first of his men were leaving. The Green Machine was finally in motion. The First Cavalry Division was beginning to roll toward war.

COLUMBUS, 14 AUGUST

Shawn sat across the dinner table from Cindy, watching her eat. She set down her fork.

"Why are you staring at me?"

"I was thinking how lucky I am to have you to look at. I think we should—"

"Don't say it, Shawn. I told you before, I'm not going to talk about it."

Shawn kept his eyes on her. "Cindy, marry me."

"No."

"Why not?"

She looked up at him for just an instant and quickly averted her eyes. "You know why."

Shawn reached across the table and took her hand. "I *don't* know why. All I know is I love you and you're having our child."

Cindy lowered her head. "I'm not losing this baby. Thinking and worrying about you all the time when you're gone will make me sick, heartsick, but sick nevertheless. You don't know what it's like and how I feel when you're away."

Shawn searched her eyes. "What's going to happen when I leave tomorrow?"

Her chin trembled. "I'll cry, but I'll get over it. I have my baby to think about. I'll put you out of my mind and think about the future."

Shawn maintained his stare. "Cindy, you are going to marry me today. Taco is going to be here in a few minutes. It's all arranged. Don't argue with me, just listen. Forget about me if it makes it easier for you. Think only of our baby. Married, you'll have an ID card, and you'll be able to go to the post hospital and be properly cared for by the Army for free. If something happens to me, there is government insurance and plenty of benefits. You'll also get money from me to live on, especially when you have to quit work when it's time for the baby to come. Cindy, I can't leave here without knowing our child will be cared for. I'm responsible, and I have to do what's right."

Cindy lifted her head and was about to speak when a knock came at the trailer door.

Shawn spoke loudly. "Come in."

John Quail walked in and nodded toward Cindy with a tentative smile. "You ready to get hitched, little lady?"

Cindy closed her tear-filled eyes and shook her head no. Quail glanced at Shawn and motioned with his head to go on to the car. Quail sat down beside the crying woman and put his arm around her shoulder. "Cindy, I have just one question for you and I want an honest answer. Do you love him?"

Cindy took in a breath and wiped her eyes with the back of her hand. "Yes, John, but—"

Quail stood. "No buts, let's go." He pulled back her chair and took her hands and pulled her to her feet.

Cindy looked into his caring eyes. "John, you don't know about me. You don't—"

"I know you, Cindy. I know you're confused and you think you'll fall apart once he's gone. You won't. I know you're much stronger than that. Come on, it's time. It's time to quit worrying about your past and begin thinking of the future."

He led her to the open door and offered his arm for support. Cindy wiped her eyes again, raised her head, and squared her shoulders. She took the sergeant major's arm and began walking down the trailer steps. She would go and they would be married, but she knew it wouldn't change how she felt or what had happened in her past. Everyone she had ever loved had left her: Todd, her first husband; Timmy, dying so young; and now, tomorrow, Shawn. When they left, they took a piece of her with them. The baby she and Shawn had made was all she had left. She had saved enough of herself to love the child. The baby was her last chance, her last hope of keeping the bad memories away. Hope was her reason for wanting to continue to live. Hope was alive inside her. Despite her love for Shawn, he would soon be like Timmy—a painful memory that had to be locked away in a special place.

15 AUGUST

Shawn gave his wife a last hug and backed up to say his farewell. Cindy raised a finger to his lips. "No, Shawn, don't say anything. Don't make any promises or tell me you love me. I know how you feel. Just go and come back to me as soon as you can. Know that I love you and I'll be here with our child when you come home."

Shawn leaned forward and gave her a last kiss, then picked up his bag and walked down the trailer steps to the waiting cab. He didn't look back until the cab was pulling away. Tears were streaming down Cindy's face as she stood in the doorway, waving good-bye. Shawn raised his hand and hoped she realized how much he loved her. The machine was rolling.

Corporal Blake Alexander escorted his platoon sergeant down a maze of passageways to the lower hangar bay. There, in the fantail, Maggie stood in a ten-by-ten-foot stall filled with hay. "We built it in a day and got Maggie in that night. We didn't have any problems . . . Well, that's not quite true. The damn swabbies have been a pain in the ass with all their wisecracks and we've taken a lotta shit from them, but all in all it's gone smooth."

Shawn nodded in approval and inspected the stall. "Ya done good." He turned his attention to the rest of the huge bay, which was filled with helicopters. "When did they stow the birds?"

Blake poured half a bucket of oats into a can for Maggie. "Half of 'em were here when we got in. They've been putting 'em in ever since. They finished up yesterday. You think they're packed in tight, wait till ya see where the platoon is sleepin'. We have hammocks strung up four high, and there's hardly any room to move . . . The food ain't bad, but you'd better warn the guys about the swabbies. They're a bunch of shitbirds and don't care much for us grunts. I almost had to tie up Vinny so he wouldn't punch one of 'em out."

Blake got no reaction in reply except a slight nod. Blake had noticed when he first met Flynn on the pier that he had seemed preoccupied.

"Sarge, you all right?" Blake asked with concern.

Shawn nodded absently and turned toward the hatchway. "Guess you'd better show me where the platoon is bunkin' and where they'll store their gear. I need to get 'em on board and get settled in. This is going to be one long, boring trip."

Blake led the way to the sleeping bay. He figured that his sergeant must have been exhausted from the train ride. With some rest, Flynn would be his old self tomorrow.

U.S.S. *BOXER*, 17 AUGUST

Blake, Vincent, Eugene, and Lee stood by the rail, watching the setting sun extinguish itself into the sea. Blake sighed. "Our first day at sea, we're finally going to war. It's hard to believe that just months ago we all sat tied together with buddy ropes, trying to learn each other's names."

Eugene spoke reflectively. "We became friends, soldiers, infantrymen, then paratroopers. Now we're cavalrymen, and in another month we can call ourselves veterans. There's not much else we could do."

Lee nodded in agreement, while Vincent gazed silently at the shimmering wake of the carrier.

Sergeant Flynn was leaning on the rail only ten feet away from the young soldiers. His mind was on a woman living in a rusted trailer.

Blake looked past his friends to the sergeant. Something was wrong with his boss. Flynn had not improved over the previous two days. He seemed to have withdrawn into himself. He had hardly even come around to check on the platoon.

Blake moved down the rail closer and spoke softly so the others wouldn't hear. "Sarge, you feeling all right? I mean you seem kinda down."

Shawn reluctantly broke from his reverie. "I'm fine. Just thinkin'."

Blake had heard about his sergeant's exploits in Korea and Vietnam and thought he might get the old vet to share some war stories. "You were probably thinkin' about when you shipped to Korea. It probably hasn't changed much, huh?"

Shawn's eyes suddenly focused. "Korea?" He backed up and looked at the young corporal as if seeing him for the first time. "Why'd you ask if I was feeling sick? You're about the hundredth troop to ask me that."

Blake was taken back by the sudden transformation from meek to mean sergeant.

Blake shrugged. "Well, you've been awfully quiet, and we haven't seen much of ya. I thought maybe you were down with some kind of bug. A lot of the guys are moping around homesick, but I know for a vet like you, that's not possible. I was hopin' maybe when ya got to feelin' better, ya'd tell us some stories about Vietnam. We haven't had much of a chance to learn about Nam, with the loading out of equipment and all."

Shawn didn't blink or move a muscle as he kept his penetrating stare fixed on the young soldier. Finally, after a full ten seconds of silence, he spoke. "You asked if I was thinking about shipping to Korea. No, I wasn't thinking of Korea, but you reminded me that I should have been. I stood on a deck like this one, with friends just like you and your squad. I was about your age and scared to death. I wasn't sure I was ready. When I got to Korea, I found out I wasn't. They had taught us by the book . . . the fuckin' book didn't even come close to what it was really like. You reminded me of something that I swore I'd never forget. I wasn't ready for combat. I wished somebody had sat me down and taught me a few simple lessons that I ended up having to learn the hard way."

Shawn glanced back to the red horizon and mentally cast overboard his image of Cindy, crying and waving good-bye. It had been tearing him up. He had missed her so much that he'd spent most of his time feeling sorry for himself.

Shawn backed away from the rail and squared his shoulders before again looking at the corporal. "I was not ready for combat, but you and this platoon will be. Alexander, inform the other squad leaders I want them and their men on the fantail after chow. Your first class will be tonight." Shawn turned to go but shot a glance at Blake. "Thanks for reminding me."

Shawn opened the hatchway and disappeared into the darkness. There was no time to think about his wife now. It was time to teach his young expendables the truth about war. They had to know that they couldn't defeat the bitch, but had to form an allegiance with her and become as cold and unforgiving as she was. They had to learn to accept confusion, uncertainty, and fear. They had to accept death because war *was* death. They had to beat the bitch at her own game and survive. They had to become killers and give her the blood she wanted.

Staff Sergeant Shawn Flynn waited until his platoon was assembled before telling them to sit down and make themselves comfortable. In their faces he saw himself as he had been years before, and he felt his confidence growing.

"Men, I was reminded today that I have been failing you. I was walking around in a daze, feeling lower than whale shit. I was caught in the trap that most of you are in right now. I was thinking of home and feeling sorry for myself. Well, ol' Irish is back and he's gonna kick ass. The first thing you all must do is clear your heads of home, girlfriends, wives, or loved ones. Put them in the back of your brains and start thinking about that bastard out there who is waiting for you. He's waiting for First Platoon. He's waiting on his own turf to put a bullet between your eyes. Picture him in your minds, respect him, hate him, then . . . kill him.

"Men, you'll be getting training schedules when I'm finished talking. The new schedule will keep you busy from the time you get up in the mornings till you hit the hammocks at night. You are about to begin Flynn's finishing school for killers. We're going to go over the basics, then move up to the finer skills on how to survive. You're going to know your weapons like you've never known them before. Tomorrow, you will draw your M-16s and carry them everywhere you go, including to bed. In Vietnam, that is what you're going to do, so we're going to learn now. Your weapon is a killer. It will kill whatever you shoot at—including yourself or your buddy if you don't think about safety. Or, if you're good, you could even shoot at the enemy. In Vietnam you're going to be issued live ammunition and your weapon will be loaded at all times. Nobody in my platoon is going to die dumb. You will know your weapon and how to handle her safely until you want to use her. You're going to be able to take her apart blindfolded, as you will the M-60s and the M-79 grenade launchers.

"We will have P.T. twice a day to keep you in shape. We will have classes on how to call and adjust artillery fire and gunships. We're going to learn how to read a map and how to talk on a radio. We are going to learn first aid that goes beyond simple life-saving steps. You'll be able to give a buddy an IV and take care of a sucking chest wound, just to mention a few things on the schedule. You're going to learn how to carry your equipment for combat and how to use munitions, like hand grenades and explosives, without killing yourselves. You're going to learn about your enemy and what weapons he carries and how he employs them.

"Men, in short, we're going to focus our minds and bodies on two things—killing and surviving. You are going to learn to hate me because

I will not let you think of anything else. The lieutenant and I are going to be relentless. We will not let you get away with anything half-assed. You will do it right or you will do it again and again until you've got it done cold. You are going to learn from me that you check everything and then check it again.

"Remember this tonight. You cannot be thinking of home or your girl while in the field or you are going to die. You will die dumb. It's the worst death there is, because it's senseless. Pick up the training schedules as you file back to your bunks. You are dismissed—but think about that bastard tonight . . . that bastard who is waiting for you."

The following morning after P.T. Shawn approached the first squad. The men were resting by Maggie's stall. "Alexander, what the hell do you think you're doing?" he barked at Blake.

Blake stood up and shrugged his shoulders. "We were just taking a break before your next class."

Shawn took two steps, grabbed Martino's weapon from his hands and tossed it at Blake. "Tell me, squad leader, what's wrong with that weapon?"

Blake looked down at the black weapon and turned it over in his hands. "Aw, shit, it's not on safe," he mumbled.

Shawn grabbed the weapon away from Blake and pointed it at Martino and pulled the trigger. To Blake the metallic click of the firing pin ramming forward seemed as loud as a real bullet being fired. Shawn swung the rifle toward Prescott.

"Squad leader, you will find that Prescott's weapon is also not on safe. *You did not check your people, and now you have two dead men! You* were thinking only of yourself and getting a little rest. *You* did not think or care for your men! You failed, squad leader! Check them! Recheck them! Think of what could go wrong and check! *You* don't rest, squad leader, until you've thought of and checked everything. Is that clear?"

Blake nodded sheepishly.

Shawn's jaw tightened, *"Don't nod at me!* Tell me what you're going to do about it!"

Blake snapped to attention. "I'm going to check and recheck, Sergeant!"

Shawn's eyes shifted from the young squad leader to the other five men who now were on their feet. *"You failed* to check your buddies! You are going to die dumb unless you start thinking, and doing something about it!"

Shawn spun around and strode down the bay like a rampaging bull.

Vincent shook his head once the sergeant was out of sight. "I'm sorry, Ace. I thought it was on safe."

Blake waved the apology away. "I shoulda checked like he said. Everybody check your weapons again and give me an up."

Ten minutes later the platoon was gathered in the weapons bay that served as the classroom. Lieutenant Owens held up a picture of a Viet Cong soldier dressed in black.

"Men, this is your enemy. He believes in what he's doing. He carries a pack with only the basic essentials, and a rifle just as good as yours. He can march all day on a handful of rice and drink nothing but paddy water. He is well-trained and knows how to survive. He is not a giant or a magician. He is nothing more than a man. If you cut him, he bleeds. If you shoot him, he dies. This man can be defeated by you if you don't fear him. *He . . . must fear you!* If he fears you, you have the advantage. Fear makes a man panic. If you panic, you don't aim and you don't squeeeeeeze the trigger, you jerk the trigger and miss your target. Fear makes a man move when he should stay hidden. Fear takes control of your mind and body and you die!

"How do you overcome fear? The answer is confidence in yourself and your weapon. *You know you are good!* You know you will kill him. You know that your buddies, squad, and platoon are like you and are good. If you *know* you're better, you are."

Owens held the picture up again. "This class is going to teach you the weakness of your enemy. It will show you what signs he leaves behind and how you can find him and kill him. First, he's like you and needs the basics to survive, food and water. He must stay close to sources of water and . . ."

During the class break, Blake checked his men's weapons before letting them go to the latrine. He checked the last man and was about to turn around when Sergeant Flynn growled, "Alexander, come here."

Blake jogged over to the sergeant, who was glaring at him with narrowed eyes. "Did I see you checking the weapons of your people?"

"Yes, Sergeant, I checked each man."

"Wrong! Have your team leaders check and give you an up. Use your team leaders. Spot check now and then, but don't do your team leader's job or he will let you do it all, and you don't have time. Got it?"

Blake looked directly into the sergeant's eyes. "Yes, Sergeant . . . thank you."

The next two weeks were a blur of classes and ass chewings. Flynn had been truthful. He and the lieutenant had been relentless in making sure everyone carried out all instructions to the letter. The first platoon was easy to spot. They were the only ones carrying weapons and always moving. During breaks they quizzed each other or read notes. When the rest of the troop laughed and joked during chow, the first platoon sat together and went over checklists and asked each other questions. Sergeant Flynn and Lieutenant Owens seemed to be everywhere, always hitting when they were least expected.

Martino was feeding oats to Maggie when Owens strode up and barked,

"Specialist Martino, if you're following an azimuth of 360 degrees, what is your back azimuth?"

Vincent closed his eyes, picturing the compass he had trained with over the past two days. "Sir, the back azimuth would be 180 degrees or due south."

"Correct," Owens blurted back. "Now, what are the things you must consider and must do before you throw a hand grenade?"

"Sir, first I check if there are branches or other stuff blocking my toss so the grenade don't go and bounce back at me. Second, I make sure I got cover so I won't get hit by no shrapnel. I pull the pin an' yell 'grenade' so my buddies know I'm throwin' it and they can hit the dirt. I throw the grenade, exposin' myself as little as I can, then hit the ground, usin' the cover to protect myself, but also makin' sure my rifle is ready to follow up if I have to."

"Eh . . . that's right," Owens said, showing his surprise. "Good job, carry on."

Later, Owens called his platoon sergeant over. "Irish, these guys are really gettin' good. I couldn't find a single trooper who didn't know his memory work or understand the principles of what we've been teaching them. What the hell we gonna do now to keep them on their toes?"

Shawn let himself smile for the first time in ten days. He had been driving himself and his men hard. The good news was that it had all paid off.

"Sir, we now start phase two of the school. So far, we've covered individual training. Now we need to teach them how to put it all together and train as a squad. I figure patrolling is next on the agenda."

Owens rolled his eyes. "Come on, how can they patrol on this tub?"

Shawn grinned. "Sir, you gotta use your imagination . . . all we gotta do is get some maps and . . ."

Corporal Blake Alexander sweated profusely as he knelt on the deck with a map spread out before him. The map was the standard military, multicolored 1:50,000 type that covered a small portion of the South Vietnam highlands. Minutes before, Flynn had told Blake to pretend he was in the village of An Khe and that he had been given a mission to ambush a trail. Flynn pointed out the trail on the map. Blake was to brief his squad on how they would accomplish their mission.

Blake finally looked up from the map and motioned his squad closer.

"Okay guys, this is what we're gonna do. We leave from here, An Khe, and go across these fields and through this forest and get to the road here. From there we go north to the ambush site, here, where we hide along the trail and wait for the V.C."

Sergeant Flynn, who had been standing behind the squad, stepped forward. "Squad leader, is that all you want to tell your squad?"

Blake glanced first at the map then back to the sergeant. "I think that pretty much covers what we would do."

Shawn pointed at Lee. "What do you think, Calhoon? Did your squad leader cover everything?"

"Well, I reckon we ought to know when we're going," Lee said thoughtfully, "and maybe how we gonna get back after we hit 'em. We might even plan us some artillery targets, if we was to run into somethin' along the way."

Shawn nodded and suddenly rattled at Blake, "Who is the compass man? Who is the point man? Who is the radioman, and what is the radio frequency you're using? What are your men carrying for the mission? Water? Food? First-aid kit? Claymores? What happens if you get ambushed along the way? What happens if you get killed or wounded, who takes over? Do they know your plan well enough to carry it off? Are you going to have a patrol base or are you going to walk right up on the ambush site and not recon first? How are you going to organize your ambush, who is your left and right security, and who is going to initiate the ambush? What happens if an enemy battalion walks down the trail instead of a squad? Who checks the bodies after you ambush the enemy? What are you looking for on the bodies?"

Blake's eyes cringed a little more with each stinging question. The thought of being responsible for the men in his squad and having missed so many important questions was like getting stabbed over and over again with a dull knife.

Shawn sat down beside the young corporal. "Squad leader, don't you think you and your men would want to know those things before your squad went out, at night, through enemy territory, to ambush some guys who didn't want to die?"

Blake lowered his head, feeling useless. "I fucked it up."

Shawn surprised Blake and the squad by laughing aloud. "Hell, Alexander, you didn't fuck up. You haven't been taught warning orders and operations orders yet. I was just making a point as a lead-in to my next class, and you made it easy for me." Shawn turned his attention to the rest of the squad. "Men, you and your squad leader are going to memorize a warning order format and operations order format. They will help you organize your thoughts so that you don't forget important information you'll need to accomplish on your mission. Let's look at the map again and talk through the mission I gave Alexander. First, we have to analyze the mission. What that means is . . ."

Blake tried to absorb every word and thanked God he was on board a ship called *Boxer* rather than in the village called An Khe.

———

Eugene motioned to the calendar by his hammock. "Check it out. We've been on board this bucket for almost three and half weeks. Now I know what prison is like."

Blake swung out of his hammock. "I wouldn't be a swabbie for all the gold in Fort Knox. They can have the Navy. The only good thing about this trip has been what we've learned. I'm glad we've had the time to get ready."

Vincent was putting on his fatigue pants and frowning. "These classes is gettin' to me. I sleep and still I hear the sergeant talkin' to me. I'm gettin' so smart I'm scarin' myself."

Lee watched his three friends as they dressed. He couldn't help but notice how different they had become over the past weeks aboard ship. They all kept their rifles at no more than an arm's length away as they put on their uniforms, and immediately picked them up when they were finished. They checked their weapons automatically every few minutes and glanced at their buddies' weapons as well. It had become second nature. All of them wore no underwear or T-shirts under the fatigues, at Flynn's guidance. The sergeant had said that in Nam the heat was so bad, the cotton underwear and T-shirts kept in all the moisture and caused chafing that could lead to infection. It had been the most difficult thing for Lee to get used to—not wearing underwear. It didn't seem natural. But neither was sleeping with an M-16. Now he wondered why he had ever worn underwear in the first place.

They were changing in other ways too. The classes had drilled them so thoroughly that they were all talking, acting, and thinking more and more alike. And they were becoming more like their teacher, Sergeant Flynn.

Blake noticed Lee's distant expression. "Yo, Reb, you ain't thinkin' of home, I hope."

Lee smiled. "Naw, I was thinkin' how much we've learned and how we all soundin' and thinkin' like Flynn."

Vincent puffed out his chest in indignation. "Not me! Flynn, he likes fuckin' with us. I ain't thinkin'a ways to fuck with you guys."

"You fucked with me yesterday, man," Eugene retorted hotly. "Just 'cause I forgot to pull the bolt back on the M-60, you got all bent outta shape and made me do it five times . . . that's fuckin' with us!"

Vincent faced his accuser with a smirk. "You can't fire unless the bolt is back. I was just tryin' to make sure you learned how to do it right. You gotta know stuff like that."

Eugene broke into a smile and raised an eyebrow. "Hey, dudes, do you hear Sergeant Flynn talkin' here? He's now got a South Philly accent."

Vincent lowered his head in defeat. The point was made.

Eugene placed another X on his calendar and laid his head back on the hammock. They had been at sea for almost a month and had finally gotten word at the evening class that the morning's training schedule was canceled. Instead they were to pack their gear. Tomorrow they would be arriving in Vietnam at a seaport called Qui Nhon.

Eugene began to close his eyes when Vincent ran into the crowded bay with a strained expression. He slid to a halt in front of Eugene and tugged at his arm.

"Come on. We got trouble."

Eugene rose up. "What's going on, man?"

Vincent tossed Eugene's boots to him. "Some fuckin' swab branded Maggie with 'USN.' We can't find the Reb, and we figure he's out lookin' for the bastard. Reb will kill 'em!"

Eugene quickly slipped on his boots and broke into a run. Minutes later, in a hatchway heading for the second-deck hangar, they heard a scream. Blake was in the lead, having joined the hunt. He darted down a side passage toward the sound.

Lee swung his rifle butt up, striking an attacking sailor's arm, diverting the blow. The sailor screamed in pain and fell on the bloody deck beside another groaning machinist's mate. Lee's head recoiled forward from a blow from the back, and he spun around to face another attacker.

"Come on! I want all of ya!"

A big yeoman wearing a filthy T-shirt held up his massive arms to halt the seven other angry sailors. *"Back off!* He's mine."

Lee glared at the huge man and snarled, "You gonna pay for hurtin' her."

The sailor snickered. "That nag deserved what she got, and you're gonna be next!"

Lee attacked with a jab of the rifle barrel to the man's midsection. The yeoman sidestepped the lunge and struck Lee in the mouth with a crunching right jab. The blow snapped Lee's head back, but he kept up his forward attack, surprising the man. Off balance now, the shocked sailor tried to recover by shifting his weight to land another blow, but it was too late. Lee viciously jammed the rifle butt directly into the sailor's exposed stomach. The yeoman expelled a rush of air as his body contorted with the blow. His eyes were bulging out of their sockets as he sunk to his knees.

Lee tried to jerk the rifle free, but the sailor had grasped the barrel in a death grip.

Two sailors were moving in to finish Lee off, when suddenly the small bay was filled with the deafening slam of the hatch door being shut. The sailors spun around to see Blake, Vincent, and Eugene standing in front of the closed hatch. The three men were holding their M-16s in the parry position.

With the distraction, Lee freed his rifle and began swinging at the closest standing sailor. Blake ran forward, seeing that the sailors were not in the mood for any more fighting.

"Lee! Lee, stop it!"

With blood trickling from cuts above his eye and mouth, he stepped menacingly toward the sailors and screamed crazily, *"Which one of ya did it!"*

Afraid that the crazed man would kill them all, a short sailor pointed to one of his mates.

"Willy did it! He made the brand and burned the—"

Lee had already spun around to deal with the man whom the sailor had pointed out. The yeoman was still on his knees, wheezing for air, when Lee struck with a knee into the man's chin. The yeoman recoiled back with the blow and banged his head on the steel bulkhead. Lee had raised his rifle to knock out the stunned man's yellow teeth when Blake grabbed him.

Lee's face contorted in rage. His eyes were wild and unseeing. He broke the grip with a vicious jerk and raised the rifle again. Blake stepped in front of the gagging sailor, blocking Lee's attack.

"Reb, it's over!"

Lee's chest heaved as his stone-cold eyes penetrated the man before him. It took him a moment to realize that it was Blake. Lee's eyes changed their expression from hatred to confusion.

Vincent sighed in relief. He had thought for an instant Lee had been going to strike Blake. He looked past his friends to the two sailors writhing on the floor and glanced back at Lee. Of all people, Lee Calhoon would have been the last he would have thought to possess such pent-up rage. Inside the quiet soldier was another man, a man he would never want to face as an opponent.

Eugene motioned for the sailors to help their downed buddies, and grabbed Lee's arm.

"Come on, we gotta get outta here before any brass shows up."

Blake turned toward the short sailor. "We're even. No use in reporting this happened, is there?"

The sailor had been warned, like everybody else on ship, that if interservice fighting broke out, the fighters would be dealt with harshly. A cell and bread and water was not his idea of spending a port call in Vietnam. He agreed with a nod.

"Yeah, I'll tell the others." He motioned toward Lee. "You'd better watch that fucker—he's crazy mean."

Blake looked at Lee, still disbelieving what he'd seen. "Yeah, I guess he is."

Eugene lay back down in his hammock and smiled. "Yo, Vinny, I think the Reb has taken the training too seriously. He thinks we're in Vietnam and the V.C. wear white sailor hats."

Vincent glanced at Lee on the lower bunk. "Yeah, he's been holdin' out on us."

Lee hurt too bad to sit up. "Lay off, y'all. I reckon it just riled me seein' Maggie with that brand. Them swabs shoulda left her be. She weren't hurtin' nobody."

Blake couldn't help but smile. "I was just thinkin'. You know those bastards who are waiting on us? Well, they'd better watch out. They don't know what fear is until they see the Reb get 'riled.'"

Eugene joined in the laughter and closed his eyes to sleep. He pictured the enemy in his mind and smirked. Blake was right. The bastards better pray they don't meet the team.

19

The thirty-eight men of Charlie troop's blue platoon stood in the semi-darkness of the lower hangar bay, M-16s and duffel bags on their shoulders. Far above, a metallic monster groaned, hissed, and clanked. Suddenly a brilliant shaft of golden light bathed the platoon. The starboard aircraft elevator had begun its descent from the flight deck. Several minutes later the platoon felt a shudder beneath their feet and the platform began rising toward the sun. The pungent oily, metallic odor of the carrier's lower decks dissipated, replaced with a new smell, the smell of land. The elevator clanked into place like a piece of a jigsaw puzzle.

The men of the blue platoon did not march off the elevator as they had been told. Instead they stood mesmerized by the sight before them. Nestled in the sunlit harbor, floating on picture-book blue water, were carriers, destroyers, and transports of every description. Beyond the gray ships were bustling piers, and beyond them, rows of royal palm trees around a pastel-colored town. After almost four weeks below decks, the assault of dazzling colors, strange smells, and frantic activity was too much for their minds to register. The scene was a perfect mental postcard, and they wanted to remember it forever.

Sergeant Shawn Flynn waited on the flight deck for his men. "Come on, Blues," he bellowed impatiently, "ya ain't tourists. Put your eyes back in your heads and *moooveit!* Form up on me!"

The platoon broke from their trance and quickly formed a semicircle around their sergeant. Shawn motioned for them to put down their bags. Lieutenant Owens stepped forward.

"Men, last night I was briefed by the troop commander on what we're going to be doing. You're gonna hear lots of rumors, so I wanted to set the facts straight. First, the good news. We are not staying here in Qui Nhon to help unload the ships. We're flying in choppers to our new base today. The bad news is that our new base is in An Khe and it's not exactly what you'd call a vacation summer camp. The First Cav sent an advance party of almost a thousand men to the base a month ago, and they've cleared a landing zone, but it's still not finished. We're going to help finish clearing the landing zone, then help finish building the base. I know it's not what you expected, but it's what we're gonna do. Any questions?"

Lee Calhoon raised his hand. Owens smiled patiently and motioned for him to lower his arm. "I know what you're gonna ask, Calhoon. What about Maggie? Maggie flies out of here in forty-five minutes on the squadron commander's bird. You and the rest of the first squad will be going with her."

"Sir," Lee spoke up worriedly, "the colonel's helicopter is a Huey. How is Maggie gonna—"

"Wait and see," the lieutenant said with a sly grin.

Forty-five minutes later the first squad sat on the vibrating floor of the colonel's UH-1 as it steadily gained altitude over the harbor. Dangling twenty feet below the Huey was Maggie, securely tied into a modified cargo net. The men of the First Cavalry who were unloading the precious cargo of helicopters and ammunition looked up at the unusual sight. Then it happened. A single soldier cheered, and then another, and then another. Soon the entire harbor was filled with the voices of cheering men. Maggie had become their symbol. A perfect symbol—a mule, a hard-headed mule, who was cantankerous, like her colonel, like all the men of the First Cav. The first airmobile division in the world was flying to its base in a foreign land by helicopter, and they were taking their mule with them, and to hell with the brass who said they couldn't.

24 SEPTEMBER

Corporal Blake Alexander closed his stinging eyes and staggered back from the small tree he was killing. Feeling faint, he grabbed a low tree branch to keep himself from keeling over. He took in several labored breaths and raised his head. He was losing the war. They were beating him. He would kill one, but behind that one were thousands more.

He heard laughter and shifted his bloodshot, stinging eyes to the source. Goddamn him! Goddamn his stupid laugh and even stupider grin. God, he hated Lee Calhoon's hick, dumb-ass grin.

Blake's head was pounding as if his cranium was a bell. The heavy striker hit one temple then swung back through his simmering brain to hit the other. Each thunderous, reverberating blow sent tremors through his entire body, causing his eyes to bulge farther and farther. The sticky heat rose from the rotting jungle floor like thick tendrils that entwined his body and squeezed out his strength. Didn't the others see what was happening? Couldn't they see they were losing?

Through a blurry cloud he heard laughter, but his eyes would no longer focus to tell him who it was. He knew anyway. It was all of them. They were watching him and laughing because he was failing. His father was right. He'd known all along his son would never be a real Alexander, never be anything but a loser.

The squad had arrived in An Khe ten days before. The helicopter ride with Maggie to the desolate outpost had been wondrous. They had flown over vibrant rice paddies displaying every possible hue of green, and beautiful mountains covered in steaming rain forests. The country had looked like a paradise from the air. When they had landed, they were filled with excitement. Then they were immediately plunged into stark reality.

Within five minutes of landing, Blake Alexander had learned the first truth—Vietnam was *no* paradise. The beauty of the flight had been a sickening joke played on his mind. It was like seeing a beautiful woman in the distance who, upon coming closer, turned out to be a warty, scab-covered old man. Vietnam, and in particular An Khe, was the hottest, ugliest, filthiest, most unmerciful place he had ever been in his life. The second truth he learned was that An Khe was no base. It was a squalid concentration camp, complete with thin, emaciated prisoners, barbed wire, and bamboo guard towers. It was right out of the movie *Bridge on the River Kwai,* except that there was no bridge. Instead there was a huge landing zone hacked out of the jungle by hand. Even now men were hacking down foliage to make the field larger.

The squad collected their bags and were shown where to bivouac by a sunburned sergeant, who gave Blake two machetes and pointed to a solid wall of small trees, brush, vines, and ant mounds.

"Make yourself at home . . . I mean, make yourself 'a' home," he said with a laugh.

It had taken the rest of the day to chop, hack, pull, and dig themselves out a large enough area in the jungle for Maggie and them to set up their shelter halves. That first night had been the worst of Blake's life. He had sweltered in the heat of his canvas tent and at the same time shivered in frozen fear from the terrifying night sounds. Gunfire, artillery, and screams were the only sounds he knew and understood. It was the other noises, the screeching, squealing, and unexplained crackling, that caused his body to stiffen and his heart to pound so hard he couldn't breathe. His imagination ran wild. He visualized man-eating tigers, bloodsucking insects, and V.C. crawling on their bellies toward his canvas shelter. Then out of the darkness came a buzzing black cloud that covered his fear-ridden, sweat-soaked body—mosquitoes. So many that when he had slapped his body, his hands had been covered in mushy carnage. The only escape from the incessant little bastards was to cover himself with his poncho. Thus wrapped in the plastic ground cloth, his body felt as if it were melting. Throughout the rest of that first sleepless night, he'd had to cough, hack, and spit out the crawling, buzzing creatures so that he could breathe. When day finally came, with it came the backbreaking work of clearing the L.Z.

For ten days he endured at An Khe, but it felt as if it were ten years. He became a veteran in that time, but not a combat veteran. He learned the lessons of being a hopeless prisoner. He learned the night sounds so that he could distinguish those that could mean trouble from those that meant nothing. He'd learned how to live on only C-rations and water. And even the water tasted as if someone had left dirty dish rags in the canteens. His blisters disappeared, replaced with thick callus. The soreness also went away, replaced with bone-weary exhaustion from swinging a machete all day. Even the mosquitoes ceased to be a threat when he learned to cover himself with the Army's insect repellent—so strong it melted plastic watch crystals.

His body hardened and darkened. He lost ten pounds, so that his uniforms didn't fit anymore. Misery and discomfort had become a way of life. The others accepted it. He did not. He couldn't accept either the conditions or the filth. Water was precious and rationed, so it was not used for washing. Shaving was still a must, but they were only allowed one-fourth of a canteen cup to shave. His body and fatigues were reddish-brown in color. In the mornings his stinking uniform was stiff with dried sweat and caked dirt, but after just a few minutes of work it turned again into a soggy rag that oozed red mud. His whole body constantly itched and seemed to exude the odors of sweat, mud, and rotting jungle. The bamboo was the worst, for it itched unmercifully. It made him feel as if he had rolled naked on a barber's floor. The filth was total. If his hands got muddy, he had no place to wipe them. Filth only covered and caked over more stomach-wrenching filth.

Blake's eyes rolled back and focused for a moment. It had not been a nightmare after all. He was truly living in hell.

"Alexander, I thought I told you to take it easy today."

Blake slowly lifted his head. The voice was familiar, too familiar.

"I—I feel better, sir," he said thickly.

Lieutenant Owens shook his head as if dealing with a dumb third grader. "Alexander, you can't lead if you're in the fuckin' hospital. Sit down right now before you fall down."

Owens led the wobbly soldier to a stump and had him sit.

"Look, Alexander, you ain't dumb—at least I didn't think you were. You can't be tryin' to be some kind of a supertrooper. I've been watching you. You've done a hell of a job leadin' your squad, but you can't keep trying to prove you're better than everybody else. Your squad knows you ain't made of steel. Take it easy and get your strength back. This heat and fuckin' work will knock ya on your ass unless ya pace yourself. Ya listening to me?"

Blake's chin had dropped to his chest. He felt ashamed of himself. Calhoon and Martino had adjusted to the horrid conditions by the second day. Eugene Day made the adjustment by the fourth, and Prescott and Lasalle by the fifth. He, their squad leader, was the only one who had not been strong enough to adjust to their new life. He had tried. God only knows how he had tried to keep up and lead his men. He was always the first one up in the mornings and the last to go to bed. He was the first to attack the jungle with his machete and the last to quit and faithfully check his men. He tried to forget the misery and heat, but he only got weaker, while his men seemed to grow stronger. He was so tired that even blinking took a conscious effort. His body seemed to move in slow motion. He often found himself forgetting what he was about to say before he could say it. It had gotten so bad that his men often had to cover for him.

Owens roughly poked the sullen soldier. "When was the last time you pissed?"

"Eh, I . . . I can't remember, sir."

"How many canteens of water have you drank?"

"Uh, I think I . . ."

Owens nodded. His suspicions were confirmed. "Alexander, when I played ball, I saw this all the time. You got a bad case of dehydration. Drink both of your canteens right now. I'm going to watch you."

"Sir, we're short on wa—"

"Do it!" the officer commanded with a glare.

Blake drank his first canteen dry and lifted his second. Owens pointed at the tree stump. "You're going to sit right there and not move for an hour. When you get up, you're to sup-per-vise and not swing a machete today. In an hour you're going to drink another full canteen—that's an order. When you start feeling better—and you will—then we're gonna talk again."

Owens looked up and barked. "Calhoon, come here!"

Lee approached the barrel-chested officer with a quizzical grin. "Yes, sir?"

"Look after your squad leader. I don't want him moving from this spot. And make sure he drinks his water. He's dehydrated."

"Yes, sir. He's been workin' twice as hard as the rest of us. I was wonderin' how long it'd be before he done went down."

"You all should have told him," Owens shot back.

"Sir, we did. He don't listen worth a hoot."

The lieutenant's glare softened. "He's just tryin' to do too much. I think he learned his lesson. Watch him and I'll be back later to check his progress. I'll send a medic over. He's gonna need an IV to get his fluid level back to normal."

After the lieutenant had gone, Lee squatted down by his friend. "Ya lookin' pretty poorly. Ya shoulda listened ta us."

Blake closed his eyes to ease the pounding between his eyes. "I—I'm sorry about lettin' you guys down."

Lee stuck his machete into the ground. "Ace, I sure wish you'd quit actin' like a damn hard-headed Yankee and see what you was doin' to yo'self. Last night you was moanin' an talkin' in your sleep like a crazy man. You was talkin' back to your daddy, I think. You ain't still tryin' to prove somethin' to him, are ya?"

Blake brought his head up sharply. "It's none of your business."

Lee arched his brow. "I'd say after listenin' to ya last night that ya got your thinkin' all wrong. You ain't got nothin' to be ashamed of. I reckon it ain't for me to say, but it seems like it's your daddy is the one who's got the problem. You got more to worry about than what your daddy thinks. He ain't here. We are."

Blake felt himself sinking in a quagmire of doubt. Was it just the heat? Could he regain his confidence again?

An hour later Blake was standing behind his men, talking to another squad leader, when he felt a raindrop lightly caress his hand. He quickly looked up and felt another strike his cheek. He frantically took off his filthy fatigue shirt. He was not alone; the entire workforce of over six hundred men had thrown down their machetes and were hurriedly stripping. A newcomer would have been shocked by their strange behavior, but anyone who had been in An Khe more than three days understood perfectly.

Blake tossed down his trousers, put on his boots again, and lifted his head and arms to the sky to let the gentle rain finally cleanse his tormented body of dirt, dried mud, caked sweat, itchy bamboo, and dead ants.

Eugene pulled out a sliver of soap from a plastic bag he'd kept in his fatigue pocket and hurriedly lathered his body. He knew he was taking a big risk, but he couldn't stand himself any longer. Five days before, when it had rained, he had seen a soldier soap himself up and the rain almost instantly stop. The angry man had to use puddle water to rinse himself.

The sky darkened quickly and the rain began coming down harder. Martino and Calhoon finished rubbing their bodies clean with the pelting rain and held their fatigues up to soak. Lee glanced over his shoulder at Blake.

"Ya gonna rub your skin off if'n ya keep that up."

Blake didn't answer, but continued rubbing furiously at his arms to get off another layer of dirt. Vincent sloshed over to him.

"Yo, Ace, it's stayin' this time. I'm gettin' clean."

Blake looked up at the dark clouds and made himself relax. This rain-cloud wouldn't go away like the one five days before. He looked at the naked Italian, then at the others, and began laughing. They all looked ridiculous, standing around bare-ass naked except for their combat boots. They had learned about ants, snakes, and centipedes from seeing victims whose bodies had swelled up to twice normal size, and so they never took off their boots.

Lee looked around at the widening puddle in which they were standing. "This ain't none too good. I'll bet our tents are floatin' by now."

Eugene held up his wet bundle of fatigues. "At least I won't smell like I shit my pants."

Blake noticed a huge welt on Lee's side, and it reminded him to start thinking like a squad leader again. "Line up and let me inspect your bods."

"Aw, come on, Ace," Vincent whined. "Don't fuck with us now."

"Shut up, Vinny, and get in line." Blake inspected the welt on Lee's side. "It's getting infected just like Flynn said it would. Get some ointment from the medic and don't be scratchin' it anymore."

He next checked Vincent and saw he had two bad red swollen places on the inside of his thighs.

"Damn it, Vinny, you're not using the salve. Use it or they'll get infected, and you know what that means."

Vincent nodded in silence, remembering Flynn's description of what happened when you didn't treat infection early. It could kill you just as dead as a V.C. bullet.

Blake finished his inspection, noting that Al Prescott would have to see the medic as soon as they finished their work. The small Texan had cut his arm four days before when a machete bounced back off of a particularly hard tree. The wound wasn't healing properly. The Texan could barely lift his arm.

The rain fell harder suddenly, and Blake ordered his men to dress. Within seconds he could barely see Vincent, who was only five feet away, trying to put on his pants. They couldn't work in these conditions.

"Follow me," Blake yelled over the pounding, "and stay close." He remembered that a truck had been parked only a hundred meters behind them. A few minutes later the squad squatted under the big engineer dump truck. At least they could breathe without sucking in water.

Eugene took off his glasses to wipe them. "We wanted rain, and boy did we get it. It's gonna be miserable tonight, sleeping in wet clothes."

Vincent smirked. "Yeah, but maybe the rain will drown the mosquitoes."

Prescott lifted his swollen arm tenderly. "Ace, why the fuck we cuttin' this L.Z. by hand? Let me on a bulldozer, and I'd clear the L.Z. in two days."

Blake sighed. He had explained all this before. "If they bring in heavy equipment, the L.Z. would become a mud pit or dust bowl. We have to cut it out by hand so that we don't fuck up the topsoil. The general says he wants it to look like a golf course. The cav has got over four hundred choppers. If it was a dirt L.Z., the rotor wash would blow up so much dust nobody could see, and there'd be accidents, to say nothing of clogged engines. The only way to do it is the way we're doing it."

"But everybody else is gettin' over while we do all the work," Prescott persisted. "It ain't fair."

Lee leaned closer to Prescott. "Al, ya know that ain't so. The engineers are clearin' the perimeter with their bulldozers and stringin' barbed wire, and buildin' bunkers and them big guard towers. They workin' just as hard as us. Remember, we at least get ta sleep at night. The Second Brigade troops is guardin' the perimeter and have to stay awake all night. They ain't gettin' over."

"They gettin' over," Prescott snarled. "Every fuckin' body is gettin' over but us."

Blake had heard enough. He glared at the surly soldier. "Quit your snivelling. It could be worse."

A man materialized out of the rainstorm and splashed over to the truck. Staff Sergeant Shawn Flynn ducked under the huge truck, wiping water from his eyes. "I figured I'd find you all here. Some gully washer, huh?"

Blake scooted back farther beneath the truck to make room for his sergeant. "Where ya been, Sarge? We haven't seen ya in days."

Shawn ran his hand through his wet hair. "I've been seeing some buddies and makin' deals so we could get out of this L.Z.-clearin' detail. It worked. I talked to the ol' man and he agrees that we need to keep the Blues fine-tuned. Soon as this rain is over, go back and pack your shit. We're gonna fly out to a Special Forces camp and learn how to do some patrolling. I convinced the ol' man that when the cav finally starts operations, us Blues gotta be ready."

Vincent was not convinced the news was good. "Sarge, where is this Special Forces camp?"

Shawn raised his hand, pointing to the east. "That way, near a village called Plei Me. It's been quiet up there, so it'll be a good training area for us until you learn the basics." Shawn put on his helmet again and stepped back in the rain. He tapped his watch. "One hour, first herd, be at the east end of the L.Z. for pick up. We're gonna start phase three of my killer school." He turned and disappeared into the wall of water.

Lee glanced at Prescott. "I reckon we're gonna get over now, huh?"

Eugene lifted his head, repeating the village name. " 'Play Me'? What kinda name is Play Me? It sounds like the name of a porno flick."

Blake stepped into the rain. "Who cares. Wherever it is, it's got to beat the shit outta this place. Come on, we got a bird to catch."

20

At a secret base camp hidden in the mountains forty-five kilometers from An Khe, Brigadier General Chu Huy Man, the division commander of the North Vietnamese Army western plateau forces, sat at a table with a map spread out before him. To his right was his chief of staff, Senior Colonel Tung, and to his left was the assistant division commander, Colonel Lee Van Quan.

General Man motioned toward the objective circled on the map. "How are the preparations coming?"

Colonel Quan took the cigarette from his lips. "The reconnaissance units are in place. In two days we begin to stock the necessary supplies. Everything is going according to plan."

The general turned and stared out of the hut door toward the pelting rain. He spoke as if talking to himself. "This is our first. We cannot fail."

Both colonels exchanged glances. Their general had reason to worry, given the decision of the politburo to change the war strategy. Their division would be the first to carry out the Dau Tranh Vu Trang—armed struggle—strategy in a campaign to liberate parts of the Central Highlands and to fight the Americans head to head. It was the belief of the politburo that the regular army could inflict so many casualties on the Yankees that political pressure in their homeland would cause an end to the massive buildup of their forces.

The colonels knew too that their leaders were not as convinced as the politicians that the strategy would work. They had no experience with division-size operations. Until now, they had fought only small-unit engagements. This campaign would be the first to use regular army regiments under the command of a division commander.

The plan their general had devised was complex and required much planning and preparation. The need for precise timing would be their greatest vulnerability. The plan had three phases. The first required the two thousand men of 32nd Regiment to surround the small outpost and attack with enough strength to make the defenders call for reinforcements. There was only one road through the mountainous terrain to the camp, and it would be along that road that the 33rd Regiment would conduct phase two of the plan. The 2100-man force of the 33rd was to ambush and wipe out the relief column. In phase three the two regiments would join and combine their power for the final assault and for overrunning of the American outpost. Preparations for phase one had been going on for days, although the attack wasn't planned until the middle of October. The problem with the plan was phase two. The 33rd Regiment had not yet arrived from the north. They were expected to appear soon, but every extra day they took meant less time to recon and prepare their ambush positions.

The general broke his trance and turned back to look at the map. "When will the 33rd arrive?"

The chief of staff leaned forward and put his finger on the map, pointing to a spot just inside the Cambodian border. "Comrade General, their lead unit is here. They will cross the border within the week. The entire unit should be in their assembly area around the village of Anta by the second day of October. They will rest for only a few days, then begin movement into their ambush positions."

The general nodded in reflection, knowing it would be risky to use exhausted men who had been marching for months. They would have no time for rehearsals or training to regain their fighting skills. It was a risk he had to take. The politburo wanted him to attack as soon as possible. American forces were pouring into the south. A victory had to be achieved to show the American people their government's efforts were in vain.

The assistant commander, Colonel Quan, tapped the table while he studied the map. He wished that the third regiment could have been included in the attack. With his favorite regiment, the 66th, victory would be assured, but the 66th was still on the infiltration trail and would not be arriving until the first week in November.

General Man could see his colonel was having second thoughts about the plan, and pointed at the map's circled objective. "We will wipe them out easily. They are too small and weak to defeat us."

Colonel Quan shook his head and stood. "General, the camp does not concern me. It is the power they can beckon that is my worry. The planes and bombs will not stop once we attack."

"We will have well-prepared positions for that contingency," Man said, defending his plan.

The colonel gave his commander a faint smile. "General, it will not be a 'contingency.' It will be a fact."

The general's eyes narrowed. "The attack goes as planned. I cannot keep the Americans waiting for the war they desire. I will give them all they want and more . . . much more. Our new war begins at their small outpost, Plei Me. That is where they will face my regulars and learn." The stern division commander looked into Quan's eyes with determination. "They will learn this is a war they cannot win. And the lesson will be brutal."

Quan nodded in brooding silence.

PLEI ME

Blake Alexander stretched his legs out and leaned back against the sand-bagged bunker. Twenty yards away Vincent and Eugene were walking toward an old man who had set up shop just outside the perimeter wire. The old man was selling canned Cokes, and they thought it would be a good chance to try out some of the new language they had picked up while in camp. The platoon had arrived the day before at the triangular Special Forces camp and had spent most of their time building themselves sleeping bunkers and learning the strange language they needed to know to communicate with the locals. Flynn had given them the morning off to rest because he'd planned classes for them that night.

Blake was about to close his eyes when Lee strolled up. "Ace, ya see them water buffalo out there? They sure is somethin', ain't they?"

From where he sat, Blake could see the small village, which was only a hundred meters past the wire. The village was like an island surrounded in a sea of green rice paddies. Dotting the sea were huge black water buffalo, occasionally prodded by farmers. "Yeah, I wish I had a camera. This is the Vietnam I saw in the pictures. I like this place."

Lee leaned back to gain the shade of the bunker. "This camp sure ain't what I thought it'd be. I thought there'd be more Americans. All them little people runnin' around with guns bigger than them ain't that comforting. Ya reckon them Montagnards know what they're doin'?"

Blake leaned his head back and looked up at the light blue sky. "According to Flynn, they're more dependable than the Vietnamese soldiers. He's been right about everything else so far. I'm just glad we're here instead of back on the damned golf course."

Lee was about to speak when Al Prescott and Jim Lasalle strode up to the bunker. Prescott was wearing his usual smirk.

"Well, if it ain't our squad leader and the slow-talkin' cracker. What's up? You been checkin' out the ville for any poontang? I hear it's real cheap over here, 'cause the gook dudes got little peckers. The word is the broads dig our big A-merican dicks. I gotta find me some pussy pretty quick 'cause Jimbo, here, is beginnin' to look awfully cute."

Jimbo Lasalle's face turned beet red. "Ah, don't say things like that, Al."

Blake motioned toward the old man talking to Vincent and Eugene. "The only action you're gonna get around here is buying a Coke from Pops. I've been sittin' here watchin' the village, and the only females I've seen are all over sixty."

Prescott took in a deep breath. "No man, I can smell it. Poontang is there. I just gotta get me some gook pussy so I can tell the guys back home."

An all-too-familiar voice boomed from behind the bunker, freezing the four men's blood. "Did I hear somebody say gook?"

Sergeant Shawn Flynn stepped into view wearing crisscrossed bandoliers and a Special Forces boonie hat. The sight of him was enough to make Al Prescott want to shrivel. 'Gook' was a word Flynn had warned them not to use in his presence. Prescott put on his "I didn't mean it" look and waited for the lecture.

Blake was just as shocked as Prescott when Flynn strode past them, heading for the barbed-wire perimeter.

Eugene Day didn't see the sergeant approaching as he pointed an accusing finger at the old man. "You dinky dau, num-ba ten papa-san."

"Yeah," Vincent Martino added hotly. "You boo-coup numba ten, dinky dau askin' that much for them Cokes!"

The small, brown-skinned old man grinned, exposing blackened teeth. "Fifty pea. G.I. have beaucoup mon-nay. No sweat. You pay, okay?"

Vincent eyed the old man with his most threatening glare. "G.I. have *tee-tee* mon-nay! You give Coke for thirty-five pea."

The old man laughed, exposing his blackened mouth again. "You funnay G.I. Pay fifty pea."

"You're wastin' your time," Flynn said. "He's not gonna come down."

Vincent cringed as he turned around to face the sergeant. Eugene saved his buddy by jerking his thumb over his shoulder at the old man. "That robber called me a Montagnard. I think he's a V.C."

Shawn nodded, as if in understanding, then yelled over his shoulder toward the bunker, "Alexander, gather up the rest of your squad and come here!"

It only took a minute for the six men to form up behind their platoon sergeant. Shawn was standing with his back to them, looking at the village. He spoke matter-of-factly. "You men know this country mostly by what others have told you." He turned slowly and looked into their faces. "I think it's time you saw for yourselves what makes up this place known as Vietnam. Come on."

Shawn led the squad to a zigzagging path that led through the wire toward the village. In minutes they were standing in the middle of a dusty road lined with clapboard, rusted tin, and thatch huts. Swayback pigs and half-naked children rooted and played alongside the hooches, which had only thin, stained material hanging in place of doors. Several older children giggled shyly as they approached the Americans. An old woman with a blackened mouth came out of a hut and tossed a pan of water onto the road at the squad's feet, without so much as a glance at the visitors.

Shawn noted the looks of his men and motioned wordlessly for them to follow him. He followed the old woman into her hooch and rattled a few words in Vietnamese. She smiled and bowed, then went back to tending the fire in the corner of the small smoky room. Shawn waited until the squad was inside before sitting down on the hard, clay-packed floor.

"Sit down and take a look around. This is a typical hooch. It doesn't have any TV or radio, refrigerators, washers or dryers, or a car parked outside. What you see is all they have." He motioned to a low, flat, bamboo table. "That's where they sleep. Probably a family of four or five sleep on that table. They don't have pillows or blankets or nightstands. The only light they have is the fire, and the oil lamp on the shelf there beside the bed. You see those thin smoking sticks stuck in the bowl above the bed? That's incense. This family is Buddhist, like most around here. The fire the old woman is tending is their stove. Take a good whiff of that smoke. You'll smell it again. That distinctive smell is burning bamboo. The kids collect it for her; it's plentiful and makes a good starter. Notice there is no bathroom or hot or cold running water. She's heating water in the pan for rice. Rice is what they eat for almost every meal." Shawn rose and bowed to the old woman, speaking to her softly. She stood, bowed, and gave her company a black smile.

Shawn led the men outside into the road and headed toward the village well. "That woman was no more than thirty-five years old. This country and her life have made her look fifty. Vietnam has been at war for over forty years with somebody—the Japanese, French, themselves, us, it doesn't matter who. That woman has lost at least five relatives over the past five years, and she knows she will lose more. She was born in war, lives in war, and will die in war. She knows more about war than you and I ever will. If we're lucky, we'll go home in a year. She is home."

Shawn halted by the well, where three wrinkled women spread rice in flat baskets to dry in the sun. "These women are doing what they will do for the rest of their lives—work. They work from sunup till sundown. Notice how they squat. They can stay that way for hours. Did you see any chairs in the old lady's hooch? That's why they squat. It's their way of sitting to keep out of dust and mud. They're wearing silklike pants and blouses 'cause it's cool and dries quick. The straw, conical hats are also cool and keep the sun and rain out of their faces. If you look at their hands, you'll find they're like a man's hands. They plant and harvest rice up to their knees in mud beside the men. They can stay bent over for hours planting rice. You would last only ten minutes, then complain that your back was breaking.

"These women's idea of a good time is walking ten miles to a market for eel and dried bananas for their family. They don't wear makeup or blue jeans. A luxury item is a store-bought comb or a metal pot."

The group of children following the squad had grown to seven. They had become bolder and stepped closer to Lee Calhoon to stare and giggle at his arms.

Shawn smiled and spoke Vietnamese to them. A little girl giggled and put out her small hand to touch the hair on the Georgian's arm.

"They think of us as long-nosed and hairy," Shawn said. "The hair on your arms is really odd to them. Vietnamese have little facial hair and almost no hair on their legs and arms. The children learn our language quickly and do most of the communicating for us with the older folks. These kids in this village are luckier than most. The camp sends out a teacher three times a week. Most children in the outlying villages or in the war zones don't have teachers. They learn from their parents. Like their mothers and fathers, they've known nothing but war since they were born. Most of their fathers are in the army. It doesn't matter much which army. They just know they're away and don't come home very often."

Shawn motioned to the well. "This is their water for cooking, cleaning, bathing, and drinking. The women carry the water to their homes four and five times a day. If you were to drink that water, you'd be in the hospital within a day. There is no safe water in this country unless it's boiled or you use your Halizone tablets. Even if you're up there"—he pointed to distant mountains over his shoulder—"still use your tablets. Snails too small to see live in the streams, and they'll eat out your insides. Up there in those mountains are sons of the people like these in this village. They are the toughest light infantry in the world. Now you know why. They have had to struggle to live every day of their lives. War is second nature; it's like breathing to them."

Shawn let his words sink in for effect, then smiled at Prescott. "I want you to take a piece of gum to that little girl riding the water buffalo out there in that rice paddy." Shawn pointed to a field no more than seventy-five meters off to his right. "She is a daughter of a Vietnamese soldier in the camp."

Prescott looked at his sergeant for a sign he was being screwed with. He didn't trust Flynn, but there was no twinkle or gleam in the sergeant's eye that told him the request was anything but legitimate.

"Sure." The slim soldier shrugged his shoulders.

Prescott began walking toward the distant paddy and soon came to the narrow dike that would lead him to the little girl. He looked over his shoulder several times to make sure it wasn't a joke of some kind. At twenty paces from the water buffalo and little girl, who had their backs to him, he held up a pack of spearmint gum. "Hey, kid, looky what I got for you!"

The girl screamed in fright and slid off the massive shoulders of the horned buffalo. Spinning around, the dark gray beast jerked its head up and bellowed. Shaking its huge head, the maddened animal bolted toward Prescott, blowing muddy water and froth from its flared nostrils. Prescott turned in a dead run, his face white and his teeth bared in a frozen silent scream of terror. The charging buffalo's stout legs churned the muddy water like a paddle wheel, and its massive head pumped up and down between its wide shoulders like a hissing piston.

To the rest of the stunned squad, watching in horror, it looked as if a half-ton miniature locomotive with horns had been turned loose to wreak havoc. A scream finally escaped Prescott's mouth. He pumped his arms and legs for all they were worth. Unknown to the Texan, the puffing beast was nowhere close, but to him it sounded as if it was breathing down his neck.

The little girl clutched her conical hat and cried out in a singsong voice. The sleepy village immediately awoke in a clamor of excited wails and cries, as if hearing a three-bell fire alarm in downtown New York. The frothing buffalo halted its rampage at the edge of the paddy dike and threw its head back, bellowing in victory. Children and old people rushed to the paddy and tried to calm their maddened pet with singsong words and consoling pats.

Prescott dared a look over his shoulder only after running to within a few yards of the squad. Seeing he was out of danger, he tumbled to the ground, relieved and out of breath. He looked at his sergeant as if wanting to kill him.

"You . . . you . . . bastard," he growled, his chest heaving.

Shawn nodded nonchalantly. He reached down, grabbed the soldier's fatigue shirt and yanked him up, then leaned forward to within inches of his face. "Don't you ever say 'gook' around me again," he snarled.

The sergeant backed up and changed his expression to one that was more benign. "You have just had a valuable lesson. Never get close to water buffalo unless you're upwind from them. You're the 'gook' to them. You're strange and you smell like death. They can tell you eat meat, they smell it, and they don't plan on being on your next meal without a fight."

Shawn couldn't help but smile to himself. He'd gained the squad's undivided attention. He motioned toward the excited people around the buffalo.

"Those people live simply. The land is their life. That buff belongs to the village. They cost too much for just one rice farmer, unless he's rich. The buffalo is their livelihood. It tills the paddies. Without buffalo, they don't get rice, and rice is what they eat and trade in order to survive. They rarely eat meat. Mostly fish, vegetables, and rice. Sometimes chicken, and lots of eggs, duck eggs. Everybody has a job in the village. The kids feed and care for the ducks, pigs, chickens, and buffalo. They gather wood for fires. The older folks work the land, harvest the rice and other food, and sell or trade what's left. Some are the builders. They cut the bamboo to make or fix the hooches and weave mats. This bamboo stand behind us belongs to the village. Don't ever cut down bamboo around a village or you'll piss them off. Everything has its purpose. Remember that. Everything has its purpose. These people don't have television and booze to forget their bosses or jobs. All they have is their work and their families. They take care of and honor their old, so be nice to the old folks. Bow and talk low, never loud. To them, American soldiers are loud and disrespectful and don't appreciate their land. They're right, you don't, and that makes you dangerous."

Shawn looked into each man's face to see if he was getting through. Their eyes told him he was.

"I didn't bring you out here to feel sorry for these people. Don't. In some ways they're better off than us. I wanted you to know them a little better. The buffalo, for instance. You learned that they go crazy when they smell us. The people know that, and that's why their pens are outside of the villages. The buffs warn them if we try to patrol the villages at night. They also stake out geese. They're the best night watchmen there are. And don't forget the dogs. One bark at night and your ambush is blown. When we patrol out farther from the larger towns, you can bet most of the villages are V.C. You can tell by the location of the buffalo pens and the dogs. Remember what I said about everything having a purpose. We're going to look again at the village, but this time I'm going to point out what you have to look out for if it's V.C. First, always watch a village before going in. See what paths the locals use and which ones they avoid. You should always . . ."

The squad followed the sergeant for thirty minutes, trying to soak in all of his knowledge and experience. He explained that if they knew how the locals lived, they would also know how their enemy lived in the jungle or in the mountains. The smells of their fires and cooking food would be the same. Their need for water, likely places to find their latrines, foods they ate, and clothing they wore were all important to remember.

At first the squad just listened, but as their interest and curiosity grew, they began to ask questions. Blake had asked the first.

"Sarge, how come all the older people have black mouths?"

Shawn pointed at the ground next to Blake's feet, where there were reddish-brown blotches that looked like dried blood. "That's betel-nut juice they've spit out. Just about every villager over twenty-five chews the stuff. It's a mild narcotic that takes the place of the dentist they don't have. When you're on patrol and you see those blotches beside a trail, you know you're not alone."

Martino nodded to the children, who were still following them. "Them kids always go barefoot like that?"

Shawn snapped his fingers. "Damn, I shoulda told ya. Good question, because it reminded me of something else. The V.C. and NVA usually wear sandals made of rubber tires. It sounds funny but it works great. You'll learn to hate your leather boots and wish you had a pair. The point is, you can pick out their sandal prints pretty easy . . . and they can pick out yours. As far as the kids go, they usually go barefoot around places they know."

Blake and the rest of the squad were shocked when Prescott spoke up. "Sarge, how can you tell a V.C. from these people in the village?"

Shawn thought a few moments before answering. "These people know the rules. There is no moving at night. They have to be inside their hooches. If someone is moving around at night, he's V.C. During the day, if you spot

young or middle-aged men in a village, you search them. Look for welts
or blisters on their backs from carrying packs. Check them for wounds or
recent scars. Find out who their family is and question the family without
the suspect, then question the suspect. If they're V.C., their stories won't
jive. Once you're away from a village, the rules change. Everybody is a
suspect, and you don't take any chances. Always keep a suspect covered,
and if he runs, he's V.C.—shoot him. It sounds cruel, but it's the rule. The
people know it."

Shawn led the squad back into the Special Forces camp and climbed up
onto the northeast corner bunker.

"Take a good look around and get a feel for the camp. You can see it's
shaped like a triangle, and the three corner bunkers are the strong points.
The airfield over there, outside the wire, is the way the camp is resupplied.
The V.C. have control of all the roads leading in. I told ya the area was
quiet, and it is, but the roads are a different matter. The camp, as I told
ya before, has 350 Montagnard strikers from the Jari tribe. Montagnards
can only be compared to our Commanche Indians. They are the best
hunters and fighters around when trained properly. Tonight, you and the
rest of the platoon are gonna meet me here. We're gonna have a class on
weapons. The S.F. team has some enemy weapons, and we're going to be
shooting them so you can learn the difference between their sounds and
ours. It's gonna be important, 'cause when you're in a firefight, you gotta
know what you're up against before you react. Remember the rules: stop,
listen, then react. Tonight you're going to learn just what it is you're
listening for. Okay, I've probably been boring you to tears, and you're
gettin' tired of my voice. Get your weapons cleaned, and get some rest.
You're gonna be up most of the night."

Green tracers cracked only a foot over the heads of the men who lay
shaking on the ground. Blake pressed his body down farther until he felt
his fatigue shirt buttons dig into his chest. Lee blew out the air from his
lungs to flatten himself even more. Vincent alternated from cussing to
praying with each bullet that passed overhead. Jimbo Lasalle cried and Al
Prescott swore.

A voice in the darkness replaced the sound of the bullets. "What weapon
was that?"

No one in the squad raised their heads or yelled back in response. They
had been concerned only about living, not about listening or watching.

"That fuckin' Flynn is gonna kill one of us with his fuckin' lessons,"
Prescott mumbled.

"I heard that, Prescott," the voice in the darkness bellowed. "Noise
travels farther at night, especially voices. In the jungle a voice is unnatural
and can easily be distinguished from other sounds. You just killed your
squad, Prescott!"

A hail of bullets cracked over the squad to sink in the point. Lee Calhoon yelled as soon as the air was again still. "RPD machine gun!"

"Right," the voice bellowed back. "What size unit usually has an RPD machine gun?"

Blake rose up slightly and yelled, "A platoon. If we were a small patrol, we'd know not to attack. They'd outnumber us three or four to one."

"Right! Now how about this one . . ." *Crack crack crackcrackcrack.*

Vincent screamed before the sound of the bullets quit ringing in his ears. "AK-47!"

"How many rounds in its magazine?"

"Thirty!" Eugene and Lasalle both yelled.

"Right! Now how about this one . . ." *Pop pop poppoppop,* the red tracers looked like ten-inch red flames passing over the squad, which yelled in unison, "M-16!"

"Right!"

Thirty minutes later the first squad was in a foxhole listening to the second squad get shot at. Flynn's class was not what they had expected. Lieutenant Owens had given the entire platoon a quick ten-minute refresher class on the enemy weapons they had studied on board the carrier. Flynn had then ordered the first squad to follow him, and made the rest of the platoon stay in the bunker. The sergeant led the squad to the perimeter fence opposite the village and told them to lie down in a shallow ditch and not to raise their heads, no matter what.

The sounds of gunfire and the sergeant's voice directed at the second squad still made Blake and the others jump. Flynn wanted them to hear the weapons shooting from different distances.

"That was the RPD machine gun, right?" Vincent whispered.

"Yep." Lee nodded in the darkness. "Ya see those green tracers?"

Eugene joined Lee and Vincent in watching the tracers streak across the barren ground. Blake felt a tingle run up his spine listening to another weapon firing. AK-47 flashed in his mind. He had no doubt. Nothing else sounded like it. The crack rather than the pop of an M-16, and not near as throaty as the RPD machine gun. The next weapon opened up, and its red tracers looked like a hose squirting out a long flame of red, continuous fire. M-60 machine gun. The thunderous rat-tat-tat was still echoing somewhere in his brain.

"The 'sixty is the worst," Lee whispered.

An hour had passed, and all the squads had been through Flynn's firing line. The platoon was gathered in a tight group close to the wire. Lieutenant Owens had them sit in total silence, listening to the darkness. Flynn had obviously enlisted help from his S.F. buddies, because from different directions they could hear men whispering, a radio crackling, something that sounded like snoring, and a weapon charging-handle sliding back and forth. After ten minutes of straining to pick out different sounds, the sound of Owens's voice seemed incredibly loud. He was not visible, but his voice seemed to come from outside the perimeter wire. Every man leaned forward instinctively to try and see him.

Blam! The brilliant flash of light blinded them an instant before the loud explosion reached their ears. No one could see anything but dull purple and bluish spots—the lingering effects of flash-blindness at night. It would take a full three to five minutes to regain their night vision.

"You're blind now, all you have is your ears," a familiar voice in the darkness called out to them. "Listen . . . learn."

"Ooooooh shit," someone whispered.

They were sitting silently when suddenly another explosion only twenty meters away covered them in dust and took away their night vision again. A pop, then a whooshing noise, made them jump. A flare popped overhead, bathing the stunned men in red light. Seconds later there came another whooshing noise, and now they were bathed in an eerie green radiance. The flares continued, alternating in color for several minutes. Then came the silence and darkness again.

"If one of you had closed just one eye during the flare show, you would be able to see what's going to happen to you . . . and it would warn you," the voice called out.

Lee Calhoon raised his head and scanned the darkness. He had closed his right eye after the first blinding explosion and had kept it closed during all that followed. On a rise only twenty yards behind the platoon, he saw what looked like ten to fifteen men rise up, holding weapons. He screamed a warning to the others and flung himself into the dirt.

"Git down!"

Shawn fired a flare first, to make sure the Montagnards knew where the platoon was gathered. The instructions to the twelve men had been very simple—shoot two magazines at least ten feet over the heads of his men. The deed was done in less than thirty seconds. Shawn let Lieutenant Owens thank the Yards while he walked down the rise to the prone platoon. "What you've learned so far tonight is simple. Night is either your friend or your enemy, depending on how you control your fear. Fear at night is a killer. You must know and understand the night to use it to your advantage. Tomorrow morning you will all sleep in until noon. The afternoon class will be on patrolling, and tomorrow night we'll be going outside the wire on our first patrol. We'll be lookin' for that bastard who is waitin' on ya . . . Hit the sack, Blues . . . tomorrow you become hunters."

21

Lee Calhoon stepped lightly off the trail. The gray wisps of smoke ahead confirmed it. His prey had made a mistake. The warm air rising from the valley had carried their campfire smoke up the slope. Lee looked over his shoulder and gave his squad leader a confident nod. Lee didn't need to get any closer to know his prey was there. Thirty minutes before, he had caught the first, faint scent of burning bamboo and had changed the planned route. The beckoning smell had led him to a narrow trail that headed down into a small valley. He had moved only ten feet along the steep path when he'd seen the first sandal prints and what looked like bicycle tire prints. The prints and location of the fire told him the three-day hunt would soon be coming to an end.

Blake Alexander ignored the sweat that trickled down his forehead and pooled in his eyebrows. He returned the nod to his point man and turned slowly to face Martino, who carried the M-60 machine gun. Blake motioned him up to cover Calhoon. He wanted the weapon's firepower where it would do the most good. Blake turned his head slightly, looking at Eugene, pointed at his own eye, then motioned to the right side of the path. The signal told Day he would be responsible for watching the flank to ensure there were no surprises from that direction. Blake then pointed at Prescott and began to repeat the signal, but Prescott immediately turned to watch the other flank. Good man, Blake thought, he knew what to do. Blake looked over his shoulder toward Jimbo Lasalle, who was waiting for his signal. Jimbo stuck his thumb up and turned around to watch their rear. Blake felt a surge of pride. The previous two weeks of training were paying off. Not a word had been spoken. Every man knew what he was supposed to do. They had truly become a team.

Ready now, Blake gave Lee a second nod. It was the go-ahead.

Though it seemed like ten hours, it took ten minutes to move thirty meters down the steep path. The trail was packed hard, so there was no worry about making noise, unless their prey could hear them sweat. But if noise was not a problem, visibility was. Sunlight was streaming down through the canopy in golden shafts, speckling the ground around them. Before they started down the slope, they had been in semidarkness. Now, on the hill, the huge trees were closer together, causing the canopy to block out almost all light. On the slope the stately trees were farther apart, allowing sunlight to penetrate to the jungle floor and feed the plants. The thick vegetation on both sides of the twisting trail allowed no more than three feet visibility to right or left. This ambush would not be like the ones they had trained for, in which they would spread out and sneak up on the elusive enemy. The thick vegetation changed things. The squad would have to get as close as possible and attack violently in a single rush. Surprise and speed would have to be their advantage.

Lee stopped a few feet from a break in the green wall of huge ferns and strangler fig vines. He concentrated on the popping and crackling of the campfire, which was only a few meters on the other side of the green curtain, then concentrated his attention on the other sounds. He could hear someone humming, another breaking branches to feed the fire, and a third running a rod down the barrel of a rifle. Their sounds told him where each man was in relation to the campfire.

Lee silently moved his selector switch from safe to semiauto and looked over his shoulder toward his squad leader. He made eye contact and signalled that he was ready. Blake took a breath to control his shaking before nodding back. The training was over. The waiting was over. It was time.

Lee motioned Martino closer and signaled that he, Lee, would be breaking right, while Martino was to break left.

Vincent winked and brought the machine gun in close to his hip. He held out the belt of ammunition with his left hand.

Lee took another step at a half crouch, then straightened up and quickly took the last two steps that would finally expose him to his prey. The Vietnamese soldier who was cleaning his rifle saw the movement, but he never had a chance to react. He had been the only one facing the trail and became Lee Calhoon's first target. The Georgian snapped off two quick shots. The first M-16 bullet hit the man below the right eye and blew out the back of his skull, taking with it blood and quivering brain. The second copper-jacketed slug struck him above the chin, tumbled downward, and ripped through his larynx.

The experienced senior sergeant, who had been putting branches on the fire, did not turn toward the rifle's report. He knew the sound all too well. He did not need to waste time in confirming what he already knew. He bolted for the protection of the stream's heavy vegetation, but got only two steps. He was suddenly knocked off his feet with a terrific blow to his back and tumbled forward to his hands and knees. He didn't understand why he fell until a split second later he felt the strange, excruciating pain.

The humming eighteen-year-old soldier sat in his hammock looking at his killer with a puzzled expression, as if to say, "I don't know you, why are you here?" Only when Vincent Martino fired his machine gun did the young man's eyes show fear, but only for an instant. Then they didn't see anything.

Lee spun to his left and fired at a movement he had noticed from the corner of his eye. The approaching khaki-clad Vietnamese soldier who had run from the stream had just begun to press back the trigger of his Chinese assault rifle when three bullets traveling faster than the speed of sound ripped through his thigh, stomach, and chest in less than a second. The impact of the burning rounds twirled him around like a ballet dancer exiting stage right, except he collapsed at the end of his performance.

Blake rushed in behind Vincent and took up a position beside the smoldering campfire. He had not fired a single shot, for it had all happened so fast and the action was already over. It had been like watching frames of a badly spliced movie flash on a large outside screen. Every detail was captured. He relaxed his grip on his rifle and flicked the selector switch back to safe. A quick glance to either side told him the situation. Prescott and Eugene were to his right. Lee and Vincent were to his left. Three uniformed enemy were down and one was inexplicably on his hands and knees. Strange-looking bicycles were leaning up against a huge, barkless tree. The bikes were loaded down with large, brown sacks, long cardboard tubes, and wooden ammunition boxes. A cooking pot half full of boiling water was resting in the coals of the campfire. The distinct smells of blood and gun smoke were overpowering.

Something was out of place. Blake didn't know what it was, and it nagged at him. He began to scan the camp again when he stiffened. Eugene jerked his rifle up as he saw them too. Blake instinctively pushed the selector off safe as he dropped to his knee and fired.

Eugene had no time to warn the others. Thirty meters on the other side of the camp was a steep ridge covered with moss and fern. Sliding down the slick embankment, carrying AK-47s, were four khaki-uniformed men. Eugene sighted in on the closest one.

The four soldiers of the third squad, first platoon, 32nd Transportation Company, were helplessly committed. They had left the rest camp ten minutes before, pushing their heavily loaded bicycles up the ridge. They had followed a trail, but when they'd heard the shooting, they dropped their bikes and jumped off the path. The young corporal in charge had ordered the others to follow him down the slope rather than take the trail. He had made a fatal mistake. The thin topsoil had given way beneath their feet, causing them to slide down as if on ice.

In the lead, the overanxious corporal was knocked backward with a hail of bullets that tore through his chest and face. Splattered with a fine spray of blood, the three other soldiers could do nothing, not even raise their weapons as they continued their downward plunge. Even the corporal, with a look of astonishment on what was left of his face, continued to slide down on his back with them.

The ancient trees seemed to wince and groan at the insanity as the squad fired at the hapless men. The increasing staccato built into a thunderous, continuous roar. Delicate ferns were uprooted and crushed under the weight of the falling bodies.

Then came the silence, eerie dead quiet, in which nothing moved except wispy tendrils of gray gun smoke. The complete silence lasted a full two seconds before, finally, the world began turning again. It was as if time had frozen for a moment, grieving.

Through a smoky haze Blake stared at the jumble of muddy bodies at the bottom of the slope. It couldn't be real, he told himself. He trembled, and when he tried to stop, he began shaking harder. He wanted to look away from the bodies, but wanted even more to savor the grotesque scene. The rush of adrenaline flowing through his body was the most incredibly exhilarating feeling he had ever experienced in his life. He screamed to himself, *I won!* I've faced the ultimate challenge and *won!* Man-to-man combat, face to face, where victory is living and losing is death, *and I won!* I don't feel guilt, I'm strong, and I can take it. The blood and horrible wounds don't bother me. *Look at me, Dad! I'm a winner!*

A guttural moan snapped Blake out of his ecstasy, as if he'd been slapped. He spun around with his weapon ready. The Vietnamese soldier on his hands and knees was rolling his head from side to side. *Shit!* screamed Blake to himself, realizing his finger was still holding back the trigger of his empty weapon. He had been so caught up in the strange, blissful feeling, he'd forgotten everything Flynn had taught him.

Blake released the trigger, hoping the others had not seen his weakness, and pushed his magazine release button. The empty magazine clanked, hitting the ground. He turned around, fighting the hazy cloud that had seemed to penetrate and paralyze his brain. He tried to sort through all the things he should do, say, and check. *Think, goddamnit!* His eyes focused. He realized that, unbelievably, only a few seconds had passed since the last round had been fired. He forced himself to think as a squad leader. Okay, all my men are—no! Lasalle is unaccounted for. The V.C. on his hands and knees hasn't moved. There could be more of them on the ridge. Gotta post security. Shit, gotta report the situation and check the bodies and . . . *Think!*

Blake slapped in a full magazine and swung his eyes to Vincent. He tried to speak, but his tongue wouldn't move. He was so tense his entire body seemed like a block of concrete. He swallowed and tried again. The sound of his voice seemed strange.

"Vinny, cover the slope," he said.

Blake's eyes shifted to Prescott, who was either grinning or grimacing, Blake couldn't tell which.

"Al? . . . *Al!* Check the one out on his hands and knees."

Blake could now see Prescott was grinning strangely, and wondered if he too had been captured by the strange feeling. Blake pointed his rifle at the V.C. on all fours.

"Al, change magazines. You're empty. Check him out, then the bodies. Collect anything of intel value."

Blake turned to speak to Eugene but suddenly remembered Lasalle. *Shit! "Lasalle!"*

A voice from behind the vegetation near the trail responded immediately. "*Yo! . . . You— You guys okay?*"

"Come here!" Blake commanded.

Eugene Day was shaking so badly his teeth were chattering. He had never killed anything bigger than a bird in his life. He had thought and dreamed of killing bad men like villains in the movies and later racist fuckers who had taunted him, but those had all been dreams. Through all the training, it had never sunk in what death really was. Now it was lying all around him. It wasn't sickening or repulsive, just sad. Sad in that death had taken away their dignity. They seemed like indistinguishable, inanimate mannequins. Nothing remained of their essence. Death had emptied life from their bodies, leaving only empty heaps of flesh.

Eugene stared at the gaping wound in the back of the seated Vietnamese who had been cleaning his weapon. Flies had already found the gore and were feasting in a gleeful buzz.

Unable to take the flies, Eugene turned his head and looked directly at Prescott, who spoke as if he were enjoying himself. "You check him out yet? Getcha any souvenirs?"

Lee Calhoon turned over the blood-splattered body of the soldier who had run from the stream. Lee wasn't curious. He was doing his job, checking the body for anything of intelligence value. He had killed over a hundred deer, as well as other animals, so he had seen plenty of death before. To him these dead men looked like the deer. Their eyes were the same—blank. The killing bothered him, but he knew it was necessary. He'd had to kill animals and he'd had to kill these men. There was no difference.

Vincent Martino closed the cover tray of his M-60, having inserted a new belt of ammunition. It was an easy task, which he'd done hundreds of times in training, but this time it had taken him twice as long as usual. He couldn't seem to concentrate or make his fingers respond, though the shaking had stopped and the electric tingling sensation had passed. The excitement and adrenaline high were wearing off. He had experienced the same blissful sensation after winning fistfights. Killing had been strangely like winning a fight, except that the tingling high was ten times better. It was as if a jolt of electricity had boosted his senses to supersensitivity, so that he saw, smelled, heard, and felt everything at once. The brain had seemed to shut down, overcome by this heightened awareness. Free of thinking, his body had become a powerful, mindless mass of energy bent on the single purpose of destruction. The M-60 had become an appendage, and he'd felt each bullet strike, tear, and rip through his enemies' flesh.

Vincent relaxed his trembling trigger finger. He was making the rush of power come back just by thinking about it. He took a deep breath and concentrated on watching the ridge.

Blake had begun to yell for Lasalle again when the small soldier stepped through a wall of ferns. He looked lost.

Lasalle's head was like a swivel as he walked toward his squad leader. His face turned pale white at the sight of the blood-splattered bodies and gorging flies. He held out the radio handset.

"I tried . . . calling but . . . I couldn't contact any . . . I . . . *Oh Jesus!*"

He noticed he had stepped into a pool of blood from one of the dead soldiers. Lasalle tentatively lifted one boot then the other, unsure of what to do.

"Come on, Jimbo, it'll wash off," Blake said gently.

He held his hand out for the handset. Lasalle blinked and forced himself to continue walking toward his squad leader.

"Ace," he said, "we're down too low to get anybody. We gotta move to higher ground to make radio contact."

Blake's eyes shifted to the bodies at the bottom of the slope. He knew he had to get the bodies checked before moving. The same lingering feeling that something was out of place nagged at him again. He looked back at Lasalle and was about to speak when he heard gagging. He turned toward the sound and saw Prescott standing beside the man who was on his hands and knees. Prescott's crazy grin was gone, replaced with a look of confusion mixed with horror.

Vincent snapped his fingers and spoke in a loud whisper, pointing to the jumble of muddy bodies on the slope. "One of those guys is movin'."

Blake motioned Lasalle toward the bodies with his rifle. "Check 'em out." He then strode toward Prescott. "What's wrong, Al?"

Prescott tried to speak, but then spun around and vomited. Blake approached the V.C. There was a cherry-red entry wound in the man's lower back, and on the ground directly beneath the man's stomach it looked as if a light bluish-pink snake had coiled its body in a pool of deep crimson blood. The snake's body was pulsating and elongating, adding another coil. Then the smell reached Blake. Jesus, he gasped to himself, and backed up a step. The soldier's intestines were oozing out of the exit wound, winding their way down his uniform shirt to the ground.

Blake breathed through his mouth and stepped around to look into the wounded soldier's face. The man's mouth was open and his eyes were rolled back. The skin around his cheeks and forehead was wrinkled back as if he were facing the blast of a hurricane wind. Blake kneeled down. He didn't know what to do, but he wanted to somehow ease the man's suffering. The soldier was shaking with the effort to keep his stiff arms from collapsing.

Eugene and Lee walked up behind him. Lee put his hand on Blake's shoulder.

"Lasalle wants ya. Go on, there's nothing ya can do for this un."

Blake stood and walked to Lasalle, trying to put the man's grimacing face out of his mind. His stomach was rumbling and churning up a rancid acid that was boiling into his throat.

Lasalle and Vincent stepped out of the way, revealing a small Vietnamese soldier with only a partial face. A bullet had hit the man's chin and tumbled through his jaw, tearing away bone and muscle. He lay staring up at the jungle canopy with a strange, almost contented look. His breathing was shallow but made a gurgling noise. Two bullet-entry holes in his chest were bubbling pink froth. The sight struck Blake in the gut as if he had been jabbed with a steel bar. It was the soldier he'd shot.

Forcing himself not to show his emotions, he leaned over and pulled back the uniform shirt to inspect the chest wounds. One glance told him both lungs were nothing but mush. The soldier's eyes flickered and suddenly locked on him. Blake shook his head. The soldier's eyes seemed to sadden in understanding and slowly shifted back to the canopy.

"What are we gonna do with them?" Lasalle whined.

Blake stood erect but kept his eyes on the man he had defeated in mortal combat. The past feeling of winning some kind of victory was gone. He now felt dirty and small. He had lied to himself, believing that killing such a man made him, Blake Alexander, better. The dying soldier was just like him, a boy trying to be a man. Blake looked down and saw the blood on his hands. It had come from the young soldier's shirt. His jaw tightened as he shut his eyes.

Vincent held up a Vietnamese pack to get Blake's attention back on his job.

"Ace, I got all their documents and other stuff."

Blake looked blankly at the pack, not understanding for a second, then suddenly focused his eyes. "Yeah . . . good. Lasalle, collect the rest of the packs and weapons and put 'em by the fire. We'll divvy up everything to carry. Make a list of what's attached to the bikes and make a sketch of this camp. Make it quick. I wanna move in five minutes."

Lasalle shifted his eyes toward the dying soldier. "What are we gonna do with the wounded?"

Blake looked up at the shafts of golden light that streamed through the canopy. "I'll take care of it. Go on and do what I said."

Minutes later the squad stood waiting on the trail leading up the ridge. They waited for their squad leader, who knelt over the dying soldier. Eugene exchanged glances with Vincent and Lee. They knew what their friend was feeling and wanted to be with him.

Blake stood and spoke in a whisper to the young corporal. "I'm sorry."

He placed his M-16 barrel on the soldier's forehead and pulled the trigger. Without looking at what he'd done, he turned and walked toward the second wounded soldier. He was still on his knees but had collapsed to his elbows. Blake raised the rifle with one hand as he walked. Coming within a few feet of the man, he fired without breaking stride and continued walking toward his waiting squad. He stared blankly straight ahead as he passed his men and took up the point position. He stopped and checked his rifle once more.

"Check your weapons," he said over his shoulder. "Keep your distance and keep your eyes open. The men we killed were not V.C.—they were North Vietnamese regulars."

Blake had finally found the missing piece of the puzzle that had been nagging at him. It had come to him while looking at that last soldier for the last time. Sergeant Flynn had told them V.C. wore peasant clothes. These men were in full uniform.

Blake squared his shoulders, narrowed his eyes, and concentrated on listening to his senses. He knew he had changed, but he wasn't sure how, except for one revelation that had become crystal clear—he knew he didn't give a shit if he ever pleased his father. Blake Alexander was not going to fight the war worrying about trying to be accepted as a true "Alexander." He was going to struggle for what really mattered—his men. He didn't want them or himself to die like those they had killed. They had died dumb. Their mistakes had killed them. Flynn had been right—dying dumb was a waste.

Blake brought his rifle up and began walking. He was no longer an "Alexander of Williamsburg, Virginia." He was just plain Alexander, a soldier.

Staff Sergeant Shawn Flynn tossed a poker chip into the center of the table. "I'm in. It looks like I might be takin' you all's money for another night. Sorry 'bout that."

Captain Harold Moss snickered as he threw a chip onto the table. "Knowin' you, Irish, I'd say you planned it. You got that lost patrol of yours hiding in some ville drinking beer."

Master Sergeant Purdue, the team's senior NCO, took a blue chip from a stack in front of him and scooted it out to the center of the table. "Irish, if you win another hand, I'm personally going out and finding your patrol so as to get rid of yo' lousy ass."

"Ditto, Top. I'm running outta beer money. I'll help ya," said Sergeant First Class Brockton, the team's demolition expert.

Shawn had known and trained with these men both at Fort Bragg and on his last tour. Team A-217 was like most teams assigned to the desolate outposts. They did a job they knew they could do better if it weren't for the policies and politics of the American and South Vietnamese governments.

While looking at his cards, Shawn stole another glance at his watch. He wasn't worried; he was just getting more embarrassed by the first squad's failure to report. It wouldn't have been such a big deal, but three hours before, Colonel Stockton had flown in with four birds. He had explained an operation was coming up for the squadron and he needed the blue platoon back. Shawn had made contact with three out of four of the squads and had told them to find L.Z.s for immediate pickup. Lieutenant Owens and the three squads had been picked up and were already back in An Khe, leaving him behind to wait for the first squad. Colonel Stockton had understood. The patrol probably had radio problems. He told Shawn he would send a chopper back the following afternoon.

Shawn threw another chip in the pot. "Bumping one up to see who's got balls."

The ruddy-faced captain studied his hand as he talked. "Don't feel bad about having lost a patrol, Irish. I had a striker unit lost for two days just a couple 'a weeks ago. I had a new platoon leader who I found out later couldn't read a fuckin' compass or map. Hell, your kids are green. The RTO is probably asleep or his radio is broke dick. They probably heard the choppers and are hightailin' it back right now to get out of this dry hole." The captain picked up a chip and tossed it in. "I'm in."

In the adjoining room the radio speaker box crackled with static, then suddenly a calm voice filled the room. "Green Base, this is Charlie One, over."

Shawn tossed down his cards, recognizing the call sign and voice of his first squad leader, Alexander.

" 'Bout damn time."

The captain smiled and held up two blue chips. "I bet they blame the radio."

Master Sergeant Purdue shook his head in disagreement. "Naw, they'll say it was a bad battery or broken antenna."

The Special Forces radio operator pressed the sidebar of his handset to respond. "Charlie One, this is Green Base, I hear you loud and clear. Stand by for message, over."

The sergeant manning the radio leaned back in his chair to see around a bamboo partition curtain. "Irish, you wanna tell 'em to come back to camp, or ya want me to do it?"

The speaker box crackled again. "Green Base, be advised I have a contact report. You prepared to copy? Over."

The radio operator quickly sat forward and picked up a pencil as he pushed the sidebar with his other hand. "Send it, Charlie One, over."

Shawn and the rest of the card players came to their feet hearing "contact" and moved into the radio room just as the squad leader's voice came over the speaker.

"Green Base, we made contact with eight enemy North Vietnamese regulars in a rest camp at grid, Sierra Uniform 784326, at 1320 hours. Patrol engaged and KIA'd all eight enemy. No friendly casualties. Enemy were carrying AK-47s and pushing modified bicycles with rice and ammunition. Patrol has moved to high ground to make this report. Advise, over."

Captain Moss had stared at the speaker with a shocked expression and grabbed the handset from the sergeant. "Charlie One, how did you determine the enemy were regulars? Over."

There was a pause for several seconds before the speaker crackled again. "This is Charlie One. All eight enemy were wearing khaki uniforms, ammo vests, and belts with stars on the buckles . . . and all of them had fresh haircuts. Over."

Master Sergeant Purdue plotted the grid on the wall map and spoke in a rush to the captain. "They hit 'em ten klicks to the east of us. Are you thinkin' what I'm thinkin'?"

The captain shifted his gaze to Shawn. "This squad of yours reliable?"

Shawn nodded. "They're young, but the strongest bunch I got."

The captain shifted his eyes back to the master sergeant. "Top, I want a reinforced strike platoon to move out within the half hour and check out that kill site. Have 'em bring back everything that ain't growin'. I wanna know what the fuck is going on in *my* neighborhood." The captain pressed the handset sidebar again. "Charlie One, send your present location and wait where you are. We have a party planned, so expect company. You roger? Over."

Shawn spoke up. He didn't like the idea of his newly trained men having to stay in an area after a kill. If any other dinks had been within hearing distance, they would be coming to investigate.

"Sir, what about getting choppers to take in the strike force?"

Moss shook his head. "It'd take us half a day to get a request approved to get just one bird. We're gonna have to go by foot and hope your boys don't run into any more surprises."

Shawn understood the dilemma of the captain, but it didn't make him feel any better. He had sent the squads out, certain that their missions would be walks in the sun. The squads going out alone without him or the lieutenant were supposed to have been training confidence builders, not real combat missions. After all, the area was supposed to have been "quiet." Either the first squad had lucked into a passing infiltrating unit, or they were in the eye of a hurricane. Shawn went over the report again in his head. They said they'd killed eight enemy. What the hell were they doing initiating on a unit larger than themselves? He'd taught them never to engage more than half the number in their own patrol. Any more than that, and the odds turned against them. How in the hell did they do it?

Minutes later the ruddy-faced captain stood in front of the operations map addressing his assembled twelve-man A-team and one visitor wearing a First Cavalry patch.

"If the report we received is true, we got us a problem. Regulars pushing bicycles loaded with rice and ammo means they're stocking cache sites somewhere locally, or else they're passing through on their way to another area. Either way, we have dinks in our territory that I don't know anything about. I want maximum patrols out tomorrow. I don't like the feeling I've got about this. If regulars were caching stocks close to us, then their reconnaissance units have already checked us out and sketched every detail of this camp. It also means that assault units are not far behind. Men, we have to know what the fuck is happening out there as soon as possible. If it's what I think it is, we're gonna need all the time we can get to get ready. We may be up to our ass in alligators."

Shawn raised his hand. "Sir, I want to go with the strike unit that's going to my squad's location."

Moss raised an eyebrow. "Go ahead. If their report is correct, I'll see to it they get a medal. If it isn't you kill 'em before I do."

Shawn could see his men were different the second he spotted them standing on the ridge. The faded fatigues and the way they carried their weapons were the first signs. When he got closer, the look in their eyes confirmed it. Shawn had seen the transformation many times before, young men becoming veterans overnight.

He smiled as he stepped off the trail to where they were waiting. He motioned behind him toward the Montagnard strike platoon.

"I brought ya some company. Looks like you troops stirred things up a bit."

Blake's eyes narrowed in anger. "They said wait here, so we've been here with our ass hanging out for the past *twenty-four fucking hours!* You taught us never to stay around a kill site, but here we are. We don't have any water or food left. What the fuck took so long?"

Shawn kept his grin and scanned the men's beard-stubbled faces, which showed all the classic effects of continuous stress. He knew they had been in a hide position only five hundred meters from the ambush site. Shawn raised an eyebrow toward Blake. "We left yesterday to get here, but ran out of daylight and had to lagger up. We took off again at first light, but kept coming across signs of fresh foot traffic. We had to slow down or run the risk of being ambushed ourselves." Shawn's voice lowered. "You ain't the only ones trying to survive this war."

"What about choppers? Why didn't you fly in?" Blake asked Shawn with less rancor.

"These guys ain't cav. They don't have slicks dedicated to their camp.

The S.F. has to request birds from district, and they seldom get them unless it's an emergency. Be thankful you're cav. Now, are you finished asking twenty questions so these strikers can go on and check out the kill site?"

Blake nodded in brooding silence. The Special Forces sergeant in charge of the strikers came up the path toward him. Blake took out his folded map to show the exact location.

"Don't show him on the map, lead him," Shawn said flatly. "You're going to take us back to the kill site."

Blake swallowed hard. It had been impossible to sleep the night before because the contact kept running through his mind over and over again. He didn't want to go back to the grisly scene and be reminded again of what war really was.

Shawn noticed the squad leader's reaction. The rest of the squad members also showed looks of discomfort at his words. He turned to Sergeant First Class Canton.

"Canny, this is Alexander, first squad leader. He'll fill you in on where and what happened. If it's all right with you, they'd prefer not to go back. I'll lead them back to camp once you get through with 'em."

Canton shook hands with Blake. "Damn fine job. Zapping eight regulars without taking any hits of your own tells me it was a professional job." The sergeant took out his map. "Show me the spot and fill me in on what happened, then you guys can go. You all could probably use a beer."

Minutes later the squad was moving. Shawn was walking behind Alexander, observing how the squad operated. It only took him several minutes to feel comfortable. They moved like pros. Every man watched their assigned sector of the trail with an occasional glance all around to keep abreast of the others and any hand signals. They moved silently and yet quickly, with the point man, Calhoon, twenty meters out to the front. Calhoon was obviously the secret to the squad's success, for he didn't walk so much as stalk, like a jungle cat. He stopped every so often to listen and smell the forest. Being far enough to the front of the squad their sounds didn't mask others that could mean danger.

Shawn felt proud that he had trained the squad, but he knew he couldn't take the credit for the skills Calhoon possessed. Point men were a special breed, born with a sort of sixth sense. It was mentioned in no Army manual or taught at any school, but anybody who had been in war knew the sixth sense to be a fact. It was a special ability to "feel" the enemy's presence. So point men were to be treated special and well cared for. They were the ones who kept you alive. The only problem was that the law of averages worked against them. A point man couldn't walk in harm's way day after day without finally missing a sign or failing to see the enemy first. The point man's worst fear was an enemy point man who was better.

Shawn shifted his gaze from Calhoon to the squad leader's back. He had made a good choice in selecting Alexander. Alexander was probably too familiar with his men, but he would learn with time. The young scar-faced leader had been blooded now, so he knew that war was not like in the movies, that there was no glory. He had obviously made some tough decisions under stress, and his men still looked at him with respect—a good sign he had made the right decisions. With a little more experience, he could be trusted with any mission like an old vet.

Shawn stumbled on a root but caught himself before falling down. He cussed under his breath, realizing he was the only one in the squad not paying attention. He had been behaving like an inspector rather than as a member of the unit.

He felt a tinge of sadness. The teaching was over now. The men of the first squad had graduated.

22

Wearing his light green field uniform, Brigadier General Chu Huy Man stood before his assembled staff and pointed at the wall map.

"Tonight, on this day, the nineteenth of October, our division makes history, here . . . at Plei Me. Colonel Khan's 32nd Regiment will conduct the first phase of the operation by attacking at 2300 hours. Colonel Khan's mission is to assault the American-led outpost with enough forces to make the enemy believe they will be overrun, so that they will call for reinforcements. The only unit capable of reinforcing the American camp is the puppet's Third Armored Cavalry Squadron, stationed thirty kilometers north of Plei Me, here . . . in Pleiku city. Their timid commander's headquarters is located in the city, and he will not allow all his forces to leave his palace, so he will only send a task force comprised of tanks, armored personnel carriers, and a few infantry battalions. There is only one road leading to the outpost, and Colonel Du's 33rd Regiment will conduct phase two of the operation by ambushing the relief force here, just ten kilometers east of the Plei Me camp. Once the relief force is wiped out, the 33rd will join the 32nd Regiment for phase three of the operation and wipe out the outpost."

The general stepped away from the map and stood before the table of staring men. "The Americans will not sit idly by while we destroy their outpost. They will react to our threat with air support. But we are ready for this and will destroy their planes with air defense units, which I have placed around the camp and ambush position. You, the staff, must keep me abreast of the situation. No man can rest until the battle is won. Our brave soldiers move into their battle positions even as I speak. Not a single soldier of this division will die because he was not properly supported by this staff. We must give our all for the fatherland. Unification is near. Let us not fail those who are prepared to give so much."

Colonel Lee Van Quan, the assistant division commander, waited until his staff had cleared the small room before approaching his commander. "General, both regimental commanders have reported they are in position. All is ready."

"Excellent!" General Man smiled to show confidence.

Quan, however, was concerned with recent intelligence reports. "Comrade, I fear the new American unit building their base in An Khe. Should they use their new helicopter infantry, they could mass their forces behind us and force us to fight in two directions."

The general snickered, having read the same intelligence reports. "They are, as you say, 'new,' untested. The Americans would not be so foolish as to throw newly arrived men into a battle. They know they have much more to lose than just lives. They would lose face. Their leaders would not dare use such an untested force unless success were assured."

The colonel kept his worried frown. "General, my other concern is with the American Air Force. Unlike the air cavalry unit, their Air Force *is* experienced. I fear our men have not had time to prepare strong enough positions for the pounding. The bombs and napalm could be too much."

General Man raised his wrist and looked at his watch. "My friend, our biggest enemy, time, is against us. We have no choice. Although our men lack experience with American air power, and the 66th has not arrived, we must continue the attack. Our men will learn . . . we all will learn from this operation." The general tapped the watch crystal. "Time is also the Americans' enemy. They must win quickly or lose support from their homeland. The battle of time is on our side. This day, time has hurt us, but tomorrow, next week, next year, time will turn against the Americans." The general put his hand on his assistant's shoulder. "It is a battle even they cannot win."

Colonel Quan nodded with a forced smile. His thoughts were on the 66th Regiment, which was still fifteen days away on the trail leading to South Vietnam. Had they left only two weeks earlier, they would have been in the battle and assured victory. He walked back to the map with one consolation. The sky was turning cloudy. Planes could not bomb what they couldn't see.

Vincent Martino sighed in bone-weary relief at the sight of the ranch-style main gate of the Plei Me Special Forces camp. Unable to make the S.F. camp in one day's march, the squad had laggered for the night only five klicks from the camp, but it had taken most of that day to cover the short distance. The terrain had been particularly hilly, and they had found seven recently deserted enemy rest camps. Each one had to be thoroughly searched and reported, causing even more of a delay.

Eugene Day wearily lifted his head, hearing Vincent's sigh. "Tell me we there, man."

Vincent motioned ahead. "Hundred more steps an' I'm gonna sleep for a week. My feets is tellin' me they hate me. I'm gonna wash off this dirt an—"

Leading the squad, Lee Calhoon glanced over his shoulder with a glare, telling Vincent to be quiet. They were not finished with the patrol until they were through the gate.

The warning glare was enough to stop Vincent in mid-sentence and make him concentrate on forcing his weary legs to take him the last fifty meters.

Minutes later the squad sat in the shade of the command bunker. Staff Sergeant Flynn had told them to wait outside, while he checked on the status of the helicopter that was supposed to have been sent from An Khe to retrieve them. He stepped out of the bunker entrance with a somber expression. "The bird came this morning and waited for an hour before leaving. It'll be back tomorrow."

Blake Alexander took the news as good. It meant that his men could fill their empty stomachs and get some much-needed rest. He was about to say so when Flynn motioned to the distant northern mountains.

"The strike force that checked out your kill site ran into some regulars this morning, but they didn't get any confirmed kills. They've seen plenty of recent signs of movement and are continuing to patrol. Captain Moss, the camp commander, has also gotten reports from some rice farmers that V.C. have been moving in south of the camp. In short, I think—and so does the captain—that we might be in for some trouble. I want you all to wash up, clean your weapons, get resupplied with ammo, and report to the alternate command post bunker. The captain wants us to be ready if he needs help. We'll rest up there and keep a man on watch. I'll take the first shift."

Blake lifted his rifle to the crook of his arm. "Let's do it, first herd. The sooner we get it done, the sooner we get some sleep."

Lee Calhoon stared at the clouds hiding the setting sun as the rest of the men slowly stood to follow their squad leader. Blake stepped closer to Lee and shifted his gaze to the hazy sunset.

"What's wrong, Reb?" he said softly.

Lee slowly turned his head toward his friend with a confused look. "I don't reckon I know. I jus' got a feelin'."

Blake felt a chill run up his spine. "What? What are ya feeling?"

Lee looked back at the sunset as if drawing power. "I can feel 'em. They're out there, Ace, and they're close."

Blake nodded. He was worn-out physically, but mentally he felt strong and confident. War, and his reaction to it, were no longer a mystery. He didn't want to kill again, but if the enemy was out there, so be it. He and his men would be ready. Blake put his hand on his point man's shoulder and walked him toward the water point.

"Let's wash off, then worry about it. If they wanna mess with the best, then let 'em come."

Shawn Flynn stepped out of the dark bunker and looked up at the threatening clouds that masked the stars. He took in a breath.

"You can't sleep either, huh?" he said.

Blake Alexander was sitting against the outside of the bunker, enjoying the fresh night air and time alone. For five days he had been within arm's reach of at least one of his men night and day. He tossed a pebble into the darkness.

"I was just doing some thinking."

Shawn leaned against the top row of sandbags. "If you're wonderin' if you'll ever be able to forget the ones you killed—you won't. They'll always be there, but after a while you get used to them. You'll remember the faces of the first ones. The others will just be blurry images."

Blake looked up at his platoon sergeant, barely seeing his features in the darkness. "Did it bother you? The first time you—"

"Not at first, but later it did. It's something you learn to live with. Right now you might not believe that, but one day you'll sleep without thinking about it."

Blake lowered his head. "We were lucky. I froze up for a while and couldn't seem to think. I made mistakes that could have gotten some of my men killed. I didn't post security fast enough and—"

"It's over. Put it behind you and carry on. Learn from your mistakes. Don't forget them, but don't worry about the past. Ya can't change it."

Blake sighed and stood up. "It's easy to say, but hard to do."

Shawn faced the young soldier. "You did a good job out there, Alexander. I'm proud of you and your team. You learned quick and you brought your men back alive. But let me tell you a simple fact. Tomorrow is another day and the odds will be a little less in your favor. To beat the odds, you and your men have to get even better. Think about that. Your job and mine is getting our men back alive so that one day they can sit in rocking chairs with their grandkids and tell 'em stories 'bout what we did."

Blake felt a tingling, warm sensation. Back home, his father talked to other men like the sergeant was talking to him, except his father talked about making money. Here, an old veteran who cared about him was talking man-to-man about surviving. Flynn had also told him he was "proud" of him. David Alexander had never said that word to his son. Maybe his father was holding back the word, waiting for him to put a trophy in the Alexander case. "Proud" was such a small word, yet it meant so much.

Blake extended his hand. "Thank you, Sergeant."

Shawn smiled as he shook the soldier's hand. "I think it's time you called me 'Irish.' I only let vets call me that. Welcome to the club."

Jimbo Lasalle stood watch outside the bunker and looked at the luminous dial of his watch. It was almost 2300 hours. Damn! He thought he'd only had a few minutes left. Shit!

He shook his head to keep awake. It was still another thirty minutes before his shift was over, and then he'd be able to wake up Prescott to take his turn at standing watch outside the bunker.

Lasalle climbed up on top of the bunker to scan the dark camp. He mentally pictured the area during daylight and tried to find distinguishing landmarks. He could barely make out the southwest corner blockhouse bunker of the triangle. The three corner bunkers were the anchors to the three two-hundred-yard legs of the defense line. The bunkers were interconnected by a zigzagging trench line and smaller fighting bunkers. Inside the camp were a dozen tin-roofed buildings that housed the ammo and medical bunkers, a chow hall, administration, and sleeping quarters for the American detachment and their Montagnard soldiers known as the CIDG, Civilian Irregular Defense Group. Between the buildings were several deeply dug, sandbagged bunkers, where command and control took place. The bunker Lasalle sat on was a smaller version of the main command bunker. Inside were several radios, in case the main C.P. was knocked out. Outside the wire were barbed-wire entanglements, ditches, and deadly claymore mines.

Lasalle shifted his stance, imagining he was in a modern version of Fort Apache in the old west. He smiled to himself and mimicked John Wayne's walk to the edge of the bunker. All I need is attacking Indians to make it perfect, he thought as he climbed down. His foot had just touched the ground when he heard several distant metallic thunks. Lasalle spun around and saw small brilliant flashes in the distance far beyond the camp. "Awww *shit!*" he screamed. *"Incoming!"*

Lasalle yelled the warning again and dove into the crowded bunker, crashing on top of the sleeping Prescott.

Shawn sat up and, hearing the all too familiar metallic pops of mortars, cussed under his breath. He sprung to his feet and scooped up his rifle with one hand and his old friend, the .45 pistol, with the other. "Everybody stay in here and keep to the sides of the firing ports. Shrapnel is going to be everywhere in just a—"

The first mortar shells burst inside the camp, showering the camp in flashes of light and cracking explosions. Shawn knelt at the bunker entrance looking at the flashes. By the number of tubes he'd heard firing, they were in for a pounding.

He spun around and yelled over the explosions, "Get a candle burning so we can see each other!"

Lee turned on his flashlight and quickly found the C-ration box they had used for a table. A candle was stuck to the top, mired in its own wax. He lit the wick and in seconds the bunker was bathed in a golden glow. An explosion ripped the air just outside the entrance, violently shaking the ground beneath them. Shawn scanned the frightened men's faces. They were all wide-eyed, looking up at the sandbagged ceiling, waiting for a round to blow them to kingdom come.

"Look at me!" he yelled. "It's lesson time again. Those are 82-millimeter mortars. If you listen close you can figure how many crews are firing. I figure about eight to ten tubes."

Another vehement explosion rocked the bunker and sent up a cloud of choking dust. Nonplussed, the sergeant continued. "This is a prep for a ground assault. You can usually tell from which direction it will come by the way the mortars shift their fires just before the attack. Once they have everybody's heads down, they'll concentrate on knocking out the corner bunkers with heavy machine guns, B-40 rockets, and recoilless rifle fire. The assault will come after the—"

A round buried its iron head into the red soil just outside the bunker and exploded, almost knocking Shawn off his feet. He wiped the dust from his eyes and continued, "The assault will come after they send in sappers to clear paths through the mines and wire. When their satchel charges go off, you'll know it by the different sound that rattles your teeth."

The squad jumped each time a round exploded close by, but one by one they unwound their fear-stiffened bodies and lowered their eyes from the ceiling to concentrate on what the sergeant was saying. Blake watched the process in fascination. Unlike the others, he didn't feel fear. Not that he wasn't afraid to die—he just figured it was a waste of time worrying about it. He couldn't help but remember how, when he was younger, he loved to walk around the estate during a thunderstorm. The excitement of the crashing thunder and flashing lightning had been intoxicating. He broke from his reverie to listen to his platoon sergeant, who was trying to calm the others.

"The command bunker is probably calling for a flare ship that will soon fly over to light the area for the Air Force. Once the team captain determines the direction of the main assault, he'll concentrate the bombing there."

Shawn motioned toward the radios and field phone resting on an ammo box table. "Lasalle, turn on the radios and hook up the speaker box. We'll be able to monitor the calls and keep up with what's happening. Calhoon, stay to the side of the right firing port; Martino, you take the left."

Vincent cautiously rose and moved to the firing port. "I don't like this. I rather be patrollin' than this."

Eugene Day lifted his eyes to the sergeant. "What can I do?"

Shawn motioned to the boxes of ammunition stacked under the table. "Inventory what ammo we've got and make sure everybody has all they can carry, especially grenades."

Between the crumpling explosions came a new sound that turned every man's head toward the bunker entrance. The throaty rattling of heavy machine guns was adding to the din. "Heavy machine guns." Shawn winked. "What'd I tell ya?"

The speaker crackled with the excited voice of a Special Forces sergeant. ". . . we're getting the shit kicked out of us from the south. Is the Air Force on station? Over."

The Plei Me camp commander, Captain Harold Moss, answered with his usual calm voice. "Negative, no contact with the FAC yet. Can you reinforce your bunker with more sandbags? Over."

"Roger, we're doing that and— Shit! That was close! We just got hit by another .57 recoilless round. The sonofabitches are tearing our bunker apart piece by piece. *Where's the fuckin' planes?*"

Shawn had spread a map on the floor of the bunker to keep up with the reports. It had been an hour since the first mortar shells had landed, and the pounding still had not let up. By the reports, it was clear the enemy ground assault would come from the south. The outposts that had been positioned outside the south side of the camp had quit reporting. Their silence meant they were dead or captured. Also, the southwest bunker was taking most of the recoilless weapon and rocket fire and a concentrated mortar barrage.

Shawn looked up from the map at Blake. "According to the reports, the aid station, ammo, and como bunkers have all been destroyed. The sappers will be coming next to blow holes in the wire. Better make sure every man is carrying all the ammo he can."

Blake had Eugene pass out more bandoliers and open another box of grenades. Blake stepped into the bunker entrance and peeked over the sandbags. Green and red tracers crisscrossed the camp, accented by bursts of white-orange light. Ear-shattering, cracking explosions followed. Dust and cordite filled the air, making the macabre scene hazy and unreal. Shawn knelt down beside the squad leader, looking at the distant command bunker which was silhouetted by the burning mess hall.

"You're in charge," he said. "I'm gonna have to go and see Captain Moss. He's gonna need help holding the south leg. Keep your men in the bunker and remember to use the grenades first."

Blake put his hand on the sergeant's shoulder. "Take care, Irish. We'll see ya later, huh?"

Shawn winked. "Yeah." He broke into a dead run for the bunker.

Blake held his breath. The mess hall fire cast an orange glow over the plowed ground, which smoked with plumes of reddish-yellow, making it look as if his sergeant were running through hell. A sudden explosion behind Flynn knocked him off his feet, and Blake bit his lip. A full five seconds passed before the dust cloud drifted away enough for Blake to look for the prone figure. He wasn't there. Blake relaxed and stepped back into the bunker.

Lee was bent over the map and listening to the radio. Captain Moss was asking for a report from the northern side of the camp.

A drawling voice came over the speaker. "We got the villagers streaming in the northwest gate. We're still gettin' hit by mortars but not direct-fire weapons. I can spare a platoon, if you need them, over."

Captain Moss responded immediately. "Have a platoon reinforce the southwest leg. Have 'em take up positions in the trench line. Move them out as soon as the barrage lifts, over."

"Roger, we'll be there, out."

Blake knelt down next to Lee. "Flynn went to the command bunker. You're now second in command. If anything happens to me, you take care of the squad."

Lee smiled. "I sure fancy that big watch of yours. Ya reckon I could have it if'n somethin' happens to ya?"

Blake grinned. "What for? They can't read time in Cusseta."

Shawn dove over the remaining five feet of earth between him and the bunker and crawled to the entrance as fast as he could. He was out of breath and soaked in sweat. He had thought of Cindy and the baby when the explosion had knocked him to the ground and temporarily stunned him. He had lain looking up at the black sky, wondering if she would understand.

Captain Moss gaped at the man entering the bunker as if he were seeing a ghost. "Irish, you're still in one piece?"

Shawn, trying to catch his breath, could only nod in reply. Moss pointed at the situation map.

"It looks like it's gonna come from the south, probably gonna try and take out the southwest bunker and then roll up the legs."

Shawn straightened up, finally able to breathe. "What . . . what can I do for you?" he gasped.

Moss began to speak when gunfire suddenly erupted. It sounded like three hundred rifles firing at once. Shawn and the captain rushed to the entrance and looked to the south. The ground seemed to rise up beneath their feet and rock them as if they were standing on springs. Then the sound wave hit. The thunderous roar of the explosion made both men wince in pain.

"Sappers just blew the wire," Shawn said flatly.

Moss began to sprint toward the south trench, but Shawn held out his arm, stopping him.

"I'll go. You've got to stay here and control this mess."

With that, Shawn slowly jogged toward the gunfire and disappeared in the smoke of the burning building.

Moss rushed back into the bunker, yelling at the radio operator, "Tell the others the assault has started! They're hitting the south leg!"

Lieutenant Colonel Nyguen Van Khan stepped up to the rise to watch his battalion attack. His three one-hundred-man companies had worked their way within three hundred meters of the camp wire during the mortar barrage and then dug shallow positions. Only a few seconds before, they had risen up and begun the long awaited assault. The colonel winced hearing the first enemy machine guns chattering their death chant.

"Where is the flank battalion? Why are they not attacking?" he asked his operations officer.

The young major lowered his head, afraid to tell his commander the news. The colonel pointed toward his charging men.

"*Where is the other battalion?*" he screamed.

The major lifted his head, staring with wide eyes. "They are not going to attack. The general has ordered that they remain in reserve."

Colonel Khan's face screwed up into a mask of horror. His battalion was attacking straight into the enemy's main defense without a supporting attacking battalion. It meant that all the enemy's fire could be concentrated at the single threat. It would devastate his men's ranks. Colonel Khan screamed in rage and pulled the pistol from his holster. He didn't need to ask why the other battalion had been ordered at the last minute not to attack. The rumors that he had heard, that he did not want to believe, were now substantiated. The general had no intention of taking the camp. He wanted only to force the enemy to call for reinforcements. The men in his battalion were pawns. They were running toward an entrenched enemy believing they had the honor of leading a regimental attack, when in fact it was merely a feint. The general had lied.

Khan broke into a slow run toward the camp. He screamed as he increased his pace and ignored the tears that stung his eyes. He would lead his men. They at least deserved that.

Shawn reached the trench line just as the reinforcements arrived from the north leg. He jumped into the five-foot ditch and ducked under and entered a small bunker. Christ, he thought, he'd stepped back fifteen years through time. A middle-aged Montagnard wearing a headband was loading a BAR with a magazine. It had been the same type of weapon his friend Quail had used in Korea. The Yard grinned despite the incoming bullets that slapped against the protective sandbags. Shawn looked out the firing port and gasped. It *was* Korea all over again. The attacking enemy were streaming toward the wire in assault waves. And they weren't V.C. Viet Cong didn't wear khaki uniforms and pith helmets. The Montagnard leaned forward, supporting himself on the sandbag ledge, and began firing. Shawn raised his rifle and joined in the killing.

Colonel Khan stepped over body after body as he approached the barbed-wire fence. The sappers had only been partially successful. They had blown a gap through two rows of the twisted barbed wire, but not the third row, which was now weighted down with dozens of his soldiers' riddled bodies. He continued forward, as did his men, trying to get over the barrier of corpses. Red tracers slapped the ground at his feet and ricocheted like fizzing rockets. A sergeant to his right pitched backward, hit in the chest. A private screamed in anguish, having been hit in the ankle. Khan climbed over his dead comrades and crossed the wire. He raised his pistol and called for his men to follow him. He took three steps and was chopped almost in half by a sweeping machine-gun burst. He crumpled to the ground, still holding his pistol.

Shawn moved out of the bunker and walked up and down the trench directing fire on the attacking waves of enemy floundering in the wire. Handheld flares popped overhead in green, white, and red star bursts, silhouetting the screaming, shooting North Vietnamese who still struggled to clear a path through the wire.

Captain Moss's face was drawn as he listened to the new reports coming in from the northwest bunker. The enemy had partially destroyed the bunker with recoilless rifles and were still attacking in strength. A minute before, he had felt joy upon hearing that the southwest bunker and southern leg were still holding. But the news of the northwest bunker's destruction had just as quickly ended his hope that the enemy's attack would remain limited to the south. The meaning was clear. He was not facing a single battalion or even two. He was fighting a full regiment, capable of striking all three legs at once! Moss turned to his radio operator.

"Call headquarters and tell 'em we can't hold without reinforcements. Tell 'em we're under attack by an enemy regiment—a North Vietnamese Army regiment!"

Master Sergeant Purdue saw Shawn in the trench and jumped down and grabbed his shoulder.

"Irish, the northwest bunker is under attack. We gotta get over there!"

Shawn slapped in a fresh magazine and climbed out of the trench. He motioned to the distant alternate C.P. bunker as he broke into a jog. "I'm gonna get my squad and I'll join you."

Seconds later he rushed into the bunker. "Lasalle, you stay and monitor the radios; the rest of you come on! We've got to plug a hole!"

Blake and the others ran hunched over, following their platoon sergeant toward the northwest bunker. With every step the firing grew louder and more intense. The air seemed alive with bullets, which cracked and zinged overhead. The green incoming tracers looked like softballs whizzing past.

An explosion to their right threw up a cloud of dust and peppered them with scorched dirt clods. Prescott threw himself to the ground, but Shawn jerked him to his feet.

"Keep moving!" Shawn yelled.

Seconds later they reached the trench and jumped in, landing on squatting villagers. Shawn cussed and fought to untangle his body from a screaming woman and called out for his men to follow him. It was like trying to move through the narrow aisle of a crowded department store during a sale. Old women held on to small pigs and little babies. Crying children huddled in groups. Wounded Montagnards sprawled all over the trench floor. The men of the squad pushed and shoved their way through the human sea of panic and desperation. When they finally reached a small fighting bunker only twenty meters from the huge blockhouse corner bunker, Shawn stopped and motioned his men inside.

"Take up firing positions! Martino, sweep the wire with the 'sixty in short bursts! Use grenades if they penetrate the wire!"

Lee pushed off his M-16's safety and moved up to the firing step. What he saw over the sandbagged ledge made his stomach shrivel into a bouncing lead marble. The wire entanglements, twenty-five meters down a slight slope, were full of hundreds of screaming, shooting men. Lee raised his rifle and began shooting back. Vincent quickly swung down the bipod legs and positioned the machine gun on the ledge.

"Gene, feed me ammo!" he yelled.

Blake frantically pulled grenades from his pockets and began tossing them toward the wire. Prescott lifted his rifle and tried to fire, but nothing happened. Panicked, he cussed and jerked the charging handle back, ejecting a cartridge. He slapped the weapon to his shoulder and pressed the trigger, but again nothing happened.

Shawn grabbed the startled soldier's weapon and pushed the selector off safe. "Think!"

Overhead, a B-40 rocket roared like a freight train. Fifty-one-caliber machine-gun bullets thudded into the bunker's lower bags, tearing open huge holes. Chicom grenades exploded outside like Chinese firecrackers. Children wailed in terror and women shrieked.

Blake threw another grenade out the portal. Bursting flares overhead flooded the wire with eerie green light. He could see the ghostly green faces of the attackers clearly as they screamed commands at each other. He joined Lee on the ledge and sighted in on a Vietnamese trying to cut the wire. He fired, and the soldier's shoulder jerked up and back. Incredibly, the man staggered back to the wire and with his good arm tried to tear it loose from its picket. Blake fired again. The red tracer disappeared into the green face, and the soldier fell backward.

Eugene calmly fed the belt of ammunition into Vincent's machine gun and reminded him to fire in short bursts. Vincent swung right and stitched two men who were carrying bamboo poles packed with explosives. He swung left and sent five bullets into a screaming sergeant who had just cut through the wire.

"They're getting through!" he screamed.

Shawn tossed two grenades, one after another, toward the newly opened gap. "Prescott, keep that gap covered!" he yelled over the shooting.

Lee could no longer hear. His ears were ringing with the pounding clamor of weapons shooting from inside the bunker. He patted his bandolier to check for a full magazine, but felt only the smaller cardboard boxes the bullets came packed in. He looked down. At his feet was the pile of empty magazines he had used and ejected. For an instant he panicked. He didn't want to take precious time to reload, but he knew he had no choice. He dropped down to his knees and tore open the small cardboard box with his teeth. He shook the twenty bullets onto his lap and quickly began to load them into an empty magazine.

Shawn felt his own bandolier. He had only two full mags left. *"Check magazines!"* he yelled.

Blake patted his chest bandolier. "I've got four!"

"Three!" Prescott blurted a second later.

Eugene took off the crossed bandoliers from around his neck and tossed them to Shawn. "Ten full."

Shawn quickly redistributed the full magazines to Blake and Prescott, then dropped down to pick up all the empties. He and Lee would have to reload them.

Captain Harry Moss had lost all patience. *"I'm tired of excuses!"* he yelled into the handsets. *"Get me planes here right fuckin' now!"*

"We're doing everything we can," an agitated voice replied over the speaker. "A C-123 is inbound from Nha Trang. Estimated ETA is thirty minutes, over."

"Where are the bombers and attack planes?" Moss snapped into the handset. "I need bombs and napalm!"

"Roger, they are standing by waiting for the C-123 to drop flares."

Moss gave up. He had been wrong to yell at the operator, but his frustration level had overflowed an hour before. The mortar attack had begun at 2300 hours, and the ground assault at thirty minutes past midnight. He looked at his watch. It was now almost one-thirty, and they still did not have a single aircraft overhead. All the promises of air support within fifteen minutes had been lies. *Goddamnit!* The fuckers were sleeping in beds with clean sheets and had refrigerators full of beer. They could haul in ice machines and liquor for their clubs, but they couldn't find time to drop a few bombs on the enemy. Maybe they had all been at a party and had to sober up first . . . Goddamnit, what the fuck kind of war was this? *Where in the fuck is the Air Force?*

Prescott waited for the next flash of light to expose the bloody gap in the wire. A pile of dead and wounded lay blocking the opening cut. He inched himself up farther, ignoring the torrent of bullets that cracked overhead.

Eugene heard a smack and turned just as Prescott reeled back and fell over Shawn, who was kneeling in the bunker floor reloading magazines. Prescott moaned but didn't move as Shawn slid from beneath the man's weight. Shawn turned on his red-filtered lens flashlight and checked for the wound. The red light made Prescott's blood look black. The bullet had struck him in the lower jaw, shattering the bone. The entry wound was small and clean, but the bullet and some crushed bone had blown out the back of his face, just below the ear. Sticky black blood and dirt matted his hair.

Shawn had just reached for the soldier's first-aid pouch when Prescott began gagging and flopping on the ground. Shawn grabbed Prescott's thin shoulders in a steel grip and turned him on his injured side.

"Calhoon, stick your finger in his mouth and clear the airway!" he yelled.

Lee picked up the flashlight Shawn had dropped and worked a dirty finger into Prescott's mouth, clearing away blood, bone, broken teeth, and skin tissue, which mixed with spit and dribbled down the wounded soldier's chin. Lee opened Prescott's first-aid pouch and pulled out a sterile bandage. He tore off the plastic with his teeth, gently placed the white absorbent material over the exit wound and exerted pressure. He passed the bandage tails to Shawn, who wrapped them around the soldier's head and tied a knot on top of the bandage to keep pressure on the wound.

Prescott moaned like a terrified animal and clawed the ground in anguish and pain. Shawn wiped his bloody hands on his fatigues and pushed Prescott against the earthen wall. He put his foot on the soldier's back, pinning him against the wall to ensure he wouldn't roll over and choke to death on his own blood. Satisfied he had done all he could, Shawn went back to work loading the magazines.

Lee crawled back to the pile of magazines feeling sick. The smell of blood in the small bunker was overpowering. Vincent's machine gun spit out more lead, which ripped and tore through more flesh. A child screamed somewhere outside in the trench, and another mortar shell exploded only twenty meters behind the bunker. Prescott's moans were soon lost among the deafening, cacophonous orchestra of war.

Captain Moss rubbed his tired eyes and looked back at the map. Things were finally looking up. The camp defenders were holding their own. The C-123 Provider had arrived on station over the camp at two A.M. and had been dropping parachute flares ever since to keep the camp and attacking enemy exposed. And the striker company that had been patrolling to the north had traveled most of the night and were now only a kilometer away.

Moss walked to the bunker entrance and looked out at the sky. The best news of all was that it was almost light. With daylight would come the fighter bombers, and at last the bastards who had attacked his camp would pay. The thoughts he'd had hours before concerning Air Force pilots were now all taken back—as long as they dropped their bombs straight and true.

Shawn awoke to a thunderous blast that shook two sandbags lose from the ceiling. They crashed on his legs and shoulder. He quickly got to his feet and stepped into the trench. The corner blockhouse bunker had received a direct hit. A recoilless shell had passed through a firing port and exploded against the back wall, setting off stored explosives. The resulting explosion left only shredded burlap bags and pieces of small brown bodies. Shawn knew there would be a follow-up ground attack and stepped back inside the squad bunker. Calhoon and Martino were in their fighting positions. The rest were sleeping in odd positions. Shawn shook Blake awake.

"The blockhouse has been destroyed. I expect an attack any time. Better get ready. I'm gonna try and get a medic for Prescott and find us some ammo. Keep your eyes and ears open."

Blake shook his head. Had he actually slept? Shawn had ordered him to try and get some rest a few hours before, but he'd thought that sleep would be impossible. He crawled on his hands and knees to Prescott. For an instant Blake thought the wounded man was dead, then he saw his chest moving. The soldier was blissfully unconscious from the pain. Blake stood and ordered his men to check their ammunition and the number of grenades they had left. They were low on everything. He checked his watch and looked out the firing port. Hope and strength rushed back into his body. Daylight was coming. Now he and his men would be able to see the bastards before they were in the wire.

Lee motioned for Eugene to take his place so he could step out into the trench and relieve himself. He walked out of the bunker and immediately froze. The body of a woman was sprawled in the dirt, her chest cavity opened as if by a meat cleaver. She was covered in a dusting of red soil, so that she looked almost like part of the trench floor. Lee saw several children huddled with their mother only a few yards away. They looked at him with great, sad eyes, as if pleading for him to save them. Lee turned around and walked down the crowded trench in the opposite direction. Those eyes had gotten to him. He had answered their pleading look with one of his own, a look that said "yes."

Vincent dusted off his machine gun and inserted a new belt of ammunition. It was the last; only two hundred rounds were left. He nodded toward the bodies littering the battlefield.

"Them guys were either dumb or brave. They wouldn't stop comin', you know?"

Eugene wiped his glasses free of dirt and put them on again. "They're soldiers like Prescott and you and me. They were doing their job."

Vincent suddenly pulled back the charging handle of the machine gun. "Well, they're back on the job. I see 'em movin' about four hundred out."

Blake rushed up to the ledge. Sonofabitch, hadn't they had enough? He could clearly see what looked like at least a company of men jogging in a loose formation toward the main gate.

"They're moving into position for an attack."

Eugene relaxed the grip on his rifle with relief. "That means we're out of it, then."

Blake backed up from the ledge, realizing they were anything but "out of it." If the regulars breached the gate and got into the trench, it would be all over. He tapped Vincent's shoulder.

"Come on, you and I are going down the trench and join the Yards protecting the gate. Gene, you stay here and tell Lee where we've gone and look after Pres."

"Hold it, Ace, the sarge said stay here and keep our eyes open, man."

Blake motioned Vincent out and looked at Eugene. "We don't have a choice, and you know it."

Eugene nodded reluctantly. "Take care of the big guy for me, huh?"

Blake nodded in silence and joined Vincent in the trench. Minutes later they were digging frantically to expand a partially destroyed firing position that sat between stacked sandbags on both exposed sides. Mortar shells were making impact behind them as they worked with their hands and the broken butt of an M-1 rifle. They had no overhead protection, but the fields of fire were perfect for covering the wire gate. Suddenly the air filled with angry cracks and pops as bullets whizzed by. Blake brought his rifle into his shoulder and pushed off the safety. Vincent dug his elbows into the ground behind his weapon.

"I wish I was home," he whispered.

Blake sighted in on his first target, a man who sprang up and rushed for the gate, carrying a satchel charge. Home had been the farthest thing from his mind. The thought struck him that he was home now. He squeezed the trigger.

Shawn turned toward the sound of gunfire. He didn't like it that Alexander and Martino had gone, but he knew they had done the right thing. He turned back and nodded toward Lee, who helped him lift Prescott. Shawn had found the S.F. medic in a bunker beside the C.P. Burned and wounded patients covered the makeshift aid station's dirt floor. Shawn knew better than to ask the medic to make a house call.

The two men carried the small soldier by locking arms and sharing the weight. They moved fast. They didn't want to be in the open any longer than they needed to be. The night barrage had cratered and plowed the ground and made covering the short distance more difficult than they had expected. When they finally made it to the aid station, they dropped off

Prescott with a Montagnard assistant medic and hurried to their old bunker, where Lasalle was still monitoring the radios.

With Jimbo Lasalle were two slightly wounded Special Forces sergeants who were using the radios to talk to an Air Force pilot flying high above the camp. The pilot was going to direct an aerial resupply drop.

Shawn and Lee threw bandoliers over their shoulders and each picked up a can of M-60 machine-gun ammunition. Shawn nodded toward Lasalle. "Come on, these guys are using the radios. Grab five of those bandoliers and a box of grenades."

Jimbo Lasalle was happy to comply. He had been miserable in the bunker, wondering all night if he was going to die alone.

Vincent swung the smoking barrel to the left and pressed the trigger. Two running soldiers pitched forward, hit in the lower legs. Vincent had quickly learned that he didn't waste as much ammunition if he fired low. If he missed, the ricocheting bullets still stopped them. He swung back to cover the gate and glanced down at the remaining belt of ammo. He had no more than fifteen or twenty rounds left. It might be just enough, he thought, looking at the bodies lying in front of the gate. The assault had lasted a full ten minutes and the small Montagnard tribesmen had risen to the occasion. They had poured devastating fire into the North Vietnamese regulars, forcing them back. The regulars had regrouped and assaulted several more times, but each attempt had been made with fewer attackers.

Blake pushed the magazine release, slapped in another, and continued firing. Individual soldiers were still trying to put a satchel charge against the gate. As soon as one would die in the attempt, another would run forward, pick up the bag of explosives, and try again. He had shot six men in succession and saw the seventh jump up. He looked like a mere boy, no older than fourteen. He ran straight for his fallen comrade. Blake closed one eye, aimed, and fired. The boy fell forward, his thigh spouting blood. He rolled over, grabbing his leg, and stared in horror at the wound. The Montagnards farther down the trench noticed the easy target and began firing. Blake saw the boy jerk once then twice and fall backward into the dust.

"*No more!*" Blake screamed. "*Please God, no more!*"

Another soldier rose from behind a rise and sprinted toward the satchel of explosives. Blake aimed and fired.

Shawn heard the barreling medevac helicopter only after it passed overhead. It banked hard right, almost standing on its side, and sank like a rock into the camp. He had just collected Blake and Vincent from the north leg and were jogging back to the others, who were now waiting inside the alternate C.P. bunker. Shawn could see the Montagnards loading the

wounded on the shaking Huey, and knew they would put Prescott on
before one of their own. It was the way they were, totally unselfish people.
A gunship passed overhead to cover the air evacuation, but the North
Vietnamese gunners had recovered from the surprise appearance of the first
low-flying chopper. The circling gunship was a big juicy target for every
gunner outside the wire to sight on. Green tracers arched upward toward
the war bird. The pilot jinked his bird left, then right, but his efforts were
futile. The chopper took hit after hit and began to smoke. Nosing over to
regain airspeed, the gunship flashed over the camp, trailing gray-white
smoke, unable to lift its nose. The bird crashed in a fiery ball just outside
the wire.

Taking advantage of the distraction, the medevac lifted off and swung
around toward the north. It picked up airspeed and skimmed only a few
meters over Shawn's head, then suddenly pulled up. The North Vietnamese gunners swiveled their weapons toward the new target, but it was
gaining altitude too quickly. Only a few gunners even tried half-hearted
bursts.

Shawn motioned his men inside the bunker and heard the radio blaring
as he entered. Captain Moss had just ordered a rescue team from the north
leg to go out and check the wreckage for survivors. Shawn sat down
wearily.

"They won't make it fifty feet outside the wire," he said.

Vincent lowered his canteen. "What do you mean? I thought the regulars pulled back. We beat 'em."

"Who do you think shot down the hog?" Shawn said. "They're out
there, all right, digging in deep and waiting. We're under siege. If they can
stop us from getting resupplied, they can walk in here in less than twenty-
four hours. All they have to do is put pressure on us till we're out of ammo.
The Air Force is going to have to win this one for us."

Blake sat in the corner, looking over his men. Their bearded faces where
gaunt and their bloodshot eyes were sunken. Filled with resolve, he got to
his feet.

"If it's gonna be a siege, we're gonna have to stock this bunker with
ammo, food, and water. Gene, check and see how much ammo and food
we have left in here. Lee, you and Vincent search the other bunkers for
extra supplies. Check the dead and get their ammo and whatever else we
might need. From here on out, we ration everything . . . especially water."

23

Blake surveyed the meager results of the search and made a note in his small, pocket-size notebook.

"We get one C-ration meal a day and a half a canteen of water," he said to the squad. "And boil the water you got from the Yards. Rest is gonna be important, so I want everybody to lie down now and get some shut-eye. The watch list and times will be posted on the bunker door. I'll stand first watch."

Vincent leaned back on the sandbags and looked up at the ceiling. "You know what I'd give for a hoagie right now?"

Eugene sat down by his friend. "Yeah, the same as I'd give for a T-bone steak. I'd give everything I had, including you."

Lee sat down beside Lasalle, stretched his long legs and closed his eyes. He wondered what the children in the trench were going to eat.

Captain Moss watched the bomber coming in from the east and cringed as green tracers rose up toward the aircraft like angry bees. The tracers crisscrossed in the sky, searching for their target. Low cloud cover was forcing the bomb runs lower than were normal. For waiting enemy gunners, it was a turkey shoot. A B-57 Cannaberra bomber had already been hit that morning, as well as an A-1E Sky Raider. The pilots had managed to get far enough away from the camp before punching out, so that all had been rescued.

Moss saw the attacking bomber shudder from the peppering fire of the heavy machine-gun bullets, but it continued its attack and dropped a five-hundred-pounder south of the camp.

Moss wished he had never thought badly of the pilots and swore to himself he'd never do it again. They had to have balls the size of watermelons to come in under the clouds. The ground shook violently with the explosion. Seconds later the shock wave caused the captain to grind his teeth in pain.

Master Sergeant Purdue yelled for the captain from inside the bunker. Purdue's face showed the strain of staying awake for over twenty-four hours. "Sir, Joe Bailey got hit bad just outside the wire as he led a rescue party to the chopper," he said as Moss entered. "Sergeant Clifford also got wounded a few minutes later, trying to pull Bailey in. The dinks have dug in machine-gun positions surrounding the camp. The strike company that was on patrol up north is within five hundred meters of the main gate, and they haven't bumped into any enemy. They're requesting us to lay down covering fire while they make a run for the gate."

Captain Moss sat down on an ammunition box. He wanted to know more about the condition of his two wounded men, but his questions would have to wait. "I don't like it. Running across that open ground in broad daylight is too dangerous."

"Sir, we don't have a choice," Purdue said evenly. "The longer they wait, the more likely it is they'll be seen. If the dinks catch them out there, they'll tear 'em to pieces. We gotta chance it."

The sergeant was right. Moss rubbed his eyes. He was just too damn tired to think anymore. "Tell 'em to execute in thirty minutes," he said. "That'll give us time to warn our people and position some covering machine guns."

Purdue nodded to the radio operator to send the go-ahead message and looked back at his team captain. "Sir, I've got some more good news. In a couple'a hours the Air Force is gonna start air droppin' resupplies into the camp. I've requested ammo, food, and water. Irish and his squad'll handle the recovery."

"Good. Now, what about a relief force? Any word from group?"

Purdue's eyes narrowed. "Them slow movin' South Vietnamese generals can't make a decision. They're gonna send a unit from Pleiku, but it's gonna take at least two days to assemble the force."

Moss looked at the team sergeant as if he'd called his mother a whore. *"Two days?* You gotta be shitting me."

Purdue kept his eyes steady. "No, sir. They're worried about an ambush between Pleiku and here. Group is talking to them, trying to push 'em, but the Viet general is balking. He don't want to leave Pleiku open for attack. Group is as upset as we are, and they've scrambled two Viet Ranger companies under the command of Major Beckwith from Project Delta. They're flying in to Pleiku sometime tomorrow night. They'll be reinforcing us the next morning."

Moss nodded absently. An additional two hundred men would help, but what they really needed was tanks. Outnumbered light infantry could do very little against dug-in positions. Losses would be extremely heavy if they tried to dislodge the enemy now.

The captain stood wearily. "I'm gonna make sure our people know about the strike company coming in. I'll be in the trench near the gate, waiting for them. Keep everything running here, Top."

"Sir, you need rest," Purdue growled at his commander. "When you get back, get some sleep."

Moss tried to smile but found the effort too difficult. He shook his head and mumbled as he walked up the bunker steps. "Sleep? What the hell is that?"

22 OCTOBER

Blake awoke at first light, after only a few hours' sleep. Four parachute air drops had come in at dusk the day before, and it had taken most of the night to uncrate and distribute the supplies. The Air Force had done a phenomenal job of keeping the parachute drops inside the camp perimeter. Whoever was calculating the winds and drop speed deserved a promotion.

Blake stood and immediately gagged. The stench that had permeated the camp was gut wrenching. He'd thought he would have gotten used to it by now, as he had the incessant bombing, but after a few days the sickening smell of the rotting flesh had only become stronger and more unbearable. Eating had become next to impossible. Steeling himself, he tied a bandanna around his nose and mouth, cowboy style, and began his routine.

He first checked with the Special Forces radio operator to get the daily schedule of air drops, and posted the times on the bunker door. He then checked with the main command post for an update on the current situation. The past two days had been mostly a standoff. The North Vietnamese had been content to mortar and snipe at the camp, while they, the defenders, dug in deeper and directed air strikes in an attempt to blow the enemy out of his stranglehold. Hundreds of bombs had turned the land outside the wire into a Martian landscape. Blake found out that a relief force led by Special Forces had helicoptered to an L.Z. four klicks away the night before, and was now poised outside the camp gate, ready to make a mad dash into the camp. He wrote the information down and jogged back to his bunker to wake his men, check their weapons, and make sure they were taking in enough water and food. Eating was the hardest task to do. The ghastly stench had permeated even the food.

Blake detoured from his route and stopped by the north defensive trench line, where he knew he would find one of his men. Lee was already up and feeding the kids, as usual. The Georgian had supervised the digging of a bunker for the children and had made sure they were supplied with food and canned milk from the air-dropped supplies. Blake hailed him.

"Lee, we got a drop in about fifteen minutes."

"I'll be there," Lee said as he spooned rice into the open mouth of a dirty four-year-old.

Blake jogged back to the bunker. Shawn waited outside for him. Like his own, the sergeant's face was partially covered by a dirty scarf.

"Major Beckwith and his relief force of two Ranger companies are going to make a run for the gate in about thirty minutes," Shawn said. "If you hear shooting, you'll know what it is."

"They want us to help cover them?"

"Naw, Captain Moss wants us to continue the drop on schedule. We need the ammo."

Blake stepped into the bunker and shook Vincent, Eugene, and Lasalle. "Wake up, it's another great day in South Vietnam. They're super-ripe this morning, so you'd better put on your bandanna before you stand up. The aroma seems to get stronger when you're standin'."

Vincent sat up with a scowl and wrinkled his nose. "If we don't get mail call soon, I'm gonna forget my Gina."

Eugene tied on his bandanna and snarled. "Write your fuckin' congressman, maybe you can get one of the North Viets to mail it for you."

Vincent tied his bandanna on and stood up. "We look like robbers in the movies, you know?" He put his hand out to Eugene and pulled him to his feet. "We oughta take a picture."

Eugene's stomach rumbled. The horrible, sickly-sweet smell made his insides feel like runny Jell-O. He stared at Vincent. How could the guy not be affected by the stink of human flesh?

"You got a fucking camera? How about fuckin' film? And who'd want a fuckin' picture of this fuckin' place? Fuck, Martino, you oughta have to listen to some of the shit you say."

Vincent's eyes narrowed. He grabbed Eugene's filthy fatigue shirt and pulled him within inches of his partially covered face. "You talking to Vincent Martino, your *fuckin'* buddy. You wanna maybe apologize to me, or what?"

Eugene glared back. "*I fuckin'* a-pologize, o-fuckin'-*kay?*"

Vincent released his grip and his eyes lost their menace. "It's gettin' you down, huh?"

Eugene backed up a step to look for his helmet. "I hate this fuckin' place, Vinny. I really fuckin' hate it."

Vincent put his arm around the smaller man. "We gonna get through it. We're a team."

Eugene relaxed his trembling body and nodded in silence. He wanted to shut his eyes, go back to sleep and dream of better times. Over the past days, he had been living in a hellish nightmare that never seemed to end. When he shut his eyes, he hoped he'd wake up and find it was all a dream. Of course, it wasn't. It was a nightmare. But it was real.

Lasalle tried to stand but fell over. Eugene offered his hand, knowing the man would never be able to get up on his own. Lasalle had not kept a meal down in two days. He was feverish and ghostly pale.

"Jimbo, just take it easy today," Blake said from across the room. "Stay in the bunker and rest. We're gettin' some medical supplies in the drop today, and the medic will fix ya right up. Lay back down and rest."

Lasalle fell back on the parachute material without saying a word.

Blake followed his two men out of the bunker and steered Eugene to the side. "You came on pretty strong to Vinny. I know this shit sucks, but don't take it out on him or the squad."

Eugene lowered his head. "I know . . . it's just that the guy is fuckin' steel. Nothing seems to bother him. It drives me crazy not being able to take it like he does."

Blake patted Eugene's back. "Hang tough. Vinny was right. We're gonna make it."

Eugene sighed behind the scarf. "You're gettin' as bad as him. Doesn't it bother you?"

"I hate it too, Gene," Blake lied. He had never felt more alive or needed in his life. "But we don't have a choice. We're in it. All we can do is face it and beat it . . . together."

Eugene lifted his rifle, making sure it was on safe. "My dad once told me he missed the war only because of the friends he made. I understand now what he meant."

Blake collapsed the camouflaged parachute and dragged the silk material back to the container. Gunfire erupted from the direction of the main gate, and he instinctively turned toward the sound. The command bunker blocked his view, but the noise told him that the reinforcements' dash would be successful. Most of the gunfire was outgoing, covering fire. He didn't hear the throaty enemy heavy machine guns that would have meant slaughter to men in the open.

Eugene cut the steel bands and turned the first wooden box on its side to read the label. "This one's got the medical supplies!" he yelled excitedly to the others.

Blake and the others left their containers and ran toward Eugene. The wounded were dying from a lack of supplies; every second counted.

Having stacked the last boxes of medical supplies into the aid station, the squad went back for the other containers. They saw small soldiers in camouflage uniforms assembling in the trench in front of the main gate.

"Them guys is Viet Rangers. I seen pictures of 'em before," Vincent said.

Eugene stopped in his tracks. The Rangers were climbing out of the trench! "Man, must be at least a hundred fifty of 'em . . . wonder what they doin' headin' for the gate?"

Shawn jogged up to his men and motioned toward the north trench. "Come on, we gotta cover the attack."

"What attack?" Blake said as he ran to catch up with the sergeant.

Shawn nodded toward the northern ridge, which lay outside the camp. "The Rangers are gonna try and take that high ground. A colonel flying in a chopper four thousand feet above us has ordered a frontal assault to try and ease the pressure off the camp."

Blake glanced up at the sky, then at the ridge. "Did anybody tell the colonel he's nuts? Doesn't he know what the hell is out there?"

Shawn slid into the trench and took up a firing position on the lip. Blake took a position beside him. "Captain Moss told him, but the colonel said to do it anyway," Shawn replied. "Those Rangers better hope the colonel knows what he's doing."

Lee shook his head as he laid out extra magazines on the trench lip. "They're out there waitin' for 'em."

Shawn's squad and a company of Montagnards waited in anticipation as the Rangers spread out just outside the gate and started toward the ridge. Many of the Rangers vomited as they marched forward, sickened by the blackened, bloated bodies of North Vietnamese killed two days before. Huge, black, buzzing flies covered the carnage and formed swarming dark clouds when disturbed by the oncoming Rangers.

An American advisor, a tall captain wearing the same camouflaged uniform as his men, led the Ranger unit toward the ridge. Behind him the smaller Vietnamese soldiers looked like children wearing U.S. Army helmets that were so big they bounced and sat at odd angles on their heads. The captain turned and signaled for his men to assemble into an assault formation. He turned around to face his objective and took two steps forward when suddenly the top of the ridge exploded with gunfire.

Blake cringed and bit his lip as miniature dust clouds kicked up by the North Vietnamese machine guns made a trail to the captain, then knocked him off his feet. The bullets had ripped through his chest. He fell on his back and reached toward the sky, as if trying to grab something. Behind the captain twenty Rangers lay on the ground, all hit in the first volley. The rest of the soldiers stood stunned for a full second before dropping to their bellies and returning fire, but the North Vietnamese outnumbered them five to one and poured lead down the ridge like a fire hose. Rangers screamed with heart-stopping fear at the impact of bullets. The captain's body jerked and bucked. Overcome with panic, a single Ranger jumped up and ran back toward the gate. Another dropped his rifle and ran. Soon a flood of men were running toward the camp entrance.

The squad fired at the dust clouds, unable to see a target. In minutes it was over.

Shawn lowered his rifle. "Cease fire!"

Blake stared over his rifle at the dead captain, whose helmet had come off, exposing his blond hair. An "all-American boy" was Blake's first impression. The crew cut was fresh. Blake had become so accustomed to seeing violent death that he had not thought it possible he had any feelings left. The sight of the young captain, however, enraged him and tore at his heart. Minutes before, the officer was a perfect example of a leader: strong, good-looking, and confident. Now he lay dead in the red dirt.

Blake looked skyward for the helicopter that held the colonel safely out of danger. "You motherfucker! *You* should have led the attack!"

Lee looked at the remaining Rangers left behind in the rout. Fifteen lay still, while another twenty-five rolled, crawled, or screamed in pain. Most of the wounded had been left behind.

Lee spoke in a monotone, as if in a trance. "My Gawd, they jus' left 'em out there."

Eugene lowered his gaze. He couldn't take the pathetic screaming and pleading of the wounded. Hearing them was horrible. Seeing them was unbearable.

Vincent shook like an enraged water buffalo. "They gotta go back an' get 'em! They gotta!"

The Rangers had gathered behind a mound inside the gate, yelling and screaming at each other. Another American captain advisor, dressed in camouflaged fatigues, stood up on the mound and screamed for their attention. He spoke forcefully and pointed at the wounded outside the gate. The translator did not have to tell the small soldiers what the captain wanted from them. They formed in squads and prepared themselves for the dash. This captain, much thinner than the first, yelled toward the trench line, "Give us covering fire in one minute!"

The squad and Montagnards responded immediately by changing magazines. Vincent put in a new belt of ammunition and got down behind his weapon.

Sweat poured from Blake's face. "Come on, come on, come on, come on," he mumbled to himself.

Shawn glanced at his watch. "Ten seconds!" he barked. "Shoot when I do. Aim just below the crest and shoot until I say stop. We wanna at least kick up dust and blind 'em . . . ready . . . *fire!*"

The recovery operation lasted only fifteen minutes. For some unexplainable reason, the North Vietnamese did not unleash the same level of lead fury as they had in the first attack. Only four Rangers were wounded. The American captain leading the operation was shot through the stomach, but he survived. All the wounded and dead were recovered.

Blake slid down the side of the sandbag wall to his buttocks. He was bone-weary. All afternoon he and his squad had carried wounded Rangers to the aid bunker and then to other bunkers. The small brown-skinned soldiers had been pathetic to see. Bullets and grenade fragments had wrought horrible damage on them.

Vincent rolled over and faced his squad leader. "Ace, I been thinkin'. If somethin' ever happens to me. I don't wanna be left like them guys out there today."

Blake forced a faint smile. "You're too mean to get hit. They wouldn't dare shoot an Italian and chance pissin' off half of Philadelphia."

Vincent's eyes remained serious. "I don't wanna be left alone, Ace. I . . . I don't wanna be alone."

Eugene rose up to his elbow beside Vincent and tapped his shoulder. "Vinny, I'd never leave you, man. You're my buddy, remember?"

Vincent stared at Blake for just a second, telling him he'd meant what he had said, and turned to Eugene. "Thanks, Gene. I promise I won't leave you either."

Blake felt uncomfortable with the morbid subject and tried to lighten the conversation. "Come on, guys, nobody is gonna get it. We're the best, remember?"

Lee was sitting against the wall listening. He went over and knelt down between Vincent and Eugene. "I don't wanna be left like them boys were either. I reckon we oughta make us a team promise." He held his hand out, palm up. "I promise I won't ever leave none of ya if you was hit."

Eugene understood immediately and slapped his hand on top of Lee's. "I promise not to leave any of you."

Vincent put his hand on top of Eugene's. "I promise too."

The three men looked at Blake, who was secretly praying he would never be in a position where he would have to fulfill the promise he was about to make. He leaned forward and put his hand on top of Vincent's. "I promise not to leave any member of the team . . . my best friends."

Later that night, as the squad slept, Blake arose and made his way through the darkness to the bunker entrance. The ground shook beneath his feet from a distant bomb explosion, but he didn't think twice about it. He had acquired "sea" legs over the past days. Even the deafening noise now seemed normal. He went outside, sat down beside the bunker wall and looked up at the stars. The Ranger attack had gotten to his men, and for that matter, to him as well. But the promise they had made to each other bothered him even more, because it made him face the unthinkable. Prescott had been wounded, but that had not affected him. There had been no time to brood about it. And though Prescott had been a member of the squad, he was not part of the team. The team was different. They *couldn't* be hurt. He knew them, loved them. Nothing could happen to the team.

Blake closed his eyes and saw the blond captain lying in the dirt. The officer had been filled with such determination, and yet . . . *no!* It couldn't happen. The team was better than that. They would make it. They had to make it.

Blake opened his eyes and looked up at the twinkling stars. "Please, God, they have to make it."

24 OCTOBER

Colonel Lee Van Quan stepped out of the thatch hut and looked up at the stars. He took in a deep breath to relax his inner shaking. The past twenty-four hours had brought nothing but bad news. The so-called Army of the Republic of Vietnam, better known as ARVNs, had finally mounted a relief operation and had fallen into the 33rd Regiment's snare. The ambush had been executed according to plan, but the ARVN force had not turned tail and run, as they had in the past. Instead, they had stood their ground and fought. Even though his brave men had surprised the ARVNs and killed exposed infantrymen, the tanks and armored personnel carriers had gotten through undamaged, and their cannons and heavy machine guns had wrought havoc. The battalion that had ambushed the lead armor element had been decimated by the awesome firepower. Obviously, the puppets had been bolstered by their American counterparts, who had given them false confidence. The only good news was that the light-skinned vehicles, carrying fuel and extra ammunition behind the armored units, had been destroyed. The armor force then had to stop its advance. Without fuel, the tanks would not be able to reinforce the Plei Me camp for at least another two days.

The colonel looked up at the stars and gave thanks to destiny for giving him the strength to convince the general he still had time to save much of the division from his failed plan. The unstoppable power of the American air support and unsuspected resolve of the ARVN armor units had taken away any hope of victory. His beloved division had paid dearly for the general's poor judgment. Colonel Khan's unit, whose men attacked the camp, had suffered almost two hundred dead, including the colonel himself, and three times that number wounded. Colonel Du's regiment, which had ambushed the enemy column, had reported only minutes before the loss of almost an entire battalion, over five hundred killed or wounded.

The colonel felt twenty years older. Each death had further stooped his shoulders and aged his breaking heart. There had been no other choice. He'd had to tell the general that he had to order the regiments from the death traps and save the men so they could fight another day.

Taking in another deep breath, Quan walked back into the hut and up to the map. Seated at the table in front of him was his chief of staff. "Ha, give orders for the withdrawal of the 32nd and 33rd. Have each of them leave one battalion behind to fight a rear-guard action and delay the enemy in his pursuit of us."

The fatigued colonel sat with a somber expression. His voice was raspy from having smoked too many cigarettes during the ordeal. "Where are we to go?"

The colonel moved his finger across the map almost due west of the Plei Me camp to a mountainous area close to the Cambodian border. "The general has ordered us to go here, the Chu Pong Massif. It is there that the 66th Regiment will assemble, and so will the division. The general believes we can rebuild in safety there. The Chu Pong has an old underground command complex that was built in the first revolution. I served as a young captain there and know the area well. The mountain's forests will shield us from the view of enemy planes. We will—" The colonel's outstretched hand suddenly began trembling. His voice cracked as the pent-up tears of remorse and failure trickled down his cheeks. "We . . . we must rebuild."

The chief of staff rose and took the colonel's arm. "My friend, you must sleep. Tomorrow you must be strong for the rest of us. The general needs you to direct him out of the failure into which he has led us. You are the only hope for our soldiers."

Quan allowed himself to be led to the bed in the corner of the hut. He wanted to sleep, though he knew that the dreams would come, the dreams of his beloved men who had died. They always came.

28 OCTOBER

Shawn and the squad watched as a long green line of slick helicopters approached the camp. The First Air Cavalry had finally been ordered in to relieve the outpost. The choppers landed just outside the camp, kicking up clouds of red dust. Through the haze came American infantrymen, running and carrying their rifles, as if they expected a fight.

Blake spoke through three layers of parachute cloth tied around his nose and mouth. "They sure are a pretty sight."

Eugene weakly leaned back on the bunker outside wall. "They're a little late."

Vincent took hold of Eugene's arm and pulled him erect. "We can't be lookin' beat. We're cav, like them."

Lee turned around for a look at the children's distant bunker. He was going to miss them. Their small faces had kept him sane through the ordeal. Easing their fears had somehow eased his. He would not forget their smiles for a long, long time.

Shawn watched the approaching First Cavalry soldiers stop one by one and vomit. The stench of the putrefying flesh had finally gotten to them.

Blake reached down and picked up a North Vietnamese pack from a man he had killed days before and put it over his shoulders. He brought his rifle up to the crook of his arm.

"Saddle up, team," he softly commanded. "We're goin' home."

In silence Vincent, Lee, and Eugene hefted their own North Vietnamese Army packs to their shoulders and followed.

Shawn turned and saluted Captain Harry Moss, who stood by the command bunker. "Sir, request permission to rejoin my unit."

Moss raised his hand in a perfect salute. "Permission granted . . . our thanks isn't enough, Sergeant."

Shawn lowered his hand. "Yes, it is, sir." He turned and followed his men to the waiting helicopters.

24

Lee stood in the shallow stream washing himself for the second time in four hours. The squad had been back at An Khe for two days, but everyone still avoided them as if they had the black plague. It was the smell. The stench of death had permeated every hair and pore of their skin. Even Maggie would have nothing to do with them. They had burned their uniforms and washed their equipment with gasoline, but the smell still lingered. So did the nightmares.

Buck naked, Eugene Day squatted in the creek and rubbed sand on his arms and hands. "Yo, Vinny, we heard they found our mail. They're gonna give it to us at noon chow."

Vincent Martino had been lying in the shallow water next to the bank like a beached whale. Wide-eyed, he sprang up. "You ain't kiddin'? They really found it?"

Blake walked down to the bank carrying his clothes. "Yeah, Gene ain't shittin' ya. We got word when you and Reb were checking Maggie. They had sent our mail back to some postal holding-unit in Nha Trang. You're gonna finally hear from Gina."

Vincent grinned like a Cheshire cat and looked over his shoulder at the lanky Georgian. "You hear that, Reb? We got mail."

Lee smiled and waded over to the bank to pick up his fatigue pants. "Ya reckon Gina sent ya some food? One'a them candy bars she used to send ya sure would be good."

"If she did, I wouldn't give you guys any," Vincent snapped back. "I need to get back to my fightin' weight."

"What the hell do you people think you're doing?"

Blake spun around. An obese sergeant major was striding down the steep trail that led to the creek. Blake didn't recognize the fat noncom. The senior sergeant stopped on the sand bank with a cold glare. "Well, what the hell you idiots think you're doing?"

Blake returned an icy stare, taking note of the overweight soldier's uniform name tape. "We're cleaning up, Sergeant Major Breed. And we're not idiots."

Breed smirked as he wiped sweat from his flushed face. "You're idiots because *no*-fuckin'-body leaves the bivouac area unless you're on a mission

305

or a work detail. My job today is to find slackers like you four and put you back to work. Get your uniforms on and follow me. I've got the perfect detail for you in my area—burning shit."

Blake shrugged his shoulders and walked into the cool water. "Sorry, we have our orders. We've been told to wash up, and that's what we're doin'."

"Who gave you that order?" Breed barked, to call the surly soldier's bluff.

Blake's eyes rolled up as if in thought. "Uh . . . I think it was Stockdale—no, that's not it. Uh . . . Reb, what's our colonel's name again?"

Lee hid his smile and played along. "Uh . . . I think it was Stockton. Yep, Colonel John Stockton. I remember now."

The sergeant shook his massive head. "You idiots gonna have to do better than that. *Get your fuckin' uniforms on and follow me!*"

Blake sat down in the ankle-deep steam and splashed water on his chest. "We can't do it. Orders."

The sergeant's jowl and second chin shook, and the folds of flaccid skin over his eyes turned white. "Get outta the fuckin' water or I'll—I'll call the M.P.s an' have your insubordinate asses burning shit for a year."

Blake looked over his shoulder at his men, who were all sitting in the stream. "Any'a you wanna disobey the colonel and go with the sergeant major to burn shit?"

"Not me." Vincent smiled. "I smelled enough stink for a lifetime."

Eugene slapped mud on his shoulder and began rubbing it over his body. "Sergeant Major, do you have some soap by any chance?"

Lee's narrowed eyes were locked on the sergeant, burning holes through his forehead. "We ain't idiots."

Breed forced a nervous smile. "I'll be back, and when I do, you four *idiots* will pay!" He spun around and marched up the path.

Blake stood and waded over to his friends. "What's he gonna do, send us to Vietnam?"

Eugene began laughing and was quickly joined by Vincent, who slapped Lee's back. "We are idiots, you know."

Lee kept his frown for only a second before the contagious laughter got to him. He chuckled first, then rolled his head back and let out a whooping rebel yell.

Blake held his stomach, he was laughing so hard. Even if the confrontation with the sergeant major wasn't that funny, he needed to laugh. They had not laughed in thirteen long, nightmarish days, and they needed the release. It was like smelling clean air for the first time when they had reached altitude in the helicopter that had picked them up from Plei Me. The simple pleasure of breathing in air that didn't make them sick had been unbelievably wonderful.

Minutes later the four men sat on the bank of the stream, leaning back on a huge boulder and enjoying the sun's rays. "I wish Jimbo and Pres were here with us," Eugene said. "I hear the malaria that got Jimbo will keep him in the hospital for at least a couple of weeks."

Vincent brushed a fly from his nose. "Pres is gonna be in the hospital a lot longer than that. I guess he'll be goin' home after he gets out."

Eugene leaned back and closed his eyes. "Home. Man, that seems a million, zillion miles away. When I get back I'm gonna use the G.I. bill and get my dumb ass in college. I don't know what I'm gonna major in, but I'm gonna go."

Vincent smiled with his eyes closed. "I wanna walk the walk down the streets'a my neighborhood, smell the smells, and get the feel."

"I wanna sit on the front-porch swing of our house and rock forever." Lee sighed. "There ain't nothin' like the smell of honeysuckle in the evenin'."

Blake could picture each of his friends doing what they described. They were all such simple wishes, yet no place but their homes could make them come true. He wished he could think of home that way.

"Ya know what I really wanna do?" Vincent said. "I wanna run my own hoagie stand when I get back. I ain't gonna make a million dollars doin' it, but . . . but at least I'll be doin' what I wanna do, you know?"

Eugene nodded in understanding and thought of what he really wanted to do. His jaw muscle rippled and his eyes became distant as he spoke almost in a whisper. "I wanna take my dad to the Carlisle Veterans Day ceremony and sit in the front row. He deserves to sit with the other veterans, and it's time they knew that." He felt the old rage building inside him and took in a deep breath to relax. Exhaling, he looked at Lee. "What about you, Reb? Whatta you really wanna do?"

Lee picked up a pebble and tossed it into the creek. "I wanna teach school back in Cusseta. I had a teacher there that really made a difference. I reckon I wanna make a difference too. It don't pay much, but at least every day I'd feel good about what I was doin'."

Eugene pushed his glasses back up on his nose. "You'd be the best, Reb."

Vincent nodded in agreement and shifted his gaze to Blake. "How 'bout you, Ace? What'ta you really wanna do?"

Blake leaned back, looking up at cloudless light blue sky. "It's funny, but I always thought I wanted to walk in the door of our house, march up the stairs to the Alexander trophy case, and put in a medal or something. I wanted to see my dad's face, ya know?" Blake shrugged his shoulders. "It's not important anymore. I'll probably go back to school, see what works out."

Lee tossed the rock into the creek. "I think you'd be a good teacher, Ace."

Blake sighed. "I don't know. Maybe."

Vincent put his arm over Blake's bare shoulder. "I know a girlfriend'a

Gina's who'd make you forget that trophy case for sure. You two oughta get together."

Blake smiled his half smile. "I'd love to meet her."

Vincent's eyes suddenly widened and he grabbed Blake's wrist, raising it up to look at his watch. "We gotta go! Mail call!"

The four men were headed down the road to their new bivouac camp when two M.P. jeeps skidded to a halt in front of them, blocking their way. Sergeant Major Breed stood up in the front seat of the open vehicle and pointed. "That's them!"

A buck sergeant with M.P. stenciled on the front of his helmet cover stepped out of the jeep. "Get out your billfolds and let me see your IDs," he ordered.

Blake shook his head, knowing he was dealing with a rear echelon type. "We don't carry billfolds. They rub your ass raw when you're humpin', plus when it rains, everything in 'em gets ruined. We keep that stuff in a locker in our company headquarters."

The sergeant raised an eyebrow. These were obviously not your normal skaters. The eyes of the men standing before him revealed self-confidence, not nervousness. They were wearing new fatigues, but they didn't carry themselves or their rifles like new replacements. The strange mustard-colored packs they wore caught his eye. He motioned to Blake's.

"What is that?"

"NVA pack," Blake answered matter-of-factly.

"Where'd you get 'em?"

Blake jerked his thumb over his shoulder toward the west. "Plei Me. We got back a couple of days ago."

The sergeant's eyes widened. "Shiiit. You guys were the ones? Well, I'll be damned. Nice to meet ya. We heard all about a squad from the cav who were up there during the attack. Me and my section were just talkin' about it last night. I heard it was a real motherfucker. I mean the NVA attacking in regimental size and all. You guys need a ride?"

The sergeant major sat down in astonishment. He had heard about the squad, as had every other man in the division.

Blake glanced at Breed, who looked sullen with disappointment, then back to the M.P. "Thanks, but looks like your jeep is already full. We'll walk. Thanks anyway."

The M.P. sergeant smiled. The young corporal had gotten a good barb into the sergeant major. "Okay, well, it was nice meetin' you guys. You made the cav proud."

Fifteen minutes later the four men strolled down a dusty path between rows of large tents. An Khe had changed since they had left. The poncho and shelter half-hooches were gone, replaced with the Army's general-purpose medium tents, which would hold fifteen men comfortably. Made of heavy canvas, the tents were supported by large wooden poles that allowed plenty of head room. Wooden crates served as flooring, to keep the bunks and inhabitants dry.

Blake walked with his shoulders back proudly, despite questioning stares from everyone they passed. The packs he and his men wore set them apart. They were a symbol that the team had been in combat.

Sergeant Shawn Flynn saw his squad approaching and excused himself from Lieutenant Owens. He faced the four men with a scowl.

"It's about time. You just about didn't make it for your own—"

A whistle blew in the distance, and the men lounging around the tents broke into a run toward the sound.

"What's goin' on, Irish? We supposed to go too?" Blake said with a puzzled expression.

Shawn smiled. "The squadron is forming up for an award ceremony. It's for us, we're the awardees."

Blake's mouth dropped open. "What?"

The last recipient, Lee Calhoon, shook hands with Colonel Stockton and looked down at the medal hanging from his own fatigue shirt pocket.

Stockton executed an about-face and positioned himself in front of the large formation of cavalrymen. "Today we honor five Silver Star recipients. They are not 'winners' of the Silver Stars. Such decorations are not 'won.' They are *earned* for gallantry in action. These five men have set an example for all of us. They fought as true cavalrymen, against overwhelming odds in the worst of conditions. They have earned the honor of receiving the first medals for heroism in the First Air Cavalry Division. It is a proud day for this squadron, for these cavalrymen have led the way."

The colonel shifted his stance. His voice grew more somber. "Men, the North Vietnamese Army has finally entered the war in strength. The attack on Plei Me was the first such battle involving NVA regiments. They were beaten at Plei Me but not defeated. Yesterday, we received the mission to find the retreating NVA regiments, fix them, and then destroy them. We have trained long and hard for just this opportunity. Today, as I speak, our scout ships are beginning the hunt. These men behind me were the first of the cavalry to face and beat the NVA. You troopers standing in ranks will soon be called upon to do the same. This unit is like no other in the history of modern warfare. We can strike farther and faster and with more deadly force than any cavalry unit in the world. Over the next few weeks, we will write new chapters in the history books of warfare. You men of the First Squadron, Ninth Cavalry, will write those pages with your skill, tenacity, and the enemy's blood."

The colonel took a step back. "I have another award for the men behind me, but it is not my place to give it. I have asked Staff Sergeant Flynn, the platoon sergeant of second platoon and two-time recipient of the award, to give his men the honor of wearing the Combat Infantryman's Badge."

Shawn stepped forward and faced his men. "If you're late again, I'll kill ya," he whispered.

The squadron sergeant major marched forward and handed four badges, emblazoned with silver-wreathed muskets, to Shawn. Shawn stepped in front of Blake and pinned the Combat Infantryman's Badge above the left pocket of Blake's fatigue shirt.

"Ace, you're now an official combat infantryman. You can't buy a cup of coffee with this award, but to men like us, it means more than all the money in the world. It stands for something only we veterans understand. Congratulations."

Standing ramrod straight, Blake shook hands with his sergeant and heard Lee whisper out of the side of his mouth, "Ace, now ya have somethin' to put in that Alexander trophy case."

Eugene Day couldn't stop the tears that trickled down his cheeks as the sergeant pinned the badge to his shirt. He could hardly wait to write to his father and tell him he now understood why the wreathed musket meant so much.

Vincent Martino swelled out his chest as Shawn pinned on the badge. It was the best day of his life, for today he was a *somebody*.

Lee Calhoon kept his eyes straight ahead as Shawn pinned on the award. In Cusseta they would wonder why all the fuss. A man didn't need to wear a badge to be respected. The team knew he had done his part, and that was enough.

Marauding mosquitoes buzzed unnoticed by the four men who sat in the darkness outside their tent unable to sleep. The awards, speeches, and countless handshakes had made it their day, and they weren't yet ready to come down from the high.

Vincent held up the star-shaped medal with the red, white, and blue ribbon. "I'm gonna send this to Gina to give to her ol' man. He ain't gonna call me a bum no more."

Eugene shook his head as he looked up at the stars. "You were never a bum, Vinny. Give me the asshole's name, and I'll send him a grenade. Hey, what did Gina have to say in her letters? She send any boxes of food?"

Vincent sighed. "She's still waitin' for me, like she said, but the brownies she sent turned green. Sorry 'bout that, buddy."

Lee patted his shirt pocket, which held the four letters he'd received from his mother. "My mama says hiya ta y'all and wants ya ta know ya have a second home in Cusseta. She sent a small package, but it was sugar cubes for Maggie. Maybe next time she'll send some of Dad's venison jerky."

Blake patted Lee's leg. "Tell your mom thanks from the team and Maggie."

Lee looked at his squad leader. "How 'bout you, Ace? You git any letters from home?"

Blake laughed to conceal his pain. He had received one from his mother that said she missed him terribly, and she'd begged for him to write. He would find paper tomorrow and write her a letter, but unlike Vincent, he would not send his medal home. He knew his mother would not understand what it meant, and his father wouldn't care.

"Yeah, my mom is worried about me gettin' enough vitamins. She sent me a box of 'em. Any of you guys want any?"

Eugene smirked. "I'll take some. Anything beats C-rations."

Lee stood and stretched. "Well, I reckon we best get us some sleep. Tomorrow we gonna have ta think about 'them' again. Like the sarge says, 'They're out there, waitin'.' "

Vincent pushed himself up. "Heroes today an' grunts tomorrow. It just don't seem fair."

Eugene smiled. "Come on, he-ro, I'll tuck you in. I wanna check out those green brownies. I think you're holdin' out on me again."

Lee put his hand out to help Blake up. "Ya ready ta call it?"

Blake nodded and grabbed Lee's hand; he was on his feet a second later. Lee had already started for the tent when Blake touched his arm.

"Reb, ya really think I'd make a good teacher?"

Lee's smile went unseen in the darkness.

The morning birds were still chirping as Lee led the rest of the team to the perimeter to find Maggie. An Khe had grown. The bunker line now extended farther to the south. Maggie had been turned loose to roam where she might, like a true cavalry mule. Lee didn't like the colonel's decision, but he understood that the commander could not afford a full-time trooper to care for the mascot.

Lee spotted the gray trooper eating grass sprouts near a bunker. He called out to her and grinned when her head came up. In seconds she was trotting toward him. Lee held out two sugar cubes, hoping his countless scrubbings had been enough to get rid of the smell from Plei Me. Maggie came up to him and, ignoring his hand, lightly butted her head against his chest.

Eugene smirked at the affectionate display. "Vinny, I bet Gina does the same thing to you when you see her."

Vincent walked forward and began scratching under Maggie's neck. "Gene, I think maybe you're gettin' jealous again. Yo, Mag, you lookin' good."

Eugene frowned as he began pulling burrs from Maggie's forequarters.

"I got a girlfriend . . . kinda. We had this kind of fallin' out before I left, but I wrote her a couple of letters makin' things right again. She'll be there when I get back."

Blake walked around inspecting Maggie's brand. "The damn Navy can't do anything right. The hair's already grown back. You can hardly see it anymore."

Vincent chuckled. "Good thing. I wouldn't wanna be a swabbie around the Reb. I heard that Navy recruits is goin' AWOL cause they heard the Reb was still 'riled.' "

Blake laughed and patted Maggie's back. "Is that true, Reb?"

Lee scowled with hate in his eyes. "Them swabs shoulda left her be."

When the team got back to their tent, Sergeant Flynn was standing outside the entrance, talking to three men in new fatigues.

"Ace, here's your replacements. They just flew in today."

Blake felt sorry for the wide-eyed boys. They were obviously tired and overcome by the change in scenery. *Boys?* He realized he had thought of them that way because they looked so young and innocent.

Shawn tossed his head toward the supply tent. "Get 'em ammo and get their weapons zeroed this morning. We're moving out this afternoon. We're going to Plei Me again. Us Blues are gonna join in the hunt."

Blake's mouth dropped open and just as quickly recovered. "Plei Me?"

Shawn smiled. "Yeah, we're gonna base out of our old stomping grounds and be a reaction force if the scout ships find something." Shawn's eyes cut to the replacements, then back to Shawn. "I just got finished telling these men how lucky they are to have the old vets of the first squad to square them away."

Blake gave his sergeant a "thanks a lot" look and turned to the replacements. "Welcome to the first squad. I'm Corporal Blake Alex—"

Shawn raised his hand, interrupting. "Sorry, I forgot ta tell ya. You're a sergeant now. The colonel signed the paperwork this morning." Shawn put two fingers to his helmet in a sarcastic good-bye salute. "See ya later on the L.Z., 'Sarge.' " He turned his back to the squad leader, whose mouth still hung open in shock, and strode to the headquarters tent.

Blake watched Vincent lead the replacements to the supply tent, then took out his small pocket notebook. He wanted to jot down some of his first impressions of the three men after talking with them.

William Bradshaw, age 19, high school wrestling star from Ames, Iowa. Flunked out his freshman year of college, drafted. Got a chip on his shoulder—watch him.

Gerry Hanslow, age 20, played drums in the high school band in Rochester, Minnesota. Was playing in rock band when he got drafted.

Says he's good with an M-79 grenade launcher. Get him one. Talks a lot, but seems willing to learn.

Robert Winsome, age 19, stutters, VERY QUIET, didn't graduate from high school. Before joining the Army, worked as a car and tractor mechanic in Tucson, Arizona. Says he joined to see Vietnam.

Blake glanced up at Lee, who was cleaning his rifle. "What do you think of 'em?"

Lee shrugged his shoulders. "They look okay, I reckon. Bradshaw t'weren't none too friendly, but Gerry an' Bob seemed trainable."

Blake nodded in agreement and closed the notebook. "You take Gerry and Bob. I'll put Vincent and Eugene with Bradshaw. Those two will either drive him crazy or make him a good cavalryman."

Lee raised an eyebrow. "That boy better change his attitude purty darn quick."

Vincent shook his head at the new member of his fire team. "Now, Billy, you don't carry your 'sixteen like that." He took the rifle off the soldier's shoulder and quickly removed the sling. "You hold the weapon like this, ready. If you walk around with it on your shoulder, the other guys is gonna know you're green, capish?"

Bradshaw sighed and took the rifle back. "Yeah, I got it, but don't call me 'Billy.' The name is William."

Eugene had been walking beside the two men. "Okay, Willie, we can do that."

Bradshaw stopped and gave Eugene a cutting stare. "I said, 'William.' The name is 'William' Bradshaw. I don't like this Army nickname shit."

Vincent exchanged glances with Eugene, then stepped closer to Bradshaw and pointed his finger at the soldier's face. "You is now Willie Billy. Got it?" he growled.

Bradshaw began to step back, but Eugene clapped his hand roughly on his shoulder. "Willie Billy has a nice ring to it, don't you think?"

Bradshaw's face turned furious red. He met Vincent's stare, then Eugene's, and then he lowered his head in seething anger. "I don't give a fuck what you call me."

Vincent smiled. "Good. Now as I was sayin', you carry your weapon always ready an' . . ."

Lee handed another 40-millimeter shell to Gerry Hanslow. Hanslow slid the round into the chamber of his new breach-loading weapon, the M-79 grenade launcher. The stubby weapon looked like a miniature single-shot shotgun, but its barrel had a much wider mouth. The shell was also stubby. Its rounded shiny metal nose made it look like a tiny bomb.

Hanslow raised the weapon to his shoulder and aimed slightly over the fifty-gallon drum a hundred meters away. He pressed the trigger. Instead of the usual bang, the weapon thunked. The minigrenade hit the barrel dead center, exploding on impact.

Lee nodded in approval. "Good un. Remember now, the maximum effective range is 350 meters, an' the minimum range is thirty-five meters. It takes so many spins before it arms itself ta explode. I think ya got the hang of it purty good."

Lee turned to Robert Winsome, who held a new M-16. "All right, Bob, your turn. Ya need to zero and fire a couple of magazines to git used ta her. In the first squad we think safety first. Always, always double-check your selector switch an' make sure you're on safe. Never load twenty rounds in your mags like they said in AIT. Load eighteen and make sure ya put three tracer rounds in first. That way when ya git ta your last bullets, ya know to change mags."

Bob opened his mouth, tried to talk, rolled up his eyes, and tried again. "Wh-Wha-What other tips youuuu have?"

Lee shifted his feet as he brought to mind some of the things he'd learned through experience. "Write the zero on your helmet cover, an' your blood type. Keep the barrel covered with one'a them aluminum foil packages ya git in C-rats. And carry at least fifteen mags, two filled with tracer."

"Wh-Whe-Where you . . . ca-ca-carry the mags?"

Lee pointed at the metal ammunition box. "M-16 bullets come in a cloth bandolier. The bandolier has ten pockets that holds ten cardboard boxes, with twenty rounds each. You take out the cardboard boxes, load your mags and put the mags in the bandolier pockets. You can tie the bandolier around your waist. I like to tie the other ones around my chest so all the weight ain't hangin' on my hips. I'll show ya how to tie it like shoulder straps."

Hanslow had been listening, and motioned to the stack of loose 40-millimeter shells. "How do I carry those?"

Lee slid off his shoulder what looked like a green canvas shoulder bag. "Ya put 'em in a claymore bag like this one. You'll be carrying two of these full. Bob, we'll get you one too, 'cause that's what you'll use ta carry your C's, poncho, and extra ammo. Y'all are gonna find the more you can carry on your shoulders, the better. When ya wear your pistol belt with three quarts of water, and put smoke and hand grenades in your ammo pouches, you're weighted down purty good."

Hanslow shook his head in wonderment. "Why in the hell didn't they teach us this stuff in the States?"

Lee shrugged. "Don't know." He turned again to Bob. "Git ta shootin'. We gotta git back and git y'all packed."

———

Blake hopped out of the helicopter into a swirling dust cloud. He held his breath as long as possible, but finally had to inhale. Most of the smell of Plei Me was gone, but traces still lingered.

Shawn led the platoon inside the Special Forces camp gate and pointed to a newly constructed row of tin buildings. "That's gonna be home for a while. First and second squads in building one, third and fourth in two. Squad leaders, I want those two tin deathtraps sandbagged halfway up by nightfall. Get weapons cleaned and come see me once you're settled. I'll be in the first building."

Minutes later, after dropping off his gear, Shawn walked over to the new command bunker. He was disappointed to find that Captain Moss and his team had been replaced.

Lieutenant Owens waved him over to a table where the troop commander was looking at a map.

The captain looked up. "Sergeant Flynn, take a look at this and tell me what you think." He pointed at the map. "The intel people can't tell us shit, so right now we don't know where the NVA regiments have gone. One troop is searching north, another south, and our troop is searching west. My scout ships are reporting ones and twos, but no large units. Division wants us to put the Blues out at dusk, along likely avenues of escape, and to set up ambushes. What do you think?"

Shawn studied the map for a moment. "They're wasting their time, if they're looking for them to go north. Too many villages in that direction, they—"

"Wait a sec," the captain interrupted. "The intel major told me north was the *most* probable direction they would go. He said the villages would supply them with food and supplies and such."

Shawn shook his head. "The major would be right if it were V.C. we were looking for, but we're talking about NVA. The regulars don't need or want local support. They have their own stockpiles, and my guess is those stockpiles are in Cambodia or close to it. The regiments that hit us here need resupply and recovery time. They're going to go where they can do both without drawing a lot of attention to themselves."

The captain looked at the map. "Where is that, Sergeant?"

Shawn drew a circle with his finger. "There, in the hilly terrain along the Ia Drang River. It's only a few klicks from the Cambodian border, and it's far enough away from villages so they're not compromised. If I was them, that's where I'd go."

The captain picked up a grease pencil and drew a red goose egg where Shawn had pointed. "That's about thirty klicks from here, and it's in our area of search, but we have to check the areas between here and there first. Take us a week before we get that far west. Right now our scout ships are ranging out about twelve klicks. The division is keeping the strings on pretty tight. Every time we expand the ring of search, we have to move our artillery forward so they can support our ground units. We have to move our refueling units as well."

Shawn understood the logistical nightmare involved in such an operation, and he could imagine all the problems presented by trying to protect, feed, and fuel an airmobile division at the end of a huge logistical tail that came from the United States, across the ocean, and across Vietnam. He had seen enough crumbling French forts to know that others had tried and failed.

The captain tapped the map at the goose egg. "Thanks, Sergeant. I knew with your experience you could shed some light on the situation. Have your Blues standing by on strip alert. I want them ready to go if the scouts kick up something."

Shawn backed away from the table and saluted. "Sir, we'll be ready."

Willie Billy Bradshaw struggled out of his heavy pistol belt and bandoliers, after walking a quick clearing patrol around the perimeter at dusk. "I'm not some fucking pack animal, for Christ's sake! Carrying all this shit is ridiculous!"

Vincent glanced at the sweat-soaked soldier without sympathy. "Better drink a lotta water. You lookin' pale."

Bradshaw angrily motioned to the two other new men, who were already eating their C-rations. "Look at them! They didn't carry as much as I did. You're fuckin' with me, Martino!"

Eugene picked up a heavy claymore bag from the stack of equipment Bradshaw had taken off. "You and I carry extra 'sixty ammo for Vinny. You better do what Vinny says and drink some water. You're gonna need it."

Bradshaw began to protest again when Blake shot up from the floor, where he had been seated cleaning his rifle. "Don't say another fuckin' word, Private. Eugene weighs forty pounds less than you and he carried the same weight. You best shut your damn mouth and start listening instead of complaining. Nobody said this was gonna be fun or exciting, 'cause it ain't. The walk was easy. You're not used to the climate or the ammo weight. Two weeks from now you'll be adapted and stronger. Now, drink water, like Vinny told ya, and eat."

Blake had begun to sit down when Bradshaw mumbled a little too loudly, "Fuckers."

Blake grabbed for the soldier, but Vincent already had his arm around Bradshaw's neck in a vice grip. Vincent winked at Blake. "Let me take care'a this. He's been askin' for it."

Blake sat back down.

Vincent dragged Bradshaw outside and turned him loose. "You bad, I know, so come on. You think you're better than ol' Vinny, don't ya, pretty boy?"

Bradshaw crouched in a wrestler's stance and began circling his lumbering opponent. "You dumb fuckin' dago. You enjoy making me look like a fool. When I get finished with you, you're gonna beg for me to stop the pain. You hear me? You're gonna beg!"

Vincent moved slowly, keeping himself squared to the soldier. "I'm waitin', pretty boy," he said evenly.

Inside the hooch Eugene nervously paced in front of the door. Unable to stand it anymore, he again began to plead to go outside, but Blake anticipated and shook his head. "No, he'll be fine."

Bradshaw faked a lunge right and dove at Vincent's feet. Vincent had seen all the moves before on the street. He hopped back, shifted his weight to his front leg, and kicked with the back. The boot caught the shocked soldier under the chin, jerking his head up. Without hesitating, Vincent dropped like a rock to his knee with his arm cocked back and shot his fist forward to the side of Bradshaw's face. The second blow wasn't needed, for the kick had knocked the soldier senseless. Vincent stood and rolled the soldier over with his foot. "You pretty boys never learn."

Vincent walked in the hooch with a fake look of concern. "I think Willie Billy passed out from the heat."

Blake motioned with his head for Eugene to check the damage. "Did he learn anything?" he asked Vincent.

Vincent winked. "I don't think he'll remember."

Gerry Hanslow leaned over to Bob Winsome. "I'm drinking my water when they say to," he whispered. "How 'bout you?"

Winsome nodded, wide-eyed, and spooned a peach slice into his mouth.

General Chu Huy Man ate the last of his fish and rice and set down his chopsticks. His assistant division commander, Colonel Quan, had waited patiently for him to finish his meal. Now, as Quan prepared to speak, the campfire cast a golden glow on his face.

"The reports are not good, my general. The Americans have unleashed their new helicopter division to hunt us. Like dogs, they smell our blood and have been snapping at our rear. The regiments have had to break down from companies into platoons and even into squads to hide from their gun-firing helicopters. They search with their smaller machines, and when our men are impatient and shoot, the bigger helicopters pounce with their rockets and machine guns. All units have reported losses and delays."

"And the wounded?" the general asked without emotion.

Colonel Quan gazed into the softly glowing coals of the fire. "They are being cared for at the aid stations we had pre-positioned for the attack. I received a report this afternoon from the 33rd Regimental hospital. It will be moving back the day after tomorrow. It was the closest field hospital to Plei Me, only twelve kilometers to the west, next to the Tae River. The 33rd has left a battalion to secure the hospital and help carry the wounded. They should join us at Chu Pong in five or six days."

The general's aide came out of the darkness and offered his commanding officer a cup of green tea. Man took a sip.

"Inform the units about the Americans' tactic of baiting our soldiers into firing. Tell them to avoid contact at all costs and to assemble as planned at the Chu Pong." Man looked intently at Quan. "You said the Americans have been unleashed and smell our blood. If we are the fox, it is time we became sly. Order the rear-guard companies north to draw the hounds away."

"And the wounded?" Quan asked softly.

Man nodded. "Yes, the wounded as well."

Quan rose, stepped away from the crackling embers and into the darkness. He knew that forwarding the general's orders meant sending many men to their deaths. The diversion to the north would be too much for the wounded to endure. They would die long before reaching the necessary medical supplies and hospitals along the northern border.

The night was still and beautiful, but he did not notice as he made his way to the communications section. His heart and mind were with those who would have to endure untold agony for the general's diversion. Even now he felt their pain as he squatted by the radioman and held his hand out for the handset. This radio message he would have to send himself, for he was going to tell young leaders their wounded were going to die.

25

Willie Billy Bradshaw sipped his C-ration chicken and noodles carefully. The chunks of chicken bumped up against his teeth, but he only sucked in the juice and soft noodles. He couldn't open his mouth wide enough to accept the chunks, and if he could have, he couldn't have chewed the meat. His jaw was so sore from yesterday's fight, he could barely swallow the noodles.

Vincent opened a can of C-ration applesauce and set it down in front of his new assistant gunner. "This is good for you."

Blake walked in the front hooch door and announced to his squad they were on standby alert. They had to be ready to leave on ten-minute notice. A scout and gun chopper team had made a sighting of NVA that morning at 0720 hours just twelve kilometers to the west. Another troop scout and gun team had spotted a second NVA unit close to the same location and took the enemy under fire.

Blake spread a map out on the floor and took out his pocket notebook. He read the grid coordinates from the notebook and pointed at the map.

"Here, next to the Tae River, is where the Whites made the first sighting of fifteen to twenty regulars. The second sighting was here, only five hundred meters from the first. They spotted twenty to twenty-five more NVA."

Hanslow gave Lee a puzzled look. "What are 'Whites'?"

Lee motioned Winsome and Hanslow over so he could give them a quick lesson on how the cav troop operated. "Whites is the scout ships, OH-13s. The Reds are the gunships that swoop in if the Whites flush somethin'. If it's big, like this sighting, they call on the Blues, us, to go in and develop the situation."

Hanslow's face turned pale. "But they saw fifty NVA. We only have thirty-one men in our platoon."

Lee waved the question away like shooing away a fly. "Naw, we got the gunships and scouts flying overhead looking for ambushes and covering every move we make."

Hanslow gulped before asking a question to which he didn't really want an answer. "Are we going in, you think?"

Lee shrugged. "The squadron has three troops, and in each troop is one blue platoon. We have a one-in-three chance of gettin' called in. Whoever is closest or most available will get the mission. It could be us."

Hanslow's eyes rolled upward and he prayed that another blue platoon would be called.

The platoon had moved from the hooches to the shade of the command bunker to listen to the speaker box the troop commander had ordered placed there. It was after twelve in the afternoon, and the anxiety of being called for the mission had long ago worn off. The blue platoon from another troop had been air assaulted into the sighting area a few minutes after eight A.M. Within twenty minutes of landing, the platoon ran into an NVA regimental hospital, complete with patients, doctors, and orderlies. The Blues had been lucky. They had surprised the hospital defenders, who had been so distracted by the buzzing helicopters that they hadn't been watching for a ground approach. The blue platoon had killed fifteen NVA and captured forty-three doctors and patients.

Shawn stepped out of the bunker and assembled his squad leaders. "Looks like we're out of this one. They have every general and VIP in the area flying out to the captured hospital to see what the cav found . . . it's gonna be a big dog and pony show. Our fly-boys and brother Blues done good. According to the reports, they captured a couple'a duffel bags full of documents, and beaucoup medical equipment, rice, and weapons. It's the first NVA regimental hospital ever captured, and the most NVA captured alive at one time. I want you guys to stand down and take it easy for the rest of the day. A few commo and medical classes will be enough. Tomorrow, we'll be flying out to the west and setting up an ambush in Indian country, so make sure your weapons and ammo are squared away. Any questions?"

Blake spoke up. "Any idea where the ambush will be?"

"Nope, not yet. It'll depend on what the scout ships find tomorrow. They'll be looking for a well-used trail. Any more questions? Good. Take charge of your men."

Blake glanced at his watch at the end of his class on radio procedures. It was after 1400 hours. He had begun to explain how to call for artillery, when he heard yelling.

"Saddle up, Blues! Squad leaders to the command bunker! Saddle up!"

Blake recognized the voice of his platoon sergeant. "Go back to the hooch and get saddled up for a mission," he quickly rattled to his three students. "I'll meet you there in a couple minutes."

Blake broke into a run toward the command bunker. With his adrenaline pumping, the sluggishness he'd felt a few minutes before disappeared. Waiting all morning on standby had been mentally and physically draining.

Outside the bunker Shawn gave his squad leaders a situation update.

"Looks like the hospital complex they found this morning had a hidden jack-in-the-box. The 'jack' just popped out a couple of minutes ago. Colonel Stockton and the assistant division commander were at the hospital site when an NVA force of undetermined size attacked. They flew out just in the nick of time, leaving the blue platoon as the only cav force defending the site, and they got pinned down. Us and the Alpha Blues are going in to help out until they get a couple of companies from one of the line battalions. The slicks will be here in five minutes to pick us up. We're closer than Alpha Blues, so we'll be inserted first. We'll use the load plan we had this morning. A guide will lead us from the L.Z. to the pinned-down platoon. Take extra water and ammo. Go back and brief your squads and meet me on the alert pad. Do it."

Lee Calhoon sat on the helicopter floor with his long legs dangling over the side as the forest twenty meters below streaked by in a blur at a hundred knots. Beside Lee sat his two new men, wearing mixed expressions of horror and exhilaration. Going on a combat air assault was like riding a heart-stopping roller coaster, except that during this ride, people might shoot at you.

Blake sat on the other side of the chopper, in the door with Vincent, Eugene, and Bradshaw. Blake leaned inside the cabin when he noticed the co-pilot signalling him. The warrant officer lifted his helmet visor and yelled to be heard over the screaming turbine engine, "Whites report! L.Z. may be hot! We're one minute out!"

Blake acknowledged with a thumbs up. "Lock and load!" he yelled to his men. "L.Z. may be hot! Remember we have friendlies on the ground! Be *sure* before you shoot!"

Vincent readied his machine gun and looked over his shoulder at Willie Billy. The handsome soldier's face was twisted into a mask of terror. Vincent smiled and motioned to Willie Billy's rifle. "Don't take it off safe unless you got a target! Stick to my left side!"

Willie Billy nodded like a robot.

Lee leaned forward into the hundred-knot winds to look ahead. He could see gunships firing rockets and smaller scout ships darting over the hogs like angry little bees.

The slick's tail suddenly dipped in a flair, slowing the ship's airspeed. A bullet exploded through the Plexiglas window behind the co-pilot and showered the passengers in slivers of clear plastic. The pilot held steady descent, ignoring the bullets that pinged off of the thin-skinned aircraft. Blake and the others ducked down and tried to make their bodies as small as possible. Beside Lee, Bob Winsome jerked, feeling as if the aircraft's floor had suddenly erupted beneath him. The pain hit him a millisecond later, and he screamed.

Ten feet from the small, grassy L.Z. the chopper dropped and landed like a broken elevator. Blake jumped to the ground in a dead run toward a soldier he saw waving to him from the edge of the treeline. He sprinted for several meters, then pitched forward into the blown-down grass and looked behind him. All of his men had gotten off, except for Winsome, who lay screaming and rolling on the blood-covered chopper floor. The crew chief grabbed Winsome's collar and began dragging him back into his door-gun compartment. Poor bastard, Blake thought. His first air assault and he gets hit.

The shaking machine lifted off and shot forward at so low an altitude that its skids clipped the tops of trees. Gunfire erupted out of the forest, and the bird darted to the right, dipped its nose, and sped away. For an instant the L.Z. was quiet. Then another whining slick popped over the treeline and began its approach.

Blake jumped to his feet, yelling for his men to follow him. He ran for the protective treeline. Seconds later he rolled behind a huge, brown ant mound. Five feet in front of him was a black soldier, a specialist, leaning against a tree and smoking nonchalantly.

The soldier said, "Not bad. We coulda done it better, but you brother Blues ain't bad."

Blake rose up to his knees and looked behind him for his squad. They were lying only a few feet behind him, staring in puzzlement. Lee's fatigue trousers were splotched with drying dark blood.

"How bad was Winsome hit?" Blake asked him.

Lee wiped blood from his hands with his shirtsleeve. "He got it in the back of the thigh. I s'pect he ain't comin' back."

Blake saw the second squad running toward him. "What the fuck is going on?" he asked the specialist, who was still enjoying his smoke.

"You are, man." The soldier grinned. "I been waitin' here forever. Da others is halfway up da ridge with NVAs every-fuckin'-where."

Blake saw Shawn jump off a slick, and stood up to wave at him. Seconds later the broad-shouldered platoon sergeant strode up, wearing his soft boonie hat instead of his helmet. He ignored the specialist and walked past him a few steps before stopping and lowering his head to listen. He stood still for several moments, until he'd heard enough.

Blake knew what his platoon sergeant was going to ask before he opened his mouth, and he cussed himself. The old vet had been listening to the gun battle in the distance, determining who had the upper hand.

"Who's doing the shooting?" Shawn asked.

Blake had already begun concentrating, trying to tune out the events around him. A fusillade in the distance confirmed his answer. "Mostly friendly outgoing, but a RPD machine gun is definitely up there banging away at our guys."

Shawn cracked a smile. "Bingo." His expression changed to all business. "Send two men back to the L.Z. to lead the fourth squad here." He turned his attention to the specialist and began grilling him with questions.

Five minutes later, Lee and Hanslow returned from the L.Z., with Lieutenant Owens and the fourth squad following.

Shawn quickly filled his platoon leader in on what he had learned from the specialist. The NVA hospital was just on the other side of the L.Z., close to the river. The NVA force had first been spotted by scout ships on a ridgeline east of the hospital complex. The blue platoon had gone out to investigate and had made it halfway up the wooded ridge when they ran into the NVA unit coming down.

Shawn took out his map and showed the officer where the unit was located. "Sir, it ain't gonna do any good going in behind the pinned-down platoon. We'll just get pinned down too. I think we oughta move up the ridge from here and hit 'em from another direction."

Owens motioned for his radioman. He took the handset and explained the plan to the troop commander, who was flying three thousand feet overhead, controlling the battle.

Owens listened for several moments and lowered the handset. "We got a go on your plan," he said to Shawn. "Move 'em out."

"First squad take point with me," Shawn barked over his shoulder. "Second, third, and fourth, follow in that order of march. Keep your eyes open. Weapons on safe until you have a target. Nice and easy now . . . mooove out."

Blake nodded at Lee, who stood and walked with Shawn toward the distant ridge. Shawn pointed toward the direction in which he wanted the point man to travel and dropped back beside Blake. "You and I will pull slack for Reb. Have your 'sixty gunner on our ass in case we need him."

Blake gave the hand signals that moved Vincent, Eugene, and Bradshaw up closer.

Lee kept the sound of shooting to his front right as he made his way up the gentle slope. The vegetation allowed for plenty of visibility, as the trees were widely spaced and formed only a thin canopy above. It was not a jungle, but rather a true forest. It reminded him of hunting in the pine forests of Georgia. He walked cautiously, listening first to the gunfire, then tuning it out and concentrating on other sounds. A little farther up the slope he heard a distant clink. He froze. Hearing it again, he dropped to his knee and raised his hand, forming a fist.

Blake's stomach knotted and his heart pounded when he saw the freeze signal. He made the same signal and glanced over his shoulder to make sure his men had seen the sign. The squad halted. Every man watched him with nervous anticipation, except for Vincent, who was slowly unwinding the belt of ammunition from around his arm to prepare for action.

Lee turned slightly to his left, the direction from which he'd heard the sound. Just a few feet in front of him the slope abruptly steepened, almost to a forty-five-degree angle. Fifty meters above him and to the left, a khaki-clad soldier wearing a pith helmet appeared and just as quickly disappeared behind trees. He appeared again, walking quickly with his AK-47 held ready. His chin strap was flopping back and forth, and the metal clasp was hitting the fiberglass helmet, making the clinking noise. Without taking his eyes from the soldier, Lee raised his rifle. It was just like hunting deer, he thought. He would let his prey come to him. Lee instinctively flicked his eyes farther up the ridge, as he did when he hunted, looking for the buck's following harem. What he saw was the top of the ridge coming suddenly alive with the mustard-brown uniforms of NVA regulars.

Ever so slowly, and always with his eyes on the approaching enemy, Lee held his arm out behind him, closing and opening his hand with fingers spread.

Blake held his breath and counted as Lee's hand opened and closed, signaling the number of enemy he had in sight—five, ten, fifteen, twenty. *Oh shit!*

Without waiting for orders from his platoon sergeant, Blake spun around and shot his arms out to his sides forming a T, then frantically waved them downward, a signal to get on line and get down, ready for action.

To the platoon's front Lee lowered himself gently to the ground and crawled back two feet to get beside a tree for more protection. He raised his rifle toward the approaching NVA regulars whose eyes were fixed on the ground ahead of them as they tried to negotiate the steep slope.

Lee judged that it was twenty meters back to his platoon. He would have to wait and shoot the lead scout when he was almost on top of him so that the platoon could see and engage the others. If he fired too soon, the enemy would be able to take cover among the trees and have the advantage of the high ground.

Lee scooted back a few more inches and waited. The scout's downward path would take him to Lee's left, and perhaps out of sight.

Shawn and Blake had crawled backward like scurrying crayfish to the squad's ragged defense line, which took advantage of the cover of trees and ant mounds. Lieutenant Owens had the second squad crawling up to the right of Blake's men, while the third squad was moved up to the left. Together, they would form a longer line of defense. Blake wiped sweat from his eyes and gulped. He could now see the line of NVA coming down the hill. Their lead scout was twenty meters ahead of the others, and only ten meters directly to Lee's left. Blake's eyes shifted anxiously. *Come on, Lee. Come on you hick bastard, shoot him!*

Lee decided to let the scout pass, to let the others get even closer. He knew it would be only a second before the scout would spot the platoon and be shot. He raised his rifle, ignoring the scout behind him, and picked out the only approaching soldier who wore a pistol. He hoped he was their leader.

Willie Billy Bradshaw realized his safety was still on and panicked. He flicked it forward. The metallic click caused the NVA scout to lift his head and weapon at the same time. Shawn shot the scout in the temple.

Lee fired a split second later, knocking the startled NVA platoon commander backward with a bullet through the heart.

Vincent's M-60 machine gun began its loud, deadly chatter, spewing out a tongue of orange flame and red tracers. Twenty-four other weapons joined in, unleashing a destructive fury.

The startled NVA, caught in the killing maelstrom, had to make the split second decision of diving for cover, turning and running, or attacking. The confused ones who stood exposed, unable to decide, died with frozen expressions of horror. Those who screamed defiantly and ran toward the platoon were cut down like stalks of wheat. They died with hate in their eyes. Those who turned around and ran were lucky, for the platoon was kept busy with fighters who had dropped to the ground, shooting, and rolled for cover.

One NVA private crawled frantically toward a nearby tree for protection, only to see a long-nosed, round-eyed Yankee roll from behind the trunk. The private gasped and tried to raise his rifle.

Lee fired at point-blank range. The small soldier's head jerked back, then flopped forward with a gaping, smoking hole that gushed blood and gray ooze. Lee saw another soldier crawling to his right and fired. The soldier grunted as if poked in the side with a pointed stick and tried to get up. Red tracers from Vincent's machine gun struck him in the chest with distinctive slapping noises and knocked him backward. Lee both smelled and heard the tracers sizzling inside the soldier's chest.

Shawn rose up, yelling, *"Second squad, bound forward. First squad, cover them!"* He wanted to hurry and flank the remaining enemy before they had time to recover from the shock.

Lieutenant Owens sprang to his feet and led the second squad. He ran like a star halfback, avoiding trees instead of tacklers. A young Vietnamese soldier lying behind an ant mound saw the huge man running toward him and jerked his weapon up, pulling back the trigger. Despite the close range, his bullets missed the intended victim because he had aimed at the running man instead of leading him.

Owens ducked left, seeing the orange flame from the rifle barrel, and hit the ground rolling. He came back up to his feet and fired from the hip as he ran straight toward the wide-eyed North Vietnamese soldier.

The soldier felt as if his shoulder were being ripped from his body. He screamed in anguish and felt more than saw the huge Yankee pass by. Still screaming, he saw more green-uniformed men coming, and closed his eyes as one man pointed his black rifle at him. Suddenly he felt a slap to the head that knocked him over. His eyes fluttered open. The pain was blissfully gone, replaced with a strange, warm tingling sensation that spread through his head, neck, and down his spine. He tried to move but couldn't. Incredibly tired, he quit fighting the strange tingling feeling and closed his eyes to rest in the forever darkness.

"Moveit!" Shawn yelled as he dashed up the ridge. Blake struggled to keep up, then suddenly pitched forward, tripped by an aboveground root. He hit the ground with the rifle under him and knocked the air out of himself.

Lee was only a few feet away and ran over to his squad leader, thinking he was hit. He rolled Blake over expecting the worst, but instead discovered his friend was only gagging for air. He grabbed Blake's collar and began dragging him toward a tree for protection.

"I thought I was gonna get that fancy watch fur sure," Lee mumbled.

Shawn stitched an NVA who bolted from behind a tree, trying to run up the ridge. He fell beside the body and turned around, yelling for his men to form a new defensive line.

Vincent fell to the ground beside the platoon sergeant and looked over his shoulder for his new assistant gunner. Bradshaw was still lying twenty meters down the slope in the initial defensive position. He had his arms over his head, as if he were trying to block out the battle sounds. Eugene had made the dash with Vincent and lay only a few feet to his right. He jumped up, tossed a belt of ammo to his friend, and started back to Bradshaw. A burst of AK bullets popped by his ear and thudded into a nearby tree. He threw himself down and belly-slid the last five feet into Willie Billy Bradshaw.

Eugene grabbed the claymore bag full of M-60 belts on the soldier's back and yanked the strap free from around Bradshaw's arm and shoulder. Bradshaw raised his head from the dirt and looked with fear and tear-filled eyes at Eugene. "I—I can't take this!"

Eugene swung the heavy bag, knocking the scared soldier's helmet off, and sneered. "I never thought you could."

Pushing himself up, Eugene ran back up the ridge toward Vincent, who was spraying the retreating NVA with burning lead.

Hanslow saw a North Vietnamese behind a tree and fired his M-79. The round exploded, hitting the tree.

Lee grabbed Hanslow's arm. "Not the tree. Hit beside it!" he yelled over the shooting.

Hanslow slapped in a new shell and raised his small weapon. He fired, and Lee immediately came up into firing position. The shell exploded just to the right of the tree, and the hiding NVA soldier rolled left from behind the trunk splattered with red splotches. The wounded soldier clawed the ground in desperation, trying to get back behind his cover, but Lee ended his attempt with a bullet in the head.

Sergeant Thomas Maynard, the third squad leader, saw movement from the corner of his eye and spun around firing. He was too late. He was stitched across the chest and fell back mortally wounded. His machine gunner twisted around to face the surprise flank attack and got off one burst before being hit in the head and neck by a flurry of AK-47 bullets.

Lieutenant Owens looked to his right, toward the new eruption of shooting, and saw to his horror a ten-man enemy squad overrunning his right-flank unit. He yelled a warning as he spun around, firing.

Vincent jerked up his machine gun and fired from the hip at the screaming men who were almost on top of him.

Four of the running NVA were shot by the lieutenant and Vincent, their bodies jerking with the impact of the tearing bullets that ripped through flesh and bones. A fifth soldier, not hit by the avenging fire, ran by Vincent and began to swing his rifle butt at the Italian's head when Eugene rose up, jamming his rifle barrel into the soldier's stomach and unloading the last half of his magazine.

The five remaining NVA jumped over their dead comrades' bodies and continued their assault. Lee and Hanslow were waiting. They fired at almost point-blank range. Lee's victim spun around, hit in the shoulder, while Hanslow's target was knocked off his feet and fell on his back with an unexploded grenade round embedded just below the rib cage.

Blake, nearly at the feet of a running NVA, rose up swinging the butt of his empty rifle. The blow glanced off the NVA's chest bandolier, which was full of magazines. The North Vietnamese soldier had whipped his rifle barrel down to fire at his attacker, when he was suddenly knocked forward with a vicious blow to the back of the head. Willie Billy Bradshaw raised his rifle butt again and bashed the North Vietnamese, who already lay on the ground, for a second time.

Shawn and the lieutenant shot the last two attackers, but not before one had sprayed the lieutenant's radio operator in the legs with a burst from his assault rifle.

Blake slapped in another magazine and immediately stitched the two wounded, who lay in front of Lee and Hanslow. He looked around for any more that could be dangerous and yelled, *"Check ammo!* Eugene, help the RTO. Bradshaw, Hanslow, help the third squad with their wounded. Vinny, Lee, keep an eye out and watch the flanks."

Shawn had been about to order the same actions. He closed his mouth and looked at the young first squad leader with pride. Alexander was thinking clearly under stress, and making others do the same. Jesus, he reminds me of me, Shawn thought. He turned around and hollered, "Fourth squad, move up here and get security out." He shifted his stance and barked for the whole platoon to hear. *"Report!"*

Blake lifted his head. "One man hit during the air assault, seven effectives, ammo okay."

The second squad leader yelled back, as he put a first-aid dressing on one of his men, "Two WIA, five effectives, ammo okay."

The Alpha fire-team leader of the third squad looked down at his dead squad leader. "Two killed, three wounded," he yelled angrily. "I'm the only effective. Ammo is . . . shit, I don't know."

"Easy, trooper, you're doing fine," Shawn said calmly. "Take care of your wounded as best you can."

The fourth squad leader had jogged up the slope and was close enough to his platoon sergeant not to yell. "Sarge, we're up on everybody, but we've got one twisted ankle. He can still walk."

Shawn quickly scanned the dead and wounded lying about him. "Post one man on each flank for security and one to the rear. Have your other men take care of the wounded."

Lieutenant Owens spoke into the radio handset while watching Eugene try and stop the radioman's thighs from bleeding. ". . . and hit us from the flank. We've got six WIA and two KIA. Over."

Owens listened to the reply as he took out his map. He moved his finger across the grid and pressed the handset's sidebar. "Roger, I understand. Fall back to the creek embankment to our rear. When will the relief unit arrive? Over."

Shawn strode over and inspected the wounds of the groaning radioman. He saw that Eugene had stopped the bleeding, but the young soldier was already in shock. Shawn gave instructions to Eugene, who had begun to tie off a tourniquet. "Get his head downhill and—"

Lieutenant Owens grabbed Shawn's shoulder. "We gotta move back to a stream embankment four hundred meters to the southeast and link up with the other Blues. The scouts spotted more NVA heading our way. We're gonna hold at the creek until a relief force comes in."

"What about our wounded?" Shawn said as he changed magazines.

"There's an L.Z. close to the embankment. We can move our wounded there for a pickup."

Shawn stepped closer, looking at the lieutenant's map to see what route they would take, then raised his head. "Break out ponchos for carrying the wounded!" he yelled. "We're moving out! First squad, you'll be staying here and covering our withdrawal till we're at the bottom of the ridge. We'll signal when we get there by shooting three single-shot M-16 rounds, followed five seconds later by two more."

Minutes later Lieutenant Owens stood beside his platoon sergeant as the wounded were carried down the slope. Owens shifted his gaze to the NVA bodies scattered about him. "Did you count 'em?"

"Twenty-two," Shawn said flatly.

"How many of them are wounded?"

Shawn lifted his bloodshot eyes to the officer. "Don't ask that question, sir. We got our hands full as it is, unless you wanna carry one down the hill."

Owens nodded tiredly. This was one subject they hadn't covered in the Law of Warfare class, back at the infantry officer basic course. Or maybe they did, but he didn't remember. Not that he felt bad about leaving behind the enemy wounded. His particular situation was a matter of simple math. He had six wounded and two dead of his own to bring along, and it took two men to carry each casualty. He also had to leave behind a security force and send a point team to lead the carrying party. The total number equaled the simple conclusion that the wounded enemy had to be left behind. He was doing his job—putting his men's lives above everything else.

Owens looked over his shoulder at the first squad. They would be staying behind to buy him and the others time. He *did* feel guilty leaving them, but his platoon sergeant seemed to read his mind and said reassuringly, "They're gonna be fine. Alexander knows his business."

Owens's jaw tightened. Being a leader at times like these ripped at his heart and insides. He glanced back again at his first squad, vowing to remember their faces and names for as long as he lived. It was the least he could do.

Shawn patted his platoon leader's shoulder. "Come on, sir, we gotta move."

Feeling old and tired, Owens turned in silence and began walking down the ridge.

Blake saw the first NVA soldier approaching cautiously. This time they won't be surprised, he thought to himself. He snapped his fingers and pointed up the slope.

Vincent nodded and pressed the machine gun's heavy butt into his shoulder, estimating the range to his target at seventy-five meters. Eugene nodded to his squad leader that he was ready, as did Willie Billy.

Blake glanced to his other side to make sure Lee and Hanslow had seen the lead NVA soldier. Both men acknowledged with small dips of their chins. Blake looked back at the scout and saw farther behind him a platoon of his comrades on line coming over the ridge. He had begun to raise his rifle when, from behind him, he heard in the distance the wonderful sound of three successive rifle shots. He counted silently to himself and smiled, hearing two more distinctive M-16 pops.

"Take the scout out, then follow me," he whispered to Lee.

Lee brought the butt up into his shoulder and laid his cheek along the black plastic stock. Aiming and taking a breath, he let out half and began a gentle squeeze of the trigger. The recoil came as a surprise, as it was supposed to. The scout fell back with the impact of the small bullet tearing through his chest and right lung.

Blake was on his feet the moment Lee fired. He waited until Vincent and his men began running before breaking into a dead run, followed by Hanslow and Lee.

Blake topped the sand creek embankment and winced. Below him along the sandy bank were the four dead and ten wounded of the other blue platoon. The small, narrow creek's slow-moving water had turned red with their blood.

Smiling with relief, Lieutenant Owens called out to Blake from up the creek and waved him to his position. Blake waved back and avoided looking at the water as he continued down the embankment.

One of the wounded, who had a bloody bandage around his head, raised his hand toward Blake. "Please help me. Please, it hurts so bad. Pleeease."

Blake kept walking, keeping his eyes on his lieutenant. He knew if he stopped, he wouldn't be able to leave the pathetic young soldier.

Owens slapped Blake's shoulder like a long-lost brother. "Damn, am I glad to see you guys. Any trouble?"

Blake glanced over his shoulder toward the ridge. "A platoon was coming down the slope when you signaled. Reb dropped their scout before we lit out."

Owens nodded and seemed to brighten. "We were lucky. When we got to the L.Z., a chopper was landing and we got all our wounded out."

Blake looked over his shoulder at the men he'd passed. "When they gonna get them out?"

Owens's face tightened. "The bird our wounded went out on got hit a couple of times. We're waitin' on the gunships to come back to cover another slick."

Blake's heart went out to the wounded who had to endure the uncertainty of getting out before bleeding to death.

Owens put his hand on Blake's shoulder to get his attention. "I want your squad to take up a defensive position to the right of the fourth squad. You're gonna be the farthest unit to our right, so watch your flank."

Blake began to march forward but stopped himself. Where was his mentor? "Where's Irish, sir?" he asked the lieutenant.

Owens saw the concern in the young squad leader's eyes and smiled to alleviate his fears. "He's posting an O.P. to our front. He'll be back in just a minute."

Blake felt a surge of relief. He was glad his sergeant was okay, and doubly glad he had not been asked to provide men from his squad for the observation post. The O.P.'s mission was to give advance warning of an attack. Most troops thought of O.P. as a nice way to say "suicide."

Minutes later Blake had his men in position along the sand embankment. "Comin' in!" a voice called out from the forest.

Blake recognized Shawn's voice. "Friendly coming in. Hold your fire!" he yelled down the defense line.

Shawn strode into the perimeter and was met by Lieutenant Owens. "I made sure the other Blues know we've got an O.P. out, and Alexander's squad is back with us," Owens told him. "I put 'em on the right flank."

Shawn nodded tiredly. "The Whites should be able to give us some warning time until it gets dark."

A gunship streaked overhead, its Gatling gun buzzing like a chain saw. Spent brass casings rained down, causing both men to duck out of the way.

Shawn turned, hearing a slick that was on its final approach into the small L.Z. to their rear. He looked for more birds in the distance but didn't see any. The landing chopper was the medevac, not the lead bird bringing in the relief force he had hoped for. He began to turn away when he saw a soldier hop out of the chopper. Shawn's face turned to stone.

"At least we don't have to worry about them anymore," Owens said of the wounded being carried to the Huey. He saw his sergeant wasn't listening and raised an eyebrow. "What's wrong?"

Shawn was so angry as he strode to meet the passenger that he had not heard the officer's question. He stopped within ten paces of the approaching soldier and pointed at the chopper. "Get your ass back on that bird right now!"

The passenger smiled. "Nice to see you too, Irish."

"Goddamnit, I mean it! Get the fuck outta here, Taco!" Shawn shouted over the turbine engine.

Sergeant Major John Quail kept his smile. He knew his old friend was worried about him, and worse, would feel obligated to protect him. "I ain't taught you worth a shit. You don't respect rank or your fuckin' elders. Shut up and come here and give your frozen chosen buddy a handshake at least."

Shawn relented. He knew Quail wouldn't leave. The two men walked forward with hands extended, but they hugged instead.

Standing behind them Owens smiled, though he felt a twinge of jealousy. Flynn was a tough professional whom he cared for as only a man can care for another man. It was a special bond, like that of brothers. He was jealous that Shawn could not look upon him in the same way he did this stranger.

Minutes later, after introductions and a tour of the defense by Lieutenant Owens, Quail and Shawn sat down in a fighting position that had been dug into the sandy bank.

Quail gave his friend a concerned look. "You lookin' awfully thin. You best start eatin' more."

Shawn raised an eyebrow. "And it looks to me like you need to be eatin' less. How is Cindy doin' and what the fuck you doin' back here?"

Quail dug in his fatigue pocket and pulled out a packet of letters. "Cindy's doin' great. I saw her a week ago, just before I left. She wanted me to give these to you and to tell you she thinks it's gonna be a boy for sure. She's due in a couple of weeks, ya know."

Shawn felt the weakness he dreaded eating at his insides. It was the feeling he got every time he thought of her, the horrible longing that brought back so many of the memories he couldn't afford to think about. The guilt he felt for not being with her when she had their child tore him up inside and left him empty and feeling helpless.

Shawn took the letters. "She really doing all right?"

Quail nodded with a look of sincerity. "Pretty as a picture and excited about having the kid. I—I gotta tell ya, I probably helped put ya into bankruptcy. The trailer was no place for her and the baby, so I did a little house huntin'. You're gonna love it."

Shawn took the news without reacting. He was too relieved to hear Cindy was doing well to worry about money. God, he missed her. He sighed, putting her image away. "Come on now, tell me about why you're here."

Quail leaned back and looked around. "The scenery. I love the fuckin' scenery around here. Oh, yeah, and also they sent me here to see how the airmobile division is working out. I've been at division headquarters for two days getting briefed with the usual bullshit. I didn't come to get smoke blown up my ass. I want to know what the real problems are so we can fix them. For some reason, the staff gave me the old 'everything is wonderful' routine. It took me a day to finally wear them down to get to the real truth."

Shawn looked puzzled. "From what I've seen, the concept is working fine."

Quail grinned. "That's right, you're nothing but a grunt, so you don't see what really goes on. The problem is maintenance and support. The division can only keep a little over half of the birds up at any given time. We're gonna have to beef up the maintenance battalion with more mechanics and equipment. It's nothin' that can't be fixed, but it's gonna take some time."

Shawn began to ask a question when a single shot rang out from the forest to their front. Shawn sprang up. The sound had come from where he had placed the O.P. Every man was looking over their readied weapons, expecting an attack.

"*We got friendlies out there!*" Shawn yelled. "*Nobody shoots unless you know they ain't ours!*"

From out of the forest came the two men of the O.P., running as fast as they could. "*They're coming!*" one was yelling. "*They're co—*"

Crack! Crack, crack crack! The soldier's arms came up as if he were balancing himself, and he crumpled to the ground. His buddy turned around and ran back to help his fellow squad member. Bullets chewed up the ground to his right. He dived to the dirt and crawled to the bleeding soldier.

The combined blue platoons sprayed the forest in covering fire, though they couldn't see any targets.

The crawling soldier reached his buddy and began dragging him to a nearby felled tree.

Shawn spun around to tell his lieutenant to get the gunships, but he heard an all-too-familiar sound.

Quail heard it too and yelled the warning, *"Mortars! Incoming!"*

Shawn knew he had at least ten more seconds. *"Sir, get the guns here fast!"* he yelled to Lieutenant Owens.

The officer popped his head up. He was holding the radio handset to his mouth, already making the call. He stuck his thumb up.

Shawn spun around and fell on top of Quail, driving him into the sand. Two seconds later, a shell exploded twenty meters behind them, throwing up dirt clods and whizzing fragments. Another exploded to the left, and a third hit just outside the perimeter and filled the air with sand.

Quail pushed Shawn off him and blew sand off his rifle. "Just like the old days, huh?"

Shawn dug in the wet sand to deepen the hole. "You shouldn't be here, goddamnit! Don't sit there, *dig!*"

Quail helped carry a wounded soldier to the waiting slick and set him down gently on the bird's floor. He patted the soldier's leg. "Ya gonna be home soon, son, drinkin' beer and tellin' war stories."

The trembling soldier's eyes said thank you. Quail knew the boy would live, but he would lose his right arm. Mortar shrapnel had sliced through it just below the elbow, leaving his wrist and hand hanging by only sinew.

Quail walked back to where the Blues had assembled into squads, waiting for their ride out of hell. A relief company from one of the battalions had already airmobiled in, and another was on the way. The blue platoons had been ordered out to refit and rearm for more missions. The hunt was still on.

Quail walked over to Shawn, who sat beside a young sergeant. "Irish, the guns musta got the mortars."

Shawn nodded tiredly. "Yeah, we ain't been hit in the last thirty minutes or so." He began to lower his head but thought of something important. "You're going out with us, right?"

Quail shrugged his shoulders. "Naw, I think I'll stick around for a while. Once the companies clear the area, I wanna take a look at that hospital. I'll see ya later, and we'll have a beer."

Shawn stood up. "Taco, you're going out with us. I don't wanna worry about you. I won't sleep if you don't."

Blake lifted his head. He couldn't believe what he was hearing. He hadn't thought his sergeant had it in him.

Quail sighed and sat down. "You're worse than an old lady, Irish."

Shawn glanced at Blake. "Ace, you and me are gonna personally escort this antique to the first bird that comes in. Watch him like a hawk, 'cause he's a slippery old cuss."

Quail shook his head as if disappointed and looked at Blake. "Son, I feel sorry for ya, having the likes of this old lady for your platoon sergeant. I taught him everything he knows, and it hurts me to see it obviously wasn't very fucking much."

Blake smiled as Shawn winked at him, but then the sergeant's expression changed, and he looked at Blake's face more closely. "You better see a doctor when we get back. Your cheek is drooping pretty bad."

Blake self-consciously touched his face. "Yeah, the guys already told me. The plastic surgeon said this might happen. I'll get it done when I get home."

Shawn nodded, trying not to show the concern he felt, and lifted his head at the whopping sound of an approaching helicopter. He glanced back at Blake. "Ya done good this afternoon. Ya made me proud."

Blake shyly avoided his platoon sergeant's eyes and stood up. "The squad did good. I guess I'd better check on 'em." He walked toward his men with his chest swelling.

Quail motioned toward the squad leader when he was out of earshot. "I take it he's one of your good ones."

Shawn glanced over his shoulder at the soldier. "Yeah, he's good people."

26

Willie Billy Bradshaw swaggered between the rows of tents, basking in the stares. He wore an NVA pack and a Combat Infantryman's Badge just like the rest of the veterans of the first squad.

Vincent walked beside the good-looking soldier with a disgruntled frown. Bradshaw had been bragging ever since they got back from the hospital relief mission the day before. Blake was worried about him. He was wearing all the symbols, but he wasn't really a veteran, not yet. He had not yet learned to keep his mouth shut and listen. Willie Billy thought he already knew everything.

Eugene tapped Bradshaw's shoulder. "Yo, Willie Billy, there was a guy back there asking about you. He wanted to know if we had a helmet big enough for your swelling head. I told him they didn't make helmets that big."

Willie Billy grinned. "Fuck 'em, they ain't seen any action like us."

"Us?" Vincent said. "You been in a one-day contact."

Bradshaw brushed nonexistent dust from the silver-wreathed infantryman's badge. "One day under fire is all I needed to get this."

Eugene exchanged glances with Vincent, and both men shook their heads.

Lee walked behind the others, totally absorbed in explaining the difference between NVA and American weapons.

Hanslow was taking it all in like a sponge. His eyes widened. "I hate the mortars more than anything else. You can get behind something if they're shooting at you, but them mortars are so . . . so unfair."

Lee agreed. "You gotta find a hole or a ditch and get away from trees. If the shell goes off in the branches, it blows the shrapnel downward."

Blake halted his squad by a small tin building that served as their hooch. "I want everybody to get as much rest as possible. Our platoon is going on standby alert tomorrow."

Willie Billy's mouth dropped open. "Already? Shit, we just got here."

Eugene took off his pack and strode by the shocked man. "What'sa matter, Willie, you already had enough 'action'?"

"Willie," Vincent chuckled, "maybe you should strut up an' down the street an' tell the other guys more of them war stories. It might be your last chance, you know?"

Minutes later Blake lay back on his pack and closed his eyes. His platoon sergeant had been right, he couldn't remember a single face of the NVA he had killed from the preceding day. At least he would be able to sleep without their lifeless eyes staring at him. The only face he could remember, and it still bothered him, was the wounded Blue's private lying on the sandy bank. He wished he had stopped and helped him.

Hanslow scooted closer to Lee. "Reb," he whispered, "how do you sleep? I mean get them out of your head?"

Lee opened one eye and whispered back, "Kill 'em again then think of home. Think of that special place where ya could always go ta git away for a while. I go back ta my front-porch swing, an' rock an' smell the honeysuckle."

Hanslow's eyes closed. "I had a treehouse like that. Thanks."

The squadron operations officer stood before the assembled troop commanders and platoon leaders, briefing them on the upcoming mission. "The search for NVA regiments is mostly our show. The rest of the division has to leapfrog its units and artillery forward, so they can't search as big an area as we can. The division G-2 has analyzed some marked NVA maps found at the captured hospital and thinks the regiments are in this area." The major turned and pointed at the wall map toward a clump of mountains just east of the Cambodian border. "It's called the Chu Pong Massif. The NVA maps indicated their infiltration routes into South Vietnam. Two of those routes are major trails that pass just north of the Chu Pong Mountain area. The trails more or less parallel this river and valley called the Ia Drang.

"As you can see, the area is a considerable distance from where our present line battalions and artillery units are located. Division wants us to fly out to the Ia Drang valley tomorrow and check it out. Colonel Stockton has agreed, but wants a rifle company on standby alert in case we get in a situation with our asses hangin' out. The hospital contact yesterday taught us all a lesson. The Blues need immediate backup if they get in over their heads. Tomorrow the Whites and Reds will fly out and conduct a recon of the area. If the trails are really there and look like they've been used recently, find us a spot for our Blues to set up an ambush. That's it, unless somebody has questions."

A mustached captain stood up. "Major, we've lost a lot of Blues the past couple of days. Any way we could get some replacements?"

The operations officer shook his head. "No, the entire division is short of people. Between the malaria that's depleting the ranks, and those rotating home, the division is at about seventy-five percent strength. We're all gonna have to go with what we've got."

"What about our birds?" another captain asked, getting to his feet. "We're flying the rotors off my scout ships. My maintenance crews are working night and day trying to keep the birds up, but we're losing the maintenance battle. I've got five ships right now that need a complete engine overhaul or replacement, and three more about to come due for overhaul. We've already thrown all the maintenance safety regulations out the window. We're flying in the red."

The major motioned over his shoulder at the map. "If the fuckers escape into Cambodia, you're gonna have plenty of time for maintenance. We've almost got the running commie bastards. We have to find 'em, fix 'em, and finish 'em, now! We've got the momentum, and we have to keep it."

The unimpressed captain sat down shaking his head. "I've heard all those speeches before, Major. I'm telling you, the birds can *not* take this kind of punishment. We might find them and even fix them, but we won't be able to finish shit."

Grumbling and nods in the group told the major the scout platoon leader was speaking for the others. He relaxed his tight jaw and sighed. "Okay, I hear you. I'll pass it on to the colonel, but tomorrow the mission goes as planned."

Shawn and John Quail were sitting in the back of the small briefing room, listening.

"It's beginning," Quail said. "The scout commander is just the first one to say it. The division isn't capable of supporting this big an operation. They're taking a risk."

Shawn looked at his old friend. "Do we have a choice?"

Quail lowered his head. "No."

Far below the triple canopy which left the forest floor in perpetual twilight, Colonel Lee Van Quan paced with his hands clasped behind his back. The reports he had been receiving from the regiments were mostly bad. The 32nd had reported that while two of its battalions had reached the Chu Pong sanctuary, their ranks had been horribly thinned. The 33rd reported that their headquarters had reached the northeast slopes of the Chu Pong, also that they had lost their hospital, doctors, and in defending the hospital site, at least half a battalion.

The colonel halted and stared at the entrance to the underground command post. He didn't have the heart to go back into the depressing darkness. The Americans had chased him and his men into hundreds of such black holes. Despite what his general had said, he did not feel like a cunning fox, but rather a scared rabbit.

Colonel Du climbed up the bunker's entrance steps and smiled at his assistant commander. "Good news at last. The 66th Regiment is one day's march away. The lead elements of their headquarters have already crossed the border."

Colonel Quan felt a tremendous weight lifted from his shoulders. The presence of the fresh regiment would breathe life into the other men and bolster their morale. He returned a faint smile. "We needed a miracle, and now we have it."

3 NOVEMBER

The scout pilot popped over the treeline at eighty knots and gasped. Directly below was a wide, red-clay, hard-packed trail. He tensed and waited for the bluish-green tracers to tear through his chopper's plastic bubble. The co-pilot had even raised his feet and tucked in his arms, expecting a hosing. Several seconds passed before the pilot relaxed and quickly offered his maker a prayer of thanks for protecting the stupid. Flying over an open area, especially an infiltration trail, would usually have guaranteed their taking a few hits. He pushed his internal talk button. "Sorry 'bout that, Ray. I didn't expect nothin' like that."

Ray eased his feet back to the floor. "We better check it out. That NVA map was off a little on where the trail was located, but that's gotta be it. Hell, it looked like Ho Chi Minh's Highway Sixty-six. That sucker has been used a lot."

The pilot brought the bird around and increased its air speed. "I think our Blues are gonna be busy tonight."

Ray kept his eyes straight ahead. "Yeah, the poor bastards."

Shawn shook Quail's hand in farewell. "Taco, promise me you won't be 'visiting' me in the field again."

Quail grinned. "Good luck, ya ol' lady. Take care of them kids ya got, and good huntin'."

Shawn kept his firm grip on Quail's hand. "Promise me."

Quail nodded. "Go on. I'll see ya when ya get back. I'm going to division headquarters and poke around a little."

Satisfied, Shawn released his friend's hand and joined his platoon, which was waiting on the alert pad.

"I've missed you, Irish," Quail called out to him. "Come back, ya hear?"

Shawn glanced over his shoulder and raised his thumb.

Blake finished inspecting his men's equipment and gathered them around him. "Okay, let's go over it one more time. We're going to be loading the second bird. We're going into an L.Z. with the rest of the platoon close to the border and near a river called the Ia Drang, but another blue platoon will already be on the ground, so no shooting. We set up the patrol base along with the other two blue platoons, a CIDG Montagnard platoon and a mortar platoon assigned to support us. We man the southern perimeter of the patrol base, and once the patrol base is set up, we march out and set up our ambush about fifteen hundred meters south along a trail. Our mission is to ambush any retreating enemy trying to get back into Cambodia."

Blake was going to ask for questions, but the roar of the approaching helicopters ended the review. Lowering his head and squinting his eyes to keep the blown-up dirt from blinding him, he leaned into the rotor wash. Once the flight of four slicks landed, he raised his head and yelled for his men to follow him.

Vincent pushed Willie Billy ahead of him. "Go on, he-row. I can tell you can hardly wait!"

Shawn watched the ground beneath the speeding chopper and patted his front fatigue shirt pocket, where he kept Cindy's letters, still unread. He wished that he'd had a chance to write her and tell her how much he missed her, but there had been no time and no envelopes. He wondered what her letters said, and thought of her sitting alone in their new house, but the vision vanished as the bird's tail suddenly dipped. He cleared Cindy and the letters from his mind and climbed out into the windstream onto the slick's skid.

Like his platoon sergeant on the lead bird, Blake and his squad climbed out onto the skids to be in position to jump. The report from the scouts had said that the L.Z. was open, but that small trees, at least five feet high, were interspersed throughout the area and would make a touchdown impossible without the chance of a tail-rotor strike.

The bird began dropping, but Blake jumped the last six feet to the ground, landing in a crouch. He stood erect and walked a few steps to get out of the way of the rest of his men. He had seen there was no need to run for cover. Men from the Alpha Blues were standing around the L.Z. next to huge ant mounds watching the show.

Shawn motioned Blake over and pointed south. "Spread your men out from that tall ant mound to that black rock. Have 'em keep an eye out and yell if they see anything."

Minutes later more slicks unloaded the Montagnard platoon. Lee looked around to get a feel for the flat terrain. The first squad would be the lead unit in the march to the ambush position, so he would be the point man again.

Blake could see his friend's eyes studying the stunted trees and flat ground covered in yellow clumps of grass and towering ant mounds made of what looked like mud-brown concrete. "What do ya think? You gonna be able to spot 'em if they're waiting out there for us?"

Lee's brow furrowed. "Don't reckon so. They could hide behind all them mounds and grass purty easy. The wind ain't right ta smell 'em either." Lee gave Blake a wink. "But I ain't worried. You gonna be backin' me up, aren't ya?"

The left side of Blake's mouth rose in a smile that looked more like a sneer. "I'll be there with you. I made you a promise, remember?"

Lee nodded with a grin and motioned toward Blake's Rolex. "Ya take care of that watch. I wouldn't want nothin' ta happen ta it."

Lieutenant Owens and the four other platoon leaders sat under a gnarled tree, watching the designated commander of the patrol base, Major Jim Anderson, draw in the dirt.

"The Ia Drang River is eight hundred meters due north of us. One of the trails parallels it a ways, and that's where Bravo Blues are gonna put in their ambush to catch any NVA trying to cross the river and slip back into Cambodia. Alpha Blues are going to put in their ambush about a klick farther up the river on a side trail, and Charlie Blues are gonna put in their ambush to the south of the patrol base on the other major trail at the foot of Chu Pong Mountain. If anybody makes contact, the mortars here at the patrol base will support you. You've all got your radio frequencies and running password. I want your units moving out in the next ten minutes. Report when you've established your ambush positions. The time now is 1640 hours. Good luck and good hunting."

General Chu Huy Man glanced up toward the sound of the helicopter passing a thousand feet overhead. It was just one of many that had flown over that day, forcing him to delay the 66th Regiment from crossing the river and joining him in the sanctuary. He stepped down into the command bunker entrance and made his way through the underground maze of dark tunnels to the radio room. The two sergeants on duty both stood as their general entered. He motioned them down with a wave of his hand. "Sit," he commanded. "Inform the commander of the 66th he can begin crossing the border with his units once darkness comes."

The senior sergeant picked up the radio mike. "Your order will be sent, my general."

Man backed out of the candlelit room and ducked his head to continue down the tunnel to his operations center. The assistant commander was placing the 66th Regiment's location on the wall battle map when the general walked in. Colonel Quan tapped the map with frustration. "All units are reporting Yankee helicopters in their area. Could the Yankees really have so many machines?"

Man walked to the map and looked over the most recent location updates from his units. "Yes, and that is why I delayed the 66th and ordered the others to remain hidden. We must have time to rebuild. We cannot let the Americans find us."

Quan lit a cigarette and sucked the smoke into his lungs, then exhaled slowly and looked through a blue cloud of smoke at his commander. "What happens if they do find us?"

Man faced his assistant commander with eyes of stone. "We would attack and destroy the fools."

Lee positioned his two crescent-shaped claymore mines in the grass so they would blow down the clay-packed trail, then carefully inserted the electric blasting caps into the fuse wells. After once more checking the alignment on both mines, he backed up and trailed the electrical firing wires to his ambush position. Blake had just returned from setting out his claymores as well. Hanslow was glad to have both men back with him, as he had been responsible for covering his fellow squad members while the other two were gone.

Lee inserted the firing wire female plug into the male plug of the small green clacker. The electrical firing device had a short arm that, once pushed down, would send a current to the blasting cap and detonate the mine. A claymore was packed with composition C-4 plastic explosive, which blew a thin panel of over seven hundred small, steel ball bearings into the kill zone.

Hanslow watched as both Lee and Blake set their clackers in front of them and took out two grenades. Straightening the pins for easy pulling, they set those beside their clackers, then took out one magazine apiece and set them beside the grenades.

Lee saw Hanslow's questioning stare and leaned over. "Do the same thing we're doin'," Lee whispered. "You gotta set everything out while it's light. Once it's dark, you don't wanna be movin' around and searchin' for stuff." He motioned to his grenades and magazine. "If they come into the kill zone, we're gonna blow the claymores, then throw the grenades, and then fire at anything that's still movin'. The extra mag is there if we need it."

Hanslow immediately reached down for his grenades.

Shawn inspected the platoon's ambush positions and each claymore's alignment. Satisfied, he moved back to the platoon command post, which was centered just behind the line of positions. The trail was only twenty meters away, and he didn't like that his men had only grass, a few trees, and folds in the ground to hide behind. The platoon had a good view of the fifty-meter kill zone, but an observant enemy point man would also be able to spot them, if anyone made a sudden movement or noise.

"We ready?" Lieutenant Owens whispered when Shawn sat down beside him.

Shawn nodded. Ten claymore mines and twenty-five weapons were trained on the kill zone. If anyone was caught on the trail when the bush was executed, he would either be dead or wounded within milliseconds.

Owens raised the radio handset to his mouth to send the codeword that would tell the patrol-base commander that Charlie Blues' ambush was established.

Blake leaned over to Lee, who lay beside him.

"It's gonna be a long night, buddy," he whispered.

"I'm just ahopin' it's a quiet one," Lee whispered back.

Vincent scooted over to Willie Billy. "If you push off your safety like you done last time, I'll kill ya. Hold it while you movin' it, capish?" he muttered.

Willie Billy swallowed his pride and nodded silently. Vincent looked at Eugene and winked. Eugene pushed his glasses back up on his nose and winked back.

Lieutenant Owens raised his wrist to see the iridescent green watch hands. It was almost eight-thirty P.M. It was going to be a long night, he thought to himself. The radio operator suddenly tugged at his arm and passed him the radio handset. Owens put the device to his ear. Bravo Blues' platoon leader was reporting to the patrol base.

". . . and we just heard horns blowing to the west of us from across the river. I have a two-man security team over there, and they just reported what sounds like a lot of people moving south along the east bank of the river. They aren't coming this way, but heading south, over."

The major's voice came back over the air. "Are you sure you heard sounds to the west of you and not the east? Over."

"I can read a fuckin' compass!" the agitated platoon leader whispered back. "We can hear 'em *west* of us, *not* east. Over."

Owens grabbed Shawn's arm, pulling him closer, and whispered, "Bravo's bush is hearing lots of movement west of their position."

"West? Are they sure?" Shawn said softly, but with urgency.

"They're sure. The C.O. just had them confirm it."

Shawn rose to his knees, cursing the U.S. Army's intelligence pukes for not warning them about the possibility of additional infiltrating enemy units. His ambush was laid out for troops trying to leave South Vietnam, not enter it! *Shit! Shit! Shit!* Why didn't he think of it? How fuckin' dumb could he get?

Shawn took a deep breath to calm himself and make himself think. He walked the ambush positions again in his mind, recalling the claymore placements. Slowly he relaxed, for the five pairs of mines had been laid so they would all overlap each other, just as he had taught his men to do it. The claymores were not going to be the problem—it was his men. They had instinctively positioned themselves toward the threat, which they thought would come from the east. Shit! He would have to crawl out and warn them.

Shawn turned around to whisper to Owens and tell him where he was going when his heart stopped beating and his breathing suddenly ceased. Only fifty meters away he heard a Vietnamese speaking in a normal tone, as if he were on a Sunday stroll. Another voice answered the first and was joined by laughter from others.

Shawn lowered himself to the ground and looked up to the stars far above. He spoke in a reverent whisper. "Thank you for dumber people than me." His fears and anger were now gone. He knew his men could hear the approaching enemy and they would have plenty of time to shift around. Shawn tapped the still stunned lieutenant, who was staring toward the voices.

"Sir, you'd better report that we got visitors."

Blake flattened himself farther down, until his buttons hurt his chest. The full moon perfectly silhouetted a group of soldiers wearing pith helmets and carrying rifles only twenty meters from where he lay. The strange thing was that the soldiers had stopped and looked as if they were taking a break. The sounds farther away, which were probably made by the clinking equipment of a large unit on the march, had ceased. He thought they must have stopped along the trail, as had the men he could see.

Lee extended his hand and patted Hanslow's arm reassuringly. "Steady now, Gerry, we're gonna wait nice an' quiet like. Things has done changed on us, and we ain't gonna be startin' the shootin' as planned. The NVA are comin' into our kill zone from the west, not east. We won't be blowin' our claymores until the fourth squad, on the other end of our ambush, fire theirs first. No shootin' till they do. Okay?"

Hanslow's whisper came out in a barely audible tweek. "Okay."

Five meters to Lee's right Vincent had a grip on Willie Billy's chin and was within an inch of his face, whispering. "Don't you fart, itch, or cough, an' don't touch your trigger till I tell ya, capish?"

Willie Billy nodded. Vincent patted his face before backing up and leaning over to Eugene. "Willie's gonna be fine."

Lieutenant Owens, his radio operator, and Shawn had crawled to the fourth squad's ambush position to take charge. It was clear by the voices that a lead element of a very large unit had stopped just outside the kill zone. When the enemy started moving again, Owens wanted to make sure his men did not execute the ambush on the first group that passed. He wanted to wait like the manual said and hit the enemy's less alert second unit. Owens raised his wrist again, looked at his watch, and saw that it had been almost twenty minutes since he'd first heard the voices. He didn't know if he could take the waiting any longer. His uniform was soaked with nervous sweat and his heart was pounding so hard he knew any passing NVA soldier would surely hear it.

When the nearby chatter rose, Shawn poked his platoon leader. "They're comin', sir."

Owens whispered into the handset, "Base, they're moving into the kill zone. I'm going to wait and initiate on the second group. Get mortars ready to fire on my command. Over."

Owens listened for a simple acknowledgment but got a question back instead. "Charlie Six, how do you know there will be a second group? Over."

Owens could now clearly see the first men walking down the trail. He murmured very softly, " 'Cause I can hear the fuckers, out."

Blake waited for what seemed like an eternity for the ear-shattering explosion that would allow him to finally push the clacker. He had counted forty-two men passing by, and more were coming, forty-three . . . forty-four . . . forty-five . . . forty-six . . . *Come on,* blow the bastards away! Forty-eight . . . Blake shifted his eyes looking for number forty-nine, but there was no one there. He began to worry when he heard more singsong chatter coming from down the trail. Within seconds the next group of soldiers appeared, like the first, in single file, but these were much closer together and holding short, thick poles on their shoulders. No, they were not poles! They were mortar tubes—it was the heavy weapons unit!

Lee kept waiting for one of the passing soldiers to look left and wonder about the dark objects lying on the ground.

Vincent removed his sleeping trigger finger and quickly opened and closed his hand several times to pump blood back into it. The effort was torture, for his entire lower arm felt like lead.

Eugene had endured buzzing mosquitoes and their bloodsucking attacks for over thirty minutes without moving. His face and hands were puffy from countless bites. He'd had enough. One bloodsucker had landed on his lower lip and was draining his blood. Ever so slowly as the NVA passed in front of him, he opened his mouth and drew his lower lip in. Suddenly he clamped his mouth shut, catching the unwary mosquito inside. Taking great pleasure in the torture, he brought his tongue up toward the roof of his mouth, reducing the prisoner's space like a moving wall. Then, smiling to himself, he pushed his tongue to the roof of his mouth and felt the creature squish. *There! You bastards, I got one of you!* And the NVA kept passing by.

It was now a test of patience between Shawn and the lieutenant as to who would finally push his clacker and begin the killing. The first two soldiers of the second group were at the end of the kill zone and getting step by step farther away. Owens could not take it anymore. He pushed down the handle of his clacker.

A senior NVA sergeant near the lead saw a blinding flash of light and was suddenly knocked backward by a thunderous explosion that seemed to make the ground rapidly jump and fall. He hit the ground hard on his side when another explosion blew over him, covering his twitching body in a thick cloud of choking dust and smoke. He felt as if he'd been impaled to the ground by a flurry of burning arrows. More explosions behind him knocked him over again, and his head rolled forward into one of his men's dirt-covered intestines. Gagging from lack of air, he tried to extricate his head from the filth, but he couldn't make his neck or shoulders respond. He thought of his wife and two sons, knowing they would never see him again. Something landed beside his face and splashed his forehead with gore.

Shawn threw another grenade and dropped to the ground. He had no idea where either bomb had landed because of the dust cloud covering the kill zone.

Vincent swung the machine gun left and right, keeping the red tracers low and hoping at least to cripple any escaping NVA. His eyes stung and his ears rang from the explosions, but his trigger finger had not failed him. As soon as the first claymore ripped the air, his finger had automatically pressed the trigger.

Eugene lowered his weapon after firing only four single unaimed shots. His glasses were so coated in thick dust that he could barely make out the tree next to him.

Willie Billy burned up a magazine and slapped in another while looking for some kind of target. Raising his rifle, he fired anyway. He liked the feeling of power when the weapon bucked in his hands.

Hanslow fell into his routine of shoot, break the breach, pop out the shell, insert a new one, close the breach, raise and fire.

Blake lowered his rifle and strained to see through the dissipating dust. The bright moon again shone through the cloud, and slowly the trail became visible, but it didn't look the same. Grotesque, torn bodies lay in heaps, as if they had been pushed together with a 'dozer blade, while others lay individually in odd positions. The overwhelming smell of fresh-tilled soil was sweet and pungent in the air, and it mixed with the tangier smell of gun smoke and plastic explosive, which left a tinny taste in his mouth.

Shawn stood. There was no use in wasting any more ammunition. The ambush had been perfectly executed. Not a single shot had been returned. He knew it wouldn't last for long. The first unit, and perhaps even more behind, would soon be coming to exact their vengeance.

"Move back to the rally point!" Shawn yelled. *"Now! Moveit! Moveit!"*

Owens stood and looked down the body-covered trail. "Jesus," he mumbled in disbelief.

Shawn grabbed his arm. "Sir, come on, we gotta move quick!"

Owens put the handset to his mouth and pushed the sidebar as he ran along with his sergeant. "Base, fire mortars in thirty seconds. Ambush was successful . . . I say again, ambush was successful. Estimated forty to fifty NVA KIA'd."

Major Anderson walked the perimeter where the Charlie Blue platoon had taken up defensive positions in the patrol base. The young excited soldiers seemed to be so charged with electricity that he could feel it emanate from their bodies. They had killed over forty men only an hour before, and now they couldn't keep from fidgeting and whispering to each other.

Anderson had begun to walk back to his command post when a squad leader rose from the ground close to him. "Sir, have we got friendlies coming in this way?"

Anderson spun around and saw in the bright moonlight a line of dark figures scurrying from tree to tree, coming toward his patrol base. He raised his head and yelled, "Those aren't ours!"

The officer's words had no sooner left his mouth than a burst of green tracers whizzed by his head. Anderson dived to the ground and crawled as fast as he could toward his C.P. to report the situation to squadron headquarters.

Shawn had just walked the perimeter, trying to calm down his men, when the distinctive sound of the Chinese-made RPD machine gun shattered the eerie silence. He dove to the ground next to Blake and rolled behind an ant mound. Bullets thudded into the ground to his right, kicking up small clouds of dust.

Blake rolled into a firing position just in time to be blinded by a brilliant flash of light from a whooshing rocket that passed within a foot of his head, showering him with sparks. Shocked both by the screeching sound and by the realization he had almost lost his head, he dropped his rifle and began digging frantically with his bare hands. Neither he nor any of his men had had time to dig fighting positions, so they lay exposed in the open field. The bright moon made them sitting ducks.

"Lee, Hanslow, come to me!" he yelled. "Vinny, get Gene and Willie next to you. Two men cover and one man dig!"

Shawn raised up to his knee behind the mound to see what was happening. The NVA had only probed them with fire, but they now knew exactly where the patrol-base perimeter was located. The mortars that fired after the ambush were a dead giveaway. Every enemy soldier within earshot had probably made a beeline toward the sound. He bet the first shots had come from their advance units. Shawn lowered himself and began crawling to find Lieutenant Owens. He knew it would not be much longer until the main force enemy units arrived and began their attack.

Major Anderson huddled behind an ant mound, trying to keep his body hidden. It had been thirty minutes since the NVA's first probe, so by now their snipers had climbed into the trees. Every time one of his men moved, he was immediately brought under fire. Crawling had been the only way to move with any chance of surviving. One of his men had been killed and two more wounded from the sniper fire. He reached for the radio handset again, and immediately a bullet glanced off the mound only inches from his face. That last shot had come from the north. His base was surrounded. He brought the handset to his mouth and began to push the sidebar when the air all around him seemed to crack and pop.

"They're attacking! Use grenades!" Shawn yelled as he pushed his safety off.

Blake rose up just enough to look over the lip of the shallow hole and toss out one of his two remaining grenades. Over the lip he had seen a line of at least six running men, only twenty meters away. He was about to rise up and shoot when he heard the throaty chatter of Vincent's machine gun. The grenade exploded in a flash of light, heat, and whizzing shrapnel. Rising up to shoot, he saw only one of the attacking soldiers remaining. He was about to fire, but Lee beat him to it and shot the attacker.

Blake saw more coming from his right and turned to shoot, but again others fired before he did. Suddenly the sky turned golden-yellow. A bright hissing flare, showering sparks, floated on a parachute overhead. Two more flares popped and cast their golden light. Blake raised up to see if there were any more attackers, and felt his heart shrivel into a tiny pulsating ball. The eerie light cast long dark shadows, both from the trees and the forty or so NVA that were approaching in a ragged line.

Mortar shells landed among the NVA, exploding in cracking flashes of light and white-hot shrapnel, yet they kept coming. Vincent's machine gun further scythed their ranks with red tracers, but a suppressing NVA machine gun swung its barrel toward Vincent's position and let loose its green tracers, which stitched the ground and air all about the Italian, forcing him down. Willie Billy Bradshaw's helmet was knocked off by a near miss, and the stunned soldier screamed like a wounded jungle cat.

Thunk! Gerry Hanslow lowered his M-79, quickly reloaded, and raised it again. He took aim, despite the slugs hitting the small tree beside him, and fired again. The spinning shell arched and came down in front of a North Vietnamese soldier who was yelling commands. The thin warhead, filled with tightly packed, notched wire, burst in a small explosion, and pieces of the red-hot steel ripped into his legs, thighs, and groin. He hit the ground grabbing for his penis, which was spouting blood into his khaki pants.

Lee, Eugene, Blake, and the rest of the platoon fired at the attacking men, whose faces were shadowed beneath their pith helmets. The crescendo grew louder as green and red tracers crisscrossed like jet-powered fireflies in a frenzy. RPG rockets as loud as freight trains flashed over the perimeter and left trails of spiraling white smoke. Drifting above it all, the swaying flares hissed and burned. Inside the perimeter, Chinese-made mortar shells began raining down, creating a storm of vehement explosions that threw up clouds of dust, black smoke, and jagged chunks of iron. Blood, tears, and urine soaked the ground beside moaning, writhing men, whose pleas could not be heard over the general din.

Major Jim Anderson clutched the handset and yelled into the black plastic for his units to report their status, but heard nothing in reply. His ears were ringing so badly he wasn't sure if they were responding or not. He gave up and called squadron operations to ask for reinforcements. Again he heard no reply. All he could do was pray they had heard his plea.

Shawn knew the NVA attack had failed. Their fire had slackened and was no longer hitting close. He rose up, ready to shoot, but saw no targets in the dancing light. He began to yell when he heard a familiar voice fill the night.

"Every other man reload magazines! Report casualties and ammo status!"

Blake lowered himself back to the ground and waited.

"We're all okay," Vincent barked, "but we're short'a 'sixty ammo an' got no more grenades."

Blake saw that Lee was not hit, and turned to Hanslow. The young soldier was shaking his head and mumbling, "No M-79 ammo left. What . . . what am I gonna do?"

The other squad leaders heard Blake's commands and yelled likewise to their men for situation reports. Information about the number of wounded and dead, as well as ammunition supplies, would tell the platoon leader who needed priority in plugging their part of the perimeter and who needed the medic first. It would also tell the platoon sergeant who to get extra ammo from and give to others who were out. Battles were won and lost by the lack of such information, for only with updated situation reports could leaders make the necessary decisions to reorganize for combat. The rules were simple: replace all the wounded and dead leaders, man the automatic weapons, and redistribute the ammo.

"Report!" Shawn yelled.

Blake lifted his head. "None hit, short 'sixty ammo, out of 'forty mike-mike and grenades!"

The second squad leader lay on his back and spoke loudly. "The lieutenant is with us, and he's hit. I've got one dead and one lightly wounded. We're short everything and out of grenades. The lieutenant is bleeding bad!"

Shawn listened to the rest of the squad reports totaling the dead and the status of the wounded in his head as he quickly crawled toward the second squad's position. He had one dead and four wounded by the time he leaned over Lieutenant Owens. The flares were still popping overhead, which made finding the officer's wounds easy. His platoon leader had been hit in the shoulder and hip by mortar shrapnel and was still bleeding, despite first-aid efforts by a second squad rifleman.

A rifle shot cracked in the distance, and a mortar round landed thirty feet away. The shock was over and the NVA were reorganizing as well. Shawn knew he didn't have much more time. He yelled toward the first squad, "Alexander, take over the platoon and get ammo redistributed. I'll take the lieutenant back and report our situation. If I'm not back in ten minutes, you're in command."

Blake was too busy to worry about the time as he crawled down the platoon's positions checking the wounded and handing out magazines. When he got back to his squad, he realized he had never been so happy to see anybody as he was his platoon sergeant lying behind an ant mound and talking to Lee.

Shawn was glad to see him too, but his expression was all business. "How bad are the wounded?"

A sniper's bullet popped over Blake's head, but he was too exhausted to care. "Two are superficial and can stay on the line. Ski got hit in the head and lost an eye. Paxton, from the fourth, is gut-shot. They both need a medevac pretty soon or it doesn't look good."

There was nothing Shawn could do for the wounded. He had left Owens at the C.P., where the major's radio operator placed him in a gully with five other badly wounded men. There was no more room in the ditch.

"What about the ammo?"

Blake rested his head on his rifle stock. "Every squad has at least two mags per man, and the 'sixty gunners have three to four hundred rounds apiece. No M-79 or grenades left."

Shawn flinched as a green tracer streaked by his shoulder. He raised his chin just a fraction and spoke with surprising softness. "Ya done good, Ace, thanks." He raised his head and spoke loud enough for the rest of the platoon to hear. "Colonel Stockton is sending in a relief force tonight. They're going to air assault right into the patrol base. They'll be here in less than an hour. Everybody hang tough and don't waste your ammo. We got the U.S. fuckin' cavalry on the way!"

Blake and his squad squatted in front of the small gully, which was full of wounded. The squad had been given the mission of carrying the wounded to the slicks that would land with the relief force.

Lee turned hearing the approaching helicopters. The first slick popped out of the darkness and began its descent into the flare-lit L.Z. NVA green tracers immediately streaked skyward from the distant treeline.

Vincent grabbed Blake's arm in a vicelike grip. "They ain't gonna make it!"

Despite the ground fire, the pilot continued the approach into the patrol base, blowing up blinding dust and shredded grass. Turning right, but maintaining its forward momentum, the bird dropped lower, which allowed the cavalrymen standing on its skids to jump the last six feet to the ground. When the last man left the skid, the bird dipped its nose, picked up speed, and banked left, seeking the protection of the darkness.

Blake watched in trembling terror the display of raw courage displayed by the pilot. The lead bird had been hit at least four times and yet never stopped its approach. He turned in time to see the second aircraft doing the same. A cavalryman about to jump from the skids suddenly jerked, as if hit by a jolt of electricity, and fell the six feet to the ground like a rag doll.

Lee clasped Blake's shoulder. "What about the wounded?" he yelled.

Blake took his eyes from the crumpled cavalryman lying on the ground and shook his head. "They can't land."

Lee motioned to the small trees in the middle of the patrol base. "We can cut down them trees and then they can!"

Blake glanced toward the mortar positions across the perimeter, where he knew the crews would have shovels and maybe axes. He stood up and yelled for his squad to follow him.

Minutes later the first tree was toppled and dragged out of the way. Each squad member had taken a turn at jumping up, taking two whacks with a dull axe, then hitting the ground. The snipers didn't seem interested in the first squad's tree-cutting operation, for no bullets cracked by their ears or thudded into the ground close by. The NVA sharpshooters were after bigger prey—one of the helicopters that were still coming in, one after another.

Soaked in sweat, the squad ran back to the wounded and dragged them on ponchos toward the newly cleared L.Z. The second to last Huey came to a hover over the cleared area and settled to the ground. Blake and Vincent lifted their lieutenant and ran toward the bird as the off-loading cavalrymen ran past in the opposite direction. The crew chief was waiting in the open door and grabbed the officer like a hunk of meat, then quickly pulled him two steps into the compartment and dropped him. Returning to the door, he grabbed the next bleeding soldier. Four more wounded were loaded in the same way before the bird lifted up and shot forward.

The last chopper began its approach. Five more wounded waited, but Blake didn't think he was capable of lifting his own arms, let alone a man. He had nothing left after the ambush, the march back, the digging in, the wood chopping, and all the running and lifting. His body was totally drained of energy. He looked at his exhausted men, who were trying to pick up the remaining wounded. They were obviously in the same condition. He was about to yell for help when the second squad ran up and gave a hand lifting the ponchos. With the last of his strength and the help of the second-squad leader and his machine gunner, Blake lifted a gut-shot screaming soldier. Awkwardly, they ran toward the chopper, ignoring the hail of biting, windblown dirt. When the weight was lifted from Blake's arms, he staggered away and sunk to his knees. Seconds later the slick lifted off, leaving four men lying on the ground.

Too exhausted to move, Lee, Eugene, and Vincent lay down beside Blake, who was facedown in the dirt, passed out.

Shawn raised up to a knee. His second squad was returning to the perimeter, supporting two men. "Are they wounded?" he called out to the approaching squad leader.

The sergeant dropped to the ground beside his platoon sergeant. "No, they're Alexander's men. They were so damn tired an' weak, they couldn't get back by themselves."

Shawn glanced worriedly over his shoulder. "Where is Alexander and the rest of his squad?"

The sergeant shook his head. "Three of the crazy bastards wouldn't leave Alexander. He's passed out cold. I told 'em we couldn't help all of them at once and that we'd go back for Alexander, but they wouldn't leave him. They're all fuckin' nuts if ya ask me."

Shawn slapped in a new magazine. "You're in charge till I get back." Pushing himself off the ground, he broke into a zigzag run toward the center of the patrol base.

Shawn fell to the ground and rolled next to the pile of dark bodies just as a flare popped overhead. He raised his head and was about to order his men to get up and follow him when he saw their faces in the golden dancing light. He knew in an instant they couldn't follow his orders if they had wanted. He crawled closer and took out his last canteen, which held only a few swallows of water. "Sorry, I ain't got more. Rest here and I'll send back a couple of men to get ya one at a time."

With a trembling hand, Vincent took the canteen and handed it to Lee. The Italian looked back to his platoon sergeant with menacing eyes. "We're all goin' together or we ain't goin'."

Lee poured the precious water into his hand, and as he rubbed it over Blake's forehead, he looked at Shawn with an almost threatening glare. "The team has gotta stay together."

Shaking with fatigue, Eugene lifted his head from the dirt and squinted through dust-covered glasses. "All . . . all or none. We're not leaving anyone behind."

Shawn understood. He lowered his head to the ground to rest a few moments to regain his own strength. A burst of green tracers whizzed over the perimeter, hitting the trees on the other side. Immediately the nervous cavalrymen from the relief company returned fire, spraying the treeline from where the enemy machine gun had fired.

"Christ!" Shawn mumbled to himself, and he rose up yelling angrily. *"Don't fire on automatic, damnit! Save your ammo!"* Shawn mumbled more obscenities as he shifted his gaze to the prone men. "So the team ain't leavin' each other? Good! At least some-fuckin'-body knows what they're doing! I'll send two squads back for you as soon as I get back." Shawn crouched low and began running toward his platoon's positions, feeling as drained as the team, thinking, I'm gettin' too old for this shit!

The sky turned gray in the east, bringing hope to the dust-covered men in the patrol base. Soon the sun would be up and so would the United States Air Force.

Blake crawled over to Vincent's position to make sure his men were all awake and ready if the enemy tried a dawn attack.

Vincent looked up from his machine gun with a faint smile. "You lookin' better, Ace. How you feelin'?"

Blake slid into the shallow foxhole and took off his helmet. "Better, since the resupply brought in water. Thanks for helpin' me last night. I guess I ran out of steam or somethin'." Blake raised his bare head. There was a new line of defensive positions dug in to his left. "If ever I see Colonel Stockton, I'm gonna give him a big kiss for bringing in the relief company last night. I think it's a first, a night air assault under fire and all. We'll have another war story to tell our kids."

Vincent glanced over his shoulder at Willie Billy to see if he was listening and looked back at Blake. "Don't tell that to super he-row. He's bad enough already."

Lying beside Vincent, Eugene raised up on an elbow and gave a tired smile. "We all made it again, didn't we?"

"Yeah, we did it again. We were lucky. Last night the relief company lost two men and had fifteen wounded." Blake noticed the black soldier's swollen face. "Looks like the ants or mosquitoes got more of ya than the NVA."

Eugene shrugged off his squad leader's look of concern. "Couple of mosquito bites isn't as bad as what happened to the lieutenant. I'm gonna miss him. He was one of us."

Vincent nodded in agreement. "He was a good one. But at least he's goin' home."

Blake didn't want to think about the loss of Owens. "I gotta go," he said. "You guys keep a lookout and be ready. I suspect we'll be getting outta here soon, so keep your heads down and no hero shit. Let the line dogs get the medals today."

Vincent smiled again. "Ace, your dad gonna have ta build another trophy case for all them medals you got comin'."

Blake patted Vincent's leg. "And Gina's gonna frame yours and hang 'em up on your hoagie stand. She's gonna call your hoagies 'Vinny's he-rows.' "

Eugene chuckled. "I can just see Gina's father reading the papers about us. Don't you know he's gettin' shit from Gina sayin' I told you so?"

Vincent grinned at the thought and suddenly clasped Eugene's shoulder.

"I been thinkin', an' I decided I'm comin' with you."

"Where?" Eugene asked.

"The Veterans Day parade with you and your dad. I wanna be there. We all oughta go, the team, together, lookin' good and struttin' like Willie Billy."

"I like it," Blake said as he began crawling out of the foxhole.

Vincent leaned over to Eugene once his squad leader was gone. "His face is gettin' worse."

Eugene turned and looked over his rifle toward the treeline. "He won't go see a doctor 'cause he knows they'll pull him out of the field."

Vincent pulled back the charging handle of his machine gun and spoke in a soft whisper. "He won't go 'cause'a us, huh?"

Eugene nodded in silence.

General Man walked up to the top of the ridge and knelt down by his waiting assistant division commander, Colonel Quan. The colonel handed his field glasses to the general and pointed to the north. "The American base is only two kilometers to the north, where you see the smoke from the Yankee bombs."

Man lifted the glasses and scanned the valley. "What were the 66th's casualties?"

Quan glanced down at the note he had received from the 66th Regiment's commander. "The battalion had forty-four men killed in the ambush and another twelve wounded. The battalion sent two companies to attack the American camp, and as of this report have another forty-two killed and over seventy wounded. The attack has ceased, as per your orders, and our soldiers are now infiltrating across the border, using other trails."

General Man lowered the glasses but kept his gaze on the distant valley. "Have the Americans reinforced their camp and begun patrolling?"

Quan shook his head. "Only during the night did helicopters bring in more soldiers, but no other reinforcements have been reported as of 1000 hours this morning. I believe the Americans only established the base temporarily for the purpose of their ambush. They do not know the division they seek is within five kilometers of their camp."

The general pondered the colonel's assessment. "Then what I suspected is true. The Americans are still searching." He smiled wryly and turned around, facing the tree-covered slopes of the Chu Pong Mountains. "We must confuse their search even more. According to the last reports we've had from the units we left behind during the withdrawal, the American battalions are still searching the Tae River valley, twenty kilometers to the east." The general shifted his distant gaze to his assistant commander. "Order the stay-behind units to engage the Americans at every opportunity. Tell them to fight, fall back to hiding positions, and then fight again and again. We must confuse the American leaders."

Without responding, Quan slipped the field glasses into their leather case. Man sensed his assistant was troubled. "Your silence tells me you do not agree."

Quan faced his general with an accusing stare. "You and I know the Americans will find us. They are searching in the east but they will eventually come west to the Chu Pong. We cannot remain here. We must move back into Cambodia and rebuild in safety."

The general's eyes became expressionless, like a man-eating shark's, and his voice became frigid. "You do not understand this war. Sentiment has made you blind to what must be done to achieve victory. *I will not withdraw!* No battle or war was won withdrawing! We must now attack!"

Quan's mouth dropped open. Attack? Attack who, where, and with what? Before Quan could ask those questions, General Man abruptly turned around and started down the slope.

The general glanced over his shoulder. "Assemble the staff," he commanded icily. "We have a new plan to prepare!"

Quan nodded mechanically, knowing all too well what the general intended. He looked back at the distant billowing smoke cloud rising up from the river valley where just under a hundred of his countrymen had died. He could not help but think about the families in small villages in the north who would soon be crying in grief at the loss of their sons and husbands.

Quan lowered his head. He and the general were responsible for those tears. So many tears, he thought. So many, and now there would be more.

27

7 NOVEMBER

Lee leaned over to Vincent, who was writing a letter. "We have done died and gone ta heaven. That's what I wrote my mama. I wish I had me a camera so I could take me some pictures."

Vincent chewed the end of his pencil as he looked at the writing pad. "I'm gonna have Gina send us one. How you spell the name'a this place again?"

Lee leaned back against the bunker wall, closing his eyes to rest. "It's the Catecka plantation. C-A-T-E-C-K-A. The biggest tea plantation in Vietnam."

Eugene and Blake lay with their shirts off on the top of the bunker, soaking up the sun to kill the fungus on their backs. Eugene scooted forward to look down at Lee. "Reb, is the mansion like the ones down in Georgia?"

Lee opened one eye and glanced to his left at the huge French-colonial plantation house. "I reckon so, except we don't grow no tea in Georgia."

Blake rose up on his elbows and savored the tranquil beauty of the surroundings. It was hard to believe they were in Vietnam, let alone a war zone. The mansion had manicured lawns and was landscaped better than the governor's mansion in Virginia. Surrounding the house were thousands of acres of four-foot-high tea bushes planted in straight rows under large trees to protect the delicate tea leaves from the blistering sun. Working the plantation were hundreds of Vietnamese who were annoyed with the intrusion by the air cavalry's first-brigade headquarters and support troops. For the past three days the blue platoon of Charlie troop had been given the mission of resting and pulling light guard duty around some helicopters parked in a nearby grassy field.

Blake felt the best he had in weeks. The rest and sun had done wonders for his morale. The brigade had set up a mess hall that had been serving real food. Well, not *really* real because it was dehydrated canned food, but close enough. Although the dehydrated eggs were pea green, they still kind of tasted like eggs, and that was better than C-rations or nothing at all. Lee had been right in his description, it was a heaven on earth.

Willie Billy swaggered up to the guard bunker and began taking off his shirt. Vincent gave Eugene a conspiratorial wink and looked back at Willie.

"What'd ya think you're doin'? You can't take your shirt off!" he said gruffly.

Willie Billy abruptly stopped unbuttoning his fatigue shirt and angrily pointed at the two men on top of the bunker. "Why? They're not wearing theirs!"

Vincent kept his rigid stare. "Yeah, that's 'cause they got orders 'cause of the fungus. You ain't got fungus or orders."

"Yeah," Eugene added, "us guys who have been here longer than you picked up this tropical shit that makes spots on our backs. It's called 'veteran spots' 'cause only *real* vets have it."

Willie Billy's eyes narrowed. They were screwing with him again. "Alexander, tell your funny buddies to lay off. I'm tired of their shit."

Blake casually turned his head. "Shut up, Bradshaw. If you don't have the spots, you're not taking off your shirt."

Seething, Willie spun around and bumped into Hanslow, who had just walked up carrying a cardboard box. Gerry Hanslow wasn't wearing a shirt. Willie spun around, glaring at Blake, wanting an explanation.

Blake ignored the glare as he spoke with dripping concern to Hanslow. "Gerry, are your veteran spots clearin' up any?"

Hanslow's expression showed he didn't understand the question, and he was doubly perplexed when Willie Billy called him an asshole and stormed off.

Laughing, Eugene reached down and slapped Vincent's hand. "Score one for the real vets, man."

Shawn listened to the required afternoon aviation briefing, all the while wishing his lieutenant was back. Owens had always attended the boring updates to keep up on events and rub shoulders with his fellow officers. Shawn felt conspicuous, being the only NCO in the stuffy room, and so he had sat in the back in the hope that no one would ask him any questions.

The young major who was giving the briefing stood on a shipping crate as he pointed to a wall map behind him. "The First Brigade is pulling out today and returning to An Khe. They have been in the field for the past eighteen days, but only in the last three days have they seen extensive action—here, in their search area around the Tae River valley. To date they have sustained fifty-nine killed and 196 wounded. The First Brigade is being replaced with the 'Gary Owen' Brigade. For those who just joined our aviation battalion, the Gary Owen Brigade is the Third Brigade, which comprises the First and Second battalions of the famous Seventh Cavalry, Custer's old regiment . . . 'Gary Owen' is the Irish beer-drinking song of the old Irish Lancers and was adopted by George Armstrong Custer as his regiment song . . ."

Shawn yawned. The young mustached aviators sitting in front of him probably needed the history lesson. Most didn't look old enough to have graduated from high school.

". . . and it's been said they sang the song as they rode into the valley of the little Bighorn. The reason I told you all that is the Third Brigade is a green unit that hasn't seen much action, but they have a lot of tradition and they're raring for a fight. They're very gung-ho and they'll be requesting a lot of off-the-wall support. Don't let them tell you how to do your business. All air support missions *must* be cleared through me."

Shawn closed his eyes and let his chin fall to his chest.

General Chu Huy Man pulled off the cloth covering the battle map. "Before you is the plan that will lead us back to victory," he announced proudly. "On the sixteenth of November we will again attack Plei Me."

The assembled regiment commanders looked at one another in disbelief. The 32nd Regiment commander was left with only sixty percent of his men still alive. The 33rd Regiment was at forty-nine percent strength and had lost all its battalion commanders and half of its company commanders—it was a regiment only on paper, not in fighting capability. The 66th was almost at full strength, but it had just finished a two-month march.

General Man tapped the map for his commanders' attention. "While the Americans search for us in the west, we will slip around them and destroy their base. We will not toy with the camp this time. We will wipe it out in one large, coordinated attack. I have already contacted our southern patriot forces, and they will begin harassing attacks immediately to disrupt the American supplies and fuel convoys. In a few days they will be striking the camps at Duc Co, Plei Bak, and Catecka to destroy the helicopters that stage there. This will cause confusion among the Americans, and they will not have the time or forces to cover every threat. It is then, my friends, that we will slip out of our staging area and do what they least expect— *attack!*"

Colonel Lee Van Quan stubbed out his half-smoked cigarette and watched the reaction of the regimental commanders. He knew by reading their expressions they thought the plan was suicide. But he knew none would say what they felt. They had been selected carefully by the party for just this type of situation. They would go back and tell their regimental staffs that unification of the fatherland was near and the attack on Plei Me would bring them one step closer. They would say the Americans were weak, confused, and would lose heart if the camp were wiped out—they would lie.

Quan looked away, unable to watch as the commanders nodded in acceptance. Too many young men would die believing the lies. Too many would die for them and a general who believed not in the fatherland, but in his own career.

12 NOVEMBER

Blake made the rounds of the guardposts and stopped by the small tent where his platoon sergeant was bunking.

Shawn looked up from a letter he was writing and motioned Blake inside. "Sit down, Ace, and make yourself comfortable." He glanced down at the half-written letter. "I was just telling my wife about this place. She's gonna have our baby any day now and—" Shawn stopped in mid-sentence. He felt uncomfortable talking about home. "You don't wanna hear this, sorry."

"No, I do, really," Blake said quickly, realizing he had imposed on his sergeant. "I wish sometimes I found someone like you did. It'd be nice to have someone to go home to."

Shawn glanced up. "You've got a family, don't you?"

"Sure, but . . . well, it's not the same. A wife isn't family, she's . . . she'd be special. Someone who you could share your feelings with . . . a very special friend."

Shawn raised an eyebrow. "Kind of like the guys in the team?"

Blake shrugged. "Yeah, kinda, but different from that too."

Shawn winked. "I know, and you're right. Cindy *is* special. But I guess my best friend in the world is the sergeant major you met a few days ago. We're kinda like you and the team are—real close. Combat does that to ya, I guess. You have to trust each other to make it. I can tell Taco anything." Shawn sighed and tapped his pencil on the writing tablet. "This becoming a daddy business is new to me. I've always wanted a kid, but hell, I don't know if I can even throw a baseball anymore."

Blake smiled at his sergeant. "You'll be great. I can just see you teaching your son to throw and how to choke up on a bat . . . hell, you'll probably raise the next Mickey Mantle."

Shawn grinned but then looked uncertain. "What if it's a girl? What am I gonna do then?"

"Teach her to fish and play baseball. Make her the best tomboy on the block," Blake said, laughing at his sergeant's look of distress.

Shawn laughed with his squad leader and set down his pencil. "I guess your ol' man was quite a dad, huh?"

Blake kept his smile and nodded. "Sure . . . he was great." Blake raised his wrist and glanced at his watch. "Guess I better wake up the next shift. See ya, Irish. Tell your wife from the team we wish her the best."

Blake got up to leave, but Shawn reached out and touched his arm. "What do the medics say about your face?"

Blake lied again. "It's just temporary. They said in a month or so it would be fine. Night, Irish."

"Night, Ace. I'll be up later and check the guards. Get some sleep."

Blake sighed as he strolled away from the tent and looked up at the stars. Why, Dad? Why couldn't you have just once smiled at me instead of always looking as if I was a disappointment? I just wanted a smile . . . just one.

Lee, waiting for his squad leader outside the bunker, only relaxed when he finally returned. "Hiya, Ace. I was waitin' on ya."

Blake took off his helmet and leaned against the sandbagged bunker. "What's up?"

Lee looked up at the stars for a moment, collecting his thoughts before shifting his eyes to his friend. "We, the rest of the team, wanted to tell ya we think ya oughta see a doctor. It's gettin' worse, Ace, and we think you oughta be checked."

Blake touched his cheek, pushing up the drooping skin. He knew he must look hideous. "I'll do it once we get back to An Khe. That's a promise."

Feeling better, Lee looked back at the stars. "I ain't got much of a way with words, but tonight is somethin', ain't it?"

Blake put his arm over Lee's shoulder, feeling closer to his friend than he had to any other man in his life. Lee was more than his friend, he was the brother he never had. There was nothing he wouldn't tell or share with him.

Blake looked up at the stars, sharing with his brother a brief respite from the war. "They don't make nights any better."

Shawn was awakened by a thunderous explosion that shook him like a rag doll and sent shrapnel through the tent's canvas just a few inches above his head. He grabbed the .45 pistol beside him, rolled over onto the ground and faced the tent opening. A flash of brilliant light followed by another ear-shattering explosion told him all he needed to know. They were under mortar attack. He brought his leg under him to make a sprint to the nearby defense line when he heard AK-47 fire from the west. Shit! A coordinated ground attack!

Blake yelled for his men to hurry, and before leaving the bunker, picked up four more bandoliers of M-16 magazines. He sprinted to catch up to his squad. They were running through the dust and smoke toward a shallow trench that served as the first line of defense in protecting the helicopters. With each mortar impact, the ground shook and the men were showered with smoking dirt clods.

Out of breath, Blake dived into the ditch just as Vincent opened up with his machine gun. Hot, expended shell casings from the M-60 clinked on Blake's helmet, causing him to roll out of the way before one burned his neck. He stopped beside Lee, who was looking down the sight of his M-16.

Lee fired and quickly aimed again. Blake looked over the lip. Five dark shapes ran toward them from only ten meters away. He jerked his rifle up and fired.

Beside Lee, Gerry Hanslow hummed aloud to get himself into the rhythm of firing his M-79. He raised up to fire, but was knocked backward by an AK-47 bullet through the neck. Feeling and smelling his own blood, he grabbed at his throat. It was spewing blood in a stream each time his heart beat. Weakening, he tried to call for help, but his larynx was shattered, as was his right carotid artery. He knew he was dying, but he kicked and jerked to steal every last breath from life.

Lee turned in time to see Hanslow's blood-covered hands fall limp to his chest and the last stream of blood pump from his neck wound. Lee flung himself toward his only subordinate and clapped his hand over the gaping wound. He could actually feel the heart's last attempt to push blood to the brain. Lee screamed at the night and gently lowered the young soldier into the bottom of the blood-covered trench floor.

Blake changed magazines and turned to see Lee sitting beside the body, rocking back and forth.

Blake quickly looked around for more enemy, then back to Lee. "Lee? Get up, Lee. There's nothing you can do for him. Lee?"

The Georgian raised his head, tears running down his cheeks. "Gawd, he was only nineteen! He was . . . was my first student. I was responsible for him!"

Blake kept his eyes on the tea bushes to his front, seeing muzzle flashes that exposed for a split second the shooters dressed in black. "Come on, brother, I need you now. Get up here with me . . . come on."

Lee picked up his rifle and gave Hanslow one last look before crawling up beside Blake. "It ain't fair," he said softly.

Blake sighted in on a muzzle flash and squeezed the trigger.

Shawn left the third squad's positions and saw to his front the gunship pilots running toward their warbirds. How stupid they were, exposing themselves like that. But he understood that they probably felt more at risk on the ground than in the air. A door gunner had already reached one of the gunships and was firing his door machine gun with a vengeance. Miraculously, all the pilots made it to their aircraft, and in seconds the birds stirred to life. Ever so slowly their large blades began rotating with the whine of turbines as green tracers crisscrossed the field.

Shawn heard the distinctive pings of bullets hitting the still-motionless aircraft. *"Get up! Get up!"* he yelled out of frustration. *"Come on, crank them fuckin' blades."*

The rotor blades began spinning faster and faster until they were blurs lost in the blown-up dust clouds. The first ship lifted off with its door gunner lying on the floor clutching his chest. In a matter of seconds the other warbirds were airborne and seeking the flashes of the mortar tubes.

Shawn shook his head in admiration of the pilots' courage and continued his run toward the first squad's positions.

Willie Billy added another belt of linked ammo to Vincent's almost expended belt and tapped his shoulder, signaling him he was good for another two hundred rounds. Eugene tossed a grenade over a row of tea bushes and quickly raised his rifle. The cracking explosion caused one Vietnamese soldier to jump up, flailing at his back where hot shrapnel had lodged. Eugene ended the soldier's agony with a single shot.

Directly overhead, a gunship roared past. Its rockets streaked like Roman candles into the tea rows. The ensuing series of explosions stopped incoming fire from in front of the first squad's position.

Shawn crawled into the trench and saw Hanslow's body in the diffuse light of a distant explosion. He reached down to feel for a pulse on the soldier's neck, but instead his fingers found the sides of the sticky open wound. Wiping his hand on his fatigue pants, he lay on the trench lip beside Blake. "What's your situation?"

Blake motioned with his rifle toward his front and the dead lying there. "We had a platoon-size attack trying to make it to the choppers. Hanslow got—"

"I know. How's your ammo?"

Blake quickly changed magazines. "We're good. The hogs will make quick work of the rest of 'em. I think they're V.C., not regulars, and they won't have the stomach for it." Blake felt confident in his estimate, knowing that four fully loaded gunships were awesome killers.

Shawn turned to Lee, who was inserting another magazine. "Sorry 'bout Hanslow. You all right?"

Lee nodded in silence.

Shawn patted the Georgian's back. "Put it behind you, Reb, and carry on. It's gonna be a long war, son." Shawn jumped out of the trench and ran to the next position to check the rest of his men.

The sun rose over the tranquil plantation. The first squad was dragging bodies from among the rows of tea. Blake dragged his V.C. to a line of corpses. He didn't want to wipe his hand on his fatigues, so he squatted and rubbed it on the grass to get rid of the stink and filth of death. The detail of cleaning up the battlefield had been a gruesome task. The black pajamaed V.C. had taken most of their dead and wounded with them during their early morning retreat, but enough had been left behind to sicken his stomach. The ones struck by gunship rocket fragments had been the worst. It looked as if they'd been hit by a cannon full of steel bolts. Their torn bodies reeked of campfires and fish mixed with blood and excrement.

Willie Billy fell to his knees to vomit a second time, but with nothing in his stomach, he mostly dry-heaved and drooled.

Eugene sat down beside Blake and tiredly motioned toward the Vietnamese plantation workers who were headed out to work the fields. "Would you look at that shit. You can't tell me those V.C. weren't moving into position yesterday. Those bastards had to have seen them."

Vincent sat down beside Eugene, looking over his shoulder at the workers. "I ain't trustin' them fuckers."

Lee walked past the squad toward the row of seven poncho-covered bodies that lay beside the grassy field. The dead American soldiers had to wait for extraction, because more than twenty wounded had priority on the slicks that would ferry them to An Khe. Lee walked along the row of covered bodies. Only their legs and scuffed boots were visible. He knelt by the fifth body. Its pant legs were black with dried blood. Taking off his helmet, he lowered his head and prayed that Gerry Hanslow's family would understand.

Blake, who was watching, took out his pocket notebook and wrote "KIA, 12 Nov." beside Hanslow's name. Gerry was the first member of the squad to die. Later he would write the family and tell them he was sorry and that their son would be missed but always remembered. For now he had to do what his sergeant had told him—carry on.

As the flight of slicks came in, Shawn turned his back to avoid the rotor wash. He had been told to meet the arriving company from First Battalion of the Seventh Cavalry Regiment and show them around the small base. After last night's attack, it had been decided that a rifle company would remain on all the forward bases to protect the support troops.

When the wind died down, Shawn found himself looking into the smiling face of John Quail, who immediately punched his shoulder and strode past. "Don't be telling me to leave, Irish. I'm here on business, so don't give me any of your old lady lectures."

Shawn was about to follow his friend when a young captain approached him. "Are you our contact?"

Minutes later Shawn led the captain and his platoon leaders around the perimeter, showing them the defensive positions. Shawn expected the tour to be short and sweet. Instead he was slowed to a snail's pace by questions from obviously green, untested officers who wanted to drain him of all his experience.

Finally running out of patience, Shawn introduced the officers to Blake. "Gentlemen, I have to attend to my platoon. This is my first squad leader, Sergeant Alexander. He's seen more action in the past month than I did all the time I was in Korea. He has at least thirty personal kills and already has one Silver Star, one pending, and two Bronze Stars for valor. He's my most experienced combat squad leader, and he can answer any questions you might have. It was nice meeting you, gentlemen."

Blake leaned over Shawn's shoulder and whispered harshly, "You're an asshole, Irish."

Shawn nodded with a faint dip of his chin and strode for the platoon command post.

Blake turned to the impressed and curious stares of the officers of Bravo Company, First Battalion of the Seventh Cavalry. "Sirs, before you ask, my face is sagging 'cause of an old facial-muscle injury. It's only temporary. Last night we defended from over here and . . ."

Quail absently looked around the small tent and poked his finger through one of the many shrapnel holes. "Ain't this paradise got any beer?"

Shawn sat down and tossed his helmet to his bunk. "No. Now, what the fuck are you doing here?"

Quail gave his friend an indulgent smile. "I guess that answers one question for me. You ain't heard from Cindy, or you'd be telling me about your new kid."

Shawn relented with a slight smile of his own and leaned back. "Good to see ya, Taco. What does bring ya out? Ya really on business?"

Quail glanced around again. "Yeah, tomorrow the First Battalion is going to airmobile into an area just a klick from the border, and I'm going in with them to see a cav operation firsthand. Colonel Hal Morris, the battalion commander, is a friend from the Korea days. He invited me along for the ride."

Shawn's jaw tightened. "I was out there close to the border on the ambush, remember? Don't be tellin' me it's just a 'ride.' You know damn well they're going into some shit."

Quail shrugged. "It's the job. Now tell me what happened last night. Did you lose any of your kids?"

Shawn lowered his head. There was no sense arguing with his friend. Quail had his job to do, and no one could report back to the Pentagon with an infantryman's perspective any better.

"They hit us with mortars first, just before midnight, and . . ."

Colonel Quan glanced at the setting sun and immediately stood. "I'm sorry, my friend. I must return now before it grows too dark. I wish you a safe journey tomorrow and a successful attack on the sixteenth."

Lieutenant Colonel Bin Ty Duc, commander of the Eighth Battalion of the 66th Regiment, rose to his full six feet and extended his hand. "And I wish you success in helping our commander to gain greater wisdom."

Feelings of friendship and concern passed unspoken between the two men as they shook hands. Quan motioned for his six-man bodyguard force to proceed, and he followed directly behind them down a ridge trail through the forest. Bin Duc and he had served together against the French, and had remained close friends ever since. Duc was one of the few who had not been selected for command by the party, for he was a Catholic. Fortunately, the party did not make the decision on all command positions, and the military leadership had not been blind to his friend's abilities and experience. Duc had been selected by General Giap himself to be the next regimental commander of the 66th.

As Quan walked along he couldn't help but think that he might have been wrong about General Man's decision to attack the base at Plei Me. For the past week no helicopters had flown over the Chu Pong, and the reports from the reconnaissance units to the east all indicated that the American search had become focused on the south. Perhaps, after all, the American leadership really *had* been confused and wasn't capable of mounting a search of the Chu Pong Massif.

Quan felt better, at least, that his friend would leave tomorrow, in command of the advance attack regiment. He relaxed and took in the beauty around him. The Chu Pong Mountains were tranquil and quiet, the perfect sanctuary for resting and rebuilding the division. The ravages of war had not yet touched the forest or scarred the land. He walked along hoping the forest could remain so beautifully virgin. In just two days the division would be gone and the threat to the peaceful Chu Pong would be over.

28

Shawn handed his friend a bandolier full of loaded magazines. "Take this with ya in case your 'ride' gets a little hot."

Quail tossed the bandolier over his shoulder and headed for the waiting helicopter. "Don't start your complainin' again, Irish. You take care, and I'll see ya in a couple of days."

Shawn patted the veteran's back. "See ya . . . and keep your butt down. You ain't no spring chicken, ya know."

Quail stepped on the skid and then up into the passenger compartment. He sat down, winked, and raised his thumb. Shawn returned the gestures. Seconds later the bird lifted off and made a lazy turn toward the west.

Blake, who had been waiting a few meters behind his sergeant, approached when the slick was out of sight. "Irish, what's going on? I just heard the company that came in yesterday is leaving today on some kind of mission. Does that mean we're tasked to pull palace guard again?"

Shawn sighed. "Sorry, Ace, I forgot to brief you. The First of the Seventh Cav is air assaulting into the mountain area just south of the Ia Drang River. The division is sending another company in this afternoon to pull the guard detail."

Blake could see by the sergeant's expression he was worried. "Is Sergeant Major Quail going with them?"

Shawn forced a weak smile. "Ya can't keep that ol' bastard from a good fight. It's in his blood."

Blake fell into step alongside his platoon leader. "You think there'll be a fight?"

Shawn's jaw muscle twitched. "You can bet on it."

Sitting quietly at a bamboo table in the operations room, Colonel Quan reached for his tea. Suddenly the porcelain cup began shaking on its saucer, spilling much of its contents. Quan's stomach instantly tightened and he took in a sharp breath. He stood and confirmed his fears. The ground was quaking beneath his feet.

He ran down the dark tunnel to the entrance and sprinted up the bunker steps into the open. He was met by the sounds of thunderous explosions coming from below the ridge to the east. A captain from the security

365

company scrambled up the slope toward the bunker. Quan stepped in front
of the frightened officer, blocking his path.

"What is happening?"

The wide-eyed captain pointed frantically to the valley. "Artillery shells
are hitting the field below the ridge! And helicopters are circling to the east!
The Americans are going to land and attack!"

Realizing that he was feeling the same panic as the young officer, Quan
fought his queasiness back and forced himself to nod calmly, as if receiving
a routine report. Fear was contagious. He had to be strong for the captain
and the others in the tunnel. The Americans had come in his dreams and
he had outsmarted them. Today would be no different.

Quan placed his hand on the captain's trembling shoulder and spoke
with confidence. "You must relax, my friend. If the Americans land, *they*
will be the ones under attack. Come, let us go below and give your report
to the general."

With the ground vibrating beneath him, Brigadier General Man listened
with a blank expression and perfect steadiness as the captain made his
report. When the young officer finished, he waited, expecting questions, but
the stone-faced general only stared blankly past him.

Quan stepped from behind the general and motioned with his eyes for
the captain to leave, then sat down and fixed his attention on the wall map.
"If the Americans land below the mountain, we must attack to buy time.
I suggest you direct the 33rd Regiment and the remaining battalion of the
66th to prepare to attack."

The general's eyes narrowed and slowly moved to the colonel. "They
dare attack me?"

Realizing that his general was shaken, and so not really listening, Quan
motioned for the signal officer, who was standing by the door.

"The general desires you to radio the 33rd Regiment. Tell the commander to prepare his unit for immediate attack, but to wait for further
orders."

The officer dipped his head in a half bow and headed out for the radio
room.

Quan glanced back at the map. "The 33rd will delay the enemy long
enough while we withdraw back to Cambodia."

The general pounded his fist on the table. *"There will be no withdrawal!
Never! Never say that word to meeee!"* He sprayed Quan with spittle as he
shouted. "Have my entire division attack now! I want the Americans
destroyed as they land!"

Gathering all the patience he possessed, Quan took out a thin cardboard
box from his shirt pocket and removed a cigarette. He waited until the
general sat down again. "General," he said soothingly, "what is left of the
33rd Regiment is located only five hundred meters from the clearing. It and

a battalion from the 66th are the only units in position to attack. It will take at least two hours or longer for our other units to prepare and move into position. We must wait and see if the Americans land, and in what strength, before we commit additional forces. The Americans may place more of their infantry around us, and if they do, we must have units available to attack or delay them." Quan lit the cigarette and exhaled the smoke before looking into the black, bottomless eyes of his general. "Shall I issue the necessary orders?"

General Man kept his distant stare for a moment before blinking and looking back at the map. "Order the 32nd Regiment to begin digging defensive positions around us here on the Chu Pong. If the Americans want a battle, I will give it to them!"

Quan's face flushed. "General, limited attacks will only buy time so that the others can withdraw. We will lose the division if we defend the Chu Pong."

Man's glistening eyes shifted to Quan. "You still do not understand do you? We *cannot* lose. Victory . . . *victory* is ours!"

Lieutenant Colonel Hal Morris pointed at the plumes of smoke two thousand feet below the helicopter. "The artillery is right on target."

Sergeant Major John Quail nodded and was about to speak when his headphones buzzed and the co-pilot spoke rapidly over the internal frequency. "Colonel, we're going down to join the slicks. The artillery is lifting its barrage in one minute, and we're going in behind the gunships' second hot pass."

The colonel pressed his talk button. "Roger."

The bird dropped like a rock, leaving Quail's stomach back at two thousand feet. He wondered if the obviously excited young soldiers beside him were crazy enough to believe this was fun.

A minute later the slick was in the lead of fifteen other heavily laden birds streaking toward the landing zone.

The two gunships fired their rockets at the distant treeline and peeled away, leaving the large field at the base of Chu Pong Mountain in a cloudy haze of smoke and dust.

Quail scooted toward the open door, and like the others, fully expected a face full of lead. Instead he was hit with ninety-knot winds. The tail of the chopper dropped, shooting up the nose. Then the slick leveled off and began to hover. It slid slightly to the right to avoid an eight-foot ant mound. Quail's heart was beating so fast he thought he might pass out as the skids lightly touched down. Jumping to the ground, he landed in waist-high grass and tried to run to the distant ant mound, but the elephant grass slowed him down. It was like running through water. He flung himself to the ground after only taking four steps and disappeared into a world of hot yellow-brown stalks that smelled of musty clothes.

Colonel Morris waded through the grass, leading a gaggle of three radiomen, an artillery forward-observer officer, a Vietnamese interpreter, and his battalion sergeant major, who was yelling for Quail.

John Quail did not get up until he was sure he heard no incoming fire. When he finally stood, he took in a deep breath and promised the heavens that he would attend church every Sunday from now on and never ever accept another offer for a "ride" on a cavalry air assault. He heard his name called out again, and he headed toward a clump of trees in the middle of the landing zone, where the colonel was establishing his command post. Feeling vaguely uncomfortable, as if somebody were watching him, Quail glanced to his left.

"Jesus H. Christ," he mumbled aloud.

What he saw was a huge, thickly forested mountain that had not looked nearly so big from the air. He hurried as best he could and tried to shake the helpless feeling that he was a walking target.

A minute later he sat down beside a small tree a few feet away from the colonel's three radio operators. He wiped sweat from his nose, took out his notebook, and tried to concentrate. The noise around him was deafening, as the turbine engines and whopping rotor blades of the other landing choppers filled every cavity of his brain. He noted the time of insertion—two minutes past eleven A.M.—and that the artillery and gunship prep had been perfectly timed. He glanced up from the pad and looked around him. The only thing missing from the perfectly executed combat operation was the enemy.

Colonel Quan tried once again to reason with his general not to waste time and men. "General, if we remain, we will be pounded by their Air Force and artillery. Our men have suffered enough. A rear-guard action is all that is called for. We can save the division and fight another day when the time is right. You must reconsider."

Man, feeling better and more in control of himself, snorted through his nose. "You have a defeatist attitude, and that is why you will never be a division commander. We have the opportunity that we have sought. The party has ordered us, *ordered* us, to wipe out an American unit. We will *not* withdraw from this fight. We will attack and attack and attack and force them to bring in more of their battalions. I want them to assault the Chu Pong, where the 32nd will be waiting to destroy them!"

Quan lifted his head after the verbal assault. "Did your orders say what costs in men would be acceptable?"

Man leaned forward with a cruel smile. "The cost is immaterial. It is the price of unification of the fatherland."

And your political career in the party, Quan wanted to say, but he clenched his teeth. There was only one way remaining to try and diminish the losses. He would personally coordinate the attack to ensure at least that the regiment was synchronized in the execution of attack.

"I will issue the orders for the 33rd to attack immediately," he said, with as much distaste in his tone as he could put into it.

Sergeant Major John Quail, like all veterans, knew there were four enemies that infantrymen could possibly face simultaneously: flesh and blood ones who tried to kill you, terrain that could beat you if your opponent held better ground, weather that could freeze your ass or fry your brains, and finally, your own fuckin' politicians. Up to now, the First Battalion of the Seventh Cavalry had to fight only the terrain, which was a bitch. The ground around the L.Z. was basically flat but covered in elephant grass, which made seeing nearby defensive positions impossible. There was no way a leader could control his men to the left or right, although they were only five feet away. The landing zone itself was oval-shaped, with a little grove of trees in the middle that split the L.Z. into two parts. Around the open grassed area were scrub trees, spaced a good distance apart. On the west side of the landing zone, however, Chu Pong Mountain loomed like a monster. Coming off the mountain was a ridge that snaked down toward the northern end of the L.Z. On both sides of the ridge were thickly vegetated stream beds that looked like bulging veins running alongside a well-developed muscle. Quail cussed that mountain.

In Korea he had learned one lesson well: whoever controlled the high ground called the shots. He knew that trying to attack up such a monster would take at least three more battalions plus supporting artillery, and that was only if no more than a small force of enemy were defending it.

Quail took out his notepad and made an assessment in simple infantryman terms, "Terrain is a motherfucker."

Colonel Hal Morris lowered the radio handset. He had kept it glued to his ear, monitoring his Bravo Company, which had flown in on the first lift. He announced to the command group that Bravo Company had captured a prisoner close to the northern ridge.

Minutes later a half-starved North Vietnamese soldier was looking in fear up at the towering colonel as an interpreter asked questions.

Quail moved closer to hear. He was not surprised to see the small soldier point to the mountain and tell the interpreter that there were three NVA battalions hidden on and around the Chu Pong.

Colonel Morris took up the handset and pushed the sidebar. "Bravo Six, this is Yellow Hair Six, I want you to move up the ridge and see what else you can flush out."

Quail felt goose bumps run up his spine as he glanced toward the mountain. He again had that strange feeling he was being watched.

Colonel Morris handed the radio handset back to his RTO and walked out from under the shade of the trees to watch the second flight of Hueys arrive at the landing zone. The birds had dropped him and the hundred men of Bravo Company off earlier, and then had returned to base to pick up Alpha Company.

The first chopper landed in a swirl of dust and dried leaves. The colonel's Alpha Company commander hopped off the lead slick and waved him over to the C.P. Moments later the two men were kneeling in the grass looking at the colonel's map, laid out on the ground.

Colonel Morris motioned to the northern ridge. "I sent Bravo up there to check it out. I want your company to secure the L.Z. until Charlie Company comes in. Once they get here, you take the—"

An exchange of rifle and machine-gun fire from the direction of the ridge stopped the colonel in mid-sentence.

John Quail checked his rifle and stood facing the mountain. The sounds told him the firefight was taking place only a few hundred meters away. Telling himself that he ought to know better, he stepped out of the shade into the blistering sun for the short walk. He had come to see the battalion in action, and that was exactly what he was going to do.

Colonel Morris saw the old veteran walking toward the ridge and yelled, "What the hell you think you're doing?"

Quail did not slow his stride as he continued across the field and barked over his shoulder, "My job, sir."

Sweating profusely, Quail crossed a dry stream bed and headed toward the sounds of the firefight. A bullet clipped the branch of a tree only a foot over his head, and he abruptly halted. "What the fuck am I doing?" he asked himself aloud. To his front, just up the ridge, he saw a lieutenant and his radioman. Beyond them the lieutenant's platoon lay down in a hasty defensive line facing up the slope.

Quail walked up and knelt down by the young officer. "Sir, could you tell me what's going on up ahead?"

The second lieutenant handed the radio handset back to the radioman. "The first platoon went up this side of the ridge and the second went up the other. The radio report says the first platoon ran into an NVA platoon coming down and they fired each other up. The company commander ordered the second platoon to try and flank the enemy, but they only made it twenty meters before they got pinned down by fire from the front and flanks."

Quail was about to ask about casualties when the Bravo Company commander came down the ridge followed by two radio operators. The captain halted in front of the lieutenant. "Charlie, we don't have much time, so listen carefully and do exactly what I say. The dinks are pouring down the ridge, and they've cut off the second platoon. I want you to move up and link up with the first platoon. Once you're there, we're gonna try and reach the second platoon and then pull back. Go ahead now and move your men up, and I'll join you just as soon as I report our situation to the old man."

Quail saw movement to his right. He yelled a warning and raised his rifle. Hearing a strange voice, the two NVA soldiers who were running toward the clearing immediately stopped and turned around, breaking into a hasty getaway sprint. Quail only got off two quick shots, which were followed by a dozen more from startled platoon members who had been looking up the ridge rather than toward their flank.

The captain rose up off the ground where he had thrown himself and grabbed the lieutenant's arm. "Charlie, move your people out, now, before we get cut off too."

The captain said a quick thanks to Quail and motioned for the handset from his RTO. He gave a situation report to his battalion commander and looked back at Quail. "Sergeant Major, it looks like we're in some deep shit. You going with me back up the ridge?"

Quail knew he should say no and go back to the C.P., but the captain's expression told him he wanted him to go up the ridge, if for no other reason than to have an additional M-16. Quail tried to sound convincing. "Lead on, sir, I ain't got nothin' else better to do."

Sergeant Shawn Flynn was briefing the newly arrived company commander and platoon leaders from the Second Battalion when he heard Blake calling his name.

"Over here!" Shawn yelled.

Blake broke into a run. Shawn met him halfway. Blake motioned over his shoulder toward the aviation battalion's C.P. "Irish, the First of the Seventh is in a firefight on the L.Z. I was just in command post and heard the first reports."

Shawn immediately bolted for the distant bunker.

"What's going on?" asked the company commander who had run over after Shawn.

Blake felt a sinking sensation in the pit of his stomach. He knew Shawn was feeling the same thing, and he wished there was something he could do.

"Sir, First Battalion is in contact, and the sergeant has a friend with the unit. I'll finish the briefing and take you around to take a look at the guard positions."

The captain nodded in acceptance, then eyed his new guide with curiosity. "What happened to your face, Sergeant?"

Quail snap-fired from the hip and fell back behind a tree to reload another magazine. It was the second time in five minutes that he'd had to kill attacking NVA soldiers who had gotten through the small perimeter.

The attempt of the company commander to reach his surrounded second platoon had failed. The captain had ordered a halt fifteen minutes earlier, after two of his men had been killed and five had been wounded by heavy fire from the top of the ridge. He had ordered the formation of a wagon-wheel defensive perimeter and called for help from Colonel Morris.

A radio operator beside Quail yelled for his captain. "Sir, Alpha Company is coming up the ridge to our rear. They want us to cease fire in that direction so they can come in."

The captain crawled next to Quail and lifted his head, hollering to his platoon, "Cease fire to the rear. We've got friendlies comin' in!"

Minutes later the lead platoon of Alpha Company walked into the perimeter. They were greeted as if they were long-lost brothers.

Quail had never in his life been so glad to see baby-faced kids carrying M-16s. He was about to stand and shake hands with the platoon leader when someone screamed, *"They're attacking!"*

Quail spun around just as a burst of AK bullets stitched the ground to his right. A platoon of NVA were running down the slope across the front of the company, like ducks in a carnival shoot. The men on the perimeter unleashed a vengeful spray of lead, beginning the slaughter. It was obvious to Quail that the hapless NVA leader had led his men in an attack without first pinpointing his enemy. Now the leader and his men would die stupidly.

The radio operator looked up after listening to a report on the radio and yelled to the captain, "Sir, the second platoon just reported he has five killed and five wounded, but they're still holding on."

The other radio operator monitoring the battalion frequency lowered his handset. "Sir, Alpha Company's two other platoons are in heavy contact behind us. Their third platoon leader and a squad leader have been killed."

The captain took both reports in silence and looked at Quail. "The dinks must be bypassing us, trying to get to the L.Z."

Quail nodded. "Yes sir, and they're running directly into Alpha Company. Sir, we need to get artillery support and break out of here so we can link up with Alpha."

"And what about my surrounded platoon?" the captain asked tersely.

Quail's eyes shifted to the dead and wounded, lying only a few feet to his left, then back to the captain. "Sir, you have to save the rest of your company. Out here you're either gonna get overrun or picked off one by one. Alpha can't call in arty without hitting us. We have to consolidate and blow the shit out of 'em with arty and air." Quail fixed the captain with a penetrating look. "Sir, your second platoon is gonna have to hang tough until we consolidate and stop the NVA's attack."

Colonel Hal Morris listened to the situation reports radioed in from his units and made grease-pencil circles on his map to indicate their locations.

Alpha and Bravo companies were involved in the firefight north of the L.Z., at the base of the ridge. Charlie Company, which had arrived ten minutes before on the third lift, was now securing the southern and western portions of the L.Z. One look at the map told him he could do nothing to help the surrounded second platoon of Bravo Company until his last unit, Delta Company, came in. Once they arrived, he would immediately have them link up with his companies in contact and push up the ridge to relieve the surrounded platoon.

Morris looked up from his map. The situation was not as bad as it could be. The only threat was to the north, and so far that had been contained.

Then firing broke out to the south.

The voice of Captain Ethan, the Charlie Company commander, whose job was to secure the southern portion of the L.Z., came over the handset. "NVA are attacking in waves! I need air support!"

Morris motioned for the handset from the radio operator. The situation had just turned critical.

John Quail saw the smoking A1-E Sky Raider streak overhead, then quickly lost sight of the wounded bird because of the trees. Seconds later he heard the explosion. He could also still hear the echoes of NVA 12.5 antiaircraft machine guns. Quail knew as soon as he had heard the heavy, enemy guns firing from the mountain that the battalion was facing more than just a few NVA companies attacking at random. The big antiaircraft guns were assigned to regiments that usually comprised three battalions. The captured NVA soldier had not lied. The First of the Seventh Cavalry was not only facing an enemy on higher ground, it was outnumbered!

A cracking explosion a few hundred meters away caused the veteran to look up the ridge. The artillery was finally getting close enough to ease the pressure. No matter how brave the NVA infantry were or how many of them there were, they could not penetrate a wall of killing, red-hot, American-made shrapnel.

The company commander, sitting beside Quail, turned to his artillery forward observer. "Have them drop the rounds fifty meters closer and fire for effect." He raised up and yelled to his men, "Get ready to pull back when the arty hits!"

Quail leaned over to a wounded soldier, who was in agonizing pain from a gaping leg wound. "We gonna get you home, son. Just a few more minutes and we'll have you on the L.Z. for a medevac."

The soldier spoke through clenched teeth. "It—It hurts so fuckin' bad."

Quail heard screams in the sky, the sound of incoming artillery rounds. He quickly dropped to the ground and covered the soldier's body with his own to protect him in case the rounds were short.

———

Above the noise of gunfire to his south, Colonel Morris heard the beating *whop-whop* of rotor blades. Slicks were bringing in the last platoon of Charlie Company and two platoons of Delta. As the lead bird began its flare into the northern portion of the L.Z., he immediately began to feel better. Having his Delta Company on the ground would give him the strength he needed to secure the L.Z. and get his surrounded platoon extracted.

On board the lead slick sat the Delta Company commander, Captain Louis Leonard. He was about to jump to the ground when he saw, to his horror, two NVA pop up from the grass shooting their AKs. The door gunner returned fire, stitching both enemy soldiers, knocking them backward into the grass. Captain Leonard jumped to the ground and glanced over his shoulder. His young radioman lay on the Huey's floor with blood oozing out of a bullet hole in his right temple. Leonard pulled the radio from the dead soldier's back and began running for the closest cover.

With bullets cracking over his head and striking the ground around him, he flung himself toward the protection of heavy bushes just ahead. Breaking through the vegetation, he found himself sliding on his stomach down a rocky embankment into a dry stream bed. He was about to get up when he was showered with gravel as the remaining men on his bird jumped over the bank, joining him. At least the rest of his men weren't hit, but Leonard's feeling of relief lasted only a split second, for he quickly realized he could hear firing on three sides of him. Then he felt relief again. Coming down the stream bed toward him was the familiar face of his friend, Captain Jerry Arhens, the Alpha Company commander, and his two radiomen.

Captain Arhens knelt down in front of Leonard and shook his head. "Lou, I wish I could tell you what the hell is happening, but I don't honestly know myself. We tried pushing up the ridge to get to a surrounded platoon of Bravo Company but never made it. Dinks are every-fuckin'-where. They must be trying to—"

Arhens's radiomen were frantically pointing up the stream bed. He rose up to see over Leonard and immediately jerked his rifle up, firing. Leonard and the rest of the small group of men spun around and joined the captain. They killed five startled NVA soldiers, who were trying to make their way to the L.Z.

Seconds later the shooting and killing were over. Leonard changed magazines with shaking hands and looked at Arhens. "This is fucking crazy!"

Arhens began to nod when a burst of AK bullets struck the gravel in front of him. The radioman beside him grunted and fell forward with a bullet through his heart.

Captain Leonard rolled right, and suddenly his left arm jerked up and seemed to explode. Screaming in pain, he continued his roll until he reached the protection of the stream bank. A soldier behind Leonard rose up to lay down covering fire for his captain, but was knocked backward as a bullet tore through his thigh.

Arhens let loose a long burst from his M-16 toward the high ground where the shooting had come from. Two NVA rushed down the hill, ignoring the danger, and fired back as they ran. Arhens dropped one with a slug in the head. The second crumpled, hit by one of the remaining radiomen.

Arhens glanced at his fellow company commander, whom he had known since the battalion was formed at Fort Benning. They had gone on a picnic at Weems pond with their wives just before they left for Vietnam. He thought of Millie, Lou's wife, and how lucky she was. Her husband, Lou, would be home soon with a debilitating wound, but at least he would be alive to enjoy other picnics.

Arhens pushed the bolt release and looked back up the slope. He hoped his wife Janice would be so lucky.

Colonel Hal Morris ducked as whizzing shrapnel tore through the trees overhead. He rolled to a nearby tree trunk and rose up again just in time to see a second slick get hit so badly it couldn't take off. "Sonofabitch!" he yelled, but his words were lost in the deafening cacophony of exploding NVA mortar rounds, helicopters trying to land, and cracking booms of artillery making impact.

He spun around looking for his radiomen. Instead he saw his medics caring for rows of wounded. The battle was no longer a matter of tactics or strategy. The fight had been reduced to basic survival, where the strongest would live.

The radioman crawled to his colonel and lifted up the lifeline to the outside world. Morris took the handset and glanced back at the wounded. He had no choice now. They and the rest of his battalion would die unless the challenge was won. He pushed the sidebar and called his brigade commander. He had to have additional forces.

John Quail struggled under the weight of the wounded soldier he was helping to carry, but the sight of the colonel's C.P. in the distance was all the incentive he needed to put his fatigue aside and keep going. Alpha and Bravo companies had finally linked up fifteen minutes before and had pulled back off the ridge toward the L.Z., taking their wounded and dead with them.

When they reached the grove in the L.Z., Quail and a radioman lowered a pale, wounded soldier to the ground, among many more such men. Dizzy with fatigue, Quail sunk to his knees. He had known the situation was bad, but not this bad. There were rows and rows of wounded and stacks of dead. It was much worse than he had thought.

As soon as he struggled back to his feet, he was almost knocked over by a huge explosion to the south. He caught his balance and saw a Sky Raider pulling up. It had dropped its five-hundred-pound bomb just outside the perimeter. Another warbird swooped in, and he braced himself and yelled into the deafening battle noises, "Get the motherfuckers!"

Shawn Flynn stood with his back to his platoon. He was watching the company from the Second Battalion, Seventh Cavalry, load up waiting helicopters. Seconds after they finished, the slicks lifted off, blowing up a cloud of dust that left the Blues covered in settling dirt.

"That's it," Shawn said to his men. "We've got the guard duty now. Squad leaders, take charge of your men and post the sentry schedules. Do it."

Blake gave Lee charge of the squad and hurried to catch up to his sergeant, who was hurrying to the aviation C.P.

"Any word?" he asked, falling in beside Shawn.

Shawn maintained his long stride. "The First Battalion commander estimates he's in contact with at least two NVA battalions but can hold on if he gets reinforcements."

Blake had already heard the situation reports. He touched Shawn's arm to slow him down. "Come on, Irish, you know what I mean. You heard anything about Sergeant Major Quail?"

Shawn stopped and glanced over his shoulder at a lone slick making its landing approach. "The battalion has sent out five slickloads of wounded and dead. It's too early to try and get the names, 'cause they're taking them all to An Khe."

Blake could feel his sergeant's pain, and did something he'd never done before—he patted the sergeant's shoulder. "He'll be all right, Irish."

The gesture of support was not lost on Shawn, who turned and looked at the squad leader. Blake seemed much older than his years. "Thanks, Ace. You're right, he's too damn mean and contrary to get himself hit. Come on, let's check the recent reports, then the squads."

Shawn clapped his hand on Blake's shoulder as they walked toward the C.P. bunker. "Don't tell your squad, but we're tagged to go in next if the situation turns any worse. I want you to make sure your squad takes extra ammo, and I want you to find some entrenching tools for yourself and your men."

"Entrenching tools?" Blake asked with a sidelong glance.

"They're gettin' hit by mortars and wave attacks."

Blake's jaw muscle rippled. "I'll make sure we have them."

Sergeant Major John Quail offered his canteen to a captain who, despite a shoulder wound, was helping to load the wounded on board the incoming slicks.

Captain Bob Metzer took only a swallow and handed the canteen back. "Thanks, Sergeant Major. It ain't as good as a Dr Pepper, but it's pretty damn close."

Quail glanced toward the remaining wounded lying on ponchos. "Looks like you've got most of them out, sir. You're gettin' on this next bird too, aren't you?"

Metzer glanced at his shoulder wound. "It doesn't hurt that bad. I think I'd better stick around and help out."

Quail heard an incoming slick and patted the tired captain's back. "Sir, I'll take over here. You get on and get yourself fixed up. You've done all you can do."

Metzer lifted his head and looked around the perimeter with sad eyes. "Is this place worth it?"

Quail's answer was drowned out by the beating rotor blades of the landing Huey. The captain helped a wounded soldier to his feet and supported him as they walked rapidly toward the bird.

Quail grabbed the corner of a poncho and lifted along with three other men. Walking quickly toward the shaking chopper, Quail saw the crew chief lean out of the passenger compartment to help Metzer and his wounded soldier. Suddenly, the crew chief's expression became a grimace, and he staggered back inside the chopper with a deep crimson spot blossoming on the front of his fatigue shirt.

Quail had not heard the incoming fire over the shrill whine of the turbine engine, but he had seen just enough to convince him and throw himself to the ground. Rolling into a slight depression, he looked up just as Captain Metzer fell back, clutching his chest, and toppled over the Huey's skid.

Knowing his bird couldn't take any more hits, the pilot began lifting off to try and escape. Metzer's body, lying over the skid, tilted the bird. The door gunner reached down, grabbed the captain's collar and pulled the body into the passenger compartment beside the wounded crew chief.

Quail lowered his head to the dirt, closed his eyes, and cursed.

Colonel Hal Morris glanced up at the darkening sky and looked back at his assembled company commanders. "We don't have much daylight left, so I'll make it quick. It digs at my guts, leaving that surrounded platoon out there tonight, but there's not a damn thing we can do until tomorrow. The defensive perimeter around the L.Z. looks good. You've done a hell of a job, but I want you all to double-check to make sure your men know who is in position to their left and right and to make sure they're tied in for mutual fire support. I expect probes tonight, with an all-out attack in the morning. Make sure your men are awake and ready an hour before daybreak. The resupply birds that came in should have taken care of the ammo and water shortages, but let me know if you need anything else. The brigade commander called me thirty minutes ago. He's bringing in another battalion tomorrow and getting another ready if we need it. Tomorrow, we're going up that damn ridge and getting the second platoon. That's it. Keep up the good work and keep me updated during the night."

Quail sat behind the officers and watched as they rose and quickly made their way back to their units. Morris walked over to Quail and sat down. "It's in their hands now."

Quail leaned back against the tree trunk, looking up at the gray sky. "It never changes, sir. It's always been a grunt's war, and all we can do is help the poor bastards. You've done all you can do."

Morris lowered his head. "I wish I could do more for the kids on the ridge. The last radio report from them said they had eight killed and twelve wounded, and the remaining seven men were all short on ammo. The arty is the only thing saving them from being overrun."

Quail kept his distant gaze. "Like you said, sir, it's in their hands now."

A little after midnight the radio messages began coming into the signal room of the tunnel complex, where Colonel Quan waited for updates. The news was tragic. The 33rd Regimental commander had reported over 250 killed and another 300 wounded. The American artillery and bombs had devastated his already depleted ranks. He had told Quan that he had no leaders left to carry out the general's orders of attack. The 66th Regimental commander had reported that two battalions not yet committed had sustained ten percent casualties from artillery and bombings. Still, they would attack in the morning as planned. He also requested authority to recall his battalion, which had departed the previous day for the east.

Quan's thoughts turned to his friend, Colonel Bin Ty Duc, who was leading the Eighth Battalion. He had not wanted to approve his recall back to the Chu Pong, but he had had no choice. The general had ordered the annihilation of the Americans at all costs. The cost already included one of his regiments and would surely mean another. Colonel Duc and his men would have to return and join the butchering to satisfy the general's lust for American blood.

Sergeant Shawn Flynn walked out of the C.P. and strode directly toward the first squad bunker. Blake was just about to go inside to get some sleep when he saw a figure approaching in the darkness. He raised his rifle. "Who's there?"

"Flynn."

Blake lowered his M-16 and relaxed. "What's up, Irish?"

Shawn took off his helmet when he got close enough to see Blake. "I just got word that me and a squad are going in tomorrow."

Blake didn't need to ask where. "We'll be ready."

Shawn stood motionless. "What makes you think I'm taking your squad?"

Blake shifted his eyes to the sergeant. " 'Cause you'd want the best. The only question I have is how come you're going, if they just need a squad?"

Shawn put his helmet back on. "I trained you too damn well for your own good. I'm going 'cause they need qualified pathfinders to relieve the ones on X-Ray. Since we're Blues, they think we can handle the job. We can, but only if I'm there, 'cause I'm the only one who knows what a pathfinder does."

Blake's brow furrowed. "What do pathfinders do?"

"See? You need me. A pathfinder is a fancy word for ground air-control-ler. They have beaucoup lifts going in tomorrow, and they need someone to talk to the pilots and keep the air pattern organized. I can do that, and you and your squad will keep the L.Z. marked so there's no blade strikes. I taught you that stuff on board the *Boxer*, the dimensions of L.Z.s and how to use panel markers. The L.Z. has some downed birds on it, so the landing area has gotten real tight."

"What time we going in?" Blake asked flatly.

Shawn looked up at the stars. "I don't want you and the team going in, Ace . . . but like you said, I need the best." Shawn lowered his head. "I wish things were different. Be ready at 0700."

Blake knew his sergeant had struggled with the decision, but if he'd been in the sergeant's place, he would have done the same thing. When it comes to life and death situations, you don't put in the second or third team. He needed the first. Blake lifted his eyes to his leader. "You heard anything from your wife? You a daddy yet?"

Shawn didn't want to think about it. He shook his head. "Naw, nothin' yet. Get some sleep, and I'll see ya in the morning." Shawn walked back into the darkness, wishing Blake had not reminded him of home. His heart wasn't big enough to hold all the worries, pain, and guilt of not being there with Cindy when she needed him.

Sergeant Major John Quail spoke softly into the handset. "Steady, son. Just keep adjusting the artillery like you've been doin'. You're gonna make it."

The scared soldier lay behind two dead friends within the tiny perimeter. "We can hear them all around us!" he whispered back. "For God's sake, come and get us out of here!"

Quail's jaw tightened. He could envision the surrounded platoon's survi-vors huddled together, trying to stay awake, and trying to put out of their minds the fact that they had to use their friends' dead bodies for protection. The fear of hearing the NVA moving around them and not knowing when the next attack would come would be unnerving. Quail pushed the sidebar. "Son, listen to the bastards. Once you've got their direction, call arty on 'em. If you can't see them, that means they can't see you. Keep down and don't let anyone move around and make noise."

"Put the forward observer back on," the whisper came back. "I hear a group to the south of us."

Quail handed the handset to the artillery officer. "Sir, the platoon has got a fire mission for you."

Colonel Morris heard Quail's voice in the darkness and walked over. "I thought you'd be trying to get some rest."

Quail shrugged. "I wanted to do somethin' useful. Your radio operators looked beat so I took a shift to monitor the platoon."

"How they doing?" Morris asked.

"Scared, but hangin' tough."

Morris turned and stared at the distant ridge, where an occasional artillery-round explosion lit the sky. His voice broke as he spoke softly. "John, I'm . . . I'm gettin' those kids out tomorrow. You can promise them that for me."

29

15 NOVEMBER

John Quail shivered with nauseous anticipation as he watched the distant treeline. It was almost light. If they were going to attack, the time was perfect. He had been awakened by the sudden quiet only thirty minutes before, but it had seemed like hours. He felt as if all the nerve endings in his body were exposed antennae.

All night long the incessant artillery had crashed around the perimeter, leaving a cloak of sound, smoke, and dust that permeated everything and everybody. The NVA had made hourly probes to pinpoint machine-gun positions. In time, Quail's senses had become dulled into almost insensibility from the chaotic sounds of battle. He had finally been able to get some sleep, though it was fitful, but then had come a nerve-racking silence.

Shawn Flynn slapped a full magazine into the butt of his trusty .45 and jacked a round into the chamber. His old friend felt comfortable. He placed the pistol in his hip holster and shouldered his NVA pack. He put on his helmet, picked up his M-16, and stepped outside to meet the new day. In the east the horizon was grayish-blue. He rolled back his shoulders and took in a deep breath. It was time to go to war again, but this time it was different. He wanted to go. A friend needed him.

Colonel Quan sat beneath an old teak tree, sipping tea and watching the eastern horizon for signs of the new day. He had come out of the tunnel to enjoy the strange silence that the security forces had reported. For the first time in over twelve hours, the ground was not shaking and the sky was not rumbling. Peace had returned to the Chu Pong, for a time at least.

He saw the first crimson and orange brush strokes paint the eastern sky. It was truly a wonder, the certainty of the sun. Always there, dependable, always a source of light and hope.

The 66th Regiment would need all the hope he could give them. It would not be long before hundreds of his countrymen would rise and follow their leaders in the attack. Then the silence would end and the horror would begin.

———

The radio operators sat watching Colonel Morris pace like a cat back and forth. He would take five steps toward the east with his head up to see the rising sun's progress, then he would spin around, lower his head, and take five steps toward the west in deep thought. The colonel was wondering what every man in the perimeter was wondering: when were the NVA going to attack?

The radiomen watched their commander's strange ritual for almost two minutes before he finally came to an abrupt halt, muttering to himself, "The bastards aren't going to do it." He faced his radiomen with narrowing eyes. "Call the company commanders. Tell them to have each platoon send out a squad-size clearing patrol two hundred meters to their front. Their mission is to sweep our front of any snipers that might have moved in during the night." Raising his wrist, he looked at his watch. "The time is now 0630. Tell them I want the patrols to move out at 0640. Once they've got the patrols out, tell the commanders to meet me for an operations order briefing in the Charlie Company C.P."

Morris strode over to Quail's shallow hole and knelt down. "I thought for sure they'd attack this morning . . . I guess they've had enough. I'm gonna give the orders for the companies to attack up the ridge and rescue the platoon."

Quail sat up stiffly and glanced toward the treeline. "It's too fuckin' quiet, sir."

Morris stood and stared at the northern ridge. "Those kids in that platoon have waited long enough. We're gettin' them out." He glanced back at Quail. "I'm going to check with the medics and see how many wounded we had last night, then I'll head for Charlie's C.P. I'll see you there." He motioned for his radioman and strode directly toward the aid station.

Quail slowly stood up to give his stiff back a chance to loosen up. Sleeping in foxholes was for younger, more flexible men. His back felt as if a bent steel bar had replaced his spine. Fighting through the pain, he forced himself erect.

Now what the hell am I gonna do? he wondered. It'll take two troopers to help me sit down again. God, what I'd give to be ten years younger and hung five inches longer.

He decided to head south, toward the Charlie Company C.P., to hear the colonel's briefing. Maybe somebody in Charlie's C.P. would take pity on him, give him a canteen cup of coffee . . . hot, U.S. Army, C-ration coffee could not be beat . . . at least not there in that fuckin' place.

Captain Jim Elkins gave his platoon leaders their mission and returned to his small dugout command post. Sergeant Major Quail was leaning against an ant mound staring at his radio operator's fresh coffee. "You want some, Sergeant Major?" the captain asked.

Quail reached for his canteen cup with lightning speed. "If it wouldn't be puttin' you out none, sir. Thanks."

Elkins, a thin officer with a rugged face, poured the steaming liquid into the veteran's cup. He noticed the star on the old veteran's Combat Infantryman's Patch. "Is this like Korea, Sergeant Major?"

Quail took a sip and shut his eyes for a full two seconds, savoring the taste, smell, and much-needed caffeine before looking at the officer. "Sir, if you was to drop the temperature about eighty degrees, then we'd be gettin' close to what it was like in Korea. In Korea I woulda give a . . ."

Twenty meters to the front of the C.P., eighteen-year-old Private First Class Leyland Harper was walking point for his squad. He fixed his eyes on a distant gnarled tree he judged to be a hundred meters away. As long as he walked straight for the tree, he wouldn't wander off course. He glanced to his rear to make sure that the five other men from the second squad were following, then started forward very cautiously. He moved only twenty-five meters, then stopped, searching left and right for a sign. Artillery rounds had hit close during the night, blowing large, circular plowed areas in the waist-high grass, but there was no sign of any recent enemy activity.

Harper looked thirty meters to his left to the first squad's patrol, which was almost even with him, and felt better. At least he and his squad were not out there alone. He began walking again, feeling more relaxed. The smell of cordite was still heavy in the morning air. Just to his left he saw something that instantly froze his blood. At first he couldn't believe his eyes. The ground to his front seemed to be moving toward him. Recognition came a split second later, and his heart skipped a beat. Crawling NVA, camouflaged with grass, were all around him.

Leyland Harper's warning yell was still in his throat when a burst of AK-47 bullets tore through his body, ending his eighteen years of living.

John Quail hit the ground before the captain and still held on to the canteen cup. He was surprised his reactions were still so finely tuned, and he was doubly proud that he had spilled only a few drops of the precious liquid. The silence of the morning had ended with the rattle of gunfire, as did his last war story to the captain. Bullets cut through the grass like a scythe, felling the dry stalks all around him. Someone screamed above the fire that the patrols were in contact, but Quail knew better. He could not hear a single U.S. weapon returning fire. The men on the perimeter couldn't see targets through the grass and they were afraid of shooting patrol members somewhere to their front. By the sound of the enemy weapons, he knew this was no "contact," but a full-scale attack. He began to yell a warning to the captain, but to his shock, the officer had already jumped to his feet to look over the grass and see what was happening. One look was all he needed. He dropped down like a rock and screamed, *"They're attacking! Fire! Fire, goddamnit!"*

Twenty-five meters in front of Charlie Company's perimeter, camouflaged scouts of the attacking Sixth Battalion began pitching their stick grenades toward the Americans. The grenades produced little killing shrapnel, but that was not their purpose. The explosions would serve to guide the attacking companies.

Crawling, Colonel Morris dragged a wounded soldier behind an ant mound and yelled for a medic who was only a few meters away. The incoming fire was merciless. It chopped the grass down only a foot above his head. Morris low-crawled into a shallow dugout position that served as his command post. There his operations officer was listening to the radios and trying to determine what the situation was. Next to the major, the artillery forward observer yelled into a handset for the firing battery, ten kilometers away, to hurry and fire their first rounds so that he could adjust the range. Next to the artillery officer was a captain clutching a radio between his legs and calling for Air Force support.

The colonel crawled beside his operations officer. "What's Charlie Company's status?"

The face of the major looked strained as he lowered the handset from his ear. "They're gettin' hit bad. None of the patrols made it back, and the two platoons on their left are not reporting. Captain Elkins can't see because of the fucking grass, but based on the shooting he hears, he thinks maybe the two platoons are in big trouble. He's asking for the reserve to be sent forward to help him repulse the attack."

Morris shook his head. "I've only got one platoon in reserve from Delta Company. If we send it now and they hit us from another direction, we won't have anything left. Tell him we have to wait and see if the attack from the south is the main one."

Captain Jim Elkins angrily tossed the handset to his radio operator and looked at Quail in disgust. "He won't send me the fuckin' reserve!" He pushed himself up to look over the grass again to see if he could spot any of his positions. Instead, to his horror, he saw three NVA soldiers creeping in a low crouch only ten meters to his left. Dropping to his knee, he pulled a grenade from his pistol belt and yanked out the pin. Standing up again, he tossed the grenade, then was suddenly knocked forward.

Quail cussed, seeing the blood on the back of the officer's fatigue shirt, and crawled out of the shallow depression. Grabbing Elkins by the shirt collar, he dragged him back into the hole with him. Elkins was breathing in painful gasps, but motioned for the radio handset.

Colonel Morris's operations officer explained that Elkins was wounded and that the enemy were overrunning Charlie Company's left defensive positions.

Morris nodded. "Okay, we'll send relief, but not the reserve. Send a platoon from Alpha Company. And notify the perimeter supply point to send Charlie Company's executive officer forward to take command from Elkins."

John Quail waited until the crawling NVA soldier looked in his direction before shooting him between the eyes. The small soldier dropped, revealing another who was on his hands and knees trying to see what was ahead. Quail shot the soldier in the temple and ducked down as a burst of fire cracked mere inches over his head. The radio operator finished bandaging his commander and grabbed Quail's leg. "The XO is coming up to take over."

Quail raised his head an inch from the ground and looked left then right. The lieutenant had better hurry up or there would be nothing left to take over.

Minutes later the young officer crawled up behind the C.P., followed by six other men. Quail felt a wave of relief, for with added firepower, they could hold the C.P. position until the relief platoon showed up.

The wounded captain weakly raised his head. "What's happening?"

Quail motioned over his shoulder. "Your XO is coming in."

Elkins's eyes seemed to brighten and he turned around. The young, blond lieutenant was ten feet away and had just rolled to his side to get a new magazine from his bandolier. RPD machine-gun fire suddenly swept over the position, grazing the top of Elkins's helmet and knocking over the lieutenant with a round in the chest.

Unable to lift his head because of the lead cracking overhead, Quail pushed himself as flat as possible and yelled for the radio operator to tell any officer left in the company to take command.

Fifty yards away Lieutenant Franks, the only remaining officer not dead or wounded in Charlie Company, heard the radio message and began crawling toward the C.P. He got ten feet when he too was hit by grazing fire that shattered his leg and hip.

Colonel Morris glanced at his watch. He figured it must have been at least noon, but he was shocked to see it was only 7:45 A.M. The attack had begun only forty-five minutes ago. It seemed like hours. Time had been lost in a flurry of reports and decisions.

It was impossible to see anything but the ground for five feet in any direction. A soldier from the supply point who had delivered new batteries for the radios crawled in front of the colonel to go back and pick up medical supplies. He acknowledged his commander with a brief nod and continued crawling. He put his hand out to push away a box of ammunition and suddenly collapsed.

Morris reached out, grabbed the soldier's foot and pulled him into the shallow hole. When he turned the young man over, he saw the bullet hole just above the trooper's nose. Morris lowered the body to the ground just as a new wave of shooting came from the east.

The operations officer lowered the handset and looked at his commander with empty eyes. "Delta Company is being attacked."

Shawn Flynn strode out of the command bunker directly toward his squad. The men were resting under the shade of a huge banyan tree.

Vincent Martino saw the sergeant approaching. "Maybe this hurry-up-an'-wait shit is over."

Eugene leaned back against the huge tree trunk. "Man, the longer we wait, the longer we stay in one piece. Don't be complainin'. I kinda like this tea plantation guard duty. I think I'll even drink tea when I get home."

Lee leaned over to Blake, who had dozed off. "Ace, the sarge is comin'."

Blake stretched and slowly got to his feet. As usual, nothing that was planned turned out the way it was supposed to. The squad had been ready to leave at first light, only to be told that the reinforcement company would not go in until after 0800. Orders had changed twice since then. The last had been to stand by and be ready when called.

Shawn took off his helmet as he reached the shade. "We're still on five-minute standby. The First Battalion is gettin' hit by NVA attacks from two directions, but holdin' their own. Once the fire slackens on the L.Z., we're going in."

Bradshaw's face turned pale. "Did you say we're going in when the fire slackens?"

Shawn took off his pack and sat down. "Yep, that's what I said."

"What happens if they just quit shooting and wait for us to come in?"

Before Shawn could respond, Eugene spoke up with a grim smile. "Then you'll be the first to know, won'tcha, he-row?"

Vincent bobbed his head. "Yo, Willie Billy, you can tell all your friends 'bout the hot L.Z. you went in on."

Lee leaned over to Vincent and Eugene with piercing eyes. "I reckon y'all better quit messin' with my new man. Willie is jus' askin' questions."

Vincent frowned apologetically. "You're right, Reb. We forgot. Sorry."

Blake had made the move several days before to give Bradshaw some breathing room away from the constant hounding by Vincent and Eugene. Lee had accepted Bradshaw with only a nod, but he had protected the soldier like a mother hen ever since.

Blake scooted closer to Shawn. "Did the other battalion get in?"

Shawn took his map from his pocket. "Yeah, the First Battalion, Fifth Cavalry got into an L.Z. about three and a half klicks south of X-Ray. It's moving to link up."

"X-Ray?" Blake repeated, not understanding.

"X-Ray is the name they're calling the L.Z. the First of the Seventh is defending." Shawn pointed at the map. "They're getting hit from the south and east according to the last reports. We'll—"

"Saddle up!" a captain yelled from across the alert pad.

Shawn stood and hefted his pack to his shoulder. "You heard him, first herd, let's do it."

John Quail's eyes burned and his head felt like a brass bell with a runaway clanger. The last bomber had dropped a five-hundred-pound bomb no more than five hundred meters away. The explosion had been earth-shattering, but the follow-up concussion wave had nearly torn his head off. His eyes had bulged so badly that he thought they were going to pop out. Never had he experienced anything so frightening. He lay huddled against the radioman, who was crying uncontrollably and stank of defecation and vomit. The soldier had done both on himself. Quail fought the incredible weakness that seemed to be robbing him of his will to survive. He had seen it happen in Korea, when men lay down in the snow to die. They had chosen death over misery, exhaustion, and pain.

Quail shook his head and growled to himself to get back control of his mind. His ears still ringing, he shook loose the grip of the crying soldier and rose up. A bullet creased the lip of his helmet, but he didn't drop back down. Directly to his front, only four feet away, was an NVA soldier on his hands and knees, looking at him with dull eyes.

Quail snapped his rifle up and pressed the trigger. Nothing happened. His magazine was empty. The NVA soldier had not moved up to that time, thinking he was going to die, but the moment he knew he had a chance of surviving, he reached for the rifle slung across his back.

Quail screamed as he lunged toward the small man. The Vietnamese had managed to bring the rifle only to his chest when he was knocked backward by the American's crushing weight.

Using his head and body to pin the writhing soldier to the ground, Quail clawed at the man's face. Raking down, he found both closed eyelids and dug his thumbs into the corners. The animal scream from the young soldier was joined with Quail's own crazed scream as his thumbs thrust deeper through the watery membrane of the eyeball to the optic nerves.

The small soldier's body went slack beneath the sergeant major, who slowly raised the man's head. Both of the soldier's eyeballs were lying on his cheeks beside his nose. Quail's thumbs were still buried to the second knuckle inside the blood-filled sockets.

Colonel Morris watched the silver F-105 Thunderchief streak in from the north, and to his horror saw the two aluminum tanks detach from under the wings and begin their tumble. He had watched several previous air strikes and knew the pilot had punched too soon. He screamed as he rolled behind an ant mound, *"Take cover, napalm!"*

The thud and ensuing whoosh sounded as if he were lying directly under the tracks of a passing freight train; then came the fire and heat. It was over in seconds, but it seemed like two eternities. The wave of flame rolled over the center of the L.Z., engulfing everything with fire. The air had been sucked from the colonel's lungs, and when he finally did manage to take a breath, it was like inhaling gasoline mixed with model airplane glue. Choking, he opened his burning eyes and gasped. Everything living around him had shriveled, blackened, and begun smoking. The back of his neck and hands were still burning. Feeling light-headed from the fumes, he rolled into the C.P. foxhole.

The operations officer looked at his colonel's blackened face and smoking fatigues as if seeing a specter. "Sir? You're alive?"

Morris took in his first normal breath and abruptly stood to survey the damage. The two canisters of napalm had miraculously hit in the one place in the perimeter where there were no positions—the center. Several men of the command group were screaming from their burns, but the number of casualties would be small. In his mind he accepted the casualties in a morbid way. He knew that the accident could have been much worse. A bullet whizzed past his ear, and he dropped back to the ground.

Pointing skyward, the operations officer tapped the colonel's leg. "Sir, the relief force is coming in."

Shawn was already standing on the skids looking ahead of the nose of the chopper. He saw the smoking, blackened L.Z. and the red-dirt fighting positions scattered in the grass along the perimeter. The pinging of bullets against the chopper caused him to duck just as the bird's tail dipped in its flare. The pilot lowered the nose and dropped the Huey to the ground. In less than two seconds the passengers were gone and the aircraft was again airborne.

Blake and the others followed their sergeant as he dashed for the C.P. Shawn motioned for his men to take up positions behind the bullet-scarred trees as he approached the command center foxhole. It bristled with radio antennae. He knelt by the depression and reported to the first officer he saw. "Sir, I'm Staff Sergeant Flynn from Charlie Blues. I have a squad with me to relieve the pathfinders."

The operations major who took the report motioned Shawn down into the hole beside him. More slicks were landing and unloading the reinforcement company from Second Battalion, Seventh Cavalry. The officer had to shout to be heard over the screaming turbines. "Good to have you here. About ten meters to our rear is the three-man pathfinder element. I want them to continue bringing in these birds. Later this afternoon, you can spell them. In the meantime, I want you to stay close and act as our command security force."

Shawn nodded and looked around the position for his old friend. "Yes, sir . . . Sir, where is Sergeant Major Quail located?"

The major motioned to the south. "Last time I saw him was early this morning walking to Charlie Company's C.P. That was just before the first big attack that hit that area. If you had a message for him, I think you might be too late. Charlie had a lot of casualties."

Shawn stared at the major with liquid eyes. "He's a close friend, sir. I request permission to find him. I'll leave my squad here to secure your C.P. and go by myself."

The major sighed tiredly. "Sorry, I didn't know or I wouldn't have sounded so fuckin' grim. Sure, go on. And good luck."

Shawn spun around and called for Blake, who raised his head from behind a small ant mound. "Ace, establish security around the C.P. I'll be back in thirty minutes. If I don't show up in that time, you take charge."

Blake began to protest that his sergeant should take at least one man with him, but Shawn had already begun running toward the southern side of the perimeter. Blake knew where he was going and prayed he would find the soldier he was looking for.

Shawn's face became more taut as he made his way through Charlie Company's positions. The fighting had obviously been at very close range, for the bodies, mostly jumbled together, were both American and Vietnamese. The hands of one young, dead G.I. were still frozen around the throat of a dead NVA. Shawn felt his hope fading as he stepped over a Charlie Company lieutenant and three of his men, all killed within an arm's reach of each other. At least the wounded were all being attended to, by the reinforcement company he had flown in with.

Shawn came to the edge of a shallow foxhole surrounded by six dead NVA. In it was the body of a lone American, lying facedown.

"I was wonderin' when you was gonna show up."

Shawn spun around, immediately recognizing the voice. John Quail was sitting against the side of an ant mound, holding a steaming canteen cup full of coffee. Quail motioned to the ground beside him. "Sit down, Irish. I taught ya better than standin' around like that. Have some coffee. I just cooked it up."

Shawn fought to keep from running over and hugging the gruff bastard. Instead, he walked over calmly and sat beside his friend. He couldn't speak yet. He wasn't in enough control of his emotions. So in silence he took out his canteen cup. The sergeant major took it, but his blood-covered hand was shaking so badly he had to put the cup down. "Sorry, Irish, you gonna have to do it. You . . . you were right. I'm too old for this." The old veteran turned his bloodshot eyes to the young soldier in the foxhole. "He died fifteen minutes ago. I tried to talk him out of it . . . but he just wouldn't listen. The kid died of shock from a fucking chest wound. I told him he'd be okay but . . ."

Shawn put his arm around his friend. "Ya did all you could do."

Quail shifted his gaze to the bodies of the NVA. "They're good, Irish. Damn good. They don't stop comin' and don't die easy."

"Neither do you," Shawn said matter-of-factly.

Quail looked at Shawn's face for the first time. "Why the fuck didn't we get out of the fuckin' Army when we had the chance? We coulda been fat farmers or lovable drunks. Fuck, Irish, anything beats this bullshit."

Shawn shrugged and took a sip of coffee. He took the cup from his lips and raised it to look it over. "It was the coffee. You always said there was nothing like Army coffee, remember?"

A smile played at the corners of Quail's mouth. He lifted his own cup and took a long drink, then leaned back against the mound and sighed at the sky. "Yeah . . . it was the coffee."

When Blake recognized the two men approaching his position, he suddenly felt light-headed. He hadn't had much hope that Quail could have survived.

Blake stood up and offered his hand. "Damn glad to see you, Sergeant Major."

Quail smiled. "Not as glad as I am to see you and ol' Irish here." The sergeant major's eyes suddenly brightened, and he turned to Shawn. "Fuck! I forgot to ask. Am I a godfather yet?"

Shawn rolled his eyes. "No. And what's this about you being my kid's godfather? You ain't nothin' but a beer-guzzlin' dinosaur that . . ."

Colonel Morris walked down the row of dead troopers from his Gary Owen Battalion. Tears trickled down his blackened cheeks. At the last soldier's feet he stopped and turned toward the northern ridge. The radio operators standing behind their commander shared his remorse. The battalion had formed at Fort Benning and most of his men knew each other by first name.

The operations officer approached and spoke softly. "Sir, we're ready."

Morris set his shoulders and faced the major. "Give the orders to move out."

The major took ten steps into the L.Z. to make his presence known to the newly arrived battalion commander who had marched his men that morning up from an L.Z. three and a half kilometers to the south. Colonel Morris ordered his Bravo Company to lead the relief battalion to the platoon on the ridge and to "bring his boys back."

The operations officer raised his hand toward the assembled relief force. "Move out!" he barked.

"The two battalions of the 66th Regiment have no leaders remaining," Colonel Quan said to his stone-faced general, "and both units report they have lost more than half of their men. The Americans have been reinforced by at least another battalion, and more artillery units have been brought into range."

The general nodded without expression. "Which of our units is in position to attack?"

"Attack?"

"Yes, attack! I am not through with them."

Quan sat stunned in disbelief at what he was hearing. Who are you not finished with? he thought. Us or them? He had to try once more. "General, I just told you the 66th is finished and that the Yankees have been reinforced. We cannot 'attack.' We must escape, now, before they bring more forces in and storm the Chu Pong and destroy the entire division."

General Man shook his head and stood. "This is the first battle between our regular armies. It is a test of wills that only we can win. We want them to attack the Chu Pong. Our 32nd Regiment is waiting for them. We can lose twenty men for every one they lose, and still we will be victorious. It is a test of wills, and 'will' is what battle is about."

Quan lowered his head. He did not want to understand the logic of such thinking. All he was capable of understanding was the suffering of the men he had helped to train. He knew all the leaders down to the platoon commanders, as well as many of their families. How would he be able to face those families and tell them their sons died for "will"?

The general tapped the wall map. "Reorganize the remaining men of the two battalions into one unit and appoint new leaders from the ranks. I want them to attack tonight. Where is the Eighth Battalion? Are they not hurrying to return?"

Quan lifted his sad eyes to the general. "The Eighth will not arrive back to the Chu Pong until tomorrow. Colonel Duc is moving his men as fast as he can."

General Man nodded, satisfied. He studied the map for a moment. "When the Eighth arrives, order them to attack immediately."

Quan lowered his head, knowing that more ghosts would be added to his nightmares.

Colonel Morris put down the handset and turned to the command group assembled in the C.P. "They have reached the second platoon, and they're bringing them back."

"Gary Owen!" barked the operations officer in a burst of emotion.

"Gary Owen, sir," the others repeated.

Twenty meters away Blake and his squad helped the medics prepare the wounded for air extraction. Vincent was assisting with the rebandaging of a soldier's shoulder wound. "How many of 'em we got?"

An exhausted medic finished tying off the bandage and wearily closed his eyes. "I stopped counting after fifty. Charlie Company had forty this morning, and there's been a bunch from Delta and some from Alpha."

Vincent slowly shook his head. Behind him were at least another fifty young troopers with ponchos over their bodies.

Eugene sat across from Vincent, talking to a young black soldier who had been stitched across the back of his legs. "Just keep thinking of home, man. You can't be going into shock on me, okay?"

The soldier was trembling, as if he were freezing to death. "I . . . I don't . . . wanna die."

"Whatcha talkin' about, man? You ain't dyin' on this brother. Shit, man, we bad motherfuckers. We be too mean for these yellow commies."

"I'm . . . I'm so cold."

Eugene took the soldier's hand and squeezed it tightly. "Talk to me, man. Where you from in the world? Got a girlfriend?"

The soldier closed his eyes. "Detroit . . . we got a little place on . . ." Eugene glanced at Vincent and nodded in victory. Vincent nodded back with a faint smile.

Lee knelt beside Bradshaw, who was sickly pale from having had to wet down a soldier's intestines, which were lying on top of the man's stomach and covered with a T-shirt. The medic had explained the soldier would probably make it once he got back, but that the exposed intestines had to be kept moist.

Lee gave his subordinate a sidelong glance. "Ya still feelin' poorly?"

Bradshaw lowered his head and his stomach rumbled. "How . . . how can you stand it?"

Lee glanced down at the glassy-eyed, wounded soldier. "I reckon if he can take it, so can we. It's the least we can do."

Bradshaw swallowed the bile in his throat and continued sprinkling his canteen water over the T-shirt.

Blake sat beside a dying lieutenant who had been shot in the head. The bullet had gone through his helmet, striking him above the corner of his right eye. He lay like a child in the fetal position with his hands curled inward and trembling. His breathing was shallow, and he seemed to be murmuring something like a nursery rhyme. Blake took the young soldier's hand into his own. He would stay with him until the end. Someone needed to be there and care that he was hurting. No one should have to die alone.

"Taco . . . Taco?"

Quail kept his eyes closed but spoke gruffly. "Go away unless you're Liz Taylor wantin' my body."

Shawn lowered the heated C-ration can of beef-and-spice sauces and passed it in front of the old soldier's nose. "Chow time, Sleeping Beauty."

Quail stirred and uncoiled his legs. "Shit. Give me a hand, will ya?"

Shawn helped Quail stand and watched in amusement as his friend tried to straighten his stiff back into a completely upright position.

"Ah, aw . . . aaah shit . . . there. Christ, my back is gettin' back at me for all them weird positions I used on all that 'strange.' You got hot sauce?"

Shawn held up a bottle of Tabasco.

"How long have I been out?"

Shawn glanced at his watch. "About six hours. I had to wake ya up 'cause you were snoring so loud the other guys thought we were being mortared."

"Fuck you, Irish. Got a spoon?"

The two men sat down in front of a sterno fire in the bottom of a freshly dug fighting position. Quail wolfed down the meat, two cans of crackers, and a can of fruit cocktail in less than five minutes. "Got any poggy?" he asked, smacking his lips.

Shawn raised an eyebrow. "Candy? Out here? You gotta be shittin'."

Quail shrugged. "Never hurts to ask. I'll have coffee instead. Got water?"

Shawn took out one of his canteens. "What'a ya gonna do without me?"

"Get laid."

"Taco, I think all those 'strange' stories are bullshit."

Quail winked. "Wanna see the scars on my back? This is a fact. If I buy it, there will be a flood at my funeral 'cause there'll be so many tears from all the strange that love me. Hell, they'll probably have to call out the National Guard for 'strange' control. I wish I could see it. It makes my dick hard just thinkin' about it."

Shawn's expression became serious. "What have we got ourselves into here, Taco? We went out with the battalion to clear the outside of the perimeter a couple of hours ago, and there must be at least five hundred dead NVA out there. Their leaders must know it's nothing but a meat grinder. I knew the chinks were capable of it, but not the Viets . . . not like what I saw out there."

Quail opened a foil pack of instant coffee and sprinkled it on top of the water in his canteen cup. "I figure they were committed. They probably didn't understand the firepower we could bring in to tear up their ass. Now they know, but it ain't over yet." Quail motioned over his shoulder toward the mountain behind him. "To finish them, we're gonna have to take that fucker. I figure we've wasted two or three battalions' worth of the little bastards. That means they have at least another regiment on the mountain. The cav found 'em, they most definitely fixed 'em, but now we gotta finish them."

Shawn glanced at the mountain. "They couldn't have many more left. This is the same bunch that hit Plei Me."

Quail put his dirty finger into the water to check if it was getting hot. "You know as well as I do it don't take many when you're in good defensive positions on a mountain like that one. The way I see it is, if we're gonna beat their ass, it might as well be now. The bastards are standing and fighting for the first time. This ain't guerrilla war. This is like Korea. We got 'em, and it's time to finish 'em."

Shawn knew that the First Battalion had suffered almost seventy dead and over 110 wounded so far in this battle. It was the equivalent of two companies. Over one-third of the battalion's strength was gone. To take the mountain would cost the rest of the First Battalion and at least one or two more. Jesus, he thought, making a quick calculation in his head. It could easily eat up a thousand American lives. He looked at Quail. "But the cost, Taco."

Quail grasped the handle of the canteen cup and removed the cup from the flames. He sipped once at the hot liquid. "I know. I'm glad it ain't me makin' the decision to finish them or not. But I gotta tell ya, Irish, if we don't it means we ain't here to win this war." Quail turned and looked at the sun setting behind the Chu Pong. "The NVA have shown us they're willing to pay to win. The question is, are we?"

30

The morning sun began to peek over the horizon, but many would never see it. Blake and his squad had to look over a human wall of bodies to see the treeline. The previous night had begun quietly, but as the darkness grew, so did the impatience of the NVA. Two of their companies had attacked in separate waves, and been stopped by the men on the perimeter and then blown to pieces by the artillery. Over eighty bodies lay in the grass, some stacked as many as four high. Blake's squad's position had been directly behind the company that had done most of the killing. He and Lee had been on watch when a trip flare went off at four A.M., revealing a formation of NVA. The company reacted immediately by pouring a wall of copper and lead into the waves of screaming attackers. A few of the tenacious Vietnamese might have gotten through the small-arms fire, but when the artillery rained in, the battle was all but over. At first light the squad had joined with a platoon to check the results of the fighting.

Lee shook his head at the carnage around him. "Them boys shoulda known better by now. They just kept on comin' and dyin'. Makes ya wonder what gets in a man's head ta do somethin' like that."

Blake rolled a shell fragment over with his foot and looked up at Lee. "Pickett's charge at Gettysburg. Hooker's attack on Fredericksburg. Verdun, the Marne, Guadalcanal. Pick a war, Lee. There's always somebody ready to die, thinking what they're doing will make a difference. These poor bastards are no different."

Bradshaw was not listening. He was searching the corpses, looking for souvenirs. When he found a belt with an NVA buckle, he held it up with a smile. "Hey, check this out. It's got a star and everything!"

Lee and Blake exchanged glances, communicating the same thought. There would always be some who would never learn.

Looking very tired, Colonel Morris stood before his remaining officers under the shade of a battered tree. He took off his helmet and ran his hand through the blond stubble of his military crew cut. "We're done here. Our sister battalion, the Second of the Seventh, is taking our place. We're flying out in a couple of hours to go back to the rear for rest and refitting." The colonel paused and gazed at his men as if they were his sons. "I'm . . . I'm

damn proud of each and every one of you. I got word from the commanding general that our battle has been heard around the world. America
knows what you and your men have done. You can walk tall, leaders of
the Gary Owen, because you've written another chapter in the Seventh
Cavalry's history."

Standing behind the small group of officers, Quail leaned over to Shawn
and whispered, "I think ya oughta name your son Gary Owen Flynn."

"Catchy," Shawn said flatly.

"As the kid's godfather I got some say," Quail persisted. "I think 'Gary'
is kinda . . . uh, 'Gary'? Naw, you're right. It don't have the right ring.
How 'bout—"

The colonel dismissed his officers and approached Shawn. "Sergeant
Flynn, I got word you and your men will be needed to support the Second
of the Seventh. They're going to spend the night here, then move to L.Z.
Albany about four klicks north of here." The colonel extended his hand.
"Thanks for all your support."

"Gary Owen, sir," Shawn said, gripping Morris's hand firmly.

The Colonel then faced Quail. "Sergeant Major, I think you've seen
enough for your report back to Washington. You want to ride back with
me?"

Quail smiled. "Sir, no offense, but I ain't never gonna 'ride' with you
again. I think I'll stick with my ol' buddy here for the night and take the
walk in the sun tomorrow. Your 'rides' seem ta always end up in full-scale
charges."

The corners of the colonel's mouth curled up in a warm smile. "Sergeant
Major, I don't blame you. In a little while I'm gonna have to talk to a bunch
of reporters that Public Affairs is flying in, so I want to shake your hand
now in case I don't see you before I go. I also want you to know I'm putting
you in for a Silver Star soon as I get back. I heard about what you did out
there with Charlie Company. Take care and the best of luck back in
Washington. You're a Gary Owen now."

Quail shook the colonel's hand. "Sir, I'll drink a beer to the Gary Owen
Battalion soon as I get back. It was an honor to be here with ya. Like you
said to your officers, you can be damn proud. They done good."

Shawn watched the colonel walk away and turned to Quail. "What's this
shit about you stayin'?"

Quail began walking to his foxhole to cook himself some coffee. "Don't
start, Irish. I don't wanna hear your bitchin'."

Shawn sighed and shook his head.

Through a small gap in the canopy Colonel Quan saw five helicopters
fly over. He did not want to admit his general was right, but it appeared
that the Americans were not going to assault the Chu Pong. He had just

completed his inspection of the 32nd Regiment's defensive positions and had found, surprisingly, that the men were in good spirits and eager for the Americans to attack. They were not fearful, for their deeply dug, well-constructed positions would protect them from most of the effects of bombs and artillery. He had thought the men would have been demoralized by the losses of the 33rd and 66th regiments, but most of the men had reasoned that such losses were necessary, if they were to buy enough time to construct a defense that would win a victory for the division.

Quan descended into the darkness of a tunnel. The defense was ready now, but all indications were that the Americans would not attack. A single Yankee battalion had been reported marching into the clearing, joining the two already there, one of which, a scout had just reported, was flying out in helicopters. If the Americans were going to attack, they would not be sending men back. They would be sending many more in.

Quan entered the operations room, where his general sat with the 33rd Regimental commander discussing the lessons learned from the battle.

". . . I agree, the Americans rely mainly on fire support rather than maneuver. We have seen it during their search for us during our withdrawal and here at the Chu Pong."

"Yes, once they have found our forces, they withdraw and call in their air support," added the regimental commander. "To avoid destruction, we must close in as near as possible to their positions and maneuver to their flanks. They are vulnerable while they wait. Also, my general, these helicopter forces depend entirely on their air machines. Their infantry does not live off the land and yet they can travel very light because their machines daily fly in their supplies, water, ammunition, and take out their wounded. The helicopters are not as vulnerable as we thought, but they have a weakness that we can take advantage of in the future. They must have an open area to land. We will be able to predict their movements by the number of landing places in a given area. They seem to move from one landing area to another and always establish their perimeters at night to receive their supplies. If we keep scouts around an American unit, they can report their direction of travel. If we know in what direction they march, we can move a unit ahead and set up ambushes around likely landing places."

General Man pondered the colonel's words for a moment and shifted his position. "Enlightening, wouldn't you say?" he asked Quan.

Quan stepped closer to the table, seeing a way to perhaps save the Eighth Battalion from the fate of the others. "Yes, very. I believe we should put to use this tactic immediately. The Eighth is scheduled to arrive tomorrow afternoon, here, at the Chu Pong. Perhaps we should contact the battalion and tell them not to come, but rather to position themselves east of the Americans and send their scouts forward to watch their movements."

General Man stood and walked to the wall map to study the terrain. Quan held his breath. Man moved his finger over the map and nodded. "Yes, that makes good sense. Order it done."

Quan sighed to himself in relief. At least his friend, Bin Duc, would be spared from the slaughter a little longer.

L.Z. X-Ray was again quiet as the sun set behind the Chu Pong. The newly arrived troopers of the Second of the Seventh Cavalry didn't appreciate the quiet or sunset. As they expanded the old defensive positions, their stomachs grew queasier and queasier from the smell of decaying corpses.

Bradshaw tied a bandanna around his nose, while the rest of the squad squatted by a small fire in the bottom of their fighting position.

"How can you people eat with that godawful stink in the air?" he asked in horror.

Eugene pushed his glasses back up on his nose, raised his head and sniffed the air. He then leaned closer to Vincent, sniffed again, and quickly backed away. "It ain't the NVAs. It's Vinny. All that Eye-tie shit he eats pours out of his skin in garlic sweat."

Vincent ignored the insult. "Gimme my hot sauce back," he said indifferently.

Eugene shook two more shakes of the red sauce on his C-ration beef and potatoes and tossed the bottle to Vincent. "I hope Gina makes you take a bath, man, or you can forget the hoagie business."

Vincent shook Tabasco over his C-ration spaghetti and looked up at Eugene with his best fuck-you stare. "Gene, you keep it up, maybe I won't go to your parade."

Eugene took a bite of his greasy beef and waved his plastic spoon at Vincent. "You wouldn't miss it, man. You promised me."

"Uh-uh. I didn't promise nothin'."

"Well, promise me now."

"Gene, do I stink?"

"Naw, you smell like a typical Eye-tie."

"Okay, I promise."

Quail, sitting on the lip of the fighting position, couldn't help himself—his curiosity was piqued. "Day," he said, "what parade are you talkin' about?"

"Sergeant Major, it ain't nothin'. Us guys was talkin' awhile back about what we were going to do when we got back. Vinny is gonna run a hoagie stand. Reb is gonna go back to school and be a teacher. Ace says he's going back to school and get laid. Stuff like that."

"What about the parade?" Quail pressed.

Embarrassed now, Eugene lowered his eyes. "It's something I've always wanted to do. My ol' man is a vet from W.W. Two, and I wanna go with him to the veteran's ceremony they have every year in my hometown. It ain't a big deal."

Vincent lifted his spoon. "I'm goin' with him, Sergeant Major. You heard him make me promise."

Lee raised his chin as he wiped dust off his rifle. "I'm goin' too."

Blake set down his empty fruit-cocktail can. "I wouldn't miss it either."

Eugene's smile got bigger. "They all lyin', but I love 'em anyway," he said to Quail.

Quail laughed. He felt comfortable with the squad. He had not thought it possible to have so much in common with these young men, but something about foxholes, stinking bodies, and C-rations made them all equals. He felt a closeness he had missed since he'd left field soldiering years ago. It was good to be back, and he had no regrets about passing on Colonel Morris's offer. He had needed to lay back and listen to grunts talk again. Things hadn't changed much. Women were still high on the list of topics, closely followed by complaining about everything. A grunt just wasn't a grunt unless he was bitchin' about the rear echelon's lack of support. He was glad to see food preparation hadn't changed much either. Preparing Army C-rations was an individual art through which each man could display his imagination and skill. The squad had mastered several of his own techniques. C-rations were terrible cold, but when heated, mixed, and spiced up with hot sauce, they could actually be quite good. Mealtime was also bullshit time, and he had always been a true master of that particular soldierly skill.

Quail scooted down into the hole beside Vincent. "Ain't ya gonna melt any cheese on that spaghetti?"

"Don't have none, Sergeant Major."

Quail reached in his leg pocket. "I got one I'll trade for your peaches."

Vincent raised an eyebrow. "You shittin' me? For peaches? You gotta do better than that."

Quail couldn't help but smile. C-ration peaches were still as prized as they ever were, and any trader worth his salt would never have made such a ridiculous offer. More had to be added to the deal. "Shit, okay, I lost my head. I'll kick in my white bread, but that's it."

"Add jelly and you got it."

Quail rolled his eyes, loving it. "You sonofabitch. Here, take the jelly, and I hope ya choke on the white bread."

Vincent smiled. "Thanks, Sergeant Major."

Shawn sat with other assembled leaders in front of the commander of the Second Battalion, Seventh Cavalry, Lieutenant Colonel Jeffrey Epson. Shawn noted immediately that the colonel was speaking from notes he'd made earlier and would not make eye contact with his men. When Epson finished reading the situation update and orders for the following morning's departure, he folded his notes quickly and got up to leave.

Shawn spoke up. "Sir, I've got some questions about the move tomorrow."

As if hurrying to a more important meeting, Epson offhandedly motioned to his executive officer. "Ask Major Tulley."

Ten minutes later Shawn took off his pack and settled beside Quail in his large fighting position. Quail had been listening to the squad bitch while he enjoyed a cup of Army coffee.

"How'd the brief go?" Quail asked.

"Shitty. You know anything about this Epson character? He seems like he's in the twilight zone. Looks like to me the XO runs the battalion and Epson just kind of pops in now and then to make appearances."

Quail tilted his head up, repeating the name, "Epson. I think I heard somebody say he used to be the division G-one."

Shawn nodded and took the canteen cup from Quail's hands. "That explains it. He's been away from the line dogs too long, and he's still thinkin' like a personnel weenie. I hope he gets his shit together soon, or this poor battalion is gonna suffer."

Quail shook his head, then leaned back and looked up at the stars. "You know, I've been askin' myself why I put up with this shit. But I guess I know. It's the kids, ain't it? Like these kids of yours. They're a damn good bunch."

Shawn took a sip of the sergeant major's coffee and glanced up at the stars. "Yeah, it's always been the troops. You can't live with the complainin' bastards, but ya can't live without 'em either. They get to ya."

Quail listened to the silence for a full minute before reaching up and taking the cup from Shawn. "Irish, when I get back, the first thing I'm gonna do is fly down and see Cindy for ya."

"Don't tell her about this shit, Taco. And don't be tellin' her I said name the baby Gary Owen either."

Quail laughed lightly. "Fuck you, Irish. I mean it, when I see her and your new kid, I'll make sure they're doin' okay."

Shawn knew no one who would do it better, and lowered his head, speaking softly. "Thanks, Taco, I'd appreciate it."

Quail leaned back again against the dirt wall. "And you know what else I'm gonna do? I'm gonna go to Eugene's parade next year. Shit, I ain't got nothin' else to do. It'd be good to see your bunch again."

Shawn furrowed his brow. "What parade you talkin' about?"

Quail smiled. "Aw, see? You don't know everything. You're the platoon leader, and you don't hear about the kids' hopes and dreams. You're too far away from them, being their leader. Today I got to be a squad member, and I know what makes these guys tick. Each of them has a dream . . . something they wanna do when . . . ."

Shawn listened. He knew more than Quail thought, but still, his friend put some of the pieces together for him. What he didn't know about was his squad leader, Alexander. Shawn had no idea Blake was living in the shadow of his father. It made sense now that the conversation the other night at Catecka had ended so abruptly after he suggested that Blake's dad had been a good one.

Shawn felt an ache in his heart. He tried hard to be a good leader and take care of his people, but even after all this time, he didn't know them completely. And that hurt.

31

17 NOVEMBER

Shawn waited until the Alpha Company's recon platoon moved ahead before allowing the squad to begin their march. The night before, the Second Battalion executive officer had told Shawn the squad was to march with the lead company so that they would be on L.Z. Albany before the rest of battalion. The officer wanted Shawn to establish an airlift command post.

Quail glanced at his watch as he stepped through the waist-high grass. "Irish, it's 0900. We'll be at the L.Z. by noon, and we'll be drinking beer by 1400. Think about that. Ice-cold beer."

"Shut up, Taco. You're makin' me thirsty already."

Quail shrugged. "Okay, let's talk about poontang . . . and don't tell me you're gettin' horny already."

Shawn gave in. His friend was in a talkative mood. Being as far back from the point as they were, and being in the fairly open terrain, it was safe enough. "Okay, what'd ya really wanna talk about?"

Quail seemed surprised his guise was so quickly seen through. "God-damnit, Irish, there you go again. You don't show any respect for your elders. You're supposed to let me ramble a bit first."

"Sorry, you're right. Nice day . . . catch any fish lately? Gotten laid lately? Now, what the fuck ya wanna talk about?"

Quail smiled. "I'm worried about you. Ya get more like me every day. I just wanted to know what you planned on doing when you get out of Nam. I can pull a few strings if you want."

Shawn stepped around an ant mound. "I wanna go back to Benning. I don't think you'll need to help me get there."

"You don't want to go back to the Special Forces?"

"Naw, just Benning. I got a kid to raise, remember? I have to figure out how to be a dad. I didn't have a teacher in that area, so it's all gonna be on-the-job training. What about you? You're up for retirement soon. Where you gonna go once ya leave Washington?"

Quail shrugged. "Someplace where the fishin' is good and the beer is cheap. Columbus wouldn't be bad. It's close to the Benning commissary and PX."

Shawn gave Quail a sidelong accusing glance. "You set me up, you old

402

bastard. You were askin' where I wanted to go so you could retire there. You wanna mooch free beer off me, don't ya?"

Quail forced a smile. "Shit, never could outsmart you, Irish." His smile turned into a frown as he stepped over a fallen tree. In fact, he was scared to death of retirement. The Army was all he knew. He had no home or family to go back to. The thought of getting up in the mornings with no place to go scared him. He had made the mistake of looking up some of his old, retired bachelor buddies, and didn't like what he had seen. They had been without purpose, wandering in a sea of civilians who didn't understand them or want to.

Shawn felt the veteran's silence and stole a glance at his rugged face. He could see his friend was troubled, and given the previous conversation, he figured he knew what it was.

Cradling his rifle in the crook of his arm, Shawn put on a thoughtful look. "You know, Taco, all kiddin' aside, I think Benning would be a good place to retire. Knowing you, a'course, you wouldn't actually retire. You'll probably work on post for the infantry school. There's a lot of old-timers who work there teaching and inspecting around post. Yeah, you'd probably like that. You wouldn't have to put up with the spit-shine bullshit, but you'd still be close enough to feel like you're in. Yeah, I can see you doin' that. Hell, on weekends we could take the kid fishin'."

Quail's brow furrowed as he gave the idea some thought. It wasn't a bad idea. He knew enough people to swing the job easy enough.

Lieutenant Colonel Bin Ty Duc sat under a tree eating rice with his staff when a young sergeant ran up, followed by a sweat-soaked scout. The sergeant motioned excitedly toward the south. "Colonel, the scout reports the Americans are coming this way."

Duc rose to his full six feet. "How far away are they?"

The sergeant cringed as he spoke. "Twenty to twenty-five minutes is all, my colonel."

Duc's eyes widened in anger. "You are just now reporting this?"

The sergeant looked over his shoulder at the scared private. "This fool took the wrong trail coming back to report and wasted an hour lost in the forest before finding his way to us."

Duc quickly lost the fire in his eyes. He stepped closer to the cringing young man. "It happens, my little brother. Find water and refresh yourself." He turned around, facing his staff. "We do not have as much time as we thought, but all is not lost. The Americans are coming here to us. Move the First Company into position in the treeline facing the clearing. That will be our blocking force. Also, have the Second Company immediately move parallel to the advancing American line of march." Duc squatted and drew an L in the dirt. "We will conduct an L-shaped ambush that we have practiced many times in training. The First Company will form the base, and the Second Company will form the leg. There will be no time for digging or preparing positions. Speed and surprise will give us the advantage. When the Americans reach the clearing, the First Company will engage. That will be the signal for the Second Company to immediately attack the American flank. I will be with the Third Company, which will form our reserve. Our position will be behind the First Company and next to the mortars. Go and issue the orders quickly."

The small staff of three men broke into a run to find the company commanders. Duc looked at his mark in the dirt and shook his head at the absurdity. All of his contingency plans had required early warning. There were five open clearings in which the helicopters could land, and he had chosen the one in the center so he could move to any of the others quickly. With only twenty minutes' notice, he would not have been able to move his unit fast enough to any of the other landing places. Now it was a moot point. The Americans were coming to the clearing where his battalion was now waiting and eating rice. Had he more time, the Americans would have walked into a death trap. Now they would simply be walking into a battle. All the plans he had made were gone because of one man's simple mistake. The only thing he had left was the drawing in the dirt representing the most basic of battle drills that any private could have explained.

"Call the command tunnel," he said to his radioman. "Tell Colonel Quan the Eighth Battalion is about to engage the enemy on clearing number three. Tell him it will be a battle, but not a killing as was planned."

Soaked with sweat, Shawn looked at his watch, then pulled out his map. It was almost twelve-thirty. They should have reached the L.Z. by now. He traced the route with his finger and sighed in relief. The stream they had crossed fifty meters back was only a couple of hundred meters from L.Z. Albany. Another couple of minutes and they would see the clearing. Then they could take a long break while they waited for the rest of battalion to close.

Quail had seen his friend take out his map. "How much farther?" he asked tiredly.

Shawn motioned ahead. "We're almost there."

Quail wiped sweat from his forehead. "You have any idea how much beer I'm gonna need after this?"

Lots, Shawn was about to say, when Eugene turned around in front of him and held out the radio handset. "Sarge, the Alpha Company commander wants ya on the horn."

Shawn took the handset. "Six, this is Blue one, over."

He listened for several seconds before responding. "Wilco, Six, out." He waved Blake over to him. "Ace, we're moving up to help the recon platoon scope out the L.Z."

Shawn stepped into the clearing and froze. The recon platoon leader was standing ten feet away with his hand up, signaling freeze. To the lieutenant's right the high grass parted and out stepped two NVA prisoners escorted by four recon troopers. Shawn moved closer to find out what the hell was going on. Not a word had come over the radio about the lead platoon's capturing prisoners.

A young sergeant forced the two NVA to their knees in front of his platoon leader. "Sir, the point man tripped over these two lying in the grass just a few minutes ago. We didn't see or hear anything else, but we held up to see if you wanted to continue searching the L.Z."

The lieutenant grabbed the radio and called his company commander. "Amazon Six this is Black Six, hold up the column. We just captured two NVA on the L.Z. I'm gonna need an interpreter up here ASAP to find out what these two know. Over."

The lieutenant listened for a few moments and looked at the recon sergeant as if to say, Now look what you've done. "The old man is coming up to see for himself."

Minutes later Shawn sat in the shade with Quail and the squad. A few meters away the battalion commander, Lieutenant Colonel Epson, grilled the interpreter, who in turn grilled the prisoners. After the first few questions it was clear to Shawn and the others that the colonel was wasting his time. The two NVA were either playing dumb or they were simpleminded. Nothing they said had made sense.

After five minutes of listening to the questioning, Quail leaned over to Shawn, whispering, "I think the heat has got to Epson. His questions sound like their answers, dumb."

Lee stood and looked around to search the distant treelines, then sat down on his pack.

"See anything?" Blake asked.

"Nope, jus' grass an' ant mounds. It sure is quiet. Ain't no birds squawkin'."

Vincent brushed dust off his M-60. "Them birds is smarter than us. They're probably at the river, swimmin'."

Eugene wiped sweat from his nose. "I wish I was swimmin' right now, man. The heat is kickin' ass."

Finally giving up, the colonel walked over to his executive officer. "Call Brigade and tell them we need a chopper to pick up the prisoners. We'll stay up here with Alpha Company while they clear the rest of the L.Z."

The tall major pulled out his map. "Sir, since we're stopped on the edge of the pickup zone, you might think about bringing the company commanders up so you can show them how you want to secure the clearing."

Epson patted the sweat from his brow with a handkerchief. "Go ahead, call them up here and show them for me. I want to write myself some notes for the after-action report."

The major nodded. He had guessed he would be put in charge. The colonel had only been in command three weeks and still didn't feel comfortable with the business of ordering battle formations and defensive positions.

The XO told the battalion radio operator to call the commanders forward. He then took the handset from the operator, who carried the radio on the brigade frequency and called the higher headquarters. A minute later he turned around and yelled for Shawn.

Shawn stepped out of the shade. "Yes, sir?"

"Sergeant Flynn, Brigade can't get a bird here for at least forty-five minutes. Have your squad take the prisoners back to Charlie Company. I'm going to have Alpha go ahead and clear the L.Z. I want you and your RTO to stay here to give me radio backup."

Shawn turned to Blake. "You and the herd take the prisoners back to Charlie Company. You'll be passing through Delta Company before you get there. Give the POWs to the first officer you see and hightail it back to"—Shawn stood and pointed toward the clearing—"that cluster of ant mounds."

Blake stood. "Saddle up first herd. Lee, tie the prisoners' hands behind them. Bradshaw, you help. Vinny, you stay at drag, in case they decide to run for it."

Minutes later, with Blake in the lead, the squad began moving back in the direction from which they had come. Vincent patted Eugene on the shoulder. "Take care till I get back," he said.

Eugene smiled. "Don't go swimmin' in that creek you gotta cross. It wouldn't be fair."

Vincent winked. "That's what I had in mind. I think of you when I get all wet."

"Fuck you," Eugene said with a fake frown.

Shawn helped Quail to his feet and walked behind the recon platoon until they passed the cluster of ant mounds in the center of the L.Z. Shawn stood in the shade of the largest one, which was at least eight feet tall. "This is just as good a place as any. Eugene, get out the long whip antenna and see if we can get any choppers on the aviation frequency."

Quail watched the clearing operation. "Look at that, Irish. The Alpha Company commander knows what he's doing. He's got his three platoons abreast clearing to his front just like the book teaches."

Shawn took a spare radio battery out of his pack. "Just 'cause the battalion commander is spacey doesn't mean his company commanders are too."

Fifty meters to the south, Blake was passing by the men of Delta Company, who were all getting to their feet after their long break. Lee increased his pace and came alongside Blake. "Ace, I don't like it. I got the feeling, bad."

Blake slowed and looked left then right, searching the woodline. "You see something?"

Lee was nervously rocking back and forth on his feet. "I don't like it a'tall. It's too quiet."

Blake spotted a lieutenant just ahead and caught up with him. "Sir, do y'all have security out to the flanks?"

"What for?" the lieutenant said.

Blake motioned behind him. "Sir, didn't you get word about the prisoners they found?"

The officer's eyes widened at the sight of the two NVA following Bradshaw. "No. No one said anything to us. We've been sittin' here in the sun sweatin' our balls off waiting to move out. Where did you find them?"

Blake exchanged worried glances with Lee, who was still nervously rocking.

At the north end of the L.Z., just inside the woodline, an NVA machine gunner from the First Company raised his head only slightly. Ten meters to his front were four approaching Yankees who had just stepped out of the head-high elephant grass. He lowered himself behind his gun and waited to see if more would appear. A second passed, then another. Then the grass parted and two more Americans strolled out. He aimed at the closest soldier, now only five meters away, and slowly pressed the trigger.

Quail swung to his right as soon as he heard the chatter of an RPD machine gun. He was about to lift his rifle when the entire treeline to his distant front seemed to explode with shooting. A bullet creased his hip as he threw himself toward the protection of the huge ant mound. Shawn was already on the ground, peering behind the mound to see where the fire was coming from. Ducking back, he heard Quail cussing and crawled over to him. The veteran was lying on his side, pawing at his first-aid packet trying to get his field dressing out.

"Shit! Shitshitshit! Goddamn, I forgot how bad the fuckers burn. Shiiiit!"

Shawn quickly inspected the wound and saw the bullet had cut a three-inch swath through the skin like a plow furrow. Blood welled up from it and dripped down the back of Quail's buttocks. Shawn tore the fatigue material away from the wound and snatched the dressing from the sergeant major's shaking hands.

"Goddamn you! You just fuckin' had to come out, didn't you? Hold still while I bandage it!"

"Easy! Christ, take it easy will ya? It hurts!"

Shawn eased the pressure. "Hold it in place, goddamnit!" Shawn tried to concentrate, but it was impossible with the roar of gunfire and the bullets cracking all around him. Eugene was huddled against the mound, trying to call for anybody who would listen so that he could report their situation.

When he realized he was getting nothing but static, he leaned forward to help Shawn.

"Couldn't get anybody on the horn."

Shawn quickly tied the bandage knot. "Just fuckin' great!"

A mortar shell exploded to their far left, covering the three men with pelting dirt clods and dust. Shawn screamed as he pulled Quail closer to the mound's protection. *"Just fuckin' great. Mortars too!"*

"Dig, damnit!" Blake yelled as he frantically tore at the ground with his entrenching tool. Vincent was having a hard time getting his blade to fully extend. He finally gave up and used the tool as a pick, chopping at the ground like a madman. The squad had moved next to a large tree as soon as firing broke out to the north, and Blake had ordered them to dig in immediately. Lee and Bradshaw were posted on both sides for security as the two others dug frantically. The two NVA prisoners sat watching by the tree, as if amused. Lee rose up beside the ant mound he was using for protection and glanced toward Charlie Company's lead platoon. It was in sight only twenty meters away. Instead of lying down, they were on one knee facing the shooting as if waiting for someone to tell them to move forward. Lee began to yell for them to get down when he saw movement from the corner of his eye. The instant he turned his head back forward, the trees seemed to come alive with NVA. He ducked behind the mound yelling *"Flank attack!"* A split second later the air was filled with the horrific sound of assault rifles and machine guns, all firing at once at the hapless men who were looking in the wrong direction. The huge tree trunk protected Blake and Vincent from the thudding bullets. Both men had crawled to the base and peered around to see if Lee was hit in the onslaught. He was pressed against the ant mound trying to make as small a target as possible. Bullets were scything the grass all around him like invisible lawn mowers.

Blake screamed above the crackling bullets. *"Don't move!"* The deafening noise of the NVA rifles and automatic weapons grew louder and louder, building to an ear-shattering roar. Blake ducked back to find Bradshaw. He was lying in the shallow hole he and Vincent had dug.

Blake had to yell at Vincent to be heard over the noise, even though he was only inches from his face. "You and Bradshaw dig! I'll keep Lee covered!"

Despite his pain, Quail dug hastily at the base of the ant mound, as Shawn and Eugene watched the front. Directly behind Quail sat the Alpha Company commander, the radio pressed against his ear. He and six of his men had made a dash for protective mounds the instant the shooting broke out. Two had been wounded during the short run and one never made it. What the company commander was hearing from his three platoons was grim. All had been hit simultaneously and had taken horrible casualties. Now they were all pinned down and could not move back, as he had ordered.

Looking up, he saw the battalion command group running toward him. He waited for enemy fire to cut them down, but when it didn't, he realized they probably were screened by the rock-hard ant mounds and tall grass. They were lucky, he thought. If they had come to the cluster from any other direction, they would have been chopped to pieces. He was about to lift the handset to his mouth when behind the approaching command group he saw four NVA running across the trail. Noooo! *"They're cutting us off!"* he screamed.

Lee jerked with the impact of a bullet tearing through his flesh. He bit his lip but didn't dare try and reposition himself. The bullet had hit the back of his arm, which had been peeking out slightly from behind the narrow mound. Feeling faint from the intense pain, he clenched his teeth harder and prayed the fire would let up before he passed out.

Blake had seen Lee wince, and felt his own insides turn to mush when his buddy's left, bloody arm fell limp. His best friend was going to be shot to pieces unless he did something. Ducking back, he was about to grab for a grenade when Vincent grabbed him and pointed to the north. Blake gasped. Bodies lay sprawled everywhere in the grass. Delta Company, to his north, like Charlie, to his south, had been strung out in column formation. The initial devastating fire from the flank had caught them in the open with no time to take cover. Blake looked back to the south and felt sick. He could not see a single soldier who looked as if he were alive. But, despite the heavy incoming fire, he could still *hear* the distinctive pops of M-16s to the north and south. At least there were *some* survivors. He put the helpless feeling out of his mind.

Bradshaw jerked his rifle up, shooting to the south where Charlie Company was located. Blake began to grab him to make him stop, but then he saw a six-man NVA squad running past, only twenty feet away. He snapped his rifle up and joined Bradshaw in the killing. All six NVA were hit, and fell beside dead Americans from Charlie Company's lead platoon. Three were only wounded, but they were put out of their misery by a sweep of Vincent's M-60.

Blake yanked a grenade from his web belt. "Cover me!" he yelled to Vincent. "I'm gonna toss it past Lee. When it goes off, I'm gettin' Lee and bringin' him in!"

Blake pulled the pin but still held down the spoon. Staying as close to the tree as possible, he stood and waited for Vincent to do the same. He took a couple of deep breaths and let the spoon fly. Counting to two, he stepped out, tossed the grenade, and jumped back. The vehement crack of the explosion was his signal. He broke into a dead sprint. As he got to Lee, he could hear Vincent's M-60 rattling as if it were next to his ear. He grabbed Lee's shirt and jerked and pulled him to his feet in a single motion. Clapping his arm around the Georgian's waist, they ran together for the tree. Within a few feet of the protection, Blake pitched forward. He felt as if someone had hit the back of his right leg with a red-hot sledgehammer. He hit the ground hard, but clawed and kicked with his good leg to make it the last few feet. Lee was screaming at him to move faster. He felt as if he were slipping backward.

Bradshaw tossed down his rifle and crawled forward, grabbing Blake's outstretched hand, and pulled him back to the tree as Vincent screamed and fired over their heads, spraying death into the woodline.

Shawn spun around, hearing, *"Cease fire! Cease fire, goddamnit, it's friendly incoming fire!"* It was Colonel Epson, on his feet and yelling at men around him. Shawn backed away from the ant mound and looked up at the colonel as he strode past to stop the shooting from his troopers to the right.

Shawn grabbed the officer's leg. "What the fuck you doin', sir?"

"It's friendly fire coming in, not NVA!" Epson snarled back. "We have to stop shooting!"

Shawn held onto the officer tightly. "Sir, the radio report said Delta Company was shooting wildly this way, *but so are the fuckin' NVA!* Get down and get hold of yourself!"

Epson kicked his leg free and strode to the XO, who was talking on the radio. "Tell them all to cease fire, goddamnit!"

The major lowered the handset, ignoring the order, and spoke loudly to be heard over the shooting. "Sir, Charlie and Delta companies have been hit by a flank assault. Charlie is reporting at least twenty KIA, and Delta says its rear platoon is overrun. I've got air support coming in about ten minutes. We've got to hold and try to consolidate till then."

Epson's face showed confusion. "NVA? It's not friendly fire causing the casualties?"

Shawn shook with rage and frustration. He had sent his men toward Charlie Company! Jesus, twenty dead already and no telling how many wounded. And the shooting had just broken out ten minutes before.

Eugene grasped Shawn's shoulder. "Sarge, we gotta go back to the team."

Shawn lowered his head. "We'd never make it."

"I'm going." Eugene released his grip.

Shawn turned and looked at the determined soldier. "You're not going . . . yet. Once the fire slackens and we get air support in here, we'll go back. Hang tough for the time being and help the sergeant major dig that hole deeper."

Eugene stared toward the bullet-swept trail that led to the team. "I promised them."

Shawn handed him an entrenching tool. "Dig."

Blake pushed up the dug-up dirt to his front to form a parapet. The pain in his leg was throbbing so badly he stopped for a moment to wipe the stinging tears from his eyes. Lee lay beside him, holding his M-16 in his right hand, watching for more attacks. Nine dead NVA lay within ten feet of their hasty fighting position. Two men from Charlie Company had crawled to the tree only minutes before, and now, despite minor wounds, were expanding the hole. The large tree was like a wall protecting them all from fire from the west. It was one of the few places a soldier could raise his head without getting a bullet between the eyes. The two men from Charlie Company had left a pocket of survivors to try and get help but had found no one else in the company who wasn't dead or wounded.

Vincent extended the M-60's bipod legs and linked another belt of ammo to the last rounds of his old one. He looked over the lip of the position. "We can hold 'em off. No sweat," he said confidently.

Blake glanced behind him. "Help will be here real soon. Don't waste ammo, and keep your grenades ready. Bradshaw, keep digging and make this mother deeper. We'll keep an—"

Lee fired and yelled, *"They comin'!"*

Blake turned and immediately pulled the trigger. A line of NVA had risen out of the grass only fifteen feet away. Bradshaw's moan was drowned out by the deafening rattle of the M-60. One of the Charlie Company soldiers pitched backward, spraying the others with blood from his face and neck. Seven of the attackers were knocked down in the barrage of bullets, but three were almost on top of the position. One fired from the hip as he approached, stitching Vincent across the back of the legs. Blake flicked his selector to auto and held the trigger back, hosing both the shooter and another one about to fire. The last soldier jumped into the hole, stabbing with his bayoneted rifle toward Bradshaw, who lay on his back with a shoulder wound. Screaming, Bradshaw threw up his hands to deflect the thin blade. It sliced through his palm. Lee stood up, jammed his M-16 barrel into the NVA's face and pulled the trigger, firing the last round in his magazine.

Blake screamed for Lee to get down. There were more NVA running toward them. Lee dropped, but not before a bullet passed through the forearm of his wounded arm. Groaning, he dug into his bandolier for another magazine. Blake had already slapped in another mag and begun to fire. The remaining soldier from Charlie Company tossed out a grenade and ducked. The shrapnel from the explosion ripped through the line of men like grapeshot. Blake finished off the standing survivors while the Charlie Company soldier screamed, "Eat it motherfuckeeeers! *Eat it!*"

Shawn saw them but didn't believe his eyes. He blinked and took the slack out of the trigger. Twenty-five meters away an NVA platoon had trotted out of the woodline in a column formation three deep. Their weapons were at port arms and they were led by an officer wearing a French slouch hat. Shawn aimed at the officer and fired. The Vietnamese officer fell face first with a bullet in the brain. The men in the C.P. joined in the shooting. The startled Vietnamese platoon members, instead of running, fell to the ground and tried to return fire. Quail gritted his teeth as he rose up and tossed one grenade after another. Every man in the NVA platoon was dead in less than thirty seconds. The cluster of ant mounds was like a signpost on the L.Z., and by now any American soldier who had not been hit had crawled there. A perimeter had been formed by over thirty men who had been waiting for just such an opportunity to get revenge.

Shawn ducked down after a bullet cracked by his ear. *"Snipers!"*

He hit the ground and rolled toward Quail, who was already at the bottom of his freshly dug fighting position. Lying beside the old vet was Eugene, talking over the handset to a gunship platoon leader who was inbound for his first firing pass.

Blake heard the sound of the beating chopper blades but was too busy with Vincent's bullet wounds to look up. The Italian had been hit three times in the back of the legs, twice in one leg and once in the other. With bloody hands Blake ripped Vincent's pant legs off and used them to cover the horrible exit wounds that had blown away large pieces of muscle. Vincent was passing in and out of consciousness from the excruciating pain.

Lee finished dressing Bradshaw's shoulder wound and inspected the moaning soldier's palm where the bayonet had passed through. The puncture wound was bleeding profusely on both sides. With his good arm Lee reached over, picked up Bradshaw's helmet and pulled the cloth cover off. He poked Bradshaw.

"Willie," he said softly, "ya gonna have to sit up and help me. Put this cover around your hand, and we'll use the elastic helmet band to keep it in place. Come on, Willie, ya gotta get up an' help me."

Bradshaw's eyes fluttered. He rose to a seated position, groaning aloud from the stabbing pain that ran up his neck and down his arm. He shuddered, but focused his tear-filled eyes, took the helmet cover in his good hand, and laid it over the bleeding wound. Grimacing from his own wound, Lee laid the helmet's elastic band across the material and wrapped it around loosely. He looked up into Bradshaw's eyes. "I'm gonna have to tighten it up. It's gonna hurt."

Bradshaw gritted his teeth and nodded. Lee began to pull the band tight when a shot rang out. Bradshaw's hand was yanked from Lee's hand as the soldier's body jerked back. He lay staring up blankly, unseeing. A small hole just below his right eye began oozing deep crimson blood. Lee fell back just as the second sniper's bullet echoed through the forest.

Blake looked up after the first shot and saw the muzzle flash of the second. He dropped behind Vincent's machine gun, aimed at the tree branches thirty meters away, and pressed the trigger.

Eugene watched the gunship's rockets streaking toward the treeline and prayed the pilot was on target. Five men had been killed within the small perimeter in the past five minutes. Nobody could as much as move their fingers without drawing fire. Wounded were screaming for medics and their mothers, but no one dared move to help.

Safe in their hole, Shawn lay huddled with Quail and Eugene. They had a good view of the chopper's gun run. The hot sun made the hole a sauna, but none of them complained.

The second gunship came directly overhead. Green tracers flashed by its nose, but that didn't stop the co-pilot from pushing the red fire button, unleashing the 40-millimeter cannon under the bird's nose. The wide-barreled swivel gun thumped out stubby little rounds that exploded in a succession of resonating *ka-boom*s.

Behind the gunship came the A1-E Sky Raiders, which swooped in and unleashed 250 pounds of iron death. Shawn rose up after the fourth bomb had shaken him almost senseless. He had to have a fresh breath of air.

Quail grabbed Shawn's web harness and pulled him back down. "Not yet! The bastards are tied in the trees!"

Shawn took his helmet off and put it on the end of his rifle, then raised it up above the lip of the hole. Nothing happened. The other men in the perimeter began stirring, and a medic jumped up to help a gut-shot screaming soldier.

Quail lifted his head, seeing the activity, and tapped Shawn. "Okay, but stay low."

Shawn looked at the treeline and saw why it was now safe. The trees that used to ring the clearing were nothing but blown and shattered sticks. Eugene brushed off his rifle and inserted a new magazine. "We gotta find the team."

Shawn glanced at Quail as he put on his helmet and inserted a new magazine. "Stay here and don't move. We'll be back."

Quail rose up and tested his movement, trying not to show the pain he felt. "I can't feel it anymore. It's just a scratch."

Shawn's face showed his rage. "Get down and stay put!"

Quail picked up his rifle and stared back just as coldly. "Fuck you, Irish. I'm senior here. You take point and take it slow and easy. Keep an eye on the trees. Eugene, you keep your eyes on the flanks. I'll take drag and cover our rear. Let's go."

Shawn's jaw muscles rippled as he stared a hole through Quail. The sergeant major ignored the stare and spoke through clenched teeth. "Move out, Sergeant."

As soon as the three men got up and began moving, the Alpha Company commander barked, "Hey, where are you going? We need that radio here."

Eugene slipped the radio backpack off his shoulders and tossed it toward the commander. "Sir, we have to find the rest of our squad."

The captain's eyes widened. "Are you all crazy! Didn't you hear the reports of what's happening back there?"

Quail patted the officer's shoulder as he passed by. "Sir, we're all fuckin' crazy for being here in the first place. See ya later."

Blake sat against the side of the shallow hole looking at Bradshaw's dull, still-open eyes. He had pushed the bodies out of the hole to form a human wall for protection. The decision had not been easy for him, but it had to be done if others were to survive. Lee sat beside Blake, listening to the sounds around them. The bombs and gunships were all working to their north, but nearby the shooting had died down to only single gunshots by snipers. The Charlie Company soldier slapped in a full magazine. "I'm Bobby Hastings," he whispered. "I . . . I wanted you guys at least to know my name . . . in case."

Feeling too weak to talk, Blake rolled his head toward the soldier and weakly lifted his hand. Hastings shook it and fell silent again.

Vincent lay on his stomach. Blake let his hand fall to the soldier's back, and he patted it while shutting his eyes and trying to will what little strength he had left into his unconscious friend.

Shawn ducked behind a tree to rest and get his emotions under control. He had passed so many dead Americans, he had lost count after fifty. The sad thing was that most had died without a chance. No one had organized a perimeter, so the men had been left to fight an unorganized, confusing battle. Some had fired wildly, shooting fellow squad members who had sought protection in the tall grass. The saddest thing was passing by the countless wounded who had begged for help and water. They lay unattended in pools of their own blood and filth. All the medics had been killed or wounded early in the ambush.

Shawn turned and glanced over his shoulder. Quail was putting on a good show, but his face couldn't hide the pain he was feeling. The old soldier's lip was bleeding where he had bitten through it, trying to contain his agony. A little way ahead, Shawn saw a huge tree surrounded by dead NVA. Surprisingly, he had not seen many enemy dead during the search.

He called out softly, as he had done during the movement back. "Friendly moving forward. Don't shoot."

Lee sat up. "Did you hear that?"

Blake bit his lip and nodded. The sound of the familiar voice was like a miracle drug. He lifted his head. "We're over here, Irish. For God's sake hurry."

"They're okay," Shawn said to Eugene. He got up and cautiously crept forward, stepping over the dead Vietnamese. As he dropped to his knee at the edge of the fighting position, he at once felt nauseated and elated. Three of his men were alive, but they were all hanging on to life by a thread.

Eugene crawled directly into the hole. He patted Blake and Lee on the shoulder and sat down in front of Vincent. With tears trickling down his face, he lifted the Italian's head. "I'm here, Vinny, just I like I promised. I'm here, man."

Quail pressed himself against the tree to make a smaller target. One look at the squad told him they couldn't carry them all back. "Irish, we're gonna have to expand the position and wait for help."

Shawn looked at the Charlie Company soldier who was staring at him wide-eyed. "I'm Flynn, the platoon leader of these men. You're now an official member of my platoon. Start digging."

Quail finished dressing Vincent's leg wounds with battle dressings. He put the thought out of his mind that the soldier would never be able to walk normally again. He was alive, and right now that was good enough. He checked Lee's shattered arm to make sure the bleeding had stopped, then inspected Blake's leg. The wound was nasty, but with proper care he would recover with a year or so of therapy. The Georgian was not as lucky. In fact, it wasn't likely that he would keep his arm, from the elbow down. The bullet had shattered the bones in his forearm, destroying all the muscles around them.

Shawn tossed down his entrenching tool. It was going to be tight, but at least they were dug in deep enough to protect themselves from the grazing fire that had gotten most of the other men he had passed by earlier.

Shawn tapped his plastic rifle stock to get the attention of Eugene and Hastings. "That's deep enough. Eugene, crawl out and get the water and ammo from the dead. Hastings, you cover him."

Blake finished making an inventory and held out three grenades. "We've got five to six magazines per man and these three grenades."

Shawn took the grenades and tossed Quail one. "We'll be okay. A relief force will be here any minute."

Shawn looked at his watch. It was almost six P.M. He had been waiting for almost two hours, and there was still no sign of a relief force. The shooting had increased again, and most of the firing was NVA, not American. He scooted next to Quail, who was looking pale and weak. He leaned close to the old soldier's ear. "They should have been here by now. Somethin' is fucked up."

Quail slowly rolled his eyes toward his friend. "I know. Maybe they put them in another L.Z. and they're moving overland."

Shawn listened to the exchange of gunfire to the north and south, and to the artillery making impact from the direction of the L.Z. A burst of AK bullets cracked overhead, shattering tree branches above him. He knew the NVA had long ago recovered from the bombing and were now probably moving in to finish off pockets of resistance. Shawn could tell the perimeter at the L.Z. was holding its own and that there must have been another such perimeter to the south. He surmised that the NVA flank attack had struck the middle of the column and had not hit the rear battalion company.

He leaned over to Quail again. "We gotta get a radio to call in arty, or they'll overrun us as soon as it gets dark."

Quail's eyes closed. "I know what you're thinkin'. You can't go. Send somebody else."

Shawn handed Eugene his pistol and gave Hastings a full bandolier. "Remember what I told ya. Stay low, and move slow. It's gettin' dark. Call out ahead of you softly so our own guys don't fire you up. I saw the dead RTO no more than fifty meters up the trail. Get his radio and spare battery, if he's got one, and get your asses back here ASAP."

Eugene stuffed the pistol in his web belt with a nod. "No sweat, we'll be back in te-te time." He leaned over to Vincent, who was now conscious. "I'll be back, man. Bank on it."

Vincent tried to put his hand up to touch his friend, but he was too weak and it fell limply to the ground. Eugene patted his shoulder and crawled up the embankment.

Five minutes later Eugene halted at the sound of a trooper screaming, *"No! No please, mother of God, noooooo!"*

A series of shots rang out, ending the plea. Eugene felt sickened, and to think of something else, he quickly double-checked his selector switch. He got up into a low crouch, then took four steps and froze. Ten feet away, five NVA were searching the dead from Delta Company. One Vietnamese was removing the dog tags from the neck of a Negro soldier, whose face was matted with blood, grass, and dirt.

Eugene placed his finger on the trigger, but he didn't fire. His mission was more important than getting revenge. He began to lower himself slowly, to hide in the grass, when one of the soldiers abruptly turned around and faced him. Their eyes met for an instant, and Eugene fired.

Hastings shot one more of the souvenir hunters before the other three spun around firing. Eugene switched to rock and roll and sprayed the men as he backed up, then turned and ran. Hastings did the same and sprinted back down the trail. Ten meters back Eugene stopped and took up a position behind a small ant mound. Having already inserted a new magazine, he let Hastings pass by before raising his rifle to blast and run again. Hastings was three steps past him when two more NVA stepped onto the trail and opened fire. Hastings never had a chance even to lift his rifle. He was almost cut in two at the waist. Eugene spun around and blasted the two men with a long burst. He began to run when he was hit in the back with three rounds from the soldiers behind him. Sinking to his knees, he tried to lift his rifle, but it fell from his hands.

The lead NVA soldier who had done the shooting stepped off the trail to change magazines and let his comrade behind him finish off the black Yankee.

Shawn charged forward screaming and shooting from the hip. His wild charge startled the three remaining Vietnamese, who bolted for the protection of the trees. Shawn dropped to his knee beside Eugene, aimed and shot one of the men in the back of the head. Grabbing Eugene, he tossed the small man over his shoulder and backed up, with rifle ready.

Blake blanched when his sergeant laid Eugene on the rim of the fighting position. Eugene was bouncing on the ground trying to breathe. Quail tore at the soldier's shirt and slapped his hand over the exit wound, which was bubbling frothy pink foam. Immediately Eugene took in a labored breath from his one uncollapsed lung.

"Plastic!" the sergeant major commanded, nodding toward the discarded cover to a field bandage. Lee scooped it up and gave it to the old veteran.

Shawn listened for more marauding NVA and heard what he prayed he wouldn't. "Get a grenade ready. Everybody get down," he whispered as he raised his rifle.

Blake took the grenade from Quail's web belt and crawled next to Shawn. The sun had set ten minutes before, leaving the forest in fading twilight. The tall grass fifteen meters to their front rustled with approaching men.

Shawn pressed himself against the tree and whispered softly, "Throw it if I fire."

Blake straightened the pin and put his finger through the ring. Shawn waited with his finger on the trigger, praying that the soldiers who appeared would be the lead elements of the relief force. The grass parted and a small Vietnamese wearing a faded pith helmet stepped forward, carrying an AK-47 at the ready. Shawn shot the soldier in the face, lowered the barrel, and fired a sweeping burst into the stalks at knee level as Blake tossed the grenade.

Both men ducked back behind the tree, and Shawn immediately changed magazines. The cracking explosion sent shrapnel into the trunk and whizzing through the branches. Shawn heard a scream and stepped out to fire. A second passed, then ten, without any more movement. He lowered his rifle and sank down to rest. He didn't want to think about their chances, and he didn't want to face his men's stares. He flicked the selector to safe and built up his courage enough to whisper, "How's Gene?"

Quail kept working on trying to make Eugene's bandage airtight while he still had enough light to see. He finished tying the knot over the wound and shook his head. "He's in trouble, Irish. He needs more help than I can give him. He's got three rounds in the back. Only one of 'em exited."

Vincent raised his head from the ground. He'd heard the sergeant major. "Huh-uh, he's gonna make it. You wait and see." He dragged himself to his friend and took Eugene's limp hand in his own. "We . . . we gonna make it together, huh, Gene. Gene? Gene, you're gonna make it. You gotta make it."

Blake turned away and stared into the deepening darkness. He knew he had to be strong, but he couldn't keep his eyes from pooling. He concentrated on the woodline. They'd pay. The bastards were gonna pay.

Quail jumped feeling the hand on his shoulder. Shawn leaned over and whispered, "They're gonna be coming."

Quail had been dozing and for a moment and thought that his dream had come true, that the relief force had finally made it. But he felt a .45 being pushed into his hand and heard Shawn whisper again, "I'm gonna try and draw them away. Keep the kids quiet."

Quail began to protest, but the sergeant was already crawling out of the position. Quail put his hand out to his front and felt along the edge of the hole to get his bearings in the pitch-blackness. He moved to his left, where he knew Blake was located. He touched the squad leader's shoulder and whispered, "Irish has crawled out to try and draw them away. Don't shoot unless I do or they're on top of us. Pass it on to the others not to fire."

Blake had heard the horrible sounds too, and knew his sergeant was trying to buy time. If anyone in the fighting position fired a weapon, the NVA would know exactly where they were. It would be only a matter of minutes before they would be overrun. Blake turned around and touched Eugene, who was still wheezing. Then he moved his hand and touched Vincent, who lay by his friend. "Vinny, you awake?"

"Yo. It . . . it hurts too bad to sleep."

"Keep real quiet. They're coming this way."

"Give me a rifle, I gotta have a rifle."

Lee was sitting beside Blake and turned around, holding an M-16. "Here, Vinny, it's Willie's. It's got a full mag an' ready ta fire."

Blake leaned closer to Lee. "Irish went out."

Lee lowered his head. "I figured he would. I reckon I oughta go out in the other direction an' do the same thing."

"You stay right where you are. I need you on the M-60," Blake commanded.

Lee reached out in the darkness and touched his squad leader's arm. "Ace . . . I been meanin' to tell ya somethin.' I . . . I just wanted ya ta know . . . when ya called me 'brother' back at Catecka, it made me feel good. I wanted ta tell ya that . . . brother."

Blake patted Lee's leg and silently crawled toward Quail.

Shawn had crawled straight out from the tree, heading east, feeling the ground in front of him and trying to commit the path to memory. He would have to find his way back if the approaching NVA stopped their search. He had heard men screaming in the distance followed by AK shots, so he knew the NVA were searching for the wounded and killing them. The only chance for his squad's survival was in not being found in the darkness. The branches and leaves of the big tree blocked out even the starlight. Shawn crawled over a torn body and breathed through his mouth so as not to gag. Artillery was hitting to the north, but he heard a blood-chilling scream that seemed only ten meters away. He stopped to regain control of his shaking. He knew that sounds carried farther in the night and that he had to concentrate more. He crawled another few feet and felt another body. He stopped. This place was as good as any. He could use the body for protection, and he was far enough away to draw whoever came searching for his men. Checking his rifle one more time, he became perfectly still and stared into the darkness.

Quail scooted next to Lee. "Reb, you gonna be able to handle the 'sixty with just one arm?"

Lee had thought it was Blake who had moved next to him. The sergeant major's voice surprised him. "I can handle it, Sergeant Major. Where's Ace?"

Quail leaned closer and touched Lee's leg with his hand. "He said to give you this."

Lee felt suddenly weak as he dropped his hand and touched the sergeant major's arm. He felt the watch and closed his eyes. "When did he go out?"

Quail put the Rolex into Lee's hand. "He had to go, son, just like Irish did. They know it's the only chance we have for the wounded."

Lee squeezed the heavy watch, praying he would be able to give it back to his brother.

Shawn heard a twig snap and stopped breathing. Pushing the safety off very gently, he turned toward the sound and raised his rifle. Suddenly a flashlight beam shone through the darkness and panned the ground only five feet in front of him. A Vietnamese voice spoke softly and he heard what sounded like five or six men approaching through the grass. The light panned left and spotlighted a dead NVA soldier. The man with the light blurted a command, and two of the other men came toward the body. Shawn could see only their feet in the yellow halo, and he heard them mumbling to each other. The flashlight wavered and began moving again. Shawn relaxed as the beam moved off to his left. He took in a deep breath and was about to lower his rifle when he heard more voices coming from behind him. He turned around and froze. Three dark figures were silhouetted against the starry sky. They were only a few meters away and moving in his direction. The first NVA soldier walked past within inches of Shawn's head. The second tripped over the feet of the NVA corpse and fell beside Shawn. Mumbling, the man got to his feet and spoke to the third soldier behind him, who stopped and turned on his flashlight.

At point-blank range Shawn shot the Vietnamese holding the light, then spun, shooting the second man in the legs. He rolled just as the lead soldier fired wildly at the ground where he had seen the blinding M-16's muzzle flashes. Shawn stopped rolling and jumped to his feet firing from the hip at the leader. The young North Vietnamese was struck three times by bullets that ripped through his heart and lungs. He toppled over his screaming, wounded comrade. Shawn closed in and snapped off another shot, ending the soldier's scream just as shots rang out from the direction of the other group that had passed by. Shawn fell to the ground searching for the AK-47s. He found one and rose, firing the entire magazine in the direction of the attacking NVA. Dropping the weapon, he ran northward ten strides and hit the ground.

Talking to each other to keep dressed on line, the Vietnamese walked forward, constantly shooting at the ground to their front. Shawn crawled backward as fast as he could to get out of their line of advance. Bullets thudded into the ground only inches from his head. He quit crawling when the flames of the weapon passed him only five feet away. He raised his rifle and cussed himself, remembering he hadn't changed magazines. The NVA soldier fired again, the muzzle flash lighting his khaki uniform and face. Shawn used the sound to cover the sound of his changing magazines. He waited until another Vietnamese fired to release the bolt that slammed forward.

Ready now, Shawn kept an eye on the line of men. He knew the tree was off to his left and that if they kept to their present direction, the NVA would miss his squad. He drew in a deep breath of cordite-filled air. He had done it. But for how much longer? he wondered.

Blake lay beside an ant mound twenty meters west of the tree. He had heard the shooting to the east and knew it was Shawn delaying the enemy. He prayed his sergeant had not been discovered. Lying still, he could hear the artillery hitting north, south, and west of him, as it had been for hours, though until now he had somehow put the noise out of his mind. He cussed the explosions, for they covered the closer, early warning sounds that would tell him if the enemy was coming. He tensed, feeling ants crawl up his pant leg toward his wound, and he began to crawl away from the mound. He had pulled himself along the ground for only two feet when he heard a Vietnamese voice directly behind him. Blake froze.

The NVA squad leader turned and ordered his men not to come forward until the shooting stopped to their front. He kneeled down by the ant mound and looked at the distant muzzle flashes.

Blake could hear the man behind him breathing and heard him slap his body. The ants, he thought.

The NVA sergeant stood, took a step forward, and felt a body beneath his foot. He stopped and felt with his foot for firm ground only inches from Blake's thigh, and took another step. Kneeling down again, he felt for the body to see if it was one of his countrymen or a Yankee. If it was a Yankee, he might be lucky and get cigarettes and a watch. All Yankees wore watches. His hand touched Blake's helmet and he scooted closer.

Blake threw his elbow up, striking the startled soldier just below the chin, knocking him back onto the ground. Throwing himself on top of the writhing man, Blake grabbed for the soldier's throat. The stunned sergeant gagged and kicked to free himself, but Blake had already dug his fingers around his larnyx, trying to rip it out. The soldier's eyes bulged as he tore frantically at Blake's face with his fingernails. Despite the excruciating pain, Blake dug his fingers deeper and squeezed as he pushed down with all his weight. He felt the cartilage crackle and suddenly give within his hand. The sergeant's hands fell limp to the ground. Blake released his grip, then yanked the man's head up and twisted until he heard a sickening pop. Breathing in labored gasps, he rolled off the body and patted around in the grass until he found his rifle. He collapsed to the ground. His stinging face felt like he had walked into a spinning propeller, and his leg wound was sending lightning bolts of pain up his back and into the base of his skull. Feeling as if he were about to pass out, he lowered his head to the dirt and lay open-mouthed, sucking in air. He knew he had to move, but he didn't have the strength even to lift his head. Biting down, he closed his eyes. Another shuddering bolt of pain tore through him.

There was a loud pop overhead.

"Motherfuckers," Quail hissed as the ground around him suddenly became golden in the flare's light. "Our guys oughta know better than to shoot those fuckin' light bulbs."

Shawn flattened himself and closed one eye. He raised his head slightly and saw to his horror that the line of NVA were coming back in his direction. They had all squatted down and were looking up at the sputtering flare. Stare, you fuckers! Blind yourselves! he screamed to himself.

Blake had moved only ten feet when the flare popped overhead. He lay totally exposed in a clearing surrounded by ant mounds and bodies, but he didn't dare move.

Quail checked Eugene and Vincent in the glow and began to turn back when he saw a line of NVA coming from the south. They were twenty feet away, walking quickly, obviously trying to make it to the shadows of the tree. He glanced at Lee, who had already put the stock of the M-60 firmly against his shoulder and had placed his finger on the trigger.

"Not yet," Quail whispered.

Shawn heard the NVA squad leader issue the command to his men and saw him point toward the tree. There was no choice. Shawn lifted his rifle. Taking aim at the squad leader, he fired a single shot. The squad leader stood for a full second with a dazed expression before sinking to his knees and falling face first to the ground. The NVA had their sides to Shawn when he had fired and hadn't seen the muzzle flash. They reacted by hitting the ground and firing wildly in every direction. Shawn pulled a grenade from his web belt and yanked out the pin. Rising, he tossed the small bomb and threw himself flat.

Seeing a grenade hit directly in front of him, the center NVA soldier jumped up and ran for the protection of the tree.

Quail raised his .45 and shook his head at Lee not to fire. He waited until the scared North Vietnamese soldier was almost on top of him before rising up and firing. The grenade exploded the same instant, throwing out its deadly shrapnel. Quail doubled over, hit with the tearing fragments, and fell over Vincent's legs. The Italian screamed in anguish.

Shawn heard the scream from the direction of the squad's position, as did the remaining NVA, who began firing toward the tree. Shawn jumped up and ran toward the prone soldiers, all of whom were facing away from him.

Blake dug his elbows into the ground and pushed himself toward the tree, having heard Vincent's scream. His leg wound sent tremors up his spine, but he kept moving.

Ten feet from the first soldier, who had just tossed a stick grenade toward the tree, Shawn fired, stitching him across the back. He flicked the selector to automatic mode, then pressed back the trigger and hosed two more NVA across their backs before running out of ammunition. He dropped to the ground, rolled, and dug into his bandolier for another magazine. The remaining two NVA spun around, firing at the exposed Yankee killer.

The smoking, bamboo-handled grenade hit between Eugene and Quail. The sergeant major was leaning against the back of the fighting position, holding his stomach with blood-covered hands. Too weak and in too much pain to try and pick up the grenade or yell a warning, the old soldier fell forward on top of the smoking explosive.

The partially muffled explosion tossed the veteran over against Eugene. Splattered with Quail's blood and pieces of sticky flesh, Lee spun around from the M-60 and winced at the sight of the veteran's open chest cavity smoking in the eerie light. He turned around and pulled the machine-gun butt into his shoulder.

Blake had risen up to his knee and seen the remaining two NVA soldiers clearly. He fired at the first one, who had just unleashed a long burst toward Shawn.

Shawn was knocked over onto his back with the hammer-blow impact of bullets tearing through his shoulder, chest, and side. He lay looking up at the hissing flare, feeling as if he were falling through space. The flare's light grew dimmer as he fell faster and faster. Struggling, he fought to keep his eyes open. He felt cold now, and he trembled as he felt his body withdrawing into itself, shriveling as he continued downward into the darkness. His eyes fluttered. He thought of his wife and child, whom he so desperately wanted to hold. Cindy's image took the place of the distant flare's light, and he closed his eyes to be with her one more time. Cindy . . . I'm . . . I'm so sorry. The image of the small woman faded like the flare's light as Shawn slipped silently into the peaceful darkness.

Blake shifted his rifle to the next target and began to press the trigger when the M-60 machine gun roared, spitting out a continuous tongue of red flame. The North Vietnamese soldier was thrown back with pounding bullets ripping through his body. Jerking, the limp body turned into crimson mush as over thirty bullets obliterated muscle, bone, and sinew. The machine gun finally ceased as the flare overhead sputtered and darkness again cloaked the land.

Blake lay back down and stiffly turned around, knowing others would be drawn to the sound of the M-60. He slapped in his last full magazine and lowered his head to wait. Staring at the darkness, he heard a defiant voice in the distance: "Gary Owen, you motherfuckeeeers."

Blake smiled a crooked smile and whispered to the night. "The team, ya dink bastards." Tears began trickling down his cheeks, but this time he didn't try to hold them back. Only the night saw, and only those in the team would understand. He felt incredibly sad, yet warm with the knowledge they had tried. His father would never understand the feeling, but it didn't matter. He, Blake Alexander, leader of the first squad, had no regrets. He had given everything. His brothers knew he had done his best.

A whistling shell tore through the stillness of the sky. The flare sent out a fountain of sparks and burst into a blossom of golden light.

Blake raised his head and saw five khaki-uniformed men creeping toward the tree.

No regrets, he whispered to himself, and rose up shooting.

Lee's chin dropped to his chest, but he snapped back up and blinked his eyes. He shook his head to try and clear the weariness for a little longer and stared into the blackness. It had been two hours since he had heard the last exchange of gunfire to the east. The only other sounds had been that of the artillery and a wounded NVA soldier who screamed until he ran out of breath, passed out, came to, and screamed again. Lee shifted his position to stretch his legs and felt damp stickiness on his knees. The bottom of the foxhole was covered in Quail's coagulated blood.

He leaned back and felt Eugene's chest to see if he was still breathing. He was, but he could hear gurgling each time his friend exhaled. Vincent was cradling Eugene in his arms, rocking back and forth. "Vinny," Lee whispered, "don't hold him so tight."

Vincent mumbled and kept rocking. Lee lifted his numbed, blood-soaked arm and bit his lip. He wanted the flash of pain to keep him awake. His eyes watered as he released his arm and leaned forward against the dirt wall.

Minutes later Vincent broke the silence with a cracking whisper. "Re-Reb?"

Lee raised his chin from the M-60's butt. "Yeah?"

"Gene's dead," Vincent said, sobbing quietly.

Lee closed his eyes. He felt empty of life. "I—I'm sorry, Vinny."

"Where's Ace? I gotta tell Ace."

"He's not here, Vinny. He'll be back soon."

"I'll tell the sergeant major. He was gonna go too."

"He's dead, Vinny."

With tears streaming down his dirty cheeks, Vincent raised his head. "But who's—who's gonna go to the parade?"

Lee rested his chin on the butt without answering. He didn't know anymore.

Vincent jerked with a spasm and moaned, waking Lee, who had drifted off. Lee opened his eyes and blinked to make sure he wasn't dreaming. The sky had turned gray in the east, and he could make out the dark forms of trees he had not been able to see for over ten hours. Sometime after the NVA soldier had finally quit screaming, he had succumbed to weariness and blood loss and had closed his eyes to go home. He had swung on the front porch of his house, smelling the honeysuckle instead of the blood of friends, and he had heard the buzzing of june bugs instead of artillery and the screams of wounded men.

A loud burst of gunfire snapped his attention toward the direction of the shooting. He heard a faint sound that tore through his heart.

"Lee . . . Lee?"

Lee rose up, looking over Bradshaw's stiff body. Blake was only five feet away, lying on his side and curled up like a baby. Dragging his useless arm, Lee crawled out of the fighting position and thanked God for the miracle he had prayed for.

Lee knelt over Blake and brushed dirt from his pale face. "I'm here, brother."

Blake's eyes clouded. "I . . . I didn't want to be alone."

Lee looked for wounds and leaned closer. "I'm here now. Take it easy and let me turn ya over."

Blake's eyes rolled up as Lee gently began to turn him onto his back. Lee gagged. A portion of his friend's abdomen was gone. "Lee, why couldn't he have smiled . . . just once smiled at me?"

Lee closed his eyes and clenched his teeth. Slowly he rolled Blake back into the fetal position. "He should have, Ace. Your daddy should have." Looking up, he screamed silently to the heavens, *Why God? Why?*

Blake raised his hand toward Lee's face. "Don't cry, brother. I'm here."

Lee took his hand and saw Blake's eyes slowly begin to close. *"Ace? . . . Ace? No! Nooooooooo!"*

Lieutenant Colonel Duc listened to the reports from his operations officer and slowly stood. There was only one decision left for him to make. "We have paid enough. Inform the companies to pull back immediately. We will take our wounded to the division hospital and march on to the assembly area and await further orders."

The operations officer lowered his head. "Should I report our losses to division headquarters?"

Duc put his hand on the tired major's shoulder. "No, my friend, only a battalion commander should tell his division commander that his unit has only thirty percent of its men remaining." The colonel sighed and stared into the darkness. "The Americans fought well, but they must make the same report to their higher command. Today, this battle has no victor. The winner of such a struggle can only be decided in time. The historians will have to write the final chapter."

The major looked up at his colonel with searching eyes. "But so many have died."

The colonel kept his distant stare. "It is just the beginning."

Sergeant Barry Devlin held his fist up to halt the men behind him. Holding his rifle ready, he cautiously moved forward past the NVA bodies. He had seen too many Seventh Cavalry soldiers shot in the head to be shocked by the sight of more. He prepared himself and looked down at the still soldier, but then sighed in relief. The sergeant's chest was rising and falling, although he was unconscious and shot up badly. Devlin turned around and yelled, "We got another live one! Medic up!"

A private behind Devlin pointed toward a large tree to his right. "Hey, there's another one over here." He ran over and knelt down beside Lee, who was sitting in the fighting position beside Vincent. "Hey, man, we came to get you out."

Lee's eyes slowly moved to the private. "We're stayin' together."

The private checked Vincent's pulse and rose, yelling, "Medic!" He quickly checked the others and stood as the medic approached, motioning to Vincent and Lee. "These two are it. The others are dead."

Lee screamed to blot out the soldier's words. He rose to his feet. "We're *all* stayin' together!"

The medic took out his morphine ampule and approached Lee, talking softly. "Take it easy, trooper, we're gonna get you all out. Sit down and let me have a look at that arm."

Lee didn't feel the prick of the needle as he nodded toward Blake's body. "He's my brother."

The medic glanced at the dead soldier and the others lying in the bloody fighting position. He patted Lee's back. "They're all our brothers now."

The stone-faced Charlie troop commander unhooked his shoulder harness and stepped out of the Huey. He tossed his flight helmet to the crew chief and faced the liaison sergeant who had called him.

"What the *fuck* happened?" he snarled.

The sergeant motioned toward the tarmac where the wounded were waiting for extraction back to An Khe hospital. "Sir, the Second Battalion walked into some kind of ambush yesterday afternoon and lost a bunch of people. I called for you 'cause some of your men are here waiting on medical extraction."

The captain began striding toward the wounded, shaking his head. "Nobody reported a battle to us. The reports we got were that it was a small firefight and there were just a few casualties. Nobody said a fucking thing about—" The captain abruptly halted, seeing that the rows of wounded extended far beyond the tarmac. "My God! How many wounded are there?"

The sergeant gulped. "Sir, this is the last bunch. We already sent two Chinook loads out. They had over 120 wounded and . . . and around 140 killed, with four missing in action. They got chopped up real bad."

Wide-eyed, the captain faced the sergeant. "You're telling me that a 500-man battalion had over 360 casualties?"

"Yes, sir, it's horrible. The commanding general didn't even know about it till this morning. The brigade fucked up. They didn't tell higher what was going on. Nobody knew the contact was that bad. Nobody."

The captain turned and looked at the rows of filthy, wounded men. "Those poor bastards did. Where are my men?"

The sergeant lowered his head and began walking toward the third row.

The captain felt faint as he walked down the row of young men covered in blood-caked bandages and pieces of uniform. Each face and wound made the captain feel smaller and more helpless. The sergeant stopped and knelt down by Shawn, who had IV needles and tubes in both arms. An exhausted private who had been lightly wounded in the neck held the two clear plastic bags above him.

The captain bit his lip. He had been told some of his Blues had been casualties of the fight, but he never expected one of them to be his platoon leader. Just yesterday he had received a Red Cross message for the sergeant and had planned a celebration when he got back. Somehow he had never thought a man with so much combat experience could lie stripped to the waist covered in bloody bandages. Flynn knew all the tricks and secrets of survival. The condition of the veteran sent shivers up his spine. A myth was shattered. Flynn was mortal and vulnerable just like the rest of them.

"Where are the others?" he asked the sergeant.

The sergeant motioned to the two men lying one man over from Shawn. The captain's eyes showed his pain.

"And the rest of them?"

The sergeant lowered his eyes and slowly shook his head. Oh God, thought the officer, and looked at Shawn's dirt-streaked face. He knelt down and spoke softly. "Sergeant Flynn, its me, Captain Gammon."

Shawn's eyes fluttered open.

"Sergeant Flynn, I came as soon as I heard. I'm sorry I wasn't here earlier. You . . . you need anything? You want me to do anything for you?"

Shawn closed his misting eyes and spoke in a haunting whisper. "Bring them back. Bring them back, sir."

Gammon held the sergeant's hand. "I can't do that. God, I wish I could, but I can't. There's nothing anybody can do for them. But there is hope for others. Life will go on, Sergeant. I got a Red Cross message for you yesterday. You have a new son. Seven pounds, eleven ounces. Your wife and baby are doing fine."

Shawn rolled his head to the side. His tears dropped to the canvas stretcher. "Sir . . . find him for me. Find Sergeant Major John Quail's body. I want it done right, sir. He was . . . was with us, and he was a friend. Find him, sir, please."

Gammon patted Shawn's leg. "I will. Take care, Sergeant. We're going to miss you . . . the cav is going to miss you." The pilot stood. "Think about your son. He's what's important now."

The captain moved down and talked to Lee for a few minutes, but couldn't speak to Vincent, for he was unconscious. Walking back toward his helicopter, Gammon spoke over his shoulder to the sergeant following behind. "If these men aren't outta here in the next ten fucking minutes, you call me on the radio. I'll send every fucking slick I've got here to get them back to the hospital. Where are the KIAs?"

"They took them to Camp Holloway, sir."

"Call Holloway's morgue. Tell them I'll be there in twenty minutes. I want to see the bodies of my men and Sergeant Major John Quail. Tell the morgue this cav commander is gonna pay his respects to his fellow cavalry-man. Got it?"

The sergeant nodded. "Got it, sir."

The captain climbed into the cockpit and put on his helmet. Grabbing for his shoulder harness, he stopped and closed his eyes. The co-pilot looked at his commander. "Sir, you all right?"

Gammon leaned back in the seat, staring at the Plexiglas. "This war sucks."

The co-pilot nodded. "They all do, sir."

Colonel Quan closed the report journal after making the last entry. He handed the book to the operations sergeant. "Pack it with the other things."

General Man put down his teacup. "What were your last words concern-ing the battle?"

Quan faced his commander. "I wrote that the 325th Division met the new American Helicopter Division and a great battle was fought. I wrote that there were many lessons learned, and that their losses were great and ours 'acceptable.' "

Man nodded with satisfaction. "The party will understand our sacrifice. The Americans have been taught that the price of winning this war will be too high."

"And what have we learned?" Quan asked, staring at the general coldly.

Man returned the icy stare. "What we have always known. Through sacrifice victory is achieved."

Quan lowered his eyes and stood. He knew all too well that the struggle was just beginning and that there would be many more of his countrymen sacrificed for the fatherland. He knew that he too must sacrifice, for he would have to give his soul to men like the general. He came to attention and raised his eyes to his commander. "What are your orders to the regiments, my general?"

1966

32

MARCH 1966

The cab rolled up the driveway to the mansion and came to a halt by the boxwood-lined walkway. The soldier in the backseat leaned forward and held out a ten-dollar bill. "Thank ya for the ride, and could ya call and tell 'em I'll need to be picked up in an hour?"

The cabbie took the bill. "I'll be back myself. It's a slow day anyway."

Lee Calhoon collected his small bag and stepped out of the cab. Looking up at the huge house, he adjusted his shoulder sling so it wouldn't bind his uniform. Then he straightened his cap and walked for the door.

A maid opened the oak doors only seconds after he rang the bell and looked over the thin soldier head to foot before speaking. "Mrs. Alexander is waiting in the sitting room."

Lee took off his cap and stepped into the spacious hallway. A leather-faced old man approached and held out his hand. "I'm Hank, the Alexanders' driver. Ace was like a—" The old man's eyes misted and he lowered his head. "Damn, I thought I didn't have any tears left . . . sorry." Taking in a breath, Hank again looked at the soldier. "I just wanted to tell ya, the Missus really appreciated your letter. It meant more than you'll ever know. Mr. Alexander thanks you too."

Lee's face tightened. "Is he here?"

Hank motioned Lee toward a room to their right. "Yes, but he's got a business meeting with his plant managers this morning. He sends his regrets. Mrs. Alexander is this way."

Lee followed the old man but stopped at the base of the staircase. "It's up there, isn't it?"

"What?" Hank asked, not understanding.

Lee began walking up the steps. "Blake told me it was on the landing."

Hank's eyes misted again. "He told ya about it? Hell, I guess y'all really were close. That boy tried his damnedest to put somethin' in that damn case."

Lee approached the glass trophy case, already hating it. He quickly glanced at the contents and walked back down the steps to meet Blake's mother.

Dana Alexander's hands shook as she poured tea. Her son's friend was polite enough to glance away.

"So, Lee, we finally meet. Is your arm healing?"

Lee lifted his casted arm. "They operated again a few weeks ago, and they'll tell me more when I get this thang off."

Dana gave him an exaggerated nod. "You let me know if I can do anything. I know some very fine doctors who will be more than willing to offer their services."

Lee forced a smile. "Thank you, ma'am."

Struggling, Dana stood, walked over to a sideboard and opened the lower door. She took out a folded flag, a small wooden box, and a scrapbook. She set the box of medals and scrapbook on the coffee table in front of Lee, but kept the flag. She sat down on the couch beside him and placed the flag in her lap.

"They gave me this after the funeral," she said, running her hand over the material reverently. "The young officer was very sweet and told me it—it—"

Lee had wondered how long it would take—he had seen the look in her eyes the instant he met her. Dana Alexander had been putting on a good show, but her heart had not been in the performance. Now she covered her face with her hands, unable to speak, and began to sob.

Lee placed his arm around her shoulder. "I loved him too, ma'am. I miss him."

Dana lowered her hands, and looking into Lee's eyes, transmitted her loss and pain. Lee nodded and they hugged each other.

Lee followed Dana into the hallway, and she motioned to the second door down on the left. "He's in there. Thank you for coming, Lee, and thank you from the bottom of my heart for telling me about my son. It meant everything to me to know."

Lee leaned over, kissing her cheek. He began to speak, but she put her finger to his lips. "I know. Do what you have to do. I understand." Turning around, Dana raised her head and walked up the stairs without looking back.

His jaw muscles rippling, Lee strode down the hallway to the second door. He slid the door back and walked into a regal office filled with oak book shelves and green leather furniture. David Alexander sat behind his seventeenth century French desk, looking at the soldier as if he were expected. Lee saw the father's resemblance to Blake in the gray eyes.

David smiled his business smile. "I was just about to see if you were still here. I finished my meeting early and—"

"You're lying," Lee said matter-of-factly. "Ya didn't wanna talk ta me, jus' like ya didn't want ta talk to your son. I reckoned ya wouldn't want ta see me." Lee reached in his blouse and took out a thick envelope. He tossed it on the desk. "While I was in the hospital, I wrote that for ya. It's your son's hopes and dreams that you never knew. I knew him . . . an' loved him and wanted ya ta at least know what you missed. I reckon you ain't gonna like it, but read it anyway. It's the son ya didn't know ya had."

Lee turned around and began to walk out, but stopped. He had one more important thing to do. He faced David again and held out his hand. "I want the key to your 'Alexander' case."

David pushed back in his chair trying to regain control of the situation. "Please, why don't you sit down. I have fifteen minutes before I have an appointment with—"

Lee spun around, marched out of the room and into the sitting room, where he picked up the flag and box of medals that the Army had given the family. He walked up the steps, taking them two at a time, and halted in front of the case. He put Blake's things on the oriental carpet and took his casted arm out of the sling.

"What do you think you're doing?" David said as he reached the top step. Lee looked at the case, then back to Blake's father. "Sir . . . I'm—I'm gonna—" Tears began trickling down his cheeks. "I'm gonna do what your son wanted more than anything in this world."

Lee winced as he smashed the glass with the cast. Glass slivers sliced his exposed knuckles, but he didn't feel a thing. Dripping blood, he picked up a large silver trophy from the center shelf and placed it gently on the carpet. Then he picked up the folded flag and laid it on the green velvet. In front of the flag he placed each medal, centering the two Silver Stars. When he was finished, he took a step back and raised his bleeding hand in a salute. "I know you're smiling up there, Ace. Ya did it."

Lowering his hand, he strode past David, who would not look at him, and walked down the stairs. He picked up his cap and bag, opened the front door, and stepped out into the cold February wind. He smiled and kept walking.

David Alexander stared at the flag and medals for a long time before reaching into the case to remove them.

"No, David! Don't touch them."

He turned to his wife, who stood at the top of the stairs with fire and remorse in her eyes. She took a step down. "I mean it. Don't touch them. I'm not hiding them or my son anymore. Blake died trying to prove himself to you . . . don't you understand that? He loved you, but he was too much like his father. He just couldn't say it."

David Alexander lowered his eyes and silently walked down the steps.

Cindy opened the door and helped Shawn to get out of the car. "Keep your eyes closed like ya promised."

The long two-day ride from Washington, D.C.'s Walter Reed Hospital had been uncomfortable for him, but wonderful. To be free at last, out of the hospital, on the open road with Cindy, after all the operations and small, yellow-painted rooms and white-uniformed nurses, was like riding through paradise. He couldn't seem to see, smell, or hear enough of his clean, abundant country. The neon signs, storefronts, clothes, restaurant food, and new cars were like drugs that stimulated his need for more. He had absorbed it all like a huge sponge. And he had enjoyed every minute, as long as Cindy was near him. Only when he was alone did he feel lost and fearful of his nagging memories.

To be back and really see the "world" again was heaven, but also troubling. Something was missing. He looked and searched during the trip but couldn't find it. The war, the war was missing in America. Nobody seemed to know or care that young men were struggling to stay alive and come home to see what he had seen these past days. The United States was not at war, only a few of her young men in fatigues were.

He had kept his hand on Cindy's shoulder and touched her silky hair while she drove, to remind himself she was real and it wasn't a dream. He couldn't stand not to be touching her or to feel her close. She was his strength, the one hope in the outside world that he had longed for. Cindy had come up to see him the first day he arrived from Camp Zama's hospital in Japan, and had been back every other weekend when the doctors had allowed her. The last week in Walter Reed she had stayed with him, and finally they had become husband and wife again. He had another six months of therapy to go, but the doctors had released him to Fort Benning's Martin Army Hospital to complete his recovery so he could go home.

Cindy was beside herself with joy and anticipation as she led Shawn down the walkway. "Keep your eyes closed a little longer. The trim needs paint, but . . . okay, open your eyes."

Shawn had already peeked as they had driven up to the house. Now, smiling in wonder, he took in every detail in seconds. The rough red-brick rancher with wood shingles sat back in the pines just like a picture-book home in a glossy magazine. It was perfect. He put his arm around his wife, needing to share his feelings. "I love it, honey. It . . . it looks like a real home."

Cindy kissed his cheek, with tears of happiness running down her cheeks. "I knew you'd like it. I just knew."

Shawn faced the house again, wanting to take it in his arms like his wife and shout out his joy. The front door opened, and he suddenly became weak. Cindy's sister came out holding his son. He had only seen the baby once, when June had come with Cindy two months before. It had been too difficult for Cindy to take the baby and get around Washington by herself.

Shawn couldn't stop the tears that began to pool as he took the little boy from June's arms and held him. Shawn loved his smell and his smallness.

Cindy hugged her two men. "Welcome home, Irish. We missed you."

Shawn kissed his son's forehead and whispered, "Did you hear that John Quail Flynn? Your daddy is home."

Vincent gripped the wheelchair's arms tighter as he looked down, cussing his emaciated thighs, which were covered in knotted pink and purple scar tissue. Because of bullet damage and infection, the doctors had removed most of both large thigh muscles.

Vincent locked the brakes of his wheelchair, clenched his teeth, and tried to stand for the second time in the past fifteen minutes. He only rose a few inches before falling back and almost blacking out from the stabbing pain. They had told him that to perform the simple act of standing up without his quadriceps was almost impossible without the aid of canes or some kind of support, but that with time and exercise, the other leg muscles would grow stronger and compensate for the loss. He'd be able to stand within six months and be able to walk in a year.

The Veterans Hospital day nurse of ward three, who was attending the patient in bed six, had watched Vincent's futile efforts. She raised a painted eyebrow and smacked her gum as she spoke. "Don'tcha think you're pushing it a little, Martino? The doc said your therapy wouldn't start till next month."

Vincent returned a scowl, his forearm muscles rippling as he clutched the wheelchair's arms with even more determination. "I'm walkin' the walk when I get back ta South Philly."

The nurse set down the tray of water pitchers and waddled over to the impatient Italian, knowing what was really bothering him. "Look, it's none'a my business, ya understand, but I think you oughta see that young girl. She drives a long way to come here every week, and I don't like telling her you don't wanna see her. It's gonna take time for you ta get back on your feet, and she might not wait that long, ya know what I mean?"

Vincent looked up at the rotund nurse whom the ward vets called "Bubble." She chewed gum as if it were a narcotic, and she had the figure of a basketball with legs. "Miss Bee, you're right. It ain't none'a your business. I don't want her to see me like this."

Bubble smirked. "Like what? Like that you're an asshole? Get off it, Martino, you're alive, and you didn't get your dick blown off like some of 'em did, so what's the problem?"

Vincent rolled his eyes. Bubble was in one of her foul lecture moods again. She was notorious for preaching with field-soldier give-a-shit language. At times it was entertaining just to get her started, but this was not one of those times. Vincent knew Gina was in the waiting room, and that was much more painful for him than trying to stand. The pain in his legs subsided in minutes, but the pain of knowing she had been only a few feet away would linger for days.

Bubble waited for a response but saw, surprisingly, that he had none. She smiled to herself, knowing that he had weakened and that she had finally gotten through his macho pride. Deciding on the hard-sell approach, she put her hands on her hips and gave him her best bitch look. "I've had it with you. I'm gonna talk ta that young girl and tell her you wanna see her."

Vincent began to protest, but she shook her three chins. "No, don't try and stop me with your self-pitying bullshit. I'm not lying to her anymore." She turned around and marched for the double doors.

Vincent frantically looked for something to cover his legs. Pushing the chair's wheels, he rolled up to his bed and pulled off the light gray blanket. He ran his hand through his long hair and faced the door in a cold sweat.

Bubble came through the entrance followed by a dark-haired vision. Her face was exactly as he remembered it in his dreams—beautiful. Her large brown eyes were wide and wild, darting left and right, searching for him. Then she saw him. He couldn't help his smile. She was angry. She always was the most beautiful when she was upset with him.

Gina marched toward him with narrowing, misting eyes. "About time you decided to see me, Vinny Martino. I'm only your girl, you know?"

Vincent kept his smile, taking her all in. "I know."

"You don't act like it."

"Come 'ere."

Gina's full lips turned up in a smile, releasing her tears. "Oh, Vinny . . ." She ran over and hugged him, rolling the wheelchair back against the radiator. Vincent felt his own tears running down his cheeks and squeezed his dream closer, knowing it was time to begin living again.

17 NOVEMBER 1966

Jewel Day heard a knock at the door and set down the morning paper. Opening the door, she felt her knees almost give way. It had been a year ago that she had opened the door and saw soldiers standing on her steps. They had told her Eugene had been killed. The uniformed white soldier on her steps now was just too much a reminder of that horrible day.

Vincent took off his overseas cap. "I'm sorry, Mrs. Day, for disturbing you. I'm Vincent Martino and I—"

Jewel raised her tearing eyes, recognizing the name. "You're Eugene's friend! He wrote about you. Come in, come in, please."

"Who is it?" came a voice from the kitchen.

"James, come in here. Eugene's Army friend is here."

Jewel turned back to the soldier and saw he was using two canes to support his awkward steps. Her eyes teared and she turned away to keep from bawling. She had forgotten the others in her grief. This boy, with such old eyes, was the same age as her son. He'd been blessed and had lived, but he was maimed for life. Her pain had dulled with time, but her son's young friend would have to live with his forever.

James Day limped into the living room, holding a cup of coffee. "What

did you say?" He abruptly halted, seeing the soldier standing in the hallway. "My God."

Vincent straightened his back and faced the old man. "Sir, you an' me
is gonna go to the Veterans Day ceremony this morning. Gene wanted ta
take you, but . . . I promised Gene I'd be here."

Jewel Day trembled as she wiped her eyes and walked up the steps to
get the uniform cap she'd found among Eugene's effects they had sent from
Vietnam. At the time, she had not understood why he had kept it. Now
she knew.

Gina, waiting in the car outside, noticed another car pull in behind her.
It would not have been unusual except that the driver and passenger were
both white and dressed in dark green uniforms like Vincent's. She turned
around in the seat to get a better look and saw a tall, thin soldier get out
of the passenger side and a stocky sergeant step out from behind the wheel.
Both men put on their caps and began walking toward the painted brick
rowhouse that Vincent had walked into.

Gina opened her door as the soldiers passed. "You guys lookin' for
Vinny?"

Lee smiled a huge grin. "You have ta be Gina."

Gina's eyes widened. "Are you Reb . . . and are you Irish?"

"Heck, yeah. Dadgum if you ain't as pretty as Vinny said."

Lee was about to introduce Shawn when the front door opened. James
Day stepped out, wearing his old uniform and holding Vincent's arm as
they began walking down the steps.

Vincent raised his head to look for Gina and froze. He thought for a split
second his eyes were betraying him. He blinked and felt his eyes moisten
again. It was them! They had remembered! God, he had missed seeing
them. The war was only in his nightmares now, but seeing Lee and his
sergeant brought it all back . . . the good times and the bad they had shared.
There was so much he wanted to say, but he could only cry.

Lee jogged up the steps and the two men embraced. Vincent pounded
Lee's back but still couldn't speak. Shawn walked up and put his arms
around both men's shoulders.

Vincent patted Shawn's back and put his arm over James Day's shoulder. The old man joined the embrace as one of them, sharing the special
moment with his son.

The sun broke through the gray clouds as the color guard approached
the reviewing stand. Standing in the first row, James Day, Vincent, Lee,
and Shawn came to attention as the color guard passed down the aisle.

The chair beside Lee had intentionally been left empty at Lee's insis-
tence. He had explained it was for Blake, who he knew was watching.

A silver-haired man wearing an expensive business suit made his way through the crowd and strode down the aisle. He saw who he was searching for and stepped toward the empty chair. Lee began to say it was reserved when he saw the man's tear-filled gray eyes.

David Alexander extended his hand. Lee ignored the gesture and stepped closer, hugging his friend's father.

The colors halted on the stage and the high school band began playing the Star Spangled Banner. James Day raised his hand in a rigid salute, feeling both incredibly sad and proud. It seemed like only yesterday that a small wide-eyed boy stood beside him and lifted his small hand in imitation of his father. Oh, Eugene . . . my son, I miss you so much. Thank you for this day, and thank you for your friends who loved you.

The music ended and a pastor approached the microphone. "Let us bow our heads in prayer and remembrance. This special day we honor the living and those who died serving our great nation of free men. Our heavenly Father, we . . ."

The crowd of veterans and families lowered their heads. They did not notice the old black man wearing an ill-fitting World War II uniform, three beribboned soldiers, and a man wearing a business suit, who had all put their arms over each other's shoulders and become as one.

Shawn smiled through his tears, knowing that if there was beer in heaven, Taco was raising his glass in a toast to them, saying, "To the expendables!"

AUTHOR'S EPILOGUE

The thirty-five-day battle of the Ia Drang was the first pitting a U.S. Army division against an NVA division. As a result of the battle, 304 names are engraved in the east wall, panel III on the Vietnam War Memorial in Washington, D.C. Five hundred and twenty-four men of the First Cavalry Division still carry the scars from the wounds of that thirty-five-day struggle. The NVA division almost ceased to exist as a unit because of the action, and required nearly a year before achieving combat effectiveness. This book is a novel, in that I have taken the liberty to put my characters in some places and battles where their unit would not have actually been. For that, I apologize to those who were there. Nevertheless, the battles were fought, and the men who fought them know all too well men like those in this story.

The battle of the Ia Drang is well documented, and of particular note are two excellent nonfiction books I strongly recommend: *Pleiku* by J. D. Coleman, and *Headhunters* by Matthew Brennan.

The war is over for most, but to those who were there, it will remain with us until John Quail toasts the last Vietnam veteran put to rest.